JOSEPH BALSAMO

"YOU OFFER ME WHAT IS NOT YOURS TO GIVE"

Dumas, Vol. Six

ALEXANDRE DUMAS

❧

JOSEPH BALSAMO

❧

ILLUSTRATED WITH DRAWINGS ON WOOD BY
EMINENT FRENCH AND AMERICAN ARTISTS

Fredonia Books
Amsterdam, The Netherlands

Joseph Balsamo

by
Alexandre Dumas

ISBN 1-58963-224-9

Reprinted from the 1902 edition

Fredonia Books
Amsterdam, The Netherlands
http://www.fredoniabooks.com

In order to make original editions of historical works available to scholars at an economical price, this facsimile of the original edition of 1902 is reproduced from the best available copy and has been digitally enhanced to improve legibility, but the text remains unaltered to retain historical authenticity.

JOSEPH BALSAMO.

INTRODUCTORY.

Near the source of the Seltz, on the left bank of the Rhine, some leagues from the imperial city of Worms, there begins a range of mountains, the scattered and rugged summits of which disappear northward like a herd of wild buffaloes vanishing in a mist.

These mountains, which from their lofty summits overlook an almost desert region, and seem but to form an attendant train to one which is their chief, have each a peculiar figure, and each bears a name indicating some tradition connected with it. One is the King's Chair—another the Wild-rose Stone; this the Falcon's Rock—that the Serpent's Crest.

The highest of all, which raises to the clouds its granite top, girt with a crown of ruins, is Mont Tonnerre.

When evening deepens the shadows of the lofty oaks—when the last rays of the sun die away on the peaks of this family of giants, we might imagine that silence descended from these sublime heights to the plain—that an invisible hand unfolded from their declivities the dark-blue veil through which we see the stars, to wrap it over the world wearied with the toil and the noise of the day. Waking gives place to sleep, and all the tenants of earth and air repose.

Even then is not heard the stream of the Seltz, pursuing its mysterious course by the fir-trees on its banks, stopping not by day or night, for it must hurry on to the Rhine, which to it is eternity. The sands of its current are so smooth, its reeds so flexible, its rocks so richly clothed with moss, that not one of its waves murmurs, from Morsheim, where it rises, to Freewenheim, where it finishes its course.

A little above its source, between Albisheim and Kircheim-Poland, a road, winding deep between two rugged walls of rock, leads to Danenfels. Beyond Danenfels the road becomes a path; it narrows, is lost, and the eye seeks in vain anything on which to rest, except the slopes of Mont Tonnerre, whose lightning-blasted summit is hidden by a belt of trees impenetrable to the eye.

In fact, once under those trees, leafy as the oaks of Dodona of old, the traveler may, in open day, continue his way unseen by any one on the plain below. Were his horse hung with more bells than any mule in Spain, not a sound would be heard ; were his trappings of gold and jewels like those of an emperor, not a ray from them would pierce through the foliage, so powerful is the density of the forest in extinguishing sound, and its darkness in dimming the brightest colors.

Even at the present day, when our highest mountains have become mere observatories for every-day tourists, on whose lips the most fearful of the legends of poetry call up a smile of doubt—even now this solitude has its terrors. A few miserable-looking houses, outposts of neighboring villages, appear here and there, but at a distance from the magic belt, to show that man is to be found in that region. Their inhabitants are millers, who carry their flour to Rockenhausen or Alzey, or shepherds, who herd their flocks around the mountain, they and their dogs trembling often to hear some enormous fir-tree fall with age, crashing in the unknown depths of the forest.

All the fireside tales of the country are gloomy, and that path which is lost beyond Danenfels, among the heath and furze of the mountains, has not always, they say, led good Christians to a safe shelter. Perhaps there yet may live one of those country people who has heard his father or his grandfather tell what we are now about to relate.

On the 6th of May, 1770, at that hour when the waters of the great river are tinged with a pale-rose color, that is to say, when the inhabitants of the Rhingau see the setting sun sink behind the spire of Strasburg Cathedral, which divides it into two hemispheres of fire—a man, who came from

Mayence, having passed through Alzey and Kircheim-Poland, appeared beyond the village of Danenfels. He followed the path so long as the path was visible, then, when all trace of it vanished, dismounting from his horse, he fastened its bridle to the first fir-tree of the pathless forest.

The animal neighed uneasily, and the woods seemed to start at a sound so unusual.

"Gently, gently, Djerid!—twelve leagues are enough for you : here you must wait my return."

The traveler tried to peer into the recesses of the forest, but in vain ; he could only see masses of dark shadows relieved upon shadows yet darker. Turning then to his horse, whose Arab name declared his race and swiftness, he took his head between his hands, approached his lips to the smoking nostrils of the animal, and said :

"Farewell, my good horse !—farewell, if it be fated that we meet not again."

As he said these words he looked quickly around as if he feared they might have been overheard, or as if he desired it. The horse shook his silky mane, pawed and neighed, as he would in the desert on the approach of the lion. The traveler stroked down his head with a smile which seemed to say, "Thou art not wrong, Djerid ; there is danger here."

Then, having decided beforehand, no doubt, not to oppose force against this danger, the unknown adventurer drew from his saddle-bow two richly mounted pistols, took out their balls, and sprinkled the powder on the ground. This done, he put them back in their place. Then he unbuckled a sword with a steel handle, wrapped the belt of it round it, and put all together under the saddle, so that the pommel of the sword was towards the horse's shoulder. After these formalities, the traveler shook off the dust from his boots, took off his gloves, felt in his pockets, and having found a pair of small scissors and a penknife with a tortoise-shell handle, he threw first the one and then the other over his shoulder, without looking where they fell. That done, he again stroked Djerid, breathed deeply, as if to expand his chest, feeling that his strength was about to be taxed, and sought a pathway among the trees.   He found none, and at last entered the forest at a venture.

It is time that we should give our readers some idea of the traveler's appearance, as he is destined to play an important part in our history.

He was a man apparently of thirty or two-and-thirty years of age, of middle height, but admirably made, and his every movement exhibited a fine combination of strength and flexibility of limb. He was dressed in a traveling-coat of black velvet, with gold buttons, under which appeared an embroidered waistcoat; tight-fitting breeches of leather, and polished boots, on limbs which might have served as a model for a sculptor, completed his costume. As to his face, whose rapid change of expression bespoke him of a southern race, there were in it both tact and power of character. His eye, which could express every feeling, seemed to read the soul of any one on whom it rested. His complexion, naturally dark, had been rendered darker by exposure to a warmer sun than ours. His mouth, large, but well formed, showed a fine set of teeth, the whiteness of which was heightened by contrast with the darkness of his skin. His foot was long, but finely formed, and his hand small, but sinewy.

Scarcely had he advanced two steps among the dark fir-trees when he heard the quick tramp of hoofs in the direction where he had left his horse. His first movement was to turn back, but he stopped himself ; however, he could not resist the wish to know the fate of Djerid—he raised himself on tiptoe and glanced through an opening. Djerid had disappeared, guided by an invisible hand which had untied his bridle. A slight frown contracted the brow of the unknown, yet something like a smile curled his chiseled lips.

Then he went on his way toward the center of the forest.

For a few steps further the twilight aided him, then it left him, and in darkness so thick, that seeing no longer where to place his foot, he stopped.

" I got on very well to Danenfels, for from Mayence to Danenfels there is a road," said he, aloud, " and from Danenfels to the Dark Heath, because there is a path, and from the Dark Heath hither, though there is neither road nor path, because I could see where I was going—but now I must stop—I see nothing."

Scarcely had he pronounced these words, in a dialect half French, half Sicilian, when a light appeared about fifty paces from the traveler.

"Thanks," said he, "now as the light moves I shall follow."

The light moved steadily on, with a gliding motion, as we sometimes see a light move over the stage of a theater.

The traveler might have gone about a hundred steps further, when he thought he felt a breathing at his ear. He started.

"Turn not," said a voice on the right, "or thou art dead."

"Good!" replied the immovable traveler.

"Speak not," said a voice on the left, "or thou art dead."

The traveler bowed without speaking.

"But if thou art afraid," said a third voice which, like that of Hamlet's father, seemed to come from the bowels of the earth, "turn back; that will declare that thou abandonest thy scheme, and thou shalt be permitted to go."

The traveler made a gesture of dissent with his hand, and went on.

The night was so dark and the forest so thick that he could not advance without occasionally stumbling, and his progress was slow. For nearly an hour the flame moved on, and he followed without hearing a murmur, and without showing a symptom of fear. All at once it disappeared.

The traveler was out of the forest. He raised his eyes, and in the dark-blue sky saw some twinkling stars.

He continued to advance in the direction of the place where the light had disappeared, and soon saw arise before him a ruin, the specter, as it were, of some ancient castle.

Next, his foot struck against some of its fragments. Then something cold passed his temples and sealed up his eyes, and he saw not even the shadows of outward objects.

A bandage of wet linen bound his head. This was only what he expected, no doubt, as he made no effort to remove it. He only silently stretched out his hand like a blind man imploring a guide. His gesture was understood. A cold, dry, bony hand grasped the fingers of the traveler.

He knew that it was the hand of a skeleton, but if that hand had been endowed with sensation it would have felt that his did not tremble.

Then the traveler felt himself rapidly drawn on for about a hundred paces. Suddenly the hand released its grasp, the bandage fell from his eyes, he stopped—he was on the summit of Mont Tonnerre.

II.

HE WHO IS.

In the midst of a glade formed by larches, bare with age, rose one of those feudal castles which the Crusaders, on their return from the Holy Land, scattered over Europe. The gateways and arches had been finely sculptured, and in their niches were statues ; but these lay broken at the foot of the walls, and creeping plants and wild-flowers now filled their places.

The traveler, on opening his eyes, found himself before the damp and mossy steps of the principal entrance ; on the first of these steps stood the phantom by whose bony hand he had been led thither. A long shroud wrapped it from head to foot, and the eyeless sockets darted flame. Its fleshless hand pointed to the interior of the ruins, as the termination of the traveler's journey. This interior was a hall, the lower part of which was but half seen, but from its vaults, heaped with ruins, flickered a dim and mysterious light.

The traveler bowed in assent. The phantom mounted slowly step by step to the hall, and plunged into the ruins. The unknown followed calmly and slowly up the eleven steps which this specter had trodden, and entered also.

With the noise of a clashing wall of brass the great gate of the portal closed behind him.

At the entrance of a circular hall, lighted by three lamps, which cast a greenish light, the phantom stopped. The traveler, ten steps farther back, stopped in his turn.

"Open thine eyes!" said the phantom.

"I see!" replied the unknown.

The phantom then drew, with a proud gesture, a two-edged sword from beneath his shroud, and struck it against a column of bronze. A hollow, metallic groan responded to his blow.

Then all around the hall arose stone seats, and numerous phantoms, like the first, appeared. Each was armed with a two-edged sword, and each took his place on a seat, and seen by the pale-green light of the three lamps, they might have been taken, so cold and motionless were they, for statues on their pedestals. And these human statues came out in strange relief on the black tapestry of the walls.

Some seats were placed in advance of the others, on which sat six specters who seemed like chiefs—one seat was vacant.

He who sat on the middle seat arose.

"Brethren, how many are present?" he asked, turning to the assembly.

"Three hundred," replied the phantoms, with one voice. It thundered through the hall, and died away among the funereal hangings on the walls.

"Three hundred," replied the president, "and each speaks for ten thousand companions. Three hundred swords, which are equal to three million of poniards!"

Then he turned to the traveler.

"What dost thou wish?" he asked.

"To see the light," replied the other.

"The paths which lead to the mountain of fire are rugged and difficult. Fearest thou not?"

"I fear nothing."

"One step forward, and you cannot return. Reflect."

"I stop not till I reach the goal."

" Wilt thou swear ? "

" Dictate the oath ! "

The president raised his hand, and, with a slow and solemn voice, pronounced these words :

" In the name of the crucified Son, swear to break all bonds of nature which unite thee to father, mother, brother, sister, wife, relation, friend, mistress, king, benefactor, and to any being whatever to whom thou hast promised faith, obedience, gratitude, or service ! "

The traveler, with a firm voice, repeated these words, and then the president dictated the second part of the oath.

" From this moment thou art free from the pretended oath thou hast taken to thy country and its laws ; swear thou to reveal to the new head whom thou acknowledgest all that thou hast seen or done, read or guessed, and henceforward to search out and penetrate into that which may not openly present itself to thine eyes."

The president stopped ; the unknown repeated the words.

" Honor and respect the *aqua toffana*, as a prompt, sure, and necessary means of ridding the world by the death or idiocy of those who would degrade the truth, or tear it from us."

An echo could not have been more exact than the unknown in repeating the words of the president.

" Flee from Spain, flee from Naples, flee from every accursed land ; flee from the temptation of revealing aught that thou shalt now see and hear ! Lightning is not more quick to strike than will be the invisible and inevitable knife, wherever thou mayest be, shouldst thou fail in thy secrecy."

Spite of the threat conveyed in these last words, no trace of emotion was seen on the face of the unknown ; he pronounced the end of the oath with a voice at calm as at the beginning.

" And now," continued the president, " put on his forehead the sacred band."

Two phantoms approached the unknown—he bowed his

head—one of them bound round it a crimson ribbon covered with silver characters, placed alternately with the figure of our Lady of Loretto ; the other tied it behind, just at the nape of the neck. Then they left his side.

"What wouldst thou ask ? " inquired the president.

"Three things."

"Name them."

"The hand of iron, the sword of fire, the scales of adamant."

"Why the hand of iron ? "

"To stifle tyranny."

"Why the sword of fire ? "

"To banish the impure from the earth."

"And why the scales of adamant ? "

"To weigh the destinies of humanity."

"Canst thou withstand the necessary trials ? "

"Courage is prepared for all trials."

"The proofs ! the proofs !" cried many voices.

"Turn !" said the president.

The unknown obeyed, and found himself face to face with a man pale as death, bound and gagged.

"What seest thou ? " asked the president.

"A malefactor or a victim."

"A traitor ! One who took the oath as thou hast done, and then revealed the secrets of our order."

"A criminal, then."

"Yes:"

"What penalty has he incurred ? "

"Death."

The three hundred phantoms repeated "Death !" and, in spite of all his efforts, the condemned was dragged into a darker part of the hall. The traveler saw him struggle with his executioners—he heard his choking voice—a dagger glimmered for an instant—a blow was struck—and a dead and heavy sound announced a body falling on the earthy floor.

"Justice is done !" said the unknown, turning to the ghastly assembly, who, from beneath their shrouds, had devoured the sight with greedy looks.

"Then," said the president, "thou dost approve what has been done ?"

"Yes, if he who has fallen was really guilty."

"Thou wilt drink to the death of every man who, like him, would betray our secrets ?"

"I will."

"Whatever be the draught ?"

"Whatever be the draught."

"Bring the cup," said the president.

One of the two executioners brought the unknown a red, tepid liquor in a human skull. He took this frightful cup, raised it above his head, saying :

"I drink to the death of every man who shall betray the secrets of this holy society."

Then, bringing it to his lips, he drained it to the last drop, and returned it calmly to him who had presented it.

A murmur of surprise ran through the assembly, and the phantoms seemed to look at each other through their half-opened shrouds.

"Good !" said the president. "The pistol !"

A phantom drew near the president, holding in one hand a pistol, and in the other a ball and a charge of powder.

"Thou promisest passive obedience to our orders ?"

"Yes."

"Even if this obedience be put to the proof against thyself ?"

"He who enters here is no longer his own ; he belongs to all."

"Then thou obeyest whatever order be given thee ?"

"I obey."

"This instant ?"

"This instant."

"No pause ?"

"No pause."

"Take this pistol—load it."

The unknown took the pistol and loaded it, all the dread assembly looking on the operation in a silence only broken by the sighs of the wind among the arches of the ruin.

"The pistol is loaded," said the unknown.

"Art thou sure?" asked the president.

A smile passed over the lips of the traveler, as he tried the pistol, showing that it was loaded. The president bowed in token of being satisfied.

"Yes," said he, "it is loaded."

"What am I to do with it?"

"Cock it."

The unknown cocked the pistol, and its click was distinctly heard in the intervals of silence in the dialogue.

"Now put it to thy forehead," said the president.

He obeyed unhesitatingly.—The silence seemed to deepen over the assembly, and the lamps to turn pale. These were real phantoms, for not a breath was then heard.

"Fire!" said the president.

The cock was heard to snap, the flint flashed, but the powder in the pan alone took fire, and no report accompanied its quick flame.

A shout of admiration burst from every breast, and the president involuntarily extended his hand to the unknown.

But two proofs were not sufficient to satisfy all, and some voices shouted:

"The dagger! the dagger!"

"You demand that, also?" said the president.

"Yes; the dagger! the dagger!" replied the voices.

"Bring the dagger," said the president.

"It is useless," said the unknown, making a disdainful movement with his head.

"Useless?" cried the assembly.

"Yes, useless," he replied, with a voice which drowned every other: "useless. You lose time, and it is precious.

"What mean you?" asked the president.

"I tell you I know your secrets—that these proofs of yours are but child's play, unworthy of men. I tell you that I know the body which lies there is not dead; that I have not drunk blood; that by a spring, the charge fell into the butt at the moment I cocked the pistol. Such things may frighten cowards. Rise, pretended corpse; thou hast no terrors for the brave."

Another shout made the vaults ring.

"Thou knowest our mysteries, then," said the president. "Thou art one of the illuminated or a traitor."

"Who art thou?" demanded the three hundred voices; and, on the instant, twenty swords, in the hands of the nearest phantoms, were pointed with a motion as precise as if directed by a military signal, at the bosom of the unknown.

He smiled, shook the thick curls of his hair, which, unpowdered, were only retained by the ribbon which had been bound round his head, and said, calmly:

"*I am he who is!*"

Then he turned his eyes slowly around the living wall which hemmed him in, and gradually sword after sword sunk before him.

"Thou hast spoken rashly," said the president. "Doubtless thou knowest not the import of thy words."

The stranger shook his head and smiled.

"I have spoken the truth."

"Whence comest thou?"

"I come whence comes the light."

"But we have learned that thou comest from Sweden."

"I might come from Sweden, and yet from the East."

"Then we know thee not. Who art thou?"

"Who am I? Aye, ye shall know more. Ye pretend not to understand me; but first I will tell you who you are."

The phantoms started, and the clang of their swords was heard, as they grasped them in their right hands and raised them to the level of the stranger's breast.

"First," said he, "thou who questionest me, who believest thyself a god, and who art but the forerunner of one, thou who representest Sweden, I shall name thee that the rest may know I can also name them. Swedenborg, how comes it thy familiars told thee not that he whom thou waitedst for was on the road?"

"They did declare it to me," replied the president, putting aside a fold of his shroud, in order to see him better who spoke, and, in doing so, contrary to all the habits of the association, he showed a white beard and the venerable face of a man of eighty.

"Good," replied the stranger. "On thy left is the representative of England or of old Caledonia. I grant you, my lord, if the blood of your grandfather flows in your veins, England's extinguished light may be rekindled."

The swords sunk—anger gave place to astonishment.

"Ah, captain," said the unknown, addressing one on the left of the president, "in what port waits thy good ship? A noble frigate of Providence. Its name augurs well for America."

Then, turning towards him on the right:

"Look, Prophet of Zurich, thou hast carried physiognomy almost to divination—read the lines on my face, and acknowledge my mission."

He to whom he spoke recoiled.

"Come," said he, turning to another, "descendant of Pelago, we must drive the Moors a second time from Spain —an easy task if the Castilians yet retain the sword of the Cid."

The fifth chief remained so still, so motionless, that the voice of the unknown seemed to have turned him to stone.

"And to me," said the sixth, "hast thou naught to say to me?"

"Aye," replied the traveler, turning on him a look which read his heart, "aye, what Jesus said to Judas—but not yet."

The chief turned paler than his shroud, and a murmur running through the assembly seemed to demand the cause of this singular accusation.

"Thou forgettest the representative of France," said the president.

"He is not here," replied the stranger, haughtily, "and that thou knowest well, since his seat is vacant. Learn, then, that snares make him smile who sees in darkness.

who acts in spite of the elements, and who lives in spite of death."

"Thou art young," replied the president, "and thou speakest as if from divine authority. Reflect! boldness overcomes only the weak or the ignorant."

A disdainful smile played over the lips of the stranger.

"You are all weak, since you have no power over me; you are all ignorant, since ye know not who I am. Boldness, then, alone might overcome you; but why should one all-powerful so overcome?"

"Give us the proof of your boasted power," said the president.

"Who convoked you?" asked the unknown, becoming the interrogator, instead of the interrogated.

"The grand assembly."

"And not without a cause hast thou," pointing to the president, "come from Sweden—thou," and he turned from one to another of the five chiefs, as he spoke, "thou from London, thou from New York, thou from Zurich, thou from Madrid, thou from Warsaw, and you all," looking round the assembly, "from the four winds of heaven, to meet in the sanctuary of the dreaded faith."

"No," replied the president, "not without cause; for we came to meet him who has founded in the East a mysterious faith, joining two worlds in one belief, entwining mankind with the bonds of brotherhood."

"Is there any sign by which you shall know him?"

"Yes," said the president, "and an angel has revealed it to me."

"You alone know it?"

"I alone."

"You have revealed it to none?"

"To none."

"Name it."

The president hesitated.

"Name it. The hour is come."

"He will bear on his breast a diamond star, and on it three letters, the signification of which is only known to himself."

"Declare the letters."

"L. P. D."

The stranger rapidly threw open his coat and vest, and on his fine Holland shirt shone like a flaming star the diamond and the three letters, formed of rubies.

"It is he!" cried the president.

"He whom we await?" asked the chiefs.

"The great Copt?" murmured the three hundred voices.

"Now," cried the stranger, triumphantly, "do you believe me when I say, "I am he that is?""

"Yes," said the phantoms, prostrating themselves before him.

"Speak, master," said the president, "speak; we shall obey."

III.

L. P. D.

There was silence for some moments, during which the unknown seemed to collect his thoughts, then he began:

"Sirs, ye but weary your arms with your swords: lay them aside and lend an attentive ear, for you shall learn much from the few words which I am about to utter."

All were profoundly attentive.

"The sources of great rivers are sacred, therefore unknown. Like the Nile, the Ganges, the Amazon, I know to what I tend, not whence I come. All that I can reveal is, that when the eyes of my spirit first opened to comprehend external things, I was in Medina, the holy city, playing in the gardens of the Mufti Salaaym. He was a venerable man, kind as a father to me, yet not my father; for though he looked on me with love, he spoke to me with respect. Thrice a day he left me, and then came another old man, whose name I may pronounce with gratitude, yet with fear. He was called Althotas, and him the seven great spirits had taught all that the angels know, in order to comprehend God. He was my tutor, my master, my friend—a friend to be venerated indeed ; for his age was double that of most among you."

His solemn tone, his majestic deportment, deeply impressed the assembly ; they seemed trembling with anxiety to hear more.

He continued :

"When I reached my fifteenth year I was initiated into the mysteries of nature. I knew botany, not as one of your learned men who has acquired only the knowledge of the plants of his own corner of the world—to me were known the sixty thousand families of plants of the whole earth. My master, pressing his hands on my forehead, made a ray of celestial light descend on my soul ; then could I perceive beneath the seas the wondrous vegetations which are tossed by the waves, in the giant branches of which are cradled monsters unknown to the eye of man.

"All tongues, living and dead, I knew. I could speak every language spoken from the Dardanelles to the Straits of Magellan. I could read the dark hieroglyphics on those granite books—the pyramids. From Sanchoniathon to Socrates, from Moses to Jerome, from Zoroaster to Agrippa, all human knowledge was mine.

"Medicine I studied, not only in Hippocrates, in Galen, and in Averrhoes, but in that great teacher, Nature. I penetrated the secrets of the Copts and the Druses. I gathered up the seeds of destruction and of scarcity. When the simoom or the hurricane swept over my head, I threw to it one of those seeds which its breath bore on, carrying death or life to whomsoever, I had condemned or blessed.

"In the midst of these studies I reached my twentieth year. Then my master sought me one day in a grove, to which I had retired from the heat of the day. His face was at the same moment grave and smiling. He held a little vial in his hand. 'Acharat,' said he, 'I have told thee that nothing is born, nothing dies in the world—that the cradle and the coffin are twins—that man wants only to see into past existences to be equal to the gods, and that when that power shall be acquired by him, he will be as immortal as they. Behold! I have found the beverage which will dispel his darkness, thinking that I had found that which destroys death. Acharat, I drank of it yesterday; see, the vial is not full—drink thou the rest to-day.

"I had entire confidence in my venerable master, yet my hand trembled as it touched the vial which he offered me, as Adam's might have done when Eve presented him with the apple.

"'Drink,' said he, smiling.

"I drank.

"Then he placed his hands on my head, as he always did when he would make light penetrate to my soul:

"'Sleep!' said he.

"Immediately I slept, and I dreamed that I was lying on a pile of sandal-wood and aloes. An angel, passing by on the behests of the Highest from the east to the west, touched the pile with the tip of his wing and it kindled into flame. Yet I, far from being afraid, far from dreading the fire, lay voluptuously in the midst of it, like the phenix, drawing in new life from the source of all life.

"Then my material frame vanished away; my soul only remained. It preserved the form of my body, but transparent, impalpable, it was lighter than the atmosphere in which we live, and it rose above it. Then, like Pythagoras, who remembered that in a former state he had been at the siege of Troy, I remembered the past. I had experienced thirty-two existences, and I recalled them all. I saw ages pass before me like a train of aged men in procession. I beheld myself under the different names which I had borne from the day of my first birth to that of my last death. You know, brethren—and it is an essential article of our faith—that souls, those countless emanations of the Deity, fill the air, and are formed into numerous hierarchies, descending from the sublime to the base; and the man who, at the moment of his birth, inhales one of those pre-existing souls, gives it up at his death, that it may enter on a new course of transformations.

He said this in a tone so expressive of conviction, and his look had something so sublime, that the assembly interrupted him by a murmur of admiration.

"When I awoke," continued the illuminated, "I felt that I was more than man—that I was almost divine. Then I resolved to dedicate not only my present existence, but all my future ones, to the happiness of man.

"The next day, as if he had guessed my thoughts, Althotas said to me, 'My son, twenty years ago thy mother expired in giving birth to thee. Since that time, invincible obstacles have prevented thy illustrious father revealing himself to thee. We shall travel; we shall meet thy father; he will embrace thee, but thou wilt not know him.'

"Thus in me, as in one of the elect, all was mysterious—past, present, future.

"I bid adieu to the Mufti Salaaym, who blessed me and loaded me with presents, and we joined a caravan going to Suez.

"Pardon me, sirs, if I give way for a moment to emotion, as I recall that one day a venerable man embraced me; a strange thrill ran through me as I felt his heart beat against mine.

"He was the Cheriffe of Mecca, a great and illustrious prince, who had seen a hundred battles, and at the raising of his hand three millions of men bent their heads before him. Althotas turned away to hide his feelings, perhaps not to betray a secret, and we continued our road.

"We went into the heart of Asia; we ascended the Tigris; we visited Palmyra, Damascus, Smyrna, Constantinople, Vienna, Berlin, Dresden, Moscow, Stockholm, Petersburg, New York, Buenos Ayres, the Cape of Good Hope, and Aden; then, being near the point at which we had set out, we proceeded into Abyssinia, descended the Nile, sailed to Rhodes, and lastly to Malta. Before landing, a vessel came out to meet us, bringing two knights of the order; they saluted me and embraced Althotas, and conducted us in a sort of triumph to the palace of the grand master, Pinto.

"Now, you will ask me, sirs, how it came that the Mussulman Acharat was received with honor by those who have vowed the extermination of the infidels. Althotas, a Catholic, and himself a Knight of Malta, had always spoken to me of one only God omnipotent, universal, who, by the aid of angels, his ministers, made the world a harmonious whole, and to this whole he gave the great name of Cosmos. I was then not a Mussulman, but a theosophist.

"My journeyings ended; but in truth all that I had seen had awakened in me no astonishment, because for me there was nothing new under the sun, and in my preceding thirty-two existences I had visited the cities before, through which I lately passed. All that struck me was some change in their inhabitants. Now I would hover over events and watch the progress of man. I saw that all minds tend onward, and that this tendency leads to liberty. I saw that prophets had been raised up from time to time to aid the wavering advances of the human race; and that men, half blind from their cradle, make but one step towards the light in a century. Centuries are the days of nations.

"'Then,' said I to myself, 'so much has not been revealed to me that it should remain buried in my soul; in vain does the mountain contain veins of gold, in vain does the ocean hide its pearls, for the persevering miner penetrates to the bowels of the mountains, the diver descends to the depths of the ocean, but better than the mountain or the ocean, let me be like the sun, shedding blessings on the whole earth.'

"You understand, then, that it is not to go through some masonic ceremonies I have come from the East. I have come to say to you, brethren, take the wings and the eyes of the eagle; rise above the world, and cast your eyes over its kingdoms.

"Nations form but one vast body. Men, though born at different periods, in different ranks, arrive all in turn at that goal to reach which they were created. They are continually advancing, though seemingly stationary, and if they appear to retreat a step from time to time, it is but to collect strength for a bound which shall carry them over some obstacle in their way.

"France is the advance guard of nations. Put a torch in her hand, and though it kindle a wide-spreading flame, it will be salutary, for it will enlighten the world.

"The representative of France is not here—it may be that he has recoiled at the task imposed on him. Well, then, we must have a man who will not shrink from it—I will go to France."

"You are in France," said the president.

"Yes; the most important post I take myself—the most perilous work shall be mine."

"You know what passes in France, then?" inquired the president.

The stranger smiled.

"I know, for I myself have prepared all. An old king, weak, vicious, yet not so old, not so weak, not so vicious as the monarchy which he represents, sits on the throne of France. He has but a few years to live. Events must be prepared to succeed his death. France is the keystone of the arch; let but this stone be unfixed, and the monarchical edifice will fall. Aye, the day that Europe's most arrogant sovereigns shall hear that there is no longer a king in France, bewildered, they will of themselves rush into the abyss left by the destruction of the throne of St. Louis!"

Here, he on the right of the president spoke, and his German accent announced that he was a Swiss.

"Most venerated master, hast thou, then, calculated all?" he asked.

"All," replied the great Copt.

"Your pardon if I say more; but on our mountains, in our valleys, by our lakes, our words are free as the winds and the waters. Let me say, then, that a great event is on the eve of arriving, and that to it the French monarchy may owe its regeneration. I have seen, great master, a daughter of Maria Theresa traveling in state toward France, to unite the blood of seventeen emperors with that of the successor of the sixty-one kings of France, and the people rejoiced blindly, as they do when their chains are slackened, or when they bow beneath a gilded yoke. I would infer, then, that the crisis is not yet come."

All turned to him who so calmly and boldly had spoken to their master.

"Speak on, brother," said the great Copt ; "if thy advice be good, it shall be followed. We are chosen of Heaven, and we may not sacrifice the interests of a world to wounded pride."

The deputy from Switzerland continued, amidst deep silence :

"My studies have convinced me of one truth, that the physiognomy of men reveals to the eye which knows how to read it their virtues and their vices. We may see a composed look or a smile, for these caused by muscular movements are in their power, but the great type of character is still imprinted legibly on the countenance, declaring what passes in the heart. The tiger can caress, can give a kindly look, but his low forehead, his projecting face, his great occiput, declare him tiger still. The dog growls, shows his teeth, but his honest eye, his intelligent face, declare him still the friend of man. God has imprinted on each creature's face its name and nature. I have seen the young girl who is to reign in France ; on her forehead I read the pride, the courage, the tenderness of the German maiden. I have seen the young man who is to be her husband ; calmness, Christian meekness, and a high regard for the rights of others, characterize him. Now, France remembering no wrongs, and forgetting no benefits, since a Charlemagne, a Louis, and a Henry have been sufficient to preserve on the throne twenty base and cruel kings ; France who hopes on, despairs never, will she not adore a young, lovely, kindly queen, a patient, gentle, economical king ? and this, too, after the disastrous reign of Louis XV.—after his hateful orgies, his mean revenges, his Pompadours and Dubarry ? Will not France bless her youthful sovereigns, who will bring to her as their dowry peace with Europe ? Marie Antoinette now crosses the frontier ; the altar and the nuptial bed are prepared at Versailles. Is this the time to begin in France your work of regeneration ? Pardon if I have dared to submit these thoughts to you whose wisdom is infallible !"

At these words, he whom the great Copt had addressed as the Apostle of Zurich, bowed as he received the applause of the assembly, and waited a reply.

He did not wait long.

"If you read physiognomy, illustrious brethren, I read the future. Marie Antoinette is proud ; she will interfere in the coming struggle, and will perish in it. Louis Augustus is mild : he will yield to it, and will perish with her, but each will fall through opposite defects of character. Now they esteem each other, but short will be their love ; in a year they will feel mutual contempt. Why, then, deliberate, brethren, to discover whence comes the light ? It is revealed to me. I come from the East, led, like the shepherds, by a star, which foretells a second regeneration of mankind. To-morrow I begin my work. Give me twenty years for it—that will be enough, if we are united and firm."

"Twenty years ?" murmured several voices. "The time is long."

The great Copt turned to those who thus betrayed impatience.

"Yes," said he, "it is long to those who think that a principle is destroyed as a man is killed with the dagger of Jacques Clement or the knife of Damiens. Fools ! the knife kills the man, but, like the pruning-hook, it lops a branch that the other branches may take its place. In the stead of the murdered king rises up a Louis XIII., a stupid tyrant ; a Louis XIV., a cunning despot ; a Louis XV., an idol whose path is wet with tears of blood, like the monstrous deities of India, crushing with changeless smile women and children, who cast garlands before their chariot-wheels. And you think twenty years too long to efface the name of king from the hearts of thirty millions of men, who but lately offered to God their children's lives to purchase that of Louis XV.! And you think it an easy task to make

France hate her lilies, which, bright as the stars of heaven, grateful as the odors of flowers, have borne light, charity, victory, to the ends of the world ! Try, try, brethren ! I give you, not twenty years—I give you a century. You, scattered, trembling, unknown each to the other, known only to me, who only can sum up your divided worth, and tell its value—to me, who alone can unite you in one fraternal chain—I tell you, philosophers, political economists, theorists, that in twenty years those thoughts which you whisper in your families, which you will write with uneasy eye in the solitude of your old somber towers, which you tell one another with the dagger in your hands, that you may strike the traitor who would repeat them in tones louder than your own—I tell you that these thoughts shall be proclaimed aloud in the streets, printed in the open face of day, spread through Europe by peaceful emissaries, or by the bayonets of five hundred thousand soldiers, battling for liberty, with your principles inscribed on their standards. You, who tremble at the name of the Tower of London ; you, who shrink at that of the Inquisition, hear me—me, who am about to dare the Bastile ! I tell you that we shall see those dreaded prisons in ruins, and your wives and children shall dance on their ashes. But that cannot be until, not the monarch, but the monarchy, is dead—until religious domination is despised —until social inferiority is extinguished—until aristocratic castes and unjust division of lands are no more. I ask twenty years to destroy an old world, and make a new one —twenty years—twenty seconds of eternity—and you say it is too long ! "

The silence of admiration and of assent followed the words of this dark prophet ; he had obtained the sympathy of the representatives of the hopes of Europe who surrounded him.

The great Copt enjoyed for some minutes his triumph ; then, feeling that it was complete, he went on :

"Now, brethren, now that I am going to devote myself to our cause—to beard the lion in his den—to risk my life for the freedom of mankind—now, what will you do for that to which you say you are ready to give up life, liberty, and fortune ? This is what I am here to demand."

A deeper silence fell on the assembly than when he last ceased to speak ; it seemed as if the motionless phantoms around him were absorbed in a fateful thought, which, when expressed, should take twenty thrones.

The six chiefs conversed for a moment apart, and then returned to the president. The president spoke:

" In the name of Sweden, I offer for the overthrow of the throne of Vasa the miners who established it, and one hundred thousand crowns. "

The great Copt made an entry in his tablets.

Another on the left spoke.

" I, sent by Scotland and Ireland, can promise nothing from England—our firm opponent—but from poor Scotland, from poor Ireland, I shall bring three thousand men and three thousand crowns yearly."

He wrote again.

" And you ? " said he, turning to one whose vigorous frame and restless spirit seemed wearied by his phantom robe, and who replied :

" I represent America, whose stones, whose trees, whose waters, whose every drop of blood are vowed to rebellion. Whilst we have gold we will give it, while we have blood we will shed it—let us but be free first. Though now divided, marked, and disunited, we are the links of a gigantic chain, and could some mighty hand join two of them, the rest will unite themselves. Begin, then, oh, great master, with us ! If thou wouldst rid France of royalty, free us from a foreign yoke first."

" It shall be so," replied the master ; " you shall first be free, and France shall help you. Wait, brother, but I promise thou shalt not wait long."

Then he turned to the Swiss deputy, who replied to his look:

" I can promise nothing. Our republic has been long the ally of the French monarchy, to which it sold its blood at Marignan and Pavia ; its sons are faithful—they will give that for which they have been paid ; for the first time, I am ashamed of their fidelity."

" So ; but we shall conquer without them, and in spite of them. And you, representative of Spain ? "

" I am poor ; I can only offer three thousand of my brothers, with a contribution of a thousand reals yearly. Our Spaniards are indolent ; they sleep on a bed of pain— provided they sleep, they care not."

" Good ! And you ? " said he to another.

" I represent Russia and Poland. My people are either discontented nobles or wretched serfs. The serf, who owns not even his life, can offer nothing ; but three thousand nobles have promised twenty louis d'ors each annually."

Then all the representatives in turn declared what those from whom they came would give for the great cause. Some were deputies from small kingdoms, some from large principalities, some from impoverished states, but all declared that they would add something to what had been offered. Their promises were written on the tablets of the great Copt, and they were bound by an oath to keep them.

"Now," said he, " you have seen and recognized the initials of our watchword—let it be placed *on* your hearts, and *in* them ; for we, the sovereign lord of the east and west, have decreed the downfall of the lily. Hear it, then, brethren—LILIA PEDIBUS DESTRUE."

Loud was their shout at this explanation of the mysterious letters—so loud that the gorges of the mountains re-echoed to it.

"And now, retire," said the master, when silence had succeeded, " retire by those subterranean passages which lead to the quarries of Mont Tonnerre. Disperse before the rising of the sun. You shall see me once more, and it will be on the day of our triumph ! Go "

His words were followed by a masonic sign, understood only by the six heads of the assembly, so that they remained around him when the rest had disappeared.

" Swedenborg," said he, " thou art truly inspired. God thanks thee by me for thy efforts in His cause. I shall give thee an address to which thou shalt send the promised money to France."

The president bowed, and departed, full of astonishment at that intelligence which had discovered his name.

"I grant thee, Fairfax," continued the master, "thou art worthy of thy great ancestor. "Remember me to Washington when next thou writest to him."

Fairfax bowed, and followed Swedenborg.

"Come, Paul Jones," said the Copt, "thou spokest bravely ; thou shalt be the hero of America. Let her be ready at the first signal."

The American thrilled in every nerve, as if the breath of some divine being had passed over him, and retired also.

"And now, as to thee, Lavater, abjure thy theories ; it is the time for action. Study no longer what man is, but what he may be. Go ! Woe to thy countrymen if they rise against us ; for our people will devour in its wrath as the wrath of God devours."

The trembling Swiss bowed and departed.

"Here, Ximenes," he went on, addressing the Spaniard, "thou art zealous, but distrustful. Thy country sleeps, but it is because none awakes her. Go ! Castile is still the country of the Cid."

The last of the six was advancing, but by a gesture the Copt forbid him.

"Scieffort of Russia, before a month thou wilt betray our cause, but in a month thou shalt be no more."

The Russian envoy fell on his knees, but a threatening movement of the master made him rise, and with tottering steps he also departed.

And now this singular man, whom we have introduced as the hero of our drama, left alone, looked around the empty, silent hall, buttoned up his black velvet coat, fixed his hat firmly on his head touched the spring of the great bronze gate which had closed behind him, and sallied out into the defiles of the mountain. Though he had neither guide nor light, he went on rapidly, as if led by an invisible hand.

Having passed the thick belt of trees, he looked for his horse; but not seeing him, he listened, and soon thought he heard a distant neighing. He whistled with a peculiar modulation, and in a moment Djerid could be seen coming forward like a faithful and obedient dog. The traveler sprang to the saddle, and quickly disappeared in the darkness, which spread over the heath extending from Mont Tonnerre to Danenfels.

CHAPTER I.

THE STORM.

EIGHT days after the scene just related, about five in the evening, a carriage with four horses and two postilions, left Pont-à-Mousson, a small town between Nancy and Metz. It had taken fresh horses at an inn, in spite of the recommendation of an attentive hostess who was on the lookout for belated travelers, and continued on its road to Paris. Its four horses had scarcely turned the corner of the street, when a score of children and half a score of gossips, who had watched the progress of their being put to, returned to their respective dwellings with gestures and exclamations expressive in some of great mirth, in others of great astonishment.

All this was because nothing like that carriage had for fifty years passed the bridge which good King Stanislaus threw across the Moselle to facilitate the intercourse of his little kingdom with France. We do not except even those curious vehicles of Alsace, which bring from Phalsbourg to our fairs two-headed wonders, dancing bears and the wandering tribes of harlequins, and gypsies.

In fact, without being either a child or a curious old gossip, surprise might have arrested one's steps on seeing this primitive machine, on four massive wheels, roll by with such velocity that every one exclaimed:

"What a strange way of traveling post!"

As our readers, fortunately for them, did not see it pass, we shall describe it.

First, then, the principal carriage—we say principal, because in front it was a sort of cabriolet—the principal carriage was painted light blue, and bore on its panels a baronial scroll, surmounting a J and a B intwined. Two windows—large windows, with white muslin curtains—gave it light, only these windows, invisible to the profane vulgar, looked frontwise into the cabriolet. A grating covered them through which one might speak to the inhabitants of the carriage.

This carriage, which was eight feet long, had no light but from the windows, and no air but from a ventilator on the top ; and then, to complete its oddity, a chimney rising about a foot above the roof offered to the passers-by the pleasant sight of a cloud of smoke lengthening into a bluish trail behind it. At the present day we should only have thought it a new invention combining the power of steam with that of horses.

This would have seemed so much the more probable that the carriage, preceded, as we have said, by four horses and two postilions, was followed by one horse, fastened to it by his bridle. His small head, slender legs, narrow chest, and silky mane and tail bespoke him of Arab race. He was ready saddled, which indicated that one of the travelers shut up in this Noah's ark sometimes enjoyed the pleasure of riding beside the carriage.

At Pont-à-Mousson the postilion who left had received, besides the pay for the horses, a double gratuity, presented by a strong but white hand, slipped through the leather curtains of the cabriolet, which shaded it as imperviously as the muslin ones did the carriage.

"Many thanks, my lord," said the astonished postilion, quickly taking off his cap and bowing low.

A sonorous voice replied in German for at Nancy German is still understood though no longer spoken), "*Schnell! Schneller!*" which means "Fast! faster!"

Postilions understand nearly all languages ; above all, when accompanied by the sound of certain metals, of which it is said they are rather fond. So the two new postilions did their utmost to keep to a gallop, but after efforts which did more honor to their arms than to the powers of their horses, wearied out, they fell into a trot, getting on at the rate of two and a half or three leagues an hour.

Toward seven they changed at St. Mihiel; the same hand passed through the curtains payment for the last stage, and the same voice uttered a similar injunction.

There is no doubt the strange vehicle excited there the same curiosity as at Pont-à-Mousson, for as night was fast approaching, its appearance was still more fantastic.

Beyond St. Mihiel there is a steep hill, and travelers must be satisfied to let the horses walk. It took half an hour to proceed a quarter of a league.

On the top the postilions stopped a moment to breathe their horses, and the travelers in the carriage, by withdrawing the curtains, might have gazed on a wide prospect, had not the mists of evening begun to veil it slightly.

The weather had been clear and warm until three in the afternoon—toward evening, however, it became oppressive. A great white cloud from the south seemed as if intentionally to follow the carriage, threatening to overtake it before it reached Bar-le-Duc, where the postilions resolved at all risks to pass the night.

The road, shut in between the hill and a rugged declivity, descended to a valley, in which was seen the winding Meuse, and was so steep that it was dangerous to allow the horses to do anything but walk, which prudent plan the postilions adopted. The cloud advanced, and as it brooded over and almost touched the ground, continually extended its limits by drawing the vapors arising from the soil; so was it observed in ill-boding whiteness to overwhelm the bluish clouds which seemed to take up their station to windward, like ships preparing for an engagement. Soon, with the rapidity of the flood-tide, it spread until it hid the last rays of the sun. A dim gray light struggled through upon the scene, and although no breeze swept along, the leaves shivered, and put on the dark tinge which they assume in the deepening twilight succeeding sunset.

Suddenly a flash illuminated the cloud, the heavens burst into sheets of flame, and the startled eye might penetrate the immeasurable depths of the firmament. At the same moment the thunder rolled from tree to tree, shaking the earth, and hurrying on the vast cloud like a maddened steed. On went the carriage, sending forth its smoke, now changed in color by the changes of the atmosphere.

In the meantime, the heavens grew darker and darker, but a purple light appeared from the carriage, as if the person within, careless of the storm, had lighted a lamp and went on with some work which he had to accomplish. The vehicle was now on a level part of the mountain, and when about to begin the descent, a peal of thunder more violent than the first rent the clouds, and the rain fell at first in large drops, then thick and smarting, like arrows darted from the heavens.

The postilions seemed to consult together, and then stopped.

"Well!" cried the voice which had before spoken, but now in excellent French. "What the devil are you doing?"

"We were consulting whether we should go on," replied the postilions.

"I think you ought to ask me—not one an other. On with you!"

The postilions obeyed, for there was that in the voice which forbade all thought of disobedience, and the carriage began to descend.

"Good!" said the voice, and the leather curtains, which had been half opened, fell between the traveler and the postilions.

But the road had become so slippery from the torrents of rain, that the horses stopped of themselves.

"Sir," said the leading postilion, "it is impossible to go any further."

"Why?" asked the voice within.

"Because the horses only slip—they cannot get on—they will fall."

"How far are we from the next place where we change?"

A good way, sir ; four leagues."

"Well, postilion, put silver shoes on your horses, and they will get on ; " and as he said this the stranger opened the curtain, and held out four crowns.

"Many thanks !" said the postilion, receiving them in his broad hand, and slipping them into his great boot.

"The gentleman spoke, I think," said the other postilion, who had heard the sound of money, and did not wish to be excluded from so interesting a conversation.

"Yes ; the gentleman says we must push on."

"Have you anything to say against that, my friend ?" asked the traveler, in a kind voice, but with a firmness that showed he would brook no contradiction.

"Why, as to myself, I have nothing to say ; but the horses won't stir."

"What is the use of your spurs, then ? "

"I have buried them in the sides of the poor jades, and if it has made them move a step, may Heaven——"

He had not time to finish his oath, for a frightful peal of thunder interrupted him.

"This is no weather for Christians to be out in," said the honest fellow. "See, sir, see ! the carriage is going of itself ; in five minutes it will go fast enough—Jesus Dieu ! there we go ! "

And in fact, the heavy machine, pressing on the horses, they lost their footing. It then made a progressive movement, and, according to the mathematical increase of forces, its velocity augmented till, with the rapidity of an arrow, it was visibly nearing the edge of a precipice.

It was not now only the voice of the traveler which was heard ; his head was seen thrust out of the cabriolet.

"Stupid fellow !" cried he, "will you kill us ? To the left ! the leaders to the left ! "

"Ah, monsieur, I wish from my heart I saw you on the left," replied the frightened postilion, vainly trying to recover the reins.

"Joseph !" cried a female voice, now first heard, "Joseph ! help ! help ! Oh, holy Virgin ! "

Indeed, danger so terrible and so imminent might well

call forth that ejaculation. The carriage, impelled by its own weight, neared the precipice—already one of the leaders appeared suspended over it ; three revolutions of the wheel, and horses, carriage, and postilions would all have been precipitated, crushed and mangled, to its base, when the traveler, springing from the cabriolet on the pole, seized the postilion by the collar, lifted him like a child, flung him two paces from him, leaped into the saddle, and, gathering up the reins, called to the second postilion :

"To the left, rascal, or I will blow out thy brains !"

The command acted like magic. By an extraordinary effort the postilion gave an impulse to the carriage, brought it to the middle of the road, on which it began to roll on rapidly, with a noise that contended with that of the thunder.

"Gallop !" cried the traveler, "gallop ! if you slacken your speed, I will run you through the body, and your horses, too !"

The postilion felt that this was no vain menace ; he redoubled his efforts, and the carriage descended with frightful speed. As it thus passed in the night, with its fearful noise, its flaming chimney, and its stifled cries from within, it might have been taken for some infernal chariot drawn by phantom horses and pursued by a hurricane.

But if the travelers escaped from one danger, they met another. The cloud which had hung over the valley was as rapid as the horses. From time to time, as a flash rent the darkness, the traveler raised his head, and then, by its gleam, anxiety, perhaps fear, might have been seen on his face—for dissimulation was not wanted then—God only saw him. Just as the carriage had reached level ground, and was only carried on by its own impetus, the cloud burst with an awful explosion. A violet flame, changing to green and then to white, wrapped the horses—the hind ones reared, snuffling the sulphurous air—the leaders, as if the ground had given way beneath their feet, fell flat, but almost instantly the horse upon which the postilion was mounted regained his feet, and finding his traces snapped by the shock, he carried off his rider, who disappeared in the darkness, while the carriage, after proceeding ten yards farther, was stopped by encountering the dead body of the lightning-stricken horse.

All this was accomplished by piercing shrieks from the female in the vehicle.

There was a moment of strange confusion, in which no one knew whether he was dead or living. The traveler felt himself all over to assure himself of his own identity. He was safe and sound, but the woman had fainted.

Although he suspected this from the silence which had succeeded to her shrieks, it was not to her that his first cares were directed. Scarcely had he lighted on the ground, when he hastened to the back of the vehicle.

There was the beautiful Arabian horse of which we have spoken—terrified—rigid—with every hair rising as if life were in it. He tugged violently at his fastening, shaking the door to the handle of which he was secured. His eye was fixed, the foam was on his nostrils, but after vain efforts to break away, he had remained, horror-stricken by the tempest; and, when his master whistled to him in his usual manner, and put out his hand to caress him, he bounded aside, neighing, as if he did not know him.

"Aye, always that devil of a horse," muttered a broken voice from the carriage. "Curse him, he has broken my wall!"

Then, with double emphasis, this voice cried, in Arabic: "Be still, demon!"

"Do not be angry with Djerid, master," said the traveler, loosing the horse, which he now tied to one of the hind wheels; "he has been frightened that is all; and indeed, one might well have been frightened at less."

Saying this, he opened the carriage door, let down the step, entered, and closed the door after him.

CHAPTER II.

ALTHOTAS.

THE traveler found himself face to face with an old man with gray eyes, a hooked nose, and trembling but busy hands. He was half buried in a great chair, and turned, with his right hand, the leaves of a manuscript on parchment, called "La Chiave del Gabinetto;" in his left he held a silver skimming-dish.

His attitude, his occupation, his face, motionless and deeply wrinkled, alive only, as it were, in the eyes and mouth, may seem strange to the reader, but they were certainly very familiar to the traveler; for he scarcely cast a look on the old man, nor on all that surrounded him, and yet it was worth the trouble.

Three walls—so the old man called the sides of the carriage—were covered by shelves filled with books. These walls shut in his chair, his usual and principal seat, while above the books had been planned for his convenience several articles for holding vials, decanters, and boxes set in wooden cases as earthen and glass-ware are secured at sea. He could thus reach anything without assistance, for his chair was on wheels, and with the aid of a spring he could raise it and lower it to any height necessary to attain what he wanted.

The room, for so we must call it, was eight feet long, six wide, and six high. Opposite the door was a little furnace with its shade, bellows, and tongs. At that moment there boiled in a crucible a mixture which sent out by the chimney the mysterious smoke of which we have spoken, and which excited so much surprise in old and young who saw the carriage pass.

Besides the vials, boxes, books, and papers strewed around, copper pincers were seen and pieces of charcoal which had been dipped in various liquids; there was also a large vase half full of water, and from the roof, hung by threads, were bundles of herbs, some apparently gathered the night before, others a hundred years ago. A keen odor prevailed in this laboratory which in one less strange would have been called a perfume.

As the traveler entered, the old man wheeled his chair with wonderful ease to the furnace, and was about to skim the mixture in the crucible attentively—nay, almost respectfully—but disturbed by the appearance of the other, he grumbled, drew over his ears his cap of velvet, once black, and from under which a few locks of silver hair peeped out. Then he sharply pulled from beneath one of the wheels of his chair the skirt of his long silk robe—a robe now nothing but a shapeless, colorless, ragged, covering. The old man appeared to be in a very bad humor, and grumbled as he went on with his operation.

"Afraid—the accursed animal! Afraid of what? He has shaken the wall, moved the furnace, spilled a quart of my elixir in the fire. Acharat, in Heaven's name, get rid of that brute in the first desert we come to."

"In the first place," said the other, smiling, "we shall come to no deserts; we are in France. Secondly, I should not like to leave to his fate a horse worth a thousand louis d'ors, or, rather, a horse above all price, for he is of the race of Al Borach.'

"A thousand louis d'ors! I will give you them, or what is equal to them. That horse has cost me more than a million, to say nothing of the time, the life, he has robbed me of."

"What has he done—poor Djerid?"

"What has he done? The elixir was boiling, not a drop escaping—true, neither Zoroaster nor Paracelsus says that none must escape, but Borri recommends it."

"Well, dear master, in a few moments more the elixir will boil again."

"Boil? See! there is a curse on it—the fire is going out. I know not what is falling down the chimney."

"I know what is falling," said the disciple, laughing—"water."

"Water?—water? Then the elixir is ruined : the operation must be begun again—as if I had time to lose! Heaven and earth!" cried the old man, raising his hands in despair. "Water? What kind of water, Acharat?"

"Pure water, master—rain from the sky. Have you not seen that it rained?"

"How should I see anything when I am working? Water? You see, Acharat, how this troubles my poor brain! For six months—nay, for a year—I have been asking you for a funnel for my chimney. You never think of anything—yet, what have you to do, you who are young? Thanks to your neglect, it is now the rain, now the wind, which ruins all my operations : and yet, by Jupiter! I have no time to lose. You know it—the day decreed is near ; and if I am not ready for that day—if I have not found the elixir of life—farewell to the philosopher! farewell to the wise Althotas! My hundredth year begins on the 15th of July, at eleven at night, and from this time to that my elixir must attain perfection."

"But it is going on famously, dear master."

"Yes, I have made some trials by absorption. My left arm, nearly paralyzed, has regained its power—then, only eating, as I do, once in two or three days, and taking a spoonful of my elixir, though yet imperfect, I have more time, and am assisted on by hope. Oh, when I think that I want but one plant, but one leaf of a plant, to perfect my elixir, and that we have perhaps passed by that plant a hundred—five hundred—a thousand times !— perhaps our horses have trodden it, our wheels crushed it, Acharat—that very plant of which Pliny speaks, and which no sage has yet found or discovered, for nothing is lost. But say, Acharat, you must ask its name from Lorenza in one of her trances."

"Fear not, master, I will ask her."

"Meantime," said the philosopher, with a deep sigh, " my elixir remains imperfect, and three times fifteen days will be necessary to reach the point at which I was to-day. Have a care, Acharat, your loss will be as great as mine, if I die, and my work incomplete. But what voice is that? Does the carriage move?"

"No, master : you hear thunder."

"Thunder ? "

"Yes ; we have nearly all been killed by a thunder-bolt ; but my silk coat protected me."

"Now, see to what your childish freaks expose me, Acharat ! To die by a thunder-bolt, to be stupidly killed by an electric fire that I would myself bring down from heaven, if I had time, to boil my pot—this is not only exposing me to accidents which the malice or awkwardness of men bring on us, but to those which come from heaven, and which may be easily prevented."

"Your pardon, master ; I do not understand."

"What, did I not explain to you my system of points—my paper-kite conductor? When I have found my elixir, I shall tell it you again; but now, you see, I have not time."

"And you believe one may master the thunder-bolt of heaven ? "

"Certainly ; not only master it, but conduct it where you choose ; and when I have passed my second half century, when I shall have but calmly to await a third, I shall put a steel bridle on a thunder-bolt, and guide it as easily as you do Djerid. Meantime, put a funnel on my chimney, I beg you !"

"I shall. Rest easy."

"I shall ; always the future, as if we could both look forward to the future. Oh, I shall never be understood !" cried the philosopher, writhing in his chair, and tossing his arms in despair. " ' Be calm !'—he tells me to be calm, and in three months, if I have not completed my elixir, all will be over. But so that I pass my second half century—that I recover my powers of motion—I shall meet no one who says, 'I shall do '—I shall then myself exclaim, 'I have done !'"

"Do you hope to say that ,with regard to our great work ? "

"Yes ; were I but as sure of—oh, heavens !—discovering the elixir as I am of making the diamond !"

" Then you are sure of that ? "

" It is certain, since I have already made some."

" Made some ? "

" Yes ; look ! "

" Where ? "

" On your right, in the little glass vase."

The traveler anxiously seized the little crystal cup, to the bottom and sides of which adhered an almost impalpable powder.

" Diamond dust ? " cried the young man.

" Yes, diamond dust—but in the middle of it ? "

" Yes, yes ; a brilliant of the size of a millet-seed."

" The size is nothing ; we shall attain to the union of the dust, and make the grain of millet-seed a grain of hemp-seed, aod of the grain of hemp-seed a pea. But first, my dear Acharat, put a funnel on my chimney, and a conductor on the carriage, that the rain may not descend through my chimney, and that the lightning may go and sport itself elsewhere."

" Yes, yes ; doubt it not. Be calm."

" Again, again, this eternal ' Be calm !' You make me swear.   Youth—mad youth ! presumptuous youth ! " cried the old man, with a laugh of scorn, which showed all his toothless gums, and made his eyes sink deeper in their hollow sockets.

" Master," said Acharat, " your fire is going out, your crucible cooling.   But what is in the crucible ? "

" Look into it."

The young man obeyed, uncovered the crucible, and found in it a heap of vitrified charcoal, about the size of a small seed.

" A diamond ! " cried he ; then, after a slight examination of it, " Yes, but stained, incomplete, valueless ! "

" Because the fire was put out—because there is no funnel on the chimney."

" Let me look at it again, master," said the young man, turning in his hand the diamond, which sometimes shot forth brilliant rays and sometimes was dull.   " Good ! pardon me, and take some food."

" It is unnecessary ; I took my spoonful of elixir two hours ago."

" You are mistaken, dear master ; it was at six in the morning that you took it."

" Well, and what o'clock is it now ? "

" Half-past eight in the evening."

" Heaven and earth ! another day past !—gone forever ! But the days are shorter than they were ; there are not twenty-four hours in them now."

" If you will not eat, sleep at least for some minutes."

" Well, yes, I will sleep two hours—yes, just two hours Look at your watch, and in two hours awake me."

" I promise to do so."

" Dost thou know, dear Acharat," said the old man, in a caressing tone, " when I sleep, I always fear it will be for eternity—so in two hours you will wake me. Will you not ? Promise it—swear it ! "

" I swear it, master."

" In two hours ? "

" In two hours."

Just then, something like the trampling of a horse was heard, and then a shout which indicated alarm and surprise.

" What does that mean ? " cried the traveler ; and hurriedly opening the carriage door, he leaped out.

CHAPTER III

LORENZA FELICIANI.

WE shall now inform the reader what passed outside, while the philosopher and the traveler were conversing inside the carriage.

At the noise of the thunder-bolt, which struck down two of the horses, and caused the other two to rear so frightfully, the lady in the cabriolet, as we have said, had fainted. She remained for some minutes motionless ; then, as fear alone had caused her to swoon, by slow degrees her consciousness returned.

"Ah, heaven !" she exclaimed, "abandoned here—helpless—with no human creature to take pity on me !"

"Madame," replied a timid voice, "I am here, if I can be of any service to you."

At the sound of this voice, which seemed close to her ear, the young lady rose, put her head out between the leather curtains, and found herself face to face with a young man, who was standing on the step of the cabriolet.

"It was you who spoke, sir ?" said she.

"Yes, madame," answered the young man.

"And you offered me your services ?"

"Yes."

"But first, tell me what has happened ?"

"The thunder-bolt. which fell almost on your carriage, broke the traces of the front horses, and one of them ran off with the postilion."

The lady looked uneasily around. "And he who rode the hinder horses ?" she asked.

"He has just got into the carriage, madame."

"Has he not been injured ?"

"Not in the least."

"Are you sure ?"

"He leaped from his horse, at least, like a man all safe and sound."

"Heaven be praised !" and the young lady breathed more freely.

"But who are you, sir, who are here so opportunely to offer me assistance ?"

"Madame, overtaken by the storm, I was down in that hollow, which is merely the entrance to a quarry, when all at once I heard a carriage coming with alarming speed. I at first supposed the horses had run off, but soon saw that they were managed by a powerful hand. Then the thunder-bolt fell with a tremendous explosion, and I thought for an instant that all was over with me. Indeed. on recovering, all that I have related seemed but a dream."

"Then you are not sure that the gentleman entered the carriage ?"

"Oh, yes, madame; I had quite recovered and distinctly saw him enter."

"Make yourself certain, I entreat you, that he is in the carriage."

"But how?"

"Listen—if he be there, you will hear two voices."

The young man jumped down from the step, and approached the door of the carriage.

"Yes, madame," said he, returning to her; "he is there."

The young lady, by a movement of her head, seemed to say, "It is well;" but she remained for some time as if plunged in deep reverie.

During this time the young man had leisure to examine her appearance. She was about three or four-and-twenty years of age; a brunette in complexion, but of that rich brown which is more beautiful than the most delicate tint of the rose; her fine blue eyes, raised to heaven, from which she seemed to ask counsel, shone like two stars, and her black hair, which she wore without powder, notwithstanding the fashion of the day, fell in jetty curls on her neck. All at once she roused herself, as if she had decided on her part.

"Sir," said she, "where are we now?"

"On the road from Strasbourg to Paris, madame."

"On what part of the road?"

"Two leagues from Pierrefitte."

"What is Pierrefitte?"

"A village."

"And after Pierrefitte what is the next stage?"

"Bar-le-Duc."

"Is it a town?"

"Yes, madame."

"A large one?"

"About four or five thousand inhabitants."

"Is there any cross-road by which one could get more directly to Bar-le-Duc?"

"No, madame; at least, I know of none."

"*Peccato!*" murmured she, falling back in the cabriolet.

The young man waited, expecting to be questioned further ; but as she kept silence, he moved a step or two away. This roused her, for, leaning out again, she called, hurriedly :

"Monsieur !"

The young man returned. "I am here, madame," said he, approaching her.

"One question, if you please."

"Speak, madame."

"There was a horse behind the carriage ?"

"Yes, madame."

"Is he there still ?"

"No, madame ; the person who got into the carriage untied him and fastened him to the wheel."

"Nothing, then, has injured the horse ?"

"I think not."

"He is a valuable animal, and I should like to be sure that he is safe ; but how can I reach him through this mud ?"

"I can bring the horse here," said the young man.

"Oh, yes ; do so, I pray—I shall be forever grateful to you."

The young man approached the horse, who tossed his head and neighed.

"Do not be afraid," said the female ; "he is as gentle as a lamb ; then, in a low voice, she murmured, "Djerid ! Djerid !"

The animal evidently knew the voice to be that of his mistress, for he snorted and stretched out his intelligent head toward the cabriolet. During this time the young man was untying him, but the horse no sooner felt his bridle in unpractised hands than at one bound he was free, and twenty paces from the carriage.

"Djerid," repeated the young woman, in her most caressing tones, "Djerid ! here, here !"

The Arabian tossed his head, snuffed the air, and came toward the cabriolet, pawing as if in time to some musical air.

The lady leaned out. "Come, Djerid, come !" said she.

And the obedient animal advanced toward the hand which she held out to caress him. Then, with her slender hand, she seized him by the mane, and sprang as lightly into the saddle as the goblin in the German ballads, who leaps behind unwary travelers, and holds on by their belts.

The young man hurried towards her, but she waved him off imperiously.

"Hearken!" said she; "though young, or rather, because you are young, you ought to be humane. Do not oppose my flight. I leave a man whom I love; but my religion is still dearer to me. That man will destroy my soul if I stay with him longer; he is an atheist and a necromancer. God has warned him by His thunders; may he profit by the warning. Tell him what I have said, and receive my blessing for what you have done for me—farewell."

At that word, light as a vapor, she disappeared, borne away by the aerial Djerid. The young man, seeing her flee, could not prevent a cry of astonishment escaping his lips. It was this cry which startled the traveler in the carriage.

CHAPTER IV.

GILBERT.

THE cry had, as we have said, aroused the traveler. He leaped out, shut the door carefully after him, and looked uneasily around.

The first object which he beheld was the young man standing there in alarm. The lightning, which flashed incessantly, enabled him to examine him from head to foot, a practise which seemed habitual with the traveler when any unknown person or thing met his eye. He was a youth sixteen or seventeen years old, little, thin, and muscular. His black eyes, which he fixed boldly on any object which attracted his attention, wanted mildness, but had a certain kind of beauty; his nose, small and turned up, his thin lip and projecting cheek-bones, betokened cunning and circumspection, and the strong curve of his chin announced firmness.

"Did you shout just now?" asked the traveler.

"Yes, sir."

"And why?"

"Because——" He stopped short.

"Because?" repeated the traveler.

"Sir, there was a lady in the cabriolet."

"Yes!"

And the eyes of Balsamo darted on the carriage, as if they could have penetrated its sides.

"There was a horse tied to the wheel."

"Yes; where the devil is he?"

"Sir, the lady has fled on the horse."

The traveler, without uttering a word, sprung to the cabriolet, undrew the curtains, and a flash of lightning showed him it was empty.

"Sang du Christ!" shouted he, loud almost as the thunder which pealed at that moment.

Then he looked round, as if for some means of recovering the fugitives, but soon felt that it was vain.

"To try to overtake Djerid," he muttered, "with a common horse, would be to hunt the gazelle with the tortoise; but I shall know where she is, unless——"

He felt hurriedly in the pocket of his vest, and drew from it a little case, opened it, and took out of a folded paper a curl of black hair. At the sight of it the traveler's face lost its anxious expression, and his manner became calm, at least, in appearance.

"Well," said he, wiping the perspiration from his forehead, "well and did she say nothing on leaving?"

"Oh, yes, sir!"

"What did she say?"

"That she quitted you, not through hatred, but fear; that she is a good Christian, and that you——" He hesitated.

"And that I?"

"I know not how to tell it!"

"Pardieu! tell it."

"That you are an atheist and an infidel—that God has given you a last warning by the storm—that she understood that warning, and conjures you not to be deaf to it."

A smile of contempt curled the lip of the traveler. "And this was all she said?"

"Yes, this was all."

"Well, let us speak of something else;" and all trace of disquietude passed away from the traveler's countenance.

The young man remarked all these emotions reflected on his face, with a curiosity indicating no deficiency on his side of powers of observation.

"And now," said the traveler, "what is your name, my young friend?"

"Gilbert, sir."

"Gilbert? That is merely a baptismal name."

"It is the name of our family."

"Well, my dear Gilbert, Providence has sent you to my aid."

"I shall be happy if I can oblige you, sir."

"Thank you. At your age one is obliging for the mere pleasure of the thing; but what I am going to ask is only a trifle—merely if you can direct me to a shelter for the night?"

"Why, in the first place, there is that rock under which I was sheltering just now."

"Yes," said the traveler; "but I should like something more like a house, where I could have a good supper and a good bed."

"That would be very difficult to find."

"Are we, then, so far from the next village?"

"From Pierrefitte?"

"It is called Pierrefitte, then?"

"Yes, sir; it is about a league and a half off."

"A league and a half!—let us see; surely there is some habitation nearer?"

"There is the Château of Taverney, about three hundred paces from this."

" Well, then——"

" What, sir ? " and the young man opened his eyes in astonishment.

" Why did you not say so at once ? "

" The Château of Taverney is not an hotel."

" Is it inhabited ? "

" Yes."

" By whom ? "

" Why, by the Baron de Taverney, of course."

" What is this Baron de Taverney ? "

" He is father of Mademoiselle Andrée, sir."

" Very pleasing intelligence, indeed ; but I mean what sort of a man is he ? "

" An old nobleman, sir, of sixty or sixty-five years of age ; he once was rich, they say."

" Ay, and poor now. That is the history of all those old barons. Well, show me the way to this baron's abode."

" To the Baron de Taverney's ? " he asked, in alarm.

" Then you refuse ? "

" No, sir ; but——"

" Well ? "

" He will not receive you."

" He will not receive a gentleman in need of shelter ?— Is he a bear, your baron ? "

" Dame ! " said the young man, with an expression which said plainly, " not much unlike one."

" Never mind ; I'll run the risk."

" Remember, I do not advise it."

" Bah ! " said the traveler, " bear as he is, he won't eat me."

" No ; but he may shut the door in your face."

" Then I'll break it open ; so, if you refuse to be my guide—"

" I don't refuse, sir."

" Show me the way, then."

" Willingly, sir."

The traveler leaped into the cabriolet and brought from it a little lantern. The young man hoped, as it was not lighted, that he should be obliged to open the carriage and that then its interior would be disclosed. But the traveler did nothing of the kind; he put the lantern into Gilbert's hand.

"What shall I do with it, sir?"

"It will light you on the way, whilst I lead the horses."

"But it is not lighted."

"I am going to light it."

"Oh, you have a fire in the carriage?"

"And in my pocket," replied the traveler.

"But in this rain the tinder won't kindle."

"Open the lantern," said the traveler, smiling.

Gilbert obeyed.

"Hold your hat over my hands."

Gilbert obeyed, regarding with curiosity what followed, for he knew no other means of procuring a light than with a flint and tinder.

The traveler took from his pocket a very small silver case, drew from it a match, which, he rubbed in some sort of inflammable paste, and it kindled instantly, with a slight crackling.

Gilbert started; the traveler smiled at his surprise, which was natural enough at that time, when phosphorus was only known to a few chemists, who kept the secret for their own advantage. The candle in the lantern being lighted by the match, he put up the little case. The young man followed his movements with greedy eyes; it was evident he would have given a great deal for such a treasure.

"Now that we have light, lead on."

"Follow, now, then, sir;" and Gilbert advanced, while his companion, taking the horse by the bit, dragged him after.

The weather was now not so bad; the rain had ceased, and the thunder was only heard muttering at a distance. The traveler seemed to wish for more conversation.

"You know this baron, then, my good fellow?"

"Certainly, sir; since I have lived in his house from my infancy."

"A relation?"

" No, sir."

" Your guardian ? "

" No."

" Your master ? "

The young man started, and colored with anger at the word master.

" I am not a servant, sir," said he.

" Well, but you are surely something or other ? "

" I am the son of an old tenant of the baron ; my mother nursed Mademoiselle Andrée."

" I understand ; being the young lady's foster-brother —for I presume she is young—you live at free quarters in the house."

"She is sixteen, sir."

Now, in the traveler's last words there was something like two questions, but Gilbert avoided any reply to that which concerned himself. The traveler seemed to observe this, and gave his interrogations another turn.

" How did you happen to be out during such weather ? "

" I was under a rock near the road."

" What were you doing there ? "

" I was reading."

" You were reading ? "

" Yes."

" What were you reading ? "

" ' Le Contrat Social,' by Rousseau."

"The traveler looked at the young man with surprise.

" Did you get that book in the baron's library ? "

" No, sir ; I bought it."

" Where—at Bar-le-Duc ? "

" No, sir ; from a pedler. They roam this way now and then, and bring us some tolerably good books."

" Who told you ' Le Contrat Social' was a good book ? '

" I soon found that out, as I read it."

" Have you read bad books, then, that you know the difference so well ? "

" Yes."

" What do you call bad books ? "

" Why, ' Le Sofa,' ' Tanzai ' and ' Néadarné,' and books of that description."

" But where the deuce did you get such books ? "

" In the baron's library."

" And how does the baron get new novels in this den of his ? "

" They are sent to him from Paris."

" So this poor baron spends his money on that sort of trash ? "

" No ; they are given him."

" Given him ?   By whom ? "

" By one of his friends, a great nobleman."

" A great nobleman ?   Do you know his name ? "

" The Duke de Richelieu,"

" What, the marshal ? "

" Yes, the marshal."

" I take it for granted he does not leave such books in Mademoiselle Andrée's way ? "

" Indeed, sir, he leaves them in everybody's way."

" Is Mademoiselle Andrée of your opinion," asked the traveler, with a sly smile, " that they are bad ? "

" She does not read them, sir," replied Gilbert, drily.

The traveler was silent for a minute—this character, a singular mixture of shame and boldness, of good and evil, interested him in spite of himself.

" And why did you read those books when you knew they were bad ? "

" Because I did not know when I began them."

" But you soon found it out ? "

" Yes."

" And nevertheless you went on ? "

" Yes."

" But why ? "

" They taught me things I did not know before."

" And ' Le Contrat Social ' ? "

" It teaches me things that I have guessed."

" How so ? "

" Why, that men are brothers—that societies in which

they are serfs or slaves are ill constituted—that one **day** we shall all be equal."

"Oh, ho!" said the traveler.　There was a short silence.

"So, my good fellow," continued the traveler, in a low voice, "you wish to be instructed?"

"Yes, sir; that is my most ardent wish."

"And what do you wish to learn?"

"Everything."

"For what purpose?"

"To raise myself in the world,"

"And how high would you rise?"

Gilbert hesitated.　No doubt he had his mind made up on that point; but it was evidently a secret, and he would not reveal it.

"As high as man can rise," he replied.

"Well, have you studied anything?"

"Nothing.　How can I study, not being rich, and living at Taverney?"

"Then you know nothing of mathematics?"

"No."

"Nor of natural philosophy?"

"No."

"Nor of chemistry?"

"No; I know only how to read and write; but I shall know all those things."

"When?"

"Some day or other."

"But how?"

"I don't know yet."

"Strange creature!" muttered the traveler.

"And then——" murmured Gilbert, speaking to himself.

"Well! then——?"

"Nothing."

They had now proceeded for about a quarter of an hour; the rain had ceased, and the earth sent up those odoriferous exhalations which in spring follow a great storm.

Gilbert seemed reflecting—all at once he said,

"Sir, do you know the cause of storms?"

"Certainly."

" You really do ? "

" Yes."

" You know the cause of the thunder-bolt ? "

The traveler smiled. " It is the meeting of two streams of the electric fluid—one from the clouds, the other from the earth."

Gilbert sighed. "I do not understand that," said he.

Perhaps the traveler would have explained the matter more clearly, but just then a light appeared through the trees.

" Ah! what is that ? " asked the stranger.

" It is Taverney."

" We have reached it, then ? "

" Yes ; this is the gate of the back entrance."

" Open it."

"And do you think the gate of Taverney, sir, can be opened with a push ? "

" Is it a fortified place, then ? Knock."

Gilbert approached the gate, and timidly gave one knock.

" Pardieu ! they will never hear that. Knock loudly."

Nothing, indeed, indicated that Gilbert's knock had been heard—all was silent.

" You must take the responsibility upon yourself, sir, then," said Gilbert.

" Don't be troubled about that."

Gilbert hesitated no longer—left the knocker, and pulled a string which made a bell sound so loud one might have heard it a mile off.

" Ma foi ! if your baron does not hear that," said the traveler, " he must be deaf."

" Hark ! I hear Mahon barking."

" Mahon ? That is no doubt a compliment from your baron to his friend, the Duke de Richelieu ? "

" I don't know what you mean, sir."

" Mahon was the last place taken by the marshal."

" Oh, sir, I told you I know nothing," and Gilbert sighed again.

These sighs revealed to the stranger some hidden ambition, some secret cause of pain.

A step was heard. "Here is some one at last," said the stranger.

"It is Master La Brie," said Gilbert.

The gate opened, but La Brie, taken by surprise at seeing the stranger and the carriage, when he expected no one but Gilbert, would have shut it again.

"Excuse me, my friend; but I have come here purposely, and you must not shut the door in my face."

"But, sir, I must tell the baron that an unexpected visitor——"

"Never mind I shall run the risk of his looking a little cross at me, but he shall not turn me out, I can tell you, until I have got warmed, dried, and fed. They say you have good wine in this part of the country. Do you happen to know?"

La Brie, instead of replying, was going to make further resistance, but it was in vain; the traveler pushed in, and Gilbert closed the gate after him, the two horses and carriage being in the avenue.

La Brie, seeing himself vanquished, proceeded as quickly as his old limbs would permit, toward the house, to announce his own defeat, shouting with all his strength, "Nicole Legay, Nicole Legay!"

"Who is this Nicole?" asked the stranger, calmly making his way to the house.

"Nicole Legay, sir?" replied Gilbert, with symptoms of some inward emotion.

"Yes; she whom Master La Brie is calling."

"Mademoiselle Andrée's waiting-maid, sir."

In the meantime, in answer to the calls of La Brie, a light appeared under the trees, borne by a beautiful young girl.

"What do you want, La Brie? What is all this fuss?" asked she.

"Quick, Nicole," cried the quivering voice of the old man. "run and tell the baron a strange gentleman is come to ask shelter."

Nicole did not wait to be told twice, but flew off toward the chateau so quickly that in a moment she was out of sight.

As to La Brie, having thus satisfied himself that the baron should not be taken by surprise, he stopped and took breath.

The message soon produced an effect. A sharp, commanding voice was heard from the house, repeating, with an accent by no means indicating a wish to be hospitable— " A strange gentleman ? Who is he ? People don't come in that way without sending up their names ! "

" Is it the baron himself ? " asked he who was the cause of all the disturbance.

" Oh, yes, sir," replied the poor frightened old man, " you hear what he says."

" He asks my name, I think."

" Yes. I forgot to ask it, sir."

" Say the Baron Joseph Balsamo. Our titles being the same, he will, perhaps, not be so angry."

La Brie, a little emboldened by the rank of the stranger, announced him as he requested.

" Well," grumbled the voice from the house, " since he is there, he must come in. Here, sir—this way—this way."

The stranger advanced quickly ; but just as he reached the foot of the stone steps leading up to the door, he turned to see whether Gilbert was there or not. Gilbert had disappeared.

CHAPTER V.

THE BARON DE TAVERNEY.

ALTHOUGH in some degree forewarned by Gilbert of the poverty of the Baron de Taverney, the person who had caused himself to be announced as the Baron Joseph Balsamo could not help being surprised at the miserable appearance of the abode, called by Gilbert, with emphasis, a château.

The house was built in the form of an oblong square of one story in height, with a square tower at each corner. Its irregular appearance had, however, something pleasing and picturesque, seen by the pale light of the moon, shining out from between the huge masses of the clouds left by the storm. There were six windows in the low building, and two in each tower—that is, one window in each of its stories. A broad flight of steps led up to the hall-door, but they were so broken and rugged that they seemed rather a sort of precipice than a staircase.

Such was the dwelling, on the threshold of which the stranger was received by the Baron de Taverney, in his dressing-gown, and holding a candlestick in his hand. The baron was an little old man of from sixty to sixty-five years of age, with a keen eye and a high, retreating forehead. He wore an old wig, which from frequent accidents with the candles on the mantelpiece had lost all the curls which the rats, which frequented his wardrobe, had left it. He held in his hand a napkin of very dubious whiteness, which indicated that he had been disturbed when going to sit down to supper.

In his malicious countenance, which slightly resembled that of Voltaire, two expressions struggled for mastery— politeness required a smile for his guest, but vexation returned it to a rather decided atrabilious sneer. And thus lighted as he was by the candle in his hand, the flickering of which disturbed his features, the Baron de Taverney could not well be called anything but a very ugly nobleman.

"Sir," said he, "may I know to what fortunate circumstance I owe the pleasure of seeing you?"

"Simply, sir, to the storm, which frightened my horses and caused them very nearly to destroy my carriage ; one of my postilions was thrown from his horse, the other galloped off with his, and I know not what I should have done, had I not met a young man who conducted me to your château, assuring me that your hospitality was well known."

The baron raised his light to endeavor to discover the unlucky wight who had, by this piece of information, been the cause of the unwelcome visit. Balsamo also looked around for his guide, but he had retired.

"And do you know the name of the young man who pointed out my château?" asked the Baron de Taverney, as if he wanted to return him thanks.

"Gilbert, I think, is his name."

"Ha! Gilbert. I scarcely thought him fit even for that—an idle dog—a philosopher, you must know, sir."

The threatening tone in which these epithets were uttered showed that there was little sympathy between the lord and his vassal.

"However, sir," said the baron, after a moment's silence, as expressive as his words, "will you be good enough to enter?"

"Allow me first, sir, to see after my carriage, which contains some very valuable articles."

"La Brie!" cried the baron, "La Brie! get some assistance, and put the gentleman's carriage under the shed in the yard; there are still some laths of a roof there. I can't answer for your horses, however, getting a good feed, but as they are not yours, but the postmaster's, you need not care very much."

"In truth, sir," said the traveler, beginning to get impatient, "I fear that I am giving you quite too much trouble."

"Not at all, sir—not at all—no trouble to me; but you will be rather poorly lodged, I warn you."

"Sir, I assure you I feel exceedingly grateful."

"Pray do not deceive yourself as to what we can do for you," said the baron, raising his candle so as to throw its rays in the direction where Balsamo was assisting La Brie to wheel his carriage under the shed, and elevating his voice in proportion as his guest retreated; "pray do not deceive yourself. Taverney is a dull abode, a wretched place."

The traveler was too busy to reply; he chose the best-covered part of the shed to shelter the carriage, and having pointed it out to La Brie, slipped a louis d'or into his hand. and returned to the baron.

La Brie put the louis in his pocket, supposing it only a crown, and thanking heaven for his good fortune.

"Heaven forbid I should think ill of your château as you speak of it," said Balsamo, bowing to the baron, who, as the only proof of the truth of his assertion, shook his head, and led the guest through a wide antechamber, grumbling as he proceeded :

"Oh, all very good ; but I know what I am saying—I know, unfortunately, my own means, and I assure you they are very limited. If you are a Frenchman, sir—but your German accent shows you are not, and yet your name is Italian, but that is no matter—if you are a Frenchman, I repeat the name of Taverney may recall some recollections of splendor—it was once called Taverney the rich !"

Balsamo expected a sigh at this conclusion, but there was none. "Philosophy !" thought he.

"This way, this way !" cried the baron, opening the dining-room door. "Hola ! Maître La Brie ! wait at supper now as if you were yourself a hundred footmen in one."

La Brie bustled about in obedience to this command.

"I have no servant but this, sir," said Taverney ; "he is a very bad one, but I have not the means of getting a better. The fool has been with me twenty years without getting a penny of wages. I feed him about as well as he waits on me. He is an ass, you see."

Balsamo continued to study this character. "No heart," thought he ; "yet, perhaps all this is merely affectation."

The baron shut the door of the dining-room, and then, as he held his light high above his head, the traveler saw distinctly its size and its furniture.

It was a large, low hall, which had formerly been the principal apartment of a small farmhouse, raised by its owner to the rank of a château. It was so scantily furnished, that, at the first glance, it appeared empty. Straw chairs, with carved backs, some engravings from the battle-pieces of Lebrun, framed in black varnished wood, and a large oak cupboard, dark with age and smoke, were all its ornaments. In the middle stood a little round table on which was a dish of partridges and cabbage. The wine was in a stone jar, and the plate, unpolished, worn, and battered, consisted of three covers, one tankard, and one salt-cellar—but this last article was very massive, exquisitely chased, and looked like a diamond among worthless pebbles.

"There, sir, there!" said the baron, offering a seat to his guest, whose scrutinizing look on all around did not escape him. "Oh, you are looking at my salt-cellar. You admire it. Good taste—and very polite, too, for you fix on the only thing here worth looking at. I assure you, sir, I am particularly obliged. But, no, I forget—I have one other valuable commodity—my daughter!"

"Mademoiselle Andrée?" said Balsamo.

"Faith, yes, Mademoiselle Andrée!" said the host, surprised that his guest was so well informed. "I shall present you to her. Andrée, Andrée! come hither, child—don't be afraid."

"I am not afraid, father," answered a sweet and clear voice; and a tall and beautiful girl entered the room, in a manner perfectly unembarrassed, and yet quite free from forwardness.

Joseph Balsamo, though, as we have seen, perfectly master of himself, could not prevent an involuntary bow at sight of all-powerful beauty like hers. Andrée de Taverney seemed indeed sent to adorn and brighten all around her. She had dark, auburn hair, of a rather lighter shade at her temples and neck, black eyes—clear, with dilated pupils—and a steady and majestic look like that of an eagle, yet the mildness of that look was inexpressible. Her small mouth, formed like Apollo's bow, was brilliant as coral; her tapering hands were antique in form, as were her arms, and dazzlingly fair. Her figure, flexible and firm, was like that of the statue of some pagan goddess to which a miracle had given life. Her foot might bear a comparison with that of the huntress Diana, and it seemed only by a miracle that it could support the weight of her body. Her dress was of the simplest fashion, yet suited her so well that it seemed as if one from the wardrobe of a queen would not have been so elegant or so rich.

All these details were perceived by Balsamo in the first glance, as the young lady passed from the door to the table. On his side, the baron had not lost a single impression produced on the mind of his guest by the rare union of perfections in his daughter.

"You were right," whispered Balsamo, turning to his host, "Mademoiselle Andrée is perfection."

"Do not flatter poor Andrée," said the baron, carelessly; "she has just returned home from her convent, and she will believe all you say—not that I am afraid of her coquetry—on the contrary, the dear child is not enough of a coquette, but, like a good father, I am cultivating in her that first and most important quality for a woman."

Andrée looked down and blushed; although she tried to avoid listening, she could not but overhear her father's words.

"Did they tell mademoiselle that at the convent?" asked Joseph Balsamo, laughing; "and was that precept part of the instructions of the nuns?"

"Sir," replied the baron, "I have my own way of thinking on particular subjects, as you may see."

This was so self-evident that Balsamo merely bowed in assent.

"No," continued he; "I do not imitate those fathers who say to their daughters, 'Be prudes, be rigid, be blind; think of nothing but honor, delicacy, devotion.' Fools! It is as if the fathers of the knights of old had sent those champions into the lists—after having taken off all their armor—to fight an adversary armed cap-a-pie. Pardieu! that is not the way I shall bring up my daughter Andrée, though she be brought up in this miserable den."

Although Balsamo perfectly agreed with the baron as to the propriety of this last epithet, yet he deemed it polite to contradict it.

"Oh, all very well!" resumed the old man; "but I know the place, I tell you; yet, though now so far from the sun of Versailles, my daughter shall know the world which I formerly knew so well myself; and if she enter it, it shall be with an arsenal of weapons forged by my experience and my recollections. But I must confess, sir, the convent has ruined all my plans. As if that was what I wanted, my daughter was the first boarder who really practised the precepts there taught, and followed the letter of the gospel. Corbleu! was not that being prettily served?"

"Mademoiselle is an angel!" replied Balsamo, "and in truth, sir, what you say does not surprise me."

Andrée bowed her thanks for this compliment, and sat down in obedience to a look from her father.

"Be seated, baron," said the host, "and if you are hungry, eat. What a horrible ragout that fool La Brie has given us!"

"Partridges! Do you call that horrible?" said the guest, smiling. "You slander your supper. Partridges in May! Are they from your own estates?"

"My estates? It is long since I had one. My respectable father left me some land, indeed, but it was eaten and digested long enough ago. Oh, Heaven be praised! I have not an inch of ground. That good-for-nothing Gilbert, who can only read and dream, must have stolen a gun, powder, and shot from some one or other, and he kills birds, poaching on the estates of my neighbors. He will be caught and sent to the galleys some day, and certainly I shall not interfere—it will be a good riddance; but Andrée likes game, so I am obliged to overlook Monsieur Gilbert's freaks."

Balsamo watched Andrée's lovely face, as this was said; but not a change, not the slightest blush disturbed it.

He was seated at table between her and the baron, and she helped him, without appearing in the least annoyed at the scantiness of the repast, to a portion of the dish procured by Gilbert and cooked by La Brie, and so heartily abused by the baron. During this time poor La Brie, who heard all the eulogiums passed on himself and Gilbert, handed the plates with a deprecating air, which became

quite triumphant at each word of praise the guest bestowed
on his cookery.

" He has not even salted this abominable ragout ! " cried
the baron, after he had devoured two wings of a partridge,
which his daughter had placed before him on a tempting
layer of cabbage, " Andrée, pass the salt-cellar to the
Baron Balsamo."

Andrée obeyed, extending her arm with exquisite
grace.

" Ah, you are admiring the salt-cellar again ! " said the
host.

" No, sir ; you are wrong this time," replied Balsamo ;
" I was admiring mademoiselle's hand."

" Ah ! very good, indeed—a perfect Richelieu. But
since you have the salt-cellar in your hand, examine it ;
it was made for the regent by the goldsmith Lucas. It
represents the loves of the satyrs and bacchantes—a little
free, but pretty."

Balsamo saw that the little figures so admirably executed were something worse than free, and he could not
but admire the unconsciousness with which Andrée had
offered him the salt-cellar.

But as if the baron had determined to put to the proof
that innocence which carries with it such a charm, he began
to point out in detail the beauties of his favorite piece of
plate, in spite of all Balsamo's efforts to change the
conversation.

" Come, eat, baron ! " said Taverney, " for I warn you
there is no other dish. Perhaps you are expecting the
roast and other removes ; if so, great will be your disappointment."

" Pardon me, sir," said Andrée, in her usual calm
manner ; " but if Nicole has rightly understood me, we
shall have another dish. I have given her the recipe for
one."

" The recipe ? You have given a recipe to your maid ?
The *femme de chambre* turned cook ! It only requires one
step more—turn cook yourself, I beg you ! Did the
Duchess de Chateauroux or the Marchioness de Pompadour

ever cook for the king ? On the contrary, it was he who dressed omelets for them. Jour de Dieu ! have I lived to see women cooking in my house? Baron, excuse my daughter, I beseech you."

"But, father, we must eat," said Andrée, quietly. "Well, Legay," added she in a louder tone, "is it done ?"

"Yes, mademoiselle," replied the maid, bringing in a dish of a very tempting odor.

"I know one, at least, who will not eat of that dish," said the baron, furious, and breaking his plate as he spoke.

"Perhaps *you* will eat some, sir ?" said Andrée, coldly ; then turning to her father, "You know, sir, we have now only seven plates of that set which my mother left me ;" and so saying, she proceeded to carve the smoking viands which Mlle. Legay, the pretty waiting-maid, had just placed on the table.

CHAPTER VI.

ANDREE DE TAVERNEY.

THE searching intellect of Balsamo found ample food for study in each detail of the strange and isolated life led by this family in a corner of Lorraine.

The salt-cellar alone revealed to him one phase of the baron's character, or, rather, his character in all its bearings. He called up all his penetration, therefore, as he scrutinized the features of Andrée, while she handed him that salt-cellar.

At length, whether moved by curiosity or some deeper feeling, Balsamo gazed on Andrée so fixedly, that two or three times, in less than ten minutes, the eyes of the young girl met his. At first she bore his look without confusion, but its intensity became by degrees so great that a feverish impatience, which made the blood mount to her cheeks, took possession of her. Then, feeling that this look had something supernatural in its power, she tried to brave it, and, in her turn, she gazed at the baron with her large, limpid, dilated eyes. But this time again she was obliged to yield; and, filled with the magnetic fluid which flowed in streams from his flaming orbs, her eyelids weighed down, sunk timidly, no longer to be raised but with hesitation.

While this silent struggle went on between the young girl and the mysterious traveler, the baron grumbled, laughed, and found fault, and swore like a true country gentleman, and pinched La Brie whenever he was within his reach, feeling that he must vent his spleen on some one. He was going to do the same to Nicole, when his eyes, for the first time, no doubt, rested on the hands of the young waiting-maid. The baron was an adorer of fine hands— all his youthful follies might be attributed to the power of a fine hand over him.

"Only see," cried he, "what pretty fingers this little rogue has—how the nail tapers !—it would bend over the tip—a great beauty, if washing bottles and cutting wood did not wear down the horn ; for it is horn you have at the ends of your fingers, Mademoiselle Nicole."

Not accustomed to compliments from her master, Nicole looked at him with half a smile, in which there was more astonishment than gratification.

"Yes, yes," said the baron, who saw what passed in the mind of the young flirt—"turn away—play the coquette, I beg of you ; but I must inform you, my dear guest, that Mademoiselle Nicole Legay, this young lady here present, is not a prude like her mistress, and is not at all afraid of a compliment."

Balsamo turned quickly toward the baron's daughter and saw an expression of supreme disdain on her handsome features. Then, thinking it right to adapt his expression to hers, he looked haughtily away, at which Andrée seemed pleased, and regarded him with less sternness, or, rather, with less uneasiness, than before.

"Would you think, sir," continued the baron, chucking Nicole under the chin, "would you think that this damsel had been in a convent with my daughter, and is

really what one might call educated ? Oh, Mademoiselle
Nicole would not quit her mistress for a moment. There
is a devotedness in her which would greatly delight the
philosophers who maintain that these creatures have
souls."

"Sir," said Andrée, displeased, "it is not devotedness
which prevents Nicole from leaving me; it is because I
order her to remain."

Balsamo raised his eyes to Nicole, to see the effect of
these contemptuous words, and he observed, from her
compressed lips, that she was not insensible to the humilia-
tions to which her position of domestic exposed her.
But the emotion was transitory ; for, in turning away to
hide it, her eyes rested with interest on a window of the
room which looked into the courtyard. Everything
roused the curiosity of Balsamo, and, as he followed her
eyes, he thought he saw what interested her—the face of
a man at the window. "In truth," thought he, "every
one has a mystery in this house, and I hope soon to know
Mademoiselle Andrée's. I have found out the baron's,
and I guess what Nicole's is." While thus communing
with himself, the baron observed his absence of mind.

"You are in a reverie, my dear guest," said he. "Well,
it is infectious here—it attacks every one. Let me reckon :
first, Mademoiselle de Taverney falls into reveries ; then
Mademoiselle Nicole does the same ; then the good-for-
nothing fellow who shot the partridges is in a perpetual
reverie, and very likely the partridges were in a reverie,
when he shot them."

"Gilbert ?" asked Balsamo.

"Yes. Oh, a philosopher, like Monsieur La Brie here.
But excuse me ! perhaps you are a friend of theirs ? If
so, I warn you you will be none of mine."

"No, sir ; I am neither for them nor against them,"
replied Balsamo. "I know nothing of them."

"Ventrebleu ! so much the better. They are wretches
as mischievous as they are ugly—the monarchy will be
ruined by their opinions ; no one laughs now ; they read
—they read—and what, I pray you ? Sentiments like

this : Under a monarchical government it is difficult for a people to be virtuous. Or this : Monarchy is an institution invented for the corruption of the morals of men, and the purpose of enslaving them. Or else this : If the power of kings comes from God, it comes as diseases and other scourges of the human race come from Him. You call that improving, I hope ! A virtuous people ! Now, I ask you, of what use would they be ? Everything has gone wrong since the king spoke to Voltaire, and read ' Diderot ' ? "

At this moment Balsamo thought he saw the pale face which he had seen before, again appear at the window ; but it vanished when he looked in that direction.

" Is mademoiselle a philosopher ? " asked Balsamo, turning to Andrée, with a smile.

" I don't even know what philosophy is," replied Andrée. " I like what is serious."

" Ha ! mademoiselle ! " cried the baron, " then, in my opinion, nothing is more serious than good living—like that, I pray you."

" But mademoiselle does not hate life, I presume ? " said Balsamo.

" That depends on circumstances," replied Andrée.

" What a stupid phrase ! " exclaimed the baron. " Would you believe it, sir, my son once made me, word for word, a similar reply ? "

" You have a son, then, sir ? "

" Oh, mon Dieu ! sir, yes. I have that misfortune. The Chevalier de Taverney, lieutenant in the body-guard of the Dauphin—a most excellent young man ! " And the baron uttered these four words as if he would have crushed each letter in them.

" I congratulate you, sir," said Balsamo, with a bow.

" Oh, yes ; another philosopher, sir. Upon the honor of a gentleman, it is sickening ! Did he not speak to me the other day about giving the negroes their freedom ? ' And what about sugar ? ' asked I, ' for I like my coffee very sweet, and so does Louis XV.' ' Sir,' replied he, ' is it not better to go without sugar than to make a whole race suffer ?' 'A race of monkeys,' said I, and I think it was saying a great deal in their praise. Well, what do you think he said next ? Ma foi! there must be something in the air to turn people's heads! He replied to me, 'that all men were brothers!' I the brother of a Hottentot!"

"Oh, that was going rather far!"

"Hey! what do you think of that ? I am in great luck with my two children, am I not ? No one will say that I shall be truly represented in my descendants. The sister is an angel—the brother an apostle! Drink, sir, drink. The wine is detestable!"

"I think it exquisite," said Balsamo, still looking at Andrée.

"Then you *are* a philosopher. Take care or I shall order my daughter to preach you a sermon. But no; philosophers have no religion. Still, religion was a very convenient thing—one believed in God and the king, and all was settled. Now people believe in neither one nor the other—they must know so much—read so much. I prefer never doubting. In my time, our only study was to amuse ourselves—to play at faro and dice, and to fence; we ruined duchesses, and were ruined by opera dancers—that was my history to a tittle. The whole of Taverney went to the opera. It is the only thing I regret, for a ruined man is not worth the name of man. You think me old, don't you ? Well, it is because I am ruined, and live in this den; because my wig is shabby, and my coat a relic of antiquity. But look at my friend the marshal, with his coats of the newest cut, and his well-curled wig, and his ten thousand a year. He looks young, fresh, and gay, and yet he is ten years older than I, sir—ten years, I assure you!"

"You speak of Monsieur de Richelieu ?"

"Yes, the same."

"The duke ?"

"Why, faith, not the cardinal, I think—I do not go quite so far back. Besides, the cardinal never did what his nephew did ; he did not last so long."

"I am surprised that, with such powerful friends at court, you should have left it."

"Oh, a temporary retreat! I shall return to it some day or other;" and the old baron cast a singular look on his daughter.   Balsamo did not allow it to pass unnoticed.

"But," said he, "the marshal might at least advance your son?"

"My son!   He hates him."

"Hates the son of his friend?"

"He is quite right."

"And do *you* say so, sir?"

"Pardieu!   I tell you he is a philosopher—he abhors him!"

"And Philip returns him the compliment," said Andrée, with perfect calmness.   "Remove these things, Legay."

The young girl, roused from her fixed contemplation of the window, hastened to obey.

"Ah," said the baron, sighing, "one used to sit after supper till two in the morning; we had what was fit to eat then, and when the eating was over, we drank.   But how drink this stuff when we are not occupied in eating? Legay, bring a flask of Maraschino, if there be one.

"Do so," said Andrée, for the maid seemed to wait for her orders before obeying those of the baron.

The baron threw himself back in his chair, shut his eyes, and sighed with a grotesque sort of melancholy.

"You were speaking of the Marshal de Richelieu," said Balsamo, who appeared not inclined to let the conversation drop.

"Yes," said Taverney, "I was speaking of him;" and he hummed an air as melancholy as his sighs.

"If he hate your son, and if he be right to hate him because he is a philosopher, he must retain all his friendship for you, since you are not one."

"Philosopher! no, heaven be praised!"

"You must surely have claims on the administration? You have served the king?"

" Fifteen years.   I was the marshal's aide-de-camp—we served together in the campaign of Mahon.   Our friendship is of long standing—let me see : it began at the siege of Philipsbourg—that was in the year 1742 or '43."

" So," said Balsamo, " you were at the siege of Philipsbourg ?   I was there myself."

The old man sat upright in his chair, and stared at the stranger.

" Excuse me ; but what is your age, my respected guest? "

" Oh, I am not old," said Balsamo, holding out his glass to be filled with Maraschino by the fair hand of Andrée.

The baron interpreted the stranger's answer in his own way, and concluded that Balsamo had some reason for concealing his age.

" Sir," said he, " allow me to say that you do not appear to be old enough to have served at Philipsbourg—that siege took place twenty-eight years ago, and you seem to be about thirty."

" Oh, anybody might be taken for thirty."

" Pardieu, then, I wish I could ; it's just thirty years since I was that age."

Mlle. Andrée gazed with increasing and irresistible curiosity on the stranger, for every word revealed him in a new light.

" You astonish me, sir," said the baron.   " Unless you are all this time mistaken in the name, and are thinking of some other town than Philipsbourg.   I should say you were not more than thirty ; would not you, Andrée, say the same ? "

" Yes, indeed," replied she, trying to bear the powerful eye of their guest, but this time again in vain.

" No, no," said the latter ; " I mean what I say—I mean the famous siege of Philipsbourg, at which the Duke de Richelieu killed his cousin, the Prince de Lixen, in a duel.   The affair took place as they were returning from the trenches, on the high-road ; he ran his sword right through his body.   I passed just as he expired in the arms of the Prince de Deux Buts : he was seated against the side of a ditch when Richelieu was coolly wiping his sword."

"On my honor, you amaze me, sir!" said the baron. "It occurred precisely as you say."

"You have heard the affair described?" asked Balsamo, coolly.

"I was there. I had the honor of being second to the marshal; he was not marshal then, but that is no matter."

"Let me think," said Balsamo, turning and gazing firmly on him. "Were you not then a captain?"

"Precisely."

"You were in the queen's regiment of light horse, which was cut to pieces at Fontenoy?"

Perhaps you were at Fontenoy, too?" asked the baron, endeavoring to jest.

"No," replied Balsamo; "I was dead at that time."

The baron stared—Andrée started—Nicole crossed herself.

"But to return to what we were saying. You wore the uniform of the light horse, I remember perfectly, at that time; I saw you as I passed; you were holding your own and the marshal's horse while they fought. I went up to you and asked you about the duel—you gave me the details."

"I?"

"Yes, you, pardieu! I recognize you now; you bore the title of chevalier—they called you *the little chevalier*."

"Mordieu!" cried the baron, all amazed.

"Excuse me that I did not sooner recognize you; but thirty years change a man. Let us drink the marshal's health, my dear baron."

He raised his glass, and drained it to the last drop.

"You saw me there?" cried the baron. "Impossible!"

"I saw you," said Balsamo.

"On the high-road?"

"On the high-road."

"Holding the horses?"

"Holding the horses."

"While the duel was going on?"

"As the prince was expiring, I said."

"Then you are fifty?"

"I am old enough to have seen what I tell you."

The baron threw himself back in his chair, but in so ridiculous a pet that Nicole could not help laughing. Andrée, instead of laughing, seemed to be in a reverie, her eyes open, and fixed on those of Balsamo. He appeared now to have attained his object. Suddenly rising, he sent from his flaming eyeball two or three lightning flashes full on her. She started, as if from an electric shock. Her arms stiffened, her neck bent, she smiled, yet as if involuntarily on the stranger, then closed her eyes.

"Do you also, mademoiselle, believe I speak falsely when I say that I was present at the siege of Philipsbourg?"

"No, sir, I believe you," she articulated, making a violent effort.

"Then it is I who am only a dotard," said the baron; "the gentleman no doubt has come back from the other world."

Nicole gazed on him with horror.

"Who knows?" replied Balsamo, in so solemn a tone that he was yet more horrified.

"Well, then, baron," resumed the old man, "to have done with jesting, are you really more than thirty? You do not look more."

"Sir," said Balsamo, "would you believe me if I told you a very incredible thing?"

"I do not promise that," said the baron, looking knowing, while Andrée listened with eager attention. "I am very incredulous, I must candidly warn you."

"What use is there, then, in putting a question, when you will not listen to my reply?"

"Well, I will believe you. There! are you satisfied?"

"Then, sir, I have only to repeat what I have told you, and to add that I knew you personally at the siege of Philipsbourg."

"Then you must have been a child?"

"Undoubtedly."

" Four or five years old at most ? "

" No ; I was forty-one."

The baron burst into a loud fit of laughter, which Nicole re-echoed.

" I told you you would not believe me," said Balsamo, gravely.

" But how is it possible to believe that ? at least, give me some proofs."

" That is easy. I was forty-one then, but I do not say that I was the man I am."

" Oh," cried the baron, " this is going back to paganism. Was there not a philosopher—for those wretches flourished in every century—was there not a Greek philosopher who would not eat beans because he pretended they had had souls, as my son says negroes have—who was he ? what the deuce was his name ? "

" Pythagoras," said Andrée.

" Yes, Pythagoras ; the Jesuits taught me that. Father Porée made me compose Latin verses on it, with little Arouet. I remember they thought mine much the best. Pythagoras ?—yes."

" Well, how do you know that I am not Pythagoras ? " replied Balsamo, quietly.

" I do not deny that you may be Pythagoras, but Pythagoras was not at the siege of Philipsbourg—at least, I did not see him there."

" No ; but you saw the Viscount Jean des Barreaux, who was in the Black Musketeers."

" Yes, I knew him well ; but he was no philosopher, although he did hate beans, and never eat them when he could help it."

" Well, do you recollect the day after the duel, Des Barreaux was in the trenches with you ? "

" Yes, perfectly well."

" For you know the Black Musketeers and the light horse always mounted guard together every seven days."

" True enough. What next ? "

" That very evening the grape-shot fell like hail, and

Des Barreaux was dull ; he asked you for a pinch of snuff, and you offered him your gold box."

"On which was the likeness of a female ? "

"Exactly. I see her now. She was fair, was she not ? "

"Mordieu ! " cried the baron, terrified, "you are right. Well, then ? "

"Well, then," continued Balsamo, "as he was taking that pinch of snuff, a ball carried off his head ; just in the same way that Marshal Berwick's was carried away formerly."

"Alas ! yes. I remember," said the baron. "Poor Des Barreaux ! "

"And now, sir, you see I must have seen and known you at the siege of Philipsbourg, since I was that very Des Barreaux."

The baron fell back once more in his chair, almost stupefied at these words, but recovering, he cried :

"Why, this is sorcery—magic ! A hundred years ago you would have been burned, my dear guest. Upon my honor, I think I can smell a sort of corpse-like odor ! "

"Sir," said Balsamo, "no true sorcerer or magician has ever yet been burned ; it is fools who have anything to do with the fagot. But a truce to this conversation, Mademoiselle de Taverney is asleep ; it seems that metaphysics and the occult sciences have few attractions for her."

In fact, Andrée, overcome by an unknown, irresistible power, felt her head sink on her breast, like a flower whose cups bends under its weight of dew.

At the last words of Balsamo, she made an effort to shake off the influence, that, like a subtle fluid, stole upon her. She shook her head, arose, seemed about to fall, but, supported by Nicole, left the dining-room. At the same moment, the face which had been looking in at the window, and which Balsamo had long ago recognized as Gilbert's, also disappeared. An instant after, he heard Andrée begin to play with vigor on her harpsichord. He had followed her with his eye as she left the room, and could not help exclaiming triumphantly, as she disappeared : "I may say, like Archimedes, *Eureka !* "

"Archimedes! Who was he?" asked the baron.

"A good sort of a fellow—a savant whom I knew two thousand one hundred and fifty years ago," said Balsamo.

CHAPTER VII.

EUREKA!

WHETHER this piece of extravagance was too much for the baron, whether he had not heard it, or whether, having heard it, he thought it best to get rid of this strange guest, we know not; but he made no reply to it; but when the sound of Andrée's harpsichord proved that she was engaged in the next apartment, he offered to procure Balsamo the means of proceeding to the nearest town.

"I have an old horse who, though on his last legs, will carry you so far, and you would at least procure good lodgings; there is, indeed, a room and a bed at Taverney. But my ideas of hospitality are rather peculiar—" *Good or none*" is my motto."

"Then you wish to send me away," said Balsamo, hiding his vexation under a smile. "That is treating me like an intruder."

"No, indeed; it is treating you like a friend, my dear guest; lodging you here would be really treating you as an enemy. I say this in all conscience, but with great regret, for I am delighted with your society."

"Then, pray, do not force me to rise when I am tired—to get on horseback when I would rather stretch my limbs in bed. Do not represent your hospitable resources as worse than they are, if you would not have me believe that I have been so unfortunate as to incur your dislike."

"Oh," said the baron, "since you view the matter in that light, you shall stay."

Then, looking round for La Brie, who was in a corner, he cried: "Come hither, you old rascal!" La Brie advanced a few steps, timidly. "Ventrebleu! come hither,

I say. Is the red room fit to accommodate a gentleman, think you ? "

"Oh, certainly, sir," replied the old servant; "you know it is occupied by Monsieur Philip, when he comes to Taverney."

"It may do very well for a poor devil of a lieutenant who comes to pass a month with a ruined father, and at the same time very unfit for a rich nobleman who travels post with four horses."

"I assure you," said Balsamo, "I shall be perfectly content with it."

The baron grinned, as if he would have said, "I know better;" then he added, aloud, "La Brie, show the stranger to the red room, since he is determined to be cured of all wish to return to Taverney. Well, you have decided to stay, I suppose?" said he, turning to Balsamo.

"Yes; if you permit it."

"Stay; there are still other means."

"Means for what?"

"To avoid having to make the journey on horseback."

"What journey?"

"To Bar-le-Duc."

Balsamo waited quietly to hear this new plan developed.

"You were brought here by post-horses, were you not?"

"Yes; unless Satan brought me."

"I at first almost suspected he did, for you do not seem to be on bad terms with him."

"You do me infinitely more honor than I deserve."

"Well, the horses that brought your carriage could not take it away?"

"No; there are only two horses left of the four, and the carriage is heavy. Besides, post-horses must rest."

"Ha! another reason. You are determined, I see, to remain."

"Because I wish to see you again to-morrow, and express my gratitude to you for your hospitality."

"That you could easily repay."

"How?"

"Since you are on such good terms with his satanic

majesty, beg him to permit me to discover the philosopher's stone."

" Why, Monsieur le Baron, if you really wish for it——"

" The philosopher's stone ? Parbleu ! if I really wish for it !"

" In that case, you must apply to another individual than the devil."

" To whom, then ? "

" To ME ! as I heard Corneille say about a hundred years ago, when he was reciting to me a part of one of his comedies."

" Ha ! La Brie, you old rascal !" cried the baron, who began to find the conversation rather dangerous at such an hour, and with such a man, " try and find a wax-candle and light the gentleman to his room."

La Brie hastened to obey, and during this search, almost as dubious in its result as that for the philosopher's stone, he desired Nicole to precede him up-stairs and air the bedroom. Nicole being gone, Andrée was delighted to find herself alone. She felt as if she required to reflect. The baron bid Balsamo good-night, and retired to bed.

Balsamo looked at his watch, for he remembered the promise he had made to Althotas—a promise now impossible to fulfil, the two hours having expired. He asked La Brie if the carriage was still in the place he had pointed out. La Brie replied that unless it would move away of itself, it must be there. He then asked what had become of Gilbert. La Brie assured him that the lazy fellow was no doubt in bed two hours ago. Then, after having studied the topography of the passage which led to the red room, Balsamo went out to waken Althotas.

The Baron de Taverney had not spoken falsely respecting the discomfort of this apartment; it was as poorly furnished as all the other rooms of the château.

An oaken bed with a faded green damask coverlet, and hangings of the same material looped up above it. An oaken table with twisted legs, a huge stone chimney-piece of the time of Louis XIII., to which in winter a fire might impart some appearance of comfort, but which now, wanting that, wanting all ornaments and utensils, wanting wood, and stuffed with old newspapers, only made the place look still more dreary. Such was the apartment of which Balsamo was for one night to be the fortunate possessor.

We must add that there were two chairs and a wardrobe painted of a gray color.

Whilst La Brie was endeavoring to give a habitable appearance to the room which Nicole had aired before retiring to her own apartment, Balsamo had wakened Althotas and returned to the house. When he reached Andrée's door he stopped to listen. From the moment Andrée left the dining-room she felt that she had escaped from the mysterious influence which the stranger exercised over her, and to rouse herself completely from its power, she continued to play on her harpsichord. Its sound reached Balsamo through the closed door, and, as we have said, he stopped to listen.

After a minute or two he made several gestures with a sweeping circular motion which might have been mistaken for a species of conjuration, since Andrée, struck again by the same sensation she had previously experienced, ceased to play, let her arms fall immovable by her side, and turned toward the door with a slow, stiff motion, as if she were obeying a command against her own free will. Balsamo smiled in the dark, as if he saw through the door. No doubt this was all he wanted, for he stretched out his left hand, and having found the balustrade of the staircase, which was deep and broad, he ascended to the red room. In proportion as he increased his distance, Andrée, with the same slow, rigid motion, returned to her harpsichord, and when Balsamo reached the highest stair he heard her resume the first notes of the air which he had interrupted,

Having entered his chamber, he dismissed La Brie. La Brie was evidently a good servant, accustomed to obey on the instant, but now, after moving a few steps toward the door, he stopped.

"Well ?" said Balsamo.

La Brie slipped his hand into his waistcoat-pocket and seemed feeling for something in its silent depths, but he did not reply.

"Have you anything to say to me, my friend?" inquired Balsamo, approaching him.

La Brie made a great effort over himself, and pulled his hand out of his pocket.

"I merely wished to say, sir, that you made a mistake this evening."

"Did I?" said Balsamo. "How so?"

"You meant to give me a crown, and you gave me a louis d'or;" and he opened his hand and disclosed to view the new shining piece.

Balsamo looked at the old servant with an expression of admiration which indicated he had not the highest opinon of men as far as probity was concerned.

"'*And honest?*'" said he, "as Hamlet says;" and, feeling in his own pocket, he drew out a second louis d'or, which he laid beside the first in La Brie's hand.

La Brie's joy at this munificence could not be described; for twenty years he had not once seen gold, and in order to convince him that he was really the happy possessor of such a treasure, Balsamo had to put the money with his own hand into La Brie's pocket. He bowed to the ground, and was retiring without turning his back on the stranger, when the latter stopped him. "At what hour does the family usually rise in the morning?" asked he.

"Monsieur de Taverney rises late, but Mademoiselle de Taverney is always up at a very early hour."

"At what hour?"

"About six o'clock."

"Who sleeps above this room?"

"I do, sir."

"And below?"

"No one; the vestibule is under this."

"Thank you, my friend. Now you may go."

"Good night, sir."

"Good night; but, by the bye, see that my carriage be all safe."

"You may depend on me, sir."

"If you hear any noise, or see any light, do not be alarmed. I have an old lame servant in it, who travels with me everywhere. Tell Monsieur Gilbert not to interfere with him, and tell him also, if you please, not to go out to-morrow morning until I have spoken to him. Can you remember all this?"

"Oh, certainly; but are you going to leave us so soon, sir?"

"I am not quite sure," said Balsamo, with a smile; "yet, strictly speaking, I ought to be at Bar-le-Duc to-morrow evening."

La Brie sighed resignedly, gave a last glance at the bed, and taking up the candle, went toward the fireplace to give a little warmth to the great damp room by setting fire to the papers, as he had no wood.

"No, never mind," said Balsamo, preventing him; "leave the old papers. If I do not sleep, I can amuse myself by reading them."

La Brie bowed and retired.

Balsamo listened until the steps of the old servant had died away on the stairs, and until he heard them overhead. Then he went to the window. In the opposite tower there was a light in the window of a garret, the curtains of which were but half closed. It was Legay's room. She was thoughtfully unfastening her gown and handkerchief, and from time to time she opened her window and leaned out to see into the courtyard. Balsamo looked at her with more attention than he had chosen to bestow on her during supper.

"What a singular resemblance!" he murmured to himself. At this moment the light in the garret was extinguished, although its occupant was not yet in bed.

Balsamo leaned against the wall, listening anxiously. The notes of the harpsichord still sounded in his ears. He assured himself that its harmony alone awoke the midnight silence around; then opening the door which La Brie had shut, he cautiously descended the stairs, and gently pushed opened the door of the saloon.

Andrée heard nothing ; her white hands continued to wander over the old yellow keys of the instrument. Opposite her was a mirror set in an old carved frame, the gilding of which had changed to a dull gray. The air she played was melancholy, or, rather, she played merely harmonies instead of an air. No doubt it was all extempore ; and she was thus reproducing in music her early recollections, or indulging in the dreams of her imagination. Perhaps her spirit, saddened by her residence at Taverney, had left the château to wander in the large shady gardens of the convent of the Annonciades at Nancy, ringing with the merry voices of troops of happy boarders. Whether such were her dreams or not, her vague gaze seemed to lose itself in the somber mirror before her, which reflected only indistinctly the different objects in the vast apartment, dimly lighted by the single candle placed on the harpsichord.

Sometimes she suddenly ceased. It was when she recalled the strange vision of the evening, and her unaccountable impressions, but before her thoughts had time to take any precise form, her heart beat, she felt a thrill run through her limbs, and she started as though a living being had come into contact with her. All at once, as she tried to account for these feelings, they returned. She felt a thrill as if from an electric shock. Her eye became fixed, her floating thoughts became embodied, as it were, and she perceived something move over the dim mirror.

The door of the saloon had opened noiselessly, and in the doorway a shadow appeared. She shuddered ; her fingers wandered involuntarily over the keys ; yet nothing could be more easily accounted for than the appearance of the figure. Might it not be her father, or Nicole, or La Brie, who, before retiring, had returned to the apartment upon some household errand ? La Brie's visits of that kind were frequent ; and on these occasions, the faithful creature never made a sound. But, no ; the eyes of her soul showed her that the being whom she did not see was none of those we have named.

The shadow drew nearer, becoming more distinct in the

mirror; and when within the circle of the light afforded by the candle the stranger was seen, his dress of black velvet increasing the ghastly pallor of his face; he had for some mysterious reason laid aside the silk one which he wore at supper.*

She would have turned and screamed, but Balsamo extended his arms, and she remained motionless. She made another effort. "Sir," said she, "in the name of Heaven, what do you want?"

He smiled—the glass reflected his smile, and she watched it with eager gaze, but he did not reply.

She tried once more to rise, but could not. An irresistible power, a paralyzing feeling, which was not without a pleasurable sensation attending it, fixed her to her chair, while her eye never left the magic mirror. This new sensation alarmed her, for she felt that she was altogether in the power of the unknown. She made another almost supernatural effort to call for aid, but Balsamo extended both his hands above her head, and no sound escaped her lips. She continued dumb, her bosom loaded with a stupefying heat which ascended slowly in invading billows to her brain. She had no longer strength or will—her head sank on her shoulder.

At this moment Balsamo thought he heard a slight noise; he turned, the face of the man he had seen before was at the window. He frowned, and, strange to say, the frown was reflected on the young girl's face.

Then, turning again to Andrée, he drew down his hands, which he had hitherto held above her head, then he raised them again gently, again drew them down, and continued thus to overwhelm her with column upon column of the electric fluid.

"Sleep!" said he.

She still struggled against his power.

"Sleep!" he repeated, in a voice of command. "Sleep; it is my will!"

* It is well known that silk is a bad conductor, and repels the electric fluid. It is almost impossible to magnetize a person who wears a dress of silk.

Then all her faculties yielded to that all-powerful will; she leaned her elbow on the harpsichord, dropped her head on her hand, and slept.

Balsamo now, without turning his face from her, left the room, closed the door, and went up to his own chamber. Scarcely had he retired when the face once more appeared at the window. It was Gilbert's.

CHAPTER VIII.

ATTRACTION.

GILBERT, whose menial position in the Château de Taverney caused him to be excluded from the saloon, watched all evening those whose rank permitted them that privilege. During supper he saw Balsamo's looks and gestures. He remarked Andrée's attention to him, the baron's unusual affability, and the respectful eagerness of La Brie.

When the party rose from table, he hid in a clump of shrubs, lest Nicole, in closing the shutters, or in going to her own room, might see him, and put an end to his espionage. Nicole had, indeed, made her round to secure all for the night, but one of the shutters of the saloon she was forced to leave open, the half-unfixed hinge of which would not permit it to close. Gilbert knew that such was the case, so he remained out certain that he could continue his watchings when Legay was gone.

His watchings, have we said? What reason had Gilbert to watch? Having been brought up at Taverney, did he not know it perfectly, as well as the habits of the family? The reason was, that on that evening he had other motives than those which usually actuated him; he not only watched, but waited.

When Nicole quitted the saloon, leaving Andrée there, after having slowly closed the doors and shutters, she walked for a few minutes up and down in front of the house, as if she expected some one. Then she looked furtively on all sides, peeped into the saloon, waited a little longer, and at length made up her mind to go to bed.

Gilbert, motionless, bending down close to the trunk of a tree, and scarcely venturing to breathe, saw every movement and gesture of Nicole; and, when she had disappeared, and when he saw a light in the windows of her apartment, he stole again on tiptoe to the window, leaned forward, and continued, although scarcely knowing why, with eager eyes, to devour Andrée, who was sitting at her harpsichord in a listless attitude.

Just then Joseph Balsamo entered the saloon. Gilbert started, and every faculty was strained to enable him to comprehend the scene which we have just described. He thought that Balsamo complimented Andrée on her musical talent, that she replied with her usual coldness, that, with a smile, he repeated his praise, and that then she stopped to reply, and to dismiss him for the night. He admired the grace with which the stranger retired backward, but he had in reality understood nothing of the scene, as it had all pass d in silence. He had heard no words, he had seen the lips and hands of the pair before him move, and, close observer as he was, he discovered no mystery in what appeared to pass so naturally.

Balsamo gone, Gilbert remained no longer in an attitude of observation, but apparently lost in observation of Andrée, so beautiful in her careless attitude; but soon, to his amazement, he discovered that she was asleep. He remained for some moments longer in the same position, to be certain that such was the case; then, when he was quite convinced, he clasped his forehead with both hands, like one who feared for his senses in the flood of thoughts and sensations which poured on his brain. " Oh," said he, wildly, " her hand! that my lips might only touch her hand! Gilbert, Gilbert, rouse thee. I WILL do it!"

As he spoke, he rushed into the anteroom, and reached the door of the saloon, which, as when Balsamo entered, opened without noise. But scarcely was it open, scarcely did he find the young girl before him without anything separating them, than he felt all the importance of the step he had taken. He, the son of a farmer and a peasant woman—he, the timid young man, who, in his lowness dared hardly raise his eyes to his haughty mistress—he was going to press to his lips the hem of the robe or the tip of the finger of this sleeping majesty, who, if she awoke, would, with a look, crush him to the dust. At this idea all that had intoxicated him and made him bold vanished: he stopped, and clung to the doorpost, for he trembled and felt as if he should fall.

But Andrée's meditation or sleep (for Gilbert could not yet decide whether she slept or was only buried in thought) was so deep that he in no way disturbed her, yet one might have heard the beating of his heart which he tried in vain to still. He remained a minute gazing on her—she stirred not ; she was so beautiful with her head gently bent forward on her hand, her long, unpowdered hair falling on her shoulders, that the flame which fear for a moment had extinguished rekindled. His madness returned ; he must at least touch something touched by her ; he made a step toward her. The floor creaked under his unsteady footstep, a cold moisture stood on his forehead—but she seemed to have heard nothing.

"She sleeps !" he murmured. "Oh, joy ! she sleeps !"

But before he advanced three steps farther, he stopped again ; it was the unusual brightness of the candle which alarmed him now, for it had burned down in the socket, and gave, as is usual, a larger flame just before it expired. But not a sound, not a breath in the house. La Brie had retired to bed, and no doubt to sleep, and the light in Nicole's chamber was extinguished.

"Courag !" said he, and he advanced anew. Strange —the floor creaked again, but Andrée stirred not, and Gilbert himself could scarcely avoid being frightened by this mysterious repose.

"She sleeps !" repeated he again, with that varying resolution peculiar to the lover and the coward—and he who is not master of his heart is always a coward. "She sleeps ! Oh, heaven ! oh, heaven !"

In the midst of all these feverish altercations of fear and hope, he still advanced, and at last found himself within two paces of Andrée. Then he felt as if fascinated; he would have fled, were flight possible; but once within the circle of attraction, of which she was the center, he felt himself rooted to the spot, and, conquered, subdued, he fell on both his knees.

Andrée remained motionless as a statue. Gilbert took the hem of her dress in both hands, and kissed it; then he looked up slowly, breathlessly—his eyes met hers, which were wide open, yet she saw him not.

Gilbert no longer knew what to think; he was overwhelmed with astonishment. For a moment the horrible idea that she was dead flashed across his mind; he seized her hand, it was warm, and the pulse beat softly; but this hand remained unresisting in his. Then, bewildered by having touched it, he imagined that she saw, that she felt, that she had discovered his maddening passion—poor, blinded heart!—that she expected his visit, that her silence indicated consent, her immovability favor. He raised her hand to his lips, and imprinted on it a long and burning kiss. Immediately a shudder ran through her frame, and Gilbert felt that she repelled him.

"I am lost," he murmured, relinquishing her hand, and throwing himself upon the floor.

Andrée rose as if moved by a spring, and not once casting her eyes to the floor, on which Gilbert lay, overcome by shame and fear, without even strength to ask a pardon, which he knew would not be granted—her head erect, her neck rigid, and with a painful and constrained step, she moved toward the door. She passed on like one drawn by a secret spell to some unseen goal, and in passing she touched Gilbert's shoulder. He raised himself on one hand, turned slowly, and followed her with eyes full of amazement. She opened the door, passed into the anteroom, and reached the foot of the stairs. Pale and trembling, Gilbert dragged himself after her on his knees.

"Oh," thought he, "she is so indignant that she would not herself deign to show her anger. She is going to the baron to relate my shameful infatuation, and I shall be turned out like a disgraced lackey!"

The thought that he should be dismissed—that he should no longer see her who was his light, his life, his soul, gave him courage; he arose and hurried after her. "Oh, pardon, mademoiselle—in the name of heaven, pardon!" murmured he.

Andrée appeared not to have heard him, passed on, but did not enter her father's apartment. Gilbert breathed more freely. She advanced toward the staircase, and began to ascend.

"Great Heaven!" murmured he, "where can she be going! That is the way to the red room which the stranger occupies, and to La Brie's loft. It may be to call him—yet she would ring—she must be going—oh impossible, impossible!" and he wrung his hands with rage at the thought that she was going into Balsamo's apartment.

She stopped before the door. A cold perspiration trickled down Gilbert's forehead; he grasped the iron of the balustrade that he might not fall, for he had continued to follow her—and all that he saw and all that he fancied filled him with horror.

Balsamo's door was half open. Andrée did not knock, but pushed it wider, and entered the room. The light within fell on her noble features, and was reflected with a golden luster from her large open eyes. Gilbert could see the stranger standing in the middle of the chamber with his eyes fixed, his brow contracted, and one hand extended with a commanding gesture.

This was all—the door was shut again.

Gilbert felt his strength abandon him. He put his hand to his head, and fell heavily on the cold stone of the upper step of the stairs, but with his eyes turned on the accursed door, which entombed his past dreams, his present happiness, his future hopes.

CHAPTER X.

CLAIRVOYANCE.

BALSAMO advanced to meet the young lady, who moved toward him in a direct line, rigid in her movement as the bronze statue of Don Juan. However strange her coming might seem to any other than Balsamo, he appeared in no degree surprised at it.

"I commanded you to sleep," said he. "Do you sleep?"

She sighed, but did not answer. Balsamo drew nearer her, imparting to her still more of the electric fluid.

"It is my will that you speak," he said.

She started.

"Have you heard my command?"

Andrée assented by a gesture.

"Then why do you not speak?"

She put her hand to her throat, as if to indicate that she could not articulate.

"Well, sit down," said Balsamo.

He took her by the hand which Gilbert had so lately kissed without her being conscious, and his touch gave her that shudder which she had then exhibited, but which had been caused by the electric fluid descending on her at that moment from the room above. Led by him, she made three steps backward and sat·down in an arm-chair.

"Do you see?" he asked.

Her eyes dilated as she tried to take in all the rays of light in the apartment.

"I do not mean to ask if you see with your eyes, do you see inwardly?" and, drawing from under his embroidered coat a little rod of steel, he touched her heaving breast; she bounded as if a dart of flame had pierced her and entered her heart, and then her eyes closed.

"And now you begin to see?" he said.

She bowed in assent.

And you will soon speak."

"Yes," replied Andrée, but at the same moment she put her hand to her head in a manner expressive of great suffering.

" What is the matter ? " asked Balsamo.

" I am in pain."

" Wherefore ? "

" Because you force me to see and speak."

He made several movements over her head, as if to lessen the influence of the electricity.

" Do you suffer now ? "

" Not so much."

" Well, then, look where you are."

Her eyes remained closed, but her face expressed great surprise.

" I am in the red chamber ! " she murmured.

" With whom ? "

" With you ! " continued she, shuddering.

" What is the matter ? "

" I am afraid—I am ashamed ! "

" Of what ? Are we not united by sympathy ? "

" Yes, certainly."

" And you know that I have caused you to come here with a pure intention ? "

" True, true," said she.

" That I respect you as a sister ? "

" I know it, indeed ! " and her face grew calm, then again was troubled.

" You do not tell me all—you do not pardon me entirely."

" Because I see that though you would not wrong me, you would another, perhaps."

" Possibly," he muttered ; " but look not at that ! " he added, in an authoritative tone.

Her face resumed its usual expression.

" Are all asleep in the house ? "

" I do not know."

" Then look and see."

"Where shall I look?"

"Let me see. First, in your father's room. What is he doing?"

"He is in bed."

"Asleep?"

"No; he is reading."

"What is he reading?"

"One of those bad books which he wishes me to read."

"And you will not read them?"

"No!" said she, with an expression of the greatest scorn on her features.

"Well, we are safe, then. Look in Nicole's room."

"There is no light in her room."

"But you do not want light to see."

"Not if you command me."

"See! it is my will."

"Ah, I see!"

"What?"

"She is half undressed—she is opening her door softly—she is going down-stairs."

"So! Where is she going?"

"She stops at the courtyard gate—she waits behind it —she watches!"

Balsamo smiled.

"Is she watching to see whether you are out?"

"No."

"Well, that is the principal matter; for when a young lady is free from her father's and her waiting-maid's eye, she has nothing to fear, unless——"

"No."

"You are replying to my thought."

"I see it."

"Then you have no lover?"

"I?" asked she, disdainfully.

"Yes; you might be in love; young people do not leave their convents to be shut up. They give liberty to their hearts when their persons are set free."

Andrée shook her head. "My heart is free," she said, sadly, and such an expression of candor and virgin modesty lighted her features that Balsamo exclaimed, with rapture :

"A lily ! a true pupil ! a clairvoyante !" and he clasped his hands with joy and gratitude.

Then, turning again to Andrée : "But if you do not love, you may be loved," said he.

"I do not know," replied she, softly.

"What, you do not know ?" he cried, imperiously. "When I question, I expect a proper answer ;" and he touched her bosom again with the steel rod. She started, but without evincing so much pain as before.

"Yes, I see," said she ; "but be gentle, or you will kill me."

"What do you see ? "

"Oh—but no ! It cannot be," said she.

"What, then, do you see ? "

"A young man who, ever since my leaving the convent, has followed me, watched me, brooded on me, yet always secretly."

"Who is the young man ? "

"I do not see his face. I see his coat ; it is like that of a workman."

"Where is he ? "

"At the foot of the stairs. He seems in sorrow—he weeps."

"Why can you not see his face ? "

"It is hidden in his hands."

"Look through his hands."

She made an effort, then exclaimed : "No ; "it is impossible—Gilbert !"

"Why impossible ? "

"He ?—he dare not love me !" cried she, with a lofty expression of disdain.

Balsamo smiled like one who knows mankind, and who is aware that there is no distance the heart will not overleap, were there an abyss between it and its object.

"And what is he doing at the foot of the staircase ? "

"Stay ; he removes his hands from his face—he seizes the balustrade—he rises—he ascends."

" Ascends where ? "

" Up here. But no matter ; he dare not come in."

" Why not ? "

" Because he is afraid," said she, with a smile of contempt.

" But he will listen ? "

" Yes ; for he is now putting his ear to the door."

" That annoys you ? "

" Yes ; he may hear what I say."

" And would he use it against her whom he loves ? "

" Yes, in a moment of passion or jealousy—in such a moment he would be capable of anything."

" Then let us get rid of him, ' said Balsamo, and he walked noisily to the door.

Gilbert's hour to be courageous was not yet come, for at the noise, fearing to be caught, he jumped astride on the balustrade, and slid down noiselessly to the bottom of the staircase. Andrée uttered a stifled cry.

" Look no more in that direction," said Balsamo, returning toward her ; " the loves of the vulgar are of no importance. Speak to me of the Baron of Taverney, will you ? "

" I will answer what you choose," said she, sighing.

" The baron is very poor, is he not ? "

" Very poor."

" Too poor to allow you any amusement ? "

" Oh, yes."

" You are heartily tired of Taverney ? "

" Heartily."

" You are ambitious, perhaps ? "

" No."

" You love your father ? "

" Yes," said the young girl, with hesitation.

" Yet I thought this evening your filial love was not very apparent," said Balsamo, smiling.

" I am vexed at him for having wasted my mother's fortune, so that poor Maison Rouge has to pass his time in garrison, and cannot worthily support the dignity of our family."

"Who is this Maison Rouge?"

"My brother Philip."

"Why do you call him Maison Rouge?"

"It is, or rather, it was the name of one of our castles, and the eldest of the family bears it until the death of the chief—then he is called Taverney."

"You love your brother, then?"

"Oh, dearly, dearly!"

"More than any one in the world?"

"More than any one in the world."

"Why do you love him so warmly, and your father so coldly?"

"Because he has a noble heart. He would die for me!"

"And your father?"

She was silent. Doubtless Balsamo thought it better not to force her against her will on this point; and perhaps, also, he already knew as much of the baron as he wished.

"And where is the Chevalier Maison Rouge at this moment?"

"Where is Philip?"

"Yes."

"In the garrison at Strasbourg."

"Do you see him there?"

"Where?"

"At Strasbourg."

"I do not see him."

"Do you know that town?"

"No."

"I know it. Let us visit it together—will you?"

"Yes; with pleasure."

"Now. Is he at the theater?"

"No."

"Is he at the coffee-house in the square with the other officers?"

"No."

"Has he gone back to his apartment? I wish that you should look for him there."

"I see nothing. I think he is not at Strasbourg."

"Do you know the road from thence?"

"No."

"I know it—follow me. Is he at Saverne?"

"No."

"Is he at Saarbruck?"

"No."

"Is he at Nancy?"

"Stay—stay!" The young girl seemed collecting all her powers—her heart beat, her bosom heaved. "I see him! I see him! Dear Philip—what joy!"

"What is he doing?"

"Dear Philip!" continued Andrée, her eyes sparkling with joy.

"Where is he?"

"On horseback, riding through a town I know well."

"What town?"

"Nancy! Nancy! where I was at the convent."

"Are you sure that it is he?"

"Oh, yes; the torches around show his face."

"Torches?" said Balsamo, with surprise. "Why, are there torches?"

"He is on horseback, at the door of a magnificent carriage, richly gilt."

"Ah!" cried Balsamo, who appeared to comprehend this, "who is in the carriage?"

"A young lady. Oh, how majestic she is! how graceful! how beautiful! Strange, I almost fancy I have seen her before—no; it is Nicole's features which resemble hers."

"Nicole resembles the young lady who is so beautiful and so majestic?"

"Yes, yes; but as a jasmine may be said to resemble a lily."

"Let us see what is passing at Nancy at this moment."

"The young lady bends forward, and makes a sign to Philip to approach; he obeys, and takes off his hat respectfully."

"Can you hear what they say?"

"I am listening," said Andrée, impressing silence on Balsamo by a gesture. "I hear, I hear!" murmured she.

"What does the young lady say?"

"She orders him with a sweet smile to hasten the pace of the horses. She says she will require her escort to be ready at six in the morning, as she wishes to stop on the road."

"To stop?—where?"

"My brother is just asking her. Heavens! she wishes to stop at Taverney to see my father. Such a great princess at our poor house! what shall we do—without plate —almost without linen!"

"Do not be uneasy; that will be provided for."

"Oh, thanks, thanks!" and the young girl, who had half risen from her seat, sunk back with a heavy sigh, completely exhausted.

Balsamo immediately approached her, and by some magnetic passes in an opposite direction, changed the course of the electric fluid.

A calm sleep then stole over her lovely frame, which had bent down exhausted, her head sinking on her palpitating bosom.

"Recover thy strength," said Balsamo, gazing at her with a stern delight. "I shall soon require thy light again. Oh, Science," continued he, with the rapture of exalted faith, "thou alone never deceivest us! to thee, then, man ought to sacrifice every feeling. This young girl is beautiful, pure as an angel, and He who made beauty and innocence knows how dear they ought to be to us. But let the creature perish—how pure, how perfect, how beautiful soever she be—if I can but make her speak the words of truth! Let all the delights of the world, love, passion, rapture, exist no longer for me, if I can only, with a firm step, advance on the path of light and science. And now, young girl—now that my will has given thee strength, awake, or, rather, sink again in the sleep which reveals all things! Speak again; but now it is for me that thou must speak."

He spread his hands over her head, and forced her to sit up by breathing upon her. Seeing her ready and submissive, he took from his pocket-book a curl of jet-black hair, which he put into Andrée's hand.

"See!" he commanded.

"Again?" said she, with anguish. "Oh, no; let me rest. It is too painful, and just now I felt so happy!"

"See!" replied Balsamo, pitilessly, touching her again with the steel rod.

She wrung her hands, struggling to evade the tyranny of the experimenter. The foam was on her lips, as formerly it gathered on those of the pythoness on her sacred tripod.

'I see! I see!" cried she, with the despair of a subdued will.

"What do you see?"

"A woman."

"Ah," exclaimed Balsamo, with wild joy, "science is not, then, a useless word like virtue. Mesmer is greater than Brutus! Describe the woman, that I may know you really see her whom I would have you see!"

"She is a brunette, tall, with blue eyes, jet-black hair, and sinewy arms."

"What is she doing?"

"She gallops—she flies forward, carried by a splendid horse reeking with sweat and foam."

"In what direction?"

"There—there!" said the young girl, pointing to the west.

"On the highway?"

"Yes."

"Toward Chalons?"

"Yes."

"Good!" said Balsamo; "she takes the road which I shall take; she goes to Paris as I do. I shall find her there. Now rest," said he, and he took from Andrée's hand the curl of hair.

Her arms fell powerless by her side.

"Now, return to your harpsichord."

Andrée arose and made a step toward the door, but overcome by inexpressible fatigue, her limbs refused to support her. She staggered.

"Renew your strength and walk !" said Balsamo, enveloping her anew with magnetic passes ; and she, like the generous steed that braces very nerve to fulfil his master's will, unjust though it be walked erect. Balsamo opened the door, and, still sleeping, she descended the stairs.

CHAPTER XI.

NICOLE LEGAY.

WHILE the scene of interrogation was passing in Balsamo's chamber, Gilbert remained under the railings at the foot of the staircase in a state of indescribable torture. Not daring to ascend again to listen at the door of the red chamber, he fell into despair, and this despair was increased tenfold by the feeling of his weakness and his inferiority.

Balsamo was only a man—for Gilbert, being a profound thinker, a philosopher in embryo, had small faith in sorcerers—but then this man was strong, and he was weak ; this man was courageous, and Gilbert was not so yet. Twenty times he arose, determined to beard the stranger, and twenty times his trembling limbs bent under him, and he sunk on his knees. Then the thought struck him that he would get a ladder used by La Brie (who was at the same time cook, butler, and gardener), for nailing the jasmine and honeysuckle against the walls, and by propping it against the balcony of the apartment, be enabled to mount to the window, and witness what he so ardently desired to discover.

He passed stealthily into the courtyard, ran to the spot where the ladder lay, but as he was stooping to take it up, he thought he heard a noise in the direction of the house, and he turned. He was almost certain that in the obscurity he saw a human form enter the dark frame of the open door, but moving so quickly and so noiselessly that it appeared rather a specter than a living being. He let the ladder fall, and, his heart beating audibly, hastened back toward the château.

Some minds are constitutionally superstitious, and these are generally the most exalted and the richest in fancy. They admit the fabulous more readily than the rational, because what is natural is too common for them, impelled as they are towards the impossible, or at least the ideal. Such spirits delight in the darkness of the forest, the depths of which they people with phantoms or genii. The ancients, who were poets in all things, saw these fantastic beings in open day; but as their sun, warmer and brighter than ours, forbade the fancy to bring forth specters and demons, they filled the forest with smiling dryads and wood-nymphs. Gilbert, born in a gloomier clime, imagined he saw a spirit. This time, in spite of his incredulity, he recalled the words of the woman who had fled from Balsamo, and the idea flashed across his mind that the sorcerer might have summoned up some evil spirit to do his bad behests. But Gilbert had always, after a first impression, a second not more encouraging, for it was the result of reflection. His recalled all the arguments of powerful minds against the belief in the return of spirits to this world, and thinking of the article "Specter" in the "Philosophical Dictionary," restored his courage, but it was only to give him another apprehension better founded and more alarming.

If he had indeed seen any one, it must have been a real individual deeply interested in watching him. Fear suggested M. de Taverney—his conscience whispered another name. He looked up to Nicole's apartment—her candle was out, not a ray of light was visible—not a whisper, not a movement, not a light in all the house, except in the stranger's room. He looked—he listened; then, seeing nothing, hearing nothing, he took up the ladder again, convinced that he had been deceived, and that this vision had been the result of a suspension of his observing faculties, rather than of their exercise.

Just as he was about to place his ladder, Balsamo's door opened and then shut. At this sound he hurried in, and saw Andrée glide out and descend the stairs without noise and without a light, as if guided and supported by a supernatural power. Having reached the landing-place, she passed by where he had now concealed himself, in the shade, her dress touching him as she passed, and continued her way. The baron was asleep—La Brie in bed—Nicole in the other turret—Balsamo's door closed—he could not be surprised by any one. He made a violent effort and followed her, adapting his step to hers, and keeping at a distance from her. She passed through the anteroom into the saloon, but although she left the door open, he stopped just before he reached it. Should he enter? He hesitated; then resolved; but just as his foot was on the threshold, an arm was stretched out in the darkness, and he was firmly grasped. Gilbert turned—his heart panting as if it would burst his bosom.

"So I have caught you at last!" whispered an angry voice, close at his ear. "Deny now, if you can, that you have meetings—that you are in love with her!"

Gilbert had not strength to shake himself loose from the gripe which detained him, yet it was only that of a young girl; it was simply the hand of Nicole Legay that held him.

"What do you mean?" whispered he, impatiently.

"Oh, I am to speak it out, then?" and Nicole raised her voice nearly to the loudest pitch.

"No—for God's sake, be quiet!" replied Gilbert, between his closed teeth, and dragging her away from the door.

"Well, come with me, then."

This was what Gilbert wanted; for by going away with her, he took her away from Andrée. He followed Nicole, who led the way into the courtyard, shutting the door behind her when he had passed.

"But," said Gilbert, "mademoiselle will be retiring to her apartment; she will call you to help her to undress, and you will not be in the house."

"Do you think I care for that now? Let her call or not, I must speak to you."

"You might put off until to-morrow what you have got to say, Nicole. You know Mademoiselle Andrée is strict."

"Yes, I would advise her to be strict—particularly with me."

"To-morrow, Nicole, promise."

"You promise. I know what your fine promises are. This very day you promised to meet me near Maison Rouge. Where were you? Why, in the very opposite direction, since you brought the traveler hither. Your promises, indeed. I believe them just as I did those of our confessor at the Annonciades, who swore to keep secret what we confessed, and then told all our sins to the abbess."

"But, Nicole, you will be dismissed if you are seen."

"And you—will you not be dismissed for being in love with my young lady? Do you think the baron too generous for that?"

"He could surely have no motive for dismissing me," said Gilbert, endeavoring to defend himself.

"Oh, none in the world. The baron, perhaps, allows you to pay your addresses to his daughter. I really did not know he was quite so great a philosopher!"

Gilbert might easily have proved to Nicole, by relating what he had just witnessed, that if he was to blame, at least Andrée was not privy to his misconduct; and incredible as her visit to the stranger's apartment would have appeared, Nicole, thanks to the good opinion women have of one another, would have believed him. But deeper reflection arrested the words on his lips. Andrée's secret was one that might serve him, as it placed her completely in his power; and as he loved Andrée infinitely more than he feared Nicole, he was silent on the singular events he had just witnessed.

"Well," said he, "since you insist on having an explanation let us understand each other."

"Oh, that is easily done. But you are right, this is a bad place for it; let us go to my room."

" To your room ?   Impossible ! "

" Why so ? "

" We might be surprised."

" Indeed ! and who would surprise us ?   Mademoiselle ? True ; she might be jealous about her sweet youth ?   Unfortunately for her since her secret is discovered, I am not afraid of her.   Mademoiselle Andrée jealous of Nicole ! What an honor ! "   And the forced laugh of the young girl frightened Gilbert more than any invective or menace could possibly have done.

" It is not mademoiselle of whom I am afraid," said he ; " I am only anxious on your own account, Nicole."

" Oh ! most anxious, no doubt.   But you are going to my room for no bad purpose, and you have often told me where there was no bad intention there should be no shame. Philosophers are Jesuits sometimes, and our confessor at the Annonciades told me all that before you.   Come, come. No more false reasons ! come to my room.   I am resolved you shall ! "

" Nicole ! " said he, grinding his teeth.

" Well, what more, pray ? "

" Take care ! " and he raised his hand.

" Oh, I am not afraid.   You struck me once, but you were jealous then ; at that time you loved me, and I allowed you to strike me, but I shall not now.   No, no, no ; for you no longer love me, and it is I who am jealous now."

" But what will you do ? " cried Gilbert, grasping her wrist.

" I shall scream, and mademoiselle will hear me.   I advise you to let go your hold of me."

Gilbert dropped her hand, then seizing the ladder and dragging it cautiously after him, he placed it against the wall of the turret, so that it reached nearly to Nicole's window.

" See how things turn in this world," said she, maliciously; " the ladder which was to assist you to climb to mademoiselle's apartment must merely serve you to descend from my humble attic.   Very flattering for me, is it not ? "

Nicole, perceiving the advantage   she had gained,

BALSAMO AND LORENZA

Dumas, Vol. Six

declared her triumph with that precipitate eagerness which women, unless indeed those of very superior minds, often exhibit—a victory which is often too dearly purchased.

Gilbert, who felt himself in a false position, was silent, and followed the young girl, reserving all his powers for the approaching contest.

In the first place, however, like a prudent general he satisfied himself on two points. The first was, in passing, before the window, that Mlle. de Taverney was still in the saloon, and the second, on reaching Nicole's chamber, that in case of necessity, he could reach the ladder without much risk of breaking his neck, and thus allow himself to slide to the ground.

Nicole's room was as simple in its furniture as the rest of the house. It was a loft, the walls of which were covered with a drab-and-green paper. A wooden bed, and a large geranium placed near the window, were its whole furniture and decorations, except a large bonnet-box, given her by Andrée, which served both for table and wardrobe. Nicole sat down on the edge of the bed, Gilbert on a corner of the box. She had had time to calm down while ascending the stairs, and now, completely mistress of herself, she felt strong in having justice on her side. Gilbert, on the contrary, was agitated, and could not recover his coolness—his anger had increased as hers decreased.

" So," said she, " you are in love with mademoiselle, and you have attempted to deceive me ? "

" Who told you I was in love with mademoiselle ? "

" Dame ! were you not going to a rendezvous with her ? "

" How do you know that I had a rendezvous with her ? "

" How do I know ? Why, there was no one else to go to but the sorcerer ! "

" Well, I might have been going to him—I am ambitious."

" Say envious."

" It is the same word taken in a bad sense."

" Don't let us dispute about words—you love me no longer."

" Yes, I do ; I love you still."

" Then why do you avoid me ? "

" Because you quarrel with me whenever I meet you.

" That is because you always avoid me."

" You know I am shy—that I love solitude."

" Yes ; and you seek solitude, ladder in hand."

Gilbert was beaten on his first move.

" Come, come ! be frank if you can, Gilbert, and confess that you no longer love me, or that you love two women at once."

" Well, and if I did, what would you say ? "

" I should say it was monstrous."

" No, no ; that there was an error somewhere."

" In your heart ? "

" No ; in our social state.   You know there are nations where every man is allowed seven or eight wives."

" They are not Christians," said Nicole, pettishly.

" They are philosophers," said Gilbert, with dignity.

" So, Master Philosopher, you would wish me to take a second lover, as you have done !"

" I would not be unjust and tyrannical ; I should not wish to repress the impulses of your heart.   Freedom, blessed freedom, respects free will.   If you change your love, Nicole, I shall not force you to a fidelity which, in my opinion, is unnatural."

" Ah, I see plainly you no longer love me !"

Gilbert was great in argument, not that he was skilful in logic, but he was an adept in paradox and, however little he knew, he still knew more than Nicole.   She had read only what amused her—he what taught him a little also —and, as they talked, he regained his presence of mind while Nicole began to lose hers.

" Has the great philosopher any memory ? " asked Nicole, with an ironical smile.

" Sometimes," replied Gilbert.

" Then you have not forgotten, perhaps, what you said to me five months ago when I came with mademoiselle from the Annonciades ? "

" I have forgotten ; tell it me."

" You said, ' I am poor ;' it was the day we were reading among the old ruins."

"Well, go on."

"You trembled very much that day——"

"Very likely; I am naturally timid; but I do all I can to correct that fault, and some others also."

"So that when you have corrected all your faults," said Nicole, laughing, "you will be perfect."

"I shall be strong; wisdom gives strength."

"Where did you read that, pray?"

"Never mind; return to what you were saying."

Nicole felt that she was losing ground every minute.

"Well, you said to me, 'I am poor—no one loves me; yet there is something here,' and you pressed your hand on your heart."

"No, Nicole; if I pressed my hand anywhere when I said that, it must have been on my forehead. The heart is merely a forcing pump, which drives the blood to the extremities of the body. Read the article 'Heart,' in the 'Philosophical Dictionary;' and Gilbert drew himself up proudly. Humble before Balsamo, he gave himself the airs of a prince before Nicole.

"You are right, Gilbert; it must have been your head which you struck. Well, striking your forehead, you said, 'I am treated here worse than a dog; indeed, Mahon is in a happier condition than I.' I replied that they were wrong not to love you; that if you had been my brother, I should have loved you also. I think, however, I said that from my heart, not from my head; but perhaps I am wrong, for I never read the 'Philosophical Dictionary.'"

"You ought to read it, Nicole."

"Then you threw your arms round me. You said, 'You are an orphan; I am one, too. Let us love each other as if we were brother and sister; no, better than if we were, for if we were, we should be forbidden to love as I wish we should;' then you kissed me."

"Very possibly."

"Did you think then as you spoke?"

"Oh, yes; one generally thinks what one says at the time one says it."

"So that now——"

"Now I am five months older than I was. I have learned things of which I knew nothing then, and I look forward to things which I do not yet know; I think differently now."

"You are a deceiver, a hypocrite, a liar!" exclaimed she, furiously.

"No more than a traveler, should he make two different answers to the same question—if you asked him in a valley what he thought of the prospect, and again when he had got to the top of a mountain which before had closed his view."

"So, then, you will not marry me?"

"I never said I would marry you," said Gilbert, contemptuously.

"And yet," cried the exasperated girl, "I think Nicole Legay fully the equal of Sebastian Gilbert."

"All human beings are equal; but nature or education makes certain faculties greater in one man than another, and according as these faculties are more or less developed, men differ from one another."

"So that your faculties being more developed than mine, you are raised above me?"

"Quite correct; you do not reason yet, Nicole, but you understand."

"Yes, yes; I understand!" cried Nicole, with redoubled passion.

"What do you understand?"

"That you are a bad man."

"It is possible. Many are born with bad inclinations. Rousseau himself had such, but he corrected them—I shall do the same."

"Oh, heavens!" cried Nicole, "how could I ever love such a man?"

"You did not love me, Nicole," replied Gilbert, coldly. "I pleased you—that was all. You had just come from Nancy, where you had only seen students whom you laughed at or soldiers who frightened you; so you took a fancy to me, and for a mouth or two we enjoyed our dream of love.

But should we, therefore, be tied together, to be eternally miserable ? You see, Nicole, if we bound ourselves for our lives in a moment of happiness, we should give up our free will, and that would be absurd."

" Is that philosophy ? " asked Nicole.

" I think so," replied Gilbert.

" Then there is nothing sacred in the eyes of philosophers ? "

" Oh, yes ; reason is."

" Yet I think you once said something about being faithful to the choice of the heart. You recollect your theory on marriages——"

" On unions, Nicole, for I shall never marry."

" You will never marry ? "

" No ; I shall be a learned man—a philosopher. Science requires perfect freedom of the mind, and philosophy that of the body."

" Monsieur Gilbert," said she, " you are a wretch ; and whatever I am, I am at least better than you."

" Now," said Gilbert, rising, " we are only losing time —you in abusing me, and I in listening to you ; let us end. You loved me because you took pleasure in loving."

" Well ? "

" Well, there is no reason in the world that I should make myself unhappy because you did a thing which gave you gratification."

" Fool ! " she exclaimed, " you think you can confound my common sense, and you pretend not to fear me ! "

" Fear you ? Why, Nicole, jealousy is turning your brain."

" Jealousy ! " she cried, stamping her foot—" and why should I be jealous ? Is there a prettier girl in the province than I ?—if I had but as white a hand as mademoiselle —and I shall have some day when I do no more hard work. You are my first lover, it is true; but you are not the first man who has paid court to me. Gilbert, Gilbert, do not force me to seek revenge on you—do not make me leave the narrow path in which a last remembrance of my mother. and the regular repetition of my prayers, have kept me.

Gilbert, if you do, you may have to reproach yourself
with bringing many evils on yourself and others."

"All in good time," said Gilbert. "So now that you
have got to the summit of your dignity, Nicole, I am perfectly satisfied on one point."

"And what may that be ?" inquired the girl.

"Simply that if I consent now to marry you——"

"What then ?"

"Why, that you would refuse me."

Nicole paused, her clinched hands and gnashing teeth
showing the workings of her mind.

"You are right!" she exclaimed, at length. "Yes;
I also begin to ascend the mountain of which you spoke.
I see a wider prospect before me. The wife of a learned
man, a philosopher! No, I am destined for something
greater than that! Mount your ladder, and don't break
your neck—though I begin to think it would be a blessing
for many persons if you would—perhaps even a blessing
for yourself."

She turned her back on him. Gilbert stood a moment
wavering and irresolute; for Nicole, excited by anger and
jealousy, was truly beautiful. But he had resolved to
break with her—Nicole could blast at once his love and
his ambition. His decision was made.

In a few seconds, Nicole, hearing no sound, looked behind her. She was alone in the apartment.

"Gone!" she murmured; "and mademoiselle—oh, I
shall know to-morrow whether she loves him or not ?"

She went to the window and looked out; all was dark,
every light extinguished. She stole on tiptoe to her lady's
door and listened.

"She is in bed—she sleeps soundly," said she; "but to-
morrow I shall know all."

CHAPTER XI.

WAITING-MAID AND MISTRESS.

THE calmness with which Nicole returned to her room was not affected. Young, strong, full of an uncultivated self-confidence, she was blessed with that faculty so important for those who would govern where they love—the faculty of forgetting ; and she could sleep after she had arranged with the little malicious sprites that dwelt in her heart her plan of vengeance.

Mlle. de Taverney appeared to her even more guilty than Gilbert. This aristocratic girl, rigid in her prejudices, elevated in her pride, who at their convent would descend to familiarity with none below the daughters of marquises —this statue, outwardly so cold, but yet with feeling in its marble bosom—this statue, warming to life for a rural Pygmalion like Gilbert, became contemptible in her estimation. For Nicole felt that Gilbert was her inferior in everything but a little reading, and thought that she had condescended very much when she, the waiting-maid of the daughter of a ruined baron, put herself on a level with the son of a poor peasant.

What, then, could she think of her mistress, if she really returned Gilbert's love ?

She calculated that, in relating what she had seen to the baron, she should fall into a great error ; first, because he would only laugh at the affair, box Gilbert's ears, and turn him out-of-doors ; next, because it would deprive her of her power over Gilbert and Andrée. What pleasure she should have—she, the waiting-maid—in seeing them turn pale or red as her eye fell on them ! This idea flattered her pride and soothed her vindictive spirit ; and, at this idea, her reflections ceased—she slept.

It was day when she awoke, fresh, light-hearted, and her mind prepared for everything. She took her usual time to dress—that is, an hour. She looked at herself in the piece of broken glass which served as her mirror ; her eyes appeared to her more brilliant than ever—her lips had not lost their brightness nor their roundness—her teeth were perfect—her neck, which she took particular care to hide from the sun, was white as a lily. Seeing herself so handsome, she began to think she could easily make her young lady jealous. Thus armed personally and mentally, she opened Andrée's door, as she was authorized to do whenever, at seven o'clock, her mistress had not rung for her.

When Nicole entered the room she stopped in amazement.

Pale, her beautiful hair damp with perspiration, Andrée lay on her bed in a heavy sleep, in which she sometimes writhed as if in pain. She was still in the dress which she had worn the day before. Her breathing was hurried, and now and then a low groan escaped her lips. Nicole looked at her for a minute, then shook her head, for she acknowledged to herself that there could be no beauty which could contest the palm with Andrée's.

She went to the window and opened the shutters. A stream of light poured in, and made Mlle. de Taverney's violet-veined eyelids quiver. She awoke, tried to rise, but felt, at the same time, such great weakness and such excessive pain, that she fell back on her pillow with a cry of suffering.

"Oh ! mademoiselle, what is the matter ?" asked Nicole.

"Is it late ?" said Andrée, rubbing her eyes.

"Very late, madame—much later than your usual hour for rising."

"I do not know what is the matter with me, Nicole," said she, looking around her, "I feel so oppressed—so ill !"

Nicole fixed her eyes on her mistress before replying : "It is the commencement of a cold that you have caught, madame, last night."

"Last night !" replied Andrée, surprised ; then, looking at her disordered dress, "Have I really lain down without undressing ? How could that be ?"

"If mademoiselle would reflect——"

" I don't recollect anything about it," replied Andrée leaning her head on her hand. "What has happened? Am I going mad?" She sat up on the bed, and looked round for the second time, all bewildered. Then, after reflecting: "Oh! yes, I remember I was very much tired—very much exhausted yesterday; it was the storm, no doubt; then I fell asleep, on the music-stool at my harpsichord—but, after that, I remember nothing. I must have come up to my room half asleep, and thrown myself on my bed without strength to undress."

"You should have called me, mademoiselle," said Nicole; "mademoiselle knows that I am always ready to wait on her."

"I either did not think of it, or had not the strength to do it"

' Hypocrite!" muttered Nicole to herself—then she added:

" But mademoiselle must have stayed very late at her harpsichord, then, for before she came up to her room, hearing a noise, I went down——" She stopped, hoping to discover in Andrée something like agitation—a blush, perhaps. No; Andrée was calm, and her countenance, that clear mirror of her soul, was undisturbed. "I went down," repeated Nicole.

" Well?"

" Well, madame, you were not at your harpsichord."

Andrée looked up, but there was only surprise to be read in her lovely eyes.

" Very strange!" said she.

" It is quite true, however."

" You say I was not in the saloon; but I never left it for a moment till I came to bed."

" Mademoiselle will pardon me for contradicting her."

" But where was I, then?"

" Mademoiselle must know that better than I," said Nicole, shrugging her shoulders.

" You must be wrong, Nicole," said Andrée, mildly; " I only remember feeling cold and stiff, and having great difficulty in walking."

"Oh, but when I saw mademoiselle, she walked very well," said Nicole, almost with a sneer.

"You saw me walk?"

"Yes, indeed, madame."

"But just now you said I was not in the saloon."

"It was not in the saloon I saw mademoiselle."

"Where, then?"

"In the vestibule, near the staircase."

"I?"

"Yes; I think I ought to know mademoiselle when I see her," said Nicole, with an affected laugh.

"I am certain, however," said Andrée, with great simplicity, after she had again tried to recall the events of the night, "that I did not stir out of the saloon."

"I am, however, quite as certain that I saw mademoiselle in the vestibule. I thought, indeed, she had just come in from a walk in the garden. It was a beautiful night, after the storm, and it is very pleasant to walk out when the air is so cool, and when the flowers smell so sweet—is it not, mademoiselle?"

"Oh, but you know I dare not walk out at night. I am too timid."

"Mademoiselle might have some one with her, and then she would not be afraid."

"And whom, pray, could I have with me?" asked Andrée, without the least suspicion that she was undergoing a cross-examination.

Nicole was afraid to proceed further in her investigation. Andrée's coolness she thought the height of dissimulation; but she judged it best to give the conversation another turn.

"Mademoiselle was saying that she felt in pain?"

"Yes, indeed, I feel in great pain—and so weak, so low. I did nothing yesterday but what I do every day, yet I am so tired—perhaps I am going to be ill."

"It may be some sorrow which causes that feeling of weariness—I have felt it myself."

"Oh, you have sorrows, have you, Nicole?"

This was said with a disdainful carelessness, which gave Nicole courage to speak more plainly.

"Oh, yes, **madame**," she replied ; " yes, I have."

Andrée got slowly out of bed, and, while proceeding to undress, that she might dress again, she said :

"Well, let me hear them."

"Indeed, I have just come to tell mademoiselle——" She stopped.

"To tell what ? You look frightened, Nicole."

"I look frightened, and mademoiselle looks tired ; so, doubtless, we are both suffering."

This piece of familiarity displeased Andrée. She frowned slightly, exclaiming, "Oh !"

The intonation of her voice might have made Nicole reflect, but she was not to be daunted.

"Since mademoiselle wishes me to speak, I shall do so."

"Well, go on."

"I wish to get married, madame."

"Oh ! Is that what you are thinking of ? Why, you are not seventeen yet."

"Mademoiselle is only sixteen, and yet does she not sometimes think of marrying ?"

"What reason have you to suppose so ?" asked Andrée, severely.

Nicole was just opening her mouth to say something impertinent, but she knew that that would cut short the conversation, which she had no desire should end yet.

"I beg mademoiselle's pardon ; I cannot certainly know her thoughts ; I am but a country-girl, I follow nature."

"That is a strange expression."

"Is it not natural for a woman to love, and to wish to be loved ?"

"Perhaps so.   Well ?"

"Well ; I am in love."

"And the person you love loves you ?"

"I think so, madame"—then, reflecting that this reply was not decided enough under the circumstances, she added : "Indeed, I am sure of it."

"You are not wasting your time at Taverney, from your own account, Mademoiselle Nicole."

"One must think of the future, madame; you are a lady, and doubtless some rich relation will leave you a fortune. I must do the best I can for myself."

All this appeared natural enough, and forgetting Nicole's little piece of impertinence, Andrée's goodness of heart began to resume the ascendency.

"Very true," said she; "but I should like to know who is your choice."

"Ah, you do know him, madame!" said Nicole, fixing her eyes on Andrée.

"I know him?"

"Yes, very well."

"Who is it, then? Do not keep me in suspense."

"I am afraid mademoiselle will be displeased."

"I displeased?"

"Yes, mademoiselle."

"Then it is some improper person whom you have chosen?"

"I do not say that, madame."

"Then tell it without fear. It is the duty of masters to take an interest in the welfare of their dependents who perform their duties satisfactorily—and you know I am satisfied with you."

"You are very kind, madame."

"Well, tell me quickly, and finish lacing me."

Nicole collected all her firmness, and all her powers of penetration, as she said:

Well, madame, it is Gilbert whom I have chosen."

To her great surprise, Andrée betrayed no emotion of any kind; she only said:

"What, little Gilbert—my nurse's son?"

"Yes, madame, the same."

"And he loves you?"

Now was the decisive moment.

"He has told me so twenty times."

"Well, marry him," replied Andrée, calmly. "I see nothing to prevent it. You have no relations—he is an orphan—you are each of you free from control."

"Certainly," stammered Nicole, quite amazed at the

matter ending so differently from what she had expected.

"Mademoiselle gives her permission, then ?"

"My full permission, only you are both very young yet."

"We shall live longer together."

"And you have neither one nor other any money."

"We shall work."

"What can he work at ?—he is good for nothing."

This dissimulation was too much for Nicole. She could not contain herself.

"Mademoiselle must allow me to say, that speaking so of poor Gilbert is treating him very ill."

"It is treating him as he deserves ; he is a lazy fellow."

"Oh, mademoiselle, he reads a great deal—he wishes to be well informed."

"He will not work."

"For mademoiselle he does all that he can."

"For me ?"

"Mademoiselle must know that, when she ordered him to procure game for her every day, and he does so."

"I ordered him ?"

"Yes ; and he often goes twenty miles for it."

"Indeed ! I confess I never thought about it."

"About the game ?" asked Nicole, sarcastically.

"What does that witticism mean ?" asked Andrée, getting a little impatient, for she felt irritable and unwell.

"I have no wit, madame ; wit is for great ladies. I am a poor girl, and tell things plainly as they are," replied Nicole, "and mademoiselle is unjust to Gilbert, who is so very attentive to all her wishes."

"He only does his duty as a servant, if it be so."

"But Gilbert is not a servant, madame ; he receives no wages."

"He is the son of an old tenant ; he is kept, he is fed, and he does nothing in return. But why defend so warmly this lad, when he was not attacked ?"

"Oh, I knew very well that mademoiselle would not attack him."

"More words that I do not understand."

"Mademoiselle will not understand."

"Enough!   Explain this moment what you mean."

"Mademoiselle must certainly have no difficulty to know what I mean."

"I know nothing—and I shall not take the trouble of finding out; you ask my consent to your marriage?"

"Yes; and I would beg of you, mademoiselle, not to be angry with Gilbert for loving me."

"What can it matter to me whether he loves you or does not love you?   You are really very tiresome."

"Perhaps mademoiselle has said the same to Gilbert?"

"I?   Do I ever speak to your Gilbert?   You are crazy, I think."

"If mademoiselle does not speak to him now, it is not very long since she did speak."

Andrée turned on her a look of ineffable scorn.

"You have been trying for an hour to let me hear some specimen of your impertinence; say it at once—I command you."

"But——" began Nicole, a little alarmed.

"You say I have spoken to Gilbert?"

"Yes, madame, I say so!"

A thought flashed across Andrée's mind, but it was so absurd that she burst into a fit of laughter.   "Heaven forgive me!" she exclaimed.   "I do believe the poor girl is jealous.   Be not uneasy, Legay, I know so little of your Gilbert, that I do not even know the color of his eyes!" And Andrée felt quite prepared to pardon what she now thought not impertinence, but mere folly.   But Nicole did not want to be pardoned, because she looked on herself as the injured person.

"It is not the way to know their color to look at them by night," said she.

"Did you speak?" asked Andrée, now beginning to understand, but scarcely willing to allow herself to entertain the thought.

"I said that if mademoiselle only speaks to Gilbert at night, she will not see very well what his features are."

"Take care!" said Andrée, turning pale, "and explain instantly what you mean."

"That is easily done. Last night I saw——"

"Be silent; some one calls me."

In fact, a voice just then called from the court in front of the house, "Andrée! Andrée!"

"It is the baron, madame," said Nicole, "with the strange gentleman."

"Go down, and say that I cannot appear, that I am indisposed, and then return and let me know the end of this extraordinary history of yours."

"Andrée!" cried her father again, "it is merely the Baron Balsamo, who wishes to bid you good-morning and inquire after your health."

"Go, I tell you," said she to Nicole, and she pointed to the door with the gesture of a queen.

But when Nicole was gone, Andrée felt a strange sensation; she had resolved not to appear, yet she was impelled by an irresistible power to the window left open by her waiting-maid. She saw Balsamo below; he bowed, at the same time fixing his eyes steadily on her. She trembled, and held by the window to prevent herself from falling.

"Good-morning, sir," said she, in reply to his salutation; and just as she pronounced the words, Nicole, whom she had sent to say she should not appear, advanced toward the gentleman, looking with open mouth at this instance of caprice at her mistress.

Andrée had scarcely spoken when she sunk, deprived of strength, on a chair. Balsamo still continued to gaze on her.

CHAPTER XII.

THE MORNING.

THE traveler had risen early in order to look after his carriage and inquire how Althotas had got on. No one was up at that hour in the castle but Gilbert, who followed with his eyes every movement of the stranger. But he could discover little, as Balsamo closed the carriage door too carefully for his inquisitive looks to penetrate its mystery.

Seeing the baron's abode by the clear light of a sunny morning. Balsamo was struck by the different impression it made on him from what it had done the preceding night. In fact the little white-and-red château—for it was built of stone and brick made a pretty picture, surrounded as it was by a grove of sycamores and laburnums of a large size, the flowers of which hung on the roof of the low building and girt the towers with a crown of gold. In front of the court there was a small piece of water surrounded by a broad border of turf and a hedge of acacias, on which the eye rested with pleasure, confined as the view was on this side by the tall chestnut and ash-trees of the avenue.

Balsamo turned along a broad walk on the left, and had scarcely advanced twenty paces when he found himself in the midst of a thick shrubbery of maples, palms, and lindens, among which the roses and syringas, steeped by the rain of the preceding night, sent forth a delicious perfume. Through the hedge of privet which bordered the walk peeped jasmine and honeysuckle, and in the distance could be seen a long alley lined with pink hawthorn and wild roses, leading to a wood.

Balsamo at last arrived at the extremity of the demesne. Here, on a slight elevation, stood the massive ruins of an ancient castle, one of the towers of which was still standing almost uninjured, and clothed from its base to its summit with luxuriant shoots of the ivy and wild vine. Viewed from this point, the demesne of Taverney, though but seven or eight acres in extent, wanted neither dignity nor elegance.

After having spent about an hour in examining the ruins, Balsamo was returning toward the house, when he saw the baron leave it by a side-door, his slight frame buried in an Indian flowered dressing-gown, and proceed to prune and arrange his little parterre. He hastened to meet him, and now having still further sounded the poverty of his host, his politeness was more decided in its expression than it had been the night before.

"Allow me, sir," said he, "to offer you my excuses for the trouble I have given you, and, at the same time, my respectful thanks for your hospitality. I should not have ventured to come down before knowing that you were up, but the view of Taverney from my window was so charming that I could not resist my desire to revisit those imposing ruins, and to see your beautiful garden."

"The ruins," said the baron, after having politely wished the stranger goodmorning—"the ruins, sir, are fine—indeed the only thing that is fine at Taverney."

"It was a large castle ?"

"Yes ; it was mine—or, rather, my ancestors'. They called it Maison Rouge, which name has long been joined to Taverney—indeed, our barony is Maison Rouge; but, my dear guest, let us not talk of things no longer in being,"

Balsamo bowed his submission.

"Allow me, rather, to make my excuses to you for your poor accommodation here. I told you beforehand what my house was."

"I have been delighted with it."

"A dog-kennel ! a dog-kennel, sir ! A very favorite place with the rats, since the foxes, lizards, and adders drove them from the other castle. Ah, pardieu ! sir, you who are a sorcerer, or something very near it, you ought certainly to raise up, with a stroke of your wand, the old castle in its glory again—above all, not forgetting the two thousand acres which formerly surrounded it. I'll wager, however, that instead of thinking of doing me such a service, you have been so polite as to go to sleep in an execrable bed ! "

"Oh, sir——"

"No—no ; don't attempt to say anything in its favor ! it's an execrable bed—it is my son's."

"You must permit me to say that such as the bed is, it appeared to me excellent. I cannot but feel ashamed of having intruded on you, and I am deeply indebted for the kindness with which you have received me. It would give me sincere pleasure to make a return, if it were in my power."

"Well, there is an opportunity," replied the old man, with a mocking smile, and pointing to La Brie who was coming with a glass of water on a splendid plate of Dresden china, "just turn this into Burgundy, Chambertin, or any other good wine, and you will do me a most essential service."

Balsamo smiled; the old man took the smile for a refusal, and at one draught swallowed the water presented to him.

"An excellent specific," said. Balsamo; "water is highest among the elements, for the Holy Spirit was borne on it before the creation of the world. Nothing can resist its action; it penetrates stone, and we may yet discover that the diamond can be dissolved by it."

"I shall be dissolved by it, I fear," replied the baron. "Will you pledge me? The water has some advantages over my wine—it is in capital order, and it is not yet exhausted. It is not like my Maraschino."

"If you had ordered a glass for me as well as for yourself, I might have been able to use it for your advantage."

"Good! explain that for me. Is it not still time?"

"Then tell your servant to bring me a glass of very pure water."

"La Brie, do you hear, you old rascal?"

La Brie hastened to obey.

"How!" said the baron, turning to his guest, "does the glass of water which I drink every morning contain any properties, any secrets which are unknown to me? Have I for ten years been making chemical experiments as Monsieur Jourdain made prose, without being aware of it?"

"I do not know what you have been doing, but you shall see what I can do. Thank you, my good fellow," said Balsamo, taking the glass from La Brie, who had brought it with marvelous rapidity.

He held the glass on a level with his eyes, and seemed

to interrogate the water which it contained; in the sunshine the little beads on its surface were bright as diamonds, and streaked with violet color.

"Oh, the deuce!" cried the baron, laughing. "Can anything beautiful be seen in a glass of water?"

"Yes, baron; to-day, at least, something very beautiful."

And Balsamo appeared doubly attentive in his occupation, the baron, in spite of himself, looking a little serious, and La Brie gazing with open mouth at what was going on.

"What do you see, pray? I am bursting with impatience to know. A good estate for me! A new Maison Rouge to set me on foot again?"

"I see something which induces me to beg you to be on the alert."

"Aye! Am I going to be attacked?"

"No; but this morning you will receive a visit."

"Then, you have yourself ordered some one to meet you here. That was wrong, sir, very wrong. There may be no partridges this morning—remember that."

"I speak seriously, my dear baron, and what I say is most important—some one is at this moment on the way to Taverney."

"Some one? What sort of a visitor, tell me, pray?—for I must confess (you must have perceived it from the rather sour reception I gave you) that every one annoys me who comes here. So, what sort of visitor? Be precise, my dear sorcerer; if possible, be precise in your description."

"I can very easily tell all you wish;" and Balsamo again raised the glass to his searching eye.

"Well, do you see anything?"

"I see everything distinctly."

"Speak, oh, speak, sister Anne."

"I see a lady of great consequence coming."

"Bah! indeed—coming without being invited?"

"She has invited herself; your son brings her."

"Philip brings her?"

" Yes, himself."

The baron laughed heartily.

" She is brought by my son ?   The great lady brought by my son ? "

" Yes, baron."

" You know my son, then ? "

" I never saw him in my life."

" And my son at this moment is——"

" Is about a mile off."

" My dear sir, he is in garrison at Strasbourg, and unless he has deserted, which he has not, I can swear, he is bringing nobody hither."

" He is bringing a great lady hither—a very exalted personage.   Ah, hold ! there is one thing I onght to tell you—you had better keep out of sight that little rogue with the horn at her finger-ends."

" Nicole Legay ?   Why, pray ? "

" Because her features resemble those of the lady who is coming."

" A great lady resemble Nicole ?   That is absurd ! "

" Why so ?   I bought a slave once, who resembled Cleopatra so much that there was some idea of sending her to Rome to pass for that queen in Octavius's triumph."

" Ah ! another attack of your malady ! "

" You must surely see, my dear baron, that this matter cannot concern me ; I only speak for your own good."

" But why should Nicole's resemblance to the great lady offend her ? "

" Suppose you were the King of France, which I am far from wishing, or the dauphin, which I wish still less, should you be flattered, on entering a house, to find among the servants one whose face was a counterpart of your august visage ? "

" Oh, the devil ! that would be a sad dilemma.   So, then, you think——"

" I think that the most high and mighty lady who is coming would not be pleased to see her living image in a short-petticoat and cotton handkerchief."

" Oh, well," said the baron. still laughing, " we must

see about it ; but, after all, my dear baron, what delights me most in this affair is, that my son is coming—that dear Philip !—without giving us a note of warning ; " and he laughed louder than before.

" So you are pleased with my prediction ? " said Balsamo, gravely. " I am glad of it ; but, in your place, I should set about giving some orders."

" Really ? "

" Yes."

" I shall think of it, my dear guest—I shall think of it."

" You have very little time."

" And you are serious, then ? "

" No one could be more serious ; if you wish to receive the great personage, who does you the honor of visiting you, properly, you have not a minute to lose."

The baron shook his head.

" You still doubt ? " asked Balsamo.

" I warn you, you have to do with a most confirmed skeptic."

And just then he turned to call his daughter, in order to communicate his guest's prediction to her, as we have before related. We have seen how the young girl replied to her father's invitation, and how Balsamo's gaze had drawn her, as if by fascination, to the window.

Nicole stood looking with amazement at La Brie, who was making signs to her, and trying to understand what had been said.

" I am dreadfully hard of belief," repeated the baron, " and unless I saw——"

" Then, since you must see, look there," said Balsamo, pointing to the avenue, where a horseman appeared galloping toward them.

" Ha ! " cried the baron, " there indeed is——"

" Monsieur Philip," said Nicole standing on tiptoe.

" My young master ! " exclaimed La Brie, joyfully.

" My brother, my brother ! " cried Andrée, stretching out her arms at the window.

" Is it your son, my dear baron ? " asked Balsamo, in a careless tone.

"Yes, pardieu, it is !" exclaimed he, stupefied with astonishment.

"This is but the beginning," said Balsamo.

"You are positively a sorcerer, then," said the baron, more submissively than before.

A triumphant smile hovered on the stranger's lips.

The horse came on at full speed, reeking with moisture —passed the last rows of trees, and, while still in motion, the rider leaped to the ground, and hastened to embrace his father, who only muttered : "What the devil ! what the devil ! "

"It is really I," said Philip, who saw his father's perplexity ; "it is indeed."

"Doubtless ; I see that plainly enough ; but what brought you hither at this time ?"

"Father, a great honor awaits our house."

The old man looked up inquiringly. Philip went on : "In an hour Marie Antoinette Josephe, Archduchess of Austria and Dauphiness of France, will be here."

The baron looked as deeply humbled as he had before looked sarcastic, and turning to Balsamo, said only, "Pardon me ! "

"Sir," returned Balsamo, "I leave you with your son ; it is long since you have met, and you must have much to say to each other."

Bowing to Andrée, who, full of joy at the arrival of her brother, had hastened down to meet him, he retired, making a sign to Nicole and La Brie, which they doubtless understood, for they disappeared with him among the trees of the avenue.

CHAPTER XIII.

PHILIP DE TAVERNEY.

PHILIP DE TAVERNEY, Chevalier de Maison Rouge, did not in the least resemble his sister, yet was as fine a specimen of manly beauty as she was of feminine loveliness. His features were noble and regular, his figure and carriage graceful in the extreme, and the expression of his eyes was at the same time mild and haughty.

Like all distinguished minds, wearied by the narrow and chilling forms of life, he was disposed to melancholy, without being sad. To this, perhaps, he owed his mildness of temper, for he was naturally proud, imperious, and reserved. The necessity of associating with the poor, his real equals, as with the rich, his equals in rank, had softened a character inclined to be overbearing and scornful.

Philip had scarcely embraced his father, when Andrée, roused from her magnetic torpor by his arrival, hastened down to throw herself on his bosom. The sobs which accompanied this action showed how dear he was to the heart of the tender girl.

Philip took her hand and his father's, and drew them into the saloon, where being now alone, he sat down between them.

"You are incredulous, my dear father—you are surprised, my dear sister," said he, "yet nothing is more true than that in a few minutes the dauphiness will be in our poor abode."

"Ventrebleu!" cried the baron. "She must be prevented, whatever it cost. The dauphiness here! We should be dishonored forever. This would be a specimen of the nobility of France to present her! No, no, it must not be. But tell me, what the deuce put my house in her head?"

"Oh, it is a complete romance."

"A romance?" said Andrée. "Relate it, brother—my dear, good brother!"

"My dear, good brother!" repeated the baron. "She seems quite pleased."

"Yes; for is not Philip pleased, my dear father?"

"Because Master Philip is an enthusiast; but for me, who look at things in a more serious manner, I see nothing very agreeable in it."

"You will be of a different opinion when I relate what has occurred."

"Well, relate it quickly," grumbled the old man.

"Yes, yes, relate it!" exclaimed Andrée, impatiently.

"Well, I was in garrison at Strasbourg, as you know. Now, you are aware that it was by Strasbourg that the dauphiness was to enter France."

"Know it—how should we know anything in this den?" asked the baron.

"Well, at Strasbourg, brother——" said Andrée.

"Well, we were waiting on the glacis from six in the morning, for we did not know positively at what hour Madame la Dauphine would arrive. It rained in torrents, and our clothes were dripping. The major sent me forward to endeavor to discover the cortége. I had galloped about a league, when all at once, at a turn in the road, I found myself close to the advance guard of the escort. I spoke a few words to them, and just then her royal highness put her head out of the carriage window, and asked who I was. It seems I had been called to to stop, but I had already set off at a full gallop—all my fatigue was forgotten in an instant."

"And the dauphiness?" asked Andrée.

"She is not older than you, and beautiful as an angel."

"But, Philip," said the baron, rather hesitatingly.

"Well, father?"

"Does she not resemble some one you have seen?"

"Some one that I have seen?"

"Yes; endeavor to recollect."

"No; I know no one like Madame la Dauphine!" he exclaimed enthusiastically.

"What! not Nicole, for instance?"

"Ha! that is most strange. Now you say so, I do think she is like her; but oh, so much inferior in beauty and grace! But how could you know that she was like her?"

"Faith! a sorcerer told me."

"A sorcerer?"

"Yes; and he predicted her coming and yours, this morning."

"The stranger?" asked Andrée, timidly.

"Is it he who was beside you, sir, when I arrived, and who retired so discreetly?"

"Yes, the same; but go on, Philip, go on."

"Perhaps it would be better to make some preparations," said Andrée.

"No; the more you prepare, the more ridiculous we shall appear. Go on, Philip, I tell you."

"I returned to Strasbourg, and told the governor, the Count de Stainville; we set out immediately to meet her royal highness, and we were at the Kehl gate when the procession came in sight. I was close to the governor."

"Stay!" said the baron; "I once knew a Count de Stainville."

"Brother-in-law to the prime minister, the Duke de Choiseul."

"It is the same. Go on, then go on."

"The dauphiness, who is young, perhaps likes young faces, for she listened very inattentively to the governor, and all the time fixed her eyes on me, although I kept respectfully in the background. Then, pointing to me, she said, 'Is not that the gentleman who was the first to meet me?' 'Yes, madame,' replied the governor. 'Approach, sir!' said she. I approached her. 'What is your name?' asked the dauphiness, in the sweetest voice I ever heard. 'The Chevalier de Taverney Maison Rouge,' I replied, stammering. 'Pray take a note of that name on your tablets, my dear friend,' said the dauphiness, turning to an old lady, who I have since learned is the Countess de Langershausen, her governess. My name was written. Then, turning again to me, she said, 'Ah, sir, you have suffered very much from your exposure to this frightful weather; I am extremely sorry for having been the cause of it.'"

"Oh, how good the dauphiness must be! what kindness and consideration!" said Andrée, with delight.

"Very well—very well, indeed!" muttered the baron, with a smile indicative of a father's partiality, and at the same time of his bad opinion of women and even of queens. But go on, Philip."

"What did you say?" asked Andrée.

"I said not a word—I bowed to the very ground. She passed on."

"What, you said nothing?" exclaimed the baron.

"I had no voice, I assure you, sir; my heart beat so rapidly—I was so much agitated."

"What the devil! do you think I had nothing to say when about your age I was presented to the Princess Leczinska?"

"But, sir, you had always a great deal of wit," Philip replied. Andrée pressed his hand.

"I profited by her royal highness's departure," continued Philip, "to hasten to my apartment and change my clothes, for I was wet to the skin, and covered with mud from head to foot."

"Poor, dear brother!" whispered Andrée.

"When the dauphiness," Philip continued, "reached the town-hall, she had to receive the congratulations of the principal inhabitants. That being over, it was announced that dinner was served. A friend of mine, the major of my regiment, since told me that while at the table she looked several times round on the officers who were present, and at last she said, 'I do not see the young officer who was sent to meet me this morning; has he not been told that I wished to thank him?' The major stepped forward. 'Madame,' said he, 'Lieutenant de Taverney was obliged to retire and change his dress, that he might present himself in a more suitable manner before you.' A moment after I entered the room, and I had not been five minutes in it when the dauphiness perceived me. She made a sign to me to approach—I obeyed. 'Sir,' said she, 'should you object to follow me to Paris?' 'Oh, madame,' I cried, 'it would only make me too happy, but I am in garrison at Strasbourg, and I am not my own master.' 'Well, I shall arrange that matter with the governor;' and she made a gesture for me to retire. In the evening she said to the governor, 'Sir, I have a vow to fulfil, and you must assist me in it.' 'I shall consider it a sacred duty, madame,' he replied. 'You must know,' she continued, 'that I made a vow to take into my own service the first Frenchman, whoever he should be, whom I should meet on touching the soil of France, and that I would make him and his family happy, if, indeed, princes can make any one happy.' 'Madame,' said the governor, 'princes are God's representatives on earth; but may I ask,' continued he, 'who was the person who had the good fortune to be the first met by your royal highness?' 'The Chevalier de Taverney Maison Rouge, a young lieutenant.' 'We shall be jealous of the Chevalier de Taverney, madame,' replied the governor; 'but we shall not place any obstacle in the way of his high fortune—the ties which engage him here shall be broken, and he shall depart at the same time as your highness.' So the day on which the dauphiness left Strasbourg I was ordered to accompany her on horseback, and since then have never left the door of her carriage."

"Oh!" said the baron, with his former singular smile, "strange enough, but not impossible!"

"What, father?"

"Oh, never mind!"

"But, brother," said Andrée, "I don't see what all this has to do with the dauphiness coming hither."

"Wait till you hear. Yesterday morning we arrived at Nancy about eleven o'clock, and were passing through the town by torchlight. The dauphiness called me to her. 'I wish,' said she, 'to depart early to-morrow morning.' 'Your highness is going to make a long march, then?' 'No; but I wish to stop on the road, and you can guess where?' she asked, smiling. 'No, madame.' 'I mean to stop at Taverney, to see your father and sister.' 'My father and sister? What! your royal highness knows——' 'I have made inquiries, and know that they live only two hundred paces from the road which we are traveling.' The perspiration broke on my forehead, and, trembling, as you may suppose, I hastened to reply, 'My father's house, madame, is not worthy to receive so great a princess—we are poor.' 'So much the better,' replied she; 'I shall, therefore, I am certain, be received more cordially and more simply ; however poor you may be, there will always be a cup of milk for a friend who wishes to forget for a moment that she is Archduchess of Austria and Dauphiness of France.' ' Oh, madame,' said I. This was all—respect forbid me to go further."

"Stupid fellow !" cried the baron.

"One might have thought that her royal highness guessed what was passing in my mind, for she added : ' Do not be afraid, I shall not stay long ; but since you think that I shall suffer any inconvenience by this visit, it is only fair, for I caused you to suffer on my arrival at Strasbourg.' Who could resist such charming words, father ? "

"Oh, it would have been impossible !" cried Andrée ; " she is so sweet, so good, she will be satisfied with my flowers and a cup of my milk, as she says !"

"Yes ; but she will not be very well satisfied with my chairs, which will dislocate her bones, and my hangings, which will disgust her. Devil take all whims ! So ! France will be well governed with a woman who takes such caprices. Plague on it ! A strange reign it will be, to judge from the commencement," said the baron angrily.

"Oh, father, how can you say such things of a princess who is honoring us so highly ?"

"Who is dishonoring us, rather !" cried the old man. "Taverney was forgotten, buried under the ruins of Maison Rouge. I intended that if it came to light again it should be in a suitable manner, and now the whims of a girl are going to drag us into day—dusty, shabby, wretched !—and the gazettes, on the watch for everything absurd, will amuse their readers with the visit of a great princess to this den of Taverney. Cordieu ! I have an idea."

The young people started at the manner in which he pronounced these words.

"What do you mean, sir ? " demanded Philip.

The baron muttered to himself, "If the Duke of Medina burned his palace that he might embrace a queen, I may well burn my kennel to get rid of the visit of a princess. Let her come ! let her come !"

Philip and Andrée only heard the last words, and they looked at each other uneasily.

"It cannot be long before she will be here, sir," said Philip. "I took the way through the wood, in order to get some minutes in advance of the cortége ; it will soon be here."

"Then I not must lose time," said the baron ; and with the agility of twenty, he left the saloon. He hastened to the kitchen, snatched a flaming piece of wood from the hearth, and proceeded to his barns ; but just as he raised his arm to throw it in to a heap of straw, he was seized by Balsamo, who flung to a safe distance the burning brand.

"What are you about, sir ?" cried he. "The Archduchess of Austria is not a Constable de Bourbon, whose presence contaminates, so that we should rather burn our house than permit her to enter it."

The old man stopped, pale, trembling, and his habitual smile banished from his lips. He had gathered all his strength to enable him to resolve on making his poverty yet greater by the destruction of his dwelling, rather than be disgraced, according to his ideas, by allowing its mediocrity to be seen.

"Come, sir, come !" continued Balsamo ; "you have only time to throw off your dressing-gown and put yourself in better trim. The Baron of Taverney, whom I knew at the siege of Philipsbourg, wore the Grand Cross of the Order of St. Louis ; any coat will be rich and elegant when decorated with that."

"But, sir, shall I show to our dauphiness that poverty which I wished to hide from you ?"

"Be not uneasy ; we shall manage to occupy her attention so that she shall not know whether your house be new or old, poor or rich. Be hospitable, sir ; it is your duty as a gentleman. What will the enemies of the dauphiness—and she has many—what will they do, if her friends burn their castles rather than receive her under their roof ?

Let us not thus anticipate that vengeance which is to come —everything in its predestined time."

The baron again showed an involuntary submission to Balsamo, and hurried to his children, who, uneasy at his absence, were seeking him on every side.

As to Balsamo, he retired in silence, like a man intent on some work which he had undertaken, and which he must complete.

CHAPTER XIV.

MARIE ANTOINETTE JOSEPHE, ARCHDUCHESS OF AUSTRIA.

As Balsamo had said, there was no time to be lost, for now on the road, generally so peaceful, which led to the Baron of Taverney's dwelling, a great sound of carriages, horses, and voices was heard.

Three carriages, one of which was covered with gilding and mythological bas-reliefs, and which, notwithstanding its magnificence, was not less dusty and bespattered than the others, stopped at the great gate of the avenue. Gilbert held it open, his eyes distended, his whole frame trembling with feverish agitation at the sight of so much magnificence. Twenty gentlemen on horseback, all young and splendidly dressed, drew up near the principal carriage, from which a young girl of sixteen, dressed with great simplicity, but with her hair elaborately piled on her forehead, got out, assisted by a gentleman in black, who wore, saltier wise, under his mantle, the ribbon of St. Louis.

Marie Antoinette, for it was she, brought with her a reputation for beauty which the princesses destined to share the thrones of the kings of France have not always possessed. It was difficult to say whether her eyes were beautiful or not, yet they were capable of every expression, more particularly of the opposite expressions of mildness and scorn. Her nose was finely formed, her upper lip beautiful, but the lower lip, her aristocratic inheritance from seventeen emperors, was too thick and prominent. Her complexion was lovely; her neck, shoulders, and bust were of marble whiteness and beautifully formed; her hands truly regal. At times, when roused to energy, her carriage was majestic, firm, and decided; at other times, when not excited, soft, undulating—one might almost say—caressing. No woman ever made a more graceful courtesy—no queen ever bowed with more tact and discrimination. This day the most expressive sweetness shone in her countenance. She had resolved to be only the woman, and to forget the dauphiness. She wore a dress of white silk, and her beautiful bare arms supported a mantle of rich lace.

Scarcely had she touched the ground, when she turned to assist one of her ladies of honor whom age had weakened a little, and, refusing the arm of a gentleman in black, she advanced, inhaling the fresh air, and looking around as if determined to enjoy to the utmost the few moments of freedom with which she was indulging herself.

"Oh, what a beautiful situation!" she exclaimed; "what magnificent trees! and such a pretty little house! How happy one might be in this healthful air, under those trees which form so sweet a retirement!"

At this moment Philip appeared, followed by Andrée, on whose arm the baron leaned. She was dressed in a simple gown of gray silk, and the baron in a coat of blue velvet, the remains of some of his old magnificence; he had not forgotten Balsamo's recommendation, and wore his ribbon of St. Louis. On seeing the three approach, the dauphiness stopped. Her escort then grouped itself around her —the officers holding their horses by the bridles, and the courtiers, hat in hand, whispering to one another. Philip drew near, pale with agitation, yet with a noble bearing.

"With your royal highness's permission," said he, "I have the honor of presenting to you the Baron de Taverney Maison Rouge, my father, and Claire Andrée de Taverney, my sister."

The baron bowed profoundly, like a man who knew how to bow to queens. Andrée showed, in her graceful timidity, the most flattering kind of politeness—sincere respect. Marie Antoinette looked at the two young people, and recalling what Philip had said of their poverty, she guessed what they suffered at that moment.

"Madame," said the baron, with dignity, "your royal highness does too much honor to the Château of Taverney —such an humble abode is not worthy to receive so much rank and beauty."

"I know that it is the abode of an old soldier of France," replied the dauphiness, "and my mother, the Empress Maria Theresa, who was a distinguished warrior, has told me that often in your country those richest in glory are the poorest in meaner treasures;" and with ineffable grace, she extended her lovely hand to Andrée, who, kneeling, kissed it.

The baron was, however, still haunted by the idea which had so much tormented him, that the train of the dauphiness was about to crowd into his little house, in which there could not be found chairs for a fourth of their number. The dauphiness hastened to relieve him from all embarrassment.

"Gentlemen," said she, turning to those who formed her escort, "I must not impose on you the trouble of following me in all my caprices. You will wait here, if you please; in half an hour I shall return. Come with me, my good Langershausen," she added, in German, to the lady whom she had assisted out of the carriage, "and you, sir," said she to the gentleman in black, "have the goodness to follow us."

This personage, though dressed thus simply, was remarkable for the elegance of his manners, and was about thirty years of age, and very handsome. He drew to one side to allow the princess to pass. Marie Antoinette took Andrée for her guide, and made a sign to Philip to come near his sister.

As to the baron, he was left to the personage of high rank doubtless to whom the dauphiness had granted the honor of accompanying her.

"So you are a Taverney Maison Rouge?" said he,

playing with his splendid ruffles of the most expensive lace, and turning to the baron with truly aristocratic impertinence.

"Must I reply, sir, or my lord?" asked the baron, with equal impertinence.

"You may say simply prince, or your eminence, which you choose," the other replied.

"Well, then, your eminence, I am a Taverney Maison Rouge—a real one," said the baron, in that tone of raillery which he so seldom abandoned.

His eminence, who had the usual tact of great nobles, felt that he had to do with no country clown, and continued, "This is your summer residence?"

"Summer and winter," answered the baron, who wished to put an end to disagreeable queries, but accompanying each reply with a low bow.

Philip could not help turning from time to time uneasily toward his father, for the house, as they drew nearer it, wore an aspect threatening and ironical, as if pitilessly determined to show all their poverty. The baron had already resignedly extended his hand to point the way to the door of his house, when the dauphiness, turning to him, said: "Excuse me, sir, if I do not enter; these shades are so delightful that I could pass my life in them. I am tired of rooms. For fifteen days I have been received in rooms —I, who love the open air, the shade of trees, and the perfume of flowers." Then, turning to Andrée: "You will bring me a cup of milk here, under these beautiful trees, will you not?"

"Your highness," said the baron, turning pale, "how should we dare to offer you such poor refreshment?"

"I prefer it, sir, to anything else. New-laid eggs and milk formed my banquets at Schoenbrunn."

All at once La Brie, swelling with pride, in a splendid livery and a napkin on his arm, appeared under an archway of jasmine, the shade of which had attracted the eye of the dauphiness. In a tone in which importance and respect were strangely mixed, he announced: "Her royal highness is served!"

"Am I in the dwelling of an enchanter?" cried the princess, as she ran rather than walked to the perfumed alley.

The baron, in his uneasiness, forgot all etiquette, left the gentleman in black, and hurried after the dauphiness. Andrée and Philip looked at each other with mingled astonishment and anxiety, and followed their father.

Under the clematis, jasmine, and woodbine was placed an oval table, covered with a damask cloth of dazzling whiteness, on which was arranged, in a brilliant service of plate, a collation the most elegant and rare. There were exotic fruits made into the most delicious confections; biscuits from Aleppo, oranges from Malta, and lemons of extraordinary size, all arranged in beautiful vases. Wines, the richest and most esteemed, sparkled like the ruby and the topaz, in decanters ornamented and cut in Persia, and in the center, in a silver vase, was placed the milk for which the dauphiness had asked.

Marie Antoinette looked around, and saw surprise and alarm imprinted on the face of her host and on the countenance of his son and daughter. The gentlemen of her escort were delighted with what they saw, without understanding it, and without endeavoring to understand it.

"You expected me, then, sir?" said she to the baron.

"I, madame!" stammered he.

"Yes; you could not, in ten minutes, have all this prepared, and I have only been ten minutes here;" and she looked at La Brie with an expression which said: "Above all, when you have only one servant."

"Madame," answered the baron, "your royal highness was expected, or, rather, your coming was foretold to me."

"Your son wrote to you?"

"No, madame."

"No one knew that I was coming here, as I did not wish to give you the trouble which I see I have done. It was only late last night that I expressed my intention to your son, and he reached this but half an hour before me."

"Scarcely a quarter of an hour, madame."

"Then some fairy must have revealed to you what was to occur. Mademoiselle's godmother, perhaps?"

"Madame," said the baron, offering a chair to the princess, "it was not a fairy who announced my good fortune to me."

"Who, then?" asked she, observing that he hesitated.

"An enchanter, madame."

"An enchanter—how can that be?"

"I know nothing of the matter, for I do not meddle with magic myself, yet to that, madame, I am indebted for being able to entertain your highness in a tolerable fashion."

"In that case we must not touch anything, since the collation is the work of sorcery. His eminence," added she, pointing to the gentleman in black, who had fixed his eye on a Strasbourg pie, "seems in a hurry to begin, but we shall assuredly not eat of this enchanted collation; and you, dear friend," turning to her governess, "distrust the Cyprus wine, and do as I do;" and she poured some water from a globe-formed caraffe with a narrow neck into a golden goblet.

"In truth," said Andrée, with alarm, "her royal highness is perhaps right."

Philip trembled with surprise, and ignorant of what had passed the evening before, looked alternately at his father and his sister for explanation.

"But I see," continued the dauphiness, "his eminence is determined to sin in spite of all the canons of the Church."

"Madame," replied the prelate, "we princes of the Church are too worldly to be able to believe that Heaven's wrath will fall on us about a little refreshment for the body, and, above all, too humane to feel the least inclination to burn an honest sorcerer for providing us with good things like these."

"Do not jest, I pray, monseigneur," said the baron. "I swear to you that a sorcerer—a real sorcerer—foretold to me, about an hour ago, the arrival of her royal highness and my son."

"And has an hour been sufficient for you to prepare this banquet?" demanded the dauphiness. "In that case you are a greater sorcerer than your sorcerer!"

"No, madame; it was he who did all this, and brought the table up through the ground, ready served as you see."

"On your word, sir?"

"On the honor of a gentleman!" replied the baron.

"Ha!" said the cardinal, in a serious tone, putting back the plate which he had taken, "I thought you were jesting. Then you have in your house a real magician?"

"A real magician; and I should not wonder if he has made all the gold on that table himself."

"Oh, he must have found out the philosopher's stone!" cried the cardinal, his eyes sparkling with covetousness.

"See how the eyes of his eminence sparkle—he who has been seeking all his life for the philosopher's stone!" said the dauphiness.

"I confess to your royal highness," replied his very worldly eminence, "that nothing interests me more than the supernatural—nothing is so curious, in my estimation, as the impossible."

"Ah! I have traced the vulnerable part, it seems!" said the dauphiness; "every great man has his mysteries, particularly when he is a diplomatist—and I, I warn your eminence, know a great deal of sorcery. I sometimes find out things—if not impossible, if not supernatural, at least incredible!" and the eye of the dauphiness, before so mild, flashed as from an internal storm, but no thunder followed. His eminence alone, doubtless, understood what this meant, for he looked evidently embarrassed. The dauphiness went on:

"To make the thing complete, Monsieur de Taverney, you must show us your magician. Where is he? In what box have you hidden him?"

"Madame," answered the baron, "he is much more able to put me and my house in a box, than I to put him."

"In truth, you excite my curiosity," said Marie Antoinette. "I must positively see him!"

The tone in which this was uttered, although still retaining the charm which Marie Antoinette knew so well to assume, forbid all idea of refusal to comply with her wish.

The baron understood this perfectly, and made a sign to La Brie, who was contemplating with eager eyes the illustrious guests, the sight of whom seemed to make up to him for his twenty years of unpaid wages.

"Tell Baron Joseph Balsamo," said his master, "that her royal highness the dauphiness desires to see him." La Brie departed.

"Joseph Balsamo!" said the dauphiness. "What a singular name!"

"Joseph Balsamo!" repeated his eminence, as if reflecting. "I think I know that name."

Five minutes passed in silence—then Andrée felt a thrill run through her frame—she heard, before it was perceptible to other ears, a step advancing under the shade of the trees—the branches were put aside—and Joseph Balsamo stood face to face with Marie Antoinette.

CHAPTER XV.

MAGIC.

BALSAMO bowed humbly, but no sooner had he raised his head than he fixed his bright, expressive eyes firmly but respectfully on the face of the dauphiness, and waited calmly until she should interrogate him.

"If it is you of whom the Baron de Taverney has been speaking to us, draw near, sir, that we may better see what a magician is."

Balsamo advanced another step and bowed.

"Your profession is to foretell events, sir?" said the dauphiness, regarding him with more curiosity than she would herself have been willing to acknowledge, and sipping some milk which had been handed her.

"It is not my profession, but I do foretell events."

"We have been brought up in an enlightened creed," said the dauphiness, "and the only mysteries in which we believe are those of the Catholic faith."

"They are to be venerated," replied Balsamo, reverently; "but here is Monseigneur the Cardinal de Rohan, who will tell your royal highness, though he be a prince of the Church, that they are not the only mysteries which deserve to be regarded with respect."

The cardinal started; he had not told his name, it had not been pronounced, yet this stranger knew it. Marie Antoinette did not appear to remark this circumstance, but continued:

"You will confess, sir, that at least they are the only mysteries which cannot be controverted?"

"Madame," answered Balsamo, with the same respect, "as well as faith there is certainty."

"You speak rather obscurely, sir; although thoroughly French in heart, I am but indifferently acquainted with the niceties of the language, and must beg you to be less enigmatical if I am to comprehend you."

"And I, madame, would entreat that all may remain unexplained. I should deeply regret to unveil to so illustrious a princess a future which might not correspond to her hopes."

"This becomes serious," said Marie Antoinette. "The gentleman wishes to excite my curiosity, that I may command him to tell my fortune."

"God forbid that your royal highness should force me to do it!"

"Yes," replied the dauphiness; "for you would be rather puzzled to do it," and she laughed.

But the dauphiness's laugh died away without meeting an echo from any of the attendants. Every one present seemed to submit tacitly to the influence of the singular man who was for the moment the center of general attraction.

"Come, confess it frankly," said the dauphiness.

Balsamo bowed.

"Yet it was you who predicted my arrival to the Baron de Taverney," resumed Marie Antoinette, with a slight movement of impatience.

"Yes, madame, it was I."

"And how did he do it?" she added, turning to the baron, as if she felt the necessity of a third party taking share in this strange dialogue.

"Very simple, madame; merely by looking in a glass of water."

"Was it so?" she asked of Balsamo.

"Yes, madame," answered he.

"Then, having read the future for the Baron de Taverney in a glass of water, surely you can read it for me in a decanter?"

"Perfectly well, madame."

"And why refuse to do so?"

"Because the future is uncertain, and if I saw a cloud on it——" He stopped.

"Well?"

"It would give me pain to sadden your royal highness."

"Have you known me before, or do you now see me for the first time?"

"I have had the honor of seeing your royal highness when a child, in your native country, with your august mother."

"You have seen my mother, then?"

"I have had that honor. She is a great and powerful queen."

"Empress, sir,"

"I used the word queen in reference to the heart and mind—and yet——"

"Reservations concerning my mother?" said the dauphiness, haughtily.

"The greatest hearts have weaknesses, madame, particularly where they think the happiness of their children is concerned."

" History, I trust, sir, will not discover one single weakness in Maria Theresa."

" Because history will not know what is known only to the Empress Maria Theresa, to your royal highness, and to myself."

" We have a secret, sir—we three ? " said the dauphiness, smiling disdainfuly.

" We three, madame," replied Balsamo, solemnly.

" Come, then, tell this secret, sir ! "

" It will then be no longer one."

" No matter. Tell it."

" Is it your royal highness's will ? "

" It is."

Balsamo bowed.   "There is in the Palace of Schoenbrunn," said he, " a cabinet, called the Dresden Cabinet, on account of the splendid vases of porcelain which it contains——"

" Yes " said the dauphiness ; " go on."

" This cabinet 1orms a part of the private suite of rooms of the Empress Maria Theresa ; in it she writes her letters."

" Yes."

" On a certain day, about seven in the morning, when the empress had not yet risen, your royal highness entered this cabinet by a door through which you alone were permitted to pass, for your highness is the favorite daughter of her imperial majesty."

" Well, sir. ? "

" Your highness approached a writing-desk, on which lay open a letter which her imperial majesty had written the night before. Your royal highness read that letter, and doubtless some expressions in it must have been displeasing to you, for you took a pen, and with your own hand erased three words."

The dauphiness blushed slightly.

" What were the words erased ? " she asked, anxiously.

" They were too condescending, doubtless, and showed too great affection for the person to whom they were addressed. This was a weakness, and to this it was I alluded in speaking of your august mother."

" Then you remember the words ? "

" Assuredly."

" Repeat them to me."

" They were, ' my dear friend.' "

Marie Antoinette bit her lip and turned pale.

" Shall I tell your royal highness to whom the letter was addressed ? "

" No ; but you may write the name."

Balsamo drew out a pocket-book with gold clasps, and having written some words on one of the leaves, he tore it out, and, and, bowing, presented it to the dauphiness. Marie Antoinette unfolded the leaf, read it, and looked with astonishment at the man who, though he bowed low before her, seemed to have it in his power to direct her fate.

The letter was addressed to the mistress of King Louis XV., "To the Marchioness de Pompadour."

" All this is true, sir," said Marie Antoinette, after a pause ; " and although I am ignorant by what means you have become acquainted with these circumstances, I cannot speak falsely, and I must declare that what you have said is true."

" Then," said Balsamo, " will your royal highness permit me to retire, satisfied with this harmless proof of my art ? "

" No, sir," replied the dauphiness ; " the more I know of your powers, the more desirous I become to have my fate foretold. You have spoken only of the past ; let me learn what the future will be."

The princess spoke these words with a feverish impatience, which he in vain endeavored to conceal from her auditors.

" I am ready, if your royal highness commands me, to declare it ; yet let me supplicate you not to do so."

" I have never expressed a command twice ; and you will recollect, sir, that I have already commanded once."

" Let me at least consult the oracle whether it may be revealed to your royal highness or not," he said entreatingly.

" Good or bad, sir," replied Marie Antoinette, " I will know it. If good, I shall take it for flattery ; if bad, I shall hold it as a warning, and shall be obliged to you for it. Begin."

Balsamo took the round caraffe with the narrow neck and placed it on a golden saucer; the rays of the sun striking on this, shone dimly yellow in the water, and seemed to offer something worthy of deep consideration to the attentive soothsayer. Every one was silent. At length he placed the caraffe again on the table, and shook his head.

"Well, sir ?" said the dauphiness.

"I cannot speak it," replied Balsamo.

"You cannot, because you have nothing to tell me," replied Marie Antoinette, a little contemptuously.

"There are things which must never be said to princes, madame," replied Balsamo, in a tone which seemed to express his determination to oppose her wishes.

"Yes, when those things, I repeat, may be expressed by the word *nothing*."

"It is not that which prevents me, madame; on the contrary, it is the very reverse."

The dauphiness smiled disdainfully, Balsamo appeared embarrassed, the cardinal began to laugh outright, and the baron drew near, grumbling :

"So ! my magician has exhausted himself; his powers have not lasted very long. It only remains for us to see all those fine things turned into vine leaves, as we have read in Eastern tales."

"I should rather have had the simple vine leaves," said Marie Antoinette, "than these fine things displayed by the gentleman for the purpose of getting himself presented to me."

"Deign to remember, madame," replied Balsamo, who was deathly pale, "that I did not solicit this honor."

"It was not difficult for you to guess, sir, that I should ask to see you."

"Pardon him, madame," said Andrée, in a low voice; "he thought he was doing right."

"And I tell you he was doing wrong," replied the princess, so as only to be heard by Andrée and Balsamo. "No one can elevate himself by humiliating an old man, and when we have the pewter goblet of a gentleman to drink in, we need not the golden one of a mountebank!"

Balsamo started as if a viper had bitten him. "Madame," he said, greatly agitated, "I am ready to let you know your destiny, since your blindness impels you to desire such knowledge."

He pronounced these words in a tone so firm and so threatening, that all present felt the blood chilled in their veins.

"*Gib im kein gehœr, mein Tochter,*"* said the old lady to Marie Antoinette.

"*Lass sie hœren, sie hat wissen wollen, und so soll sie wissen,*"† replied Balsamo.

These words, spoken in German, a language which was understood by only a few present, seemed to render more mysterious what was going on.

"No," said the dauphiness, resisting the entreaties of her venerable governess; "let him say what he desires to say; were I now to permit him to be silent, he would believe me afraid."

Balsamo heard these words, and a dark, furtive smile played for a second on his lips. "It is as I said," he muttered to himself; "the courage of bravado merely."

"Speak!" said the dauphiness, "speak, sir."

"Then your royal highness is decided?"

"I never go back from a decision once made."

"In that case, madame, I would entreat that we may be alone."

She made a sign which those around understood—all retired.

"This is not a bad plan for obtaining a private audience," said the dauphiness, turning to Balsamo; "is it not, sir?"

"I would beg your royal highness not to irritate me!" replied Balsamo; "I am but an instrument of Providence to enlighten you on those sorrows which await you. In-

---

* "Do not listen to him, my daughter."

† "Let her; she wishes to know, and she shall know."

sult Fortune, if you will—she can revenge herself ; but for me, I am but the gloomy herald of the misfortunes she has in store for you."

"Then it appears that misfortunes await me ?" said the dauphiness, mildly, touched by Balsamo's respectful manner.

"Yes ; terrible misfortunes."

"First, will my family be happy ?"

"That which you have left, or that to which you are going ?"

"Oh, my own family—my mother, my brother Joseph, my sister Caroline."

"Your misfortunes will not reach them."

"They are mine alone, then ?"

"They are yours, and those of your new family."

"The royal family of France includes three princes, the Duke de Berry, the Count de Provençe, and the Count d'Artois—what will be their fate ?"

"They will all reign."

"Then I shall have no children ?"

"You will have children."

"Not sons ?"

"Some of them sons."

"My sorrows, then, will be caused by their death ?"

"You will grieve that one is dead, but most will you grieve that the other lives."

"Will my husband love me ?"

"Yes, too well."

"Shall I not, then, be able to bear my grief, supported by my husband and my family ?"

"Neither will support you."

"The love of my people will still be mine ?"

"The people !—the ocean in a calm !—have you seen the ocean in a storm, madame ?"

"By doing good I shall prevent the storm ; or, if it rise, I shall rise above it."

"The higher the wave, the deeper the abyss."

"God will defend me."

"Alas ! there are heads which He himself foredooms."

" What mean you, sir ? " " Shall I not, then, be queen ? "

" Yes, madame ; but would to Heaven that you were not to be ! "

She smiled disdainfully.

" Did you remark," he continued, " the tapestry of the first room in which you slept after having entered France ? "

" Yes, sir."

" What did it represent ? "

" The slaughter of the innocents."

" Have not the grim faces of the murderers haunted your memory ? "

" I confess that they have."

" Had you not a storm on the way hither ? "

" Yes ; a thunder-bolt fell, and nearly on my carriage."

" Were not those omens ? "

" Fatal omens ? "

" It would be difficult to interpret them as happy ones."

The dauphiness let her head fall on her bosom, and raising it after a minute's silence, " Speak," said she ; " in what manner shall I die ? "

He shook his head.

" Speak ! "

" I dare not."

" It is my will that you should," she said, imperiously.

" Have mercy—have mercy on yourself ! "

" Speak, sir, or I shall say that all this is but an absurd fable. Take care ! the daughter of Maria Theresa is not to be jested with ! the woman who holds in her hand the destiny of thirty millions of men is not to be trifled with ! "

He continued silent.

" You know no more," she said, contemptuously ; " your imagination is exhausted."

" My knowledge of the future is not exhausted, madame ; and if you will force me—— "

" Yes ; I will hear all."

He seized the caraffe on the golden saucer, placed it in a dark hollow, where some rocks formed a sort of grotto ; then he took the hand of the archduchess, and drew her under the vault.

"Are you ready?" he asked the princess, who was alarmed by his rapid movements.

"Yes."

"On your knees, then! on your knees! and pray to God to spare you the dreadful end of all your greatness, which you are now to witness!"

She obeyed mechanically, and fell on both knees.

He pointed with a wand to the glass globe, in the center of which must have appeared some dark and terrible form, for the dauphiness, in trying to rise, trembled and sunk again to the ground with a shriek of horror—she had fainted.

The baron hastened to her assistance, and in a few minutes she came to herself. She put her hand to her forehead, as if to recall her thoughts, then suddenly exclaimed: "The caraffe! the caraffe!"

The baron presented it to her. The water was perfectly limpid—not a stain mingled with it. Balsamo was gone.

CHAPTER XVI.

THE BARON DE TAVERNEY THINKS HE SEES AT LAST A SMALL OPENING INTO THE FUTURE.

THE baron was the first to perceive that the dauphiness had fainted; he had kept on the watch, more uneasy than any one else at what might take place between her and the sorcerer. Hearing her cry of terror, and seeing Balsamo spring out of the grotto, he ran to the spot.

The dauphiness's first request was to see the caraffe; her second, that no injury should be done the magician; and it was well she made this request, for no sooner had Philip heard her cry than he bounded after him like an angry lion.

When her lady of honor came near, and ventured to question her in German, she only drew from her that Balsamo had in no way been wanting in respect to her—

that she thought the storm of the preceding night and her long journey had fatigued her and brought on a nervous attack. Her replies were translated to the Cardinal de Rohan, who stood by, but dared not himself ask for information. In courts, people are obliged to be satisfied with half answers, so what the dauphiness said satisfied nobody, but every one appeared perfectly satisfied. Philip then drew near and said :

"I am obliged to obey your royal highness's orders, yet it is with regret that I do so ; the half hour during which you intended to stay is past, and the horses are ready."

"Thanks, sir," said she, with a smile full of fascinating languor ; " but I must alter my determination—I do not feel able to set out just now. If I could sleep for a few hours, I should be quite restored."

"Your royal highness knows what a poor abode ours is," the baron stammered out.

"Oh, sir, any place will do ; a little rest is all I want !" She said this as if again fainting, and her head sunk again on her bosom.

Andrée disappeared to prepare her room for her, and having in a few minutes returned, she stood beside the dauphiness, not daring to speak until some indication was given that she might do so. At length Marie Antoinette raised her head, smiled to Andrée, and, with her hand, made a sign to her to draw nearer.

"The room is ready for your royal highness. We entreat only——"

But she was not permitted to finish her apology—the dauphiness interrupted her.

"Thank you ! thank you ! May I ask you to summon the Countess of Langershausen, and to lead us to the apartment ?"

Andrée obeyed. The old lady of honor advanced. "Give me your arm, my dear friend," said the dauphiness to her, in German, "for indeed I have scarcely strength enough to walk without support."

The baroness obeyed ; Andrée approached to assist her. Turning soon after to Andrée, the dauphiness asked :

" Do you understand German, then, mademoiselle ? "

" Yes, madame ; I even speak it a little," replied Andrée, in German.

" That is delightful ! " exclaimed the dauphiness ; " that makes my plan still more agreeable."

Andrée dared not ask her august guest what her plan was, although she longed to know it. The dauphiness leaned on the arm of the Countess de Langershausen, and advanced slowly, her limbs trembling under her. As she issued from the trees in front of the grotto, she heard the cardinal's voice.

" What ! " said he, " Count de Stainville, do you mean to insist on speaking to her royal highness notwithstanding her orders to the contrary ? "

" I must insist on doing so," replied the governor of Strasbourg, in a firm voice ; " her royal highness will pardon me, I am certain."

" And I, sir, on the contrary, insist——"

" Let the governor come forward," said the dauphiness, appearing at the opening of the trees, which formed a verdant arch above her head. " Come forward, Count de Stainville."

Every one bowed at her command, and drew back to allow free passage to the brother-in-law of the then all-powerful minister who governed France. The count looked around, as if to request a private audience. Marie Antoinette understood that he had something important to say to her, but before she could express a wish to be left alone, all had withdrawn.

" A despatch from Versailles, madame," said the count, in a low voice, and presenting a letter which he had kept concealed under his plumed hat.

The dauphiness took it, and read the address. " It is for you, sir, not for me," she said ; " open it and read it, if it contains anything that concerns me."

" The letter is addressed to me," he replied, " but in the corner is a mark agreed on between my brother, Madame Choiseul, and myself, indicating that the letter is for your royal highness."

"True ; I did not observe it."

She opened the letter, and read the following lines :

"The presentation of Madame Dubarry is decided on, if she can only procure some noble lady to present her. We still hope she may not find one ; but the only sure means to prevent the presentation will be for her royal highness the dauphiness to make all speed. Her royal highness once at Versailles, no one will dare to offer such an insult to the court."

"Very well," said the dauphiness, folding up the letter, without the slightest symptom of emotion, or even of interest.

"Will your royal highness now retire to repose a little ?" asked Andrée, timidly.

"No, I thank you, mademoiselle ; the air has revived me ; I have quite recovered ; " and abandoning the arm of her lady of honor, she walked forward firmly and rapidly. "My horses immediately ! " said she.

The cardinal looked with inquisitive surprise at the count.

"The dauphin is becoming impatient," whispered the latter ; and this falsehood appearing a secret confided to him alone, his eminence was satisfied. As to Andrée, her father had taught her to respect the whims of crowned heads, and she was not at all surprised at the change in Marie Antoinette's intentions. The latter, therefore, turning, and seeing no alteration in the sweet expression of her countenance, said :

"Thanks, mademoiselle ; your hospitable reception has made a deep impression on me."

Then, turning to the baron, she continued :

"Sir, you must know that, on leaving Vienna, I made a vow to advance the fortune of the first Frenchman whom I should meet on the frontiers of France. That Frenchman was your son. But I do not intend to stop there ; your daughter shall not be forgotten either."

"Oh, your highness ! " murmured Andrée.

"Yes, I mean to make you one of my maids of honor.

You are noble, are you not ? " she added again, addressing
the baron.

" Oh, your highness ! " cried the baron, with delight,
for all his dreams seemed realized by what he heard ;
" although poor, our descent is unblemished ; yet so high
an honor——"

" It is only due to you. Your son will defend the king
as you have done ; your daughter will serve the dauphiness
—the one you will inspire with every loyal sentiment, the
other with every virtuous one. Shall I not be faithfully
served, sir ? " she said, now turning to Philip, who knelt in
gratitude at her feet, without words to express his emotion.

" But," murmured the baron—for his feelings did not
prevent him from reflecting.

" Yes, I understand," said the dauphiness , " you have
preparations to make, yet they cannot take long."

A sad smile passed over the lips of Andrée and Philip, a
bitter one over those of the baron, and Marie Antoinette
stopped, for she felt that she might unintentionally have
wounded their pride.

" At least," she resumed, " if I may judge by your
daughter's desire to please me. Besides I shall leave you
one of my carriages ; it will bring you after us. I must
call the Count de Stainville to my aid."

The count approached.

" I shall leave one of my carriages for the Baron de Taverney, whom I wish to accompany me to Paris with his
daughter. Appoint some one to accompany their carriage,
and to cause it to be recognized as belonging to my suite.'

" Come forward, Monsieur de Beausire."

" This very moment, madame," answered the count.

A young man of about five-and-twenty years of age, with
an easy and graceful carriage, and a lively and intelligent
eye, advanced, hat in hand, from the ranks of the escort of
the dauphiness.

" Let one of the carriages remain behind," said the
count, " for the Baron de Taverney ; you will accompany
the carriage yourself."

" And, sir," said the dauphiness, " join us again as soon

as possible. I authorize you to have double relays of horses, if necessary."

The baron and his children were profuse in their acknowledgments.

"This sudden departure will not put you to much inconvenience, I hope, sir," said the dauphiness.

"We are too happy to obey your royal highness's orders," replied the baron.

"Adieu! adieu!" said she, with a smile. "Gentlemen, conduct me to my carriage. Chevalier de Taverney, to horse!"

Philip kissed his father's hand, embraced his sister, and leaped lightly into his saddle.

The glittering train swept on, and in a quarter of an hour had disappeared like an evening vapor; there remained no human being in the avenue of Taverney but a young man, who, sitting on one of the lower pillars of the gate, pale and sorrowful, followed with a longing eye the last cloud of dust which was raised by the horses' feet, and which served to show the road they had taken. This young man was Gilbert.

Meanwhile, the saloon of Taverney presented a singular scene. Andrée, with clasped hands, reflected on the unexpected and extraordinary event which had so suddenly interrupted the course of her calm life, and she believed herself in a dream. The baron was pulling some hairs, which were rather too long, out of his gray eyebrows, and settling the bosom of his shirt. Nicole, leaning against the door, looked at her master and mistress, and La Brie with his arms hanging down and his mouth open, looked at Nicole.

The baron was the first to rouse himself from his reverie.

"Scoundrel!" cried he to La Brie, "are you standing there like a statue, and that gentleman, one of the king's body-guard, waiting without?"

La Brie made a bound toward the door, got one leg hooked in the other, staggered to his feet, and disappeared. In a short time he returned.

"What is the gentleman doing?" asked the baron.

"Making his horses eat the pimpernels."

"Leave him alone, then.   And the carriage?"

"It is in the avenue."

"The horses harnessed?"

"Yes, sir—four horses; such beautiful animals! they are eating the pomegranates."

"The king's horses have a right to eat whatever they like.   By the bye, the sorcerer?"

"He is gone, sir. '

"And has left all the plate on the table!   It is not possible.   He will return, or will send some one for it."

"I don't think he will, sir.   Gilbert saw him set out with his wagon."

"Gilbert saw him set out with his wagon?" the baron repeated, in a thoughtful tone.

"Yes, sir."

"That wretch Gilbert sees everything.   Go and pack my trunk."

"It is packed, sir."

"What—it is packed?"

"Yes; as soon as I heard what her royal highness the dauphiness said, I went into your room and packed your clothes and linen."

"Who told you to do so, you officious rascal?"

"Dame! sir, I thought I was only anticipating your orders."

"Fool!   Go, then, and help my daughter."

"Thank you, father; but I have Nicole."

The baron began to reflect again.

"But, zounds! scoundrel?   it is impossible."

"What is impossible, sir?"

"What you have not thought of, for you think of nothing."

"But what is it, sir?"

"That her royal highness would go without leaving something with Monsieur de Beausire, or the sorcerer without leaving a message with Gilbert."

At this moment a low whistle was heard from the courtyard.

"What is that?"

"It is a call for me, sir," replied La Brie.

"And who calls, pray?"

"The gentleman, sir."

"The gentleman left by the dauphiness?"

"Yes, sir. And here is Gilbert coming as if he had got something to say to you."

"Go, then, stupid animal."

La Brie obeyed, with his usual alacrity.

"Father," said Andrée approaching him, "I know what troubles you. Recollect, I have thirty louis d'ors, and that beautiful watch set with diamonds, which Queen Marie Lezinska gave my mother."

"Yes, my dear, yes!" replied the baron; "but keep them, keep them. You must have a handsome dress for your presentation. I may discover some means—hush! here is La Brie."

"Sir," cried La Brie, as he came in, holding in one hand a letter, and in the other some money, "see what the dauphiness left for me—ten louis d'ors, sir—ten louis d'ors!"

"And that letter, rascal?"

"Oh, the letter is for you, sir—from the sorcerer."

"From the sorcerer? Who gave it you?"

"Gilbert, sir."

"I told you so, stupid animal! Give it me—give it me!"

He snatched the letter, tore it open, and read these words:

"SIR,—Since a hand so august has touched the plate I left with you, it belongs to you; keep it as a relic, and remember sometimes your grateful guest,

"JOSEPH BALSAMO."

"La Brie!" cried the baron, after a moment's reflection, "is there not a good goldsmith at Bar-le-Duc?"

"Oh, yes, sir; the one who soldered Mademoiselle Andrée's silver brooch!"

"Very well. Andrée, lay aside the goblet out of which her royal highness drank, and let the rest of the service be put up in the carriage with us. And you, beast that you are, help the gentleman outside to a glass of what remains of our good wine."

"One bottle, sir," said La Brie, with deep melancholy.

"That's enough."

"Now, Andrée," said the baron, taking both his daughter's hands, "courage, my child. We are going to Court; there are plenty of titles to be given away there— rich abbeys, regiments without colonels, pensions going to waste. It is a fine country, the Court! The sun shines brightly there. Put yourself always in its rays, my child, for you are worthy to be seen. Go, my love, go!"

Andrée went out, followed by Nicole.

"Hallo! La Brie, you monster!" cried the baron, "attend to the gentleman, I tell you."

"Yes, sir," answered La Brie, from a distant part of the cellar.

"I," continued the baron, going toward his room, "must go and arrange my papers. We must be out of this hole in an hour. Do you hear, Andrée? And we are leaving it in good style, too. What a capital fellow that sorcerer is! I am becoming as superstitious as the devil. But make haste, La Brie, you wretch!"

"I was obliged to go feeling about, sir, in the cellar; there is not a candle in the house."

"It was time to leave it, it appears," said the baron.

CHAPTER XVII.

NICOLE'S TWENTY-FIVE LOUIS D'ORS.

In the meantime, Andrée made active preparations for her departure, and Nicole assisted her with an ardor which quickly dissipated the little cloud that had arisen between them in the morning.

"She is a good girl," said Andrée to herself, "devoted and grateful; she has faults, but what human creature has not? Let me forget them."

Nicole was not a girl who was slow to observe the expression of her mistress's face. "Fool that I was!" said she to herself; "I was nearly quarreling with my young lady, and all about that young good-for-nothing Gilbert! and she going to Paris, and will take me with her! One is sure of making one's fortune in Paris."

Andrée was the first to speak.

"Put my lace in a band-box," said she.

"What band-box, mademoiselle?"

"Really, I don't know. Have we one at all?"

"Oh, yes; the one you gave me; it is in my room."

And Nicole ran to bring it with an obliging air which disposed Andrée still more in her favor.

"But this band-box is your own," said Andrée, when she reappeared with the article in her hand, "and you may want it yourself, my poor Nicole."

"Oh, you have more need of it, mademoiselle; and, besides, it ought to be yours—you lent it me."

"When people get married and set up housekeeping, they require many little things; so just now you have most need of the box. Keep it to put your bridal finery in."

"Oh, mademoiselle!" said Nicole, gaily, shaking her head, "my finery will not take up much room."

"But if you marry, Nicole, I should wish you to be happy—and rich."

"Rich?"

"Yes, rich, according to your rank."

"Then you have found some fermier-general for me, mademoiselle?"

"No; but I have found a dowry."

"Indeed, mademoiselle?"

"You know what is in my purse?"

"Yes, madame; twenty-five shining louis d'ors."

"They are yours, Nicole."

"Twenty-five louis d'ors!" cried Nicole, with rapture, it is indeed a fortune!"

"My poor girl, I am glad you think so!"

"And you really give them to me, madame?"

" I wish I could give you more."

Nicole felt surprised—moved ; the tears came to her eyes ; she seized her young lady's hand and kissed it.

" Do you think your husband will be satisfied ? "

" Oh, quite satisfied ! " said Nicole.   " At least, I hope so."

She reflected that Gilbert had doubtless refused her hand through fear of poverty, and that now, when she was rich, matters would turn out differently.   Then she determined immediately to offer him a share of her young lady's generous gift, and to attach him to her by gratitude. Such was Nicole's generous plan.   Andrée looked at her as she reflected.   " Poor girl ! " sighed she, " may she be happy in her simple life ! "

Nicole heard the words, and started from her reverie. They opened to her fancy a whole Eldorado of silks, diamonds, lace, and love—things of which Andrée had not thought.   But Nicole turned away her eyes from the gold-and-purple cloud brightening her horizon, and resisted the temptation.   " After all, madame," said she, " I shall be happy here—in an humble way."

" Reflect seriously on what you are going to do."

" Yes, mademoiselle ; I shall reflect on it."

" That is right.   Make yourself happy in the way you propose, if you can ; but do not be foolish."

" You are very kind, mademoiselle.   And let me say now that I was very foolish this morning ; but I hope mademoiselle will forgive me.   When one is in love——"

" Then you are really in love with Gilbert ? "

" Yes, mademoiselle ; I—I love him," said Nicole.

" Is it possible ? " said Andrée, smiling.   " What can you see to admire in the young man ?   The first time I meet him I must take a look at this Monsieur Gilbert, who steals young girls' hearts."

" Is he not going with us to Paris, mademoiselle ? " inquired Nicole, who wished to be fully informed on every point before taking the step she meditated.

" Of what use would he be there ?   He is not a domestic, and could not take charge of a horse in Paris.   Idle people at Taverney live like the birds; however poor the soil, it feeds them. But in Paris an idle person would cost too much—we could not support him."

" But if I marry him ?" stammered Nicole.

" Well, if you marry him, you shall live here with him at Taverney. You shall take care of this house which my mother was so fond of."

Andrée pronounced these words in so firm a voice, that Nicole could no longer doubt. Yet she hesitated before speaking again. Andrée, seeing her hesitation, thought that her mind was wandering from the pleasures of a Parisian life to those of the quiet country, and that she knew not how to decide. So she went on, gently : " Nicole, the decision which you are now to make will affect all your future life. Be not hasty ; 1 shall give you one hour ; it is little, but you are prompt, and I think it will be sufficient to enable you to choose between continuing to serve me or having a husband—between me and Gilbert."

" An hour ! Oh, yes, mademoiselle, I can decide in an hour."

" Collect all my clothes, and my mother's ; I would not leave behind these relics so dear to me. Then go, and return in an hour fully decided ; but whatever your determination be, here are your twenty-five louis d'ors. If you marry, they shall be your dowry ; if you continue in my service, your wages for two years."

Nicole took the purse from Andrée's hands and kissed it. Then she completed her task—not a great one, certainly— hurried down-stairs, and Andrée saw her cross the court-yard and enter the avenue. Not finding Gilbert there, she flew to a window on the ground floor, which was that of his room, and tapped at it. He was bustling about with his back to the window ; but hearing her drumming, he turned, and, like a thief caught in the act, he quickly abandoned his occupation.

" Oh, is it you, Nicole ?" said he.

" Yes, it is," she replied, smiling, but with something very decided in her tone.

" You are welcome," said he, coming forward and opening the window.

Nicole felt that there was kindness in his reception of her, and held out her hand ; he took it, pressed it. " This is a good beginning," thought she. " Farewell, my journey to Paris ! " and to Nicole's praise it must be said, she did not sigh at this thought.

" You know," said the young girl, leaning her elbows on the window, " you know, Gilbert, that the family are leaving Taverney and going to Paris."

" Yes, I know."

" Well, I am to go to Paris, too."

" I did not know that ; but I congratulate you if you are pleased at going."

" How you say that ! "

" I say it plainly, I think—if you are pleased at going."

" My being pleased depends——"

" Why do you stop ? depends——? "

" My being pleased or not depends on you."

" I don't understand you," said Gilbert, seating himself on the window so that his knees touched Nicole's arm, and they could thus converse unseen and unheard.

Nicole looked at him tenderly : he shook his head, insinuating that he understood her look no more than her words.

" Well," said she, " since all must be told, listen to what I am going to say."

" I hear you, " replied Gilbert, coldly.

" In plain words, my young lady offers to take me to Paris with her——"

" Very well ; go on."

" Unless——"

" Unless what ? "

" Unless I get married here."

" Then you still think of getting married ? " he answered, quite unmoved.

" Yes ; more particularly since I have become rich."

" Oh, you have become rich ? " he asked, so phlegmatically that Nicole knew not what to think.

" Very rich, Gilbert."

" Indeed ? "

" Yes, indeed."

" And how did that miracle come about ? "

" My young lady has given me a marriage portion."

" You are very fortunate. I congratulate you, Nicole."

" Look ! " said she, pouring out of the purse into her hand the twenty-five louis d'ors, and watching Gilbert's eyes to discover some r..y of pleasure or covetousness in them.

Gilbert moved not a muscle. " On my word, it is a nice little sum," said he.

" And that is not all," continued Nicole; " the baron will be rich once more. The old castle will be rebuilt, and the care of it given——"

" To the fortunate husband of Nicole," said Gilbert, with an irony not so well concealed but that it grated on Nicole's fine ear ; yet she restrained her anger.

" And Nicole's husband—do you not know him ? "

" I ? No."

" Have you, then, grown stupid, or do I no longer speak French ? " cried the young girl, who began to show symptoms of impatience.

" I understand you perfectly," replied Gilbert. " You offer to make me your husband—do you not, Mademoiselle Legay ? "

" Yes, Monsieur Gilbert."

" And it is since you have become rich that you have thought of this," returned Gilbert, hastily. " I am truly grateful to you, indeed—I am, indeed ! "

" Well," said Nicole, frankly, and holding out her hand, " take it. You accept it, do you not ? "

" No ; I refuse it."

Nicole sprung up from her leaning position. " Gilbert," said she, " you have a bad heart ; and, trust me, what you now do will not bring you happiness. If I felt any warmer sentiment in making the offer I have just done, than a sense of duty and honor, trust me, I would now be miserable indeed ; but, having become rich, I did not wish it to be said that Nicole would look down on her

old friend Gilbert.   However, all is now over between us."
Gilbert made a gesture of indifference.

"What I think of your conduct in the matter, you must
be well aware.   I, whose character you know to be as free
and independent as your own, had decided to bury myself here, from an old prepossession for you, when I had it
in my power to go to Paris, which may be for me a scene
of triumph.   I would have borne to see before me, every
day of the year, for a whole lifetime, that cold and impenetrable face, the mask of so many wicked thoughts.
You have not felt that there was any sacrifice in this.   So
much the worse for you, Gilbert !   I do not say that you
will regret me ; but remember, you may yet feel remorse
for the contempt and scorn you have shown me.   Guided
by you, I should have been a virtuous, happy, and contented woman ; now, I am abandoned on the ocean of life,
without a keeping or protecting hand !   Gilbert, if I fall,
God will not hold you as the cause of my fall !   Farewell !"

And the proud young girl turned away without anger or
impatience, but having shown, as all impassioned natures
do in the time of trial, true generosity of soul.

Gilbert shut his window quietly and returned to the mysterious occupation in which she had interrupted him.

CHAPTER XVIII.

FAREWELL TO TAVERNEY.

NICOLE, before entering her mistress's apartment,
stopped on the staircase to subdue some gathering emotions of resentment rising in her bosom.   The baron encountered her as she stood motionless, thoughtful, her
brows contracted and leaning on her hand, and, seeing
her so pretty, he kissed her, as the Duke de Richelieu
would have done at thirty years of age.   Roused from her
reverie by this piece of gallantry, Nicole hurried up to
Andrée's room, and found her just closing her trunk.

"Well," said Mlle. de Taverney, "have your reflections ended?"

"Yes, madame," replied Nicole, very decidedly.

"You will marry?"

"No, madame."

"What! after all your first love?"

"My love will never do for me what the kindness of mademoiselle has done for me. I belong to you, mademoiselle, and wish always to belong to you. I know the mistress I have; I do not know the master I might have."

Andrée was touched with this unlooked-for exhibition of affectionate feeling in the giddy Nicole, and was far from suspecting that this choice had been a forced one. She smiled, pleased to find one human being better than she had expected.

"You do well, Nicole," she replied, "to attach yourself to me. I shall not forget this trust to me; and if any good fortune befall me, you shall share it."

"Oh, mademoiselle, I have quite decided I will go with you."

"Without regret?"

"Blindly."

"I do not like that answer, Nicole. I should not wish you, at some future day, to reproach yourself with having blindly trusted me and followed me."

"I shall never have to reproach any one but myself, mademoiselle."

"Then you have had an explanation with your lover? I saw you talking with him."

Nicole blushed, then bit her lip. She forgot that Andrée's window was opposite that at which she had spoken to Gilbert.

"It is true, mademoiselle," replied Nicole.

"And you told him all?"

Nicole thought Andrée had some particular reason for this question, and, all her former suspicions returning, she answered: "I told him I would have nothing more to do with him."

It was plain that the two women would never understand each other—the one pure as a diamond, the other
without any fixed principle of conduct, though having
occasional impulses of goodness.

In the meantime, the baron had completed all his arrangements. An old sword, which he had won at Fontenoy, some parchments establishing his right to travel in
his majesty's carriages, and a litter of old papers, formed
the most bulky part of his baggage. La Brie followed,
tottering under the weight of an almost empty trunk.
In the avenue they found the gentlemen of the king's body-
guard, who, while waiting, had drained to the last drop
his bottle of wine. The gallant had remarked the fine
waist and pretty ankle of Nicole, who was going back and
forward with messages, and he had kept peeping about in
the hope of exchanging a word with her. He was roused,
however, to more active occupation by the baron's request
that he would order the carriage to the door. He started,
bowed, and in a sonorous voice summoned the coachman.

The carriage drew up ; La Brie put the trunk on behind with an indescribable mixture of joy and pride in his
looks. " I am, really," murmured he, carried away by
his enthusiasm, and thinking he was alone, " going to get
into the king's carriage ! "

" Behind it, behind it, my worthy friend," replied
Beausire, with a patronizing smile.

" What, sir, are you going to take La Brie with you ? "
said Andrée. " Who will take care of Taverney ? "

" Why, pardieu ! the good-for-nothing philosopher."

" Gilbert ? "

" Yes ; has he not a gun ? "

" But how will he live ? "

" By his gun, to be sure. Don't be uneasy, he will have
excellent fare ; blackbirds and thrushes are not scarce at
Taverney."

Andrée looked at Nicole ; the latter began to laugh.
" And is that all the compassion you show for him, un-
grateful girl ? "

" Oh, mademoiselle ! " replied Nicole, " he is very clever with his gun ; he will not die of hunger."

" But, sir," continued Andrée, " we must leave him two or three louis d'ors."

"To spoil him ? Very fine, indeed ! He is vicious enough as he is."

" He must have something to live on," persisted Andrée.

" The neighbors will help him, if he is in want."

. " Don't be uneasy, madame," said Nicole ; " he will have no cause to ask their assistance."

" At all events," replied Andrée, " leave him two or three crowns."

" He would not accept them."

" He would not accept them ? Then he is proud, this Mr. Gilbert of yours ? "

" Oh, mademoiselle, he is not mine—Heaven be praised ! "

" Come, come ! " said the baron, " let Gilbert go to the devil ; the carriage is waiting ; get in, my love."

Andrée did not reply. She cast a farewell look on the old château, and then got into the heavy and ponderous carriage. The baron seated himself beside her. La Brie, still wearing his splendid livery, and Nicole, who seemed never to have known such a person as Gilbert, mounted on the box ; the coachman rode one of the horses, as postilion.

" But Monsieur l'Exempt, where shall he sit ? " exclaimed the baron.

" On my horse, sir, on my horse," replied Beausire, still eying Nicole, who colored with delight at having so soon replaced a rude peasant admirer by an elegant gentleman.

The carriage, drawn by four strong horses, started into rapid motion. The trees of the avenue glided away on each side, and disappeared one by one, sadly bending before the east wind, as if to bid farewell to their owners who abandoned them. The carriage reached the gate. Gilbert stood there, upright, immovable, his hat in his hand ; he did not seem to see Andrée, and yet he watched her least movement. Her eyes were fixed on the dear home she was leaving, so as to keep it in view as long as possible.

"Stop an instant!" cried the baron to the postilion. The carriage stopped.

"So, Monsieur Good-for-nothing, you are going to be happy—quite alone, like a real philosopher! Nothing to do—nobody to scold you. Don't let the house take fire —and, hark ye, take care of Mahon."

Gilbert bowed, but did not reply. He felt as if Nicole's looks were a weight too great to be borne—he feared to meet her triumphant ironical smile, as he would the touch of red-hot iron.

"Go on, postilion!" cried the baron.

Nicole did not smile; it even required more than her habitual power over herself to prevent her expressing aloud her pity for the poor young man thus heartlessly abandoned. She was obliged to keep her eye on M. de Beausire, who looked so well on his prancing horse.

Now, as Nicole kept her eyes fixed on M. de Beausire, she did not see that Gilbert was gazing, his soul in his eyes, on Andrée. Andrée saw nothing but the house in which she was born—in which her mother died. The carriage disappeared. Gilbert, a moment before of so little importance in the eyes of the travelers, was now nothing to them.

The baron, Andrée, Nicole, and La Brie having passed through the gates of the avenue, entered a new world. Each had a peculiar subject for reflection. The baron thought that at Bar-le-Duc he could easily raise five or six thousand crowns on Balsamo's plate. Andrée repeated a prayer her mother had taught her, to keep away the demon of pride and ambition. Nicole covered her neck more closely with her handkerchief, to the great chagrin of M. de Beausire. La Brie, with his hand in his pocket, counted over the ten louis d'ors of the dauphiness and the two of Balsamo. M. de Beausire galloped at the side of the carriage.

Gilbert closed the gates of Taverney, whose hinges, as usual, creaked with a melancholy sound. Then he ran to his little room, pulled out his oaken chest of drawers, behind which he found a bundle ready tied up in a napkin, and slung it on his stick. After this, pushing his hands into his hay-stuffed mattress, he drew out something wrapped in a piece of paper—it was a shining crown piece—his savings for three or four years. He opened the paper, looked at his crown to assure himself that it had not been changed, and then put it in his pocket, still wrapped in its paper.

Mahon, on seeing Gilbert, began to howl loudly, making furious leaps the whole length of his chain. Seeing one by one his friends leave him, his fine intellect told him that Gilbert was also about to abandon him, and he howled louder and louder.

"Hush!" cried Gilbert, "hush, Mahon!"

Then smiling bitterly at the parallel which occurred to his mind, he muttered, "Have they not abandoned me like a dog? Why should not I abandon thee like a man?" But after a minute's reflection, he added, "They abandoned me free, at least—free to seek for food. Well, then, Mahon, I will do for thee what they did for me, neither more nor less;" and going to the hook to which the dog's chain was fastened, he slipped it off. "You are free!" said he; "provide for yourself as you like."

The dog bounded toward the house; but, finding the doors all closed, he sprung toward the ruins and disappeared.

"And now," said Gilbert, "we shall see which has most instinct—the dog or the man."

So saying, he went out by the small gate, closed it, double locked it, and threw the key over the wall.

But nature speaks with the same voice in almost all hearts. Gilbert felt something like what Andrée experienced in leaving Taverney, only with her sentiments mingled regret for the quiet past, with his hopes for a more stirring future.

"Farewell!" said he, turning to look for the last time at the château, whose pointed roof appeared peeping over the sycamores and laburnums—"farewell! abode in which I have suffered so much, where every one hated me and threw me food grudgingly, as if I had been a hungry hound. Be cursed! my heart bounds with joy at my free-

dom, for thy walls inclose me no more !   Farewell, prison !
hell, den of tyrants !   Farewell forever !"

And after this imprecation, Gilbert sprung forward on
the road which the carriage had taken, fancying that he yet
heard the roll of its distant wheels.

CHAPTER XIX.

GILBERT'S CROWN-PIECE.

After half an hour's headlong race, Gilbert uttered a
wild shriek of joy ; he saw the carriage about a quarter of
a league before him, slowly ascending a hill. He felt his
heart dilate with pride, as he thought that he, with only
youth, strength, spirit, was about to do all that wealth,
power, and rank could accomplish.   Then, indeed, might
the baron have called Gilbert a philosopher, had he seen
him, his stick on his shoulder, his small bundle slung on it,
walking on with rapid strides, leaping down every slope
which could shorten his path, and stopping at every ascent,
chafing with impatience, as if saying to the horses, " You
do not go fast enough for me ; see, I am obliged to wait
for you."

Philosopher ? Yes ; and he deserved the name, if it be
philosophy to despise all that contributes to ease and to
enjoyment.   It was an interesting spectacle, one worthy of
the Creator of energetic and intelligent creatures, to see
the young man bounding forward on his way, all dusty and
panting, for an hour or more, until he had overtaken the
carriage, and then resting with delight when the horses were
compelled to pause for breath.   Gilbert that day must have
inspired every one with admiration who could have followed him in spirit as we do ; and who knows but that even
the proud Andrée might have been moved, could she have
seen him, and that her contempt for his indolence would
have changed to admiration of his energy.

The day passed on in this manner.   The baron stopped

an hour at Bar-le-Duc, which gave Gilbert time to get in advance of him. He had heard the order to stop at the goldsmith's; so, having passed the town, by a détour, without entering it, he hid in a thicket until he saw the carriage coming, and when it had passed, followed it as before. Toward evening it came up with the train of the dauphiness, at the little village of Brillou, the inhabitants of which were crowded on a neighboring hill, and made the air resound with their shouts of welcome. Gilbert had not eaten a morsel during the entire day, except a morsel of bread which he had brought with him from Taverney; but, in return, he had drunk plentifully from a rivulet which crossed the road, and the water of which was so fresh and limpid, that Andrée had requested that the carriage might stop, and alighted herself to fill the chased cup, the only article of Balsamo's service which the baron could be persuaded to retain. Gilbert saw all this, hidden by some trees on the roadside. Then, when the carriage had passed on, he emerged from his hiding-place, and advancing to the stream, at the same spot where Mlle. de Taverney had stood, he lifted the water in his hand, and drank from the same source.

Evening came on, shrouding the landscape in her dusky mantle, until at last he saw nothing but the light from the large lanterns which were fastened on each side of the carriage; this pale gleam, ever hurrying onward in the distance, looked like a phantom impelled forward by some strange destiny. Then night came on. They had traveled twelve leagues; they were at Combles. The equipages stopped—Gilbert was sure that it was for the night, that he should have time to stop for a couple of hours in a barn, and how vigorously should he afterward pursue his way! He approched to listen for Andrée's voice—the carriage still continued stationary. He glided into a deep doorway; he saw Andrée by the glare of the torch-light, and heard her asking what hour it was. A voice replied, "Eleven o'clock." At that moment Gilbert no longer felt fatigue and would have rejected with scorn an offer of a seat in a vehicle. Versailles already appeared in view—Versailles, all gilded, shining, the city of nobles and kings !—and beyond appeared Paris, grim, immense—the city of the people !

Two things roused him from his ecstasy—the noise of the carriages setting out again, and the complaints of his stomach, which cried " hunger ! " very distinctly. On went the carriages, Gilbert following, his hunger unappeased. At midnight they stopped at St. Dizier. For the night ? No ; only to change horses ; while, in the meantime, the illustrious travelers took a little refreshment by torchlight.

Gilbert had need of all his courage, and he sprung to his feet from the bank where he had seated himself, as he heard them depart, with an energy of determination which made him forget that, ten minutes before, his wearied legs had bent under him in spite of all his efforts.

" Well," cried he, " go, go ! I shall stop also for refreshments at St. Dizier ; I shall buy some bread and a slice of bacon ; I shall drink a glass of wine, and for five sous I shall be refreshed as well as the masters."

Gilbert entered the town. The train having passed, the good folks were closing their doors and shutters ; but our philosopher saw a good-looking inn not yet shut up, where the large dishes of fowls and other things showed that the attendants of the dauphiness had only had time to levy a very slight contribution. He entered the kitchen resolutely ; the hostess was there, counting what her gains had been.

" Excuse me, madame ; but can I have some bread and ham ? " said Gilbert.

" We have no ham, but you can have fowl."

" No, thank you ; I ask for ham, because I wish for ham —I don't like fowl."

" That is a pity, my little fellow, for we have only fowl ; but it shall not be dearer," she added, smiling, " than ham. Take half a one, or, indeed, take a whole one for tenpence, and that will be provision for you for to-morrow. We thought her royal highness would have stayed all night, and that we should have sold all these things to the attendants ; but as she only just passed through, they will be wasted."

One would have thought that the offer being so good, and the hostess so kind, Gilbert would have gladly embraced it ; but that would be to have misunderstood his character entirely.

" No, thank you," replied he ; " I shall satisfy myself in a more humble manner ; I am neither a prince nor a footman."

" Well, then," said the good woman, " I will give you the fowl, my little Artaban."

" I am not a beggar either," replied he, in a mortified tone ; " I buy what I wish, and pay for it."

And he majestically plunged his hand into his breeches pocket ; it went down to the elbow—in vain he fumbled in his vest pocket, turning paler and paler. That paper in which the crown had been he found, but the crown was gone. Tossed about by his rapid movements, it had worn the paper, then the thin lining of his pocket, and had slipped out at his knee ; for he had unfastened his garters, to give freer play to his limbs.

His paleness and trembling touched the good woman. Many in her place would have rejoiced at his pride being brought down ; but she felt for him, seeing suffering so powerfully expressed in the changes of his countenance.

" Come, my poor boy," said she, " you shall sup and sleep here ; then, to-morrow, if you must go on, you shall do so."

" Oh, yes, yes !" exclaimed Gilbert, " I must go on— not to-morrow, but now—now !"

And snatching up his bundle, without waiting to hear more, he darted out of the house, to hide his shame and grief in the darkness. He rushed on, alone, truly alone in the world ; for no man is more alone than he who has just parted with his last crown—more particularly if it be the only one he ever possessed.

To turn back to look for his crown would have been to begin a hopeless task ; besides, it would make it impossible for him ever to come up with the carriages. He resolved to continue his way. After he had gone about a league, hunger, which his mental suffering had made him forget for a time, awoke more keen than ever. Weariness also seized on every limb—on every sinew; yet, by incredible efforts, he had once more come in sight of the carriages. But fate, it would seem, had decided against him. They stopped only to change horses, and so quickly that he had not five minutes to rest himself.

Again he set out. The day began to dawn—the sun appeared above a broad circle of dark clouds, foretelling one of those burning days of May which sometimes precedes the heats of summer. How could Gilbert bear the noon of that day? In his pride he thought that horses, men, destinies had united against him—him alone! Like Ajax, he shook his clinched fist at the heavens; and if he did not say, like him, "I shall escape in spite of the gods," it was because he knew by heart "The Social Contract" better than the Odyssey. At last, however, as Gilbert had dreaded, the moment arrived when he found the utter impossibility of proceeding much further. By a last and almost despairing effort, he summoned up all his remaining force, and once more overtook the carriages, of which he had previously lost sight, and which, under the influence of his heated and feverish imagination, he fancied were surrounded with a strange, fantastic halo. The noise of the wheels sounded like thunder in his ears, and almost maddened his brain; he staggered on, his blackened lips wide apart, his eyes fixed and staring, his long hair clinging to his forehead bathed in perspiration, and his movements seeming rather the effect of some clever piece of mechanism than those of a thinking being. Since the evening before he had traveled upward of twenty leagues, and his weary and fainting limbs now refused to carry him further A mist overspread his eyes, strange noises sounded in his ears, the earth seemed to reel under him; he endeavored to utter a cry, and staggered forward, beating the air wildly with his arms. At last his voice returned to utter hoarse cries of rage against his conquerors. Then, tearing his hair with both hands, he reeled forward, and fell heavily to the ground—with the consolation of having, like a hero of antiquity, fought the battle to the last.

"Halloo, there ! halloo, madman !" cried a hoarse voice, just as he fell, accompanying his shouts with the loud cracking of a whip.

Gilbert heard him not—he had fainted.

"Halloo, I say—halloo ! Morbleu ! the fellow will be smashed !" And this time his words were accompanied by a vigorous lash, which reached Gilbert's waist, and cut into the flesh.

But Gilbert felt nothing ; he remained immovable under the feet of the horses of a carriage which was issuing into the high-road from a by-way between Thieblemont and Vauclere.

A shrill cry was heard from the carriage, which the horses carried along like a whirlwind. The postilion made an almost superhuman effort, but could not prevent one of the horses, which was placed as a leader, from leaping over Gilbert. The other two, however, he succeeded in pulling up. A lady stretched her body half out of the carriage. "Heavens !" cried she, "you have killed the poor boy !"

"Why, faith, madame," replied the postilion, endeavoring to discover the body amid the cloud of dust which the horses' feet had raised, "I am almost afraid we have."

"Poor creature—poor boy ! Do not move a step further ;" and opening the door of the carriage herself, she sprung out.

The postilion had already alighted, and dragging Gilbert's body from between the wheels, he expected to find it bruised and bloody. The lady assisted him with all her force.

"What an escape !" he cried, "not a scratch—not a kick !"

"But he has fainted," said the lady.

"Only from fear. Let us place him against the bank ; and since madame is in haste, let us go on."

"Impossible. I would not leave any creature in such a state."

"Pooh ! it is nothing, madame ; he will soon recover."

"No, no ; poor fellow ! he is some runaway lad from

college, and has undertaken a journey beyond his strength. See how pale he is; he might die. No, I will not leave him. Lift him into the carriage, on the front seat."

The postilion obeyed; the lady got in. Gilbert was laid lengthwise on a good cushion, his head supported by the well-stuffed side of the carriage.

"And now," cried the lady, "we have lost ten minutes —a crown if you make up for them."

The postilion cracked his whip above his head; the horses knew what this threatened, and set off at a gallop.

CHAPTER XX.

GILBERT RECOVERS THE LOSS OF HIS CROWN.

WHEN Gilbert returned to consciousness, he was in no small degree surprised to find himself placed as he was, with a young lady watching him anxiously.

This young lady was about five-and-twenty, with large gray eyes, a nose slightly *retroussé*, cheeks imbrowned by a southern sun, and a delicately formed, little mouth, which added to the naturally cheerful and laughing expression of her face something of circumspection and finesse. Her neck and arms, which were beautifully formed, were displayed to advantage by a closely fitting bodice of violet-colored velvet with golden buttons, while the skirt of her dress of gray silk was so enormously wide as to fill almost the entire carriage.

Gilbert continued for some time to gaze on this face, which looked on his smilingly and with much interest, and he could scarcely persuade himself that he was not in a dream.

"Well, my poor fellow," said the lady, "are you not better now?"

"Where am I?" asked he, languidly.

"You are in safety now, my little fellow," replied the lady, who spoke with a strong southern accent; "but just now you were in great danger of being crushed under the wheels of my carriage. What could have happened to you, to make you fall in that manner, just in the middle of the highway ?"

"I was overcome by weakness, madame, from having walked too much."

"Then you have been some time on the road ?"

"Since yesterday, at four in the afternoon."

"And how far have you walked ?"

"I think about eighteen leagues."

"What, in fourteen hours ?"

"Oh, I ran all the way."

"Where are you going, then ?"

"To Versailles."

"And you came from—— ?"

"From Taverney."

"Taverney ? Where is that ?"

"It is a château, situated between Pierrefitte and Bar-le-Duc."

"But you have scarcely had time to eat on the way ?"

"I not only had not time, but I had not the means."

"How so ?"

"I lost my money on the way."

"So that since yesterday you have eaten nothing ?"

"Only a few mouthfuls of bread, which I brought with me."

"Poor fellow ! But why did you not beg something ?"

"Because I am proud, madame," said he, smiling scornfully.

"Proud ! It is all very fine to be proud, but when one is dying of hunger——"

"Better death than dishonor."

The lady looked at the sententious speaker with something like admiration.

"But who are you, my friend," said she, "who speak in this style ?"

"I am an orphan."

"What is your name ?"

"Gilbert."

"Gilbert what ?"

" Gilbert nothing."

" Ha !" said the lady, still more surprised.

Gilbert saw that he had produced an effect, and felt as if he were another Rousseau.

" You are very young to wander about in this way," continued the lady.

" I was left deserted and alone, in an old château, which the family had abandoned. I did as they had done—I abandoned it in my turn."

" Without any object in view ?"

" The world is wide ; there is room for all."

" And you lost your purse ? Was it well filled ?"

" There was only one crown in it," said he, divided between the shame of confessing his poverty and the fear of naming a large sum, which might have excited the suspicion that it had not been fairly obtained.

" One crown for such a journey ! Why, it would scarcely have been sufficient to purchase bread for two days ; and the distance !—good heavens ! from Bar-le-Duc to Paris is nearly sixty-five leagues !"

" I never counted the leagues, madame ; I only said, I must get to Paris."

" And, thereupon, you set out, my poor simpleton ?"

" Oh, I have good legs."

" Good as they are, they failed, you see. "

" Oh, it was not my legs—it was hope which failed me."

" Why, indeed, you looked before you fell as if in great despair."

Gilbert smiled bitterly.

" What was passing in your mind ? You struck your forehead with your clinched hand, and tore out your hair by handfuls."

" Indeed, madame ?" asked Gilbert, rather embarrassed.

" Oh, I am certain of it ; and it was that which, I think, prevented you hearing or seeing the carriage."

Gilbert's instinct told him that he might increase his consequence, and still more awaken the interest of the lady, by telling the whole truth.

" I was, indeed, in despair," said he.

" And about what ? " said the lady.

" Because I could not keep up with a carriage which I was following."

" Indeed," said the young lady, smiling ; " this is quite a romance.   Is there love in the case ? "

All Gilbert's resolution could not prevent him from blushing.

" And what carriage was it, my little Roman ? "

" A carriage in the train of the dauphiness."

" What do you tell me ?   Is the dauphiness before us ? "

" She is, indeed."

" I thought her scarcely yet at Nancy.   Are no honors paid her on the way, that she advances so rapidly ? "

" Oh, yes, madame ; but her royal highness seems to have some reason for being in haste."

" In haste.   Who told you so ? "

" I guessed it."

" On what grounds ? "

" Why, she said at first she would stay two or three hours at Taverney, and she only stayed three quarters of an hour."

" Do you know if she received any letters from Paris ? "

" I saw a gentleman in a dress covered with embroidery, who had one in his hand as he entered ? "

" Did you hear his name mentioned ? "

" No ; I merely know that he is the governor of Strasbourg."

" What ! the Count de Stainville, brother-in-law to the Duke de Choiseul ?   Horrible !   Faster, postilion, faster ! "

A vigorous lash was the reply, and Gilbert felt the speed of the carriage increase.

" But she must stop to breakfast," said the lady, as if speaking to herself, "and then we shall pass her.   Postilion, what is the next town ? "

" Vitry, madame."

" How far are we from it ? "

" Three leagues."

" Where shall we change horses ? "

" At Vauclere."

"Well, drive on, and if you see a train of carriages on the road before us, let me know."

While the lady was exchanging these words with the postilion, Gilbert had again nearly fainted. When she once more turned toward him, he was pale, and his eyes were closed.

"Poor child!" said she, "he is fainting again. It is my fault: I made him talk when he was dying of hunger, instead of giving him something to eat."

She took from the pocket of the carriage a richly carved flask, with a little silver goblet hanging round its neck by a chain, and poured out some of the contents for Gilbert. On this occasion he did not require to be asked twice.

"Now," said the lady, "eat a biscuit; in an hour or so you shall breakfast more solidly."

"Thank you, madame," said Gilbert, gladly taking the biscuit as he had done the wine.

"As you have now recovered a little strength," said she, "tell me, if you are disposed to make a confidante of me, what induced you to follow a carriage in the train of the dauphiness?"

"Well, madame, you shall hear the truth. I was living with the Baron de Taverney when her royal highness came. She commanded him to follow her to Paris—he obeyed. I was an orphan, and, consequently, nobody thought of me—they left me there, without food and without money; so I resolved, since everybody was going to Versailles, with the assistance of good horses and fine coaches, I, with the assistance of only my legs, would go to Versailles, and as soon as the horses. But fate was against me—if I had not lost my money, I should have had something to eat last night, and if I had eaten last night, I should have overtaken them this morning."

"Very well. You showed courage, and I like that; but you forgot that at Versailles people cannot live on courage alone."

"I shall go to Paris."

"But in that respect Paris resembles Versailles exceedingly."

"If courage will not support me, labor will."

"A good answer, my little fellow ; but what sort of labor ? Your hands do not seem those of a workman or porter."

"I shall study."

"I think you seem to know a great deal already."

"Yes ; for I know that I know nothing," replied Gilbert, remembering the aphorism of Socrates.

"And may I ask, my young friend, what branch of study you would choose ? "

"I think, madame, that the best is that which teaches man to be most useful to his fellows. Besides, man is so frail a being, that he should learn the cause of his weakness, in order that he may know his strength. I should like to know some day why my stomach prevented my legs from carrying me any further this morning, and if it was not that weakness of my stomach which summoned up the phantoms which distressed my brain."

"Really, you would make an excellent physician, and you speak already most learnedly on the science of medicine. In ten years you shall have me for a patient."

"I shall try to deserve that honor, madame."

They had now reached the place where they were to change horses. The young lady asked for information respecting the dauphiness, and found that she had passed through that place a quarter of an hour before ; she intended to stop at Vitry to change horses and to breakfast.

A fresh postilion took the place of the former one. The lady allowed him to leave the village at the usual speed ; but when they had got a little beyond the last house :

"Postilion," said she, "will you undertake to come up with the carriages of the dauphiness ? "

"Certainly, madame."

"Before they reach Vitry ? "

"Diable ! they are going full trot."

'Yes ; but if you were to go at a gallop ? "

The postilion looked at her.

"Treble pay," said she.

"If you had said so at first," replied he, "we should have been a quarter of a league further by this time."

"Well, here is a crown on account—make up for lost time."

The postilion's arm was stretched back, the lady's forward, and their hands met. The horses received a sharp lash, and the carriage started off like the wind.

During the change of horses, Gilbert had alighted and washed his face and hands at a fountain, had smoothed down his hair, which was very thick, and had altogether improved his appearance very much.

"In truth," said the lady to herself, "he is handsome enough for a physician;" and she smiled.

Having finished her dialogue with the postilion, she turned once more to Gilbert, whose paradoxes and sententious humor amused her exceedingly. From time to time she interrupted herself in a burst of laughter, which his philosophizing caused her, to lean out of the carriage and look anxiously before her, They had gone about a league in this way, when she uttered a cry of joy—she had caught a sight of the last wagons of the dauphiness's train as they were slowly ascending a steep hill, and now there appeared in advance of them about twenty carriages, from which many of the travelers had got out and were walking beside them. Gilbert slipped out his head also, desirous to catch a glimpse of Mademoiselle de Taverney in the midst of the crowd of pygmies, and thought he discovered Nicole by her high cap.

"And now, madame," said the postilion, "what must we do?"

"We must get before them."

"Get before them? But you know we cannot pass the carriage of the dauphiness."

"Why not?"

"Because it is expressly forbidden. Peste! Pass the king's horses! I should be sent to the galleys!"

"Now, listen, my good fellow; manage it as you please, but I must positively get before those carriages."

" I thought you belonged to the train of her royal highness ? " said Gilbert, inquiringly.

" It is very proper to wish for information," replied she ; " but we should not ask indiscreet questions."

" I beg your pardon, madame," said he, reddening.

" Well, postilion, what are we to do ? "

" Why, faith, this—keep behind till we reach Vitry, and then if her highness stops, obtain her permission to go on before her."

" Aye ; but then it would be asked who I was—I should have to tell. No, no, that will not do. We must find out some other way."

" Madame," said Gilbert, " if I might give an opinion ? "

" Yes, yes, my young friend ; if you have any good advice, give it."

" Could we not take some by-road which would bring us round to Vitry, and so get before the dauphiness without having been wanting in respect to her ? "

" Excellent ! The boy is right," cried the young lady.

" Postilion, is there a by-road ? "

" To go where ? "

" Where you like, provided you leave the dauphiness behind."

" There is, in fact, a by-road leading round Vitry, and joining the high-road again at Lachaussée."

" That is it, that is the very thing ! " cried the lady.

" But, madame, if I take that road, you must double the pay."

" Two louis d'ors for you, if we get to Lachaussée before the dauphiness."

" Madame is not afraid, then, of her carriage being broken ? "

" I care for nothing. If it breaks I shall proceed on horseback."

And turning to the right, they entered a cross-road, full of deep ruts, bordered by a little river, which falls into the Marne between Lachaussée and Martigny.

The postilion kept his word ; he did all that human power could do to break the carriage, but, at the same time, to arrive before the dauphiness. A dozen times Gilbert was thrown into the lady's arm, and a dozen times she into his. Intimacy springs up quickly from jolting on in the loneliness of a carriage ; and, after two hours' traveling on this by-road, it seemed to Gilbert as if he had known his companion ten years, and she, on her part, would have sworn she had known him since his birth. About eleven o'clock, they came again on the high-road between Vitry and Chalons. A courier whom they met told them that the dauphiness was not only staying to breakfast at Vitry, but that she meant to take two hours' repose. He added that he had been sent forward to desire those who attended to the horses to have them in readiness between three and four o'clock. This news filled the lady with joy. She gave the postilion the two louis d'ors which she promised him ; and, turning to Gilbert : " So now," said she, " we shall be able to dine at the next stopping-place."

But fate had decided that Gilbert should not dine there.

CHAPTER XXI.

IN WHICH A NEW PERSONAGE MAKES HIS APPEARANCE.

FROM the top of the hill which the lady's carriage was ascending, the village of Lachaussée might be seen ; it was there she was to change horses and stop to dine. It was a lovely little village, with its thatched cottages scattered here and there at the caprice of the owners ; some in the very middle of the road, some half hidden under the shade of a little grove which bordered the highway, and some following the course of the little river which we have mentioned, over which the inhabitants had placed temporary and rustic bridges to reach their dwellings.

At that moment, however, the most remarkable feature in the village was a man who, looking down the brook, was standing right in the middle of the road, as if he had been ordered to keep watch there. Sometimes he looked up, sometimes down the road ; then he turned a longing eye toward a beautiful gray horse with long mane and tail, which was fastened to the window-shutter of a cabin, which he shook in his impatient tossing of his head—an impatience which was the more excusable, as, from the fact of his being saddled, it might be presumed he was waiting for his master who was inside.

From time to time the stranger ventured to approach the horse to pat his side, or pass his hand down his slender legs ; and then when he luckily escaped the kick which was always vouchsafed him at each attempt, he returned to his occupation of watching the road. Wearied at last by this fruitless watching, he knocked on the window-shutter.

"Halloo ! In there !" he shouted.

"Who is there ?" replied a man's voice—and the shutter was opened.

"Sir," said the stranger, "if your horse is to be sold, the buyer is here at hand."

"You can see he has no wisp at his tail," answered the other, who appeared to be a countryman ; and he shut the window.

This answer did not appear to satisfy the stranger, so he knocked again.

He was a tall, stout man, with a ruddy complexion, a black beard, and large, sinewy hands peeping out from fine lace ruffles.

He wore a hat edged with gold lace, and set on crosswise like those officers of the provinces who try to look fierce in the eyes of the poor Parisians.

He knocked a third time, but no answer.

He got impatient.

"Do you know, my honest fellow," cried he, "you are not very polite, and if you don't open your shutter I'll break it in !"

At this threat the shutter opened and the same face as before appeared.

"But when you were told the horse is not for sale," replied the peasant, for the second time, "what the devil—is not that enough ?"

"But when I tell you that I want a fast animal !"

"Well, if you want one, can you not go to the post-house ? There are sixty of the king's there; you surely can choose from among them. But leave a man who has only one, that one."

"I tell you this is the very one I want."

"A nice proposal, indeed ! An Arabian——"

"That is the reason I want it."

"Very possibly ; but it is not for sale."

"Whose is it ?"

"You are very curious."

"And you mighty discreet."

"Well, it belongs to a person asleep in the house."

"A man or woman ?"

"A woman."

"Tell the woman, then, that I will give her five hundred pistoles for her horse."

"Oh, ho !" said the peasant, staring ; "five hundred pistoles ! That is a sum !"

"Tell her it is the king who wants her horse."

"The king ?"

"Yes, in person."

"Oh, come ! you are not the king, are you ? "

"No ; but I represent him."

"You represent him ?" said the peasant, taking off his hat.

"Come, come, make haste ! The king is in a hurry !" and the burly stranger cast another impatient glance toward the highway.

"Well, when the lady awakes I will tell her."

"Yes, but I can't wait till she wakes."

"What is to be done, then ?"

"Parbleu ! awaken her."

"Awaken her ? Certainly not."

"Well, I shall do it myself."

But just as the stranger, who pretended to be the representative of his majesty, advanced to knock at the window of the upper story with the handle of his long whip, he caught a glimpse of a carriage coming along at the utmost speed of the worn-out horses. His quick eye recognized it instantly, and he sprang forward to meet it— it was that in which were Gilbert and his guardian angel. On seeing this man, who made signs for him to stop, the postilion gladly obeyed, for he scarcely knew whether the horses could take him to the post-house.

"Chon! my dear Chon! is it you at last?"

"It is, Jean," replied the lady addressed by this singular name. "And what are you doing here?"

"Pardieu! a pretty question. I am waiting for you."

And he leaped on the step of the carriage, and putting in his long arms, seized her, and covered her with kisses.

"Ha!" said he, all at once observing Gilbert, who looked on with surprise at these strange proceedings. "What the deuce have you here?"

"Oh, a little philosopher, and very amusing," replied Mlle. Chon, little caring whether she hurt or flattered the pride of her new acquaintance.

"And where did you pick him up?"

"On the road; but that is not the question."

"True," said the person who was called Jean. "What about our old Countess de Bearn?"

"All settled."

"What, settled?"

"Yes; she will come."

"But what did you say to her?"

"That I was her lawyer's daughter—that I was passing through Verdun, and that my father desired me to tell her the lawsuit was coming on. I merely added that her presence in Paris had now become indispensable for its success."

"What did she say to that?"

"She opened her little gray eyes—took a long pinch of snuff—said that Monsieur Flageot was the cleverest man in the world, and—gave orders for her departure."

"Admirable, Chon! I shall make you my embassador extraordinary. And now, shall we breakfast?"

"With all my heart, for this poor child is dying of hunger. But we must be quick, for she will soon overtake us."

"Who, the old countess? Nonsense!"

"No, the dauphiness."

"Bah! The dauphiness is scarcely at Nancy yet."

"She is at Vitry, three leagues off."

"Peste! That alters the case. Drive on, drive on, postilion!"

"Where, sir?"

"To the post-house."

The carriage drove off, with the stranger still standing on the step, and soon drew up before the inn door.

"Quick, quick!" said Chon. "Let us have some cutlets, a fowl, some eggs, and a bottle of Burgundy. We must set out again instantly."

"Excuse me, madame," said the innkeeper, stepping forward, "but in that case it must be with your own horses."

"How!" said Jean, leaping heavily down from the step of the carriage. "With our own horses?"

"Certainly; or, at least, with those that brought you."

"Impossible!" said the postilion; "they have already done a double stage. See what a state they are in."

"In good earnest," said Chon, "it would be utterly impossible to proceed further with them."

"But what prevents you giving us fresh horses?" asked Jean.

"Merely that I have none."

"What, the devil! you know the regulations—it is your duty to have horses."

"By the regulations, sir, I ought to have fifteen horses; now, I have eighteen."

"Why, all we want is three!"

"Yes, but they are all out."

"What, all the eighteen?"

"Yes, sir."

"Damnation!" thundered the traveler.

"Oh, viscount, viscount!" cried Chon.

"Yes, yes, Chon; don't be afraid, I will keep calm.

And when will your miserable hacks be in?" continued the viscount, turning to the host.

"Faith, sir, I don't know; it all depends on the postilions. Perhaps in an hour, perhaps in two hours."

"Now, my good fellow," said Viscount Jean, placing his hat on one side, and setting out his right leg, "I wish you just to understand this—I never jest."

"I am sorry for it, sir. I should like you much better if you did."

"Now, take my advice. Let the horses be harnessed before I get angry."

"Go into the stable yourself, sir; and if you find a horse there, you shall have it for nothing."

"Indeed? and what if I should find sixty?"

"It would be just the same as if there were none; for these sixty horses are the king's."

"Well, what then?"

"What then? they are not to be hired out."

"What the devil are they here for, then?"

"For the use of her royal highness, the dauphiness."

"Mon Dieu! sixty horses, and we cannot get one."

"But you know, sir——"

"I know one thing, and that is that I am in a hurry——"

"It is a pity."

"And," continued the viscount, without heeding the postmaster's interruption, "as the dauphiness will not be here before the evening——"

"What do you say?" exclaimed the host, all alarmed.

"I say that the horses will be back before she arrives."

"Can it be possible you would propose——"

"Parbleu!" said the viscount, going into the stable, "I will have three horses. I don't want eight, like royal personages, although I have a right to them—by alliance, at least."

"But I say you shall not have one!" said the host, throwing himself, in desperation, between the stranger and his horses.

"Scoundrel!" cried the viscount, turning pale with anger, "do you know who I am?"

" Viscount, viscount ! in Heaven's name, no broils ! "
cried Chon.

" You are right, my good little Chon ; " then, after a
moment's thought, he turned with his most charming
smile to the host : " My good fellow, no more words, now
for deeds. I shall take the responsibility off your shoulders."

" How so ? " asked the host, by no means satisfied even
with the stranger's now gracious visage.

" I shall help myself ; these three horses suit me exactly."

" And you call that freeing me from all responsibility ? "

" Certainly ; you have not given them to me—it was I
who took them."

" I tell you the thing is impossible."

" We shall see that. Where is the harness ? "

" Let no one stir, at his peril ! " cried the host to two or
three grooms loitering about.

" Scoundrels ! " cried the viscount.

" Jean, my dear Jean ! " exclaimed Chon, " you will
only bring us into some disagreeable situation. When on
a mission like this we must endure——"

" Everything except delay," said Jean, with the utmost
coolness ; " and since these rogues won't help me, I shall
do the business myself." And Jean coolly took from the
wall three sets of harness and fitted them on three of the
horses.

" Jean, Jean, I entreat you, do not be rash ! " cried
Chon, clasping her hands.

" Do you wish to arrive in Paris, or not ? " said the
viscount, grinding his teeth.

" Of course I do. All is lost if we do not hasten on."

" Well, then, leave me alone." And separating three
horses—not the worst—from the others, he led them to
the carriage.

" Take care, sir, take care ! " cried the host ; " it is high
treason to steal those horses."

" I am not going to steal them, you fool ; I'm only going
to borrow them. Come on, my little pets."

The host sprung forward to catch the reins ; but before

he could touch them, he was rudely repulsed by the stranger.

"Brother, brother!" cried Mlle. Chon.

"Ah! he is her brother!" muttered Gilbert to himself, breathing more freely.

At this moment a window was opened on the opposite side of the way, and a lovely female face was seen. She appeared quite alarmed at the noise.

"Oh, is it you, madame?" cried Jean, who immediately perceived her.

"How, sir, me?" she replied, in bad French.

"Yes; you are awake now. Will you sell your horse?"

"My horse?"

"Yes, the gray Arabian tied to the window-shutter there. You know I offered you five hundred crowns."

"My horse is not for sale, sir," said she, shutting the window.

"Well, I am not in luck to-day; people will neither sell nor hire. But, corbleu! I'll take the Arabian, if she won't sell it, and I'll drive these hacks to the devil, if they won't hire them. Come, Patrice!"

The footman on his sister's carriage jumped down.

"Harness them," said Jean.

"Help, help!" shouted the host.

Two grooms ran forward.

"Jean! viscount!" cried poor Chon, writhing in the carriage, and endeavoring in vain to open the door. "You are mad! we shall all be slaughtered."

"Slaughtered? It is we who shall slaughter them, I hope. We are three against three. Come out, my young philosopher!" thundered Jean, adressing Gilbert, who never stirred, so great was his astonishment—"come out, and do something—sticks, stones, or fists—anything will do. Morbleu! you look like a saint carved on stone."

Gilbert gave an inquiring and supplicating glance at his protectress, but she held him by the arm. The host, in the meantime, bawled incessantly, dragging the horses to one side, while Jean pulled them to the other. But the struggle could not last forever.   Jean, wearied and heated, dealt the defender of the horses such a blow with his clinched fist that the latter fell back into the horse-pond, among his frightened ducks and geese, shouting as he plunged in : "Help ! murder ! murder !"

The viscount, thus rid of his adversary, lost no time in harnessing the horses.

"Help, in the name of the king ! help !" cried the host, rising and endeavoring to rally his frightened grooms.

"Who calls for help in the name of the king ?" cried a cavalier, riding at full speed into the yard of the post-house, and reining up his horse bathed in sweat and foam, in the very midst of the actors in this tumultuous scene.

"The Chevalier Philip de Taverney !" muttered Gilbert to himself, sinking down in the carriage to escape observation.

Chon, who lost no opportunity of acquiring information, heard the young man's name.

CHAPTER XXII.

VISCOUNT JEAN.

THE young lieutenant of the body-guard of the dauphin, for it was he, leaped from his horse at the aspect of this strange scene, which began to collect about the post-house all the women and children of the village.   On seeing Philip, the postmaster was ready to throw himself on his knees before his protector, whom Providence had sent him so opportunely.

"Sir, sir," cried he, "do you know that this person is about to take by force some of the horses of her royal highness the dauphiness ?"

Philip drew back, as if he heard what was absolutely incredible.

"And who has made this attempt ?" he inquired.

"I, sir ! mordieu !—I, myself !" said Jean.

"It cannot be, sir; otherwise you are either mad or not a gentleman."

"Excuse me, sir. I am in my perfect senses, and have the *entrée* at court."

"How! You are in your perfect senses, and are received at court, and yet you dare to take the horses of the dauphiness?"

"In the first place, there are sixty horses: her royal highness can only employ eight, and it would be strange, indeed, if I should unluckily pitch upon the very ones she wanted."

"True, sir; there are sixty horses," replied the young man, "and her royal highness will only employ eight; but that does not hinder every horse, from the first to the sixtieth, being for her service; and between these horses no distinction can be made."

"You are mistaken, sir; it is made!" said the viscount, contemptuously, "since I have taken these three for myself. Shall I go on foot, when rascally lackeys are drawn by four horses? Mordieu! let them be satisfied, as I am, with three, and there will be enough for us all."

"If the lackeys have four horses, sir, it is by the king's order; and now have the goodness to order your footman to take those horses back to the stable."

These words Philip pronounced firmly, but with so much politeness that none but a ruffian would have answered otherwise than respectfully.

"You may be right, my dear lieutenant," answered Jean, "to speak in this manner, if it be a part of your duty to attend to the cattle; but I did not know that the gentlemen of the dauphin's body-guard had been raised to the rank of grooms. Therefore, take my advice, shut your eyes, tell your people to do the same, and—a good-day to you."

"Sir, whether I have been raised or lowered to the rank of groom is not the question. What I do is my duty, and I am commanded by the dauphiness herself to attend to the relays."

"Oh, that alters the case; but allow me to tell you that

you are filling a sorry office, Mr. Lieutenant, and if this is the way the young lady begins to treat the army——"

"Of whom do you speak, sir?" interrupted Philip.

"Why, parbleu! of the Austrian."

The chevalier turned as pale as death.

"Do you dare," he exclaimed, "to speak——"

"I not only dare to speak," interrupted Jean, "but I dare to act. Come, Patrice, hasten; we are pressed for time."

Philip seized the first horse by the bridle.

"Sir," said he, in a perfectly calm voice, "do me the favor to give your name."

"Do you wish particularly to know it?"

"Yes."

"Well, then, I am the Viscount Jean Dubarry."

"What! you are the brother of her——"

"Who will send you to rot in the Bastile if you say one word more," and Jean jumped into the carriage.

Philip approached the door.

"Viscount Jean Dubarry," said he, "you will do me the honor to come out."

"Yes, ma foi! I have a great deal of time for that!" said the viscount, endeavoring to shut the door.

"If you hesitate one instant, sir," replied Philip, preventing him with his left hand from closing the carriage door, "I give you my word of honor I will run you through the body!" and as he spoke he drew his sword.

"Oh!" cried Chon, "we shall be murdered! Give up the horses, Jean—give them up!"

"What, you threaten me!" shouted Jean, grinding his teeth and snatching up his sword, which he had laid on the seat of the carriage before him.

"And the threat shall be followed up—do you hear?— in a moment," and the young man's sword glanced before Jean's eyes.

"We shall never get away," whispered Chon, "if you do not manage this officer by gentle means."

"Neither gentleness nor violence shall stop me in the discharge of my duty," said Philip, who had overheard the advice, bowing; " I recommend you, madame, to advise Monsieur le Viscount to submit in time, or in the name of the king whom I represent, I shall be forced to kill him if he resists, or to arrest him if he does not."

" And I tell you I shall have the horses in spite of you !" shouted Jean, leaping out of the carriage and drawing his sword.

" That remains to be proved, sir," said Philip, putting himself on his guard. " Are you ready ?"

"Lieutenant," said the brigadier commanding under Philip, " there are six of our men near ; shall I——"

" Do not stir—do not stir ! this is a personal quarrel. Now, sir, I am at your service."

Mlle. Chon shrieked, and Gilbert wished the carriage had been as deep as a well, to hide him.

Jean began the attack ; he was a good swordsman, but anger prevented him from turning his skill to advantage. Philip, on the contrary, was as cool as if he had been playing with a foil in the fencing-school. The viscount advanced, retired, leaped to the right, to the left, shouting in making his passes like the fencing-master of a regiment ; while the chevalier, with closed teeth and steady eye, immovable as a statue, watched all his adversary's movements and divined his intentions. Every one in the yard was silent, attentively looking on ; even Chon ceased to scream. For some minutes the combat continued without Jean's feints, shouts, and movements producing any effect, but also without his having permitted Philip, who was studying his opponent's play, to touch him once. All at once, however, the viscount sprung back, uttering a cry of pain, and at the same moment his ruffles were stained with blood, which ran down his fingers in large drops—he was wounded in the arm.

" You are wounded, sir," said Philip.

" Sacrebleu ! I feel it well enough," said he, turning pale and letting his sword fall.

The chevalier took it up and restored it to him. " Take it, sir," said he, " and never again be guilty of a similar folly."

"Plague take it ! if I have my follies, I pay for them," growled the viscount. "Come and dress this scrape, dear Chon," added he to his sister, who sprung from the carriage and hastened to his assistance.

"You will do me the justice, madame," said Philip, "to acknowledge that all this has not been caused by my fault. I deeply regret having been driven to such extremities before a lady," and bowing, he retired. "Let those horses be unharnessed and taken back to the stable," he said to the postmaster.

Jean shook his fist at him.

"Oh !" cried the host, "this is just in the nick of time ; three horses coming in that have been out ! Courtin, Courtin ! quick ! put them to the gentleman's carriage."

"But, master," said the postilion.

"Come, come ! no reply ; the gentleman is in a hurry. Don't be uneasy, sir, you shall have the horses."

"All very fine ; but your horses should have been here half an hour ago," growled Dubarry, stamping with his foot, as he looked at his arm, pierced through and through, which Chon was binding up with her handkerchief.

Meantime, Philip had mounted his horse again and was giving his orders as if nothing had occurred.

"Now, brother, now ! let us go," said Chon, leading him toward the carriage.

"And my Arabian ?" said he. "Ah, ma foi ! let him go to the devil, for I am in for a day of ill-luck," and he got into the carriage.

"Oh," said he, perceiving Gilbert, "I cannot stretch my legs with this fellow."

"Let me out, pray," said Gilbert, "and I will walk."

"In the devil's name, go, then !" replied Jean.

"No, no," said Chon ; "I must keep my little philosopher. Sit opposite me, and you will not annoy him ;" and she held Gilbert by the arm. Then, bending forward, she whispered to her brother : "He knows the man who wounded you."

A gleam of joy flashed from the viscount's eyes. "Oh, very well ! let him stay. What is the fellow called ?"

"The Chevalier Philip de Taverney."

Just then the young officer passed the carriage.

"Oh, you are there, my little gendarme," shouted the viscount ; "you look wonderfully fierce just now, but my turn will come some day."

"I shall be at your service, sir, whenever you please," answered Philip, calmly.

"Yes, yes, we shall see that, Monsieur Philip de Taverney," said the viscount, leaning forward to see what effect the mention of his name would have on the young man, when he must be so far from expecting to hear it.

Philip looked up with surprise, and indeed with a slight feeling of uneasiness, but immediately recovering his self-possession, and taking off his hat, with the utmost grace, "A pleasant journey, Viscount Jean Dubarry," said he.

The carriage rolled on rapidly. "Thousand devils !" said the viscount, making a horrible grimace, "do you know, my little Chon, I am suffering dreadful pain ?"

"The first place where we change I shall send for a doctor for you, while this poor fellow breakfasts," replied Chon.

"Ah! true, true ; we have not breakfasted, but the pain I suffer—and I am in agony with thirst—takes away all appetite."

"Will you bring a glass of wine from my flask ?"

"Certainly ; give it me."

"Sir," said Gilbert, "will you allow me to remark that wine is very bad for you in your present condition ?"

"Really, you are quite a physician, my little philosopher."

"No, sir ; but I hope to be so one day. I have read, however, in a treatise written for people in the army, that the first things forbidden the wounded are spirits, wine, and coffee."

"Ah, you read that ? Well, I shall not drink the wine."

"But if Monsieur le Viscount would permit me to take his handkerchief and dip it in that brook, and then wrap it round his arm. I am sure it would ease his pain."

"Do, do," said Chon; "stop, postilion!"

Gilbert got out to follow up his proposition. "This boy will be a horrid plague to us," said the viscount. "I have a great mind to tell the postilion to drive on, and to leave him there, handkerchief and all."

"You would be wrong; that boy can be very useful to us."

"How so?"

"He has already given me some important information about the dauphiness, and did he not just now tell you the name of your adversary?"

"True; well, let him stay."

Gilbert returned, and the application of the wet bandage to the viscount's arm, as he had foretold, relieved him greatly.

"Faith, he was right; I feel much better," said he; "let us have a little chat." Gilbert opened his ears to their utmost extent. The conversation which ensued, and which was conducted in the lively and brilliant patois of Provençe, would have sadly puzzled a Parisian ear, and Gilbert, master of himself as he was, could not avoid a slight movement of impatience which Mlle. Chon having perceived, quieted with a gentle smile. This smile reminded the poor boy of the kindness with which he was treated. Circumstances had brought him in contact with a nobleman honored with the royal favor. "Ah," thought he, "if Andrée saw me in this magnificent carriage!" and his heart swelled with pride. New ideas and hopes took possession of him, and Nicole no longer cost him a thought.

In the meantime, the brother and sister resumed their conversation; still, however, in the Provençal dialect.

Suddenly the viscount leaned forward. "See, there he is!" cried he.

"What?"

"The Arabian which I wished to buy."

"Oh!" exclaimed Chon, "what a splendid woman the rider is!

"Call her, Chon; she will not, perhaps, be so much

afraid of you. I would give a thousand crowns for the horse."

"And how much for the woman?" said Chon, laughing.

"I would give all I have for her; but call her."

"Madame!" cried Chon, "madame!"

But the stranger appeared not to hear, or not to understand. Wrapped in a long white mantle, and her face shaded by a large beaver hat with drooping feathers, she flew past them like an arrow, crying: "*Avanti, Djerid, avanti!*"

"She is an Italian," said the viscount. "Mordieu, what a splendid woman! If it were not for the pain of my arm, I would jump out and run after her."

"I know her," said Gilbert.

"Why, the little fellow is a directory for the whole province; he knows every one."

"Who is she?" asked Chon.

"Her name is Lorenza, and she is the sorcerer's wife."

"What sorcerer?"

"The Baron Joseph Balsamo!"

The brother and sister looked at each other with an expression which said: "We did well to keep him."

CHAPTER XXIII.

THE COUNTESS DUBARRY'S MORNING LEVEE.

WHILE Mlle. Chon and Viscount Jean are traveling post on the Chalons road, let us introduce the reader to another member of the same family.

In the suite of rooms at Versailles which the Princess Adelaide, daughter of Louis XV. had once occupied, his majesty had installed his mistress, the Countess Dubarry, not without keenly studying beforehand the effect which this piece of policy would produce on his court. The favorite, with her merry whims and her careless, joyous humor, had transformed that wing of the palace, formerly so quiet, into a scene of perpetual merriment and tumult, and every hour she issued thence her commands for a banquet or a party of pleasure.

But what appeared still more unusual on these magnificent staircases, was the never-ceasing stream of visitors ascending them, and crowding an ante-chamber filled with curiosities from all parts of the globe—certainly containing nothing so curious as the idol worshiped by this crowd.

The day after that on which the scene which we have just described occurred at the little village of Lachaussé, about nine in the morning, the countess, lovely as an eastern houri, was at the important duties of the toilet.

"No news of Chon?" asked one of her tiring women.

"No, madame."

"Nor of the viscount?"

"No, madame."

"Do you know has Bischi received any?"

"A message was sent to your sister's, madame, this morning, but there were no letters."

"It is very tiresome waiting in this way," said the countess, pouting her lovely mouth. "I am in a wretched humor—I pity all who may come near me to-day. Will some means never be invented of conversing at a hundred leagues' distance? Is my ante-chamber passably filled this morning?"

"Can madame think it necessary to ask?"

"Dame! but listen. Dorée—the dauphiness is coming; I shall be abandoned for that sun, I who am only a little twinkling star. But tell me, who is there this morning?"

"The Duke d'Aiguillon, madame, the Prince de Soubise, Monsieur de Sartines, the President Maupeou——"

"And the Duke de Richelieu?"

"Not yet, madame."

"How! neither to-day nor yesterday? He is afraid of compromising himself. You must send one of my servants to the Hotel du Hanover to inquire if the duke be ill."

"Yes, madame; will you receive all who are waiting at once, or do you wish to give any one a private audience?"

"Monsieur de Sartines first; I must speak to him alone."

The order was transmitted by the countess's woman to a tall footman who waited in the corridor leading from her bed-chamber to the anterooms, and the minister of police immediately appeared, dressed in black, and endeavoring, by an insinuating smile, to moderate the severe expression of his gray eyes and thin lips.

"Good morning, my dear enemy!" said the countess, without looking round, but seeing him in the mirror before her.

"Your enemy, madame?"

"Yes; my world is divided into only two classes—friends and enemies; I admit no neutrals, or class them as enemies."

"And you are right, madame; but tell me how I, notwithstanding my well-known devotion to your interests, deserve to be included in either one or other of these classes?"

"By allowing to be printed, distributed, sold, and sent to the king, a whole ocean of pamphlets, libels, verses— all against me. It is ill-natured, stupid, odious!"

"But, madame, I am not responsible."

"Yes, sir, you are; for you know the wretch who wrote them."

"Madame, if they were all written by one author, we should not have the trouble of sending him to the Bastile —Hercules himself would sink under such a labor."

"Upon my word, you are highly complimentary to me!"

"If I were your enemy, madame, I should not speak the truth thus."

"Well, I believe you. We understand each other now. But one thing still gives me some uneasiness."

"What is that, madame?"

"You are on good terms with the Choiseuls."

"Madame, Monsieur de Choiseul is prime minister; he issues his orders, and I must obey them."

"So, if Monsieur de Choiseul orders that I am to be

vexed, tortured, worried to death, you will allow me to be vexed, tortured, worried ?   Thank you !"

" Let us discuss matters a little," said Sartines, sitting down without being asked to do so, but without any displeasure being exhibited on the part of the favorite, for much must be pardoned in the man who knew better than any other all that was doing in France.   " Let us discuss this a little—and, first, what have I done for you these three days past ?"

" You informed me that a courier had been sent from Chanteloup to hasten the arrival of the dauphiness."

" Was that done like an enemy ?"

" But about the presentation on which you know my heart is set—what have you been doing for me ?"

" Doing all I possibly could."

" Monsieur de Sartines, you are not candid ! "

" Ah, madame ! I assure you you are unjust.   Did I not find and bring you Viscount Jean from the back room of a tavern in less than two hours, when you wanted him in order to send him I don't know where, or, rather, I do know where ? "

" I had much rather you had allowed my brother-in-law to stay there," said Mme. Dubarry, laughing, " a man allied to the royal family of France ! "

" Well, but was that not a service to be added to my many other services ?"

" Oh, very well ; but just tell me what you did for me yesterday."

" Yesterday, madame ? "

" Oh, you may well endeavor to recollect—that was your day for obliging others."

" I don't understand you, madame."

" Well, I understand myself.   Answer, sir, what were you doing yesterday ?"

" Yesterday morning I was occupied, as usual, writing with my secretary."

" Till what hour ?"

" Till ten."

" What did you do then ?"

" I sent to invite a friend of mine from Lyons, who had made a wager he would come to Paris without my knowing, and my footman met him just at the barrier."

" Well, after dinner ? "

" I sent to the Austrian lieutenant of police information of the haunt of a famous robber whom he could not discover."

" And where is he ? "

" At Vienna."

" So you are not only the minister of police at Paris, but perform the same duties for foreign courts ? "

" Yes, madame—in my leisure moments."

" Well, I shall take a note of that. Then, after having despatched the courier to Vienna ? "

" I went to the opera."

" To see the little Guimard ? Poor Soubise ! "

" No—to arrest a famous pickpocket, whom I did not disturb so long as he kept to the fermiers-general, but who had the audacity to rob two or three noblemen."

" You should say the indiscretion. Well, after the opera ? "

" After the opera ? "

" Yes. That seems to be rather a puzzling question, is it not ? "

" No. After the opera? Let me think——"

" So ! How much your memory has failed of late ! "

" Oh ! after the opera—yes, I remember——"

" Well ? "

" I went to the house of a certain lady who keeps a gaming-table, and I myself conducted her to Fort-l'Eveque."

" In her carriage ? "

" No, in a fiacre."

" Well ? "

" Well, that is all."

" No, it is not."

" I got into my fiacre again."

" And whom did you find in it ? "

He reddened.

"Oh!" cried the countess, clapping her hands, "I have really had the honor of making a minister of police blush!"

"Madame——" stammered Sartines.

"No; I shall tell you who was in the fiacre—it was the Duchess de Grammont!"

"The Duchess de Grammont?"

"Yes, the Duchess de Grammont—who came to ask you to contrive to get her admitted to the king's private apartments."

"Ma foi, madame!" said the minister, shifting uneasily in his chair, "I may give up my portfolio to you. It is you who manage the police of Paris, not I."

"To tell the truth, sir, I have a police of my own. So beware! Oh, the Duchess de Grammont in a fiacre with the minister of police at midnight! It was capital! Do you know what I did?"

"No; but I am afraid it was something dreadful—fortunately it was very late."

"But night is the time for vengeance."

"And what, then, did you do?"

"As I keep a police of my own, I keep a body of writers also—shocking, ragged, hungry scribblers."

"Hungry? You must feed them badly."

"I don't feed them at all. If they became fat, they would be as stupid as the Prince de Soubise; fat, we are told, absorbs the gall."

"Go on; I shudder at the thought of them."

"I recollected all the disagreeable things you have allowed the Choiseuls to do against me, and determined to be revenged. I gave my legion of famishing Apollos the following program: First, Monsieur de Sartines, disguised as a lawyer, visiting an innocent young girl who lives in a garret, and giving her, on the thirtieth of every month, a wretched pittance of a hundred crowns."

"Madame, that is a benevolent action which you are endeavoring to misconstrue."

"It is only such actions which can be misconstrued. My second scene was Monsieur de Sartines, disguised like a reverend missionary, introducing himself into the convent of the Carmelites of the Rue St. Antoine."

"I was taking those good nuns some news from the Indies."

"East or West Indies—which? My third scene is Monsieur de Sartines, disguised as lieutenant of the police, driving through the streets at midnight in a fiacre with the Duchess de Grammont."

"No, madame," exclaimed he; "no—you would not bring ridicule on my administration in that manner!"

"Why, do you not bring ridicule on mine?" said the the countess, laughing. "But wait. I set my rogues to work, and they began like boys at college, with exordium, narration, and amplification—and I have received this morning an epigram, a song, and a ballad, of which you are the subject."

"You are not serious?"

"Perfectly so; and to-morrow you shall receive them, all three."

"Why not to-day?"

"I must have some time to distribute them. Is not that the way? Besides, the police ought always to hear last about any new affair. I assure you, you will be very much amused. I laughed three-quarters of an hour at them this morning, and the king was nearly dead with laughing—it was that which made him so late."

"I am ruined!" cried Sartines, clasping his hands.

"Ruined? Nonsense! You are only celebrated in song. Am I ruined by all the verses made on me? No; I only get in a passion at them, and then for revenge I determine to put somebody else in a passion, too. Ah! what delightful verses. I have ordered some wine to my literary scorpions, and I expect by this time their senses are wrapped in happy oblivion."

"Ah! countess, countess!"

"But, pardieu, you must hear the epigram:

> " 'Oh, France, how wretched is thy fate,
> When women hold the helm of state!'

No, no ; I am wrong ; that is the scandal perpetrated against myself.   But there are so many, I confound them. Listen, listen ; here it is :

> " ' A perfumer once sought of a painter a sign,
>   His skill than his genius was duller,
>   For in a huge bottle, with knavish design,
>   He makes Boynes, Maupeou, and Terray to shine,
>   Displayed in their own proper color.
>   But for Sartines still room in the vessel he leaves,
>   And he labels the mixture the essence of thieves.' "

" Cruel woman, you will set me mad ! " cried Sartines.

" Now, we must look at the poem.   You must know it is Madame de Grammont who speaks :

> " ' Dear minister, you know my skin
>   Is to the purest snow akin ;
>   Then grant to me this single thing—
>   Oh, say so, say so to the king.' "

" Madame, madame ! " cried Sartines, more furious than ever.

" Nonsense," said the countess.   " You need not be so uneasy about these little poems.   I have only had ten thousand copies of them struck off."

" You have a press, then ? "

" Certainly.   Has not the Duke de Choiseul one ? "

" Let your printer take care ! "

" Oh, it is kept in my own name ; I am the printer."

" Shocking—shocking !   And the king laughs at these calumnies ? "

" Laughs ?   He sometimes gives me rhymes himself, when my own inspiration fails."

" You know how I serve you, and you treat me thus ? "

" I know that you are betraying me—the Duchess de Grammont wishes to ruin me."

" Madame, I declare to you she took me quite unawares."

" You confess, then, that I was informed correctly ? "

" I am forced to confess it."

" Why did you not tell me ? "

"I came now for that purpose."

"I don't believe you."

"Upon my honor."

"I bet two to one against that pledge."

"Behold me at your feet?" and he fell on his knees.
"I beg forgiveness."

"You are in the position in which you ought to be."

"Let us make peace, countess, in Heaven's name!"

"So are you afraid of a few bad verses! You, a man—
a minister! Yet you never reflect how many wretched
hours such things make me spend—I, a poor, weak
woman!"

"You are a queen."

"A queen—not presented at court."

"I swear to you I have never done anything hurtful to
your interests."

"No; but you have allowed others to do so. The matter
however, is now, not the doing nothing against them, but
the doing all in your power to forward them. Are you on
my side? Yes or no?"

"Certainly, on your side."

"Will you assist me? Will you allow nothing to inter-
pose to hinder my presentation?"

"For myself, I promise everything."

"No," said the countess, stamping with her foot.
"Punic faith; I will not accept that. There is a loophole in it to creep out at. You will be supposed to do
nothing against me yourself, but the Duke de Choiseul
will do all. Give me up the Choiseul party, bound hand
and foot, or I will annihilate you—destroy you! Take
care; verses are not my only weapons."

"Do not threaten me, madame," said Sartines, thoughtfully; "there are difficulties about this presentation which
you cannot understand."

"Obstacles have purposely been thrown in the way of it.
You can remove them."

"It would require a hundred persons to do so."

"You shall have a million."

"The king will not give his consent."

" He shall give it."

" And, when you have got it, how get a lady to present you ?"

" I am seeking for one now."

" It is quite useless ; there is a league against you."

" At Versailles ?"

" Yes. All the ladies have refused, in order to pay their court to the Duke de Choiseul, the Duchess de Grammont, the dauphiness, and the whole prudish party."

" Do not fear. I have nearly obtained what I want."

" Ha ! it was for that you sent your sister to Verdun ?"

" So you know that, do you ?" said she, angrily.

" Oh, I have also my police, you know," said Sartines, laughing.

" And your spies ?"

" And my spies."

" In my apartments ?"

" In your apartments."

" In my stable, or in my kitchen ?"

" In your ante-chamber, in your saloon, in your bedroom, under your pillow."

" Now, as the first pledge of our peace," said the countess, " give me the names of those spies."

" No, countess ; I should not wish to embroil you with your friends."

" But name only the last who told you a secret."

" What would you do ?"

" I would turn him out."

" If you begin in that way, you will soon have to live in an empty house."

" This is frightful !"

" Yet perfectly true. Oh, you know we could not govern without spies. So excellent a politician as you must have discovered that long ago."

Mme. Dubarry leaned her elbow on a table, and seemed to reflect for some minutes, then she said : " You are right. Let us say no more on the subject. What are to be the conditions of our treaty ?"

" Make them yourself. You are the conqueror."

"I am as magnanimous as Semiramis. Let me hear what you wish."

"Well, then, you are never to speak to the king about petitions on the subject of wheat ; for, traitress ! you have promised your support to those petitions."

"Very well. Take away all the petitions with you ; they are in a box there."

"As a reward, here is a document drawn up by the peers of the kingdom respecting presentations and the right of sitting in the royal presence."

"A document which you were charged to give his majesty ?"

"Yes."

"But what will you say to them ?"

"That I have given it. You will thus gain time ; and you are too clever in your tactics not to take advantage of it."

At this moment the folding-doors were thrown open, and a negro announced, "The king !"

The two allies hastened to hide their mutual pledge of peace and good understanding, and turned to salute his majesty, Louis—the fifteenth of that name.

CHAPTER XXIV.

KING LOUIS THE FIFTEENTH.

The King entered with head erect, with a firm step, his eye full of life, and a smile on his lips. As the doors were opened, a double file of bowing heads was seen belonging to the courtiers who had been long waiting in the ante-chamber, and who were now more desirous of admittance than ever, since they could thus pay their court to two powers at once ; but the doors closed on them, for the king made a sign that no one should follow him. He found himself alone, therefore, with the countess and the minister of police—for we need not reckon the waiting-maid or the little negro boy.

"Good morning, countess," said the king, kissing Mme. Dubarry's hand. "Ha! fresh as any rose, I see. Good morning, Sartines. Is this your cabinet, where you write your despatches? Heavens! what heaps of papers! Hide them—hide them! Ha! what a beautiful fountain, countess."

And, with the versatile curiosity of one always in search of something to amuse him, he fixed his eyes on a large china ornament which had been brought in since the evening before and placed in a corner of the countess's bedroom.

"Sire," replied the countess, "it is a Chinese fountain: by turning this cock, the water comes out, and makes these birds sing and these fishes swim; then the doors of the pagoda open, and there comes out a procession of mandarins."

"Very pretty! very pretty, indeed!"

At this moment the little negro walked across the room, dressed in the fantastic fashion in which, at this period, they dressed their Osmans and Othellos. He wore a little turban, ornamented with a lofty plume of feathers, on one side of his head, a vest embroidered with gold, which permitted his ebony arms to be seen, and slashed breeches of white brocaded satin; round his waist was a scarf of various bright colors, which connected the breeches with a richly embroidered jacket, and a dagger, ornamented with precious stones, was stuck in the scarf bound around his waist.

"Peste!" cried the king, "how splendid Zamore is to-day!"

The negro stopped to admire himself before a mirror.

"Sire, he has a favor to ask of your majesty."

"Madame," replied the king, with a courtly smile, "I am afraid Zamore is very ambitious."

"How so, sire?"

"Because he has already been granted the greatest favor he can desire."

"What is that?"

"The same that has been granted me."

"I do not understand you, sir."

" You have made him your slave."

" Oh, how charming, sire !" cried the countess.

The minister of police bowed in assent, and bit his lip to prevent himself from smiling.

" But," asked the king, " what can Zamore desire ? "

" The reward of his long and numerous services."

" Yes ; he is twelve years old."

" His long and numerous future services."

" Oh, very well."

" Yes, indeed, sire ; past services have been rewarded long enough ; it is now time to begin and reward future ones. There would not then be so much ingratitude."

" Ha ! not a bad idea," said the king. " What do you think of it, Sartines ? "

" That it would benefit all devoted servants of your majesty, sire ; therefore, I support it."

" Well, countess, what does Zamore want ? "

" Sire, you know my little country seat of Luciennes ? "

" I have merely heard it spoken of."

" It is your own fault ; I have invited you to it a hundred times."

" You know the etiquette, dear countess—unless on a journey the king can only sleep in a royal château."

" And for that very reason I wish you to make Luciennes a royal château, and Zamore its governor."

" But, countess, that would be a burlesque."

" I love burlesques, sire."

" The governors of the other castles would all exclaim, and this time with reason."

" Let them exclaim ; they have often done so without reason   Kneel down, Zamore."

The little fellow knelt.

" For what is he kneeling ? " asked the king.

" For the reward you are going to give him for bearing my train, and putting all the prudes of the court in a rage."

" He is really a hideous creature," said the king, bursting into a fit of laughter.

" Rise, Zamore," said the countess ; " you are appointed governor of Luciennes."

"But, indeed, madame——"

"I shall send Zamore all the writings necessary for his governorship. And now, sire, you may come to Luciennes, you have one more royal château from this day."

"Is there any way of refusing her anything, Sartines?"

"There may be a way, sire," replied Sartines, "but it has not yet been discovered."

"And if it should be found out, sire, there is one thing certain—it is Monsieur de Sartines who will be the discoverer."

"How can you think so, madame?" asked Sartines, trembling.

"Sire, only imagine that I have requested a favor of Monsieur de Sartines for three months past, and it is not yet granted."

"And what is it?" asked the king.

"Oh, he knows very well!"

"I—I swear to you, madame——"

"Does it fall under the duties of his office?"

"Yes; either in his or those of his successor."

"Madame," cried Sartines, "you really make me uneasy."

"What is the request?" again inquired the king.

"To find me a sorcerer."

Sartines breathed more freely.

"To burn him?" said the king. "It is rather too hot, countess; wait till the winter."

"No, sir; I wish to present him with a golden wand."

"Then the sorcerer foretold you some misfortune which has not befallen you."

"On the contrary, sire, he predicted a piece of good fortune which has come to pass."

"Let us hear it, then, countess," said the king, throwing himself back in an armchair, like one who was not quite sure whether the tale would tire him or amuse him, but who must run the chance.

"With all my heart; but if I tell the tale, you must contribute the half of the sorcerer's reward."

"The whole, if you like."

"Royally said. Now, listen."

"I am all attention."

"There was once——"

"It begins like a fairy tale."

"It is one, sire."

"Delightful! I love enchanters."

"There was once a poor young girl, who, at the time my story commences, had neither page, nor carriage, nor negro, nor parrot, nor monkey——"

"Nor king," added Louis.

"Oh, sire!"

"And what did your poor young girl do?"

"She trotted about through the streets of Paris like any other common mortal, only she always went very quick; for it was said she was pretty, and she was afraid of meeting some rude man."

"The young girl was a Lucretia, eh?"

"Oh, your majesty knows there have been no Lucretias since the year—I don't know what—of the foundation of Rome."

"Oh, heavens! countess, are you going to become learned?"

"No; if I were learned, I should have given you a wrong date; now, I gave you none."

"True," said the king; "go on."

"The young girl one day was trotting along, as usual, when all at once, while crossing the Tuileries, she discovered that a man was following her."

"Oh, the deuce! Then she stopped, I presume?"

"Ah, sire, what a bad opinion you have of women! It is easy to see you have only associated with marchionesses and duchesses."

"And princesses, eh?"

"I am too polite to contradict your majesty; but what frightened the young girl was, that a fog came on which became every moment denser."

"Sartines, do you know what causes fogs?"

The minister, thus taken unawares, started.

"Ma foi! no, sire."

"Nor I.   Well, go on, dear countess."

"She ran as fast as she could, passed through the gate, and found herself in the square which bears your majesty's name when she found the unknown, from whom she thought she had escaped, face to face with her.   She uttered a cry——"

"Was he so very ugly, then?"

"No, sire; he was a handsome young man of six-or-eight-and-twenty, of a dark complexion, with large, speaking eyes, and a pleasing voice."

"And the heroine was afraid?   Peste! how easily she was frightened!"

"She was not quite so much so when she looked at him; still, it was not a pleasant situation in that dense fog.   So, clasping her hands, she said: 'I implore you, sir, not to do me any harm.'   The unknown shook his head, smiled, and replied : 'Heaven is my witness, I have no evil intentions toward you.'   'What, then, do you want?' I asked. 'To obtain a promise from you.'   'What can I promise you, sir?'   'Promise to grant me the first favor I shall ask when——'   'When?' repeated the young girl likewise. 'When you are queen.'"

"And what did the young girl do?" said the king.

"Sire, she thought it would be engaging herself to nothing; so she promised."

"And what became of the sorcerer?"

"He disappeared."

"And Sartines refuses to find him?   He is wrong."

"Sire, I do not refuse; but I cannot find him."

"Oh, sir," said the countess, "those words, *cannot*, should never be in the dictionary of the police."

"Madame, we are on his track."

"Yes; what you always say when you are baffled."

"It is the truth; but consider what trivial directions you have given."

"How, trivial?—young, handsome, dark complexion, black hair, splendid eyes, a pleasing voice."

"Oh, the devil! how you speak of him, countess!   Sartines, I forbid you to find that young man," said the king.

" You are wrong, sire ; for I only wish to ask one simple question."

" Is it about yourself ? "

" Yes."

" Well, what is it ?   His prediction is accomplished."

" Do you think so ? "

" Yes ; you are queen."

" Very nearly."

" What has the sorcerer, then, to tell you more ? "

" He has to tell me when the queen will be presented ? "

" That is no concern of his ; " and the king made a grimace which showed that he thought they were getting on dangerous ground.

" And whose concern is it ? "

" Your own."

" Mine ? "

" Yes ; you must find a lady to present you."

" Oh, very likely, among the prudes of the court !   Your majesty knows they are all sold to Choiseul and Praslin."

" What ! was there not an agreement made between us that the ministers should never be named here ? "

" I did not promise, sire."

" Well, I request you to leave them in their places, and keep your own place.   Believe me, the best is yours."

" Alas ! then, for foreign affairs and the navy."

" Countess," interrupted the king, " in Heaven's name, no politics ! "

At this moment Dorée entered, and whispered a word or two in her mistress's ear.

" Oh, certainly, certainly ! " cried she.

" What is it ? " asked the king.

" Chon, sire, who has just returned from a journey, and wishes to pay her respects to your majesty."

" Let her come in, let her come in !   Indeed, for some days past, I felt that I wanted something, without knowing exactly what it was."

" Thanks, sire," said Chon, as she entered ; then, going up to her sister, she whispered : " It is all settled."

The countess uttered an exclamation of joy.

"Well, what now?" asked the king.

"Nothing, sire. I am only glad to see her again."

"I am glad, too. How do you do, little Chon?"

"May I say a word or two, sire, to my sister?"

"Yes, yes, my child; and while you are talking together, I shall ask Sartines where you have been."

"Sire," said the minister, wishing to avoid being questioned on that point, "may I beg your majesty to allow me a few moments on business of the utmost importance?"

"Oh, I have very little time now, Monsieur de Sartines," said the king, beginning to yawn.

"Only two words, your majesty."

"About what?"

"About those people with the second sight—these illuminati—these workers of miracles——"

"Pooh! jugglers. Give them permission to exercise their trade, and there will be nothing to fear from them."

"The matter is more serious than your majesty supposes. Every day we have new masonic lodges formed; they are now a powerful sect, attracting to them all the enemies of monarchy—the philosophers, the encyclopedists. Voltaire is to be received by them in great state."

"He? He is dying."

"He, sire? Oh, no, sire, he is not such a fool!"

"He has confessed."

"Merely a trick."

"In the habit of a Capuchin."

"That was an impiety, sire. But with regard to these freemasons, they are always active—they write, they talk, they form associations, correspond with foreign countries; they intrigue, they threaten—even now they are full of expectation of a great chief or head of the whole body, as I have learned from some words which escaped from one of their number."

"Well, Sartines, when this chief comes, catch him and put him in the Bastile, and the whole affair is settled."

"Sire, these persons have great resources."

"Have they greater than you, sir, who have the whole police of a large kingdom?"

"Your majesty was induced to expel the Jesuits; it was the philosophers whom you should have expelled."

"Come, come; no more about those poor quill-drivers!"

"Sire, those quills are dangerous which are cut by the pen-knife of Damiens."

Louis XV. turned pale.

"These philosphers, sire, whom you despise——"

"Well, sir?"

"Will destroy the monarchy, sire."

"How long will they take to do that?"

Sartines stared at his coolness.

"How can I tell, sire? Perhaps fifteen, twenty, or thirty years."

"Well, my dear friend, in fifteen or twenty years I shall be no more; so talk of all these things to my successor."

And the king turned to Mme. Dubarry, who, seeming to have waited for this movement, said, with a heavy sigh:

"Oh, heavens! what is it you tell me, Chon?"

"Yes; what is it?" asked the king, "for you both looked very wretched."

"Oh, sire, there is good cause for it!"

"Speak! let me hear what has happened."

"My poor brother!"

"Poor Jean!"

"Do you think it must be cut off?"

"They hope not."

"Cut off—what?" asked the king.

"His arm, sire."

"Cut off the viscount's arm? Why, pray?"

"Because he has been seriously wounded."

"Wounded in the arm?"

"Oh, yes, sire."

"Aye, in some drunken squabble, in a filthy tavern."

"No, sire; on the highway."

"But how did that happen?"

"It happened because an enemy wished to assassinate him, sire."

"Ah, the poor viscount!" exclaimed the king, who had very little feeling for the sufferings of others, although he could look wonderfully compassionate. "But to assassinate him! This is a serious matter, is it not, Sartines?"

The minister looked much less moved than the king, but was, in reality, a great deal more uneasy on the subject. He drew near the sisters.

"Can it be possible," asked he, anxiously, "that such a misfortune has occurred?"

"Oh, yes, sir, it is but too possible," said Chon, very mournfully.

"Assassinated? But how?"

"He was waylaid."

"Waylaid? Ha! Sartines, this is an affair for you," said the king.

"Relate all the circumstances, madame," said the minister, "and do not, I entreat you, allow your just resentment to exaggerate them. We shall, by being strictly just, be most severe; and, where things are looked at closely and coolly, they are often not so very serious as we at first apprehended."

"Oh," cried Chon, "this is not an affair which has been related to me. I saw the whole."

"Well, but what did you see, Chon?" inquired the king.

"I saw a man fall on my brother, and, having forced him to draw in self-defense, wound him shockingly."

"Was the man alone?" asked Sartines.

"No, indeed; he had six others with him."

"The poor viscount!" said the king, looking at the countess, that he might know exactly what degree of grief to exhibit. "Forced to fight? Poor fellow!" But, seeing that she did not relish this pleasantry: "And he was wounded?" he added, in a compassionate voice.

"But how did the quarrel come about?" asked the minister of police, trying, if it were possible, to betray her into telling the truth.

"Oh, in the most trifling way in the world. All about post-horses which I wanted in order to hasten back to my sister, as I had promised to be with her this morning."

"Ha! Sartines, this merits punishment, does it not?" said the king.

"It does, sire, and I shall take all the necessary information on the subject. What was the name of the aggressor, madame, his condition, his rank ?"

"His rank ? He is a military man—an officer in the body-guard of the dauphin, I think. As to his name, he is called Baverney, Faverney, Taverney—yes, Taverney, that is it."

"Madame, to-morrow he shall sleep in the Bastile."

"Oh, no !" said the countess, who until now had very diplomatically kept silence—"oh, no !"

"Why, oh, no ?" asked the king ; "why should not the fellow be imprisoned ? You know I detest the military."

"And I repeat, sire," said the countess, doggedly, "that I am quite sure nothing will be done to the man who assassinated the viscount."

"Ha ! countess, this is very curious ! Explain it, if you please."

"That is easily done ; he will be protected."

"And who will protect him ?"

"The person at whose instigation he acted."

"And that person will protect him against us ? Oh, that is rather too much, countess !"

"Madame——" stammered the Count de Sartines, for he felt that a blow was coming, and he was not prepared to ward it off.

"Yes !" exclaimed the countess ; "he will be protected against you, and there will be nothing said. Do you suppose you are the master, sire ?"

The king felt the blow which the minister had foreseen, and he determined to bear it.

"I see that you are going to plunge into politics," said he, "and find out some reasons of state for a paltry duel."

"There, now ! you abandon me already ; the assassination has become nothing but a duel, now that you suspect the quarter whence it comes !"

"So ! I am in for it !" said the king, going to the great Chinese fountain, turning the cock, and making the birds sing, the fishes swim, and the mandarins come out.

"And you don't know who aimed this blow ?" asked the

countess, pulling the ears of Zamore, who was lying at her feet.

"No, on my word!" said the king.

"Or suspect?"

"I swear I don't! Do you, countess?"

"No, I don't suspect, I know positively; I am going to tell you, and it will be no news to you, I am certain!"

"Countess, countess, do you know that in what you said you gave the lie to your king?" and Louis tried to look dignified.

"Sire, I know I am a little warm, but if you think I shall quietly allow my brother to be killed by the Duke de Choiseul——"

"Yes; there it is—Choiseul again!" exclaimed the king, in a loud voice, as if he had not expected this name, which for the last ten minutes he had been dreading.

"Well, it is because your majesty is determined not to see that he is my worst enemy; but I see it plainly, for he does not even take the trouble to hide his hatred from me."

"He is far from hating any one to that degree that he would cause him to be assassinated."

"There, you see, when Choiseul is mentioned, you are on his side immediately."

"Now, my dear countess, politics again!"

"Oh, Monsieur de Sartines!" cried she, "is it not dreadful to be treated thus?"

"No, no; if it be as you think——"

"I know what I think," she interrupted, passionately, "and what I am sure of—the affair will be given up."

"Now, do not get angry, countess," said the king, "it shall not be given up. You shall be defended, and so well——"

"So well, what?"

"So well that he who attacked poor Jean shall pay dearly for it."

"Yes, the instrument will be broken, but the hand that directed it will be taken and kindly pressed."

"Well, but is it not right to punish this Monsieur Taverney, who actually committed the assault?"

"Oh, certainly; but it is not right that what you do for me is no more than would be done to a soldier who should give a blow to a shop-keeper at the theater. I will not be treated like every common person. If you do not do more for those whom you love than for those who are indifferent to you, I had rather remain alone in obscurity like these latter—their relations, at least, are not assassinated!"

"Oh, countess!" said the king, imploringly, "I got up for once in such good spirits, disposed to be gay, happy, and pleased with every one, and now you are spoiling my morning completely."

"Very fine, indeed! It is a delightful morning for me, of course, when my relations are being massacred!"

The king, in spite of his internal fears of the terrible storm that was gathering, could not help smiling at the word "massacred." The countess started up in a towering passion.

"Ah, is that the way you pity me?" said she.

"Now, now—do not get angry."

"Yes, I will get angry."

"You are very wrong; you look lovely when you smile—but really ugly in a passion."

"What matters it to me how I look, when my beauty does not prevent me from being sacrificed to state intrigues."

"Now, my dear countess——"

"No, no. Choose between me and Choiseul."

"Dear creature, it is impossible to choose—you are both necessary to me."

"Well, then, I shall retire and leave the field to my enemies; I shall die of grief, but the Duke de Choiseul will be satisfied, and that will console you."

"I swear to you, countess, that he has not any dislike to you; on the contrary, he admires you. He is an excellent man, after all," added the king, in a louder tone, that the minister of police might hear him.

"An excellent man! Sire, you wish to drive me to desperation. An excellent man who causes people to be assassinated?"

"Mere suspicion!" said the king.

"And, besides," Sartines ventured to say, "a quarrel, a duel between military men is so common—so natural!"

"Ha! Monsieur de Sartines, and are you also against me?" cried the countess.

The minister of police understood this *tu quoque*, and retreated before her anger. There was a moment of deep and ominous silence.

"Ah! Chon," said the king, in the midst of the general consternation, "you see your handiwork!"

"Your majesty will pardon me," said she, "if the grief of the sister has made me forget for a moment my duty as a subject."

"Kind creature!" murmured the king. "Come, countess, forget and forgive."

"Yes, sire; I shall forgive—only I shall set out for Luciennes, and thence for Boulogne."

"Boulogne-sur-Mer?" asked the king.

"Yes, sire; I shall quit a kingdom where the king is afraid of his minister."

"Madame!" exclaimed Louis, with an offended air.

"Sire, that I may not any longer be wanting in respect to you, permit me to retire;" and the countess rose, observing with the corner of her eyes what effect her movement had produced.

The king gave his usual heavy sigh of weariness, which said plainly, "I am getting rather tired of this." Chon understood what the sigh meant, and saw that it would be dangerous to push matters to extremity. She caught her sister by the gown, and approaching the king:

"Sire," said she, "my sister's affection for the poor viscount has carried her too far. It is I who have committed the fault—it is I who must repair it. As the humblest of your majesty's subjects, I beg from your majesty justice for my brother. I accuse nobody—your wisdom will discover the guilty."

"Why, that is precisely what I wish myself," said the king : "that justice should be done. If a man have not committed a certain crime, let him not be reproached with it; but if he have, let him be punished." And Louis looked toward the countess as he spoke, with the hope of once more catching the hopes he had entertained of an amusing morning—a morning which seemed turning out so dismally. The good-natured countess could not help pitying the king, whose want of occupation and emptiness of mind made him feel tired and dispirited except when with her. She turned half round, for she had already made a step toward the door, and said, with the sweetest submission : "Do I wish for anything but justice ? Only let not my well-grounded suspicions be cruelly repulsed."

"Your suspicions are sacred to me, countess," cried the king ; "and if they be changed into certainty, you shall see. But now I think of it—how easy to know the truth ! Let the Duke de Choiseul be sent for."

"Oh, your majesty knows that he never comes into these apartments. He would scorn to do so. His sister, however, is not of his mind ; she wishes for nothing better than to be here."

The king laughed. The countess, encouraged by this, went on : "The Duke de Choiseul apes the dauphin ; he will not compromise his dignity."

"The dauphin is religious, countess."

"And the duke a hypocrite, sire."

"I promise you, my dear countess, you shall see him here, for I shall summon him. He must come, as it is on state business, and we shall have all explained in Chon's presence, who saw all—we shall confront them, as the lawyers say. Eh, Sartines ? Let some one go for the Duke de Choiseul."

"And let some one bring me my monkey. Dorée, my monkey ?" cried the countess.

These words, which were addressed to the waiting-maid, who was arranging a dressing-box, could be heard in the anteroom when the door was opened to despatch the usher for the prime minister, and they were responded to by a broken, lisping voice.

"The countess's monkey! that must be me. I hasten to present myself."

And with these words entered a little hunchback, dressed with the utmost splendor.

"The Duke de Tresmes!" said the countess, annoyed by his appearance. "I did not summon you, duke."

"You asked for your monkey, madame," said the duke, bowing to the king, the countess, and the minister, "and seeing among the courtiers no ape half so ugly as myself, I hastened to obey your call;" and the duke laughed, showing his great teeth so oddly that the countess could not help laughing also.

"Shall I stay?" asked the duke, as if the whole life could not repay the favor.

"Ask his majesty, duke; he is master here."

The duke turned to the king, with the air of a suppliant.

"Yes, stay, duke, stay!" said the king, glad to find any additional means of amusement. At this moment the usher threw open the doors.

"Oh," said the king, with a slight expression of dissatisfaction on his face, "is it the Duke de Choiseul already?"

"No, sire," replied the usher, "it is Monseigneur the Dauphin who desires to speak to you."

The countess almost started from her chair with joy, for she imagined the dauphin was going to become her friend; but Chon, who was more clear-sighted, frowned.

"Well, where is the dauphin?" asked the king, impatiently.

"In your majesty's apartments; his royal highness awaits your return."

"It is fated I shall never have a minute's repose," grumbled the king. Then, all at once remembering that the audience demanded by the dauphin might spare him the scene with M. de Choiseul, he thought better of it. "I am coming," said he, "I am coming. Good-by, countess. See how I am dragged in all directions!"

"But will your majesty go just when the Duke de Choiseul is coming?"

"What can I do? The first slave is the king. Oh, if those rogues of philosophers knew what it is to be a king! but, above all, a king of France."

"But, sire, you can stay."

"Oh, I must not keep the dauphin waiting. People say already that I have no affection except for my daughters."

"But what shall I say to the duke?"

"Oh, tell him to come to my apartments, countess."

And, to put an end to any further remonstrance, he kissed her hand and disappeared, running, as was his habit whenever he feared to lose a victory gained by his temporizing policy and his petty cunning. The countess trembled with passion, and clasping her hands, she exclaimed: "So, he has escaped once more!"

But the king did not hear those words; the door was already closed behind him, and he passed through the anteroom, saying to the courtiers, "Go in, gentlemen, go in, the countess will see you; but you will find her very dull on account of the accident which has befallen poor Viscount Jean."

The courtiers looked at one another in amazement, for they had not heard of the accident. Many hoped that the viscount was dead, but all put on countenances suitable to the occasion. Those who were best pleased looked the most sympathetic, and they entered.

CHAPTER XXV.

THE SALOON OF TIME-PIECES.

In that large hall of the palace of Versailles which was called the Saloon of Time-pieces, a young man walked slowly up and down with his arms hanging and his head bent forward. He appeared to be about seventeen years of age, was of a fair complexion, and his eyes were mild in their expression ; but it must be acknowledged that there was a slight degree of vulgarity in his demeanor. On his breast sparkled a diamond star, rendered more brilliant by the dark, violet-colored velvet of his coat, and his white satin waistcoat, embroidered with silver, was crossed by the blue ribbon supporting the cross of St. Louis.

None could mistake in this young man the profile so expressive of dignity and kindliness which formed the characteristic type of the elder branch of the house of Bourbon, of which he was at once the most striking and most exaggerated image.   In fact, Louis Augustus, Duke de Berry, Dauphin of France (afterward Louis XVI.), had the Bourbon nose even longer and more aquiline than in his predecessors.   His forehead was lower and more retreating than Louis XV.'s, and the double chin of his grandfather was so remarkable in him, that, although he was at the time we speak of young and thin, his chin formed nearly one third of the length of his face.

Although well made, there was something embarrassed in the movement of his legs and shoulders, and his walk was slow and rather awkward. Suppleness, activity, and strength seemed centered only in his arms, and more particularly in his fingers, which displayed, as it were, that character which in other persons is expressed on the forehead, in the mouth, and in the eyes. The dauphin continued to pace in silence the Saloon of Time-pieces—the same in which, eight years before, Louis XV. had given to Mme. de Pompadour the decree of the Parliament exiling the Jesuits from the kingdom—and as he walked he seemed plunged in reverie.

At last, however, he seemed to become impatient of waiting there alone, and to amuse himself he began to look at the time-pieces, remarking, as Charles V. had done, the differences which are found in the most regular clocks. These differences are a singular but decided manifestation of the inequality existing in all material things, whether regulated or not regulated by the hand of man. He stopped before the large clock at the lower end of the saloon —the same place it occupies at present—which, by a clever arrangement of machinery, marks the days, the months, the years, the phases of the moon, the course of the planets —in short, exhibiting, to the still more curious machine called man, all that is most interesting in his progressive movement through life to death.

The prince examined this clock with the eye of an amateur, and leaned now to the right, now to the left, to examine the movement of such or such a wheel. Then he returned to his place in front, watching how the second hand glided rapidly on, like those flies which, with their long, slender legs, skim over the surface of a pond, without disturbing the liquid crystal of its waters. This contemplation naturally led him to think that a very great number of seconds had passed since he had been waiting there. It is true, also, that many had passed before he had ventured to send to inform the king that he was waiting for him.

All at once the hand on which the young prince's eyes were fixed, stopped as if by enchantment, the wheels ceased their measured rotation, the springs became still, and deep silence took possession of the machine, but a moment before so full of noise and motion. No more ticking, no more oscillations, no more movement of the wheels or of the hands. The time-piece had died.

Had some grain of sand, some atom, penetrated into one of the wheels and stopped its movements? Or was the genius of the machine resting, wearied with its eternal agitation? Surprised by this sudden death, this stroke of apoplexy occurring before his eyes, the dauphin forgot why he had come thither, and how long he had waited. Above all, he forgot that hours are not counted in eternity by the beating of metal upon metal, nor arrested even for a moment in their course by the hindrance of any wheel, but that they are recorded on the dial of eternity, established even before the birth of worlds, by the unchangeable hand of the Almighty.

He therefore opened the glass door of the crystal pagoda, the genius of which had ceased to act, and put his head inside to examine the time-piece more closely. But the large pendulum was in his way; he slipped in his supple fingers and took it off. This was not enough. The dauphin still found the cause of the lethargy of the machine hidden from him. He then supposed that the person who had the care of the clocks of the palace had forgotten to wind up this time-piece, and he took down the key from a hook and began to wind it up, like a man quite accustomed to the business. But he could only turn it three times—a proof that something was astray in the mechanism. He drew from his pocket a little file, and with the end of it pushed one of the wheels; they all creaked for half a second, then stopped again.

The malady of the clock was becoming serious. The dauphin, therefore, began carefully to unscrew several parts of it, laying them all in order on a console beside him. Then, drawn on by his ardor, he began to take to pieces still more and more of the complicated machine, and to search minutely into its hidden and mysterious recesses. Suddenly he uttered a cry of joy—he discovered that a screw which acted on one of the springs had become loose, and had thus impeded the movement of the motive wheel.

He immediately began to screw it; and then, with a wheel in his left hand, and his little file in his right, he plunged his head again into the interior of the clock.

He was busy at his work, absorbed in contemplation of the mechanism of the time-piece, when a door opened, and a voice announced, "The king!"

But the dauphin heard nothing but the melodious sound of that ticking, which his hand had again awakened, as if it were the beating of a heart which a clever physician had restored to life.

The king looked around on all sides, and it was some minutes before he discovered the dauphin, whose head was hidden in the opening, and whose legs alone were visible. He approached, smiling, and tapped his grandson on the shoulder.

"What the devil are you doing there?" said he. The dauphin drew out his head quickly, but at the same time with all the care necessary to avoid doing any harm to the beautiful object which he had undertaken to mend.

"Sire, your majesty sees," replied the young man, blushing at being surprised in the midst of his occupation, "I was amusing myself until you came."

"Yes, in destroying my clock—a very pretty amusement!"

"Oh, no, sire, I was mending it; the principal wheel would not move—it was prevented by this screw. I have tightened the screw, and now it goes."

"But you will blind yourself with looking into that thing. I would not put my head into such a trap for all the gold in the world."

"Oh, it will do me no harm, sire—I understand all about it. I always take to pieces, clean, and put together again that beautiful watch which your majesty gave me on my fourteenth birthday."

"Very well; but stop now, if you please, and leave your mechanics. You wish to speak to me?"

"I, sire?" said the young man, coloring again.

"Of course, since you sent to say you were waiting for me."

"It is true, sire," replied the dauphin, with downcast eyes.

"Well, what is it? Answer me; if it is of no importance, I must go, for I am just setting off for Marly." Louis XV., as was his custom, already sought to escape.

The dauphin placed his wheel and his file on the chair, which indicated that he had really something important to say, since he interrupted his important work for it.

"Do you want money?" asked the king, sharply; "if so, I shall send you some; and he made a step toward the door.

"Oh, no, sire; I have still a thousand crowns remaining of the sum I received last month."

"What economy!" said the king, "and how well Monsieur de la Vauguyon has educated him. I think he has precisely all the virtues I have not."

The young prince made a violent effort over himself.

"Sire," said he, "is the dauphiness yet very far distant?"

"Do you not know as well as I how far off she is?" replied the king.

"I?" stammered out the dauphin.

"Of course; you heard the account of her journey yesterday. Last Monday she was at Nancy, and she ought to be now about forty-five leagues from Paris."

"Sire, does not your majesty think her royal highness travels rather slowly?"

"By no means," replied the king; "I think she travels very fast for a woman; and then you know there are receptions and rejoicings on the road. She travels at least ten leagues every two days, one with another."

"I think very little, sir," said the dauphin, timidly.

Louis XV. was more and more astonished at the appearance of impatience which he had been far from suspecting.

"Come, come!" said he, smiling slyly, "don't be impatient—your dauphiness will arrive soon."

"Sire, might not these ceremonies on the road be shortened?" continued the dauphin.

"Impossible; she has already passed through two or three towns where she should have made a stay, without stopping."

"But these delays will be eternal; and then, sire, I think, besides——" said the dauphin, still more timidly.

"Well, what do you think? Let me hear it—speak!"

"I think that the service is badly performed."

"How? what service?"

"The service for the journey."

"Nonsense! I sent thirty thousand horses to be ready on the road, thirty carriages, sixty wagons—I don't know how many carts. If carts, carriages, and horses were put in file, they would reach from this to Strasbourg. How can you say, then, there is bad attendance on the road?"

"Well, sire, in spite of all your majesty's goodness, I am almost certain that what I say is true; but perhaps I have used an improper term, and instead of badly performed I should have said badly arranged."

The king raised his head and fixed his eyes on the dauphin. He began to comprehend that more was meant than met the ear, in the few words which his royal highness had ventured to utter.

"Thirty thousand horses," he repeated, "thirty carriages, sixty wagons, two regiments. I ask you, Mr. Philosopher, have you ever heard of a dauphiness entering France with such an attendance as that before?"

"I confess, sire, that things have been royally done, and as your majesty alone knows how to do them; but has your majesty specially recommended that these horses and carriages should be employed solely for her royal highness and her train?"

The king looked at his grandson for the third time. A vague suspicion began to sting him, a slight remembrance to illuminate his mind, and a sort of confused analogy between what the dauphin was saying and a disagreeable circumstance of late occurrence began to suggest itself to him.

"A fine question!" said he; "certainly everything has been ordered for her royal highness, and for her alone; and there, I repeat, she cannot fail to arrive very soon. But why do you look at me in that way?" added he, in a decided tone, which to the dauphin seemed even threatening. "Are you amusing yourself in studying my features as you study the springs of your mechanical works?"

The dauphin had opened his mouth to speak, but became silent at this address.

"Very well," said the king, sharply, "it appears you have no more to say? Hey? Are you satisfied now? Your dauphiness will arrive soon. All is arranged delightfully for her on the road. You are as rich as Crœsus with your own private purse, and now, since your mind is at ease, be good enough to put my clock in order again."

The dauphin did not stir.

"Do you know," said the king, laughing, "I have a great mind to make you the principal watch-maker for the palace, with a good salary?"

The dauphin looked down, and, intimidated by the

king's look, took up the wheel and file which he had laid on the chair. The king, in the meantime, had quietly gained the door. "What the devil," said he, looking at him, "did he mean with his badly arranged service? Well, well! I have escaped another scene, for he is certainly dissatisfied about something."

In fact, the dauphin, generally so patient, had stamped with his foot as the king turned away from him.

"He is commencing again," murmured the king, laughing; "decidedly I have nothing for it but to fly." But just as he opened the door, he saw, on the threshold, the Duke de Choiseul, who bowed profoundly.

CHAPTER XXVI.

THE COURT OF KING PETAUD.

THE king made a step backward at the sight of this new actor in the scene, come, no doubt, to prevent him from escaping as he had hoped. "Ha!" thought he, "I had forgotten him; but he is welcome, and I will make him pay for what the others have made me suffer."

"Ha! you are there?" cried he; "I sent for you—did you know that?"

"Yes, sire," replied the minister, coldly; "I was dressing to wait on your majesty when your orders reached me."

"I wished to speak to you on serious matters," said the king, frowning in order, if possible, to intimidate his minister. Unfortunately for the king, M. de Choiseul was one of the men least likely to be daunted in his dominions.

"And I, also, if it please your majesty," said he, bowing, "I have serious matters to speak of;" at the same time he exchanged a look with the dauphin, who was still half hidden by the clock.

The king stopped short. "Ha!" thought he, "now I am caught between two fires; there is no escape."

"You know, I presume," said the king, hastily, in order to have the first word, "that poor Viscount Jean has had a narrow escape from assassination—that is to say, that he has received a wound in his arm."

"I came to speak of that affair to your majesty."

"I understand—you wished to prevent unpleasant reports?"

"I wished, sire, to anticipate all remarks."

"Then you know the whole particulars, sir?" inquired the king, in a significant manner.

"Perfectly."

"Ha!" said the king, "I was told so in a place likely to be well informed."

The Duke of Choiseul seemed quite unmoved. The dauphin continued turning the screw in the clock, his head bent down, but he lost not a syllable of the conversation.

"I shall now tell you how the affair happened," said the king.

"Does your majesty think that you have been well informed?" asked M. de Choiseul.

"Oh, as to that——"

"We are all attention, sire."

"We?" repeated the king.

"Yes; his royal highness the dauphin and I."

"His royal highness the dauphin?" repeated the king, turning his eyes from the respectful Choiseul to the attentive Louis Augustus, "and pray in what does this squabble concern his royal highness?"

"It concerns his royal highness," said the duke, bowing to the young prince, "because her royal highness the dauphiness was the cause of it."

"The dauphiness the cause?" said the king, starting.

"Certainly; if you are ignorant of that, sir, your majesty has been very badly informed."

"The dauphiness and Jean Dubarry!" said the king; "this is likely to be a curious tale. Come, explain this, Monsieur de Choiseul; conceal nothing, even though it were the dauphiness herself who pierced Dubarry's arm."

"Sire, it was not the dauphiness," replied Choiseul, still calm and unmoved ; "it was one of the gentlemen of her escort."

"Oh," said the king, again becoming grave, "an officer whom you know."

"No, sire, but an officer whom your majesty ought to know, if you remember all who have served you well—an officer whose father's name was honored at Phillipsbourg, at Fontenoy, at Mahon—a Taverney Maison Rouge."

The dauphin seemed to draw a deeper breath, as if to inhale this name, and thus preserve it in his memory.

"A Maison Rouge," said the king ; "certainly I know the name. And why did he attack Jean, whom I like so much ? Perhaps because I like him. Such absurd jealousies ! such discontents are almost seditious !"

"Sire, will your majesty deign to listen to me," said M. de Choiseul.

The king saw there was no other way for him to escape from this troublesome business but by getting in a passion, and he exclaimed, "I tell you, sir, that I see the beginning of a conspiracy against my peace, an organized persecution of my family."

"Ah, sire," said M. de Choiseul, "is it for defending the dauphiness, your majesty's daughter-in-law, that these reproaches are cast on a brave young man ?"

The dauphin raised his head and folded his arms. "For my part," said he, "I cannot but feel grateful to the man who exposed his life for a princess who in a fortnight will be my wife."

"Exposed his life ! exposed his life !" stammered the king. "What about ? Let me know that—what about ?"

"About the horses of her royal highness the dauphiness," replied the duke. "Viscount Jean Dubarry, who was already traveling very fast, took upon him to insist on having send of those horses which were appropriated to the use of her royal highness—no doubt that he might get on still faster."

The king bit his lip and changed color—the threatening

plantom from which he had so lately hoped to escape now reappeared in all its horrors. "It is not possible," murmured he, to gain time. "I know the whole affair; you have been misinformed, duke."

"No, sire, I have not been misinformed; what I have the honor to tell your majesty is the simple truth. Viscount Jean Dubarry offered an insult to the dauphiness by insisting on taking for his use horses appointed for her service. After having ill-treated the master of the posthouse, he was going to take them by force, when the Chevalier Philip de Taverney arrived, sent forward by her royal highness to have horses in readiness for her, and after he had several times summoned him in a friendly and conciliating manner——"

"Oh, oh!" grumbled the king.

"I repeat, sir, after he had several times, in a friendly and conciliating manner, summoned the viscount to desist, he was at length obliged to draw his sword."

"Yes," said the dauphin, "I pledge myself for the truth of what the duke asserts."

"Then you also know of this affair?" said the king, exceedingly surprised.

"I know all the circumstances perfectly, sire," replied the dauphin.

The minister bowed, delighted at having such a supporter.

"Will your royal highness deign to proceed?" said he. "His majesty will doubtless have more confidence in the assertions of his august son than in mine."

"Yes, sire," continued the dauphin, without testifying for the Duke de Choiseul's zeal in his cause all that gratitude which might have been expected; "yes, sire, I know the circumstances, and I had come to tell your majesty that Viscount Dubarry has not only insulted the dauphiness in interfering with the arrangements made for her journey, but he has also insulted me in opposing a gentleman of my regiment, who was doing his duty."

The king shook his head. "We must inquire," said he: "we must inquire."

" I have already inquired, sir," said the dauphin, gently,
" and have no doubt in the matter ; the viscount drew his
sword on my officer."

" Did he draw first ? " asked the king, happy to seize
any chance of putting his adversary in fault.

The dauphin colored, and looked to the minister for
assistance.

" Sire," said the latter, " swords were crossed by two
men, one of whom was insulting, the other defending, the
dauphiness—that is all."

" Yes, but which was the aggressor ? " asked the king.
" I know poor Jean ; he is as gentle as a lamb."

" The aggressor, in my opinion, sire," said the dauphin,
with his usual mildness, " is he who is in the wrong."

" It is a delicate matter to decide," replied the king ;
" the aggressor he who in is the wrong ?—in the wrong ?
But if the officer was insolent ? "

" Insolent ! " cried the Duke de Choiseul—" insolent
toward a man who wanted to take by force horses sent
there for the use of the dauphiness ? Is it possible you
can think so, sire ? "

The dauphin turned pale, but said nothing. The king
saw that he was between two fires.

" I should say warm, perhaps, not insolent," said
he.

" But your majesty knows," said the minister, taking
advantage of the king's having yielded a step to make a
step forward, " your majesty knows that a zealous servant
never can be in the wrong."

" Oh, perhaps ! But how did you become acquainted
with this event, sir ? " said he, turning sharply to the
dauphin, without ceasing, however, to observe the duke,
who endeavored vainly to hide the embarrassment which
this sudden question caused him.

" By a letter, sire," replied the dauphin.

" A letter from whom ? "

" A letter from a person concerned for her royal highness
the dauphiness, and who thinks it singular that any one
should dare to affront her."

"Ha!" cried the king, "more mysteries, secret correspondences, plots! Every one is beginning again to plan annoyances for me, as in the time of the Marchioness de Pompadour!"

"No, sire," said the minister; "this affair is no plot, and can be settled very simply. It is the crime of treason in the second degree. Let the guilty person be punished, and all will be settled."

At this word, punished, Louis XV. saw in fancy the countess furious, and Chon in a rage—he saw peace flying from his dwelling (peace which he had been seeking all his life, but had never been able to find), and intestine war with crooked nails and eyes red with tears entering in her stead.

"Punished!" cried he, "without the accused having been heard? without knowing which side is in the right? You make a very extraordinary proposal to me, duke—you wish to draw odium on me!"

"But, sire, who will henceforward respect her royal highness the dauphiness if a severe example is not made of the person who first insulted her?"

"Certainly, sire," added the dauphin, "it would be a scandal."

"An example? a scandal?" cried the king. "Mordieu! if I make an example of all the scandalous things that go on around me, I may pass my life in signing arrests for the Bastile. I have signed enough of them as it is, Heaven knows!"

"In this case it is necessary, sire," said the duke.

"Sire, I entreat your majesty," said the dauphin.

"What, do you not think him punished already, by the wound he has received?"

"No, sire, for he might have wounded the Chevalier de Taverney."

"And in such a case, what would you have done?"

"I should have demanded his head."

"But that was only what was done in the case of Monsieur de Montgomery, for killing King Henry II.," said the king.

" He killed the king by accident, sire.   Viscount Dubarry insulted the dauphiness intentionally."

" And you, sir," said the king, turning to the dauphin, " do you wish to have Jean's head ? "

" No, sir ; I am not in favor of the punishment of death, as your majesty knows ; I shall merely demand from you the viscount's banishment."

The king started up.

" Banishment for a tavern quarrel ?   Louis, you are severe, notwithstanding your philanthropical notions ; it is true that before becoming philanthropist you were a mathematician, and——"

" Will your majesty deign to proceed ? "

" A mathematician would sacrifice the universe to his problem."

" Sire," said the dauphin, " I have no ill-will toward Viscount Dubarry, personally."

" With whom, then, are you angry ? "

" With the insulter of her royal highness the dauphiness."

" What a model for husbands !" cried the king, ironically ; " but I am not so easy of belief.   I see very well who is attacked under all this—I see to what people would lead me with their exaggerations."

" Sire," said M. de Choiseul, " do not be misled ; nothing has been exaggerated ; the public are indignant at the insolence which has been shown in this affair."

" The public ?   There is another monster with which you frighten yourself, or, rather, with which you would frighten me.   Shall I listen to this public, which by the thousand mouths of libelists, and pamphleteers, and ballad-mongers, tell me that I am robbed, tossed in a blanket, betrayed on all hands ?   No, no; I let the public talk, and I laugh.   Do as I do.   Pardieu ! close your ears—and when your great public is tired of bawling, it will stop. There you are again, making your discontented bow—and Louis is putting on a sulky face !   Heavens ! is it not singular that what is done for the lowest individual can not be done for me ?   I cannot be allowed to live quietly in my own fashion.   Everybody hates what I love, and eternally loves what I hate. Am I in my sense or am I a fool? Am I the master, or am I not?"

The dauphin took up his file, and returned to his work in the clock. The Duke de Choiseul bowed exactly as before.

"There, now—no answer! Answer something, will you? Mordieu! you will kill me with vexation—first at your talk, then at your silence—with your petty hatred and your petty fears!"

"I do not hate the Viscount Dubarry," said the dauphin, smiling.

"And I do not fear him, sir," said the minister, haughtily.

"You are both very ill-natured," cried the king, pretending to be in a great passion when he was in reality only out of temper; "you wish to make me the laughing-stock of all Europe—to give my cousin of Prussia something to make jests on—to make me realize the Court of King Petaud, which that rascal, Voltaire, has described; but I will not be what you wish—no; you shall not have that satisfaction. I know what concerns my own honor, and I shall attend to it in my own way, and only as I choose myself."

"Sire," said the dauphin, with that immovable mildness which characterized him, but at the same time with that constant perseverance of his, "this is not a matter which concerns your honor—it is the dignity of the dauphiness which has been attacked."

His royal highness is right, sire," said the duke; "let but your majesty speak the word, and no one will again dare to insult her!"

"And who would insult her? No one intended to insult her. Jean is a stupid fellow, but he is not malignant."

"Well, then, sir," continued the minister, "let it be placed to the account of stupidity, and let him ask pardon of the Chevalier de Taverney for his mistake."

"I said before," cried the king, "that I have nothing to do in the affair; let Jean ask pardon, he is at liberty to do so; or let him decline, he is at liberty also."

"The affair given up in that way, sire, I must take the liberty to inform vour majesty, will be talked about."

"So much the better!" exclaimed the king; "let it be talked about until I am deafened with it, provided I don't hear all this nonsense of yours."

"Then," replied the minister, with his imperturbable coolness, "I am authorized by your majesty to say that Viscount Dubarry did right?"

"Authorized by me—authorized by me? and in an affair of which I understand nothing! You mean, I see, to drive me to extremities; but take care, duke! take care; and, Louis, I advise you to be more cautious how you conduct yourself toward me. I shall leave you to think of what I have said, for I am tired out—I cannot bear this any longer. Good-by, gentlemen. I am going to see my daughters, and then I shall take refuge at Marly, where I may hope for some tranquillity, if you do not follow me."

At this moment, and as the king was going toward the door, it was opened, and an usher appeared.

"Sire," said he, " her royal highness the Princess Louise is awaiting your majesty in the gallery to bid you farewell."

" To bid me farewell?" exclaimed the king, in alarm, "where is she going?"

" Her royal highness says that she has had your majesty's permission to leave the palace."

" Ha! another scene. This is my bigot daughter going to show off some of her follies. In truth, I am the most wretched of men!" And he left the apartment, running.

" His majesty has given us no answer," said the Duke de Choiseul; "what has your royal highness decided on?"

" Ah! there it strikes!" said the young prince, listening with either a real or a pretended joy to the clock which he had made to go once more.

The minister frowned and retired backward from the Saloon of Time-pieces, leaving the dauphin alone.

CHAPTER XXVII.

MME. LOUISE OF FRANCE.

THE king's eldest daughter awaited him in the great gallery of Lebrun, the same in which Louis XIV., in 1683, had received the Doge Imperiali and the four Genoese senators sent to implore pardon for the republic.

At the further end of the gallery, opposite the door by which the king must enter, were three or four ladies of honor, who seemed in the utmost consternation. Louis arrived just at the moment when groups began to form in the vestibule, for the resolution which the princess had taken only that morning was now spreading on all sides through the palace.

The Princess Louise possessed a majestic figure, and a truly regal style of beauty, yet a secret sadness had left its lines on her fair forehead. Her austere practise of every virtue, and her respect for the great powers of the state —powers which for the last fifty years had only obtained a semblance of respect from interest or from fear—had caused her to be regarded with veneration by the court. We must add that she was loved even by the people, although a feeling of disaffection toward their *masters* was now general. The word tyrants had not yet been heard.

She was loved because her virtue was not stern. She was not loudly talked of, but all knew that she had a heart. She manifested this every day by works of charity, while others only showed it by shameless self-indulgence. Louis XV. feared this daughter for the simple reason that he esteemed her. There were even times when he went so far as to be proud of her ; and she was the only one of his children whom he spared in his sharp raillery or his silly familiarities. He called her madame, while the Princesses Adelaide, Victoire, and Sophie he named Loque, Chiffe, and Graille.*   Since the period when Marshal Saxe carried with him to the tomb the soul of the Turennes and the Condés, and with the Queen Maria Lezinska passed away the governing mind of a Maria Theresa, all became mean and worthless around the throne of France. The Princess Louise, whose character was truly regal, and, compared with those around her, seemed even heroic, alone remained to adorn the crown, like a pearl of price amid false stones and tinsel. We should be wrong in concluding from this that Louis XV. loved his daughter. Louis, it is well known, loved no one but himself ; we only affirm that he preferred her to all his other children.

When he entered, he found the princess in the center of the gallery, leaning on a table inlaid with crimson jasper and lapis lazuli. She was dressed entirely in black, and her beautiful hair, which was without powder, was covered by a double roll of lace. A deeper shade of sadness than usual rested on her brow She looked at no one in the apartment, but from time to time her melancholy gaze wandered over the portraits of the kings of Europe, which ornamented the gallery, at the head of whom were those of her ancestors, the kings of France.

The black dress which she wore was the usual traveling costume of princesses. It concealed large pockets, still worn as in the times of the good house-wife-like queens, and the Princess Louise, imitating them in that, also, had the numerous keys of her chests and wardrobes suspended at her waist by a gold chain.

The king's face assumed a serious expression when he saw how silent all in the gallery were, and how attentively they awaited the result of the interview between him and his daughter. But the gallery was so long that the spectators at either end might see but they could not hear what passed ; they had a right to see—it was their duty not to hear.

The princess advanced a few steps to meet the king, and taking his hand, she kissed it respectfully.

---

* Tag, rag, and scrap.

"They tell me you are setting out on a journey, madame," said he, "are you going into Picardy?"

"No, sire," she replied.

"Then, I presume," said he, in a louder voice, "that you are about to make a pilgrimage to Noirmoutiers?"

"No, sire. I am going to retire to the convent of the Carmelites at St. Denis, of which you know I have the right to be abbess."

The king started, but he preserved his countenance unmoved, although in reality his heart was troubled.

"Oh, no, no, my daughter!" he said; "you will not leave me. It is impossible you can leave me!"

"My dear father, it is long since I decided on abandoning the world. Your majesty permitted me to make that decision; do not now, I entreat you, my dear father, oppose my wishes."

"Yes, certainly, you wrung from me the permission of which you speak. I gave it, but still hoped that when the moment of departure came, your heart would fail you. You ought not to bury yourself in a cloister; by acting so, you forget what is due to your rank. It is grief or want of fortune which makes the convent besought as a refuge. The daughter of the King of France is certainly not poor; and, if she be unhappy, the world ought not to know it."

The king's thoughts, and even his language, seemed to become more elevated as he entered more and more into the part he was called on to play—that of a king and a father. This is, indeed, a part never played ill, when pride and regret inspire the actor.

"Sire," replied the princess, perceiving her father's emotion, and fearful that it might affect her more deeply than she desired at that moment, "sire, do not, by your tenderness for me, weaken my resolution; my grief is no vulgar grief, therefore, my resolution to retire from the world is not in accordance with the usual customs of our day."

"Your grief?" exclaimed the king, as if from a real impulse of feeling. "Have you, then, sorrows, my poor child?"

"Heavy, heavy sorrows, sire."

"Why did you not confide them to me, my dearest daughter?"

"Because they are sorrows not to be assuaged by any mortal hand."

"Not by that of a king?"

"Ah, no, sire!"

"Not by a father's hand?"

"No, sire, no!"

"But you are religious, Louise; does not religion give you strength?"

"Not sufficient strength yet, sire; therefore I retire to a cloister in order to obtain more. In silence God speaks to the heart of man—in solitude man communes with God."

"But, in acting thus you are making a sacrifice for which nothing can compensate. The throne of France casts a majestic shadow over the children of is kings. Ought not this reflected greatness to be sufficient for you?"

"The shadow of the cell is better, sire; it refreshes the weary spirit; it soothes the strong as well as the weak—the humble as well as the proud—the high as well as the low."

"Do you fear any danger by remaining? In that case, Louise, cannot the king defend you?"

"Sire, may God, in the first place, defend the king!"

"I repeat, Louise, that mistaken zeal leads you astray. It is good to pray, but not to pray always—and you so good, so pious! can you require such constant prayers?"

"Oh, my father! never can I offer up prayers enough to avert from us the woes which threaten us. If God has given me a portion of goodness—if for twenty years my only effort has been to purify my soul—I fear, alas! that I am yet far from having attained the goodness and the purity necessary for an expiatory sacrifice."

The king started back and gazed at the princess with surprise.

"Never have I heard you speak thus before, my dear

child," said he ; "your ascetic life is making your reason wander."

"Oh, sire, do not speak thus of a devotion the truest that ever subject offered to a king, or daughter to a father, in a time of need. Sire, that throne, of which you but now so proudly spoke as lending a protecting shade to your children—that throne totters. You feel not the blows which are dealt at its foundations, but I have seen them. Silently a deep abyss is preparing, which will ingulf the monarchy ! Sire, has any one ever told you the truth ? "

The princess looked around to discover whether the attendants were far enough to be out of hearing of her words, then she resumed :

" Well, sir, I know the truth. Too often have I heard the groans which the wretched send forth, when, as a Sister of Mercy, I visited the dark, narrow streets, the filthy lanes, the dismal garrets of the poor. In those streets, those lanes, those garrets, I have seen human beings dying of cold and hunger in winter, of heat and thirst in summer. You see not, sire, what the country is—you go merely from Versailles to Marly, and from Marly to Versailles. But in the country there is not grain—I do not say to feed the people, but even to sow for a new harvest—for the land, cursed by some adverse power, has received, but has given nothing back. The people wanting bread, are filled with discontent. The air is filled in the twilight and at night with voices telling them of weapons, of chains, of prisons, of tyranny ; and at these voices they awake, cease to complain, and commence to threaten. The parliaments demand the right of remonstrance—that is, the right to say to you openly what they whisper in private, " King, you are running the kingdom—save it, or we shall save it ourselves." The soldiers with their idle swords furrow the land in which the philosophers have scattered the seeds of liberty. Men now see things which they formerly saw not, for our writers have laid all open to them ; they know all that we do, and frown whenever their masters pass by. Your majesty's successor is soon to be married. When Anne of Austria's son was married, the city of Paris made presents to the new queen ; now it is not only silent, and offers nothing, but you have been obliged to use force to collect the taxes, to pay the expense of bringing the daughter of Cæsar to the palace of the son of St. Louis. The clergy have long ceased to pray to God ; but, seeing the lands given away, privileges exhausted, coffers empty, they have begun again to pray for what they call the happiness of the people. And then, sire, must I tell you what you know so well—what you have seen with so much bitterness, although you have spoken of it to none ? The kings, your brothers, who formerly envied us, now turn away from us. Your four daughters, sire, the princesses of France, have not found husbands, and there are twenty princes in Germany, three in England, sixteen in the States of the North, without naming our relations, the Bourbons of Spain and Naples, who forget us, or turn away from us like the others. Perhaps the Turk would have taken us had we not been daughters of his most Christian majesty. Not for myself, my father, do I care for this, or complain of it. Mine is a happy state, since it leaves me free, since I am not necessary to any one of my family, and may retire from the world—in meditation and in poverty pray to God to avert from your head, and from my nephew's, the awful storm I see gathering on the horizon of the future."

"My child, my daughter ! it is your fears which make the future appear so dreadful."

"Sire, sire, remember that princess of antiquity, that royal prophetess. She foretold to her father and to her brothers war, destruction, conflagration, and her predictions were laughed at—they called her mad. Do not treat me as she was treated. Take care, oh, my father !—reflect, my King !"

Louis XV. folded his arms, and his head sunk on his bosom. "My daughter," said he, "you speak very severely. Are those woes which you announce caused by me ?"

"God forbid that I should think so ! They are the fruit of the times in which we live. You are whirled on in the career of events as we are all. Only listen, sire, to the applause in the theater which follows any allusion against royalty. See, in the evenings, what joyous crowds descend the narrow stairs of the galleries, while the grand marble staircase is deserted. Sire, both the people and the courtiers have made for themselves pleasures quite apart from our pleasures. They amuse themselves without us ; or, rather, when we appear in the midst of their pleasures, they become dull. Alas !" continued the princess, her eyes swimming with tears, "alas ! poor young men, affectionate young women ! love, sing, forget, be happy ! Here, when I went among you, I only disturbed your happiness. Yonder, in my cloister, I shall serve you. Here, you hid your glad smiles in my presence, for fear of displeasing me. There, I shall pray—oh, God ! with all my soul—for my king, for my sisters, for my nephews, for the people of France—for all whom I love with the energy of a heart which no earthly passion has exhausted."

"My daughter," said the king, after a melancholy silence, "I entreat you not to leave me—not at this moment, at least ; you will break my heart."

The princess seized his hand, and fixing her eyes, full of love, on his noble features, "No," said she, "no, my father—not another hour in this palace ! No ; it is time for me to pray. I feel in myself strength to redeem, by my tears, those pleasures for which you sigh—you, who are yet young. You are the kindest of fathers, you are ever ready to pardon !"

"Stay with us, Louise—stay with us !" said the king, pressing her to his heart.

The princess shook her head. "My kingdom is not of this world," said she, disengaging herself from her father's embrace. "Farewell, my father ! I have told you to-day what for ten years has lain heavy on my heart. The burden became too great. Farewell ! I am satisfied--see, I can smile ; I am now, at length, happy—I regret nothing."

"Not even me, my daughter ?"

"Ah, I should regret you, were I never to see you again, but you will sometimes come to St. Denis ? You will not quite forget your child ?"

" Oh, never, never ! "

" Do not, my dear father, allow yourself to be affected. Let it not appear that this separation is to be a lasting one. My sisters, I believe, know nothing of it yet ; my women alone have been my confidantes. For eight days I have been making all my preparations ; and I wish the report of my departure should only be spread when the great doors of St. Denis shall have closed on me ; their heavy sound will prevent me from hearing any other."

The king read in his daughter's eyes that her resolution was irrevocable. He wished, therefore, that she should go without disturbance. If she feared that sobs might shake her resolution, he feared them still more for his nerves. Besides, he wished to go to Marly that day, and too much grief at Versailles might have obliged him to put off his journey. He reflected, also, that, when issuing from some orgies unfit both for a king and a father, he should never more meet that grave, sad face, which seemed always to reproach him for the careless, worthless existence which he led ; and this thought was not disagreeable to him.

" Be it then, as you wish, my child," said he ; " but at least receive, before you go, the blessing of a father whom you have always made perfectly happy."

" Give me your hand only, sire, and let me kiss it. Bestow your precious blessing on me in thought."

To those who knew the decision of the princess, it was a solemn spectacle to see her at every step she made advancing, yet in life, to the tombs of her ancestors—those ancestors who, from their golden frames, seemed to thank her that she hastened to rejoin them.

At the door of the gallery the king bowed, and returned without uttering a word. The court, according to etiquette, followed him.

CHAPTER XXVIII.

LOQUE, CHIFFE, AND GRAILLE.

THE king passed on to what was called the Cabinet of the Equipages. It was there that he was accustomed, before going to hunt or to drive out, to pass a few minutes in giving particular orders concerning the vehicles and attendants he should require during the rest of the day.

At the door of the gallery he bowed to the courtiers, and, by a wave of his hand, indicated that he wished to be alone. When they had left him, he passed through the cabinet to a corridor which led to the apartments of the princesses. Having reached the door, before which hung a curtain, he stopped for a moment, shook his head, and muttered between his teeth :

" There was but one of them good, and she is gone ! "

This very flattering speech, for those who remained, was answered by a shrill chorus of voices; the curtain was raised, and the furious trio saluted their father with cries of :

" Thank you, father, thank you ! "

" Ha, Loque ! " said he, addressing the eldest of them, the Princess Adelaide, " you heard what I said—so much the worse for you. Be angry or not, just as you like—I only spoke the truth."

" Yes," said the Princess Victoire, " you tell us nothing new, sire. We always knew that you preferred Louise to us."

" In faith, quite true, Chiffe ! "

" And why do you prefer Louise ? " asked the Princess Sophie, in a sharp voice.

" Because Louise never gave me any trouble," replied the king, showing that good-humored frankness of which, when he was perfectly pleased, Louis XV. was so complete a type.

"Oh, but she will give you trouble yet, rest assured," replied the Princess Sophie, with such a peculiar emphasis that it drew the attention of the king more particularly to her. "I should be rather surprised if she did not, for she is not very fond of you."

"And pray, what do you know about her, Graille?" said he. "Did Louise, before going away, make you her confidante?"

"I can say most truly," answered the princess, "that I return her affection with interest."

"Oh, very well! Hate one another—detest one another as much as you choose; I am perfectly content; only do not summon me to restore order in the kingdom of the amazons. However, I should like to know how poor Louise is to give me trouble."

"Poor Louise!" repeated the three princesses, making different grimaces at the words. "You wish to know how she will give you trouble? Well, I shall tell you," said the Princess Sophie.

The king stretched himself in a large easy-chair, placed near the door so that he could at any moment make his escape.

"Louise is retiring to a convent because she wishes to carry on some experiments which she cannot make so well in the palace."

"Come, come!" said the king, "no insinuations against the virtue of your sister. No one beyond these walls has ever dared to sully that, though many things are said of you for which it were well there were no grounds. Do not *you* begin this subject!"

"I?"

"Yes, *you!*"

"Oh, I was not going to attack Louise's virtue," said the Princess Sophie, very much hurt by the peculiar accent her father had given to the *you*, and by the marked repetition of it; "I only said she was going to make experiments."

"Well, and if she does make experiments in chemistry, if she does make fire-arms, and wheels for chairs, if she does play on the flute, the drum, or the harpsichord, or even the violin, what harm would there be in it ?"

" The experiments to which I alluded were experiments in politics."

The king started. The princess on :

"She is going to study philosophy and theology. She will continue the commentaries on the bull 'Unigenitus' —indeed, we must seem very useless beings when compared with her—a lady who writes theories concerning governments, systems of metaphysics, and theology."

" And if these pursuits lead your sister to heaven, what harm can you see in them ?" said the king, struck, however, with the connection there was between what the Princess Sophie was saying and the manner of the Princess Louise's departure, accompanied as it had been by a political exhortation. " If you envy her happiness, you are very bad Christians."

" No, on my honor !" said the Princess Victoire, "she has my full permission to go ; but I shall take care not to follow her."

" Nor I," responded the Princess Adelaide.

" Nor I," said the Princess Sophie.

" Besides, she always detested us," said the first.

" You all ?" the king asked.

" Yes, detested us all," they replied.

" Oh, then, I see," he said, " poor Louise has chosen to go to heaven that she may not meet any of her family again."

This sarcasm made the three sisters laugh, but rather constrainedly, and Adelaide, the eldest, brought all her wit into play, in order to deal her father a more weighty blow than he had given them.

" Ladies," said she, with the sneering tone which was peculiar to her when roused from that habitual indolence which had procured for her the name of Loque, "you have either not found out, or you do not dare to tell the king, the real cause of Louise's departure."

" Come, Loque, come ! you have got some wicked tale to tell. I see. Let us hear it."

"Sire, I fear it might vex you a little."

"No, no; say you hope it will vex me, that would be nearer the truth."

Mme. Adelaide bit her lips.

"Then I shall tell you the truth, sire."

"Very fine! If you ever do tell the truth cure yourself of the habit. The truth? Do I ever tell it? and yet you see I am not the worse for it, Heaven be praised!" and he shrugged his shoulders.

"Speak, sister, speak," said the other two sisters, impatient to hear anything that might wound their father.

"Sweet little creatures!" growled the king; "see how they love their father!"

But he consoled himself by thinking that he returned their love in kind.

"Well," continued the Princess Adelaide, "what Louise dreaded most—for she was very precise on the score of etiquette—was——"

"Was what?" exclaimed the king. "Come, finish, since you have gone so far."

"It was, sire, then, the intrusion of new faces at court."

"Do you say intrusion?" asked he, by no means pleased with this beginning, for he saw to what it tended. "Intrusion? Are there intruders, then, in my palace? Am I forced to receive persons against my will?"

By this adroit turn he hoped to change the course of the conversation. But the Princess Adelaide felt herself on the right scent, and she was too cunning and too malicious to lose it, when she had so good an end in view as the annoyance of her father.

"Perhaps I was not quite correct—perhaps I used the wrong word; instead of intrusion, I should have said introduction."

"Oh, ah!" said the king, "that is an improvement. The other word was a disagreeable one, I confess; I like introduction better."

"And yet," continued the princess, "that is not the right word either."

"What is it then?"

"It is presentation."

"Yes," cried the other sisters, "yes, you have found the right word now."

The king bit his lip. "Oh, do you think so?" said he.

"Yes," replied the Princess Adelaide; "my sister was very much afraid of new presentations."

"Well," said the king, feeling what must come, and thinking it best to have done with it as speedily as possible —"well, go on."

"Well, sire, she was consequently afraid of seeing the Countess Dubarry presented at court."

"Ha!" cried the king, with a burst of passion which he could not repress; "so you have been all this time getting this out! Mordieu! Madame Tell-truth, how you beat about the bush!"

"Sire," replied the princess, "if I have so long delayed in telling your majesty this, it is because respect closed my lips, and I should not have opened them but by your own command."

"Yes, yes, you would never have opened them, I suppose, to yawn, or to speak, or to bite."

"I am quite certain, however, sire, that I have discovered the real motive which has made my sister retire into a convent."

"Well, you are wrong."

"Oh, sire!" they all three repeated, shaking their heads. "Oh, sire, we are quite certain of what we say."

"Pshaw! You are all of a tale, I see. There is a conspiracy in my family. This is the reason the presentation cannot take place—this the reason the princesses can never be seen when persons wish to visit them—that they give no answers to petitions or requests for an audience."

"What petitions? what requests for an audience?" asked the Princess Adelaide.

"Oh, you know," replied the Princess Sophie, "the petition of Mademoiselle Jean Vaubernier." (This was the Countess Dubarry's name in the days of her poverty.)

" Yes," added the Princess Victoire, " the requests for an audience of Mademoiselle Lange." (Another name which she had borne.)

The king started up, furious with passion ; his eye, generally calm and mild, now flashed in a manner rather alarming for the three sisters, and as none of this royal trio of heroines seemed courageous enough to bear the paternal wrath, they bent their heads before the storm.

" And now," cried he, " was I wrong when I said the best had left me ? "

" Sire," said the Princess Adelaide, " you treat us very ill—worse than you treat your dogs ! "

" And justly, too. My dogs, when I go near them, receive me kindly—caress me ; they are real friends. So adieu, ladies. I shall go to Charlotte, Bellefille, and Gredinet. Poor animals ! Yes, I love them ! And I love them more particularly because they do not bark out the truth."

The king left the apartment in a rage ; but had not taken three steps in the anteroom, when he heard his daughters singing in chorus the first verse of a ballad ridiculing the Countess Dubarry, which was then sung through the streets of Paris.

He was about to return—and perhaps the princesses would not have fared well had he done so—but he restrained himself, and went on, calling loudly that he might not hear them, " Hola ! the captain of the greyhounds ! the captain of the greyhounds ! "

The officer who bore this singular title hurried forward.

" Let the dogs be loosed ! "

" Oh, sire," cried the officer, placing himself in the king's way, " do not advance another step."

" What now ? what now ? " said the king, stopping before a door, from under which was heard the snuffing of dogs, aware that their master was near.

" Sire," said the officer, " pardon me, but I cannot permit your majesty to enter here."

" Oh, I understand—the kennel is out of order. Well, then, let Gredinet be brought out."

"Sire," continued the officer, with alarm depicted on his face, "Gredinet has neither eaten nor drunk for two days, and it is feared he is mad."

"Oh," cried the king, "I am really the most wretched of men! Gredinet mad? This alone was wanting to complete my vexation."

The officer of the greyhounds thought it his duty to shed a tear, to make it seem more perfect. The king turned on his heel, and retired to his private cabinet, where his valet was waiting. He, seeing the king's face so disturbed, hid himself in the recess of a window—and the king, looking upon him rather as a piece of furniture than a man, strode up and down his room talking to himself.

"Yes, I see it—I see it plainly," said he; "the Duke de Choiseul laughs at me; the dauphin looks upon himself as already half master, and thinks he will be wholly so when he has his little Austrian beside him on the throne. Louise loves me—but so sternly, that she preaches me a sermon and leaves me. My three other daughters sing songs, in which I am ridiculed under the name of Blaise. My grandson, the Count de Provençe, translates Lucretius; and his brother, the Count d'Artois, is a dissipated scapegrace. My dogs go mad, and would bite me. Decidedly, there is only the poor countess who loves me. To the devil, then, with those who would annoy her!"

Then, with a sort of settled despair, he seated himself at that table on which Louis XV. wrote his proudest letters and signed his latest treaties.

"I know now," continued he, "why every one wishes to hasten the arrival of the dauphiness. They think when she shows herself, I shall become her slave, and be governed by her family. I' faith, I shall see her soon enough, that dear daughter-in-law of mine, particularly if her arrival is to be the signal for new troubles. Let me be quiet as long as I can, and for that purpose the longer she is delayed on the road the better. She was to have passed through Rheims and Noyon without stopping, and to come immediately to Compiegne. I shall insist on the first arrangement. Three days at Rheims, and one—no, faith!

two! Bah! *three* days at Noyon! That would be six days I should gain—yes, six good days!"

He took a pen, and wrote in person an order to the Count de Stainville, to stop three days at Rheims and three days at Noyon. Then, sending for a courier, " Don't draw bridle," said he, " until you have delivered this according to its address."

Then, with the same pen, he wrote:

" DEAR COUNTESS,—To-day we install Zamore in his government. I am just setting out for Marly. This evening, at Luciennes, I shall tell you all I now think.

"FRANCE."

" Here, Lebel," said he to the valet, " take this letter to the countess, and keep on good terms with her—I advise you."

The valet bowed and left the room.

CHAPTER XXIX.

THE COUNTESS DE BEARN.

THE principal object of all the fury of the court, and their stumbling-block on this dreaded occasion—the Countess de Bearn—was, as Chon said, traveling rapidly to Paris. Her journey thither was the result of one of those bright ideas which sometimes came to Viscount Jean's assistance in his times of trouble.

Not being able to find among the ladies of the court one who would present the Countess Dubarry, and since she could not be presented without a lady to introduce her, he cast his eye on the provinces. He examined country-seats, searched carefully in the towns, and at last found what he wanted on the banks of the Meuse in an old, Gothic-looking country-seat, but one kept in good order.

Now, what he wanted was an old lady fond of law, and having a lawsuit on hand.

The old lady with the lawsuit was the Countess de Bearn.

The lawsuit was an affair on which all her fortune depended, and which was to be heard before M. de Maupeou, who had lately taken up the cause of the Countess Dubarry, having discovered what had remained hidden, until then—that he was related to her, and now called her cousin. Looking forward to the appointment of lord chancellor through her interest, he showed the king's favorite all the warmth of a friendship naturally arising from such a substantial basis. This friendship and this interest had procured for him from the king the office of vice-chancellor, and from the world in general the pithy denomination of—*the Vice.*

The Countess de Bearn was a thin, angular, agile little woman, always on the alert, always rolling her eyes like those of a frightened cat, from under her gray eyebrows. She still wore the dress which had been fashionable in her youth, and as the capricious goddess of fashion has sensible fits now and then, it so happened that the costume of the young girl of 1740 should be precisely that of the old woman or 1770.

Broad guipure, pointed mantelet, an enormous coif, an immense bag, and a neck-handkerchief of flowered silk—such was the costume in which Chon, the well-beloved sister and confidante of the Countess Dubarry, found the Countess de Bearn arrayed when she presented herself before her as Mlle. Flageot, the daughter of the lawyer in Paris who had the management of her suit. The old countess wore the costume of her early days as much from taste as from economy. She was not one of those persons who blush for their poverty, because her poverty had not been caused by her own fault. She regretted, indeed, not being rich for her son's sake, to whom she would have wished to leave a fortune worthy of his name. The young man was thoroughly country-bred, timid to a fault, caring much more for what belonged to the substantial things of life than to the honors of renown.

The countess's sole consolation was in calling the lands that were contested with the Saluce family, "my estate;" but as she was a woman of sense, she felt that if she wanted

to borrow money on that estate, not a usurer in France—
and there were some bold enough in running risks at that
period—would lend it her ; not an attorney—and there were
some not very scrupulous then, as there have been at all
times—would procure her the smallest sum on such a
guarantee.

Forced, then, to live on the annual rents of those lands
that were not disputed, the Countess de Bearn, having
only one thousand crowns a year, kept very far from court;
for there she must have spent nearly twelve livres a day in
the hire of a carriage to take her to her lawyer's and to
the judge's.   She was still more determined in keeping
aloof, since she had despaired of her cause being heard for
four or five years at least.   Lawsuits, even in the present
day, are, in truth, tedious affairs; but still, without
living to the age of the patriarchs, a person who commences one has some hope of seeing it to an end ; but,
formerly, a suit extended through two or three genera-
tions, and was like those fabulous plants of the Arabian tales, which blossomed only at the end of two or
three centuries.

The Countess de Bearn, therefore, did not wish to lose
the remains of her patrimony in recovering the ten twelfths
of it which were disputed.   She was, what is always called,
" a woman of the old school," sagacious prudent, firm, ava-
ricious.   She could certainly have managed her suit much
better herself than any advocate, lawyer, or attorney ; but
she was called Bearn, and that name prevented her from
doing many things which economy might have prompted.
Like the divine Achilles in his tent, suffering a thousand
deaths when he heard the trumpet, although feigning to
be deaf to it, she, in her retirement, was devoured by
regret and anguish.   She passed her days in deciphering
old parchments, her spectacles on her nose ; and at night,
on her pillow, she pleaded with such eloquence the cause
of the estate claimed by the Saluces, that she was always
successful—a termination of the affair which she could
but wish her advocate to arrive at.

It may readily be imagined that in such a temper of mind

the arrival of Chon, and the news she brought, were very agreeable to Mme. de Bearn.

The young count was with his regiment.

We always believe what we wish to believe ; so Mme. de Bearn was very easily caught by the young lady's tale.

There was, however, a shadow of suspicion in the countess's mind. She had known Master Flageot twenty years, and had visited him two hundred times in his narrow, dark street ; but she had never seen a child playing on the square bit of carpet which looked so little on the floor of his large office ; and had there been children there, they would surely have found their way into it to get a toy or a cake from the clients.

But what was the use of thinking about the lawyer and his office and his carpet ? What was the use of trying to remember anything about it ? Flageot's daughter was Flageot's daughter—and there she was. Moreover, she was married, and, what banished the last shadow of suspicion, she had not come on purpose to Verdun, she was going to join her husband at Strasbourg.

Perhaps the countess ought to have asked Mlle. Flageot for a letter from her father, to assure herself of her identity ; but if a father could not send his own child without a letter, to whom could he intrust a confidential mission ? Then why such fears ? What could cause such suspicions ? Why should any one travel sixty leagues to tell her a tale without any foundation on fact ?

If she had been rich, a banker's or a financier's wife, taking with her carriages, plate, and diamonds, she might have thought it was a plot got up by robbers. But she laughed to herself when she thought what a disappointment any robbers would experience who should be so ill-advised as to attack her.

So Chon having disappeared with her plain dark dress, and her shabby little one-horse chaise which she had taken at the last post leaving her carriage behind her, the countess, convinced that the time was come for her to make a sacrifice, got into her old coach, and urged on the postilions

so well that she passed through Lachaussée an hour before
the dauphiness, and reached the gate of St. Denis five or
six hours after Chon herself.

As she had little luggage, and as the most important
thing for her was to receive information from her lawyer,
she ordered her coach to drive to the Rue de Petit Lion and
stop before Master Flageot's door. The vehicle, we may
be assured, did not stop there without attracting a great
number of curious spectators—and the Parisians are all
curious—who stared at the venerable machine which seemed
to have issued from the coach-house of Henry IV.—so
antique was it in its solidity, its monumental form, and its
scalloped leather curtains which ran with a disagreeable
creaking on a copper rod covered with verdigris.

The Rue de Petit Lion was not wide, and the countess's
equipage filled it up very majestically. Having alighted
and paid the postilions she ordered them to take it to the
inn where she usually stopped—Le Coq Chantant, in the
Rue St. Germain des Pres.

She ascended M. Flageot's dark stairs, holding by the
greasy cord, which served instead of a hand-rail. The
staircase was cool, and it refreshed the old lady, who was
tired by her long and rapid journey. When Margaret, his
servant, announced the Countess de Bearn, Master Flageot
pulled up his stockings, which he had allowed to fall
nearly to his ankles on account of the heat, with one hand,
fixed on his wig with the other, and then hastily threw on
a dimity dressing-gown, and so adorned, advanced smiling
to the door. In this smile, however, there was such an
expression of surprise, that the countess could not help
saying, "Well, well, my dear sir, it is I."

"Yes, indeed," replied he, "I see plainly enough, madame, that it is you."

Then, modestly wrapping his dressing-gown round him,
he led the countess to a large leather armchair, in the
lightest corner of the apartment, carefully putting aside
the papers which covered his desk, for he knew the old
lady to be curious in the extreme.

"And now, madame," said Master Flageot, gallantly,

"permit me to express my pleasure at this agreeable surprise."

The countess had leaned back in her chair, and raised her feet from the floor to allow Margaret to slip between it and her brocaded satin shoes a leather cushion ; but at this phrase he started up hastily. "How ?" exclaimed she, drawing her spectacles from their case, and putting them on, so that she might see his face the better—"surprise ?"

"Most assuredly ; I thought you at your estates, madame," replied the lawyer, adroitly flattering the old lady by bestowing this title on the countess's three acres of kitchen-garden.

"Well, I was there ; but on the first intimation from you, I left them."

"Intimation from me ?" said the astonished advocate.

"Yes ; at your first word of counsel, or advice, or whatever you please to call it."

Flageot's eyes looked as large as the countess's glasses.

"I have been very expeditious," continued she, "and I hope you are satisfied."

"I am delighted to see you, madame, as I always am ; but allow me to say that I do not see how I have been the cause of your visit."

"Not the cause ? Most certainly you have been the entire cause of it !"

"I ?"

"Yes, you, undoubtedly. Well, have you no news to tell me ? "

"Oh, yes, madame ; it is said the king is meditating some great stroke of policy with regard to the parliament. But may I offer you some refreshment ?"

"But what does it matter to me about the king and his strokes of policy ?"

"About what, then, did you inquire, madame ?"

"About my suit, of course. Is there anything new about it ?"

"Oh, as to that," said Flageot, shaking his head sorrowfully, "nothing, absolutely nothing."

" That is to say, nothing——"

" No—nothing, madame."

" You mean nothing since your daughter spoke to me about it ; but as that was only the day before yesterday, I can readily understand that there may not be much new since then."

" My daughter, madame ? "

" Yes."

" Did you say my daughter ? "

" Yes, your daughter whom you sent to me."

" Pardon me, madame ; but it is quite impossible that I could send my daughter to you."

" Impossible ? "

" Yes, for a very simple reason—I have no daughter."

" Are you sure ? " asked the countess.

" Madame," replied Flageot, " I have the honor to be a bachelor."

" Come, come ! " said the countess, as if she supposed him jesting.

M. Flageot became uneasy ; he called Margaret to bring in some refreshment, but, more particularly, that she might watch the countess. " Poor woman ! " said he to to himself, " her head is turned."

" What ! " said she, returning to the charge, " you have not a daughter ? "

" No, madame."

" Not one married at Strasbourg ? "

" No, madame, by no means."

" And did you not send that daughter," pursued the countess, " on her way thither to tell me that my suit was called on ? "

" Nothing of the kind, madame."

The countess started from her chair, and clasped her hands.

" Drink a little of something, madame ; it will do you good," said M. Flageot ; and at the same time he made a sign to Margaret to bring a tray, on which were two glasses of beer. But the old lady was not thinking of her thirst, and she pushed away the tray so rudely that Dame Margaret, who appeared to be a privileged sort of person, was affronted.

"But let us understand each other," said the countess, eying Master Flageot over her spectacles; "explain all this, if you please."

"Certainly, madame. Margaret, you need not go; the countess will perhaps drink something presently. Let us explain."

"Yes, let us explain; for, upon my honor, my dear sir, you are quite incomprehensible to-day. I begin to think the hot weather has turned your brain."

"Do not be angry, dear madame," said Flageot, maneuvering with the hind feet of his chair, so that he got by degrees further from the countess. "Do not get angry, and let us talk over the matter quietly."

"Yes, yes, certainly. You say you have not a daughter?"

"No, madame, I have not one, and I regret it deeply, since it appears you would be pleased that I had, although——"

"Although what?" repeated the countess.

"Although, for my own part, I should prefer a son. Boys succeed better in the world, or, rather, don't turn out so ill as girls in the present day."

The countess looked more and more alarmed.

"What!" said she, "have you not sent for me to Paris, by a sister, a niece, a cousin—by some person, in short?"

"I never thought of such a thing, madame, knowing how expensive it is staying in Paris."

"But my suit?"

"I should always have taken care to let you know in time before the pleading came on."

"Before it came on?"

"Yes."

"Has it not come on, then?"

"Not that I know of, madame."

"It has not been called?"

"No."

"And it is not likely to come on soon?"

"Oh, no, madame; certainly not."

"Then," cried the old lady, rising, "I have been tricked! I have been most basely deceived!"

Flageot pushed back his wig, muttering, "I fear it indeed, madame."

"Master Flageot!" cried the countess.

The lawyer started on his seat, and made a sign to Margaret to keep near, in order to defend him.

"Master Flageot," continued the countess, "I will not submit to such an indignity as this; I will address the minister of police, to discover the impudent creature who insulted me thus!"

"Oh!" said Flageot, "it is a very doubtful affair."

"And when she is found," continued the countess, almost speechless with anger, "I shall bring an action against her."

"Another lawsuit?" said the lawyer, sorrowfully.

These words made the poor lady fall from the height of her passion, and a heavy fall it was.

"Alas!" said she, "I came here so happy."

"But what did that woman say to you, madame?"

"First, that she was sent by you."

"Shocking intriguer!"

"That you desired her to say that the trial was coming on—was very vear—that I could scarcely be in time with all the speed I could make."

"Alas! madame," repeated Flageot, in his turn, "the trial is very far from coming on."

"Yes; so far from it, I suppose, that it is quite forgotten."

"Forgotten!—sunk, buried, madame; and unless a miracle were to happen—and you know miracles are very rare nowadays——"

"Oh, yes!" mumured the countess, with a sigh.

M. Flageot replied by another sigh, a faithful echo of the countess.

"Well, sir, one thing is certain," added she.

"What is it, madame?"

"I shall not survive this."

"Oh, don't say so—you would be quite wrong."

"Oh, Heaven! oh, Heaven!" exclaimed the poor countess; "my strength is completely exhausted."

"Courage, madame, courage!" said Flageot.

"But have you no advice to give me—none?"

"Oh, yes; my advice is to return to your estates, and after this never believe anybody who does not bring you a letter from me, in my own hand."

"I must return, indeed."

"It will be the wisest plan."

"Well, sir," said the countess, with a groan, "believe me, we shall never meet again—at least not in this world."

"What an infamous affair!"

"I must have some very cruel enemies."

It has been a trick of the opposite party, I would swear!"

"It is a very mean trick, I must say!"

"A mean, sorry trick, indeed!"

"Justice! Justice!" cried the countess; "my dear sir, she is the cave of Cacus!"

"And why is it?" he replied; "because justice is not what it was—because the parliament is opposed—because Monsieur de Maupeou must be chancellor, forsooth, instead of remaining what he ought to be, president."

"Monsieur Flageot, I think I could drink something now."

"Margaret!" cried the lawyer—for Margaret had left the room, seeing the peaceable turn affairs were taking. She now entered with the tray and the two glasses which she had carried away.

The countess drank her glass of beer very slowly, after having touched the lawyer's glass with hers, then she gained the anteroom after a sad and solemn courtesy and a still more sorrowful leave-taking.

The lawyer followed her, his wig in his hand. She was in the lobby, and was reaching out her hand for the cord to aid her in her descent, when a hand was laid on hers and a head gave her a thump on the chest. The head and the hand were those of a clerk, who was mounting the stairs four steps at a time.

The old lady, muttering and grumbling, arranged her petticoats and continued on her way, while the clerk, having reached the lobby, pushed open the lawyer's door, and with the open and joyous voice for which the clerks of the parliament were noted, cried out, " Here, Master Flageot ! here ! it is about the Bearn business ; " and he held out a paper.

To rush up the stairs at that name, push by the clerk, to throw herself on Flageot, to snatch the paper from him, to shut herself up with him in his office—all this, was effected by the countess before the clerk had recovered from two boxes on the ear which Margaret bestowed, or seemed to bestow, on him, in return for two kisses.

" Well," cried the old lady, " what is it ?   Master Flageot, what is it ? "

" Faith, I can't tell, madame ; but if you will give me back the paper I shall let you know."

" True, true, my good Master Flageot ! Read it— read it ! "

He looked at the signature.

" It is from Guildon, our attorney," said he.

" Good heavens ! "

" He desires me," continued Flageot, with surprise amounting almost to bewilderment, " he desires me to be ready to plead on Tuesday, for your affair is to come on ! "

" To come on ? " cried the countess.   " Take care, Master Flageot, take care ! No more tricks. I should never recover from another."

" Madame," replied Flageot, still bewildered at the intelligence, " if there be any trick, any jest in this, Guildon is the author of it ; and it is certainly the first time in his life that he has jested."

" But are you certain the letter is from him ? "

" It is signed Guildon—see ? "

" I see it is.   To be called this morning and pleaded on Tuesday.   Well, then, you see, my dear sir, the lady who came to me was not a cheat."

" It appears not."

"Then, since she was not sent by you—but are you sure she was not ?"

"Pardieu ! am I sure of it ?"

"By whom was she sent, then ?"

"Yes, by whom ?"

"For she must have been sent by some one."

"It is a complete riddle to me."

"And to me also. Let me read the paper again. Yes, my dear Flageot, the pleading is to come on ; it is written so—and before the president, Maupeou."

"The devil ! is that there ?"

"Yes, certainly."

"That is vexatious."

"How so ?"

"Because Monsieur Maupeou is a great friend of your opponents."

"You know that ?"

"He is always with them."

"Ha ! I am truly unfortunate. Now we are more embarrassed than ever."

"But for all that," said the lawyer, "you must wait on him."

"He will receive me very badly."

"That is probable."

"Oh, Master Flageot, what do you tell me ?"

"The truth, madame."

"What ! you not only lose courage yourself, but you try to deprive me of mine ?"

"With the Chancellor Maupeou you must not hope for anything favorable."

"You, so timid—you, a Cicero !"

"Cicero would have lost the cause of Ligarius had he pleaded before Verres instead of Cæsar," replied Master Flageot, finding nothing more humble to say in return for the high compliment of his client.

"Then you advise me not to wait on him ?"

"Heaven forbid, madame, I should advise anything so irregular ; but I pity you sincerely for having to undergo such an interview."

"You really speak like a soldier who meant to desert his post. One would think you feared to undertake the business."

"Madame," replied the lawyer, "I have lost causes which seemed much more likely to be gained by me than this of yours does."

The countess sighed, but summoning all her energy, she said with a kind of dignity which made a complete contrast to all that had been comic in the scene, "I shall carry the matter through ; it shall not be said that, having right on my side, I gave way before a cabal. I shall lose my cause, but I shall at least act as a woman of rank and character, such as there are few at court in the present day. You will accompany me, will you not, Monsieur Flageot, in my visit to the vice-chancellor ?"

"Madame," replied the lawyer, also calling up all his dignity to his aid, "we opposition members of the parliament of Paris have sworn to have no intercourse beyond necessary audiences with those who betrayed the parliament in the affair of Monsieur d'Aiguillon. 'Union is strength,' and as the vice-chancellor tacked about perpetually in that business, we have determined to keep aloof until he shows his true colors."

"My suit is doomed, I see," sighed the countess ; "the lawyers quarrel with the judges, the judges with the clients. No matter ; I shall persevere to the end."

"May Heaven assist you, madame !" said Flageot, flinging his dressing-gown over his left arm as a Roman senator might have done his toga.

"This is but a poor sort of an advocate," murmured she to herself. "I am afraid I shall have less chance with him before the parliament than I had at home on my pillow ;" then, aloud, with a smile under which she strove to hide her uneasiness. "Adieu. Monsieur Flageot, adieu ; study the case thoroughly, I entreat you—we know not how things may turn out."

"Oh, madame," said Master Flageot, "do not fear as to the pleading. I shall do you justice, I shall make some terrible allusions."

" Allusions to what, sir ? "

" To the corruption of Jerusalem, madame, which I shall compare to the accursed cities on which the fire of Heaven descended. You understand—no one can mistake —by Jerusalem I mean Versailles."

" Monsieur Flageot," exclaimed the old lady, " do not compromise yourself, or, rather, do not compromise my cause."

" Oh, madame, with Monsieur de Maupeou for judge, your cause is lost. But then let the world hear of us ; since we cannot obtain justice, let us at least strike terror to the wicked."

" Sir, sir——"

" Let us be philosophic—let us thunder——"

" Deuce take you, with your thunder !" muttered the countess. " Fool of a lawyer ! you are thinking only of making a figure with your fag-ends of philosophy. Come, I will go to the vice-chancellor ; he at least is no philosopher. I may do better with him than with you, after all."

And the old countess left M. Flageot, having, poor old lady, in two days, mounted all the degrees of the scale of hope, and descended all those in that of disappointment.

CHAPTER XXX.

THE VICE.

THE old countess trembled in every limb as she proceeded toward M. de Maupeou's residence. However, one thought had quieted her a little on the road—it was so late that in all probability she would not be admitted, and she should merely have to tell the porter when she should come again.

In fact, it was about seven in the evening, and although it was still light, the habit of dining at four, which the nobility had adopted, had caused all business to be suspended from dinner until the next day. Although Mme. de Bearn anxiously longed to see the chancellor, she was, nevertheless, consoled by the thought that she should not see him. This is one of the frequent contradictions of the human mind which we can always understand but never explain.

The countess presented herself, therefore, quite certain that the porter would refuse her admittance ; and had even prepared a crown to offer the Cerberus to induce him to put her name on the list of those who requested an audience. On reaching the house, she found an usher talking to the porter, as if giving him an order. She waited discreetly that she might not interrupt these two personages ; but on perceiving her in her hackney-coach, the usher withdrew. The porter approached and demanded her name.

" Oh, I know," said she, " that it is not probable I shall have the honor of seeing his excellency."

" No matter, madame," replied the porter, " have the goodness to tell me your name."

" The Countess de Bearn," she replied.

" My lord is at home," answered he.

" What did you say ? " asked the countess, almost dumb with astonishment.

" I say that my lord is at home," repeated he.

" But of course he will not receive visitors ? "

" He will receive you, madame."

Mme. de Bearn got out of the coach, hardly knowing whether she was asleep or awake.

The porter pulled a cord—a bell rang twice. The usher appeared at the top of the steps, and the porter made a sign to the countess to enter.

" You wish to speak to my lord ? " asked the usher.

" I wish for that honor, but I scarcely hoped to attain it."

" Have the goodness to follow me, madame."

" And yet people speak so ill of this chancellor," said the countess to herself, as she went along, following the usher, " yet he has certainly one good quality—he admits persons on business at all hours. A chancellor—it is strange ! "

Yet still she shuddered at the idea that she should find him so much the more stern, so much the more ungracious, because he was assiduous at his duties. M. de Maupeou, buried under a great wig, and dressed in a suit of black velvet, was waiting in his cabinet, with the doors open. The countess, on entering, cast a rapid glance around. She saw with surprise that he was alone—that the mirrors reflected no other face than her own and that of the meager, yellow, busy chancellor.

The usher announced, "Madame the Countess de Bearn." The chancellor rose up stiffly, as if he had no joints, and, by the same movement, leaned his back against the chimney-piece.

The countess made the necessary three courtesies.

Her short, complimentary speech which followed the courtesies was rather embarrassed ; she did not expect the honor, she did not think that a minister who had so much to do would deprive himself of the hours necessary for recreation, etc., etc.

The chancellor replied that time was no doubt, as precious to his majesty's subjects as to his majesty's ministers —that, nevertheless, he admitted there were distinctions to be made as to the importance of the affairs brought before him ; consequently, he always gave the greater part of his time to those whose business was most urgent.

Fresh courtesies on the part of the countess, then an embarrassed silence, for compliments were ended, and her request must now be made.

The chancellor waited, stroking his chin.

"My lord," said she, "I have presented myself before you to explain to you an affair on which my whole fortune depends."

The chancellor bowed, as if to intimate that she should go on.

"My lord," she continued, "you must know that all my property, or, rather, my son's, is at stake in a suit now pending between us and the family of the Saluces."

The vice-chancellor continued to stroke his chin.

"But your equity is so well known to me, my lord, that, although I am aware of your interest in—indeed I may say your friendship for—the adverse party, I have not hesitated an instant in coming to entreat you to hear me."

The chancellor could not help smiling on hearing himself praised for his equity, a quality for which he was about as famous as Dubois was for the apostolical virtues on which he had been complimented fifty years before.

"You are right, madame," said he, "saying that I am afraid of your opponents, but you are also right in thinking that, when I accepted the seals, I laid aside all friendship. I shall reply to you, then, without any bias, as becomes the supreme head of justice."

"Heaven bless you, my lord!" cried the old countess.

"I shall examine your affair as a simple jurisconsult," continued the chancellor.

"I thank your lordship; your skill in these matters is well known."

"Your cause comes on soon, I think."

"Next week, my lord."

"In the meantime, what are your wishes respecting it?"

"That your lordship would look into the documents."

"I have already done so."

"Well," asked the old countess, trembling, "and what do you think of it, my lord?"

"I think that there is not a doubt on the subject."

"Not a doubt of my gaining."

"No—of your losing."

"Then, you think, my lord, I shall lose?"

"Undoubtedly; I shall, therefore, give you one piece of advice."

"What is it?" asked the countess, with the last ray of hope.

"It is—if you have any payments to make, the cause being tried, and sentence pronounced, to have your funds ready."

"Oh, my lord, we shall be ruined then!"

"Surely you know, madame, that justice never takes into account anything respecting the consequences of her decrees."

"But, my lord, there should be mercy as well as justice."

"And, for fear of justice being influenced by mercy, she is made blind, madame."

"But your lordship will not refuse me your advice?"

"Certainly not; ask it, madame. I am ready."

"Is there no means of entering into an arrangement by which the sentence might not be so harsh?"

"Do you know any of your judges?"

"Not one of them, my lord."

"That is unfortunate. Messieurs de Saluces, your opponents, are connected with three fourths of the parliament."

The countess shuddered.

"But observe," continued the chancellor, "that that does not alter the main grounds of the question, for a judge does not permit himself to be influenced by private feelings."

This was about as true as that he possessed the virtue of equity, or Dubois the apostolic virtues, but it made the poor countess nearly faint.

"But, after all," continued the chancellor, "the judge having done all that integrity demands, of course leans more to a friend than to a person about whom he is indifferent—that is only just, when it is just—and as it will be just that you should lose your cause, they may, in their sentence, make the consequence of that loss very unpleasant to you."

"But all that your lordship says is very alarming."

"As far as I am concerned, I shall refrain from saying anything that might have an influence on the minds of others; but, as I am not a judge myself, I may speak to you of the state of affairs."

"Alas! my lord, I suspected one thing."

The vice-chancellor fixed on her his little gray eyes.

" I suspected that the adverse party, living in Paris, they might become connected with the judges, and thus be all-powerful."

" Because, in the first place, they have justice on their side."

" How painful it is, my lord, to hear such words from the lips of a man infallible as you are ! "

" I merely say all this to you, because it is the truth, and yet," continued M. de Maupeou, with an affected frankness, " I should like, upon my word, to serve you."

The countess started ; she thought that she saw some hidden meaning, if not in the chancellor's words, at least in his thoughts, which concealed behind it something favorable to her.

" Besides," he proceeded, " the name you bear is one of the noblest in France, and that is, in itself, a powerful recommendation to me."

" Ah, my lord, it will not prevent me from losing my suit."

" As to that, I have no power either one way or the other."

" Oh, my lord ! my lord ! " cried the countess, shaking her head, " how things go on in this world now ! "

" You seem to infer, madame, that in the good old times they went better."

" Alas ! my lord, I cannot but think so. I recall with pleasure the time when you were merely a king's advocate in the parliament, and when you made those beautiful speeches which I, then a young woman, went to listen to, and which I applauded with such enthusiasm. What fire ! what eloquence ! what virtue ! Ah, my lord, in those times there were no plots, no cabals, no favoritism ! I should have gained my suit then."

" Yet we had Madame de Phalaris then, who tried to resign occasionally when the regent shut his eyes ; and we had, too, La Souris, who went about picking up what crumbs she could manage to gather."

" Oh, my lord, but Madame de Phalaris was really a lady of rank, and La Souris was such a good-natured girl."

" Yes ; so nothing was refused them."

" Or, rather, they could refuse no one."

"Come, madame," said the chancellor, laughing in a manner that astonished the old lady more and more, it was so open and natural, "come, do not make me speak ill of my own administration, through affection for my youthful days."

" But, my lord, when I think of those days, I must lament my lost fortune, my ruined family."

" You see, countess, what it is not to go with the times, not to sacrifice to the idols of the day."

" Alas ! my lord, those idols care not for worshipers who come with empty hands."

" What can you know about them ? "

" I ? "

" Yes ; you have never tried them, I think."

" My lord, you speak to me really like a friend."

" Well, are we not about the same age, countess ? "

" Oh ! why am I not twenty, and you, my lord, a simple advocate again ? you would plead for me, and I should gain my cause."

"Unhappily, we are not twenty, countess," said the vice-chancellor, with a gallant sigh ; " we must only, therefore, beg those who are twenty to assist us, since you confess that that is the age to have influence. What, do you know no one at court ? "

" Some old noblemen who have left it now, I once knew, but they would blush for their old friend in her poverty. Stay, my lord, I have still the privilege of being received at court. I might go to Versailles ; yet of what use would it be ? Oh, had I again only my two hundred thousand crowns of income, people would come to visit me—perform that miracle for me, my lord !"

The chancellor pretended not to hear this last phrase. "In your place," said he, " I should forget the old, as they have forgotten me. I should apply to the young, and beat up for recruits among them. Do you happen to know the princesses at all ? "

" They must have forgotten me."

"And, besides, they have no influence. Do you know the dauphin ?"

"No."

"And, after all, he is so busy about his archduchess, who is about to arrive, that he can think of nothing else. Let me see—among the favorites—is there any one——"

"I don't even know their names."

"Monsieur d'Aiguillon ?"

"A cockscomb of whom such shameful things are said—that he hid in a wall while others were fighting ! Fy ! fy !"

"Pooh ! we must not believe the half of what we hear. But stay, let me think——"

"Do—do, my lord ; think of some one !"

"Yes ; why not ? Yes—ha ! yes."

"Who, my lord—who ?"

"Why not apply to the countess herself ?"

"To the Countess Dubarry ?" said the old lady, spreading out her fan.

"Yes ; she is really a kind creature."

"Indeed !"

"And anxious to be useful."

"I am of too ancient a family to please her, my lord."

"You are mistaken, countess ; she tries to attach high families to her."

"Do you think so ?" asked the old countess, already beginning to waver in her opposition.

"Do you know her ?" said the chancellor.

"Oh, good heavens ! no."

"Ah, there is the mischief ! She is the person who has real influence."

"Yes, yes, she has influence ; but I never saw her."

"Nor her sister Chon ?"

"No."

"Nor her sister Bischi ?"

"No."

"Nor her brother Jean ?"

"No."

"Nor her negro Zamore ?"

"What, her negro, my lord?"

"Yes; her negro is one of the governing powers."

"What, that little fright whose picture is sold in the streets, which looks like that of a dressed-up pug-dog?"

"Yes, the same."

"I know that African!" cried the countess, with offended dignity. "How should I know him, my lord?"

"Well, well! I see you do not wish to keep your estates, countess."

"How is that?"

"Because you speak contemptuously of Zamore."

"But what has Zamore to do in the matter?"

"He might have gained your suit for you—that is all."

"He? That Moor—that Hottentot! How could he gain it for me?"

"By saying to his mistress that he wished you to gain it. You know what influence is; he makes his mistress do what he chooses, and she makes the king do what she chooses."

"Then Zamore governs France, my lord?"

"Hum!" replied the chancellor, nodding his head. "He has a great deal of influence; and I had rather quarrel with—with the dauphiness, for instance—than with Zamore."

"Great Heaven!" exclaimed the countess, "if it were not a grave person like your lordship who told me such things, I could not believe them."

"Oh, I am not the only one who will tell them you. Everybody can tell them. Ask any of the dukes and peers if they ever forget, when going to Marly or Luciennes, to take comfits for Zamore to put in his mouth, or pearls for him to hang in his ears. I, who speak to you, am I not the Chancellor of France, or something very near it? Well, what was I doing when you came in? I was drawing up a governor's commission for Zamore."

"A governor's commission?"

"Yes; Monsieur Zamore is appointed Governor of the Castle of Luciennes."

"The very same title with which they rewarded the Count de Bearn after twenty years' service."

"Yes; he was made Governor of the Castle of Blois. I remember that."

"But what a degradation! Good heavens! the monarchy is dead.'

"It is very ill, at least; and you know, countess, when an invalid draws near his end, people try to get all they can from him."

"No doubt—no doubt; but the question is, how to get near this invalid."

"Do you know what you must do to be well received by the Countess Dubarry?"

"What?"

"You must get admitted by being the bearer of this commission for her negro."

"I?"

"It will be an excellent beginning."

"Do you think so, my lord?" said the poor countess, all alarmed.

"I am sure of it; but——"

"But what?"

"Do you know any one acquainted with her?"

"No one but yourself, my lord."

"Oh, as for me, it would be difficult for me to introduce you."

"Assuredly," said the poor old lady, tossed to and fro by alternate hopes and fears, "assuredly, fortune is hostile to me! Your lordship has received me in a manner quite unexpected, for indeed I did not expect to be admitted to an audience; then, you have inclined me to pay my court to Madame Dubarry—I, a Bearn!—and I am ready to undertake the hateful task of delivering the commission for her wretch of a negro, and now I cannot even get an introduction to her!"

The chancellor began again to stroke his chin, and appeared very thoughtful, when suddenly the usher announced, "Monsieur le Viscount Jean Dubarry."

At this name the chancellor made a gesture of amazement, and the countess sank back breathless in her chair.

"Now, say that fortune has abandoned you! Ah, countess, countess, Heaven is working in your favor!"

Then, turning to the usher, without giving the old lady time to recover, he desired that the viscount should be admitted instantly. The usher withdrew, and in a moment after our old acquaintance, Jean Dubarry, entered, with his arm in a sling.

After the usual number of bows were made on both sides, and as the countess, trembling and undecided, was trying to rise in order to take leave—for the chancellor, by a slight movement of the head, had indicated to her that her audience was ended—"Pardon me, my lord," said the viscount, "pardon me, madame—I interrupted you, I fear; but I beg of you not to go away; I have only two words to say to his lordship."

The countess sat down again without requiring to be pressed, her heart full of joy and expectation.

"But, perhaps, sir, I shall be in your way?" she stammered.

"Oh, madame, not at all—not at all. I merely wish to lodge a short complaint with his lordship."

"A complaint? Against whom?" exclaimed the chancellor.

"An attack upon me, my lord! an assassination! One cannot pass over such things as that. Let them abuse us, make ballads about us, blacken us; we can survive all that; but when it comes to cutting our throats—mordieu! we die."

"Explain the affair, I beg," said the chancellor, pretending to be very much horrified.

"It is easily done; but I fear I am interrupting this lady's audience."

"The Countess de Bearn," said the chancellor, introducing the old lady to the Viscount Jean Dubarry.

Dubarry retreated gracefully to make his bow, the countess to make her courtesy; and both saluted as ceremoniously as if they had been at court.

" After you, sir," said she.

" Madame, I would not be guilty of such treason against gallantry for the world."

" Oh, sir, my business only concerns money, in yours honor is concerned ; yours is, therefore, more urgent."

" Then, madame," said the viscount, " since it is your wish, I shall take advantage of your obliging permission." And he related his tale to the chancellor, who listened very gravely.

" You will require witnesses," said M. de Maupeou, after a moment's reflection.

" Ah," cried Dubarry, " how easily one discovers even in those worlds the upright judge who can only be influenced by irrefutable truth ! Well, I can procure witnesses."

" My lord," said the countess, " the viscount has found one already."

" What witness ? " they both asked.

" I, myself," the countess replied.

" You ? " exclaimed the chancellor.

" Sir," said she, addressing the viscount, " did not this affair happen at the village of Lachaussée ? "

" Yes, madame."

" At the post-house ? "

" Yes."

" Well, I shall be your witness. I passed through the place where the attack was made on you, two hours after it happened."

" Really, madame ? " said the chancellor.

" Yes," continued the countess; " and everybody was talking of what had just taken place."

" Take care ! " said the viscount, " take care, madame ; if you consent to aid me in this matter, very likely the Choiseuls will find some means of making you repent of it."

" Ah," said the chancellor, " and the more easily that the Countess de Bearn is engaged in a lawsuit, her chance of gaining which is very doubtful, I am afraid."

" Oh, my lord," cried the old lady, putting her hand to her head. " I sink from one difficulty to another ! "

"Lean upon the viscount," said the chancellor, in a half whisper; "he has a powerful arm to assist you."

"Only one at present," said Dubarry, with a simper. "But I know a certain person who has two good arms—they can reach far, and I offer you their aid."

"Oh, Monsieur le Viscount, are you serious in making me such an offer?"

"It is only service for service, madame. I accept your aid—you accept mine. Is it agreed?"

"Do I accept yours? Oh, sir, you do me too much honor!"

"Then, madame, will you take a seat in my carriage? I am just going to pay a visit to my sister."

"Without any reason—without any preparations? Oh, sir, I dare not——"

"You have a reason, madame," said the chancellor, slipping into her hand Zamore's commission.

"My lord, you are my tutelary genius!" cried the old lady, taking the document. "Monsieur le Viscount, you are the flower of the French nobility."

"At your service," said the viscount, pointing the way to the countess, who was as quick as a bird to take it.

"Thanks for my sister," whispered Jean in the chancellor's ear—"thank you, cousin. But did I play my part well, eh?"

"Admirably," said Maupeou; "but pray make the countess laugh by telling her how I played mine. But take care; the old lady is as sharp as a needle!"

At that moment the countess turned; the two gentlemen bowed formally to each other, as if taking a ceremonious adieu.

A splendid carriage, with attendants in the royal livery, waited at the door; the old lady took her place in it quite elated, Jean seated himself beside her, and they departed.

After the king left Mme. Dubarry, as we have formerly related, after a very cold and constrained reception, the countess was left alone with Chon and her brother, who had not appeared at first, for fear of his wound being examined—it being, in reality, very trifling. The result of this family council was, that the countess, instead of going to Luciennes, as she had told the king, set off for Paris. She had there, in the Rue de Valois, a snug little house which served as a place of rendezvous for all her family, every member of which was constantly running backward and forward, hither and thither, as business or pleasure led them.

The countess being installed in this domicile of hers, took a book and waited. Meantime, the viscount prepared his battery.

It might be about half-past seven by the large dial of the Church of St. Eustache, when the Countess de Bearn and Viscount Dubarry passed by on their way to his sister's.

The conversation on her side expressed great reluctance to avail herself of the good fortune which had fallen in her way. On his, there was the assumption of a sort of dignity in being her patron, with repeated exclamations at the happy chance which enabled him to introduce her to the Countess Dubarry. In return, the old lady never ceased praising the politeness and affability of the chancellor. All these fits on both sides, however, did not prevent the horses from going as fast as they could, and they reached their place of destination a little before eight.

" Permit me, madame," said the viscount, leaving the old lady in an anteroom, " to inform the Countess Dubarry of the honor you have done her."

" Oh, sir," said the countess, " do not, I entreat you, allow my unseasonable visit to disturb her."

Jean approached Zamore, who was watching for his return out of one of the windows, and whispered something in his ear.

" What a dear little negro ! " cried the countess. " Is he your sister's, sir ? "

" Yes ; he is one of her favorites, madame."

" I congratulate her on having such a one."

At this moment a footman opened the folding-doors of the saloon where Mme. Dubarry usually granted audiences, and requested the countess to walk in there. While the old lady was sighing over the luxurious furniture of the apartment, Jean was with his sister, announcing his prize.

"Is it really she?" asked Mme. Dubarry.

"Flesh and blood."

"Does she suspect anything?"

"Nothing in the world."

"And how did the Vice behave?"

"Admirably; everything conspired to favor us."

"Do not let us leave her too long alone, lest she should suspect something."

"You are right; for I assure you, she seems to me cunning enough."

"Where is Chon?"

"At Versailles, you know."

"Well, she must not, by any means, let herself be seen."

"Oh, I warned her!"

"Now, princess, enter."

Mme. Dubarry gently pushed opened the door of her boudoir and entered the saloon.

All the ceremonials necessary to the etiquette of those days was scrupulously gone through by the two actresses mutually desirous of pleasing. Mme. Dubarry was the first to speak.

"I have already thanked my brother, madame, for having procured me the honor of this visit; allow me now to thank you also for having consented to his wish."

"I know not, madame," replied the old lady, "in what terms to thank you for this gracious reception of me."

"Madame," said the countess, in her turn, with a courtesy of profound respect, "it is only due to a lady of your rank to place myself at your disposal, if I can be of service to you in any way."

And three more courtesies having been made on each side, the countess invited Mme. de Bearn to be seated.

CHAPTER XXXI.

ZAMORE'S COMMISSION.

" MADAME," said the favorite, " pray let me hear your wishes—I am all attention."

" Permit me, sister," said Jean, who continued standing, " to disabuse your mind of the idea that the Countess de Bearn comes with a petition—not at all—the chancellor has simply asked her to perform a little office for him."

The old lady turned a grateful look on the viscount, and held out to the countess the patent signed by the vice-chancellor declaring Luciennes a royal castle, and Zamore its governor.

" Then it is I who am the person obliged," said the countess, glancing at the document. " If I could only be so fortunate, madame, as to be of any service to you in return."

" Oh, that you can readily be ! " exclaimed the old lady, with a frankness which enchanted the brother and sister.

" Pray let me know how, madame."

" You were kind enough to say that my name is not quite unknown to you, madame."

" Unknown !—a Bearn ? "

" Then you have perhaps heard of a lawsuit which threatens my whole property."

" Oh, yes—a suit between you and the family of the Saluces ? "

" Alas, madame, yes."

" I know all about it, madame. I heard his majesty the other evening speak of it to my cousin, the chancellor."

" His majesty speak of my lawsuit ? "

" Yes, madame."

" And in what terms, pray ? "

" Alas ! my dear madame ! " and Mme. Dubarry shook her head.

" As lost, as lost—was it not ? " exclaimed the old lady, with anguish.

" If I must speak the truth, madame, it was."

" His majesty said so ? "

" His majesty had too much prudence and delicacy to pronounce sentence decidedly, but he seemed to look upon the adverse party as already in possession of the estate."

" Oh, heavens ! madame, if his majesty were but rightly informed on the subject—if he knew that all this was about a bond really discharged—yes, madame, the two hundred thousand francs have been paid. I have not a receipt for the money, certainly ; but I have a moral certainty that it was paid. I could, if I was allowed to plead in person before the parliament, demonstrate it by inference."

" By inference ? " exclaimed Mme. Dubarry, who. did not understand one word of what she said, but who appeared to pay the most serious attention.

" Yes, madame, by inference."

" The proof by inference is admissible," said Jean.

" Do you think so, sir ? " asked the old lady.

" Yes, I think it is," replied the viscount, with profound gravity.

" Well, then, by inference I could prove that the bond for two hundred thousand francs, with the interest accumulated, amounting to a total of about one million—I could prove that this bond, bearing date 1406, was discharged by Guy Gaston, the fourth Count of Bearn, on his death-bed, in 1417 ; for there it is written by his own hand in his will : " Being on my death-bed, and owing nothing to any man, and ready to appear before God——' "

" Well ? " said Mme. Dubarry.

" Well, madame, if he owed nothing to any man, he owed nothing to the family of the Saluces, otherwise he would have said, ' owing two hundred thousands francs, instead of saying ' owing nothing to any man.' "

"Most undoubtedly he would have said so," exclaimed Jean.

"But you have no other proof?" asked the favorite.

"Than his word—none, madame; but he was called Gaston the Irreproachable."

"And your opponents have the bond?"

"Yes; they have, and that is just what makes the affair more intricate."

She should have said: "That is just what clears up the matter;" but she looked at things from her own point of view.

"So your conviction is, madame, that the bond was discharged?" said Jean.

"Yes, sir, that is my decided conviction," exclaimed Mme. de Bearn, warmly.

"Do you know," said the countess, turning to her brother, as if deeply penetrated by that conviction, "the proof by inference, as the Countess de Bearn calls it, changes the face of things wonderfully?"

"Oh, wonderfully!" returned Jean.

"And very unpleasantly for my opponents," continued the countess; "the terms of Gaston IV.'s will are most positive—'owing nothing to any man——'"

"It is not only clear, it is logical," said Jean; "he owed nothing to any man, therefore of course he had paid what he owed."

"Therefore he had paid what he owed," repeated the Countess Dubarry.

"Oh, madame, why are you not my judge?" ejaculated the old lady.

"Formerly," said the viscount, "we should not have had recourse to the tribunals to settle an affair of that kind —the judgment of Heaven would have been enough. For my part, I am so convinced of the goodness of your cause that, did the old custom still exist, I should willingly offer myself for your champion."

"Oh, sir!"

"Yes, I should act as did my grandfather, Dubarry-Moore, who had the honor of being connected with the royal family of the Stuarts, when he fought in the lists for the beautiful Edith of Scarborough, and made his adversary confess that he lied in his throat. But unhappily," continued the viscount, with a sigh of disdain for the degeneracy of the age, " we live not in those glorious times; and gentlemen, when they claim their rights, must submit their causes to the judgment of a set of pettifoggers, who have not the sense to understand a phrase so clear as 'owing nothing to any man.'"

" But, brother," said the countess, " it is three hundred years since those words were written, so you must allow that the gentlemen of the long robe may well pause a little before deciding on them."

" Oh, no matter—no matter—I am certain that if his majesty heard the Countess de Bearn state her case herself as she has done to us——"

" I should convince his majesty, should I not, sir ?"

" I am certain of it."

" Yes ; but how am I to obtain an audience of his majesty ?"

" You must come and visit me at Luciennes ; and as his majesty does me the honor of coming sometimes to see me there——"

" My dear," interrupted the viscount, " that is all very well, but it depends on chance."

" Viscount," replied the favorite, with a sweet smile, " you know that I depend a good deal on chance, and I have no reason to complain."

" Yes ; but the Countess de Bearn might go to Luciennes for a week or a fortnight, and yet not meet his majesty."

" That is true."

" In the meantime, her cause is to come on Monday or Tuesday."

" On Tuesday, sir."

" And this is Friday evening."

" Ah, then," said Mme. Dubarry, with a countenance all disappointment, " we must not reckon upon that."

" What shall we do," said the viscount, as if in deep thought.

"What a devil of a business!"

"I might have an audience at Versailles," suggested the old lady timidly.

"Oh, you will not obtain it."

"But through your influence, madame?"

"Oh, my influence would be of no avail. His majesty detests business matters—and, besides, his mind is now full of one thing only."

"The parliament?" asked Mme. de Bearn.

"No—my presentation."

"Ah!" said the old lady.

"For you know, madame, in spite of the opposition of Monsieur de Choiseul and Madame de Grammont, the king has decided that I shall be presented."

"I was not aware, madame."

"It is a settled affair," said Jean.

"And when will the presentation take place, madame?"

"Oh! very soon. You see, the king wishes it to be before the arrival of the dauphiness, that he may invite my sister to share the festivities at Compiegne."

"Ah—I understand. Then you have all the arrangements made for your presentation," said the old countess, sighing.

"Oh, yes," replied the viscount, "the Baroness d'Alogny—do you know the Baroness d'Alogny?"

"No, sir. Alas! I scarcely know any one now. It is twenty years since I was at court."

"Well, it is the Baroness d'Alogny who is to present my sister. The king loads her with favors—her husband is chamberlain—he is to be raised from a baron to a count—the son is to go into the guards—her orders on the king's privy purse are to be made payable by the city of Paris, and the day of the presentation she is to receive twenty thousand crowns paid down; so she is eager for it, you may be sure!"

"Yes, I can readily understand that," said the old lady, smiling.

"Oh, but now I think of it——" cried Jean.

"Of what?" asked the Countess Dubarry.

"What a misfortune—what a misfortune!" continued he, "that I did not meet madame a week sooner at our cousin the vice-chancellor's."

"Why, pray?"

"Why, he had no positive engagement then with the Baroness d'Alogny."

"Dear brother, you speak like a sphinx—I do not understand you."

"You do not understand?"

"No."

"I will wager something the Countess de Bearn understands!"

"No, sir, I do not, indeed."

"Last week you had not decided who should present you?"

"Undoubtedly."

"Well—the Countess de Bearn—but perhaps, madame, I am taking too great a liberty?"

"No, sir—no."

"Then madame could have presented you, and the king would have done for her what he is going to do for the Baroness d'Alogny."

"Alas!" said the old lady, opening her eyes to their utmost extent

"Oh, if you knew," continued Jean, "all the favors his majesty heaped on the family of the baroness, as soon as he knew she had offered to introduce Jeanne! There was only one thing in the affair that vexed him——"

"Ah, one thing vexed him?"

"Yes, one single thing; "one thing vexes me," said he.

"The lady who presents the Countess Dubarry I should wish to bear a historical name," and as he said that he looked at the picture of Charles I. by Vandyck.

"Yes, I understand," said the old lady, "his majesty turned to that picture on account of the alliance between the Dubarry-Moores and the Stuarts, of which you spoke just now."

"Precisely."

"The fact is," said the old lady, with a slight air of hauteur, "I never heard of the family of D'Alogny."

"A good family, however," said the countess ; "they have brought forward all the necessary proofs, or nearly all."

"Pardieu !" cried Jean, suddenly starting in his chair.

"Well, what is the matter ?" said Mme. Dubarry, scarcely able to refrain from laughing outright at the contortions of her brother-in-law.

"Monsieur has hurt himself, perhaps ?" asked the old lady, anxiously.

"No," said Jean, sinking slowly back again into his chair ; "it was an idea which just then occurred to me."

"What idea ?" said the countess, laughing ; "it almost overturned you."

"It must certainly have been a good one," said Mme. de Bearn.

"Excellent."

"Well, we are all anxiety to hear it."

"It has only one fault."

"Well ?"

"It is impossible."

"No matter ; let us hear it."

"Suppose we were to tell the Baroness d'Alogny the king's remark when he looked at Charles I.'s portrait."

"Oh, brother, that would not be politics ; we cannot think of it."

The old lady sighed.

"It is vexatious, too," continued the viscount, as if speaking to himself ; "the affair could have been so easily arranged. The Countess de Bearn, who not only bears such an ancient name, but is besides a woman of distinguished talent, would offer herself in the place of the Baroness d'Alogny ; she would have gained her lawsuit ; her son would have got a commission as lieutenant in the guards, and as madame must, of course, have been put to considerable expense in her frequent visits to Paris, there would have been an adequate compensation allowed. Such an opportunity does not occur twice in a lifetime."

"Alas, no!" exclaimed the old lady, quite overcome by this unforeseen blow.

The fact is, that any one in the position of the old litigant would have felt inclined to echo her exclamation, and like her would have sunk back overhelmed in her easy-chair.

"Now, brother," said the countess, in a tone of great compassion, "you see you are giving pain to Madame de Bearn; was it not enough that I was forced to tell her I could do nothing for her with the king before my presentation? Oh, If I could delay my suit!" sighed the countess.

"For only eight days," said Dubarry.

"Yes, in eight days," resumed Mme. de Bearn—"in eight days madame will be presented."

"Yes; but the king will be at Compiegne in eight days —he will be in the midst of festivities—the dauphiness will have arrived."

"Stop! I have another idea. No—yes—no—yes, yes —I have hit it!"

"What is it, sir?" said Mme. de Bearn, whose whole soul seemed to hang upon the viscount's lips, and who repeated mechanically the monosyllables he uttered.

"Your presentation is still a secret; no one knows that you have got a lady to present you."

"No; for the king wishes it to fall like a thunderbolt on the court."

"Well, the Countess de Bearn will demand an audience, as she is not supposed to know any more about your presentation than others, for the purpose of offering to present you. The king, at such an offer from a lady of her rank, will be delighted; he will receive her, thank her, will ask her what he can do for her. She will introduce the subject of her lawsuit, and explain her views respecting it—his majesty will give them a favorable consideration, and the suit which she thought lost—is gained."

The favorite fixed her eager gaze on the old lady, who probably began to suspect that there was some snare laid for her.

"I'm a poor unknown creature," said she; "his majesty would not, perhaps——"

"Enough. I merely wished to give you a friendly advice on the matter," said Jean.

"Oh, sir, I am only too sensible——" said the countess, hesitating.

"It is not a bad idea," replied Mme. Dubarry, smiling; "but perhaps madame would not like to descend to anything like a trick, even to gain her lawsuit."

"Quite true, madame," said the old lady, hoping to get off by this means; "I had much rather do you some real service to obtain your friendship."

"Indeed, nothing could be more condescending," said the favorite, with a slight shade of irony which did not escape the penetration of Mme. de Bearn.

"Well, I have still another means," said Jean.

The old lady listened anxiously.

"Really, brother, your imagination is as fertile in resources as that of Monsieur de Beaumarchais. Let us hear this last idea."

"It is that the Countess de Bearn shall render you the real service which she wishes to do. Can you not persuade the Baroness d'Alogny to yield her rights to the countess? You need not tell her plumply the king's observation, but you could with your tact make her understand that he preferred the countess's ancient name."

This time the attack was direct; he thought there could be no evasive answer, but the countess found one.

"I should not like to interfere with that lady's arrangements," said she—"among persons of quality a certain attention to these engagements must be observed."

Mme. Dubarry made a gesture of anger and disappointment, but the viscount, by a look, restrained her.

"Observe, madame," said he, "I insist on nothing. Like many in the world, you have a lawsuit, which very naturally you wish to gain. It appears, however, that on the contrary you are likely to lose it; you are in despair; just at that moment I arrive; I feel for you; I take an interest in the affair which does not in the remotest degree concern me;

I endeavor to make it turn out favorably for you. I am wrong—let us say no more about it !" and Jean rose from his seat.

"Oh, sir," exclaimed the old lady in despair, for she now saw that the Dubarrys, who had been till then indifferent, were going to use their influence against her—"oh, sir, believe me, I am truly grateful to you ! I feel how benevolent have been your intentions."

"As for myself," replied Jean, playing to the life the part of a person perfectly unconcerned, " it matters not whether my sister be presented by the Baroness d'Alogny, the Countess de Polastron, or the Countess de Bearn."

"Oh, certainly, sir."

"Only I confess I felt annoyed that the royal favor should be bestowed on some mean spirit actuated by sordid interest—a spirit yielding to our power, because it is impossible to undermine it."

"Oh, that is what will most probably happen," said the favorite.

"While," continued Jean, " the Countess de Bearn, almost an entire stranger to us, and coming forward without any solicitation on our part, and prompted solely by her kindness and good nature to offer her services, appears to me worthy of all the advantages which thereby accrue to her."

The old lady was probably about to disclaim that good-will which the viscount did her the honor to attribute to her, but Mme. Dubarry did not give her time.

"The fact is," said she, " the king would not refuse anything to a lady who would act as you describe."

"What ! the king would not refuse anything, do you say?"

"Even more—he would say with his own lips to the vice-chancellor, ' Monsieur de Maupeou, I wish that everything should be settled about the lawsuit as the Countess de Bearn wishes but it seems, however, as if you saw some difficulty in the matter. Very good. But you will at least do me the justice, I hope, to believe that I was actuated by a sincere wish to serve you, madame ;" and the viscount bowed.

"Indeed, sir, my heart is filled with gratitude to you !"

"Pray do not speak of it," said the gallant viscount.

"But the Baroness d'Alogny would not yield up her right," resumed the old lady, after a short pause.

"Still, her majesty would not be the less grateful to you for your offer."

"But supposing," persisted the old lady, who was determined to view the matter in the worst light, in order to see to the bottom of the affair—"supposing the baroness would yield her privilege to me, she would not so readily give up the accompanying advantages."

"The king's kindness is inexhaustible, madame," said the favorite.

"If I offered my services, madame," replied the old lady, drawn on more and more both by her interest and by the clever manner in which they played their parts, "I should leave out of view the gaining of my cause—for, to say the truth, a suit which every one thinks lost to-day will not be easily gained to morrow."

"Oh—but if the king were favorable ?" exclaimed Jean, eager to combat her new doubts.

"Well," said the favorite, "I confess I am of the countess's opinion, viscount."

"You are ?" said he, staring at her with open eyes.

"Yes—I think it would be more honorable for a lady of her ancient name to allow her suit to go as it may. Then there would be nothing binding on the king—nothing to impede his munificence to her ; and if he did not wish, in the present state of the parliament, to interfere with the course of justice, he might offer her compensation for the loss of the suit."

"Ah," sighed the old lady, "how could he offer anything to compensate for the loss of two hundred thousand francs ?"

"Why, in the first place," replied Mme. Dubarry, "there might, for instance, be a royal gift of one hundred thousand francs."

The partners in this scheme looked at their victim with eager eyes.

"I have a son——" said she.

"So much the better! One more loyal servant of the state."

"But do you think, madame, there would be anything done for my son?"

"I can answer for it," said Jean, "that the least he might expect would be a lieutenancy in the guards."

"Have you any other relations?" inquired the Countess Dubarry.

"I have a nephew."

"Well, we should find out something for your nephew," said the viscount.

"I think we may leave that in your hands, viscount," said the favorite, laughing, "as you have just given us proofs of so brilliant an imagination."

"Well," continued the viscount, apparently determined to bring matters to an issue, "if his majesty did all these things for you, would you think it tolerably well?"

"I should think him extremely generous, and should offer you, madame, all my thanks, convinced that it is to you alone I should be indebted for his generosity."

"Then," asked the favorite, "you really take our proposal seriously into consideration?"

"Yes, madame, most seriously," replied the old lady, turning pale at the very thought of the obligation to which she pledged herself.

"And you permit me to mention you to his majesty?"

"Pray do me that honor," replied she, with a deep sigh.

"Madame, I shall do so with the least possible delay—indeed, this every evening," said the favorite, rising to terminate the interview. "And in the meantime, I trust that I have secured your friendship."

"I feel so highly honored by yours, madame," said the old lady, beginning her courtesies again, "that I almost feel as if all this were a dream."

"Let us see, once more," said Jean, wishing to fix the matter so firmly in the old countess's mind, that it might be secure from all change. "One hundred thousand francs first, to make up for the loss of the suit, a lieutenancy for the young count, and something for a nephew."

"Something ?"

" I shall find out something good—that is my affair."

" And when shall I have the honor of seeing you again, madame ?" asked the old lady.

"To-morrow morning my carriage shall be at your door to take you to Luciennes—the king will be there. To-morrow, at ten o'clock, I shall have fulfilled my promise—his majesty will be informed, and will expect you."

"Allow me to accompany you, madame," said Jean, offering his arm.

" By no means, sir."

" Well, then, to the top of the stairs ?"

"Since you insist on it ; " and she took the viscount's arm.

"Zamore !" cried the countess.

Zamore appeared.

" Light this lady down-stairs, and order my brother's carriage forward to the door."

The two ladies exchanged a last courtesy. At the top of the staircase Jean bid the old countess adieu, and returned to his sister, while Mme. de Bearn majestically descended the grand staircase. Zamore marched first—then came two footmen with lights, and then the old lady, her train (rather a short one) borne by a third footman.

The brother and sister watched at the window, following with their eyes to the very carriage the precious chaperon sought with so much care and found with so much difficulty. Just as she reached the door a chaise entered the courtyard, and a young lady sprang out.

" Ah, Mistress Chon !" cried Zamore, opening his enormous mouth to its widest extent with delight. " How do you do this evening, Mistress Chon ?"

The Countess de Bearn stood petrified ! In the new arrival she recognized her visitor—the false daughter of Master Flageot. Dubarry hurriedly opened a window, and made frantic signs to his sister, but she did not see them.

"Has that little fool, Gilbert, been here?" inquired Chou of a lackey, without perceiving the countess.

"No, madame," replied one of the footmen; "we have not seen him."

It was just then that, looking up, she saw her brother, and following the direction of his hand, discovered Mme. de Bearn. Chon recognized her, hastily pulled down her hood, and rushed into the vestibule.

The old lady, without appearing to have remarked anything, got into the carriage, and gave her address to the coachman.

CHAPTER XXXII.

THE KING GETS TIRED.

THE king, who had gone to Marly, as he had said he would, ordered his carriage at three o'clock in the afternoon, and drove from that to Luciennes. He supposed that Mme. Dubarry, on receiving his note, would immediately leave Versailles, and hastened there to wait for him.

He was rather surprised, therefore, on entering the château, to find Zamore—looking very little like a governor—occupied in plucking out the feathers of a parrot, which, in return, was endeavoring to bite him.

The two favorites were rivals, like the Duke de Choiseul and the Countess Dubarry.

The king installed himself in the small saloon, and dismissed his attendants. Although the most inquisitive gentleman in his kingdom, he was not in the habit of questioning servants or lackeys; but Zamore was neither a servant nor lackey; he occupied a middle place between the monkey and the parrot. The king therefore questioned Zamore.

"Is the countess in the garden?"

"No, master." This word the favorite, in one of her whims, had ordered to take the place of majesty at Luciennes.

" Is she at the lake, feeding the carp ? "

This lake had been dug at a vast expense out of the side of the hill. It was fed with water from the aqueduct, and filled with great numbers of the finest carp, brought from Versailles.

" No, master," again answered Zamore.

" Where is she, then ? "

" In Paris, master."

" What ! Did the countess not come to Luciennes ? "

" No, master ; but she sent Zamore."

" What to do ? "

" To wait for the king."

" Ah, ha ! so you are delegated to receive me ? Very agreeable indeed ! Thank you, countess ! Thank you ! I am to have the society of Zamore ! " And he rose from his chair rather piqued.

" Oh, no, the king is not to have the society of Zamore," said the negro.

" Why not ? "

" Because Zamore is going away."

" Where are you going ? "

" To Paris."

" Then I am to be left alone ? Better and better. But why go to Paris ? "

" To find Mistress Dubarry and tell her the king is at Luciennes."

" Oh, the countess desired you to tell me that, then ? "

" Yes, master."

" And did she tell you what I was to do till she came ? "

" She said you were to sleep."

" Ah ! " said the king to himself, " she will not be long, and she has some surprise for me "—then he added, aloud : " Go, then, and bring back the countess. But how will you travel ? "

" On the great white horse with the scarlet housings."

" And how long does it take for the great white horse to go to Paris ? "

" I do not know," said the negro boy, " but he goes fast, fast, fast ! Zamore likes to go fast."

"Indeed ! I am extremely fortunate to find that Zamore likes to go fast."

And he stationed himself at the window to see Zamore depart.

A tall footman lifted him on the horse, and, with the happy ignorance of childhood, the little negro set off at a gallop on his gigantic steed.

The king, being left alone, asked the footman at last if there were anything new at Luciennes. The servant replied that there was only Monsieur Boucher, who was painting the countess's boudoir.

"Oh, Boucher, poor Boucher, is he here ?" said the king, with a slight appearance of satisfaction—"and where is he ? '

"In the summer-house. Shall I show your majesty the way to it ?"

"No, no; I should rather go and see the carps. Give me a knife."

"A knife, sire ?"

"Yes, and a large loaf."

The valet returned carrying a large loaf, with a long knife stuck in it, on a china plate. The king made a sign to the valet to accompany him, and with a pleased air led the way to the pond.

The feeding of carps was a traditional occupation in the Bourbon family, the Grand Monarque never missing it for a single day. Louis XV. seated himself on a mossy bank, from which the view before him was charming.

There lay the little lake, with its velvet slopes of turf ; beyond it a village nestled between two hills ; further off the towers of Saint Germain with their wooded terraces, and further still the blue declivities of Saunois and Cormeilles ; while above all this the gray and rose tinged sky hung like a magnificent cupola. The weather had been stormy, and the foliage of the trees looked dark and heavy against the pale green of the meadows ; the waters of the lake, glassy and immovable as a vast surface of oil, were disturbed from time to time by some silvery flashing fish springing up to seize the unwary fly, and checkering it with

wide-spreading circles of alternate black and white.   At
the margin might be perceived the enormous snouts of a
number of fish, which, fearless of hook or net, sucked the
leaves of pendant plants, and with their huge fixed eyes,
which seemed incapable of sight, stared at the gray lizard
and green frogs sporting among the bulrushes.

When the king, like a man profoundly skilled in the
art of killing time, had looked at the landscape on all
sides, when he had counted the houses in the village, and
the villages in the distance, he took the plate with the
loaf, placed it beside him, and began to cut off large pieces
of the bread.

The carps heard the sound of the knife in the crust,
and accustomed to that noise, which announced their
dinner-hour, they immediately flocked as close as possible
to the bank, to show themselves to his majesty and solicit
their daily meal.   They would have done the same for
any footman in his service, but the king naturally thought
that all this trouble was for him alone.

He threw in one after another the pieces of bread, which
first disappearing for an instant and then returning to the
surface, were contented for some time; then gradually
crumbling away by the action of the water, were seized
and seen no more.   It was, indeed, a curious and amusing enough sight to see all these crusts pushed hither and
thither by the invisible snouts, and tossed on the surface
of the water until the moment when they were swallowed.

At the end of about half an hour, his majesty having
in that time patiently cut one hundred bits of crust, had
the satisfaction of seeing that not one remained floating.
He began now, however, to feel rather tired of the sport,
and he remembered that M. Boucher might amuse him a
little ; he would certainly be as good a resource as the
carps, but in the country we must take what we can
get.

Louis therefore turned toward the summer-house.
Boucher had heard that he was at Luciennes, and though
he went on painting, or seeming to paint, he followed the
king with his eyes, saw him turn in the direction of the

summer-house, and radiant with joy, he adjusted his ruffles and mounted on his ladder, for he had been warned not to appear to know that the king was there. He heard a step on the floor of the room, and began to daub a fat Cupid stealing a rose from a shepherdess in a blue satin gown and straw hat. His hand trembled, his heart beat. The king stopped on the threshold.

"Ah, Boucher," cried he, "how you smell of turpentine!" and he walked on.

Poor Boucher, although he knew the king had no taste for the fine arts, did expect some other kind of compliment, and was nearly falling from his ladder. He came down and went away with the tears in his eyes, without scraping his palette or washing his brushes, which in general he was so careful to do.

His majesty pulled out his watch—it was seven o'clock.

Louis returned to the house, teased the monkey, made the parrot speak, pulled out the drawers of the cabinets, one after the other, and ransacked their contents.

Evening drew on. The king was not fond of darkness, and the apartments were lighted up. But he did not like solitude either.

"My horses in a quarter of an hour!" said he. "Ma foi!" added he, "I shall just give her one quarter of an hour—not a minute longer."

As he said this, he stretched himself on a sofa opposite the fireplace, to watch the course of the fifteen minutes— that is, of nine hundred seconds. At the four hundredth beat of the time-piece, which represented a blue elephant carrying a pink sultana, he was asleep.

As may be supposed, the footman who came to announce his majesty's carriage, took care not to awake him. The result of this attention of his august slumber was, that when he awoke of his own accord, he found himself face to face with the Countess Dubarry, who was looking at him with her eyes wide open. Zamore stood in a corner, waiting for orders.

"Ah! you are here at last, countess," said the king, sitting up on the sofa.

"Yes, sire, here I am," said the countess, "and here I have been a pretty long time."

"Oh, a pretty long time?"

"An hour and a half at least. But how your majesty does sleep!"

"Faith, countess, you were not here, and I was getting shockingly tired—and then I sleep so badly at night. Do you know I was on the point of going away!"

"Yes, I saw your majesty's carriage at the door."

The king looked at his watch.

"Half-past ten—then I have slept nearly three hours!"

"After that, sire, say that you cannot sleep well at Luciennes."

"Oh, faith, very well—but what the devil do I see there?" said he, looking at Zamore.

"You see the governor of Luciennes, sire."

"Not yet, not yet," said the king, laughing. "The little wretch has put on his uniform before having been appointed—he reckons on my word, then?"

"Sire, your word is sacred, and he is right in reckoning on it. But Zamore has something more than your word, or rather something less—he has his commission; the vice-chancellor sent it to me. The oath is now the only formality which is wanting—make him swear quickly, and then betake himself to his post."

"Approach, governor," said the king.

Zamore came forward. He was dressed in a uniform, with an embroidered collar and a captain's epaulets, with short breeches, silk stockings, and a sword like a spit. He walked with a stiff, measured step, an enormous three-cornered hat under his arm.

"Can he swear?" asked the king.

"Oh, yes, sire—try him."

"Advance," cried he, looking curiously at the black puppet.

"On your knees," said the countess.

"Swear!" said the king.

The child placed one hand on his heart, the other in the king's hand, and said: "I swear fealty and homage to my master and mistress—I swear to defend to the death the castle in my keeping, and to eat the last pot of sweet-meats, rather than surrender, should I be attacked."

The king laughed, as much at the form of the oath as at the gravity with which Zamore pronounced it.

"In return for this oath," he replied, with suitable gravity, "I confer on you the sovereign rights of justice on high and low, on all inhabiting air, earth, fire and water, in this castle."

"Thank you, master," said Zamore, rising.

"And now," said the king, "go and show off your fine clothes in the kitchen, and leave us alone—go!"

As Zamore went out at one door, Chon entered by another.

"Ah, and you there, too, my little Chon! Come, I shall hear the truth from you."

"Take care, sire, that you are not disappointed in your expectations!" said Chon; "the truth is, it would be for the first time in my life. If you wish to learn the truth, apply to my sister—she is incapable of speaking falsely."

"Is that true, countess?"

"Sire, Chon has too flattering an opinion of me—bad example has ruined me—and from this evening forth I am determined to lie like a real countess, if the truth will not serve me."

"Oh, ho!" said the king; "I suspect Chon has something to conceal from me. I must get from the police a report of what has occurred to-day."

"From the police, sire—Sartines' or mine?"

"Oh, from Sartines'."

"What will you pay him for it?"

"If he tell me anything worth hearing, I shall not be niggardly."

"Well, then, give my police the preference, and take my report. I shall serve you royally."

"You will even sell your own secrets?"

"Why not, if I am well paid?"

"Come, then, let me hear the report—but no fibs, remember!"

" Sire, you insult me."

" I mean no equivocations."

" Well, sire, get your funds ready—I am about to begin my report."

" They are ready," said the king, jingling some money in his pocket.

" In the first place, the Countess Dubarry was seen in Paris, in the Rue de Valois, about two o'clock in the afternoon."

" Well, I know that—go on !"

" About six o'clock Zamore proceeded to join her there."

" Very possibly ; but what did Madame Dubarry go to Paris for ? "

" Sire, to meet the lady who is to present her."

" Pooh," said the king, with a grimace which he could not altogether conceal, " she is very well as she is, without being presented."

" You know the proverb, sire : nothing is so dear to us as that which we have not."

" So she is absolutely determined to find this lady to present her ? "

" We have found her, sire."

The king started, and shrugged his shoulders.

" I like that movement, sire ; it shows that your majesty would be annoyed at the defeat of the Grammonts, the Guemenees, and all the hypocrites of the court," said the countess.

" I beg your pardon ; did you speak ? "

" Yes—I am sure you are in league with those persons."

" In league ? Countess, learn one thing, that the king only leagues with kings."

" True—but all your kings are friends of the Duke de Choiseul."

" Let us return to your chaperon, countess."

" With all my heart, sire."

" You have succeeded in manufacturing a lady, then ? "

" I found one ready made, and very well made—a Countess de Bearn—a family who have numbered princes among their ranks. She will not dishonor the relative of the relatives of the Stuarts, I hope."

"The Countess de Bearn!" exclaimed the king, with surprise. "I know only of one, who lives somewhere near Verdun."

"It is the very same—she has come to Paris on purpose to present me."

"Ha! And when is the affair to take place?"

"To-morrow, at eleven o'clock in the morning, I am to give her a private audience, and at the same time, if it be not too presumptuous, she will request the king to name a day—and you will name the earliest—will you not, dear France?"

The king burst into a forced laugh.

"Certainly, certainly," said he, kissing the countess's hand. Then all at once—"To-morrow, at eleven," added he.

"Yes—at breakfast."

"Impossible, my dear countess."

"Impossible! why?"

"I shall not breakfast here; I must return this evening."

"What!" said the countess, who felt an icy pang shoot through her heart at these words; "you are going to leave us, sire?"

"I am forced to do so, dear countess—I have to meet Sartines on very important business."

"As you please, sire; but you will at least sup here, I hope?"

"Oh, yes—I shall sup, I think—yes, I am rather hungry —I shall sup."

"Order supper, Chon," said the countess, making at the same time a private signal to her, which no doubt referred to some previous arrangements. Chon left the room. The king had seen the signal in a mirror, and although he could not comprehend its meaning, he suspected some snare.

"Ah," said he, "on second thoughts, I think it will be impossible to stay even for supper. I must not lose a moment; I have some papers to sign; to-day is Saturday."

"As you please, sire ; shall I order the horses ? "

"Yes, fairest."

"Chon !"

Chon reappeared.

"His majesty's horses," said the countess.

"Very well," said Chon with a smile, and she left the room again.

A moment afterward her voice was heard in the anteroom ordering the king's carriage.

CHAPTER XXXIII.

THE KING IS AMUSED.

THE king, delighted at this exercise of his authority, which punished the countess for leaving him alone so long, at the same time that it freed him from the trouble of settling the affair of her presentation, walked toward the door of the saloon.

Chon entered.

" Well, are my attendants there ? "

" No, sire ; there is not one of them in the anteroom."

The king advanced into the anteroom himself.   " My attendants !" cried he.   No one answered ; there seemed not to be even an echo in the silent château.

" Who the deuce would believe," said the king, returning to the saloon, "that I am the grandson of the man who once said, 'I was very nearly having to wait !'" and he wentto the window, opened it, and looked out.

The space in front of the château was as deserted as the anterooms—no horses, no attendants, no guards.   Night alone displayed to the eyes and to the soul all its calmness and all its majesty.   The lovely moon shone brightly on the woods of Chatou, whose lofty summits rustled gently, like the waves of the sea rippled by the breeze.   The Seine, on whoseb osom glittered a long line of light, looked like a gigantic serpent trailing its slow length along, its windings being visible from Bougival to Maisons—that is, for four or five leagues ; and then, in the midst of this heavenly scene, a nightingale burst forth with such a sweet and varied song as she only gives in the month of May, as if she felt that nature was worthy of her music in the early days of spring alone—days which are scarcely come ere they are gone.

All this beauty and harmony were lost on Louis XV.— a king not much of a dreamer, a poet, or an artist, but, on the contrary, a good deal of a sensualist.

" Come, countess," said he, considerably annoyed, " give the necessary order, I entreat—what the deuce !—this jest must have an end."

" Sire," replied the countess, with that charming pouting air which became her so well, " I do not command here."

" Nor do I," replied the king, " for you see how I am obeyed."

" It is neither you nor I who command."

" Who is it, then ? Is it you, Chon ? "

" I ? " said the young lady, who was seated on a couch on the other side of the apartment exactly opposite the countess, who occupied a similar one on the near side—" I find the task of obeying so difficult, that I have no inclination for that of commanding."

" But who is the master, then ? "

" The governor, sire, certainly."

" Monsieur Zamore ? "

" Yes."

" Ah, very true ! Well, let some one ring for him."

The countess stretched out her arm with a most graceful air of nonchalance to a silken cord ending in a tassel of beads. A footman, who had no doubt received his lesson beforehand, was ready in the anteroom and appeared.

" The governor," said the king.

" The governor," replied the valet, respectfully, " is on guard, watching over his majesty's precious life."

" Where is he? "

" Going his rounds, sir."

" Going his rounds ? " repeated the king.

" Yes, with four officers, sire."

The king could not help smiling.

" That is droll enough," said he ; " but it need not prevent my horses from being harnessed immediately."

" Sire, the governor ordered the stables to be closed, lest some marauder might enter them."

" And where are my grooms ? "

" Gone to bed, sire."

" Gone to bed—by whose orders ? "

" The governor's, sire."

" And the gates of the castle ? "

" Are locked, sire."

" Very well—then you mus get the keys."

" The governor has them at his belt, sire."

" A well-guarded castle, indeed !   Peste ! what order is kept."

The footman, seeing that the king ceased to question him, retired. The countess, reclining gracefully on a couch, continued to bite off the leaves of a beautiful rose, beside which her lips seemed like coral. " Come, sire," said she at length, with a fascinating smile, " I must take compassion on your majesty—give me your arm and let us set out in search of some one to help you—Chon, light the way."

Chon went before, ready to apprise them of any danger which they might encounter. At the very first turn in the corridor the king's nose was saluted by an odor quite sufficient to awaken the appetite of the most fastidious epicure.

" Ha ! ha ! what is that, countess ? " said he stopping.

" Oh, only supper, sire !   I thought your majesty intended doing me the honor of supping at Luciennes, and I made arrangements accordingly."

The king inhaled the gastronomic perfume two or three times, while he called to mind that his stomach had already given him certain tokens of its existence ; then he thought what a fuss there must be before his grooms could be awakened, that would take half an hour at least, a quarter more to harness the horses, ten minutes to reach Marly, and when at Marly, where he was not expected, he could get only a put-off of a supper. All these things passed through his mind as he stood at the dining-room door, inhaling the seductive steam of the viands. Two covers were placed on the table, which was splendidly lighted and sumptuously laid out.

"Peste!" said Louis, "you have a good cook, countess."

"Oh, sire, this is merely his first effort; the poor devil has been doing wonders to deserve your majesty's approbation. Indeed, he is so sensitive, that he might perhaps, in his disappointment, cut his throat, as poor Vatel did."

"Really—do you think so?"

"There was to be an omelet of pheasants' eggs on which he especially prided himself."

"An omelet of pheasants' eggs—I adore omelets of pheasants' eggs!"

"What a pity you must go."

"Well, countess, we must not vex your cook," said the king, laughing; "and, perhaps, while we are supping, Master Zamore may return from his rounds."

"Ah! sire, a capital idea," said the countess, unable to conceal her delight at having gained this first step. "Come, sire, come!"

"But who will wait on us?" said the king, looking round in vain for an attendant.

"Ah! sire," said Mme. Dubarry, "is your coffee less grateful when presented to you by me?"

"No, countess; and still more when you make it for me."

"Well, come, then, sire."

"Two covers only! Has Chon supped, then?"

"Sire, I did not venture without your majesty's express command——"

"Come, come," said the king, taking a plate and cover from a sideboard himself, "come, my little Chon; sit there opposite us."

"Oh, sire!" said Chon.

"Yes, yes; play the very humble and very obedient subject, you little hypocrite. Sit here, countess, near me —beside me. What a beautiful profile you have!"

"Is this the first time you have observed it, dear France?"

"How should I observe it when I am so happy in looking at your full countenance? Decidedly, countess, your cook is first-rate. What soup!"

"Then I was right in sending away the other?"

"Quite right—quite right."

"Sire, follow my example—you see it will be to your advantage."

"I do not understand you."

"I have turned off my Choiseul—turn off yours."

"Countess, no politics. Give me some Madeira."

The king held out his glass; the countess took up a decanter to help him, and as she raised it up, her white fingers and rosy nails were seen to advantage.

"Pour gently and slowly," said the king.

"Not to shake the wine, sire?"

"No; to give me more time to admire your hand."

"Assuredly, sire," said the countess, laughing, "your majesty is in the vein of making discoveries."

"Faith, yes," said the king, now in perfect good humor again; "and think I am in the fair way of discovering——"

"A new world?"

"No; I am not so ambitious; besides, I find a kingdom as much as I can manage. No, only an isle—a little nook —an enchanted mountain—a palace of which a certain fair lady will be the Armida, and the entrance to which will be defended by all kinds of monsters."

"Sire," said the countess, presenting the king with a glass of iced champagne, a luxury quite new at that period, "here is some water just drawn from the river Lethe."

"The river Lethe, countess, are you sure?"

"Yes, sire; it was poor Jean who brought it from the shades below, from which you know he has just narrowly escaped."

"Countess, I drink to his happy resurrection. But no politics, I beg."

"Then I don't know what to talk about, sire. If you

would relate something—you who have such a happy gift of telling a story."

"No—but I shall repeat you some verses."

"Verses?"

"Yes, verses. Is there anything surprising in that word?"

"I thought your majesty detested them?"

"Parbleu! out of each hundred thousand manufactured, ninety thousand are against myself."

"And these which your majesty is going to give me, belong to the ten thousand which cannot even make you look favorably on the ninety thousand."

"No, countess—these are addressed to you."

"To me? By whom?"

"By Monsieur de Voltaire."

"He charged your majesty to deliver them?"

"Not at all; he sent them direct to your highness."

"How?—without a cover?"

"No; inclosed in a charming letter."

"Ah, I understand; your majesty has been at work this morning with the postmaster. But read the verses, sire; read Monsieur de Voltaire's verses."

Louis XV. opened the paper, and read:

" ' Goddess of pleasure, soft queen of the graces,
    Why blend with the fêtes which make Paphos to ring,
Foul threat'ning suspicions and hideous disgraces—
    The fate of a hero, oh! why should'st thou bring?
Still our dear Ulysses his country shall hold,
    The State's mighty bulwark—the monarch's delight,
None wiser in council, in battle more bold,
    And Illion can tell how restless his might!
Fair Venus, thy throne all the gods shall surround,
    Thy beauty celestial all tongues shall declare,
The roses of joy in thy path shall abound—
    Then calm the rough waters and smile on our prayer,
Ah! why should thy anger burn fiercely and high
    'Gainst the hero whom foemen still tremble to meet,
For how can he draw from such beauty a sigh,
    Save in breathing his vows as he kneels at her feet?' "

"Decidedly, sire," said the countess, more piqued than

gratified by this poetical offering. "Monsieur de Voltaire wishes to recommend himself to your favor."

"He loses his pains, then," said the king. "He is a firebrand who would burn Paris if he returned to it. Let him stay with his friend, my cousin, Frederick II. ; we can do very well with Monsieur Rousseau. But take the verses, countess, and study them."

She took the paper, made a match of it, and laid it beside her.

"Some tokay, sire," said Chon.

"From the vaults which supply his majesty, the Emperor of Austria," said the countess.

"From the emperor's vaults?" said the king. "Pardieu! no one is supplied from them but myself."

"Very true, sire," said the countess ; "so I had it from your butler."

"Ah!" said the king, "and you have seduced——"

"No, sire, I have ordered."

"Well answered, countess ; I was a fool."

"Will the king take coffee?" asked Chon.

"Oh, certainly."

"And will his majesty burn it, as usual?" asked the countess.

"If the lady of the castle permit." The countess rose. "But what are you doing?"

"I am going to wait on you myself."

"Well," said the king, leaning back in his chair like a man who had made an excellent supper, and whose humors were, therefore, in a happy state of equilibrium—"well, I see that my best plan is to let you do as you like, countess."

The countess brought a silver stand, with a little coffee-pot containing the boiling mocha ; she then placed before the king a plate on which was a silver cup and a caraffe of Bohemian glass, and beside the plate she laid the match which she had just folded.

The king, with that profound attention which he always bestowed on this operation, calculated his sugar, measured his coffee, and, having gently poured on it the brandy, so that it swam on the surface, he took the little roll of paper, lighted it at a candle, and communicated the flame to the liquor. Five minutes afterward he enjoyed his coffee with all the delight of a finished epicure.

The countess looked on till he had finished the last drop ; then she exclaimed :

" Oh, sire, you have burned your coffee with Monsieur de Voltaire's verses ! That is a bad omen for the Choiseuls."

" I was wrong," said he, laughing ; " you are not a fairy ; you are a demon."

The countess rose.

" Does your majesty wish to know whether the governor has returned ?"

" Zamore ? Bah ! for what purpose ?"

" To allow you to go to Marly, sire."

" True," said the king, making a great effort to rouse himself from that state of comfort in which he found himself. " Well, countess, let us see—let us see !"

The countess made a sign to Chon, who vanished.

The king began his search for Zamore again ; but, it must be confessed, with very different feelings from those which had before influenced him. Philosophers say that we behold things either dark or bright, according to the state of our stomachs, and, as kings have stomachs like other men—in general, indeed, not so good as other men, but still communicating the sensation of comfort or discomfort to the rest of the body in the same manner—our king appeared in the most charming humor which it was possible for a king to be in ; and his search ended without his discovering Zamore, and without his being displeased at his want of success.

CHAPTER XXXIV.

VOLTAIRE AND ROUSSEAU.

AT ten o'clock the next morning, the king, though he had supped so well, began to think of breakfast ; but, going to a window, he saw his carriage and all his attendants ready for his departure. Zamore, with folded arms, was giving, or pretending to give, orders.

"What is this, countess ?" said he ; "are we not to breakfast ? One would think you were going to send me away fasting !"

"Heaven forbid, sire ! but I thought your majesty had to meet Monsieur de Sartines at Marly."

"Pardieu !" said the king, "could not Sartines be told to come here ?—it is so near !"

"Your majesty will do me the honor to believe that that idea occurred to me before your majesty."

"And, besides, the morning is too fine for work ; let us breakfast."

"Your majesty must give me a few signatures for myself."

"For the Countess de Bearn ?"

"Yes ; and then name the day and the hour."

"What day and hour ?"

"The day and hour for my presentation."

"Ma foi !" said the king, "it must be so, I suppose ; fix the day yourself."

"Sire, the sooner the better."

"Is all ready ?"

"Yes."

"You have learned to make your three courtesies ?"

"I have practised them for more than a year."

"You have your dress ?"

"In twenty-four hours it will be ready."

"And you have your chaperon ?"

"In an hour she will be here."

" And now, countess, for a bargain ! "

" What is it ? "

" That you will never again speak of that affair of the Viscount Jean with the Baron de Taverney."

" Must I sacrifice the poor viscount ? "

" Yes, faith ! "

" Well, sire, I shall speak no more of it. The day ? "

" The day after to-morrow."

" The hour ? "

" Half-past ten at night, as usual."

" It is settled ? "

" It is settled."

" On your royal word ? "

" On the word of a gentleman."

" Give me your hand on it, France ! " and Mme. Dubarry held out her pretty little hand, in which the king placed his own.

This morning all Luciennes felt the gaiety of its master. He had yielded on one point on which he had long before determined to yield ; but then he had gained another. This was certainly a decided advantage. He would give one hundred thousand crowns to Jean on condition that he went to drink the waters of the Pyrenees, in Auvergne ; that would pass for banishment in the eyes of the Choiseul party. There were louis-d'ors that morning for the poor, cakes for the carps, and praises for Boucher's paintings.

Eleven o'clock struck. The countess, although attending assiduously to the king, at his breakfast, could not help looking, from time to time at the clock, which moved too slowly for her wishes. His majesty had taken the trouble to say, that when the Countess de Bearn arrived, she was to be shown into the breakfast-room. The coffee was served, tasted, drunk, still she came not. Suddenly the tramping of a horse's feet was heard. The countess ran to a window. It was a messenger from the viscount, who leaped from his horse reeking with foam. At sight of him she felt a chill run through her veins, for she knew all could not be right ; but it was necessary to

hide her uneasiness in order to keep the king in good
humor.   She returned to his side and sat down.

A moment afterward, Chon entered with a note in her
hands.   There was no means of escape ; it must be read
before the king.

" What is that, sweet Chon ? " said the king—" a love
letter ? "

" Oh, certainly, sire."

" From whom ? "

" From the poor viscount."

" Are you quite certain ? "

" Look at it, sire."

The king recognized the writing, and thinking the note
might contain something about the Lachaussée affair,
" Very well," said he, pushing it aside, " very well—that
is enough."

The countess was on thorns.

" Is the note for me ? " she asked.

" Yes, countess."

" Will your majesty permit me——'

" Oh, yes—read it—read it ; and in the meantime, Chon
will repeat ' Maitre Corbeau ' to me."   So saying, he pulled
her on his knee, and began to sing ; sadly out of tune,
indeed—for Rousseau has recorded that Louis had the
worst ear in his kingdom.

The countess retired into the recess of a window, and
read the following epistle :

" Do not expect the old wretch ; she pretends that she
scalded her foot yesterday, and is obliged to keep her
room.   You may thank Chon's most opportune arrival
yesterday for this.   The old wretch recognized her immediately, and so put an end to our little comedy.

" It was fortunate that that little wretch, Gilbert, who
is the cause of this misfortune, was lost.   I would have
wrung his neck about !   However, he may be assured it is
in store for him, if ever he cross my path.

" But to return to the point—come to Paris at once, or
we are lost.   JEAN."

" What is the matter ? " inquired the king, surprised at the sudden paleness which overspread the countess's face.

" Nothing, sire ; it is only a bulletin of Jean's health."

" Does not the dear viscount get better, then ? "

"Oh, yes, thank you, sire, much better," said the countess. "But I hear a carriage enter the courtyard."

" Oh, our old countess, I suppose ! "

" No, sire ; it is Monsieur de Sartines."

" Well, what then ? " exclaimed the king, seeing that Mme. Dubarry was moving toward the door.

" Well, sire, I shall leave you with him, and go to dress."

" And what about the Countess de Bearn ? "

" When she comes, sire, I shall let your majesty know," replied the countess, crumpling the viscount's note in the pocket of her dressing-gown.

"Then you abandon me ?" said the king, with a melancholy air.

"Sire, remember this is Sunday ; you have papers to sign." So saying, she presented her fresh and rosy cheeks to the king, who kissed them, and she left the room.

" Devil take all signatures," said the king, " and those who bring them ! Who was it that invented ministers and portfolios ? "

He had scarcely finished this malediction, when the minister and the portfolio entered by a door opposite that by which the countess had departed. The king sighed again more deeply than before.

" Ah ! are you there, Sartines ? " said he. " How very punctual you are."

This was said in a tone which left it very doubtful whether the words were intended as a eulogium or a reproach.

The minister opened his portfolio, and busied himself in taking out and arranging his papers. Just then the sound of the wheels of a carriage was heard grating on the sand of the avenue.

"Wait a little, Sartines," said the king, and he ran to the window.

" What ! " said he. " the countess is driving off ? "

"It is she indeed, sire," said the minister.

"But is she not going to wait for the Countess de Bearn?"

"Sire, I am inclined to think she is tired of waiting, and goes to find her."

"Yet the old lady had decided on coming this morning."

"Sire, I am almost certain that she will not come."

"Then you know something about the matter, Sartines?"

"Sire, I am obliged to know a little about everything, otherwise your majesty would be dissatisfied with me."

"Well, what has happened? Tell me, Sartines."

"To the old countess, sire?"

"Yes."

"A very common case, sire—difficulties have arisen."

"Then the Countess de Bearn really will not come?"

"Hum! there was rather more certainty of it yesterday evening than there is this morning."

"Poor countess!" said the king, unable, in spite of himself, to conceal a gleam of satisfaction which sparkled in his eyes.

"Ah, sire, the quadruple alliance and the family compact were trifles, in comparison with this presentation!"

"Poor countess!" repeated the king, shaking his head, "she will never accomplish her purpose."

"I fear it, sire, unless your majesty concerns yourself about it."

"She was so certain that now all was in the right train."

"And what makes the matter worse for the countess," said M. de Sartines, "is, that if she be not presented before the arrival of the dauphiness, it is probable she never will be presented at all."

"More than probable! Sartines, you are right. They say that my daughter-in-law is very strict, very devout, very prudish. Poor countess!"

"It will certainly annoy her very much, sire, if she be not presented; but, on the other hand, it will relieve your majesty from many annoyances."

"Do you think so, Sartines?"

"Oh, yes, sire! The envious, the libelers, the ballad-mongers, the flatterers, the journalists, will not have so much to say. If she was presented, sire, it would cost us at least one hundred thousand francs additional for the police."

"Indeed—poor countess! and yet she wishes so much to be presented."

"Your majesty knows you have only to command, and her wishes will be gratified."

"What do you mean, Sartines? Do you imagine that I could meddle in such an affair? Can I by signing an order make people polite to Madame Dubarry? Is it you, Sartines, a man of sense, who advise such an innovation to satisfy the whims of the countess?"

"Oh, by no means, sire! I merely say as your majesty says, poor countess!"

"Besides," said the king, "her position is not so desperate, after all. You always look at things on the dark side, Sartines. Who can tell whether the Countess de Bearn may not change her mind? Who can be certain that the dauphiness will arrive so soon? It will take four days yet before she can reach Compiegne, and in four days much may be done. Let me see. Have you anything for me to do this morning, Sartines?"

"Oh, your majesty, only three papers to sign;" and the minister of police drew out the first from his portfolio.

"Oh!" said the king, "a lettre-de-cachet."

"Yes, sire."

"And against whom?"

"Your majesty may see."

"Oh! against the Sieur Rousseau? What Rousseau is that, Sartines, and what has he done?"

"Done, sire?—written 'Le Contrat Social.'"

"Oh, then, it is Jean Jacques whom you wish to shut up in the Bastile?"

"Sire, he disturbs the public peace."

"And what the deuce did you expect he would do?"

"Besides, I don't propose to shut him up.

"Of what use is this letter, then ?"

"Sire, merely to have a weapon ready."

"Not that I am at all fond of your philosophers, mark ye."

"Your majesty has good cause not to love them."

"But people will exclaim against us. Besides, I think we authorized him to come to Paris."

"No, sire ; we said we should tolerate him on condition that he did not appear in public."

"And does he appear in public ?"

"He is always to be seen."

"In his Armenian dress ?"

"Oh, no, sire. We ordered him to lay it aside."

"And he obeyed ?"

"Yes, but complaining loudly all the time of our persecution."

"And how does he dress now ?"

"Oh, like other people, sire."

"Then he cannot be so much remarked ?"

"What, sire ! a man who has been forbidden to appear in public not remarked ! And then, only guess where he goes every day !"

"To the Marshal de Luxembourg's, to Monsieur d'Alembert's, to Madame d'Epinay's ?"

"To the Café de la Regence, sire ! He plays chess there every evening. He must be mad upon that point, for he always loses ; and it requires every evening a company of soldiers to keep order among the crowds around the house."

"Well," said the king, "the Parisians are even greater fools than I thought them. Let them go on amusing themselves in that way, Sartines ; while they do so they will not shout starvation !"

"But, sire, if some fine day he should take it into his head to make a speech as he did in London ?"

"Oh ! in that case, as there would be criminality and public infringement of the laws, you would not require a lettre-de-cachet, Sartines."

The minister saw that the king did not wish the arrest of Rousseau to rest on the royal responsibility, so he did not press the matter further.

"But, sire," said he, "there is another philosopher."

"Another!" replied the king, languidly; "shall we never have done with them?"

"Ah, sire, it is they who have never done with us!"

"And who is this one?"

"Monsieur de Voltaire."

"Has he also returned to France?"

"No, sire; it would be much better, perhaps, that he had, for then we could watch him."

"What has he been doing?"

"It is not he who has been doing anything, it is his partisans; they are actually going to have a statue erected in his honor!"

"Equestrian, I suppose?"

"No, sire; and yet I assure you he is a famous captor of towns!"

The king shrugged his shoulders.

"Sire, there has not been seen such a one since Poliorcetes,' continued Sartines. "He obtains information from all quarters; his writings reach all quarters; the highest persons in your kingdom turn smugglers for the sake of his books. I seized, the other day, eight boxes full of them; two were addressed to the Duke de Choiseul."

"It is very amusing!"

"Sire, only reflect that they are now doing for him what is only done for kings—they are decreeing him a statue."

"Sartines, statues are not decreed by others for kings, they decree them to themselves. And who is to make this fine work of art?"

"The sculptor Pigale. He has set out for Ferney to execute the model. In the meantime, subscriptions are pouring in; and observe, sire, it is only authors who are permitted to subscribe. All come with their offerings, they make quite a procession every day. Even Rousseau brought his two louis-d'ors."

" Well," said the king, "' what can I do in the matter ? I am not an author ; it does not concern me."

"Sire, I thought of proposing to your majesty to put an end, by royal command, to this demonstration."

"I shall take good care not to do any such thing, Sartines. Instead of decreeing him a bronze statue, they would then decree him one of gold. Let them alone. Mon Dieu ! he will look even uglier in bronze than in flesh and blood !"

" Then your majesty desires that the matter should take its own course ? "

" Let us understand each other, Sartines. Desire is not the word. I should be very glad to put an end to these things, certainly ; but how can I ? it is impossible. The time is past when royalty could say to the spirit of philosophy, as God says to the ocean, ' Thus far shalt thou go, and no further !' To blame loudly but uselessly, to aim a blow, but strike short of our aim, that would only serve to show our own weakness. Let us turn away our eyes, Sartines, and pretend not to see."

" The minister sighed.

" At least, sire," said he, " if we do not punish the men, let us suppress their works. Here is a list of books, which, in my opinion, should instantly be proscribed, some attack the throne, some the altar ; some teach rebellion, others sacrilege."

The king took the list, and read in a languid voice :

"The Sacred Contagion ; or, the Natural History of Superstition."

"The System of Nature ; or, Laws of the Physical and Moral World."

"Instructions of the Capuchin at Ragusa, to Brother Pediculoso, on His Setting Out for the Holy Land."

He had not read one fourth of the list, when he let it fall, while an expression of sadness and dejection overspread his usually unmoved countenance. He remained thoughtful, and for some minutes seemed quite overcome.

" Sartines," said he at last, " one might as well undertake to move the world. Let others try it."

The minister looked at him with that perfect understanding of his wishes, which the king loved in those who approached him, as it saved him the trouble of thinking and acting.

"A tranquil life, sire," said he—"a tranquil life—is not that what your majesty wishes?"

The king nodded.

"Oh, yes!" said he. "I ask for nothing else from your philosophers, encyclopedists, thaumaturgi, illuminati, poets, economists, journalists—tribes that come one knows not whence, that are always bustling, writing, croaking, calumniating, calculating, preaching, complaining. Let them be crowned; let statues be raised to them; let temples be built to them, but let them leave me in peace."

Sartines arose, bowed, and left the apartment, muttering as he went, "It is fortunate we have on our money—*Domine salvum fac regem.*"

Then the king, now left to himself, took a pen, and wrote to the dauphin the following lines:

"You have requested me to hasten the arrival of her royal highness the dauphiness, and I wish to gratify you.

"I have ordered that there shall be no stay made at Noyon—consequently, on Tuesday morning she will be at Compiegne.

"I shall be there myself precisely at ten o'clock—that is to say, a quarter of an hour before her."

"Thus," said he to himself, "I shall get rid of that foolish affair of the presentation, which annoys me more than Voltaire and Rousseau, and all the philosophers, past, present, and to come. The affair will then be between the poor countess, the dauphin, and the dauphiness. Ma foi! it is only fair that young maids, with strength for it, should contend with these vexations, hatreds, and revenges. Children should early learn to suffer—it is an excellent part of education."

Delighted at having thus got rid of the difficulty, and certain that he would not be reproached with either favoring or hindering this presentation, about which all Paris was occupied, the king entered his carriage, and drove off to Marly, where the court was waiting for him.

CHAPTER XXXV.

CHAPERON AND DEBUTANTE.

THE poor countess !—let us continue to apply the epithet which the king had given her, for at this moment she truly deserved it—the poor countess hurried, like one in despair, to Paris. Chon, terrified by Jean's paragraph concerning Gilbert, shut herself up in the boudoir at Luciennes to hide her grief and anxiety, lamenting the fatal whim which induced her to pick up Gilbert on the highroad.

Having reached the outskirts of Paris, the countess found a coach awaiting her. In the coach were Viscount Jean and a lawyer, with whom he seemed to be arguing in the most energetic manner. The moment he perceived the countess he leaped out, and made a sign to his sister's coachman to stop.

"Quick, countess !" said he. "Quick, get into my carriage, and drive to the Rue St. Germain des Pres !"

"Is the old lady going to give us the slip ?" said Mme. Dubarry, changing carriages, while the lawyer, on a sign from the viscount, followed her example.

"I fear it, countess," replied Jean—"I fear she is giving us a Roland for our Oliver."

"But what has happened ?"

"You shall hear. I stayed in Paris because I am always suspicious, and in this case I was not wrong, as you will see. At nine last night I went prowling about the inn of the Coq Chantant. All quiet—no movement—no visitors ; all looked well. Consequently, I thought I might go home to bed, and to bed I went. This morning I awoke at break of day. I roused Patrice, and ordered him to go and keep watch at the corner of the street. Well, at nine—observe, that was an hour sooner than I had appointed—I drove up to the hotel. Patrice had seen nothing to cause the least anxiety, so I boldly walked upstairs. At the door of the countess's room a maid-servant stopped me, and told me that the countess could not leave the house to-day, and perhaps it would be eight days before she could move from her apartment. I confess that, although prepared for some rebuff, I was not for that! 'What,' cried I, 'she cannot go out! What is the matter?' 'She is ill.' 'Ill? Impossible! Yesterday she was perfectly well.' 'Yes, sir, but madame likes to make her own chocolate; and this morning, when it was boiling, she spilled it over her foot, and she is scalded. On hearing the countess's cries I hastened in, and I found her nearly, fainting. I carried her to bed, and I think she is at present asleep. I was as white as your lace, countess, and could not help crying out, 'It is a lie!' 'No, my dear Viscount Dubarry,' replied a sharp voice, which seemed to pierce the very wall, 'it is not a lie! I am in horrible pain.' I sprung to the side whence the voice came, and burst through a glass door which I could not open—the old countess was really in bed. 'Ah, madame!' I exclaimed—but it was all I could utter, I was in such a rage! I could have strangled her with pleasure. 'Look there,' said she, pointing to an old kettle which was lying on the floor, 'there is the coffee-pot that did all the mischief.' I flew to the coffee-pot, and stamped on it with both feet; it will make no more chocolate, I can answer for it. 'What a misfortune!' cried the old lady, piteously; 'it must be the Baroness d'Alogny who will present your sister. But what can we do? It was so written, as the Easterns say.' "

"Heavens! Jean, you drive me to despair!" exclaimed the countess.

"Oh! I do not despair yet, if you go to her; it was for that that I sent for you."

"But why do you not despair?"

"Why! because you are a woman, and can do what I cannot; you can make the dressing be taken off; and, if you discover that it is an imposture, you can tell her that her son shall never be anything but a clown—that she shall never touch a farthing from the estate of the Saluces —in short, you can play off the imprecations of Camilla on her much better than I the fury of Orestes."

" Is this all a jest ?" cried the countess.

" No, I assure you."

" And where does our sybil lodge ? "

" At the Coq Chantant, Rue St. Germain des Pres, a great black house, with a monstrous cock painted on an iron plate ; when the iron creaks, the cock crows."

" I shall have a dreadful scene with her."

" No doubt of it ; but you must take your chance. Shall I go with you ? "

" No, you would spoil all."

" Just what our lawyer said ; I was consulting him on that point when you drove up. For your information, I may tell you, that he says to beat a person in his own house renders you liable to fine and imprisonment, while to beat him out of it——"

" Is nothing !" said the countess. " You know that better than any one else."

Jean grinned an ugly smile.

" Debts," said he, " that are long in being paid, are paid with interest ; and if ever I meet my man again——"

" I would much rather, at present, speak of my woman."

" I have nothing more to tell you, so be off."

" But where will you wait for me ? "

" In the inn itself. I shall ask for a bottle of wine, and be there, in case you want a helping hand."

" Drive on, coachman," cried the countess.

" Rue St. Germain des Pres, at the sign of the Coq Chantant," added the viscount.

In a quarter of an hour they were in the street honored by possessing the Coq Chantant. At some distance from the inn Mme. Dubarry left her carriage and proceeded on foot. She feared that the noise of the wheels might put the old lady on the alert, that she might suspect what visitor was coming, and might have time to hide.

Alone, then, she entered the gaping porch of the inn. No one saw her until she was at the foot of the staircase; there she encountered the hostess.

"The Countess de Bearn?" said she.

"She is very ill, madame, and cannot see any one."

"Yes, I am aware; and I came to know exactly how she is."

And light as a bird, she was at the top of the stairs in a moment.

"Madame, madame!" cried the hostess, "a lady is going to force her way into your room."

"Who is she?" asked the old lady, from a distant part of the room.

"I," said the favorite, appearing on the threshold with a face perfectly suited to the occasion, for she first smiled out of compliment, and then looked sad, by way of condolence.

"You here, madame?" exclaimed the old lady, turning pale.

"Yes, dear madame, I came to express my sympathy for your misfortune, of which I have just heard. Pray, tell me how this accident happened."

"But, madame, I dare not ask you to sit down in such a miserable place as this."

"I know, madame, that you have a castle in Touraine, and can excuse your being obliged to receive your friends here in an inn." And she sat down so determinedly that the old lady saw she must allow her to have her way.

"You seem in great pain, madame," said the favorite.

"Oh, in dreadful pain?"

"The right leg? But, good heavens, how did you manage to scald it?"

"Nothing more simple—I held the chocolate kettle in my hand, the handle gave way, and I received the boiling water on my ankle."

"How shocking!"

The old lady sighed. "Yes, shocking, indeed," said she; "but this is always the case, misfortunes never come singly."

" You are aware that the king expected you this morning ? "

" Oh ! madame, that intelligence makes my sufferings infinitely greater."

" His majesty is far from satisfied, madame, that you did not pay your visit."

" But the pain I am in will be a sufficient apology, and I trust yet to be able to offer to his majesty my very humble excuses."

" I do not tell you that to cause you any vexation," said the countess, seeing that the old lady was assuming a little formality, " but merely to let you know that his majesty felt grateful for the offer that you made me."

" You see, madame, that it is now impossible for me to fulfil it."

" Certainly ; but may I ask you a question ? "

" I shall be delighted to hear it."

" Does not your present state arise from your having experienced some sudden agitation ? "

" Very possibly," said the old lady, bowing slightly ; " I must acknowledge that I was deeply moved by your gracious reception of me."

" Yes ; but there was another thing besides."

" Another thing ? nothing that I know of, madame."

" Oh, yes, an unepexcted meeting with a person on leaving my house."

" I did not meet any one ; I was in your brother's carriage."

" Before getting into the carriage ? "

The old lady seemed to be tasking her memory.

" Just as you were going down the stairs to the vestibule ? "

The old lady seemed more intent in trying to recall the events of yesterday.

" Yes," said the favorite, rather impatiently ; " some one entered the court as you left my house."

" I am so unfortunate, madame, as not to be able to recollect any one entering."

" A lady—now do you remember ? "

" I am so short-sighted, that at two paces from me, madame, I cannot distinguish any one."

" Oh, ho !" said the favorite to herself ; " she is too cunning for me ! I shall never succeed by these means. Come—to the point at once. Then, since you did not see the lady," she continued, aloud, " I must tell you that is my sister-in-law, Mademoiselle Dubarry."

" Oh, very well, madame ; but as I have never had the pleasure of seeing her——"

" Yes," interrupted the other, " you have seen her— only when you saw her it was under the name of Flageot."

" So !" cried the old lady, with a bitterness which she could not dissemble. " So, that pretended Mademoiselle Flageot, who caused me to undertake the journey to Paris, is your sister-in-law ?"

" She is, madame."

" And who sent her to me ?"

" I did."

" To mystify me ?"

" No ; to serve you, while at the same time you should serve me."

The old lady bent her thick gray eyebrows. " I do not think," said she, " her visit will turn out very profitable to me."

" Did the vice-chancellor receive you ill, then, madame ?"

" Empty promises."

" But it seems to me that I offered you something more tangible than promises."

" Madame, God disposes though man proposes."

" Come, madame, let us view the matter seriously. You have scalded your foot ?"

" Scalded it very badly."

" Could you not, in spite of this accident—painful, no doubt, but, after all, nothing dangerous—make an effort to bear the journey to Luciennes in my carriage, and stand before his majesty for one minute ?"

" It is quite impossible, madame."

" Is the injury so very serious ?"

" Serious, indeed "

" And pray, who dresses it for you, and nurses you ? "

" Like all housekeepers, I have excellent recipes for burns, and I dress it myself."

" Might I take the liberty of requesting to see your specific."

" Oh, yes ; it is in that vial on the table."

" Hypocrite ! " though the countess, " to carry dissimulation to such a point ! She is as cunning as a fox, but I shall match her. Madame," she added, aloud, " I also have an excellent oil for accidents of this kind ; but before applying it it is necessary to know what kind of scald it is —whether it is inflamed, or blistered, or the skin broken."

" Madame, the skin is broken," said the old lady.

" Oh, heavens ! how you must suffer. Shall I apply my oil to it ? "

" With all my heart, madame. Have you brought it ? "

" No, but I shall send for it. In the meantime, I must see the state of your leg."

" Oh, madame ! " exclaimed the old lady, " I could not think of permitting you to see such a spectacle. I know too well what is due to good manners."

" Delightful ! " thought Mme. Dubarry, " she is now fairly caught." Then she added, " Where we can serve our fellow-beings, madame, we must not stand upon etiquette ; " and she stretched out her hand toward the old lady's leg, which was extended on the sofa.

Mme. de Bearn uttered a scream of pain.

" Very well acted," said Mme. Dubarry to herself, watching her every feature distorted with anguish.

" How you frightened me, madame," said the old lady— " it is almost death to me to touch it ; " and, with pale cheeks and half-closed eyes, she leaned back as if nearly fainting.

" Do you allow me to look at it ? "

" If you choose, madame," said the old lady, in a weak and suffering voice.

Mme. Dubarry did not lose an instant ; she took out the pins in the bandages, and rapidly unrolled them. To her great surprise, she was permitted to go on. " When it comes to the last covering," thought she, " she will scream, and try to prevent me from seeing it; but, though she kill herself calling on me to stop, I will see the leg !" and she proceeded in her task.

Mme. de Bearn groaned, but offered no resistance.

At last the bandages were untied, the last covering was removed, and a real wound caused by a scald lay before Mme. Dubarry's eyes. Here ended the old lady's diplomacy. Livid and inflamed, the wound spoke for itself. The Countess de Bearn might have seen and recognized Chon ; but if so, her courage and determination raised her far above Portia and Mutius Scevola. Mme. Dubarry gazed at her in silent admiration. The old lady, now somewhat recovered, enjoyed her victory to the utmost ; her inflamed eye brooded with satisfaction on the countess kneeling at her feet. Mme. Dubarry replaced the bandages with that delicate care which women exercise toward the suffering, placed the limb once more on its cushion, and took her seat beside the couch.

"Come, madame," said she, "I see of what you are capable, and I beg your pardon for not having begun this subject in the way in which I ought with such a woman as you. Make your own conditions."

The eyes of the old lady sparkled, but it was only for a moment. "In the first place," said she, "state what your wishes are, and then I shall see if I can be of any service to you."

"Madame, I wish to be presented at Versailles by you, though it cost you another hour of the horrible suffering which you have endured this morning."

The Countess de Bearn listened unflinchingly. "Anything else, madame ?" said she.

"That is all. Now for your turn."

"I must have," replied Mme. de Bearn, with a decision which showed clearly that she treated with the countess as one power with another—" I must have the two hundred thousand francs of my lawsuit secured to me."

"But if you gain your cause, you will then have four hundred thousand "

JOSEPH BALSAMO.

"No; for I look on the disputed two hundred thousand as mine already, and the other two hundred thousand I shall reckon as merely an additional piece of good fortune to that of possessing the honor of your acquaintance."

"You shall have them, madame. Well?"

"I have a son, whom I love tenderly, madame. Our house has already been distinguished by military genius; but, born to command, we make but indifferent subalterns. My son must have a company immediately, and next year a colonel's commission."

"Who will pay all the necessary expenses, madame?"

"The king. You perceive that if I expended on my son the sum which I am to receive from you, I should be as poor to-morrow as I am to-day."

"At the lowest, I may reckon that at six hundred thousand francs."

"Four hundred thousand, supposing the commission worth two hundred thousand, which is a high estimate."

"This shall be granted you also."

"I have now to request from the king payment for a vineyard in Touraine, containing four acres, which the engineers deprived me of eleven years ago in making a canal."

"But they paid you then?"

"Yes, they paid me according to the valuator's estimate, but I value it at just double the sum."

"Well, you shall be paid a second time. Is that all?"

"Excuse me. I am out of cash, as you may suppose, madame, and I owe Master Flageot something about nine thousand francs."

"Nine thousand francs?"

"Yes; it is absolutely necessary to pay him—he is an excellent lawyer."

"I have not the least doubt of it, madame. Well, I shall pay these nine thousand francs out of my own private purse. I hope you will acknowledge that I am accommodating."

"Perfectly accommodating. But I think I have also proved that I wish to serve you."

"I have only to regret that you scalded yourself," replied the favorite, with a smile.

"I do not regret it, madame, since in spite of the accident, my devotion to your interests will, I trust, give me strength to be useful to you."

"Let us sum up," said Mme. Dubarry.

"Pardon me one moment. I had forgotten one thing. Alas, it is so long since I have been at court that I have no dress fit for it."

"I foresaw that, madame, and yesterday, after your departure, I ordered a dress for you. To-morrow, at noon, it will be ready."

"I have no diamonds."

"Bœmer & Bossange will give you to-morrow, on my order, a set of ornaments worth two hundred and ten thousand livres, which, the following day, they will take back at two hundred thousand. Thus your indemnity will be paid."

"Very well, madame ; I have nothing more to wish."

"I am delighted to hear it."

"However, about my son's commission ?"

"His majesty will give it to you himself."

"And for the attendant expenses ?"

"The order will be given with the commission."

"Quite right. There now only remains about the vineyard—four acres——"

"How much were they worth ?"

"Six thousand livres an acre ; it was excellent land."

"I will not subscribe an obligation to pay you twenty-four thousand livres, which will be about the whole."

"There is the writing-desk, madame."

"I shall do myself the honor to hand the desk to you."

"To me ?"

"Yes ; that you may write a little letter to his majesty, which I shall dictate—a fair return, you know."

"Very true," replied the old lady ; and arranging her paper, and taking a pen, she waited. Mme. Dubarry dictated :

"Sire,—The happiness which I feel on learning that your majesty has accepted my offer to present my dear friend, the Countess Dubarry——"

The old lady made a grimace, and her pen began to spit.

"You have a bad pen," said the favorite; "you must change it."

"It is unnecessary, madame; I shall get accustomed to it."

"Do you think so?"

"Yes."

Mme. Dubarry continued:

—"Emboldens me to solicit your majesty to look on me with a favorable eye, when I shall appear at Versailles to-morrow, as you have designed to permit me to do. I venture to hope, sire, that I merit your majesty's favor, inasmuch as I am allied to a house, every chief of which has shed his blood for the princess of your august race,"

"Now sign, if you please," said the favorite.

And the countess signed:

"Anastasie Euphemie Rodolphe,
"Countess de Bearn."

The old lady wrote with a firm hand, in great letters half an inch long, and sprinkled her letter with a sufficient quantity of aristocratic mistakes in orthography.

When she had signed, still holding the letter fast with one hand, she passed with the other the paper, pen, and ink to Mme. Dubarry, who, in a little, straight, sharp hand signed the obligation to pay the sums above stated.

Then she wrote a letter to Bœmer & Bossange the crown jewelers, requesting them to give the bearer the set of diamond and emerald ornaments called "Louise," because they had belonged to the Princess Louise, aunt to the dauphin, who sold them to obtain funds for her charities.

That done, the ladies exchanged their papers.

"Now," said Mme. Dubarry, "give me a proof of your friendship, my dear countess."

"With all my heart, madame."

"I am sure that if you come to me, Tronchin will cure you in less than three days. Come, then, and you can at the same time try my oil, which is really excellent."

"Well, but do not let me detain you, madame," said the prudent old lady, "I have some matters to settle here before I can set out."

"Then you refuse me?"

"On the contrary, madame, I accept your invitation, but not at this moment. It is just now striking one o'clock by the abbey clock; give me until three, and at five precisely I shall be at Luciennes."

"Permit my brother then to return with the carriage at three."

"Certainly."

"In the meantime take care of yourself."

"Fear nothing; you have my word, and though my death should be the consequence, I shall present you to-morrow at Versailles."

"Good-by, then, my dear madame."

"Good-by, my charming friend."

And so saying, they parted, the old lady, with her foot still on the cushion, and her hand on her papers; the countess in better spirits than on her arrival, but certainly rather vexed that she had not been able to make better terms with an old woman from the country; she, who could outwit the king of France when she chose.

Passing by the door of the principal saloon, she saw Jean, who, doubtless merely to prevent any one harboring suspicions as to the cause of his long stay, was taking a second bottle of wine. Perceiving his sister, he jumped from his chair and ran after her.

"Well?" cried he.

"Well, I may say, as Marshal Saxe once said to his majesty in the battle-field of Fontenoy, 'Sire, learn from this spectacle how dearly a victory may be purchased.'"

"Then we have conquered?"

"Yes; only it costs us about a million!"

Jean made a frightful grimace.

"Why, I had no choice ; I must either take her at that or give her up."

"But it is abominable."

"It is as I tell you ; and perhaps if you make her angry, she will make us pay double."

"Pardieu ! what a woman !"

"She is a Roman !"

"She is a Greek !"

"Never mind ! Greek or Roman, be ready to bring her to Luciennes at three o'clock. I shall never be easy until I have her under lock and key."

"I shall not stir from this," said Jean.

"And I, on my side, shall hasten to prepare everything," said the countess.

She sprang into her carriage.

"To Luciennes !" said she. "To-morrow I shall say, to Marly !"

Jean followed the carriage with his eyes. "We cost France a pretty little sum," said he. "No matter ; it is very flattering for the Dubarrys !"

CHAPTER XXXVI.

MARSHAL RICHELIEU'S FIFTH CONSPIRACY.

THE king returned to hold his court at Marly, as usual. Less the slave of etiquette than Louis XIV., who sought, even in the evening parties of his courtiers, means of exhibiting his power, Louis XV. sought in them only news, of which he was inordinately fond, and, above all, a variety of faces around him, a gratification which he preferred to all others, particularly if they were smiling ones.

In the evening of the day on which the interview just related took place, and two hours after the Countess de Bearn (who this time kept her promise faithfully) was comfortably installed in Mme. Dubarry's cabinet, the king was playing cards at Marly, in the drawing-room. On his left sat the Duchess d'Ayen, on his right the Princess de Guemenée. His majesty appeared very absent, losing, in consequence of inattention to his game, eight hundred louis-d'ors. Rather sobered by his loss—for, like a true descendant of Henry IV., Louis loved to win—the king left his cards, and retired into the recess of a window to talk to M. de Malesherbes, son of the ex-chancellor, while M. de Maupeou, who was conversing with the Duke de Choiseul in an opposite window, watched the interview with an anxious eye. In the meantime, after the king left the card-table, a circle was formed near the fireplace. The Princesses Adelaide, Sophie, and Victoire, attended by their ladies of honor and their equerries, had placed themselves there on their return from a walk in the gardens.

Around the king, who must certainly have been talking of some matter of importance, as the gravity of M. de Malesherbes was well known, were grouped, but at a respectful distance, generals, admirals, great dignitaries of the state, noblemen, and judges. The little court at the fireplace, therefore, was left a good deal to itself, and seemed bent on more lively conversation, if one might judge by the skirmishing with which they began.

The principal bodies of the group, beside the three princesses, were the Duchess de Grammont, the Princess de Guemenée, the Duchess de Choiseul, the Marchioness de Mirepoix, and the Duchess de Polastron.

At the moment when we approach this group, the Princess Adelaide had just ended an anecdote of a bishop banished from his diocese by the grand penitentiary. It was tolerably scandalous, and it is as well unrelated here.

" Well," said the Princess Victoire, " it is only a month since that bishop was sitting here among us ! "

" Oh, we shall have worse than he sitting among us," said the Duchess de Grammont, "if his majesty receive those who, not having been yet received, are now determined to be received."

Every one understood, from the tone in which these words were uttered, who was meant, and at once felt what turn the conversation was taking.

"Fortunately, wishing to be received, and being received, are two different things, duchess," said a little, elderly man, joining in the conversation. He was seventy-four years of age, but looked only fifty, so elegant was his shape, his voice so unbroken, his leg so well shaped, his eye so lively, his skin so fair, and his hand so beautiful.

"Ah, here is Monsieur de Richelieu," said the duchess, "advancing his scaling-ladders, and going to take our conversation by assault, as he did Mahon. Still something of the soldier, my dear marshal!"

"Still *something* of the soldier! Ah, duchess, you are very severe!"

"Well! But did I not speak the truth?"

"The truth! When?"

"Just now when I said that a certain person wished to force the king's doors?"

"Oh, you know, countess, I am always of your opinion, even when you speak ill of all my friends."

Some laughed, although it had already been whispered that the marshal's wit was on the wane.

"If you say such things," continued the duchess, "I shall not go on with my history, and you will lose a great deal, I assure you."

"Heaven forbid that I should interrupt it! I am all attention."

The circle drew closer around the duchess. She cast a glance toward the window to be certain that the king was still there. He was still in the same position; but, although he continued to converse with M. de Malesherbes, he kept a watchful eye on the group at the fireplace, and just at that moment his eye met that of Mme. de Grammont. The duchess felt somewhat intimidated by its expression, but she had made a beginning, and would not be stopped.

"You must know," she continued, addressing herself particularly to the three princesses, "that a certain lady —her name is of no consequence, is it?—has lately taken it into her head that she will see us, the privileged of the land, sitting in our glory."

"See us—where?" asked the marshal.

"Oh, at Versailles, at Marly, at Fontainebleau."

"Very well—very well!"

"The poor creature knows nothing of our meetings, except from having seen, with the rest of the mob, the king at dinner with his guests. How disagreeable, with a barrier between them and the great, and an usher with his rod driving them before him!"

The marshal took snuff noisily out of his box of Sèvres porcelain. "But," said he, "in order to join our circle at Versailles, at Marly, at Fontainebleau, one must be presented."

"Precisely; the lady in question has requested to be presented."

"Then I'll wager the king has consented, he is so kind."

"Unfortunately, something more is necessary than the king's permission; there must be a chaperon to present the *lady*."

"Yes; but chaperons are rather scarce," said the Marchioness de Mirepoix; "witness the fair Bourbonnaise, who has sought but has not found one."

"Pardon me," replied the duchess; "she has sought so well that she has found what she wants. But what a chaperon! a frank, sincere, real country dame! She was brought away from her dovecot, petted, and caressed, and dressed——"

"It is perfectly shocking," interrupted the Princess de Guemenée.

"But just when the dear dame had been sufficiently petted, and caressed, and dressed, she fell down-stairs, from the top to the bottom, and broke her leg."

"So there can be no presentation?" exclaimed the Princess de Guemenée.

"Not a shadow," said the duchess.

"See how gracious Providence is!" said the marshal, raising his hands and eyes to heaven.

"Gracious!" said the Princess Victoire, "not to the poor country dame; I really pity her."

"On the contrary, your royal highness may congratulate

her," said the duchess ; " of two evils she has chosen the
lesser." She stopped short, for again her eyes met the
king's.

" If the ladies who have been presented," said the Princess de Guemenée, " were courageous and faithful to the
sentiments of honor of the ancient nobility of France, they
would go in a body to return thanks to the lady from the
country who showed so much sublimity of mind as to break
her leg."

" Yes, faith," said the marshal, " that is a great idea !
But what is the name of the excellent lady who has saved
us in this great danger ? We have nothing now to fear ;
have we, duchess ? "

" Oh, nothing ; she is in her bed, her leg bound up, and
unable to move a step."

" But if the lady should find another chaperon ? " said
the princess ; " she is so indefatigable."

" Oh, do not be afraid ; it is not so easy to find chaperons."

At this moment the throng of courtiers separated, and
the king approached ; the group became silent. A moment afterward his clear and well-known voice was heard :
" Adieu, ladies. Good night, gentlemen."

Every one rose.

The king advanced toward the door, then turning before
leaving the room, he said : " By the bye, there will be a
presentation to-morrow at Versailles."

These words fell like a thunderbolt on the assembly.
The king glanced round the group of ladies, who looked
at one another and turned pale ; then he left the apartment without adding another word. Scarcely had he
crossed the threshold with the long train of gentlemen who
attended him, when there was a general explosion among
the princesses and the ladies around them.

" A presentation ! " stammered the Duchess de Grammont, her lips quite livid. " What does his majesty
mean ? "

" Eh ! duchess," said the marshal, with one of those
smiles which even his best friends could not pardon, " can

this be the presentation you have just been speaking of ?"

The princesses bit their lips with vexation.

" Oh, it is impossible," murmured the duchess.

" Ah, duchess," said the marshal, " they do set legs so well nowadays."

The Duke de Choiseul approached his sister, the Duchess de Grammont, and pressed her arm as a warning not to go too far ; but she was too deeply wounded to attend to him.

" It would be an insult to us all," she exclaimed.

" Yes ; an insult indeed !" repeated the Princess de Guemenée.

M. de Choiseul saw he could do nothing more, and walked a short distance off.

" Oh, your royal highnesses," cried the duchess, ad-dressing the king's three daughters, " there is no resource for us now but in you ! You, the highest ladies in the kingdom, will you endure it ? Must we be exposed, in the only asylum remaining for ladies of rank, to meet a person with whom we should not allow our chambermaids to associate ?"

The princesses, instead of replying, hung down their heads.

" Oh, your royal highnesses, in Heaven's name !" ex-claimed she, " save us."

" The king is master in this as in everything else," said the Princess Adelaide, sighing.

" That is true," said the Duke de Richelieu.

" But the entire court of France will be compromised in the affair," cried the duchess. " Gentlemen, have you then no regard for the honor of your families ? "

" Ladies," said the Duke de Choiseul, trying to laugh, " as this seems bordering on a conspiracy, you must allow me to retire, and to take with me Monsieur de Sartines. Will you come, marshal ?"

" I ?—faith, I adore conspiracies ! I shall certainly stay," replied Marshal Richelieu.

The two ministers departed.

There now remained around the princesses eight or ten of the ladies who had espoused most warmly the league against the presentation. Richelieu was the only gentleman. The ladies looked at him suspiciously, as if he had been a Trojan in the Grecian camp.

"I represent my daughter, the Countess d'Egmont," said he; "go on, ladies, go on."

"Your royal highnesses," the Duchess de Grammont began, "there is a means by which we can show our sense of the infamous nature of the proceedings, and for my part I shall make use of the means."

"What is it?" all exclaimed.

"We have been told that the king is master," she continued.

"And I reply it is just and right that he should be," said the marshal.

"He is master in his own palace, but we are mistresses in our own houses. Now, what is to prevent me from giving my coachman directions to drive to Chanteloup to-night, instead of to Versailles?"

"Or what is to prevent others from imitating you?" said the Princess de Guemenée.

"Why should we not all imitate the duchess?" asked the Marchioness de Mirepoix.

"Oh, your royal highnesses," exclaimed the duchess, again addressing the princesses, "what a noble example it would be for you to give the court!"

"The king would be very angry with us," said the Princess Sophie.

"No, your royal highness; I am certain he would not. On the contrary, it would make him reflect; and he has such exquisite sense, such perfect tact, that he will afterward acknowledge you to be in the right, and he will be grateful to you."

"It is true," said the Princess Victoire, encouraged by the general spirit of rebellion; "the king said nothing when we refused to admit the visits of the countess, but on a public occasion like this he might not be disposed to forgive us."

"No, certainly," replied the duchess : " if you were the only ladies who absented yourselves, but when he sees that we have all left the court !"

" All !" exclaimed the party.

" Yes, all," repeated the old marshal.

" Then you are of the plot ?" said the Princess Adelaide.

" Certainly, I am, and therefore I wish to speak."

" Speak, marshal, speak !" said Mme. de Grammont.

" We must proceed methodically," said he. " It is not enough all to shout in chorus this or that. I have known people say, ' This is what I shall do,' but at the moment of action they have done the very contrary. Now, as I have the honor to make one in this conspiracy, I do not wish to be left by myself, as I always was when I took part in the conspiracies under the late king and under the regency."

" Upon my word, marshal, you forget yourself. Among the Amazons you take upon you the airs of a leader," said the duchess.

" Madame, I beg you to consider that I may have some right to that position. You hate Madame Dubarry—there, I have let the name slip out, but nobody heard it—you hate her more than I, but I am more compromised than you."

" How is that ?"

" I have not been at Luciennes for eight days, nor at her apartments at Versailles for four. The affair has gone so far that a footman was sent to ask if I was ill—so I am already looked upon with suspicion. However, I am not ambitious—I yield the leadership to you ; you have set the affair on foot, you have stirred us all, you revolutionize our consciences—yours must be the baton of command."

" No ; I must follow their royal highnesses," said the duchess, respectfully.

" Oh, pray let us remain passive," said the Princess Adelaide ; we are going to St. Denis to see our sister Louise ; she will keep us there, and of course there can be nothing said."

" Nothing, nothing at all, unless by some very ill-disposed person," said the marshal.

"As for me," said the Duchess de Grammont, "I have to go to Chanteloup, because it is hay-making season."

"Bravo!" cried the duke; "an excellent reason."

"I must stay at home; one of my children is ill, and I have to nurse him," said the Princess de Guemenée.

"I," said the Duchess de Polastron, "have felt a giddiness all this evening—I am sure I shall be dangerously ill if Tronchin does not bleed me to-morrow."

"And I," said the Marchioness de Mirepoix, majestically, "I shall not go to Versailles because, I shall not—that is my reason."

"Excellent! excellent!" said the marshal; "all this is quite logical; but we must swear."

"What! we must swear?"

"Yes; conspirators always swear, from the plot of Catiline down to that of Cellamare, in which I had the honor of participating. We always swore—it is true, the thing did not succeed at all the better for it, still, let us respect old customs. Let us swear, then—you shall see how solemn it is."

He extended his hand in the midst of the group of ladies, and said, with proper dignity, "I swear."

All the ladies repeated the oath, with the exception of the princesses, who slipped away.

"Now that all is over," said the marshal, "when once people have sworn in conspiracies, they never do anything more."

"Oh, what a fury she will be in," said the Duchess de Grammont, "when she finds herself all alone in the grand saloon!"

"Hum!" said the marshal; "the king will most probably banish us for a little time."

"Ah!" cried the Princess de Guemenée, "what kind of court would it be if we were banished? The king of Denmark is expected—who will be presented to him? The dauphiness is expected—to whom will she be presented? Besides, a whole court is never exiled—a selection is made."

"I know that very well. and I fear I run a great risk of

being chosen for the distinction of banishment !" said the marshal. "I have always been distinguished in that way. Four times have I been selected for it, at the lowest reckoning—this is my fifth conspiracy, ladies."

"Do not be afraid, marshal," said the Duchess de Grammont; "if any one be marked out for banishment, I shall be the person."

"Or your brother, the Duke de Choiseul. Take care, duchess," replied the marshal.

"My brother is of my mind—he could submit to misfortune, not to an insult."

"It will be neither you, marshal, nor you, duchess, who will be banished," said the Marchioness de Mirepoix; "I shall be the victim. The king will never pardon me for being less condescending to the countess than I was to the marchioness."

"That is true," said the marshal : "you were always called the favorite of the favorite. I am sorry for you now —we shall be banished together."

"Let him banish us all," said the Princess de Gueenée, rising ; "for I trust none of us will draw back from the resolution which we have taken."

"We cannot draw back after our oath," said the marshal.

"Besides," said the Duchess de Grammont, "I have still other resources."

"You !"

"Yes ; she cannot be presented to-morrow evening without three things."

"What three ?"

"A hair-dresser, a dress, and a carriage."

"Certainly."

"Well, she shall not be at Versailles at ten o'clock—the king will become impatient—he will dismiss the court, and the presentation will be postponed until the Greek Kalends, on account of the arrival of the dauphiness."

A burst of delight followed this new episode in the conspiracy, but while applauding even more loudly than the others, the Duke de Richelieu and the Marchioness de Mirepoix exchanged glances—the same idea had occurred simultaneously to the two old courtiers.

At eleven o'clock all the conspirators, lighted by a lovely moon, were speeding along the roads to Versailles and St. Germain.

Marshal Richelieu, however, mounted his groom's horse, and while his carriage, with the blinds drawn closely down, bore him ostensibly to Versailles, he reached Paris by a cross-road.

CHAPTER XXXVII.

NO HAIR-DRESSER, NO DRESS, NO CARRIAGE.

It would have been in bad taste for the Countess Dubarry to have gone merely from her apartment in the palace of Versailles to the grand saloon where the presentation took place. Besides, at Versailles there were not the necessary appliances and means for such an important day.

But a better reason than any of these was, that it was not the custom. The highly favored being who was to be presented, always arrived with the noise and state of a foreign embassador, whether it was from her house in the town of Versailles, or in Paris. Mme. Dubarry chose to arrive from the latter place.

At eleven o'clock in the morning, therefore, she was at her house in the Rue de Valois, with the Countess de Bearn, whom she kept under lock and key when she did not keep her under her smiles, and whose burn was attended to most carefully—every secret of medicine and chemistry being exhausted on it.

From the preceding evening Jean, Chon, and Dorée had been at work; and any one who could have seen them at work, would have formed an exalted idea of the power of gold or the greatness of human intellect.

The one made sure of the hair-dresser, the other harassed the seamstress. Jean took the department of the carriage to himself, but also cast an eye occasionally on the hair-dresser and the dress-makers. The countess, occupied with flowers, diamonds, and lace, was buried in boxes, cases, and caskets, and gave audiences every hour to couriers from Versailles, who informed her how matters were going on. Orders had been given for lighting the queen's drawing-room, and no change had taken place in the king's intentions.

About four the viscount came in, pale, agitated, but joyful.

"Well?" asked the countess.

"Well, all will be ready."

"The hair-dresser?"

"I went to him myself; Dorée was with him; but, to make sure of him, I slipped fifty louis-d'ors into his hand. He will dine here at six o'clock precisely, so you may be quite easy on that score."

"My dress?"

"It will be a perfect wonder! Chon is superintending it, there are six-and-twenty workwomen at it, sewing on the pearls, the ribbons, and the trimmings. They go on breadth by breadth at the work, and it would certainly require eight days for any other persons than ourselves to have it finished. It is a prodigious undertaking!"

"But did you say they are doing it breadth by breadth?"

"Yes, my dear—there are thirteen breadths of the stuff; two workwomen at each breadth—one works at the right, and the other at the left, putting on the jewels and trimmings; then at the last they will all be joined together. It will take them two hours yet; at six you will have it."

"Are you quite sure, Jean?"

"Yesterday I made a calculation with an engineer about it. There are ten thousand stitches in each breadth; that is, five thousand for each workwoman. In such thick stuff, a woman can only make one stitch in five seconds; that is, twelve in one minute, seven hundred and twenty in one hour, and seven thousand two hundred in ten hours. I leave out two thousand two hundred for needle-threading and slipped stitches, and this leaves four good hours of work."

"And what about the carriage ?"

"Oh, I'll answer for it. The varnish is now getting dry in a large store heated to fifty degrees. It is an elegant vis-à-vis, compared with which the carriages sent for the dauphiness are a mere trifle. Besides the coats of arms on the four panels, there is the war-cry of the Dubarrys— 'Boutés en avant !' on each side. Besides that, I made them paint on one place two doves billing and cooing, and in another a heart pierced with a dart, the whole surrounded by bows and arrows, quivers and torches. There is such a crowd of people at Francian's to see it ! It will be here exactly at eight."

At this moment Chon and Dorée came in, and confirmed all that Jean had said.

"Thank you, my brave aids-de-camp !" said the countess.

"My sweet sister," said the viscount, "your eyes look a little dim—had you not better sleep for an hour ?—it would quite revive you."

"Sleep !—no ! I shall sleep to-night, and that is more than some will do."

While these preparations were going on, the report of the intended presentation had spread through all Paris. Idle and careless as they appear, no people love news more than the Parisians. None knew better all the courtiers and all the intriguers of Versailles than the Parisian cockney of the eighteenth century, though debarred from the festivities of the palace, and seeing only the hieroglyphics on the carriages and the curious liveries of the footmen. At that period such or such a nobleman was known to the whole city. The reason was simple. The court at that period formed the principal attraction in the theaters and in the gardens. Marshal Richelieu in his place at the Italian opera, Mme. Dubarry in a coach rivaling that of royalty itself, were constantly before the public, like some favorite comedian or admired actress of the present day.

People are much more interested in faces that are well

known to them. Every one in Paris knew Mme. Dubarry's face, constantly shown where a rich and pretty woman likes to be seen—in the theaters, in the public walks, in the shops. Besides, she was easily recognized by means of portraits, caricatures, and by her negro page Zamore. The affair of the presentation, therefore, occupied the city nearly as much as the court. This day there was a crowd near the Palais Royal; but, poor Philosophy! it was not to see Rousseau playing chess at the Café de la Regence; it was to see the favorite in her fine coach and her handsome dress, of which they had heard so much. There was something deep in Jean Dubarry's expression, "We cost a pretty little sum to France!" And it was natural that France, represented by Paris, should wish to enjoy the sight for which it had paid so dearly. Mme. Dubarry knew her people well, for they were much more her people than they had been Queen Maria Lezinska's. She knew that they loved to be dazzled by magnificence; and, as she was good-natured, she labored to make the spectacle correspond to the expense to which she put them.

Instead of sleeping, as her brother advised her, she took a bath about five o'clock. Then, about six o'clock, she began to expect her hair-dresser; and, while she waits, we shall explain, if we can, what hair-dressing then was.

It was building a complete edifice. This was the commencement of the castles which the ladies of the court of the young king, Louis XVI., erected with towers and bastions on their heads. May we not, even in this frivolity of fashion, discover something presaging that a mine was dug beneath the feet of all who were, or all who pretended to be, great? Or that by some mysterious divination, the women of the aristocracy had learned they should have a short time to enjoy their titles—that they, therefore, made the most of them, bearing them aloft on their heads; and as if—fatal omen—not having long to keep their heads, they must decorate those heads to the utmost point which extravagance can attain, and raise them as high as possible above the vulgar.

To plait the hair; to elevate it on a silken cushion; to

roll it about a hoop of whalebone ; to adorn it with diamonds, pearls, and flowers ; to sprinkle it with powder,
which made the eyes brilliant and the complexion fresh ;
to blend into harmony with the complexion, pearl, ruby,
opal, diamond, flowers of all hues and of all forms—to do
all this, a man must be not only a great artist, but the
most patient of his race.

As a proof that such a man was esteemed great, the
hair-dresser was the only tradesman allowed to wear a
sword.

This explanation may account for the fifty louis-d'ors
given by Jean Dubarry to the hair-dresser of the court.
It may account, also, for some fears lest the great Lubin
(the court hair-dresser of that day was called Lubin)
—some fears, we say, lest the great Lubin might not be so
punctual or skilful on the occasion as was desirable.

The fears about his punctuality were, alas ! too well
founded. Six o'clock struck, and the hair-dresser did not
appear ; then half-past six came ; then a quarter to seven.
One thought inspired some hope in the anxious hearts of
all ; it was, that a man of M. Lubin's importance would
naturally make people wait a little.   But seven struck.
The viscount feared that the dinner prepared for the hair-
dresser might be cold when he came, and the great artist
might be dissatisfied.   He sent a servant to say that dinner
waited.

The servant returned in a quarter of an hour.   Those
only who have waited under similar circumstances can tell
how many seconds there are in such a quarter of an hour.

The servant had spoken to Mme. Lubin herself, who
assured him that M. Lubin had set out for the countess's,
that if he were not then there, he must be on the way.

"Perhaps," said Jean, "he has been delayed in consequence of not getting a carriage.   We will wait a
little."

"Besides," said the countess, "there will be no time
lost ; my hair can be attended to when I am half dressed ,
the presentation does not take place until ten ; we have
still three hours, it will only take one to go to Versailles.

In the meantime, to employ me, Chon, show me my dress. Where is Chon ? Chon ! Chon ! my dress, my dress ! ''

"Your dress has not come yet, madame," said Dorée, " and your sister went ten minutes ago to see about it herself."

"Oh," exclaimed the viscount, "I hear a noise of wheels ! It is the carriage brought home, no doubt."

The viscount was mistaken ; it was Chon, who had come back at full speed.

"My dress !" cried the countess, while Chon was still in the vestibule—" my dress ! "

"Has it not come ? " asked Chon, terror-struck.

"No."

"Oh, well, it can't be long.   When I got to the dressmaker's she had just set out in a fiacre with two of her women, bringing the dress to fit it on."

"It is a good way from her house to this, and as you drove very fast no doubt you have passed her," said Jean.

"Yes, yes ! certainly !" replied Chon ; yet she could not suppress a vague feeling of apprehension.

"Viscount," said the countess, "you had better send about the carriage, that there may be no disappointment on that side at least."

"You are right, Jeanne," and Dubarry opened the door. "Let some of you," cried he, "take the new horses to Francian's for the carriage, so that they may be all ready harnessed when it arrives."

The coachman and the horses set off. As the sound of their trampling died away, Zamore entered with a letter.

"A letter for Mistress Dubarry," said he.

"Who brought it ? "

"A man."

"A man ?   What sort of a man ? "

"A man on horseback."

"And why did he give it to you ? "

"Because Zamore was at the door."

"But read it !   Read it rather than question him !" cried Jean.

"You are right, viscount."

"Aye, provided there be nothing annoying in the letter," he muttered.

"Oh, no! it is some petition for his majesty."

"It is not folded like a petition."

"Really, viscount, you are full of fears," said the countess, smiling, and she broke the seal. At the first line she shrieked, and fell back in her chair, half dead.

"No hair-dresser, no dress, no carriage!" she cried. Chon sprung toward her. Jean seized the letter. It was evidently the writing of a woman, and ran thus:

"MADAME,—Be not too confident. This evening you shall have no hair-dresser, no dress, no carriage. I hope this information will reach you in time to be useful to you. As I do not desire your gratitude, I do not give you my name. Guess who I am, and you will have discovered
                                        A SINCERE FRIEND."

"Oh!" shouted Dubarry, "all is over! Sang bleu! I must kill somebody! By all the devils! I'll run Lubin through the body! It is half-past seven, and he not here! Confound him! Damn him!"

And as Dubarry was not to be presented that evening, he did not care about his hair, but tore it out unmercifully in handfuls.

"But the dress! Good heavens! the dress!" cried Chon; "a hair-dresser could easily be found!"

"Oh, I defy you to find one! What sort of wretch would he be? A murderer! A slaughterer! Oh, death and damnation!"

The countess said nothing, but sighs burst from her bosom, which might have softened the Choiseuls themselves could they but have heard them.

"Let us think, let us think!" said Chon; "a little calmness only. Let us find out another hair-dresser, and send to the dressmaker to ask what has become of the dress!"

"No hair-dresser!" murmured the almost fainting countess; "no dress, no carriage!"

"Yes, no carriage!" cried Jean; "it does not come, either! It is a plot, countess, it is a plot! Cannot Sartines find out the authors of it? Cannot Maupeou hang them? Can they not, with their accomplices, be burned in the market-place? I will have the hair-dresser broken on the wheel! the dressmaker torn to pieces with pincers! the coach-maker flayed alive!"

At length the countess recovered a little from her stage of stupefaction, but it was only to feel more poignantly all the horror of her situation.

"All is lost!" she exclaimed. "Those who have bought over Lubin are rich enough to remove all the good hair-dressers from Paris. None are left me but wretches who would destroy my hair—and my dress! my poor dress! and my new carriage. I thought the sight of it would have made them burst with envy!"

Dubarry did not answer—but, rolling his eyes fearfully, strode up and down the room, striking himself against the angles of the apartment; and as often as he encountered any ornament or small article of furniture, abandoning his hair, he dashed them into the smallest morsels possible, and then stamped on them with his feet.

In the midst of this scene of horror, which, spreading from the boudoir to the anterooms, and from the anterooms to the court, caused all the domestics to run hither and thither with twenty different contradictory orders, a young man in a light green coat, a satin waistcoat, lilac breeches and white silk stockings got out of a cabriolet, crossed the court, stepping from stone to stone on the tips of his toes, entered the open door abandoned by all the servants, mounted the stairs, and tapped at the countess's dressing-room door.

Jean was just stamping on a tray with a set of Sèvres porcelain, which he had pulled down with the tail of his coat while he was dealing a blow with his fist to a great Chinese mandarin. When the noise of these feats had subsided a little, three gentle, discreet, modest taps were heard.

Then followed profound silence; all were in such a

state of expectation, that no one could ask who was there.

"Excuse me," said an unknown voice, "but I wish to speak to the Countess Dubarry."

"Sir, people do not enter here in that way!" cried a servant, who had discovered the stranger, and had run after him to prevent his further advance.

"Never mind! never mind!" cried Jean, flinging open the door with a hand which might have driven in the gates of Gaza. "Worse cannot happen to us now. What do you want with the countess?"

The stranger avoided the shock of this sudden meeting by springing backward, and falling into the third position.

"Sir," said he, "I came to offer my services to the Countess Dubarry."

"What services, sir?"

"My professional services, sir."

"What is your profession?"

"I am a hair-dresser," and the stranger bowed a second time.

"Oh," cried Jean, falling on his neck, "a hair-dresser. Come in! come in!"

"Come in! Come in, my dear sir!" cried Chon, almost taking the astonished young man in her arms.

"A hair-dresser?" cried Mme. Dubarry, raising her hands to heaven. "A hair-dresser? An angel! Were you sent by Monsieur Lubin, sir?"

"I was not sent by any one. I read in the gazette that the Countess Dubarry was to be presented this evening; then, said I to myself, suppose that the Countess Dubarry had no hair-dresser?—it is not probable, but it is possible— so I think I shall try."

"What is your name, sir?" asked the countess, a little cooled by this account.

"Leonard, madame."

"Leonard? You are not known to any one?"

"If you accept my services, madame, to-morrow every one will know me."

"Hum!" said Jeanne, "there are two kinds of hair-dressing."

"If madame distrusts my skill, I shall retire."

"We have no time to try you," said Chon.

"Why make any trial?" cried the young man, walking round the countess in a fit of enthusiasm. "I know, madame, that all eyes must be drawn to you by the style of your hair, and already, in contemplating you, I have invented a head which will have a most powerful effect."

And the young man made a gesture with his hand so full of confidence in himself, that the countess's resolution was a little shaken, and hope sprung up in the hearts of Chon and Jean.

"Have you, really?" said she, quite astonished at the young man's ease—for he was now leaning back, hand on hip, as the great Lubin himself would have done.

"Yes—but, madame, I must see your dress, that I may make the ornaments harmonize with it."

"Oh, my dress! my dress!" cried the countess, recalled by his words to the terrible reality.

Jean struck his forehead fiercely. "Oh, imagine, sir," cried he—"imagine what a horrid trick! They have carried off dress—dressmaker—all! Chon, Chon, dear Chon!" and Dubarry, tired of tearing out his hair, gave way to a downright fit of sobbing.

"Suppose you were to go back to the dressmaker's, Chon," said the countess.

"For what purpose? You know she had set out to come hither."

"Alas! alas!" murmured the countess, falling back in her chair, "of what use is a hair-dresser when I have no dress?" At this moment the door-bell rung; all the doors had been carefully shut, and even bolted, by the porter, lest any other should slip in as the hair-dresser had done.

"Some one rings," said the countess.

Chon sprung to a window.

"A bandbox!" cried she.

"A bandbox?" cried the countess.

"Coming in?" cried Jean.

" Yes—no—yes. It is given to the porter—run, Jean, run !"

He dashed down the stairs, got before all the footmen, and snatched the bandbox from the porter.

Chon looked through the window.

He pulled off the lid, plunged his hand into the depths of the bandbox, and uttered a yell of joy. It contained a beautiful dress of Chinese satin, with flowers put on, and a complete trimming of lace of immense value.

" A dress ! a dress!" shouted Chon, clapping her hands.

" A dress ?" repeated the countess, almost sinking under her joy, as she had before under her grief.

" Who gave it you, rogue ?" asked the viscount of the porter.

" A woman, sir, whom I don't know."

" Where is she? "

" Sir, she laid it on the step of the door, cried, ' For the countess,' and disappeared."

" Well, we have got a dress, that is the main thing ! "

" Come up, Jean, come up ! " called Chon ; "my sister is dying with impatience."

" Look !" said Jean, returning to the room ; " look ! admire ! See what fate sends you !"

" But it will not go on—it will not fit—it was not made for me. Mon Dieu ! mon Dieu ! what a misfortune, for it is beautiful !"

Chon quickly measured it.

" The same length, the same width in the waist!" she exclaimed.

" What admirable stuff !" said Jean.

" It is miraculous !" said Chon.

" It is terrible !" said the countess.

" Not at all," replied the viscount, " for it proves that although you have great enemies, you have also devoted friends."

" It cannot be sent by a friend," said Chon ; " for how should a friend know of the plot formed against us ? It must be sent by a sylph."

" Let it be sent by his satanic majesty !" exclaimed the

countess, " I care not, provided it assists me to oppose the Choiseuls ! Whoever sent it, he cannot be so much of a demon as they."

" And now," said Jean, " I am sure that you may confidently submit your head to this gentleman."

" Why do you think so ? "

" Because he has been sent by the same person who sent the dress."

" I ? " said Leonard, with the most innocent surprise.

" Come, come, my dear sir ! acknowledge that it was all a tale about the gazette ! "

" The simple truth, sir. Here is the paper—I kept it for curl papers," and he drew out the gazette in which the presentation was announced.

" Now," said Chon, " let him set to work—it is eight o'clock."

" Oh, we have time enough," said the hair-dresser, " it will only take an hour to go to Versailles."

" Yes, if we have a carriage," said the countess.

" Oh, Mordieu! that is true! " exclaimed Jean. " That wretch, Francian, does not come."

" You know we have been warned ; no hair-dresser, no dress, no carriage ! " repeated the countess.

" Now, if the coach-maker should not keep his word ? " said Chon.

" No ; here he is, here he is ! " cried Jean.

" And the carriage, the carriage ? " exclaimed the countess.

" It is at the door, no doubt. But what is the matter with the coach-maker ? "

At that moment Francian rushed in, all in alarm.

" Oh, viscount ! " cried he, " the carriage was on its way hither, when, at the corner of a street, it was seized by four men ; they knocked down my young man, who was bringing it, seized the reins, and set off with it at a gallop."

" I told you so ! I told you so ! " said Dubarry, sitting down resignedly in his chair.

" But, brother," exclaimed Chon, " exert yourself ! do something ! "

"What for?"

"To get a carriage; the horses here are done out, and the carriages dirty. Jeanne cannot go in any of them."

"Bah! the little birds find food when they don't expect it, and we got a hair-dresser and a dress in our need. Yes, our unknown friend will not forget a carriage!"

"Hush!" cried Chon, "surely I heard carriage wheels."

"Yes, it is stopping," he replied.

Then springing to a window, which he opened, he shouted to the servants, "Run, rascals, run! Quick, quick! Find out our benefactor!"

A carriage, lined with white satin, and drawn by two splendid bay horses, stood before the door. But neither coachman nor footman was to be seen; a common street porter held the horses by the head. A crown had been given to him by a person unknown to him at the end of the street, with orders to lead the carriage to the countess's door.

They looked at the panels; the arms were replaced by a simple rose.

The whole of this counterplay against the miseries with which the evening had commenced lasted about an hour.

Jean had the carriage taken into the yard, and the gates locked on it; he carried up the key with him. On returning to the dressing-room, he found the hair-dresser about to give the countess the first proof of his profound knowledge of his art.

"Sir," cried the viscount, seizing him by the arm, "if you do not declare who is our protecting genius, that we may make known our eternal gratitude to him, I swear——"

"Allow me," said the young man, interrupting him very phlegmatically, "allow me to say, sir, that you are doing me the honor of squeezing my arm so tight, that I fear my hand will be quite stiff when I shall have to dress the countess's hair, and it is now eight o'clock."

"Leave him alone, Jean, leave him alone!" cried the countess.

Jean sank down in his chair.

"A miracle!" exclaimed Chon; "it is a perfect fit—

only an inch too long in front ; but ten minutes will alter that."

"And what is the carriage like ? " asked the countess.

"It is in the best style," replied Jean ; "I got into it ; it is lined with white satin, and perfumed with essence of roses."

"All is right—all is right ! " cried the countess, clapping her little hands with delight. "Now, Mcnsieur Leonard, if you succeed on this occasion, your fortune is made ! "

Leonard took possession of her head, and the very first touch of the comb revealed a skilful hand. Rapidity, taste, marvelous precision, a complete knowledge of the relation between the moral and the physical—all these he displayed in the accomplishment of his important duty.

When he had, at the end of three quarters of an hour, given the finishing touch to the splendid edifice which he had reared on the countess's head, he would have modestly retired, after having washed his hands in a basin which Chon presented to him, as if he had been a king.

"Now, sir," said Dubarry, "you must know that I am as ardent in my loves as in my hatreds—as you have gained my esteem, pray tell me who you are."

"You know already, sir, who I am—my name is Leonard—I am only a beginner."

"A beginner ? Sang bleu ! you are a thorough master of your profession ! "

"You shall be my hair-dresser, Monsieur Leonard," said the countess, looking at herself in a little glass which she had in her hand ; "and I shall pay you on each occasion like this fifty louis-d'ors. Chon, count now one hundred for this time—he shall have fifty of earnest money."

"I told you, madame, that you would make my reputation."

"But you must dress no one's hair but mine."

"Keep your hundred louis-d'ors, then, madame—I prefer my liberty—to it I owe the honor of having this evening dressed your hair. Liberty is the first of human blessings."

"A philosophical hair-dresser ! " exclaimed Dubarry, raising his hands to heaven ; "to what shall we come at last ? Well, my dear Monsieur Leonard, I shall not quarrel with you—take your hundred louis-d'ors and keep your secret and your liberty. Now, countess, to your carriage !"

These last words were addressed to the Countess de Bearn, who entered, stiff and stately, and dressed like an image in a shrine. She was brought out of her room just when she was to be made use of.

"Now," cried Jean to the servants, "let four of you take her and carry her down-stairs, and if you hurt her, so as to make her heave one sigh, I'll flay you alive !"

While he was superintending this delicate and important operation, assisted by Chon, the countess turned to seek for M. Leonard—he had disappeared.

" But how did he go ?" murmured Mme. Dubarry, who had not yet quite recovered from the influence of the many surprises of the evening.

"How did he go ? Why, through the floor, or up through the ceiling, of course, as all genii do. Take care, countess, that your head-dress does not turn into a heap of mud, your dress into a spider's web, and your coach into a pumpkin drawn by two rats."

Having given utterance to this last fear, Jean took his place beside the Countess de Bearn and her fortunate god-daughter.

———

CHAPTER XXXVIII.

THE PRESENTATION.

VERSAILLES, like everything really great, is and will long be a fair and lovely scene. Though moss should cover its moldering walls—though its gods of marble, bronze, and lead should lie shattered around their broken fountains—though its broad alleys of clipped trees should remain in all the wild luxuriance of nature—though it should become but a heap of ruins—it will always present to the thinker and the poet a great and touching spectacle.

Let such look from its circle of ephemeral splendor to the eternal horizon beyond, and it will be long ere thought and fancy sink to rest again.

But it was, above all, in its days of pomp and splendor that Versailles was fairest to look upon ; when its gay and thoughtless population, restrained by a crowd of soldiers still more gay than themselves, thronged its gilded gates ; when carriages lined with velvet and satin, blazoned with armorial bearings, thundered over its pavements at the full speed of their prancing steeds, when every window, blazing with light, like those of an enchanted palace, exposed to view the moving throng, radiant with diamonds, rubies, sapphires, and bending to the gesture of one man, as bends before the wind a field of golden corn, with its bright flowers of crimson, white, and blue—yes, Versailles was brilliant indeed when its gates sent forth couriers to all the powers of the earth—when kings, princes, nobles, generals, learned men from all parts of the civilized world trod its rich carpets and its inlaid floors.

But when, for some great ceremony, all its furniture was displayed and its sumptuousness doubled by the magic of a thousand lights, even the coldest imagination must have glowed on beholding what human invention and human power could do. Such was the ceremony observed on the reception of an ambassador, or the presentation of the nobles attending the court.

Louis XIV., the creator of etiquette, a system which shut up each individual within bounds beyond which he could not pass, desired that the favored few, initiated into the magnificence of his regal life, should be struck with such veneration that ever afterward they could only regard the palace as a temple, and the king as its presiding deity, to whose presence some had the right of approaching nearer than others.

Versailles, then, still magnificent, although already showing symptoms of degeneration, had opened all its doors, lighted all its chandeliers, and exhibited all its splendor for the presentation of Mme. Dubarry. The people, inquisitive, though hungry and wretched, forgetting, strange anomaly, both their hunger and wretchedness, that they might gaze on so much grandeur, filled the Place d'Armes and the avenues leading to the palace. Every window of the château poured out floods of light, and the lusters from a distance looked like stars gleaming in an atmosphere of golden dust.

The king left his private apartments exactly at ten. He was dressed rather more richly than usual ; that is, his lace was finer, and the buckles alone of his garters and his shoes were worth a million.

The Count de Sartines had informed him of the conspiracy entered into by the ladies the evening before, so that there was a shade of anxiety on his brow, and he trembled lest he should see only gentlemen in the grand saloon. But he was soon reassured, when, on entering the saloon set apart for presentations, he saw, amid a cloud of lace and powder, mingled with the blaze of diamonds, first, his three daughters, then the Marchioness de Mirepoix, who had talked so loudly among the plotters —in short, all the turbulent spirits who had sworn not to come were there.

Marshal Richelieu, like a general on the eve of an engagement, hurried from one to another, saying to this one, " Ah, I have caught you, perfidious one ! " whispering to another, " I was certain you would not keep your oath ! " and to a third, " Remember what I told you about conspiracies ! "

" But, marshal," replied the ladies, " you are here yourself ! "

" Oh, I represent my daughter ! I represent the Countess d'Egmont. Look around, you will not find Septimanie ! She alone has kept faith with the Duchess de Grammont and the Princess de Guemenée, so I am pretty certain what my fate will be. To-morrow I shall enter on my fifth banishment or my fourth trip to the Bastile. Most certainly I shall never again conspire."

The king entered. There was a profound silence, during which ten o'clock struck—the hour fixed for the ceremony. His majesty was surrounded by a numerous court, and was attended by about fifty gentlemen, who not having sworn to come to the presentation, were, probably, for that reason present.

The king observed, at the first glance, that the Duchess de Grammont, the Princess de Guemenée, and the Countess d'Egmont were wanting in this splendid assembly.

He approached the Duke de Choiseul, who affected great calmness, but in spite of all his efforts was somewhat disturbed.

"I do not see the Duchess de Grammont here," said the king.

"Sire, my sister is ill," replied the Duke de Choiseul, "and desired me to present her very humble respects to your majesty."

"So much the worse!" said the king, and he turned his back on the duke. In doing so, he found himself face to face with the Prince de Guemenée.

"And the Princess de Guemenée," said he, "where is she? have you not brought her, prince?"

"It was impossible, sire; when I called at her hotel, in order to accompany her here, I found her in bed."

"Oh! so much the worse, so much the worse!" said the king. "Ah, here is the marshal! Good evening, marshal."

The old courtier bowed with all the suppleness of a youth.

"*You* are not ill, at least"! said the king, loud enough for De Choiseul and De Guemenée to hear him.

"Whenever, sire, I have in prospect the happiness of seeing your majesty, I am perfectly well," replied Richelieu.

"But," said the king, looking round, "I do not see your daughter, the Countess d'Egmont; how comes it that she is not here?"

The duke's features assumed an expression of deep regret.

"Alas! sire, my poor daughter is really not able to lay her humble homage at your majesty's feet—this evening, above all others—ill, sire, ill!"

"So much the worse!" said the king. "Ill! The Countess d'Egmont, who enjoys the finest health in France?

So much the worse, so much the worse!" And the king left the marshal as he had left M. de Choiseul and M. de Guemenée.

Then he completed the circuit of the saloon, and particularly complimented the Marchioness de Mirepoix, who did not feel altogether at her ease.

"You see what the price of treachery is," whispered the marshal in her ear; to-morrow you will be loaded with honors, while we—I shudder to think of it!" and he sighed.

"But I think you have rather betrayed the Choiseuls yourself, since you are here, and yet you swore——"

"For my daughter, for my poor Septimanie, marchioness; she will be disgraced for being too faithful!"

"To her father," replied the marchioness.

The marshal pretended not to hear this remark, which might have passed for an epigram.

"Do you not think," said he, "that the king is uneasy?"

"I think he has reason to be so; it is a quarter past ten."

"True—and the countess is not here! Shall I tell you what I think?"

"Yes."

"I have some fears."

"Fears about what?"

"Fears that something disagreeable may have happened to that poor countess. You know whether I am right or not, marchioness."

"I! how should I know?"

"Yes; you were up to the neck in the conspiracy."

"Well, I may tell you in confidence, marshal, that I cannot help sharing your fears."

"Oh, our friend the duchess is a fierce antagonist; she has fled, and like the Parthians, she wounds in fleeing. See how restless the Duke de Choiseul is, although he wishes to appear calm; he cannot stay a moment in one position, and he keeps his eye always on the king. Come —confess that there is some plot in the wind."

"I know nothing of it, duke; but like you, I have suspicions."

"But what can they gain by their plot?"

"Time, my dear marshal; and you know the proverb, 'He who gains time, gains all.' To-morrow something may occur to put off the presentation *sine die*. The dauphiness may reach Compiegne to-morrow instead of four days hence; perhaps they only wished to gain to-morrow."

"Do you know, marchioness, this little tale of yours has all the appearance of truth. There is no sign of her coming."

"And see, the king is becoming impatient!"

"That is the third time he has approached the window; he is really annoyed."

"Things will be much worse presently."

"How so?"

"It is twenty minutes past ten, is it not?"

"Yes."

"Then I may now tell you——"

"What?"

"The marchioness looked around, then whispered, "She will not come."

"Oh, heavens! But, marchioness, it will be a scandalous affair."

"It will perhaps cause a lawsuit—a criminal suit. I know from good authority that there will be in the case robbery, abduction, treason. The Choiseuls have played a bold game."

"Very imprudent in them."

"Passion rendered them blind."

"You see what an advantage we have over them in not being governed by our passions; we are cool, and can look at things calmly."

"Observe, the king is going again to the window."

Gloomy, anxious, and irritated, Louis had drawn near a window, leaned his head on a carved frame, and pressed his forehead to the cool glass.

During this time the conversation of the courtiers sounded like the rustling of the leaves of a forest before a tempest.

All eyes wandered from the king to the time-piece, and from the time-piece to the king. The half-hour struck the clear, vibrating sound died away in the vast saloon.

M. de Maupeou approached the king.

"Delightful weather, sire," said he, timidly.

"Very fine, very fine! Do you understand anything of this matter, Monsieur de Maupeou?"

"Of what, sire?

"About this delay—the poor countess."

"She must be ill, sire," replied the chancellor.

"I can comprehend that the Duchess de Grammont may be ill, that the Princess de Guemenée may be ill, that the Countess d'Egmont may be ill, but not that she should be ill."

"Sire, very great emotion often causes illness, and the countess's joy was so great."

"Ah! there is no longer any hope," said Louis, shaking his head; "she will not come now."

Although the king had uttered these words in a low voice, there was so profound a silence in the saloon that every one heard them. No one, however, had time to reply, even in thought, for just then the noise of a carriage was heard in the court of the palace. All heads moved; eyes interrogated eyes.

The king came forward to the middle of the saloon, that, through the open doors, he might see the whole length of the gallery.

"I am afraid," whispered the marchioness to the marshal, with a meaning smile, "that some bad news is coming."

But suddenly the king's face brightened, and his eyes flashed with pleasure.

"The Countess Dubarry! the Countess de Bearn!" cried the usher to the grand master of ceremonies.

These two names made all hearts beat, many with very opposite emotions. A crowd of courtiers, impelled by ungovernable curiosity, drew near the king.

The Marchioness de Mirepoix was nearest him; clasping her hands, she exclaimed, as if ready to fall down and worship: "Oh, how beautiful she is! how beautiful she is!"

The king turned a gracious smile on her.

"She is not a woman," said Richelieu; "she is a fairy."

The king sent the remainder of the smile in the direction of the old courtier.

In fact, the countess never had appeared more lovely; never had such a perfect representation of gentle agitation and modesty, never had a more charming figure or more noble carriage, graced the queen's saloon at Versailles, which, nevertheless, as we have said, was the saloon of presentations.

Lovely in the extreme, dressed with the most perfect taste, and above all, her hair dressed exquisitely, the countess advanced, conducted by Mme. de Bearn, who, notwithstanding her suffering, did not betray it by the slightest gesture; yet every movement caused each fiber of her frame to quiver, while from her dry and fevered cheeks the rouge dropped atom by atom.

Every eye was fixed upon the pair who represented such a strange contrast. The old lady, her neck uncovered, as in the time of her youth, her head-dress standing up a foot above her head, and her large eyes glittering in their deep sockets like those of an osprey, seemed, in her splendid dress, with her skeleton appearance, the type of the past leading forward the present.

So striking was the contrast that it seemed to the king as if his favorite had never looked so beautiful as now, when receiving her from the hand of the old Countess de Bearn.

Just as the countess, according to the etiquette, sunk on her knees to kiss the king's hand, Louis seized her arm, raised her up, and in a few words rewarded her for all she had suffered during the last fortnight.

"You, at my feet, countess!" said he. "It is I who should be, and who always wish to be, at yours."

Then he extended his arms to her, following the usual ceremonial, but on this occasion the embrace was not a pretended, but a real, one.

"You have a lovely goddaughter, madame," said the king to the Countess de Bearn; "but she has as noble a chaperon, and one whom I rejoice to see again in my court."

The old lady bowed.

"Go and pay your respects to my daughters," whispered the king to Mme. Dubarry, "and show them that you know how to make a courtesy. I hope you will have cause to be satisfied with their reception of you."

The two ladies advanced in the space which was formed around them, while the eager looks of all followed every movement which they made.

The king's three daughters, seeing them approach, rose as if moved by springs, and remained standing. Their father fixed a look on them which commanded them to be polite.

The princesses, a little agitated, returned Mme. Dubarry's courtesy, which she made much lower than etiquette demanded, and this they thought such good taste that they embraced her as the king had done, and delighted him by their cordiality.

From that moment the countess's success became a triumph, and the slower and less adroit courtiers had to wait an hour before they could get their bow made to the queen of the night.

She, free from coldness or any feelings of recrimination, received all advances favorably, and seemed to forget all the treachery used against her. Nor was this mere pretense; for her heart was too full of joy to be anything but magnanimous, or to have room for a single unamiable feeling.

Marshal Richelieu showed a knowledge of tactics worthy of the victor of Mahon. While vulgar courtiers waited in their places, the result of the presentation, in order to decide whether they should offer incense to the idol or turn their backs on her, he took up a position behind the countess's chair, like a fugelman who serves as a guide by which to deploy a troop of cavalry on a given point. The result was that at last he found himself close to Mme. Dubarry, without being troubled by the crowd. The Marchioness de Mirepoix knew that her old friend had been successful in war; she therefore imitated his tactics, and gradually drew her seat near that of the favorite.

Conversation now commenced among the different groups. The countess was criticized from head to foot. She, supported by the love of the king, by the gracious reception of the princesses, and by the high rank of the lady who had presented her, looked round less timidly on the men, and sought out her enemies among the women.

An opaque body obscured her view.

"Ah! Marshal Richelieu," said she, "I was obliged to come here in order to meet you."

"How so, madame?"

"Is it not eight days since I have seen you, either at Versailles, or in Paris, or at Luciennes?"

"I wished to render the pleasure greater of seeing you here this evening," replied the old courtier.

"You guessed that I should be here?"

"I was certain of it."

"Oh, marshal, you knew it, and you did not tell your poor friend who knew nothing about it."

"What! madame, you did not know that you were to be here?"

"No; I was like Æsop when a magistrate arrested him in the street—'Where are you going?' said he. 'I don't know,' replied the fabulist. 'Then you shall go to prison,' the other replied. 'You see plainly,' said Æsop, 'that I did not know where I was going.' In like manner, duke, I had some idea that I should go to Versailles, but I was not sure. That is why you would have done me a great service had you come and told me that I should be here. But you will come to see me now—will you not?"

"Madame," replied Richelieu, without being moved by her raillery, "I really do not understand how it was that you were not sure of being here."

"I shall tell you: it was because snares were laid on all sides for me;" and she looked steadily at him; but he bore her look without wincing.

" Snares ! Good heavens ! How could that be ? "

" First, they stole my hair-dresser."

" Stole your hair-dresser ? "

" Yes."

" But why did you not inform me ? I could have sent you—but let us speak low—I could have sent you a treasure ; my daughter, Madame d'Egmont, found him out. He is quite a superior artist to all others, even the royal hair-dressers—my little Leonard."

" Leonard ? " cried Mme. Dubarry.

" Yes, a young man whom she hides from every one. But you have no reason to complain, countess ; your hair is charmingly dressed ; and, singular enough, the design is exactly like the sketch which the Countess d'Egmont ordered from Boucher for her own head-dress, and which she intended to have used this evening had she not been ill. Poor Septimanie ! "

The countess started, and again fixed a searching look upon the marshal ; but he continued smiling and impenetrable.

" But pardon me, countess, for interrupting you," said he ; " you were speaking of snares."

" Yes, after having carried off my hair-dresser, they stole my dress—a most beautiful dress."

" How shocking ! However, it was not of much consequence, as you had another dress so wonderfully beautiful as that you wear. It is Chinese silk, with flowers embroidered on it. Well, if you had applied to me in your trouble, as you must always do for the future, I could have sent you a dress which my daughter had ordered so like that, that I could swear it was the same."

Mme. Dubarry seized both the duke's hands, for she now began to suspect who was the enchanter who had befriended her in her difficulties.

" Do you know in whose carriage I came, marshal ? " said she.

" In your own—no doubt."

" No—they stole my carriage as well as my hair-dresser. Why, it was a regular ambuscade ! "

" In whose carriage, then, did you come ? "

" Will you tell me first what the Countess d'Egmont's carriage is like ? "

" I think that for this evening she had ordered one lined with white satin ; but there was not time to paint the coat of arms."

" Yes," exclaimed the countess, " and .they substituted a rose instead ! Marshal, marshal, you are an adorable man !" and she held out to him both her hands, which he covered with kisses. All at once he felt her start.

" What is the matter, countess ? " inquired he, looking round.

" Marshal," said the countess, with an alarmed air, " who is that man near the Prince de Guemenée ? "

" In a Prussian uniform ? "

" Yes—the dark man with black eyes, and such an expressive countenance."

" He is some officer of rank, countess, whom his Prussian majesty has sent, no doubt, to do honor to your presentation."

" Do not jest, marshal. I know that man. He was in France three or four years ago ; I have sought him everywhere, but could never discover him."

" I think you must be mistaken, countess. He is the Count de Fenix, a foreigner, and only arrived in France yesterday or the day before."

" Observe how he looks at me."

" Every one looks at you, you are so beautiful."

" He bows to me—he bows to me—do you see him ? "

" Every one bows to you, at least all who have not already done so."

But the countess, who seemed greatly agitated, paid no attention to the duke's gallant speeches, but kept her eyes riveted on the stranger who had attracted her attention. Then rising, as if involuntarily, she advanced a few steps toward the unknown.

The king, who kept his eye fixed on her, observed this movement, and thought that she desired to be near him ;

and as etiquette had been sufficiently attended to in keeping so long from her side, he approached to congratulate her on her success. Her thoughts were, however, too much engaged to be turned from their object.

"Sire," said she, "who is that Prussian officer with his back to the Prince de Guemenée?"

"And who is looking at us this moment?" asked the king.

"Yes."

"That strongly marked face, that square head, framed, as it were, in the gold collar?"

"Yes—yes—the same."

"He is an accredited agent of my cousin of Prussia—some philosopher like himself, I think. I desired him to be here this evening, as I wished Prussian philosophy to enhance, by its embassador, the triumph of Cotillon III."

"But what is his name, sire?"

"Let me think—ah!—yes—the Count de Fenix."

"It is the same," murmured she to herself; "yes, I am sure it is he."

The king waited a few minutes, in order to give Mme. Dubarry time to ask further questions if she wished to do so; but finding that she did not speak, he said, in a loud voice, "Ladies, her royal highness, the dauphiness, will arrive to-morrow at Compiegne; we shall meet her precisely at noon. All the ladies who have been presented will go, except, however, those who are ill, for the journey might be fatiguing, and her royal highness would be sorry to aggravate their indisposition."

As the king pronounced these words, he looked sternly at the Duke de Choiseul, the Prince de Guemenée, and the Marshal de Richelieu.

There was a profound silence; every one understood the meaning of the royal words—they carried disgrace in their front.

"Sire," said Mme. Dubarry, who had remained near the king, "may I request your gracious pardon for the Countess d'Egmont?"

"Why so, may I ask!

" Because she is the daughter of Marshal Richelieu, who is my most faithful friend."

" Richelieu ? "

" I am certain he is, sire."

" I shall do what you wish, countess," said the king.

The king then approached the marshal, who had watched every movement of the countess's lips, and if he had not heard her words, had at least guessed their meaning.

" I hope, my dear marshal," said he, " that the Countess d'Egmont will be better to-morrow."

" Certainly, sire ; if your majesty desire it, she will even come out this evening."

And Richelieu made a bow which expressed at once respect and gratitude.

The king then whispered a word in the countess's ear.

" Sire," replied she, with a courtesy accompanied by a charming smile, " I am your majesty's obedient servant."

The king, by a wave of his hand, saluted all the assembly and retired.

Scarcely had he crossed the threshold when the countess's eyes turned again on the singular man who had before attracted her so strongly.

This man bowed like the rest as the king passed along, but even as he bowed there was something haughty, almost threatening, in the expression of his countenance. When Louis XV. had disappeared, he made way for himself through the different groups, and stopped within two paces of Mme. Dubarry. The countess, attracted by an inexpressible curiosity, made one step forward, so that, as the unknown bowed to her, he could say in a low voice, so as not to be overheard, " Do you know me again, madame ? "

" Yes, sir ; you are the prophet whom I met in the Place Louis XV."

The stranger fixed his clear, penetrating glance on her.

" Well, did I speak falsely, madame, when I predicted you should be Queen of France ? "

" No, sir ; your prediction is accomplished, or at least

nearly so, and I am ready to fulfil my part of the engagement. Speak, sir, what do you desire ? "

" This place is ill-chosen for such a purpose : besides, the moment for me to make my request is not yet come."

" Whenever it does come, you will find me ready to grant it."

" May I, at any time, in any place, at any hour, have liberty to be admitted to your presence ? "

" I promise it."

" Thanks."

" But under what name shall I expect you ?   Under that of the Count de Fenix ? "

" No ; under that of Joseph Balsamo."

" Joseph Balsamo," repeated the countess to herself, while the mysterious stranger disappeared among the groups of courtiers—" Joseph Balsamo—I shall not forget it."

CHAPTER XXXIX.

COMPIEGNE.

THE following morning Compiègne awoke, transported, intoxicated with joy ; or, rather, to be more exact, Compiègne never went to rest.

The evening before the first detachment of the king's guards had entered the town, and while the officers took up their position, the magistrates, assisted by the lord high steward and other functionaries, prepared the town for the distinguished honor which was to be conferred on it.   Triumphal arches, composed of evergreens, roses, and lilacs ; inscriptions in Latin, French, and German ; composition in verse and prose, occupied the sub-magistracy of Picardy from night till morn.

Young girls, dressed in white, according to immemorial usage ; municipal officers clad in black ; monks attired in gray ; the clergy in their richest vesture ; officers and soldiers in their new uniforms—all were at their posts ready to advance at the first signal of the arrival of the dauphiness.

The dauphin had arrived incognito with his two brothers, about eleven o'clock the night before. Very early in the morning he mounted his horse, as if he had been a private gentleman, and followed by his brothers, the Count de Provençe and the Count d'Artois, the one fifteen and the other thirteen years of age, he galloped off in the direction of Ribecourt, the road by which the princess was to approach. It was not to the young prince, we must confess, that this gallant idea had first occurred ; it was suggested by his tutor, M. de Lavanguyon, who had been desired by the king to instruct his august pupil in all the duties which the next twenty-four hours would impose on him. The tutor, therefore, had thought right, in order to maintain the honor of the monarchy, to cause him to follow the traditional example of the kings of his race—Henry IV., Louis XIII., Louis XIV., and Louis XV. —who desired to see their future wives without any of the illusions of dress and ornament, and therefore met them when not expected on the road.

Mounted on swift horses, the three brothers accomplished three or four leagues in half an hour ; the eldest had set out serious, the two others laughing. At half-past eight they returned ; the dauphin still serious, the Count de Provençe almost ill-tempered, the Count d'Artois more gay than before. The dauphin was uneasy, the Count de Provençe envious, and the Count d'Artois enchanted about one and the same thing—the beauty of the dauphiness. The grave, jealous, and careless character of each prince respectively was written on his face.

At ten o'clock the lookout employed to watch for the expected train announced that a white flag was displayed on the steeple of the church of Claives, which was to be the signal that the dauphiness was approaching. The bells of the church commenced to ring, and were answered by the firing of cannon.

At that instant, as if he had only waited for this signal, the king entered Compiègne in a carriage drawn by eight horses, between a double file of his body-guards, and followed by the immense train of the carriages of the court. The guards and dragoons at a gallop opened a passage through the crowd, which was divided between two feelings —desire to see the king and curiosity with regard to the dauphiness. One hundred carriages, drawn by four horses, extending nearly a league in length, contained four hundred ladies, and as many lords of the noblest families in France. These hundred carriages were escorted by outriders, heiducs, footmen, and pages. The gentlemen of the king's household were on horseback, and formed a brilliant army, glittering like a sea of velvet and gold, waving plumes, and silk, in the midst of the dust raised by the horses' feet.

They halted an instant at Compiègne, then slowly proceeded to the spot agreed upon for the meeting, and marked by a cross, near the village of Magny. All the young nobility thronged around the dauphin, and all the old around the king.

On the other side the dauphiness was also slowly approaching the appointed place.

At length the two parties met. On both sides the courtiers left their carriages : two only remained occupied—that of the king and that of the dauphiness. The door of the dauphiness's carriage was open, and the young archduchess sprung lightly to the ground, and advanced to the royal carriage. The king, on perceiving his daughter-in-law, ordered the door to be opened, and hurriedly got out.

The dauphiness had calculated her time so well that just as the king put his foot to the ground she was close to him, and she sunk on her knee. He raised the young princess and embraced her tenderly, yet casting a look upon her which made her blush.

" His royal highness the dauphin," said the king, introducing his grandson, who had kept behind the dauphiness without being seen by her, at least ostensibly.

The dauphiness made him a graceful courtesy ; he bowed, blushing in his turn.

Then, after the dauphin came his two brothers, then

the three princesses ; the dauphiness had something gracious to say to each.

While these introductions were going on, Mme. Dubarry stood anxiously behind the princesses. Would she be thought of ? Would she be forgotten ?

After the introduction of the Princess Sophie, the last of the king's daughters, there was a pause ; every breath was suspended. The king seemed to hesitate ; the dauphiness seemed to expect some incident concerning which she had been previously informed.

The king looked round, and seeing the countess within reach, took her hand ; all near him stepped back, and he found himself in the midst of a circle with the dauphiness.

"The Countess Dubarry," said he, "my very dear friend."

The dauphiness turned pale, yet a gracious smile appeared on her white lips. "Your majesty is happy," said she, "in possessing so charming a friend ; and I am not surprised at the attachment which she inspires."

Every one heard these words with astonishment amounting to stupefaction. It was evident that the dauphiness followed the instructions of the court of Austria ; perhaps the very words she repeated were dictated by Maria Theresa.

The Duke de Choiseul then thought his presence was necessary. He advanced to be presented in his turn ; but the king made a sign with his head, the trumpets sounded, the drums beat, the cannon was fired. His majesty took the young princess's hand, to conduct her to her carriage. She passed close to the Duke de Choiseul. Did she see him or did she not ? It was impossible to say ; but it is certain that she made no sign of recognition. At the moment when she entered her carriage, the bells of the town pealed out, and their clear tones were heard above all the other festive sounds.

The countess returned to her carriage, all radiant with delight and pride.

There was a halt for about ten minutes, while the king was reentering his carriage and giving his orders to return to Compiègne. During this time, conversation, which had been suspended from respect or by the interest of the scene, again became general. Dubarry drew near his sister's carriage—she received him with smiles, expecting his congratulations.

"Jeanne," said he, pointing to a gentleman on horseback, who was talking at the door of a carriage in the train of the dauphiness, "do you know that young man?"

"No," replied the countess: "but do you know what the dauphiness said when the king presented me to her?"

"I am not thinking of that. That young man is the Chevalier Philip de Taverney."

"He who wounded you?"

"Yes; and do you know who that beautiful creature is with whom he is talking?"

"The young girl so pale and so majestic?"

"Yes, she whom the king is looking at this moment—I think he is asking the dauphiness her name."

"Well, what then?"

"That young girl is Taverney's sister."

"Ah!" exclaimed the countess.

"Jeanne, I don't know why, but I think you have as much reason to fear the sister as I the brother."

"You are a fool!"

"No, I am tolerably wise; and I shall, at all events, look after the youth."

"Well, then, I shall keep an eye on the girl."

"Hush, here is our friend, Marshal Richelieu!"

The marshal drew near, shaking his head.

"What is the matter, my dear marshal?" inquired the countess, with her most fascinating smile; you seem dissatisfied with something."

"Don't you think, countess," said the duke, "that we all seem very grave, not to say sorrowful, for such a joyous occasion? Formerly I know, we were much more gay when we went to meet a princess as amiable and as beautiful as this, the mother of his royal highness, the dauphin. Was it because we were younger then?"

"No," answered a voice behind the marshal ; "no, my dear marshal, but because the monarchy was not so old."

"Heaven and earth !" exclaimed the marshal, "it is the Baron de Taverney ! Countess, one of my oldest friends, for whom I solicit your kindness—the Baron de Taverney Maison Rouge."

"The father," whispered Jean and the countess to each other as they stooped to salute the baron.

"To your carriages, gentlemen—to your carriages !" cried the major of the guards commanding the escort.

The two old gentlemen bowed to the countess and to the viscount, and both entered the same carriage, delighted to meet once more after so long a separation.

"And now," said the viscount, "shall I tell you another thing, my dear ? I have as little love for the father as the children."

"What a pity !" replied the countess, "that that little wretch, Gilbert, ran away. He was brought up in their house, and could have told us so much about them."

"Pshaw ! I shall find him again, now that I have nothing else to think about."

The conversation was interrupted by the carriages being again put in motion.

After having passed the night in Compiègne, the two courts—the one the sunset, the other the dawn of an age —set out on the following day for Paris—that yawning gulf which was to entomb them both.

CHAPTER XL.

THE PATRONESS AND THE PATRONIZED.

IT is now time that we should return to Gilbert, of whose flight the reader has been made aware by an imprudent exclamation of his protectress, Mlle. Chon, but of whom we have since heard nothing.

Our philosopher had cooled very much in his admiration of his patroness from the very moment that he had, during the preliminaries of the duel between Philip de Taverney and Viscount Jean, become aware that her name was Dubarry.

Often at Taverney, when hidden by some hedge, he had followed Andrée and her father in their walks, he had heard the baron explain, at great length, all about the Dubarry family. The hatred of the old baron to Mme. Dubarry—a feeling which in him, however, sprung from no dislike to what was in itself vicious—found a ready echo in Gilbert's heart, arising principally from her conduct being regarded by Andrée with contempt and reprobation, sentiments which may be taken as expressing the general opinion of the nation toward her whole family.

During the journey Chon was too much occupied with matters of a more serious import to pay attention to the change of feeling which the knowledge of who were his traveling companions had produced in Gilbert. She reached Versailles, therefore, only thinking of how the viscount's wound, since it would not redound to his honor, might be turned to his greatest profit.

As to Gilbert, scarcely had he entered the capital—if not of France, at least of the French monarchy—than he forgot every unpleasant thought, and gave free scope to his undisguised admiration. Versailles, so majestic and stately, with its lofty trees already beginning to show symptoms of decay, touched his heart with that religious sadness which poetic minds always experience in contemplating the mighty works of nature, or those erected by the perseverance of man.

From this impression—a very novel one to Gilbert, and one against which his innate pride struggled in vain—he became silent and submissive, overcome by wonder and admiration.

The feeling of his inferiority crushed him to the earth. When the great lords, in their stars and ribbons, passed by him, how deeply did he feel the wretchedness of his attire! How inferior did he feel, even to the porters and footmen! How did he tremble when, in his hob-nailed shoes, he had to walk over the shining marble or polished inlaid floors!

At such times he felt that the protection of his patroness was indispensable to him, unless he wished to sink into absolute nothingness. He drew near her, that it might be seen he belonged to her; yet it was for this very reason that he needed her, that he disliked her.

We are already aware that Mme. Dubarry occupied at Versailles the magnificent suite of rooms formerly inhabited by the Princess Adelaide. The gold, the marble, the perfumes, the carpets, the hangings, at first intoxicated Gilbert; and it was only after these had become somewhat familiar to him, that his understanding—dazzled by the reflected light which so many marvels cast on it—roused itself in the end to a clear perception of surrounding objects, and he found that he was in a little attic room, hung with serge—that there had been placed before him a basin of soup, some cold mutton, and a custard. The servant who had brought these eatables had said, with the tone of a master, "Remain here!" and then left him.

But Gilbert soon found that the picture had its sunny side. From the window of his garret he could see the park of Versailles, studded with marble statues, and ornamented with fountains. Beyond, were the dense and lofty summits of the trees, rolling like a sea of verdure; and, further still, the checkered plains and the blue horizon of the neighboring mountains. The only subject which occupied Gilbert's mind while eating his dinner was that, like the greatest lords of France, without being either a courtier or a lackey, without having been introduced there either by birth or baseness, he was living in Versailles, in the palace of the king.

His dinner, too, was an excellent one, when compared with those to which he had been accustomed. When it was over, he returned to his contemplation at the window. Meantime, Chon had, as the reader may remember, joined her sister, had whispered that her business with Mme. de Bearn was happily executed, and then related aloud the accident which their brother met with at Lachaussée. This accident, although it made a great noise at first, was lost, as the reader has seen, in that great gulf which swallowed up so many things much more important—the king's indifference.

Gilbert had fallen into one of those reveries to which he often gave way, while meditating on what was beyond his comprehension, or on what was impracticable for him to accomplish, when he was told that his patroness requested his presence. He took his hat, brushed it, compared by a glance his old worn coat with the new one of the footman, and saying to himself that that of the latter was a livery coat, he followed him. Yet, notwithstanding this philosophic reflection, he could not help blushing with shame to observe how little he resembled the men who elbowed him, and how much out of keeping he was with everything around him.

Chon was descending to the court at the same time as himself, with this difference, that she took the grand staircase, he a little back one more resembling a ladder. A carriage was waiting for them. It was a kind of low phaeton, containing seats for four persons, and resembled that historical vehicle in which the great king used to drive out with Mme. de Montespan, Mme. de Fontanges, and frequently with them the queen.

Chon got in and took the front seat, with a large box and a little dog beside her ; the other seat was for Gilbert, and a kind of steward called M. Grange. Gilbert hastened to take the place behind Chon, in order to keep up his dignity ; the steward, without thinking there was any degradation in the matter, placed himself behind the box, and the dog.

As Mlle. Chon, like all who inhabited Versailles, felt joyous on leaving the great palace to inhale the air of the woods, and the meadows, she became communicative, and was scarcely out of the town, when she turned half round and said, "Well, what do you think of Versailles, Mr. Philosopher ? "

"It is very beautiful, madame ; but we are quitting it already ? "

"Yes ; now we are going to our own home."

" That is to say, to *your* home, madame," said Gilbert, with the tone of a half-tamed bear.

" That is what I meant. I shall introduce you to my sister ; try to please her. All the greatest noblemen in France are only too happy if they can succeed in doing so. By the bye, Grange, you must order a complete suit for this boy."

Gilbert blushed up to the eyes.

" What kind of a suit, madame ? " asked the steward. " The usual livery ? "

Gilbert half started from his seat.

" Livery ! " cried he, with a fierce look at the steward.

Chon burst into a laugh.

" No," said she ; " you will order—but no matter, I will tell you another time. I have an idea on which I wish for my sister's opinion. But take care to have the suit ready at the same time as Zamore's."

" Very well, madame."

" Do you know Zamore ? " asked Chon, turning to Gilbert, who began to be very much alarmed by the conversation.

" No, madame ; I have not that honor," replied he.

" He will be a young companion of yours ; he is going to be governor of the château of Luciennes. Endeavor to gain his friendship—for Zamore is a good creature, in spite of his color."

Gilbert was about to ask of what color he was ; but recollecting the reproof he had already received on the subject of curiosity, he refrained, for fear of another reprimand.

" I shall try," he answered, with a dignified smile.

ney reached Luciennes. The philosopher saw everything ; the road, lately planted, the shady slopes, the great aqueduct, which resembled a work of the Romans, the dense wood of chestnut-trees, the varied and the magnificent prospect of plains and woods, stretching away on both sides of the Seine to Maisons.

" This, then," said he to himself, " is the country-seat which costs France so much, and of which I have heard the baron often speak."

Bounding dogs and eager domestics ran out to welcome Chon, and interrupted Gilbert in the midst of his aristo-cratico-philosophical reflections.

" Has my sister arrived ? " asked Chon.

" No, madame ; but there are visitors waiting for her."

" Who are they ? "

" The chancellor, the minister of police, and the Duke d'Aiguillon."

" Well, run quickly and open my sister's private cabinet, and tell her when she arrives that I am there ; do you understand ?   Oh, Sylvia," added she, addressing a *femme de chambre* who had taken from her the box and the little dog, " give the box and Misapouf to Grange, and take my little philosopher to Zamore."

Sylvia looked all round, doubtless to find out what sort of animal Chon was speaking of ; but her eyes and those of her mistress, happening to rest on Gilbert at the same moment, Chon made a sign that the young man was the person in question

" Come," said Sylvia.

Gilbert, still more and more surprised at all that he saw, followed the *femme de chambre*, while Chon, light as a bird, disappeared by a side door of the pavilion.

Had it not been for the commanding tone in which Chon addressed her, Gilbert would have taken Mlle. Sylvia for a great lady, rather than a *femme de chambre*, as her dress resembled Andrée's much more than Nicole's.   The young and handsome waiting-woman took him by the hand with a gracious smile ; for her mistress's words showed that, if not an object of affection, he was chosen at least through some new whim.

" What is your name, sir ? " said she.

" Gilbert, mademoiselle," replied the young man, in a gentle voice.

" Well, sir, I am going to introduce you to my Lord Zamore."

" To the governor of the château of Luciennes ? "

" Yes, to the governor."

Gilbert pulled down his sleeves, dusted his coat a little, and wiped his hands with his handkerchief. He was in reality rather intimidated at the idea of appearing before so important a personage; but he recalled Chon's remark, "Zamore is a good creature," and recovered his courage. He was already the friend of a countess and a viscount; he was going to be the friend of a governor. "Well," thought he, "surely people calumniate the court; it is certainly easy enough to find friends in it; at least, as far as me experience goes, I have found every one kind and hospitable."

Sylvia threw open the door of an anteroom, which, from its splendor, might rather have been supposed a boudoir. The panels of the walls were of tortoise-shell, inlaid with copper gilt; and one might have imagined himself in the atrium of Lucullus, but that that ancient Roman used pure gold to decorate his walls.

There, in an immense armchair, half buried in cushions, sitting cross-legged, and gnawing chocolate cakes, reposed my Lord Zamore, whom we already know, but whom Gilbert till now had never seen. The effect, therefore, which the governor of Luciennes produced on the mind of the philosopher was rather curiously depicted in his face. He stared with all his might at the strange being, for it was the first time he had ever seen a negro.

"Oh, oh!" cried he, "what is that?"

As for Zamore, he never raised his head, but continued to munch his cakes, rolling his eyes and showing the whites of them in the excess of his enjoyment.

"That," said Sylvia, "is my Lord Zamore."

"That person?" said Gilbert, almost dumb with amazement.

"Yes, to be sure," answered Sylvia, laughing in spite of herself at the turn the scene was taking.

"He the governor?" continued Gilbert. "That ape the governor of the château of Luciennes? Oh, mademoiselle, you are certainly jesting with me!"

At these words, Zamore raised his head and showed his white teeth.

"Me governor," said he; "me not ape."

Gilbert looked from Zamore to Sylvia, and his glance, at first uneasy, became wrathful, when the young woman, in spite of all her efforts, burst into a fit of laughter. As for Zamore, grave and solemn as an Indian fetish, he plunged his black claw in a satin bag, and took out a handful of his cakes.

At this moment the door opened, and the steward entered, followed by a tailor.

"Here," said he, pointing to Gilbert, "is the person for whom you are to make the suit; take the measure according to the directions I gave you."

Gilbert mechanically submitted his arms and shoulders to be measured, while Sylvia and Grange were talking in another part of the room, and at every word of the steward the chambermaid laughed louder and louder.

"Oh, it will be delightful!" she said. "And will he wear a pointed cap like Sganarello?"

Gilbert heard no more; he rudely pushed the tailor aside, and absolutely refused to submit to the rest of the ceremony. He knew nothing about Sganarello; but the name, and particularly Sylvia's mirth, plainly declared that he was some preeminently ridiculous personage.

"It is of no consequence," said the steward to the tailor. "Don't hurt him. I suppose you can do very well with the measure you have taken?"

"Certainly," replied the tailor, "for width does no harm in such suits. I shall make it very wide."

Whereupon Sylvia, the steward, and the tailor, walked off, leaving Gilbert with the little negro, who continued to gnaw his cakes and roll his great eyes. What an enigma was all this to the poor country lad! What fears, what anguish did the philosopher experience, in seeing his dignity as a man evidently more compromised at Luciennes than ever it had been at Taverney!

However, he tried to talk to Zamore. It occurred to him that he might be some Indian prince, such as he had read of in the romances of M. Crebillon the younger. But the Indian prince, instead of replying, made the circuit of the apartment from mirror to mirror, admiring his splendid clothes like a bride in her wedding-dress. After that he got astride on a chair with wheels, and impelling it with his feet, he whirled round the ante-chamber some dozen times with a velocity which showed that he had made a profound study of that ingenious exercise.

Suddenly a bell rang. Zamore jumped up from his chair, and hurried through one of the doors in the direction of the sound. This promptness in obeying the silvery tinkling convinced Gilbert that Zamore was not a prince.

For a moment he entertained the idea of following him; but on reaching the end of the passage which led into a saloon, he saw so many blue ribbons and red ribbons, guarded by lackeys so bold, impudent, and noisy, that he felt a chill run through his veins, and, with a cold perspiration on his forehead, he returned to his anteroom.

An hour passed. Zamore did not return; Sylvia was seen no more. Any human face would have seemed then to Gilbert better than none, were it even that of the dreaded tailor who was to complete the mystification with which he was threatened.

Just at that moment the door by which he had entered the room opened, and a footman appeared and said, "Come!"

CHAPTER XLI.

THE PHYSICIAN AGAINST HIS WILL.

GILBERT felt it rather disagreeable to be obliged to obey a footman; nevertheless, he lost no time in following him, for he thought that now there was some prospect of a change in his condition, and it seemed to him that any change must be for the better.

Chon, now completely her own mistress, after having initiated her sister into the whole affair of the Countess de Bearn, was breakfasting very much at her ease in a

charming morning-dress, beside a window shaded with
acacias and chestnut-trees.

She was eating with an excellent appetite, and Gilbert
remarked that a pheasant and truffles justified the relish
with which she enjoyed her breakfast.

The philosopher, having entered the apartment, looked
around to discover his place at the table, but there was no
plate for him, and he was not even asked to sit down.

Chon merely cast a glance on him; then, after swallowing
a little glass of wine, as clear and yellow as a topaz:

"Well, my dear doctor," said she, "how have you got
on with Zamore?"

"How have I got on with him?"

"Yes; I hope you have become acquainted with him?"

"How could one make acquaintance with an animal
like that who never speaks, and who, when one speaks to
him, only rolls his eyes?"

"Really you frighten me!" said Chon, without stopping one moment in her repast, and without her countenance showing any expression at all corresponding
to her words. "Your friendship is difficult to gain,
then?"

"Friendship presupposes equality, madame."

"A noble maxim," said Chon. "Then you don't think
yourself the equal of Zamore?"

"That is to say, that I do not think him my equal,"
replied Gilbert.

"In truth," said Chon, as if talking to herself, "he is
charming."

Then, turning to Gilbert, she remarked his stately
air.

"So, my dear doctor," said she, "you do not easily
bestow your affections?"

"No, madame, not easily."

"Then I was mistaken when I thought you held me as
your friend, and as a good friend, too?"

"Madame," said Gilbert, very stiffly, "I feel for you
naturally a liking——"

"Oh, a thousand thanks for your condescension! You

really overwhelm me ! And how long do you think, my scornful young gentleman, it would require to gain your affection ? "

" A long time, madame ; and there are even persons who, whatever they did, could never obtain it."

" Oh! then that explains the reason why, after having been eighteen years in the Baron de Taverney's house, you left it all at once. The Taverneys were not so fortunate as to obtain your affections—that was it, was it not ? "

Gilbert blushed.

" Well, you don't answer," continued Chon.

" I have nothing to reply, madame, but that friendship and confidence must be merited."

" Oh! it appears, then, that your friends at Taverney did not merit your friendship and confidence ? "

" Not all of them, madame."

" Ah ! and what had those done who were so unfortunate as not to please you ? "

" I did not complain of them, madame," answered he, proudly.

" Well, well ! I perceive, Mr. Gilbert, that I am also one of the unfortunates excluded from your confidence ; yet, believe me, it is not from any want of a desire to obtain it, but from my not knowing the right means of doing so."

Gilbert bit his lip.

" But to shorten the matter," added she, with an inquisitiveness which he felt must be for some object, " the Taverneys did not behave quite satisfactorily to you. Tell me, if you please, what was your occupation in their establishment ? "

This was rather an embarrassing question, as Gilbert certainly could not say that he held any particular office at Taverney.

" Madame," said he, " I was—I was their confidential adviser."

At these words, which he pronounced most phlegmatically and philosophically, Chon was seized with such a fit of laughter that she threw herself back in her chair.

"Do you doubt my words?" asked Gilbert, frowning.

"Heaven preserve me from such a rash act, my dear friend! Really, you are so fierce, that one can scarcely venture to speak to you. I merely asked what sort of people the Taverneys were. Believe me, it was with no other intention than that of serving you, by assisting you to be revenged on them."

"If I am revenged, madame, it must be by myself."

"All very well; but we have a cause of complaint against the Taverneys ourselves; and, as you have one, or, perhaps, indeed, several, we are naturally allies in our wish for revenge."

"You are quite mistaken, madame. Should I think of vengeance, mine could have no connection with yours. You speak of all the Taverneys, while I have different shades of feeling toward different members of the family."

"The Chevalier Philip de Taverney, for instance, is he of the number of your friends or enemies?"

"I have nothing to say against the chevalier. He never did me either good or ill. I neither love him nor hate him; I am quite indifferent to him."

"Then you would not give evidence before the king, or before the Duke de Choiseul, against Monsieur Philip de Taverney?"

"Give evidence about what?"

"About the duel with my brother."

'I should say all that I know about it, if I were called upon to give evidence."

"And what do you know about it?"

"The truth."

"But what do you call truth? That is a word whose meaning is very vague."

"No; not by the man who can distinguish between good and evil—between justice and injustice."

"I understand you; justice is on the side of the Chevalier de Taverney, injustice on that of Viscount Dubarry?"

"Yes, madame; so I think, if I must speak conscientiously."

"So this is the creature I picked up on the highway!"

said Chon, sharply. "I am rewarded in this way by one who owes it to me that he is living."

"That is to say, madame, who does not owe you his death."

"It is all the same."

"On the contrary, madame, it is very different."

"How, different ?"

"I do not owe my life to you ; you merely prevented your horses from depriving me of it; besides it was not you, but the postilion."

Chon fixed a penetrating look on the young logician, who showed so little scruple in the choice of his terms.

"I should have expected," said she, in a milder tone, and allowing a smile to steal over her features, " a little more gallantry from you. Come, come, you will give evidence against the chevalier, will you not ?"

"No, madame—never !"

"And why not, you foolish fellow ?"

"Because the viscount was in the wrong."

"And, pray, how was he in the wrong ?"

"By insulting the dauphiness ; while, on the contrary, the chevalier——"

"Well, what ?"

"Was right in defending her."

"Oh, ho ! then it appears you belong to the dauphiness's party ?"

"No ; I am only for justice."

"Hold your tongue, Gilbert ; you are a fool ! Do not let any one hear you talk in that way here."

"Then, permit me to remain silent when I am questioned."

" In that case, let us change the subject."

Gilbert bowed in token of assent.

" And now, my little friend," said the young lady, in rather a harsh tone of voice, " what do you intend to do here, if you refuse to make yourself agreeable ?"

"Must I perjure myself in order to make myself agreeable ?"

"Perjure ? Where did you learn all those grand words ?"

" In the knowledge that I have a conscience to which I must be faithful."

" Pshaw ! " said Chon. " When we serve a master, the master takes all the responsibility from our conscience."

" But I have no master," growled Gilbert.

" Indeed ? Well, answer my question. What do you intend to do here ? "

" I did not think that I required to study to be agreeable when I could be useful."

" You are mistaken ; we can get useful people anywhere ; we are tired of them."

" Then I shall go away."

" You will go away ? "

" Yes, of course. I did not ask to come here ; 1 am, therefore, free."

" Free ? " exclaimed Chon, who began to get angry at this resistance to her will, a thing to which she was by no means accustomed.

" Free ? Indeed, you are not ! "

Gilbert's brow contracted.

" Come, come ! " said she, seeing by his frown that he would not easily renounce his freedom, " let us be friends. You are a handsome lad, and very virtuous, which makes you very amusing, were it only for the contrast which you will present to everybody else about us. Only keep a guard upon that love of truth of yours."

" I shall take care to keep it," said Gilbert.

" Yes ; but we understand the word in two different senses. I mean to keep it to yourself. You need not exhibit it in the lobbies and anterooms of Luciennes or Versailles."

" Hum ! " said Gilbert.

" There is no occasion for ' hum ' ! You are not so learned, Mr. Philosopher, but that you may learn something from a woman ; and let this be your first maxim, ' to hold your tongue is not to lie ' —remember that ! "

" But if any one questions me ? "

" Who would question you ? Are you mad, my friend ? Who in the world would ever think about you but myself ?

You have not yet founded a school, Mr. Philosopher, I presume. It will require some little searching and trouble before you happen upon a body of followers. You shall live with me; and before four times four-and-twenty hours, I shall transform you into a perfect courtier."

"I doubt that," replied Gilbert, majestically.

Chon shrugged her shoulders.

Gilbert smiled.

"Now," said Chon, "to settle the matter at once, you have only to endeavor to please three persons."

"What three?"

"The king, my sister, and myself."

"What must I do to please?"

"Have you not seen Zamore?" asked the young lady, avoiding a direct reply.

"The negro?" said Gilbert, with the utmost contempt.

"Yes, the negro."

"What similarity is there between him and me?"

"Try to make a similarity of fortune, my good friend. That negro has already two thousand livres per annum from the king's privy purse. He is to be appointed governor of Luciennes; and even those that laugh at his thick lips and black face call him sir, and even my lord."

"I shall not be one of those," said Gilbert.

"Oh! I thought that the first principle of you philosophers was that all men are equal."

"That is the very reason that I shall not call Zamore my lord."

Chon was beaten with her own weapons. It was her turn to bite her lips.

"So you are not ambitious?" said she.

"Oh, yes, I am!" replied Gilbert, with sparkling eyes.

"And if I remember rightly, your ambition was to be a physician."

"I look upon the mission of soothing the pain and suffering of our fellow-creatures as the noblest in the world."

"Well, your dream shall be realized."

"How so?"

"You shall be a physician—and the king's physician, to boot."

"I ?" cried Gilbert, "I, who know not even the first principles of medical science ? You jest, madame !"

"Well, and what does Zamore know about portcullises, and drawbridges, and counterscarps ? He does not trouble his head about such things, yet that does not prevent him from being governor of Luciennes, with all a governor's privileges."

"Ah, yes, yes ; I understand !" said Gilbert, bitterly. "You have only one buffoon, and that is not sufficient. The king is getting tired, and wishes for another."

"There," said Chon, "you are putting on your long face again. You make yourself so ugly, my little man, it is really quite delightful to see you. Keep all those ridiculous faces till the wig is on your head, and the sugar-loaf hat over the wig, then, instead of being ugly, they will be comical."

Gilbert frowned more darkly still.

"I should think you might be glad of the post of the king's physician, when the Duke de Tresmes solicits that of my sister's monkey."

Gilbert made no answer. Chon thought of the proverb, "silence gives consent."

"As a proof that you are in favor," said she, "you shall not eat with servants."

"Ah ! thank you, madame," replied Gilbert.

"I have already given orders to that effect."

"And where shall I eat ?"

"Along with Zamore."

"I ?"

"Yes ; the king's governor and his physician may surely eat together. Go now to your dinner."

"I am not hungry," answered Gilbert, rudely.

"Very well," said Chon, quietly ; "you are not hungry now, but you will be in the evening."

Gilbert shook his head.

"To-morrow, then, or the day after to-morrow you may be. Oh, we know how to tame rebels here ; and if you con-

tinue obstinate, we have, besides, the corrector of our pages
to do our will."

Gilbert shuddered and turned pale.

"Go to my Lord Zamore now," she added, sharply;
"you will be very well treated with him; his table is excellent. But no ingratitude, remember, or we shall teach
you to be grateful."

Gilbert let his head fall on his breast, an invariable symptom that, instead of going to reply, he was going to act.

The footman who had showed him to Chon's apartment
waited at the door, and on his dismissal conducted him to
a little dining-room adjoining the anteroom.

Zamore was at table. Gilbert took his place at the table,
but he could not be made to eat.

Three o'clock struck; Mme. Dubarry set off for Paris.
Chon, who was to join her there a short time after, left
instructions for the taming of her bear. Plenty of sweet-
meats were to be his reward if he became docile; plenty of
threats, and at last the dungeon if he continued rebellious.

At four o'clock a complete suit, such as that worn by
the *médecin malgré lui*, was brought into Gilbert's apartment. There was the pointed cap, the wig, the black
jacket, and the long black robe; in addition to these, they
sent him a collar, a wand, and a large book. The footman
who carried them in exhibited the various articles one
by one.

Gilbert no longer manifested any disposition to rebel.
Grange entered after the footman, and instructed him how
all the different parts of the dress should be worn. Gilbert
listened most patiently.

"I thought," said he, at length, "that doctors formerly
carried a little writing case and a roll of paper?"

"Yes, faith, he is right," replied the steward; "go and
bring him a long writing-case, which he can hang at his
girdle."

"With pen and paper," added Gilbert; "I must have
every part of my costume complete."

The footman hastened to execute the order, and at the
same time to tell Chon how obliging Gilbert had become.

Chon was so much delighted, that she gave the messenger a little purse with eight crowns in it, to hang with the writing-case at the girdle of this model of a physician.

"Thank you," said Gilbert to the person who brought it. "Now may I be left alone to dress?"

"Well, make haste," replied Grange, "so that mademoiselle may see you before she goes to Paris."

"Half an hour," said Gilbert, "I only ask half an hour."

"You may take three quarters, if you like, my dear doctor," said the steward, shutting the door carefully, as if it had been that of his money-box.

Gilbert stole on tiptoe to the door, to be certain that the footsteps were dying away in the distance; then he glided to the window and looked down. There was a terrace about eighteen feet below him, covered with fine gravel, and bordered by lofty trees, which shaded the balconies of the windows.

Gilbert tore his long robe into three pieces, which he tied length-wise together, placed the hat on the table, and near it the purse and the following note:

"MADAME,— Liberty is the first of blessings. Man's most sacred duty is to preserve it. You endeavored to enslave me. I set myself free.   GILBERT."

This letter he folded, and addressed to Mlle. Chon, then he tied his twelve feet of serge to the bars of the window, slipped between them with the suppleness of an eel, and when at the end of his cord, dropped down to the terrace, at the risk of breaking his neck. Though a little stunned by the leap, he lost not a moment in gaining the trees, among which he glided stealthily, and running as fast as his limbs would carry him, he disappeared in the direction of Ville d'Avray.

When, at the end of half an hour, they came to seek for him, he was already far beyond their reach.

CHAPTER XLII.

THE OLD MAN.

GILBERT had avoided the highway through fear of pursuit ; he glided from one plantation to another, until he reached a sort of forest, and there he stopped. He had traveled a league and a half in about three quarters of an hour.

The fugitive looked around him, and finding himself quite alone, he felt so much courage that he thought he might venture nearer the high-road. He therefore turned in the direction which, according to his calculation of his position, he supposed would lead to Paris.

But some horses which he saw near the village of Roquencourt, led by grooms in orange liveries, frightened him so much, that he was cured of all desire to be on the public road, and he returned to the woods.

" Let me keep in the shade of the trees," said he to himself ; " if I am pursued, it will certainly be on the high-road. In the evening, from tree to tree, from one opening to another, I shall steal on to Paris. They say Paris is very large, and, as I am little, I can easily hide there."

This idea was rendered still more agreeable to him by the fineness of the weather, the shade of the forest, and the softness of the mossy sward. The sun was now disappearing behind the hills of Marly, and the vegetation, dried by the scorching heat of the day, exhaled the sweet perfume of the spring—a mingled odor of the plant and of the flower.

Evening came on. It was the hour when, beneath the darkening skies, silence falls more softly and more deeply on all things, when the closing flower-cup shuts in the insect sleeping on its bosom. The gilded flies return with constant hum to the hollow oak which serves them as an

asylum ; the birds hurry silently to their nests, their wings
rustling through the foliage ; and the only song which is
heard is the clear whistle of the blackbird, and the timid
warble of the redbreast.

Gilbert was familiar with the woods ; he was well acquainted both with their sounds and with their silence.
Without giving way, therefore, to reflection, or to idle
fear, he threw himself at full length on the heath, on
which there yet remained here and there a red leaf of the
preceding winter.

Far from feeling anxious or disturbed, he experienced
rather a vague and boundless sense of joy. He inhaled
with rapture the pure and free air, feeling, with the pride
of a stoic, that he had once more triumphed over the
snares laid for human weakness. What, though he had
neither bread, nor money, nor shelter, had he not his be-
loved liberty ? Was he not the free and uncontrolled
master of his destiny ?

He stretched himself, therefore, at the foot of a gigantic
chestnut-tree, where between two of its moss-covered roots
he found a luxurious couch ; then, gazing up at the calm
and smiling heavens, he gradually sunk to sleep.

The warbling of the birds awoke him ; it was scarcely
day. Raising himself on his elbow, stiff and painful from
contact with the hard wood, he saw, in the dawning light,
an opening from which three paths branched off through
the wood. Here and there a rabbit scudded past him with
its ears drooping, and brushing away the dew in its course,
or a stag bounded past, with its sharp, quick leaps, stopped
to gaze at the unknown object under the tree, and then,
alarmed, darted off with a more rapid flight.

Gilbert jumped to his feet, but no sooner had he done
so than he felt he was hungry. The reader may remember that he had refused to dine with Zamore, so that
since his breakfast in the attic at Versailles he had eaten
nothing. On finding himself once more under the leafy
arches of a forest, he who had so boldly traversed the
great woods of Lorraine and Champagne, he almost
thought himself beneath the trees of Taverney, or among

the brakes of Pierrefitte, surprised by the morning beams after a nocturnal expedition to procure game for his fair mistress.

But at Taverney he had always found by his side a partridge or a pheasant which he had shot, while here he found only his hat, rather the worse for his journey, and now nearly unfit to wear after the damps of the night.

It was not, then, all a dream, as he had, on first awakening, supposed. Versailles and Luciennes were realities, from his triumphant entry into the first till his forcible evasion from the last.

But what more than all else served to recall him to his real position was his hunger, now becoming sharper and sharper every moment.

Then he mechanically sought around for some of those delicious mulberries, those wild cherries, or pungent roots, which, though acrid like the radish, the woodman loves to find as he plods in the morning to his labor with his tools on his shoulder. But this was not the season for such things, and, besides, he saw around him only the ash, the beech, and other trees which bear no fruit.

" Well," said he to himself, " I will go direct to Paris. I cannot be more than three or four leagues from it—five, at most ; I can be there in two hours. What matter is it to suffer for a couple of hours, when I am sure, after that, of not having to suffer any longer ? In Paris every one has bread, and the first artisan whom I meet will not refuse me bread for my work when he knows that I am honest and industrious. In Paris I shall be able in one day to procure food for the next. What do I want more ? Nothing, except that every succeeding day may see me increase in strength, in elevation of character, in greatness of mind, and approach nearer and nearer the object of my wishes."

Gilbert redoubled his speed ; he now wished to find the high-road, but he had lost all means of directing his course. At Taverney, and in the woods around it, he knew the east and the west ; every ray of light was to him an index of the hour. At night, every star, although unknown to him by its name of Venus, Lucifer, or Saturn, served him as a guide. But here he was in a new world ; he knew neither places nor objects, and was forced to seek his way, groping by chance.

"Fortunately," said he, "I saw the finger-posts on which the roads were pointed out."

He proceeded toward an opening where one of these directing-posts was placed. It pointed to three roads ; one road led to Marais-Jaune, another to Champ-de-l'Alouette, a third to Trou-Sale. Gilbert was not much assisted by this ; he ran for three hours from one place to another, very often finding himself in the same spot from which he set out, and as far from the high-road as ever.

The perspiration poured down his face. A dozen times he threw off his coat and vest to climb some colossal chestnut-tree ; but when he had reached its summit he saw nothing but Versailles—Versailles now on his right, now on his left—Versailles, toward which, by some fatality, he seemed constantly impelled. He was half frantic with rage ; but at last his efforts were so far successful that he first passed Viroflay, then Chaville, then Sèvres.

Half-past five sounded from the clock-tower of Meudon when he reached the Capuchin Convent, between Sèvres and Bellevue ; there, climbing on a cross, at the risk of breaking it, and of being himself broken on the wheel by order of the parliament, as Sirven had been, he saw, from that height, the Seine, the village, and the smoke of the nearest houses. Beyond this he saw a great mass of buildings on the horizon, dimly distinguished in the morning vapors. That must be Paris, he thought ; so, feeling no longer either fatigue or hunger, he directed his course thither, and only stopped when out of breath from his excessive speed.

He was now in the woods of Meudon, between Fleury and Plessis-Piquet.

"Come," said he, looking around, "no false shame ! I shall no doubt soon meet some early workman going to his day's labor with a loaf under his arm. I shall say to him, 'All men are brethren, and ought to help one another. You have more bread there than you will want this day, while I am dying of hunger'; and then he will give me the half of his loaf."

Hunger rendering Gilbert more and more philosophical, he continued his reflections.

"In truth," said he, "should not everything be in common among men on this earth? Has the Eternal Source of all things given to this man or that the air which fertilizes the soil, or the soil which produces the fruits? No. Some, it is true, have usurped a power over these things; but in the eyes of their Maker, in the eyes of the philosopher, no one possesses them. He who holds them is only the man to whom the Creator has lent them."

Gilbert, in all this, was but condensing, by a natural instinct, the vague and indefinite ideas of the period, which men felt, as it were, floating in the air and hovering above their heads, like clouds impelled in one direction, and forming a threatening mass from which at length the tempest would burst.

"Some," continued he, "retain by force what should belong to all. Well, then, from such we should tear by force what by right they should share with us. If my brother, who has too much bread, refuse me a portion of that bread, why, then, I shall take it from him by force; I shall follow the law of nature, the source of all sound sense and of all justice, since it arises from our natural wants. But I must yield if my brother say to me, 'the portion you ask for is that of my wife and of my children,' 'or if he should say, 'I am stronger than you, and I shall keep what I have in spite of you.'"

He was in this temper of mind, which bore a striking resemblance to that of a hungry wolf, when he reached an open space among the trees; in its center was a pond of muddy water, margined with reeds and water-lilies, on the surface of which sported myriads of flies, dotting its glassy bosom with innumerable circles. The grassy slope which descended to the water's edge was closely studded with bunches of myosotis, and resembled a bed of turquoise and emeralds. The background of the picture, that is, the

circle around the pool and the bank, was formed of a
hedge of tall aspens, the interstices between whose golden
trunks were filled up with the thick and leafy branches of
the alder. Six paths led down to this spot ; two of which,
radiant with golden light, might have seemed to the imagination avenues to the palace of the glorious luminary of
day ; the four others, diverging like rays of a star, were
lost in the blue depths of the forest.

This verdant saloon seemed fresher and more flowery
than any other part of the wood. Gilbert entered it by
one of the dark alleys.

The first object which he perceived, when, after having
at a glance taken in its extent and circumference, his eye
rested on nearer objects, was a man seated on the fallen
trunk of a tree, near a deep ditch. The expression of his
face was mild, yet refined and penetrating, and he was
dressed in a coat of coarse brown cloth, breeches of the
same, and a waistcoat of gray jean. His well-made sinewy
legs were incased in gray cotton stockings, and his shoes
with buckles were dusty here and there, yet showed on
the sol :s and points traces of the morning dew.

Near him, on the grass, was placed a box, painted green,
wide open, and filled with plants recently gathered. He
had between his legs a stout stick, with a smooth round
handle, and terminated at the opposite end by a little spade
about two inches broad and three long.

Gilbert embraced, in one rapid glance, all these details
which we have given ; but what first drew his attention
was a piece of bread, from which the old man, from time
to time, broke off small pieces to eat, sharing them
benevolently with the linnets and the wrens, who fixed
from afar a longing eye on the food, swooped on it the
moment it was thrown to them, and then flew with joyful
twittering to their thick foliage above.

The old man watched them with an eye at once gentle
and animated, then, extending his hand to a checked handkerchief beside him, he drew from it a cherry from time to
time, as a relish with his mouthful of bread.

" Ha ! this is the man for me," said Gilbert, brushing

aside the branches of the trees and making four steps toward the solitary, who looked up as he approached : but he had not advanced a third of the distance which separated them, when, perceiving the calmness and gentleness of the old man's countenance, he stopped and took off his hat.

The old man, finding himself no longer alone, cast a hurried glance on his box, and then on his coat. He shut the former and buttoned up the latter.

———

CHAPTER XLIII.

THE BOTANIST.

GILBERT took courage and walked close up ; but he opened his mouth and shut it again before he could utter a word. His philosophy wavered, and it seemed to him that he was about to entreat alms, and not to demand a right.

The old man observed this timidity, and it seemed to banish, on his side, all feelings of apprehension.

"Do you wish to speak to me, my friend ?" said he, smiling, and laying down his bread on the trunk of the tree on which he sat.

"Yes, sir," replied Gilbert.

"What do you wish to say ?"

"Sir, I see you throw your bread to the birds, as if we were not told that God feeds them."

"Doubtless He does feed them, young man ; but the hand of man is one of the means which He employs for that purpose. If you mean your words as a reproach, you are wrong ; for, neither in the silent wood nor in the crowded street, is the bread ever lost which we cast from our hand. In the one place the birds pick it up, in the other the poor."

"Well, sir," said Gilbert, singularly moved by the soft, penetrating voice of the old man, "although we are in the woods, I know a man who would dispute your bread with the birds."

"Can it be you, my friend ?" cried the old man ; "are you, then, hungry ?"

"Very, very hungry, sir ; and if you will permit me——"

The old man seized his bread again with eager compassion. Then, reflecting for a moment, he looked at Gilbert with a keen and searching glance.

In fact, Gilbert so little resembled a starving man, that some consideration might be permitted. His coat was clean, except where it was in some places stained by its contact with the ground ; his shirt was white, for at Versailles the evening before he had taken a clean one from his bundle, yet it was rendered damp by the dews ; it was quite evident that he had passed the night in the wood.

Besides all this, his hands were white and slender, like those of a man of thought rather than of labor.

Gilbert did not want tact ; he read the stranger's distrust and hesitation in his countenance, and hastened to anticipate further conjectures which he readily saw would not be favorable to him.

"We are always hungry, sir," he said, "when we have not eaten for twelve hours, and it is now twenty-four since I have had any food."

The emotion expressed on the young man's face, his tremulous voice, and his extreme paleness, all declared that his words were true. The old man hesitated, or, rather, feared, no longer ; he held out to Gilbert his bread and the handkerchief containing his cherries.

"Thank you, sir, thank you," said Gilbert, gently pushing aside the handkerchief containing the cherries ; "nothing but the bread ; it is quite sufficient."

And he broke it in two, keeping one half for himself and returning the other to the old man ; then he sat down on the grass a couple of paces from his companion, who looked at him with increasing wonder.

The repast did not last very long. There was but little bread, and Gilbert was very hungry. The old man did not disturb his occupation by a word ; he continued to observe him furtively but silently, bestowing, apparently, great attention on the plants and flowers in his box, which, when he opened it again, raised their odoriferous heads to the level of the edge, as if to inhale the air. But seeing Gilbert approach the pond, he cried, hastily, "Do not drink that water, young man, it is rendered unwholesome by the remains of last year's plants, and by the spawn of frogs now on its surface. Take instead a few of these cherries, they will refresh you as much as the water. Take them, I beg of you, for you are not a forward guest, I see."

"It is true, sir, forwardness is the reverse of my nature, and I fear nothing so much as being intrusive. I have just experienced that at Versailles."

"Oh, you come from Versailles?" said the stranger, eying Gilbert with a strong expression of curiosity.

"Yes, sir."

"It is a rich town; one must be either very poor or very proud to be starving there."

"I am both, sir."

"You have had a quarrel with your master, perhaps?" said the stranger, while he apparently arranged the plants in his box, yet giving Gilbert a rapid, interrogating glance.

"I have no master, sir."

"My friend," replied the old man, putting on his hat, "that is too ambitious a reply."

"It is the truth, however."

"No, young man. Every one has his master here below; we do not place our pride on a proper object when we say we have no master."

"How?"

"Yes. Whether old or young, it is so ordered that we must submit to some ruling power. Some are ruled by men, others by principles; and the severest masters are not always those who order with the voice or strike with the hand."

"Be it so," said Gilbert. "Then I am governed by principles, I confess. Principles are the only masters which a reflecting mind can recognize without shame."

"And what are your principles? Let me hear them. You seem to be very young, my friend, to have any decided principles."

"Sir, I know that all men are brethren, and that every man, from his birth, is bound to fulfil certain duties toward his fellow-men. I know that God has bestowed on me a certain amount of value in society; and as I acknowledge the worth of other men, I have a right to exact from them that they should acknowledge mine, if I do not exaggerate its importance. So long as I do nothing unjust and dishonorable, I merit some regard, even were it only as a human being."

"Oh, ho!" said the stranger, "you have studied, I perceive."

"Alas! sir, I have not; but I have read the "Discours sur l'Inégalité des Conditions,' and 'Le Contrat Social.' From those two books I have learned all I know, and even all I have dreamed."

At these words the eyes of the stranger flashed, and by an involuntary movement he was nearly destroying a beautiful chrysanthemum, which he was trying to place securely in his box.

"And such are the principles which you profess?" said he.

"They may not be yours, sir," replied the young man; "but they are those of Jean Jacques Rousseau."

"But," said the stranger, with a distrust so apparent that it was rather humbling to Glibert's vanity, "but are you sure you have rightly understood those principles?"

"I understand French, I think, sir, particularly when it is pure and poetical."

"You see that you do not," said the old man, smiling; "for what I ask you, if not poetical, is, at least, quite plain. I mean, have your philosophical studies enabled you to understand the groundwork of the system of——"

He stopped, almost blushing.

"Of Rousseau, sir?" continued Gilbert. "Oh, sir, I have not studied my philosophy in a college; but there is an instinct within me which revealed the excellence and utility of 'Le Contrat Social,' above all other books that I had read."

"A dry book for a young man, sir—a barren subject for

reverie at twenty years of age—a bitter and unfragrant flower for fancy in its spring-time ! " said the old man, with gentle sadness.

" Misfortune ripens man before his time, sir," answered Gilbert ; " and as to reverie, if we give it a free and unrestrained course, it very often lends to ill."

The stranger opened his eyes, which he usually kept half closed in his moments of calmness and reflection, a peculiarity which gave an indefinable charm to his countenance.

" To whom do you allude ?" asked he, reddening.

" Not to any one, sir," said Gilbert.

" Oh, yes, you do."

" No ; I assure you I do not."

" You appear to have studied the philosopher of Geneva. Did you not allude to his life ? "

" I know nothing of his life," replied Gilbert, frankly.

" Do you not ? " and the stranger sighed. " Young man, he is a wretched creature."

"Impossible ! Jean Jacques Rousseau wretched ? Then there is no justice on earth. Wretched ? The man who has devoted his life to the happiness of mankind ? "

" Well, well ! I see that you do know nothing about him. Let us speak of yourself, my friend, if you please."

" I should prefer going on with our present subject. What, can I tell you of myself worth hearing, sir—I who am a mere nobody ? "

" And, besides, you do not know me, and are afraid of trusting a stranger."

" Oh, sir, what have I to fear from any one ? Who can make me more wretched than I am ? Recollect in what guise I came before you—alone, poor, hungry."

" Where were you going ?"

" I was going to Paris. Are you a Parisian, sir ? "

" Yes ; that is to say, no."

" Which of the two am I to believe ? " asked Gilbert, smiling.

" I abhor falsehood, and every moment I perceive how necessary it is to reflect before speaking. I am a Parisian, if by that is meant a man who has lived in Paris for a long time, and has mixed in its society ; but I was not born in that city.   But why do you ask ?"

"It was from an association of ideas arising out of our conversation.   I thought, if you lived in Paris, you might have seen Rousseau, of whom we were speaking just now."

"I have, indeed, seen him sometimes."

"People look at him as he passes by, do they not ?   He is admired, and pointed out as the benefactor of the human race ? "

"No ; children, incited by their parents, follow him and throw stones at him."

"Good heavens !" exclaimed Gilbert, with the most painful astonishment.   "But at least he is rich ?"

"He has sometimes to ask himself, as you asked yourself this morning, 'Where shall I procure a breakfast ?'"

"But, poor as he is, he is esteemed, has influence, is respected ?"

"He knows not at night, when he lies down, whether he may not awake in the morning in the Bastile."

"Oh, how he must hate mankind !"

"He neither loves them nor hates them : he is disgusted with them—that is all."

"How can we avoid hating people who treat us ill ?" cried Gilbert : "I cannot comprehend that."

"Rousseau has always been free, sir—Rousseau has always been strong enough to rely on himself alone.   It is strength and freedom which make men mild and kind— slavery and weakness alone can make them malevolent."

"Those are my reasons for wishing to be free," said Gilbert, proudly.   "I have long thought what you have just so well explained to me."

"But one may be free even in prison, my friend," replied the stranger.   "Suppose Rousseau were in the Bastile to-morrow—and he certainly will be in it one day or other— he would think and write as freely as among the mountains of Switzerland.   I have never thought, for my part that man's freedom consists in his being able to do whatever he wills, but that he should not, by any human power, be forced to do what is against his will."

"Has Rousseau written what you have just said, sir?"

"I think he has."

"It is not in 'The Social Contrat.'"

"No; it is in a new work of his, called 'The Reveries of a Solitary Walker.'"

"Sir," said Gilbert, warmly, "I think we shall agree on one point."

"What is that?"

"That we both love and admire Rousseau."

"Speak for yourself, young man; you are still in the age of illusions."

"We may be deceived about things, but not about men."

"Alas! you will learn at a later period that it is in the characters of men more than in aught else that we are deceived. Rousseau may be a little more just than other men, but, believe me, he has faults, and very great ones."

Gilbert shook his head in a way which showed that he was far from being convinced; but, notwithstanding this rather uncivil demonstration, the stranger continued to treat him with the same kindness.

Let us return to the point at which we set out," said the stranger. "I was saying that you had quitted your master at Versailles."

"And I," replied Gilbert, but more mildly than before, "I answered that I had no master; I should have added that it depended entirely on myself to have one, and a very illustrious one, too, and that I had refused a situation which many would have sought eagerly."

"A situation?"

"Yes; one in which I should only have had to serve for the amusement of great lords in want of such an occupation; but I thought that being young and able to study and push my way in life, I ought not to lose my most precious years, and compromise in my person the dignity of man."

"And you decided well. But have you any fixed plan of pursuing your career?"

"Sir, I should wish to be a physician."

"A noble profession. In it you may choose between

real science, ever modest and self-sacrificing, and quackery, ever noisy and empty.   If you would become a physician, young man, study ; if a quack, nothing but impudence and effrontery are necessary."

"But it requires a great deal of money to study, does it not, sir ?"

"It certainly requires some money ; I should not say a great deal."

"In fact, I believe that Jean Jacques Rousseau, who knows everything, studied at no expense."

"At no expense ?   Oh, young man !" said the stranger, with a sad smile, "do you call it no expense when we expend the most precious of God's gifts—innocence, health, sleep ?   These are what it has cost the philosopher of Geneva to acquire the little that he knows."

"The little ?" repeated Gilbert, almost angrily.

"Yes ; ask any one about him, and you will hear him spoken of as I speak of him."

"In the first place, he is a great musician."

"Oh, because King Louis XV. sung a song out of an opera of Rousseau's composing, that does not make it a good opera."

"But he is a great botanist ; I have only seen a few odd sheets of his letters on botany, but you, who gather plants in the woods, have read them, I dare say."

"Oh, sometimes a person thinks himself a botanist, and is only——"

"Only what ?"

"Only a herbalist—and even——"

"And which are you—herbalist or botanist ?"

"A very humble herbalist, and a very ignorant one, when I contemplate those marvels of God's creation, plants and flowers."

"He is a Latin scholar."

"A very bad one."

"But I read in a newspaper that he translated an ancient author called Tacitus."

"Because, in his pride—alas ! every man has his moments of pride—because, in his pride, he thought he could undertake anything. In the preface, however, to the first book—the only one which he translated—he says he does not understand Latin well ; and Tacitus, who is a rude antagonist, soon wearied him. No, no, my good young man, in spite of your admiration, there is no such thing as a man of universal knowledge ; and, believe me, almost all men lose in depth what they gain in superficies. A little river, when swollen by the rains, may overflow its banks till it looks like a lake, but try to sail on it, and your boat will soon touch the ground."

"Then you think Rousseau a superficial man ? "

"Yes ; perhaps he presents a greater superficies than other men, but that is all."

"There are some, I think, who would be very glad to be superficial in his fashion."

"Do you intend that for me ? " asked the stranger, with a good-natured frankness, which quite disarmed Gilbert.

"Oh, no, sir ! I am too much delighted to converse with you to say anything disagreeable to you."

"In what way does my conversation delight you ? Let me hear, for I do not think you would flatter me for a morsel of bread and a few cherries."

"You do me justice ; I would not flatter to obtain the empire of the world. You shall hear why I am pleased ; you are the first person who has ever spoken to me without haughtiness—who has reasoned with me in a tone of kindness, as if speaking to a young man and not to a child. Although we did not agree about Rousseau, there has been, in all that you have said, something so calm and elevated that it attracted me. I seem, when talking to you, to be in a richly furnished saloon, the window-shutters of which are closed, but of which, notwithstanding the darkness, I can guess the richness and magnificence. I know that you could, if you wished, permit a ray of light to penetrate into your conversation which would dazzle me."

"But you yourself speak with a certain degree of refinement, which might lead me to think that you had received a better education than you have confessed."

"It is the first time, sir, that I have spoken so, and I am surprised myself at the terms which I have employed, there are even some of them of which I do not quite understand the signification, and which I have only heard once. I have met with them in books, but I did not comprehend them."

"Have you read much?"

"Too much: but I shall re-read."

The old man looked at Gilbert in astonishment.

"Yes; I read all that fell in my way, whether good or bad; I devoured all. Ah, if I had only had some one to direct me what I ought to forget, and what I ought to remember! But excuse me, sir; I was forgetting that, although your conversation is delightful to me, it does not therefore follow that mine must be so to you. You are herborizing, and I, perhaps, interfere with your occupation."

Gilbert made a movement as if to withdraw, but at the same time with the greatest desire to be detained. The little gray eyes of the stranger were fixed on him, and they seemed to read his heart.

"No," said he, "my box is almost full; I only want a few mosses; I have been told that there are some very beautiful hair-mosses in this quarter."

"Stay, stay," said Gilbert. "I think I have seen what you want on a rock just now."

"Far from this?"

"Not more than fifty paces."

"But how do you know that description of moss?"

"I have lived almost all my life in the woods, sir; and then the daughter of the gentleman at whose house I was brought up was fond of botany; she had a herbal, and under each plant the name was written in her own hand. I have often looked at the plants and the writing, and then I knew them when I saw them again in the woods."

"Then you felt a taste for botany?"

"Oh, sir, whenever I heard Nicole say—Nicole was the waiting-maid of Mademoiselle Andrée—when I heard Nicole say that her mistress had been trying in vain to find some particular plant I asked her to get me the form of that plant. Then, without knowing why I had asked for it, Mademoiselle Andrée would frequently sketch it in a moment, and Nicole would bring the drawing to me. I would then scour the fields, meadows, and woods until I had found the plant in question. When found, I dug it up and planted it in the lawn, where Mademoiselle Andrée could see it, and, full of joy, she would exclaim, on discovering it, 'How strange! Here is the very plant which I have been searching for everywhere.'"

The old man looked at Gilbert with even more attention than he had yet bestowed on him; and if Gilbert, on reflecting on the purport of what he had said, had not cast down his eyes and blushed, he would have seen that this attention was mingled with an expression of tender interest.

"Well, young man," said he, "continue to study botany; it will lead by a short route to a knowledge of medicine. God has made nothing in vain, and one day or other the utility of each plant will be distinctly marked in the book of science. Learn first to know simples, afterward you can study their properties."

"Are there not schools in Paris?"

"Yes, and even some gratuitous ones. The school of surgery, for instance, is one of the benefits which we owe to the present reign."

"I shall follow the course prescribed in it."

"Nothing can be more easy, for your parents, seeing your inclinations, will no doubt provide you an adequate maintenance."

"I have no parents; but I am not afraid, I can provide for myself by my labor."

"Certainly; and as you have read Rousseau's works, you know that he says that every man, even a prince, ought to be taught some manual trade."

"I have not read 'Emile.' I think it is in 'Emile' he has made that recommendation?"

"It is."

"I have heard the Baron de Taverney turn that advice

into ridicule, and regret that he had not made his son a carpenter."

"And what did he make him?"

"An officer."

The old man smiled.

"Yes, our nobles are all so. Instead of teaching their children any trade by which life might be preserved, they teach them the trade of killing. When a revolution comes, and exile after revolution, they will be forced to beg their bread from foreigners, or sell them their swords, which is still worse. You, however, are not the son of a noble; you know a trade, I presume?"

"Sir, I have already told you I know nothing. Besides, I must confess that I have always had an invincible repugnance for all labors requiring strong, rough movements of the body."

"Ah!" said the old man, "you are lazy."

"Oh, no, I am not lazy. Instead of putting me to the labor of a mechanic, place me in a room half dark, and give me books, and you shall see whether I will not work day and night at the labor of my own choosing."

The stranger looked at the young man's white and slender hands.

"It is a sort of predisposition or instinct," said he. "Sometimes this repugnance for manual labor leads to a good result; but it must be well directed. Well," continued he, "if you have not been at college, you have at least been at school?"

Gilbert shook his head.

"You can read and write?"

"My mother had just time, before she died, to teach me to read. My poor mother, seeing that I was not strong, always said, 'He will never make a good workman; he must be a priest or a learned man.' When I showed any distaste for my lessons, she would say, 'Learn to read, Gilbert, and you will not have to cut wood, drive a team, or break stones.' So I commenced to learn, but unfortunately I could scarcely read when she died."

"And who taught you to write?"

"I taught myself."

"You taught yourself?"

"Yes, with a stick which I pointed, and with some sand which I made fine by putting it through a sieve. For two years I wrote the letters which are used in printing, copying them from a book. I did not know that there were any others than these, and could soon imitate them very well. But one day, about three years ago, when Mademoiselle Andrée had gone to a convent, the steward handed me a letter from her for her father, and then I saw that there existed other characters. Monsieur de Taverney, having broken the seal, threw the cover away; I picked it up very carefully, and when the postman came again I made him read me what was on it. It was, 'To the Baron de Taverney Maison Rouge, at his Château, near Pierrefitte.' Under each of these letters I put its corresponding printed letter, and found that I had nearly all the alphabet. Then I imitated the writing, and in a week had copied the address ten thousand times, perhaps, and had taught myself to write. You see, sir, that I am not extravagant in my expectations, since I can read and write—have read all that I could—have reflected on all that I read—why may I not, perhaps, find a man who requires my pen, a blind man who wants eyes, or a dumb man who wants a tongue?"

"But you forget that then you will have a master, and that is what you do not want. A secretary or a reader is only a sort of upper servant after all."

"That is true," replied Gilbert, a little downcast, "but no matter, I must accomplish my object. I shall stir the paving-stones of Paris, I shall turn water-carrier if necessary, but I will attain my object, or I shall die in attempting it—and that will also be accomplishing an object."

"Well," replied the stranger, "you seem indeed full of ardor and courage—excellent qualities."

"But have you not a profession yourself, sir? You are dressed like a man employed in the finances."

The old man smiled sadly.

"I have a profession," said he; "every man ought to have one, but mine is a complete stranger to everything connected with finance. A financier would not come out herborizing."

"Are you a herborist by profession, then?"

"Almost."

"Then you are poor?"

"Yes."

"It is the poor who are charitable, for poverty makes them wise, and good advice is better than a louis-d'or. Give me your advice, then."

"I shall do more than that."

Gilbert smiled.

"I suspected that," said he.

"On how much do you think you could live?"

"Oh, very little."

"But perhaps you do not know how expensive living is in Paris?"

"Yesterday I saw Paris for the first time from the hills near Luciennes."

"Then you are not aware that living in great towns is dear?"

"How much does it cost? Give me an idea."

"Willingly. For instance, what costs a sou in the country costs three sous in Paris."

"Well," said Gilbert, "if I got any kind of shelter to rest in after my work, I should only need for my food six sous a day."

"Ah!" cried the stranger, "that is what I like, young man. Come with me to Paris, and I shall find you an independent profession by which you may live."

"Oh, sir!" cried Gilbert, with rapture; then, after a moment's reflection, "But it must really be an occupation, I must not live on alms."

"Do not be afraid of that, my child. I am not rich enough to bestow much in charity, and not foolish enough to do it without knowing the object better."

This little sally of misanthropy pleased Gilbert instead of giving him offense. "That is right!" said he. "I like such language. I accept your offer and thank you for it. What shall I have to do with you ? ”

“ So you decide upon coming to Paris with me ? ”

“ Yes, sir, if you have no objection.”

“ Of course I have no objection, since I make you the offer.”

“Nothing—but to work. But you shall regulate the quantity of your work yourself. You are young, you ought to be happy and free—even idle if you like, after you have gained the privileges of leisure,” said the stranger, smiling in spite of himself ; then raising his eyes to heaven, he exclaimed, with a deep sigh, “ Oh, youth ! oh, vigor ! oh, freedom ! ” Then he rose with the assistance of his stick.

As he said these words, an expression of deep and poetic melancholy overspread his fine features.

“ And now,” he continued, in a more cheerful voice, “ now that you have got an employment, will you object to help me to fill another box with plants ? I have some sheets of paper here in which we can class the others according to their orders. But, by the bye, are you hungry ? I have still some bread.”

“ Keep it for the afternoon if you please, sir.”

“ Well, but at least eat the cherries, they will be troublesome to carry with us.”

“ On that account I shall eat them. But allow me to carry your box ; you will then be more at your ease, and I think, thanks to habit, my legs will tire yours.”

“ Ah, see ! you bring me good fortune. There is the *vicris hieracioïdes* which I sought in vain until now, and just under your foot—take care !—the *cerastium aquaticum*. Stop, stop ! Do not gather them. Oh, you are not a herborist yet. The one is too moist to be gathered now, the other not advanced enough. We can get the *vicris hieracioïdes* in the afternoon when we pass this way, and the *cerastium* a week hence. Besides, I wish to show it growing to a friend whose patronage I mean to solicit for you. And now, show me the place where you saw the beautiful mosses.”

Gilbert walked on, the old man followed him, and both disappeared in the shades of the forest.

CHAPTER XLIV.

MONSIEUR JACQUES.

GILBERT, delighted at his good fortune, which had hitherto befriended him in his utmost need, walked on, turning from time to time toward the stranger, who had, by a few words, made him at once so submissive and docile. In this manner he led him to the spot where the mosses grew; they were really splendid specimens, and when the old man had made a collection of them they went in search of other plants.

Gilbert was a much better botanist than he thought himself. Accustomed to the woods from his infancy, he was familiar with all the plants that grew in them; but he knew them only by their vulgar names. When he named them in that manner his companion told him the corresponding scientific term, which Gilbert, on finding another plant of the same family, would endeavor to repeat. If he miscalled the Greek or Latin term, the stranger repeated it in syllables and gave him its derivation. Then he explained how it was adapted to the nature of the plant; and thus Gilbert learned not only its botanical name, but the Greek or Latin one by which Pliny, Linnæus, or Jussieu had distinguished it.

From time to time he said, "What a pity, sir, that I cannot gain my six sous by botanizing every day with you! Oh, I should never rest a moment, and indeed I should not want even the six sous; a piece of bread such as you gave me this morning would be sufficient for the whole day. I have just drunk from a spring of excellent water, as good as that at Taverney, and last night I slept under a tree here, and I am sure that I slept better than I should have done under the roof of a château."

"My friend," replied the stranger, with a smile, "winter

will come; the plants will be withered, and the spring frozen; the north wind will whistle through the naked trees, instead of this gentle breeze which agitates their leaves. You will then require a shelter, clothes, and fire, and you must be economical with your six sous that you may obtain them."

Gilbert sighed, gathered more plants, and asked more questions.

They spent thus the greater part of the day in the woods of Almay, Plessis-Piquet, and Clamart-sous-Mendon.

Gilbert, according to his usual custom, soon became familiar with his companion, who questioned him with admirable address; but there was in the young man something distrustful and circumspect, and he revealed as little as possible of his past life.

At Chatillon the stranger bought some bread and milk, but it was with difficulty he prevailed upon Gilbert to take the half of his purchase. Then, refreshed, they set out for Paris, that they might enter it while it was yet daylight.

The young man's heart beat high at the mere thought of being in Paris, and he could not conceal his emotion when, from the hill of Vanvres, he perceived St. Geneviève, the Invalides, Notre Dame, and that vast sea of houses whose rolling billows seemed to lave the declivities of Montmartres, Belleville, and Menil Montant.

"Oh, Paris! Paris!" murmured he.

"Yes, Paris, a mass of houses, an abyss of ills!" said the old man. "If the griefs and crimes which those houses inclose were to appear on their exteriors, from every stone would ooze a tear or a drop of blood!"

Gilbert heard and repressed his enthusiasm, and, thus checked, it soon died away of itself.

The suburb by which they entered the city was filthy and squalid; sick persons on litters were carried past him to the hospitals; children, half naked, were playing in the dirt among dogs, cows, and pigs. His brow grew dark.

"You think all this hideous," said the stranger; "well, in a short time you will not even see these things. People are rich who have a pig or a cow ; they will soon have neither one nor other. Their children give them pleasure ; soon they will bring them only sorrow. As to filth, you will always find that everywhere."

Gilbert had been inclined to look on Paris with a gloomy eye ; the picture of it which is companion drew did not, therefore, displease him. The old man, at first prolix in his declamation, gradually sank into abstraction and silence as they approached the center of the city. He seemed so full of anxious thoughts that Gilbert had not courage to ask him the name of a large garden which he saw through a railing, nor of a bridge by which the Seine was crossed. The garden was the Luxembourg—the bridge, the Pont Neuf. At last, however, as they still proceeded onward, and as the stranger's meditation appeared to have changed into uneasiness he ventured to say, "Do you live far from this. sir ?"

"Not very far," answered the stranger, whom this question evidently made more morose.

They proceeded along the Rue du Four, passing the magnificent Hotel de Soissons, the windows and the principal entrances of which look on the street, but whose splendid gardens extend to the streets of Grenelle and Deux-Ecus.

They passed by a church, which Gilbert thought very beautiful ; he stopped a moment to gaze at it.

"That is a beautiful building," said he.

"It is St. Eustache," replied the old man ; then, looking up.

"Eight o'clock ! Good heavens ! make haste, young man, make haste !"

The stranger strode on faster ; Gilbert followed him.

"By the bye," said he, after some minutes of a silence so ungenial that Gilbert began to feel uneasy, "I forgot to tell you that I am married."

"Oh !" said Gilbert.

"Yes ; and my wife, like a true Parisian housekeeper, will scold us, I dare say ; for coming in so late. Besides, I must tell you, she is very suspicious of strangers."

"Do you wish me to leave you, sir?" said Gilbert, whose heart was chilled by these words.

"Not at all, not at all! I invited you to come home with me and you shall come."

"I follow you, then," answered the young man.

"Now, here we are—down this street—to the right."

Gilbert raised his eyes, and, by the last gleams of expiring day, he read at the corner of the street, above a grocer's shop, the words:

"Rue Plastrière."

The old man continued to hurry on faster, for the nearer he approached his house his feverish agitation seemed to increase. Gilbert feared to lose sight of him, and, in his haste, knocked against the passers-by, the burdens of the porters, and the poles of carriages and litters. His companion seemed to have completely forgotten him in his hurried progress, absorbed as he was by one disagreeable thought.

At last he stopped before a door, in the upper part of which was a grating. A little string hung out through a hole; the stranger pulled it, and the door opened. He then turned, and seeing Gilbert standing undecided whether to enter or not, he said, "Come on!" Gilbert obeyed, and the old man shut the door.

After a few steps forward in the dark, Gilbert's foot struck against a narrow, steep staircase; but the old man, accustomed to the place, had already mounted half the flight. Gilbert overtook him, ascended with him, and stopped when he stopped. This was an old half-worn out mat in a lobby with two doors in it.

The stranger pulled a cord near one of these doors, and a sharp tinkling bell rang; then, from the interior of one of the rooms was heard the shuffling of slip-shod feet dragging along the floor. The door opened, and a woman of from fifty to fifty-five years of age appeared.

Two voices immediately arose together—one, that of the stranger; the other, that of the woman who opened the door.

"Am I too late, dear Therese?" he murmured, timidly.

"A pretty hour, Jacques, to sup at!" she replied, rudely.

"Come, come; we shall soon make all that right!" replied the stranger, affectionately, shutting the door, and then turning to receive the tin box from Gilbert's hands.

"Oh, a porter to carry your box!" cried the old woman; "it only wanted that. So you could not carry all that nasty stuff of grass and herbs yourself. Indeed! a porter for Monsieur Jacques! I beg pardon; he is becoming quite a great gentleman!"

"Well, well, be calm, Therese," quietly replied he whom she addressed so insolently by the name of Jacques, arranging his plants on the mantelpiece.

"Pay him, then, and send him away; we don't want a spy here."

Gilbert turned as pale as death, and sprang to the door. Jacques stopped him.

"This gentleman," said he, with less timidity than he had shown at first, "is not a porter, still less a spy. He is a guest whom I have brought."

The old woman's arms fell powerless by her side.

"A guest," said she. "Certainly we are in great need of guests."

"Come, Therese," said the stranger, in a tone still affectionate, but in which a shade of derision might be detected, "light a candle; I am heated, and we are thirsty."

The old woman still grumbled, loudly at first, but gradually subsiding. Then she proceeded to strike a light.

While the dialogue lasted, and the murmurs succeeding it, Gilbert remained silent and immovable, nailed to the floor within a step or two of the door, which he deeply regretted having entered.

Jacques perceived what the young man was suffering.

"Come forward, Monsieur Gilbert," said he, "come forward, I beg of you."

The old woman turned to see the person to whom her

husband spoke with this affected politeness, and Gilbert had thus an opportunity of seeing her yellow, morose face by the first light of the miserable candle, which she had placed in a copper candle stick.

That face awoke in him, at the first glance, a violent antipathy. It was wrinkled, pimpled, and filled, as it were, with gall ; the eyes were sharp, but meaningless ; there was also a pretended softness spread over those vulgar features at that moment, which the old woman's voice and manner so completely contradicted, that Gilbert's dislike was, if possible, increased.

The old woman, on her side, found the thin, pale face, circumspect silence, and stiff demeanor of the young man little to her taste.

" I see, gentlemen," said she, " that you are hot, and I am sure you must be thirsty. Indeed, passing a day in the shade of the woods is so fatiguing, and stooping from time to time gather a plant so laborious an occupation !—for this gentleman is a botanist, also, no doubt—that is the trade of people who have no trade ! "

" The gentleman," replied Jacques, in a voice becoming every moment firmer, " is a kind, good young man, who did me the honor to bear me company all the day, and whom my Therese will, I am sure, receive like a friend."

" There is enough of supper for two, but not for three," grumbled she.

" He is easily satisfied, and so am I."

" Oh, yes—all very fine ! I know what that means. I tell you plainly there is not bread enough for your double moderation, and I am not going down three flights of stairs to get any more, I assure you. Besides, at this hour, the baker's would be shut."

" Then I shall go down myself," replied Jacques, frowning." Open the door, Therese."

" Oh, but——"

" I will go down, I tell you ! "

" Well, well," said the old woman, in a discontented voice, but at the same time yielding to the absolute tone which her opposition had called forth from Jacques ; " am

I not always ready to sstisfy your whims? I think we can do with what we have. Come to supper."

" Sit by me," said Jacques, leading Gilbert into the next room, where a little table was prepared for the master and mistress of the house. On it were laid two plates, beside one of which a napkin folded and tied with a red ribbon, and beside the other, one tied with white, pointed out where each took his seat.

The walls of the room, which was small and of a square shape, were covered with a pale-blue paper, with a white pattern, and its only ornaments were two large maps. The rest of the furniture consisted of six straw-seated chairs. the aforesaid table, and a kind of cabinet filled with stockings to be mended.

Gilbert sat down. The old woman placed a plate before him, then she brought a spoon, worn thin by use, knife and fork, and a brightly polished pewter goblet.

" Are you not going down ? " asked Jacques.

" It is not necessary," she replied, in a sharp tone, showing the spite which filled her heart at his having gained a victory over her.

" It is not necessary. I found half a loaf in the pantry. That makes a pound and a half of bread for us all—we must make it do."

So saying, she put the soup on the table.

Jacques was helped first, then Gilbert, and the old woman eat out of the tureen. All three were very hungry. Gilbert, intimidated by the discussion on domestic economy to which he had given rise, kept his appetite as much within bounds as possible ; but, notwithstanding, he had finished his soup first. The old woman cast a wrathful look on his plate so prematurely empty.

" Who called to-day ? " inquired Jacques, in order to change the current of her thoughts.

" Oh, everybody, as usual !" replied she. " You promised Madame de Boufflers her four pieces, Madame d'Escars two airs, Madame de Penthièvre a quartet with an accompaniment—some persons came themselves, others sent for what they wanted. But what of that ? Monsieur was botanizing, and as people cannot amuse themselves and do their work at the same time, the ladies had to go without their music."

Jacques did not say a word, to the great astonishment of Gilbert, who expected to see him get angry ; but as it only concerned himself, it did not disturb him.

To the soup succeeded a morsel of boiled beef, served on a common earthenware dish, scraped and cracked by the edge of the knife. Jacques helped Gilbert moderately enough, for Therese had her eye upon him ; then he took a piece about the same size for himself, and handed the dish to her.

The old woman seized on the loaf and cut a slice for Gilbert—so small a slice that Jacques blushed. He waited until she had helped him and herself—then he took the loaf into his own hands.

" You shall cut your own bread, my young friend," said he ; " and cut it according to your appetite, I beg of you. Bread ought to be doled out only to those who waste it."

A moment afterward appeared a dish of kidney-beans stewed in butter.

"Look how green they are ! " said Jacques. "They are of our own keeping—we have an excellent method for that." And he passed the dish to Gilbert.

" Thank you, sir," said the latter, " but I have eaten quite enough—I am not hungry."

" The young gentleman is not of your opinion about my kidney-beans," said Therese, angrily. " He prefers, no doubt, fresh-gathered ones, but they are early vegetables, and rather above our means."

" No, madame. On the contrary, I think these appear very nice, indeed, and I am sure I should like them ; but I never eat of more than one dish."

" And you drink water ? " said Jacques, handing him the jug.

" Always, sir."

Jacques poured out a small glass of wine for himself.

" And now, wife," said he, " you will begin and get this young man's bed ready ; he must be tired, I am sure."

Therese let her knife and fork fall from her hands, and fixed her angry eyes upon her husband.

"Bed ? Are you mad ? If you bring any one to sleep here, he must sleep in your own bed, I can tell you. You are really becoming deranged ! Or, perhaps, you are going to take up a boarding-house ? If you are, you may get a cook and waiting-maid ; it is quite enough for me to be your servant, without being servant to other people !"

"Therese," replied Jacques, resuming his serious and firm tone, "Therese, pray listen to me. It is only for one night. This young man has never set foot in Paris before. He came under my protection, and I will not permit him to sleep in an inn ; I will not, though I should, as you say, have to resign him my own bed."

After this second exhibition of firmness and resolution, the old man awaited the result.

Therese, who had watched him while he spoke, appearing to study every muscle of his face, seemed now to understand that she must give up the contest—and she suddenly changed her tactics. She was certain of being beaten if she continued Gilbert's enemy ; she therefore began to fight for him, but certainly like an ally who intended treachery.

"Well, well," said she, "since the young gentleman has come home with you, he must be a friend of yours, and it is better, as you say, that he should remain under our roof. I shall make him a bed as well as I can in your study, near the bundles of papers."

"No, no," said Jacques, quickly ; "a study is not a fit place to sleep in—he might set fire to the papers."

"A great misfortune, truly !" muttered Therese to herself. Then she added, aloud : "In that case, I can put him in front of the cupboard in the anteroom."

"No, no !"

"Well, you see, however much I wish it, I can't manage it, unless he take your bed or mine."

"I do not think, Therese, you are looking in the right quarter."

" What do you mean ? "

" Why, we have the garret, you know. "

" The garret ? The loft, you mean. "

" No, it is not a loft. It is a room, a little garret-like, I confess, but wholesome, and with a splendid view of the neighboring gardens—a thing very unusual in Paris. "

" Oh, what matters it, sir, " exclaimed Gilbert, " whether it be a loft or not ? Even if it were, I should be but too glad of it, I assure you. "

" But stay—that cannot be ! " cried Therese. " It is there that I dry our linen. "

" The young man will not disturb it, Therese. You will take care, will you not, my young friend, that no accident happens to my good housekeeper's linen? We are poor, and any loss is serious to us. "

" Oh, do not be afraid, sir. "

Jacques rose and approached Therese. " I do not wish, my dear Therese, " said he, " that this young man should be ruined. Paris is a dangerous place for a stranger ; while here, we can watch over his conduct. "

" Then you have taken him to educate? He will pay for his board, this pupil of yours? "

" No ; but I answer for it he shall cost you nothing. From to-morrow he will provide for himself. As for lodging, since the garret is almost useless to us, let us do him this slight service. "

" How well idle people understand one another! " muttered Therese, shrugging her shoulders.

" Sir, " said Gilbert, more wearied even than his host of this struggle for a hospitality which was so humbling to him, and which was only gained by fighting for every inch of ground, " sir, I have never yet given trouble to any one, and I shall certainly not begin with you, who have been so good to me. Permit me, therefore, to leave you, if you please. I saw, near the bridge which we crossed, some trees with benches under them. I shall sleep very well, I assure you, on one of those benches. "

" Yes, " said Jacques, " to be taken up by the watch as a vagabond. "

"Which he is," muttered Therese to herself, as she removed the supper things.

"Come, come, young man," Jacques added, "there is, as well as I can remember, a very good straw mattress upstairs, and that is surely better than a bench."

"Oh, sir, I have never slept on anything but a straw mattress," said Gilbert; then, correcting this truth by a slight fib, "a feather-bed always overheated me," added he.

Jacques smiled. "Straw is certainly cool and refreshing," said he. "Take that bit of candle which is on the table and follow me."

Therese did not even look at them. She sighed—she was defeated.

Gilbert rose gravely and followed his protector. Passing through the anteroom, he saw a cistern of water. "Sir," asked he, "is water dear in Paris?"

"No, my friend; but were it dear, water and bread are two things which no man has a right to refuse his fellow-man who begs for them."

"Oh, the reason I asked is, that at Taverney water costs nothing, and cleanliness is the luxury of the poor."

"Take some, my friend," said Jacques, pointing to a large earthenware pitcher; and he preceded the young man to his sleeping apartment, surprised to find united in a youth of his age all the strength of mind of the lower classes with all the refined tastes of the higher.

CHAPTER XLV.

M. JACQUES' GARRET.

THE staircase, narrow and steep even at its commencement in the hall below, became still more narrow and more steep from the third story, on which Jacques lived, to the rooms above. It was, therefore, with considerable difficulty that they reached what was really a loft. Therese was right for once; it was neither more nor less than a loft, divided into four compartments, three of which were uninhabited. To say the truth, they were all, except the one destinedfor Gilbert, uninhabitable.

The roof sloped precipitately down and formed an acute angle with the floor. In the middle of the slope, a sky-light in a broken frame, without glass, admitted both light and air ; the former rather scantily, the latter superabundantly, particularly during high winds in winter.

Fortunately, summer was near ; and yet, in spite of the approaching warm weather, the candle which Jacques held was nearly blown out on entering the loft.

The mattress of which Jacques had spoken so boastingly lay on the floor, and at the first glance seemed to be in itself the whole furniture of the place. Here and there were piles of old printed papers, which had turned yellow at the edges from age, and in the midst of them were some books half gnawed away by rats.

From two cords which were stretched from one side of the loft to the other, and the first of which was nearly strangling Gilbert, hung, dancing in the night breeze, several paper bags containing kidney-beans dried in their pods, a few bundles of aromatic herbs, some household linen, and several articles of female attire almost in rags.

" It is not a very handsome place," said Jacques, " but sleep and darkness make an humble cabin equal to a sumptuous palace. Sleep, my young friend, as you ought to sleep at your age, and to-morrow morning you may believe that you have slept in the Louvre. But, above all things, take care of fire."

" Yes, sir," said Gilbert, a little bewildered at all that he had heard and seen.

Jacques left the room smiling, then returned.

" To-morrow we shall have some conversation," said he ; " you will have no objection to work, will you ? "

" You know, sir, that, on the contrary, to work is my strongest wish."

" That is right," said Jacques, and he turned away.

" To work in an honorable way, you understand, sir," added the punctilious Gilbert.

" I know of no other, my young friend ; so, then, good night."

" Good night, and thank you, sir."

Jacques retired, closed the door, and Gilbert was left alone in his garret.

At first amazed, then stupefied at the thought that he was in Paris, he asked himself could this really be Paris ? could there be in Paris such rooms as his ?

He then reflected that, in reality, M. Jacques was bestowing charity on him, and as he had seen alms bestowed at Taverney, not only did his surprise subside, but gradually gave way to gratitude, so much difference was there in the manner of performing the two acts.

Then, candle in hand, and taking every precaution against fire, as recommended by Jacques, he went over all parts of his garret ; thinking so little of Therese's clothes that he would not take even an old gown to serve him for a quilt.

He stopped at the piles of printed papers. They roused his curiosity to the utmost ; but they were tied up, and he did not touch them.

With outstretched neck and eager eye, he passed from these parcels to the bags of kidney-beans. The bags were made of very white paper, also printed, and were fastened together by pins.

In making rather a hurried movement he touched the rope with his head and one of the bags fell. Paler and more frightened than if he had been discovered breaking open a strong-box, Gilbert hastened to gather up the beans scattered on the floor and to return them to the bag.

During this process he naturally looked at the paper, and mechanically read a few words. These words excited his interest ; he pushed aside the beans, and sitting down on his mattress he read with eagerness, for the words were so completely in unison with his own character and feelings that he could almost imagine them to have been written, not only for, but by myself. They were as follows ·

'Besides, grisettes, tradesmen's daughters, and *filles de chambre* never presented any temptation to me ; I was influenced by ladies alone. Every one has his whim, and this was mine. I do not agree with Horace on this point. It is not, however, mere admiration of rank or wealth which induces this preference ; it is the superior delicacy of complexion, the soft white hands, the becoming attire, the air of delicacy and order exhibited in the whole person, the taste which appears in every gesture and every expression, the dress so much finer and better formed, the shoes of more delicate workmanship, the more judicious blending of ribbons and laces, the hair arranged with superior care. Thus adorned, I should prefer the plainest features to beauty without them. This preference may be—and I feel that it is—very ridiculous, but my heart has made it almost in spite of me."

Gilbert started, and the perspiration burst from his forehead—his thoughts could not be better expressed, his desires more clearly defined, nor his tastes more perfectly analyzed. But Andrée, though thus adorned, did not require these auxiliaries to set off " the plainest features." All these were subservient to her peerless beauty.

After this came a delightful adventure of a young man with two young girls. Their setting out all together on horseback was related, and all the pretty little fears of the ladies were described. Then their nocturnal return was told in the most charming style.

Gilbert's interest increased ; he unfolded the bag and read all that was in it ; then he looked at the pages that he might, if possible, go on regularly with what was so interesting. The paging was not regular, but he found seven or eight bags which seemed in the narrative to have some connection. He took out the pins, emptied the beans on the floor, put the sheets together, and proceeded to read.

He was thinking of the happiness he should have, passing the whole night in reading, and the pleasure he should find in unpinning the long file of bags yet untouched, when suddenly a slight crackling was heard; the candle being low, had heated the copper around it; it sunk in the melted grease, a disagreeable odor filled the loft, and in a moment all was darkness.

This event took place so quickly that Gilbert had no time to prevent it, and he could have wept with vexation at being interrupted in the middle of his reading. He allowed the paper to slip from his hands on the heap of beans near his bed, threw himself on his mattress, and, in spite of his disappointment, soon slept profoundly.

He did not awake until aroused by the noise of taking off the padlock with which Jacques had closed the door the night before. It was broad daylight, and as Gilbert opened his eyes, he saw his host enter softly.

His eyes immediately rested on the kidney-beans scattered on the floor, and the bags turned into their original form, Jacques' glance had taken the same direction.

Gilbert felt the blush of shame covering his cheeks, and, scarcely knowing what he said, he murmured, "Good morning, sir."

"Good morning, my friend," said Jacques, "have you slept well?"

"Yes, sir."

"Are you a somnambulist?"

Gilbert did not know what a somnambulist was, but he understood that the question referred to the beans no longer in their bags, and to the bags despoiled of their contents.

"Ah, sir," said he, "I understand why you ask me that question. Yes, I have been guilty of this misconduct; I humbly confess it, but I think I can repair it."

"Yes. But why is your candle burned out?"

"I sat up too late."

"But why sit up?" asked Jacques, distrustfully.

"To read, sir."

The old man's eyes wandered with increasing interest all round the garret.

"This first leaf," said Gilbert, taking up the first page which he had unpinned and read, "this first leaf, which I looked at by chance, interested me so much—but, sir, you who know so much—do you know what book this is taken from ?"

Jacques glanced carelessly at it and said. "I don't know."

"It is a romance, I am sure," said Gilbert, "and a charming romance, too."

"A romance ? Do you think so ?"

"Yes ; for love is spoken of here as in romances, only much better."

"Well, as I see at the foot of this page the word ' confessions,' I think that it may be a true history."

"Oh, no. The man who speaks thus does not speak for himself. There is too much frankness in his avowals, too much impartiality in his judgments."

"You are wrong," answered the old man, quickly ; "the author wished to give an example of that kind to the world."

"Do you know who is the author ?"

"The author is Jean Jacques Rousseau."

"Rousseau ?" cried the young man, impetuously.

"Yes ; these are some leaves from his last work."

"So this young man, as he speaks of himself here, poor, unknown, almost begging on the highway, was Rousseau —that is to say, the man who was one day to write ' Le Contrat Social ' and ' Emile ' ?"

"The same—or, rather, not the same," said the old man, with an expression of deep melancholy—"no, not the same ; the author of ' Le Contrat Social ' and ' Emile ' is the MAN disenchanted with the world, life, glory, almost with the Deity himself ; the other—the other Rousseau is the CHILD entering a world rosy as the dawn—a child with all the joys and all the hopes of that happy age. Between the two Rousseaus lies an abyss which will forever prevent them from being one—thirty years of misery !"

The old man shook his head, let his arms sink by his side, and appeared lost in reverie.

Gilbert was delighted, not saddened, by what he heard. "Then," said he, "all that I read last night was not a charming fiction ?"

"Young man, Rousseau has never lied; remember his motto, *vitam impendere vero!*"

"I have seen it, but as I do not know Latin, I did not understand it."

"It means to give one's life for the truth. But my wife must have risen by this time; let us go down; a man determined to work can never begin the day too early. Rouse, young man, rouse."

"And so," said Gilbert, "it is possible that a man of such an origin as Rousseau may be loved by a lady of rank? Oh, heavens! what it is to inspire with hope those who, like him, have dared to raise their eyes above them."

"You love," said Jacques, "and you find an analogy between your situation and that of Rousseau."

Gilbert blushed, but did not answer this interrogation.

"But all women," said he, "are not like those of whom I read. How many are proud, haughty, disdainful, whom it would be only folly to love!"

"And yet, young man," replied the other, "such occasions have more than once presented themselves to Rousseau."

"That is true, sir; pardon me for having detained you; but there are some subjects which intoxicate me, and some thoughts which make me almost mad."

"Come, come, I fear you are in love!" said the old man.

Instead of replying, Gilbert commenced to make up the bags again, with the help of the pins, and fill them with the kidney-beans. Jacques looked on.

"You have not been very splendidly lodged," said he, "but, after all, you have had what was necessary, and if you had been earlier up, you might have inhaled through your window the perfume of the garden trees which, in the midst of the disagreeable odors that infest a great town, is certainly very agreeable. The gardens of the Rue Jussienne are just below, and to breathe in the morning the fragrance of their flowers and shrubs is to a poor captive a happiness for all the rest of the day."

"It certainly conveys an agreeable sensation to me," said Gilbert, "but I am too much accustomed to those things to pay any particular attention to them."

"Say, rather, that you have not yet been long enough the inhabitant of a town to know how much the country is to be regretted. But you have done; let us go down."

And motioning Gilbert to precede him, he shut the door and put on the padlock.

This time Jacques led his companion directly to the room which Therese the evening before had named the study. Its furniture was composed of glass cases, containing butterflies, plants, and minerals, a bookcase of walnut-tree wood, a long, narrow table, with a green-and-black baize cover, worn out by constant use, on which were a number of manuscripts arranged in good order, and four arm-chairs, stuffed and covered with hair-cloth. Every article was waxed and shining, irreproachable as to neatness and cleanliness, but chilling to the eye and the heart, so dim and gray was the light admitted through the drab curtains, and so far removed from comfort were the cold ashes on the black hearth.

A little harpsichord of rosewood on four straight legs, the strings of which vibrated as the carriages passed in the street, and the slight ticking of a time-piece placed over the fireplace, were all that seemed to give life to this species of tomb.

But Gilbert entered it with profound respect. The furniture seemed to him almost sumptuous, since it was, as nearly as possible, the same as that of the château of Taverney, and the polished floor, above all, struck him with awe.

"Sit down," said Jacques, pointing to a second little table placed in the recess of a window, "and I shall explain what occupation I intend for you."

Gilbert eagerly obeyed.

"Do you know what this is?" asked the old man, showing him some paper ruled with lines at equal distances.

"Certainly," said he; "it is music paper."

"Well, when one of these leaves has been filled up prop-

erly by me, that is, when I have copied on it as much
music as it will contain, I have earned ten sous; that is
the price which I fixed myself. Do you think you can
learn to copy music ? "

" Oh, yes, sir ! I think so. "

" But does not all this little black dotting of spots joined
together by single, double, and triple strokes, swim before your eyes ? "

" Yes, sir. At the first glance I cannot distinguish
them well, but on looking more closely I shall be able to
separate one note from another; for instance, here is a
Fa. "

" And the note above that, crossing the second line ? "

" That is Sol. "

" Then you can read music ? "

" I know only the names of the notes ; I do not understand their value. "

" Do you know when they are minums, crotchets, qua-
vers, and semiquavers ? "

" Oh, yes ; I know that. "

" And that mark ? "

" It is a rest. "

" And that ? "

" A sharp. "

" And that ? "

" A flat. "

" Very well. And so, with this ignorance of yours, "
said Jacques, his eye beginning to darken with distrust
which seemed natural to him, " with this ignorance of
yours, you speak of music as you spoke of botany, and as
you would have spoken of love, had I not cut you
short. "

" Oh, sir, " replied Gilbert, blushing, " do not ridicule
me ! "

" No, my child ; I am only surprised at you. Music is
an art which is seldom learned until after other studies,
and you told me you had received no education ; in fact,
that you had been taught nothing. "

" That is the truth. sir. "

"But you could not have found out of yourself that this black point was a Fa."

"Sir," said Gilbert, looking down with an embarrassed air, "in the house where I lived there was a—a—young lady—who played on the harpsichord."

"Oh! the same who studied botany?"

"Yes, sir; and she played very well."

"Indeed?"

"Yes; and I adore music."

"All that does not account for your knowing the notes."

"Sir, Rousseau says that the man who enjoys the effect without seeking to know the cause, allows half his powers to lie dormant."

"Yes; but he also says that man in acquiring that knowledge loses his joyousness, his innocence, and his natural instincts."

"What matters it if he find in the search itself an enjoyment equal to all the pleasures which he loses?"

Jacques turned toward him, still more surprised. Ha!" said he, "you are not only a botanist and a musician, but also a logician."

"Ah, sir, I am unfortunately neither a musician, a botanist, nor a logician. I can distinguish one note from another, one sign from another, that is all."

"You can sol, fa, then?"

"No—not in the least, sir."

"Well, no matter. Will you try to copy this? Here is some ruled paper, but take care of wasting it, it is very dear; and now I think of it, it would be better for you to take some common paper, rule it yourself, and make a trial on it."

"Oh, sir, I shall do whatever you recommend. But allow me to say that this is not an occupation for my whole lifetime. It would be much better to become a public writer than copy music which I do not understand."

"Young man, young man, you speak without reflection. Is it by night that a public writer gains his bread?"

"No, certainly."

"Well, listen to me : with practise a man can copy in two or three hours at night five or even six of these pages ; for that he will get three francs. A man can live on that sum ; you will not contradict that, you, who would be content with six sous? Thus, you see, with two hours' work at night you could earn sufficient to enable you to attend the school of surgery, of medicine, and of botany."

"Oh," cried Gilbert, " now I understand, and I thank you from my very heart." And so saying, he seized eagerly the paper which the old man offered him.

CHAPTER XLVI.

WHO M. JACQUES WAS.

GILBERT set to work with the greatest ardor, and his paper was soon covered with careful copies of what was placed before him. The old man looked at him for some time, and then sat down at the other table to correct printed sheets like those of which the bags containing the kidney-beans had been made.

They had passed three hours in this way, and the time-piece had just struck nine, when Therese entered hurriedly. Jacques raised his head.

"Quick! quick!" said she, "come into the other room. Here is another prince come to visit you. When will this procession of grandees be over? I only hope he will not take it into his head to breakfast with us, as the Duke de Chartres did the other day."

"Who is the prince?" asked Jacques, in a low voice.

"Monseigneur the Prince de Conte."

At this name Gilbert let fall on his paper a *sol* which looked much more like a dinner-plate than a note.

"A prince! a grandee!" he muttered to himself.

Jacques left the study, smiling ; Therese followed, and closed the door behind her.

Then Gilbert looked around, and finding that he was alone, sat bolt upright with astonishment.

"But where am I, then?" exclaimed he. "Princes, highnesses, calling on Monsieur Jacques! The Duke de Chartres, the Prince de Conte, calling on a copier of music!"

He approached the door to listen; his heart beat strangely.

The first greetings were over between Jacques and the prince, and the latter was speaking.

"I should have liked," he said, "to take you with me."

"Why so, monseigneur?" asked Jacques.

"To introduce you to the dauphiness. A new era is opening for philosophy, my dear philosopher."

"A thousand thanks for your kindness, my lord, but it is impossible for me to accompany you."

"Yet six years ago you accompanied Madame de Pompadour to Fontainebleau."

"I was six years younger then. Now I am chained to my armchair by infirmities."

"And by misanthropy."

"And if it were so, my lord, you must allow that the world is not worth the trouble of putting one's self out of the way for it."

"Well, I shall let you off for St. Denis, and the grand ceremonial, but I must take you to Muette, where her royal highness will sleep the night after to-morrow."

"Then her royal highness arrives at St. Denis the day after to-morrow?"

"Yes, with all her retinue. Come, two leagues are easily traveled. Report bespeaks her highness an excellent musician; a pupil of Gluck's."

Gilbert heard no more.

The day after to-morrow the dauphiness and all her retinue would be at St. Denis; these words suggested only one idea to him, that the next day but one Andrée would be two leagues distant from him.

Of the two feelings which he experienced, the stronger overcame the weaker. Love put an end to curiosity. For

a moment it seemed to him as if he had not room to
breathe. He ran to a window to open it, but it was
fastened inside with a padlock, no doubt to prevent those
on the opposite side of the street from ever having an
opportunity of seeing what passed in the study.

He sank on his chair.

"Oh, I will never listen at doors again," said he; "I
must not try to penetrate the secrets of this man, apparently so humble, whom a prince calls his friend and
wishes to present to the future Queen of France, to the
daughter of emperors, whom Mademoiselle Andrée addressed almost kneeling at her feet. And yet, perhaps,
I might hear something of Mademoiselle Andrée. No,
no; I should seem like a lackey; La Brie used to listen
at doors."

And he courageously retired from the door. But his
hands trembled so much that he could not write, and indeed he required some more exciting pursuit to divert his
thoughts; he therefore seized a book on the other table.

"'The Confessions!'" he read, with joyful surprise,
"'embellished with a likeness of the author, Jean Jacques
Rousseau,' and I have never yet seen a likeness of Rousseau!" and he hastily turned the silk paper which covered
the engraving.

No sooner did it meet his eye than he uttered a cry of
amazement. At that moment Jacques opened the door.

Gilbert compared his face with the likeness in the book
which he held in his hand, then, pale and trembling, he
let the volume fall, exclaiming, "I am in the house of
Jean Jacques Rousseau!"

"Let me see, my child, how you have copied your
music," said Rousseau, smiling, and inwardly better pleased
with this involuntary homage than with many of the thousand triumphs of his glorious life. And passing by the
trembling Gilbert, he approached the table and commenced
to examine his work.

"Your notes are not badly formed," said he, "but they
are carelessly joined together. Here, there should be a
rest to make the time complete. Then, see, the bars

which divide it are not quite straight. Make the semi-breves by two semicircles; it is not important that they should join. The note made perfectly round is ungraceful, and the stalk does not join with it so well. Yes, my friend, you are indeed in the house of Jean Jacques Rousseau."

"Oh, pardon me, sir, for all the foolish words which I have uttered!" exclaimed Gilbert, clasping his hands and ready to fall on his knees.

"Was it necessary that a prince should come to visit me," said Rousseau, shrugging his shoulders, "to enable you to discover in me the unhappy, persecuted philosopher of Geneva? Poor child! Happy in your ignorance of persecution!"

"Oh, yes, I am happy, very happy! But it is in seeing you, in knowing you, in being near you!"

"Thanks, my child, thanks. But it is not enough to be happy; you must work. Now that you have made a trial, take this rondeau and copy it on some proper music-paper; it is short and easy—above all things, observe neatness. But how did you discover——"

Gilbert, with a swelling heart, took up the volume and pointed to the portrait.

"Oh, yes; my likeness burned in effigy on the first page of the 'Emile!' However, the auto-da-fé diffuses light as well as the rays of the sun."

"Ah, sir, my wildest dreams never exceeded this! To live with you. My highest ambition never hoped for more!"

"You cannot live with me, my friend," said Jean Jacques, "for I do not take pupils. As for guests, you perceive that I am not rich enough to entertain them—certainly not to receive them as regular inmates."

A cold perspiration stood on Gilbert's forehead. Rousseau took his hand.

"However," said he, "do not despair. From the moment I first saw you, I have been studying your character. In it there is much which requires to be corrected, but there is also much to esteem. Learn to subdue your inclinations. Distrust your pride, that gnawing worm which is the bane of philosophy. Copy music, and wait patiently for better times."

"Oh, heavens!" said Gilbert, "I feel bewildered when I think of what has happened me!"

"What has happened you is very simple and very natural, my child. You were flying I know not whence, for I did not seek to know your secret; and in your flight you met a man gathering plants in a wood. He had bread, you had none; he shared his with you. You did not know where to seek an asylum for the night; he offered you the shelter of his roof. The man might have been called by any name; he happened to be called Rousseau. That is the whole affair. This man said to you, the first precept of philosophy is—man, suffice for thyself. Now, my friend, when you have copied your rondeau, you will have gained your bread for this day. Copy your rondeau, therefore."

"Oh, sir, what kindness!"

"As for your lodging, that is yours into the bargain; only—no reading at night, or if you must have a candle, let it be your own; otherwise, Therese will scold. In the meantime, are you hungry?"

"Oh, no, sir," replied Gilbert, in a choking voice.

"There is enough left from our supper of last night to serve for this morning's breakfast. Do not stand on ceremony; this repast is the last you will get at my table, unless by invitation, if we remain friends."

Gilbert made a movement as if to speak, but Rousseau interrupted him.

"There is in the Rue Plastrière," continued he, "a modest eating-house for mechanics; you can dine there on moderate terms, for I shall recommend you to the proprietor. In the meantime, come and breakfast."

Gilbert followed Rousseau without daring to reply. He was completely subdued; but at least it was by a man superior to most other men.

After a few mouthfuls he left the table and returned to his task. He spoke truly; his emotion was so great that it had taken away his appetite. During the whole day he never raised his eyes from the paper, and at eight in the evening, after having torn three sheets, he had succeeded in copying legibly and neatly a rondeau of four pages.

" I will not flatter you," said Rousseau, " it is not yet well done, but it is legible ; what you have done is worth ten sous ; here is the money."

Gilbert took it with a low bow.

"There is some bread in the cupboard, Monsieur Gilbert," said Therese, on whom the young man's modest demeanor, mildness, and industry had produced a favorable impression.

" Thank you, ma'am," replied Gilbert ; " believe me I shall never forget your kindness."

" Here," said she, holding the bread out to him.

He was about to refuse, but, looking at Rousseau, he saw by the slight frown which contracted his piercing eye and the curl which hovered on his delicately formed lips, that the refusal would wound him.

"I accept your kind offer," said he.

He then withdrew to his little chamber, holding in his hand the six silver sous and the four copper ones he had just received.

" At last," said he, on entering his garret, " I am my own master. But stay—not yet, since I hold in my hand the bread of charity."

And although he felt hungry, he laid down the piece of bread on the sill of the skylight, and did not eat it. Then, fancying that sleep would enable him to forget his hunger, he blew out his candle and stretched himself on his straw pallet.

He was awake before daybreak on the following morning, for, in truth, he had slept very little during the night. Recollecting what Rousseau had said about the gardens, he leaned out of the skylight, and saw below him the trees and shrubs of a very beautiful garden, and beyond the trees the hotel to which the garden belonged, the entrance to which was from the Rue Jussienne.

In one corner of the garden, quite surrounded by shrubs

and flowers, there stood a little summer-house, the windows of which were closed. Gilbert at first thought that the windows were closed on account of the earliness of the hour ; but observing that the foliage of the trees had grown up against the shutters, he was convinced that the summer-house must have been unoccupied since the preceding winter at least. He returned, therefore, to his admiring contemplation of the noble lime-trees, which partially concealed from view the main body of the hotel.

Two or three times during his survey, Gilbert's eyes had turned toward the piece of bread which Therese had cut from the evening before ; but although hunger pleaded loudly, he was so much the master of himself that he refrained from touching it.

Five o'clock struck. Gilbert was persuaded that the door of the passage must now be open; and washed, brushed, and combed, for Rousseau had furnished his garret with all that was necessary for his modest toilet, he descended the stairs, with his piece of bread under his arm.

Rousseau, who this time was not the first afoot, and who from a lingering suspicion, perhaps, and the better to watch his guest, had left his door open, heard him descend and narrowly observed his movements. He saw Gilbert leave the house with the bread under his arm ; a poor man came up to him, and he saw Gilbert give him the bread, and then enter a baker's shop which was just opened, and buy some more.

" Now," said Rousseau, " he will go to a tavern, and his poor ten sous will soon vanish."

But he was mistaken. Gilbert eat his bread as he walked along, then, stopping at a fountain at the corner of the street, he took a long draught, eat the rest of the bread, drank again, rinsed his mouth, washed his hands, and returned toward the house.

" Ha !" said Rousseau, " I fancy that I am luckier than Diogenes, and have found a man !" And hearing Gilbert's footsteps on the stairs, he hastened to open the door.

The entire day was spent in uninterrupted labor. Gilbert brought to his monotonous task activity, intelligence, and unshrinking assiduity. What he did not perfectly comprehend he guessed, and his hand, the slave of his iron will, traced the notes without hesitation and without mistake. By evening he had copied seven pages, if not elegantly, at least with scrupulous correctness.

Rousseau examined his work with the eye both of a critical judge and a philosopher. As a critical judge, he criticized the form of the notes, the fineness of the joinings, the spaces for the rests and dots; but he acknowledged that there was a decided improvement since the day before, and he gave Gilbert twenty-five sous.

As a philosopher, he admired the strength of resolution which could bend the ardent temperament and active and athletic frame of a young man of eighteen to such constant and unceasing labor. For Rousseau had discovered that in that young heart there lurked an ardent passion; but whether ambition or love, he had not yet ascertained.

Gilbert gazed thoughtfully at the money which he had received—it was a piece of twenty-four sous and a single sou. He put the sou in his pocket, probably with the other sous which were remaining from the little sum of the day before, and grasping the silver with evident satisfaction in his right hand, he said:

"Sir, you are my master, since you give me work and also lodge me in your house gratis, I think it only right, therefore, that I should communicate to you all my intentions, otherwise I might lose your regard."

Rousseau looked at him with a lowering eye. "What are you going to do?" said he. "Have you any other intention than that of working to-morrow?"

"Sir, for to-morrow, yes. With your permission, I should like to be at liberty to-morrow."

"What to do?" said Rousseau, "to idle?"

"Sir," said Gilbert, "I wish to go to St. Denis."

"To St. Denis?"

"Yes; her highness the dauphiness is to arrive there to-morrow."

"Ah! true; there are to be festivities in honor of her arrival."

"That is it, sir."

"I thought you less of a sight-seer, my young friend," said Rousseau. "I gave you credit, at first, on the contrary, for despising the pomps of absolute power."

"Sir——"

"Look at me—me, whom you pretend to take for a model. Yesterday one of the royal princes came to invite me to court. Well, observe, citizen as I am, I refused his invitation; not to go as you would go, my poor lad, on foot, and standing on tiptoe to catch a glimpse over the shoulder of a guardsman of the king's carriage as it passes, but to appear before princes—to be honored by a smile from princesses."

Gilbert nodded his approbation.

"And why did I refuse?" continued Rousseau, with vehemence. "Because a man ought not to have two faces; because the man who has written that royalty is an abuse ought not to be seen bending before a king. Because I—who know that every festivity of the great robs the people of some portion of that comfort which is now scarcely sufficient to keep them from revolt—I protest by my absence against all such festivities."

"Sir," said Gilbert, "believe me, I comprehend all the sublimity of your philosophy."

"Doubtless; and yet since you do not practise it, permit me to tell you——"

"Sir," said Gilbert, "I am not a philosopher."

"Tell me, at least, what you are going to do at St. Denis."

"Sir, I am discreet."

Rousseau was struck by these words; he saw that there was some mystery concealed under this obstinate desire, and he looked at this young man with a sort of admiration which his character inspired.

"Oh, very well!" said he. "I see you have a motive; I like that better."

"Yes, sir, I have a motive; one, I assure you, in no way connected with an idle love for pomp or show."

"So much the better. Or, perhaps, I should say so

much the worse. There is something unfathomable in your look, young man, and I seek in vain in its expression for the frankness and calm of youth."

"I told you, sir, that I have been unhappy," replied Gilbert, sorrowfully, "and for the unhappy there is no youth. Then, you consent to give me to-morrow to myself?"

"Yes."

"Thank you, sir."

"Remember, however," said Rousseau, "that while you are gazing at the vain pomps of the world defiling in procession before you, I shall, in one of my herbals, be passing in review the splendor and variety of nature."

"Sir," said Gilbert, "would you not have left all the herbals in the world the day when you went to visit Mademoiselle Galley after having presented her with the bouquet?"

"Good!" said Rousseau. "True, you are young. Go to St. Denis, my child."

Then, when Gilbert, with a joyful countenance, had left the room:

"It is not ambition," said he; "it is love!"

CHAPTER XLVII.

THE SORCERER'S WIFE.

At the moment when Gilbert, after his hard day's labor, was munching in his loft his bread dipped in cold water, and inhaling with delight the pure air of the gardens below him, a woman mounted on a magnificent Arabian horse was advancing at full gallop toward St. Denis, along that road which was now deserted, but which on the morrow was to be crowded with so much rank and fashion. She was dressed with elegance, but in a strange and peculiar style, and her face was hidden by a thick veil. On entering the town she proceeded straight to the Carmelite Convent, and dismounting, she knocked with her deli-

cately formed finger at the wicket, while her horse, which
she held by the bridle, snorted and pawed the ground with
impatience.

Several inhabitants of the town, struck with curiosity,
gathered around her. They were attracted, in the first
place, by her foreign attire, then by her perseverance in
knocking.

"What is it you want, madame?" said one of them, at
length.

"You see, sir," she replied, with a strongly marked
Italian accent, "I wish to obtain admittance."

"In that case, you are taking the wrong way. This
gate is only opened once a day to the poor, and the hour
is now past."

"What must I do, then, to gain an audience of the
superior?"

"You must knock at that little door at the extremity of
the wall, or else ring at the grand entrance."

Another person now approached.

"Do you know, madame," said he, "that the present
abbess is Her Royal Highness Madame Louise of France?"

"I know it, sir, thank you," she replied.

"Vetudieu! What a splendid animal!" exclaimed a
dragoon, gazing in admiration at the foreigner's steed.
"Now, that horse, if not too old, is worth five hundred
louis-d'ors, as sure as mine is worth a hundred pistoles!"

These words produced a great effect on the crowd.

At that moment, a canon, who, unlike the dragoon,
looked only at the rider, to the exclusion of her steed,
made his way toward her, and by some secret known to
himself alone opened the wicket of the tower.

"Enter, madame," said he, "and lead in your horse,
if you please."

The woman, eager to escape from the gaze of the crowd,
which seemed to terrify her, hurried in, and the gate was
closed behind her.

The moment the foreigner found herself alone in the
large courtyard she shook the bridle loose on the horse's
neck, and the noble animal, rejoiced to feel himself at

liberty, made his trappings clash, and pawed the ground so loudly that the portress, who happened for the moment to be off her post, hastened out from the interior of the convent.

"What do you want, madame?" cried she; "and how did you gain admittance here?"

"A charitable canon opened the gate for me," said the stranger. "As for my business, I wish, if possible, to speak to the superior."

"Madame will not receive any one this evening."

"Yet I have been told that it is the duty of superiors of convents to admit, at any hour of the day or of the night, their sisters of the world who come to implore their succor."

"Possibly so in ordinary circumstances; but her royal highness, who only arrived the day before yesterday, is scarcely installed in her office yet, and holds this evening a chapter of our order."

"Oh, madame!" replied the stranger, "I come from a great distance—I come from Rome. I have traveled sixty leagues on horseback, and am almost exhausted."

"What can I do? The orders of the superior are positive."

"My sister, I have to reveal to your abbess ma rs of the highest importance."

"Return to-morrow."

"It is impossible. I have stayed one day in Paris, and already during that day—besides, I cannot sleep at an inn."

"Why so?"

"Because I have no money."

The man gazed in amazement at this woman, covered with jewels, and mistress of a fine horse, who pretended that she had no money to pay for a night's lodging.

"Oh, do not heed my words! Do not examine my dress!" said the young woman. "Perhaps I did not speak the precise truth when I said I had no money, for no doubt I could obtain credit in any inn. But what I want is not a lodging, but a refuge."

" Madame, this is not the only convent in St. Denis, and each convent has an abbess."

" Yes, yes, I know that well ; but it is not a common abbess who can protect me."

" I think you are wrong in persisting thus. The Princess Louise no longer takes any interest in affairs of this world."

" What matters it to you ? Only just tell her that I wish to speak to her."

" She is holding a chapter, I tell you."

" After it is over, then."

" It has scarcely begun."

" I can go into the church and wait there in prayer."

" I am sorry, madame, that I cannot permit you to wait there."

" Oh, then I am mistaken ! I am not in the house of God !" cried the stranger, with such vehemence of voice and look that the nun, alarmed, dared no longer oppose her wishes.

" If you be really in great distress," said she, " I shall try what I can do."

" Oh, tell her royal highness," added the foreigner, " that I come from Rome, that I have made only two halts on the road, one at Mayence, the other at Strasbourg ; that during the last four days I have only taken the time absolutely necessary for myself and my horse to regain strength to continue our journey."

" I shall tell her, sister ;" and the nun hastened off.

A moment after, a lay sister appeared, followed by the portress.

" Well ? " exclaimed the stranger, impatient to know what reply had been sent.

" Her royal highness says, madame," replied the lay sister, " it is quite impossible to give you an audience this evening , but that, nevertheless, the hospitality of the convent shall be extended to you, since you are in such urgent want of an asylum. You may follow me, therefore, sister, and if you have made so long a journey as you say, and are fatigued, you can retire to rest at once."

" But my horse ?"

"Rest assured he shall be taken care of, my sister."

"He is as gentle as a lamb. He is called Djerid, and comes when addressed by that name. I entreat you will take care of him, for he is a most valuable animal."

"He shall be treated as if he were one of the king's horses."

"Thanks."

"In the meantime, conduct madame to her apartment," said the lay sister to the portress.

"Not to my apartment—to the church. I do not require sleep, but prayer."

"The chapel is open, my sister," said the nun, pointing to a little side-door which gave admittance to the church.

"And I shall see the superior in the morning?" asked the stranger.

"To-morrow morning? That is also impossible."

"Why so?"

"Because to-morrow morning there will be a grand reception."

"And for whom can a reception be more necessary than for an unfortunate like me?"

"Her royal highness the dauphiness will do us the honor to spend two hours here on her way through town to-morrow. It is a great honor for our convent, and a high solemnity for us poor nuns; so that, you understand, the abbess is most anxious that everything should be worthy of the royal guests we expect."

"But in the meantime," said the stranger, looking around with a shudder, "while I wait the leisure of your august superior, shall I be in safety here?"

"Undoubtedly, my sister. Our house is a refuge even for the guilty, much more for——"

"For fugitives," said the stranger. "It is well; then no one can enter here?"

"No one—that is, not without an order."

"Oh, but if he procures an order! Good heavens! He who is so powerful that his power at times terrifies me."

"He—who?" asked the nun.

"Oh, no one—no one."

"The poor creature is deranged, I fear," murmured the nun to herself.

"The church! the church!" repeated the stranger, so wildly as in some degree to justify this suspicion.

"Come, my sister, let me lead you to it."

"Yes, yes; I am pursued, look you. Quick! the church!"

"Oh, the walls of St. Denis are strong," said the nun, with a compassionate smile. "Believe me, after such a journey as you have described, you had much better go and rest in a good bed than bruise your knees on the stones of our chapel."

"No, no; I wish to pray—I wish to pray that God will rescue me from my pursuers!" cried the young woman, hurriedly entering the church by the door which the nun pointed out, and shutting the door behind her.

The nun, curious as all nuns are, hastened round to the principal entrance, and, advancing softly, saw the unknown praying and sobbing before the altar, her face bowed to the ground.

CHAPTER XLVIII.

PARISIANS.

THE nuns had informed the stranger correctly, when they told her that the chapter of the convent was assembled in conclave. Mme. Louise of France presided at the meeting, her first exercise of supreme authority, and assisted in their deliberation as to the best means of giving the daughter of the Cæsars a reception worthy of her august character and station.

The funds of the convent were rather low. The late abbess, on resigning her functions, had carried away with her a large portion of the lace, which was her private property, as well as the reliquaries and ostensoirs, which it was the practise of superiors, who were all taken from the highest families, to lend to their convents on devoting themselves to the service of God, from the most worldly motives.

Mme. Louise, on learning the intended visit of the dauphiness, had sent an express to Versailles, and the same night a wagon had arrived loaded with hangings, lace, and ornaments, to the value of six hundred thousand livres.

Consequently, when the tidings were spread of the royal splendor, which was to be exhibited at the reception of the dauphiness, all the ardent curiosity of the Parisians was redoubled—those same Parisians whom Mercier describes as provoking only a smile when seen in private life, but when, assembled in masses, arousing reflections more calculated to make us weep and tremble.

Therefore, from earliest dawn, the citizens of the capital, having learned from public report the route which the dauphiness was to take, began to issue from their dens, and at first, in parties of ten or twenty, then in hundreds, and finally in thousands, poured out toward St. Denis.

The French and Swiss guards, the regiments stationed at St. Denis, were under arms, and formed a line on each side of the road to keep back the waves of the living tide which rolled on toward the gates of the cathedral, and mounted even to the sculptured projections of the building. A sea of heads appeared everywhere, children's peeping from above the porches of doors, men's and women's thronging the windows. Besides these, thousands of curious spectators, who had arrived too late to secure places, or who, like Gilbert, preferred their liberty to the constraint and inconvenience of being shut up during the whole day in one spot, swarmed like ants on every side, climbing the trees which bordered the road from St. Denis to Muette, or dispersed here and there waiting for the procession.

The cortége, although still possessing a numerous train of sumptuous equipages, and troops of domestics in splendid liveries, had considerably diminished after leaving Compiègne ; for, except for the great lords, it was found impossible to keep pace with the king, who doubled and trebled the usual stages by means of relays posted on the road.

Those of lesser note had, therefore, remained at Compiègne, or had taken post-horses and returned to Paris to give their stud a breathing interval. But after a day's repose at their own domiciles, masters and domestics now thronged toward St. Denis, both to witness the preparations, and to get another glimpse of the dauphiness, whom they had already only partially seen. And then, besides the court carriages, were there not those of the parliament, the financiers, the rich merchants, the ladies of fashion, and those of the opera? Were there not, in addition, hired horses and carriages, as well as the caravans, which rolled toward St. Denis, crammed with the good citizens of Paris, both male and female, who managed to arrive by this means somewhat later than they could have accomplished the distance on foot? It may easily be imagined, therefore, what a formidable army directed its march toward St. Denis on the morning of the day when the gazettes and placards announced that the dauphiness was to arrive, forming into a dense mass before the convent of the Carmelites, and, when no more room could be obtained within the privileged inclosure, stretching away in long lines on the roads by which the dauphiness and her suite were to arrive and depart.

Now, let any one picture to himself in this crowd, which was the terror even of the Parisian, Gilbert, insignificant in appearance, alone, undecided, ignorant of the localities, and too proud even to ask a question—for since he was in Paris he had determined to pass for a Parisian—he who had never seen a hundred people assembled together in his life.

At first he saw pedestrians thinly scattered along the road; at La Chapelle they began to increase, and at St. Denis they seemed to rise out of the ground, and presented much the appearance of an immense field bristling with ears of corn. For a long time past Gilbert had seen nothing, lost as he was in the crowd; he could not look over the heads of those around him, and, swept along in the throng, he blindly followed where the concourse of spectators led him.

At last he saw some spectators perched on a tree, and longed to imitate their example, but he dared not take off his coat. He made his way, however, to the foot of the tree, just as one of those unfortunates, who, like himself, were deprived of all view of the horizon, and who staggered onward, trampling others and being trampled on themselves, was struck by the bright idea of questioning their lucky neighbors perched in safety on the branches, and learned from one of them that there was a large space vacant between the convent and the guards. Gilbert, emboldened by this intelligence, ventured, in his turn, to ask whether the carriages were yet in sight.

They had not yet appeared ; but on the road, about a quarter of a league beyond St. Denis, a great cloud of dust was plainly visible. This was what Gilbert wished to know ; the carriages not being in sight, it was now his business to ascertain precisely by what route they would approach ; but nevertheless he held on his way, traversing the crowd in perfect silence—a mode of procedure which, in Paris, leads irresistibly to the conclusion that the person practising it is either an Englishman or deaf and dumb.

Scarcely had Gilbert extricated himself from the multitude, when he perceived, seated behind a ditch, the family of an humble tradesman at breakfast.

There was a blue-eyed daughter, tall and fair, modest and timid.

There was the mother, a fat, laughing little woman, with white teeth and rosy cheeks.

There was an aunt, tall, bony, dry, and harsh.

There was the father, half buried in an immense camlet coat, which was usually brought out of his chest only on Sundays, but which he ventured to put on on so grand an occasion as the present, and of which he took more care then he did of his wife and daughter, being certain that the latter could take care of themselves.

There was the servant-maid, who did nothing but laugh. She carried an enormous basket containing everything necessary for breakfast, and even under its weight the stout lass had never ceased laughing and singing, encouraged as she was by her master, who took the burden when she was fatigued.

In those days a domestic was one of the family, and occupied a position in it very analogous to that of the house-dog, beaten sometimes, excluded never.

Gilbert contemplated by stealth this group which was so new to him. Shut up at Taverney from his birth, he had hitherto seen only the lord and the lackey; the citizen was altogether a novelty to him.

He saw these honest people employ in their domestic economy a system of philosophy, which, although not drawn from the teachings of Plato and Socrates, was modeled much after that of Bias, a little extended.

They had brought with them as much food as they possibly could, and were determined to make the most of it.

The father was carving one of those appetizing pieces of roast veal so much in vogue with the Parisian trades-man. Nicely browned, dainty, and tempting, it reposed amid a bed of carrots, onions, and bacon, in the dish in which the day before it had been baked, carefully placed there by the good housekeeper. The maid had then carried it to the baker, who, while baking his loaves, had given it an asylum in his oven along with a score of such dishes destined to assist the enjoyments of the following day.

Gilbert chose out a place for himself at the foot of a neighboring elm, and dusted it carefully with his checked pocket-handkerchief. He then took off his hat, spread his handkerchief on the ground, and seated himself. He paid no attention to his neighbors, which, they remarking, naturally directed a good deal of their own to him.

"That is a careful young man," said the mother.

The daughter blushed. She always did so when a young man was mentioned before her, a trait in her character which gave the highest gratification to her parents.

The father turned, "And a handsome lad, too," said he.

The daughter blushed still more deeply than before.

"He looks tired," said the servant maid, "and yet he has not been carrying anything."

"Rather say lazy," said the aunt.

"Sir," said the mother, addressing Gilbert, with that familiarity which is found nowhere but among the Parisians, "are the carriages still far off?"

Gilbert turned, and seeing that these words were addressed to him, rose and bowed.

"A most polite young man," said the mother.

This remark added a still deeper dye to the daughter's cheeks.

"I do not know, madame," answered Gilbert; "I only heard that a cloud of dust was seen about a quarter of a league off."

"Draw nearer, sir," said the honest tradesman, "and if you have not breakfasted——" and he pointed to the excellent repast which was spread on the grass.

Gilbert approached the group. He had not breakfasted, and the seducing odor of the viands tempted him strongly; but he jingled his twenty-five sous in his pocket, and reflecting that for the third of this sum he could purchase a breakfast almost as good as that which was offered to him, he would not accept any favor from people whom he saw for the first time.

"Thank you, sir," said he, "a thousand thanks, but I have already breakfasted."

"Ah!" said the good woman, "I see that you are a prudent young man. But from where you are seated you will see nothing."

"Why," replied Gilbert, smiling, "in that case you will not see anything yourselves, as you are in the same position as myself."

"Oh, it is a very different matter with us. We have a nephew, a sergeant, in the French guards."

The young girl looked like a peony.

"His post this morning will be before La Paon Bleu."

"If I am not taking too great a liberty," said Gilbert, "may I ask where Le Paon Bleu is?"

"Just opposite the Carmelite Convent," replied the mother. "He has promised to keep places for us behind his detachment. He will then give us his bench, and we shall see at our ease all the company get out of their carriages."

It was now Gilbert's turn to redden; he had refused to eat with the good people, but he longed to be of their party.

Nevertheless, his philosophy, or, rather, his pride whispered: "It is very well for women to require some one to assist them, but I, a man, have arms and shoulders of my own."

"All those who do not get placed like us," continued the mother, as if guessing his thought, "will only see empty carriages—no great sight, in truth, for empty carriages can be seen everywhere, and certainly are not worth the trouble of coming as far as St. Denis."

"But, madame," said Gilbert, "it seems to me that many besides yourself will endeavor to secure the place you speak of."

"Yes, but every one has not a nephew in the guards to assist them."

"Ah! true!" murmured Gilbert.

As he said this, his face wore an expression of disappointment which did not escape Parisian penetration.

"But," said the husband, well skilled in divining the wishes of his wife, "this gentleman can accompany us if he pleases."

"Oh, sir, I fear I should be troublesome," replied Gilbert.

"Bah! not at all," said the good woman; "on the contrary, you will assist us in reaching our places. We have only one man now to depend on, and then we should have two."

No other argument could have had so much weight in determining Gilbert. The idea that he could be useful, and by so doing pay for the favor which was offered him, put him quite at his ease and relieved every scruple.

He accepted the offer.

" We shall see to whom he will offer his arm," said the aunt.

This assistance was indeed a real God-send to Gilbert. How, without it, could he have passed through a barrier of thirty thousand persons, each more favored than himself by rank, wealth, or strength, and, above all, by the practise they had acquired in obtaining places at fêtes, where every one seizes the best he can procure ?

Had our philosopher been less of a theoretical and more of a practical man, the present occasion would have furnished him with an admirable opportunity for studying the dynamics of society.

The carriage with four horses, burst like a cannon-ball through the mass; all fell back on each side before its running footman, with his plumed hat, his gaily striped jacket, and his thick stick, who rushed on in advance, frequently preceded by two formidable coach-dogs.

The carriage with two horses advanced more slowly, and whispered a sort of password in the ear of a guardsman, after which it proceeded to take its place in the cortége before the convent.

Single horsemen, although overlooking the crowd from their elevated position, were forced to advance at a foot-pace, and only gained a good position after a thousand jostlings, interruptions, and oaths.

Lastly, the poor pedestrian, trodden, trampled on, and tossed about, was driven forward like the foam of the wave by a thousand waves rolling on behind. Sometimes raising himself on tiptoe to see over the heads of his neighbors ; sometimes wrestling like Antæus, to fall like him to his mother earth ; seeking his way through the multitude, and when he had found it, dragging after him his family —almost always a troop of women—whom the Parisian alone ventures to attempt conducting through such scenes.

Lowest of all, or rather superior to all, in such circumstances, was the man of the very dregs of the people. With unshaven beard and ragged cap, his arms naked to the elbow, and his garments held together by some fragment of a cord, indefatigably working with elbows, with shoulders, and with feet, and ever and anon uttering a savage and sardonic laugh, he made his way among the crowds as easily as Gulliver amid the Lilliputians.

Gilbert, who was neither a great lord with a carriage and four, nor a member of Parliament with two, nor a soldier on horseback, nor a Parisian, nor a man of the people, must have infallibly been trampled under foot by the throng, had he not been under the protection of the tradesman. Backed by him, he felt powerful, and boldly offered his arm to the mother of the family.

" Impertinent fellow ! " said the aunt.

They set out ; the father gave his sister and his daughter each an arm, and the maid-servant followed behind with the huge basket.

" Gentlemen, may I trouble you ? " said the good woman, with her ready laugh. " Gentlemen, if you please, a little room—gentlemen, be good enough——"

And every one fell back and yielded a passage to her and Gilbert, while in their wake glided the rest of the party.

Foot by foot, step by step, they managed to advance five hundred paces, and then found themselves close to that formidable line of French guards on which the tradesman and his family rested all their hopes. The daughter had by this time regained her natural color. Once there, the citizen mounted on Gilbert's shoulders to look over the soldiers' heads, and perceived at twenty yards' distance from him his wife's nephew twisting his mustache. The good man made such outrageous gestures with his hat, that at last his nephew's attention was attracted to him ; he came forward, asked his comrades to make way a little, and obtained a slight opening in the ranks.

Through this chink slipped Gilbert and the good woman, then the citizen himself, the sister and daughter, and after them the stout lass with the basket. Their troublesome journey was over, and mutual thanks were exchanged between Gilbert and the head of the family. The mother endeavored to detain him by their side, the aunt said he had better go, and they separated, not to meet again.

In the open space in which Gilbert now found himself, none but privileged persons were admitted, and he therefore easily reached the trunk of a large linden-tree, mounted upon a stone near it, and supporting himself by a low branch, waited patiently.

About half an hour after he had thus installed himself, the cannon roared, the rattling of the drums was heard, and the great bell of the cathedral sent forth its first majestic peal.

CHAPTER XLIX.

THE KING'S CARRIAGES.

A DULL heavy sound was heard in the distance which became stronger and deeper as it advanced. As Gilbert listened, he felt every nerve in his body vibrate painfully.

The people were shouting "God save the king!" It was the fashion then.

Onward came a cloud of prancing horses covered with housings of gold and purple; these were the musketeers, the gendarmes, and Swiss horse-guards. Then followed a massive carriage magnificently decorated.

Gilbert perceived in it a blue ribbon and a majestic head not uncovered; he saw the cold, penetrating light of the royal look, before which every form bent and every head was uncovered. Fascinated—motionless, breathless, he forgot to take off his hat.

A violent blow roused him from his trance; his hat rolled on the ground.

He sprung forward, lifted it up, and looking round, saw the tradesman's nephew looking at him with that truculent smile which is peculiar to the soldier.

"Well," said he, "so you don't take off your hat to the king?"

Gilbert turned pale and looked at his hat covered with dust.

"It is the first time I ever saw the king," said he, "and I forgot to salute him, it is true. But I did not know——"

"You did not know?" said the soldier, frowning.

Gilbert feared that he should be driven from the spot where he was so well placed for seeing Andrée, and love conquered pride.

"Pardon me," said he, "I am from the country."

"And you have come to Paris to be educated, my little man?"

"Yes, sir," replied Gilbert, swallowing his rage.

"Well, since you are seeking instruction," said the sergeant, arresting Gilbert's hand as he was just going to put his hat on his head, "learn this: you must take off your hat to the dauphiness as well as to the king, and to their royal highnesses the princes as well as to the dauphiness; in short, you must take it off to all the carriages on which you see the fleur-de-lis. Do you know the fleur-de-lis, my little fellow, or must I show you what it is?"

"Quite unnecessary, sir; I know it."

"It is well you know even that much," grumbled the sergeant.

The royal carriages continued to file past. As each reached the door of the convent, it stopped to permit its occupants to alight. This operation caused, every five minutes, a general halt along the whole line.

At one of these halts, Gilbert felt as if a fiery sword had pierced his heart. He became giddy; everything swam before his eyes, and he trembled so violently that he was forced to grasp his branch more firmly to prevent himself from falling.

About ten paces from him, in one of the carriages with the fleur-de-lis, to which the sergeant had desired him to take off his hat, he had just perceived Andrée. Dressed in white, and dazzling with beauty, she seemed to his excited eyes some angelic being from a higher sphere.

He uttered a stifled cry; but immediately afterward, conquering his agitation, he commanded his heart to be still and his gaze steady; and so great was his self-control that he succeeded.

Andrée, on her side, wishing to know why the procession had stopped, leaned forward out of the carriage, and directing her clear and limpid gaze around, she perceived Gilbert, and at once recognized him. Gilbert feared that on seeing him she would be surprised, and would point him out to her father.

He was not mistaken. With an air of astonishment, she turned toward the Baron de Taverney, who, decorated with his red ribbon, sat with great dignity beside her, and directed his attention to Gilbert.

"Gilbert?" cried the baron, starting; "Gilbert here? And who, pray, will take care of Mahon at Taverney?"

The young man heard these words distinctly, and with the most studied respect he bowed to Andrée and the baron. It required all his strength to accomplish this feat.

"It is really he!" continued the baron, on perceiving our philosopher. "It is the little rascal himself!"

The idea of Gilbert being in Paris was one so far removed from his thoughts, that at first he would not believe his daughter's assertions, and could hardly credit even his own eyes. As for Andrée, whom Gilbert examined closely, after the first slight shade of surprise had passed away, her countenance resumed an expression of most perfect calm.

The baron leaned out of the carriage window and signed to Gilbert to approach; but as he attempted to obey the sergeant stopped him.

"You see that I am called," said he.

"By whom?" demanded the sergeant.

"The gentleman in that carriage."

The sergeant's eyes followed the direction of Gilbert's finger, and rested on the Baron de Taverney's carriage."

"Pray allow him to come this way, sergeant," said the baron. "I wish to speak to the lad—two words only."

"Four, sir, four, if you like," replied the soldier. "You have plenty of time: they are now reading an address at the gate, and I dare say it will occupy half an hour. Pass through, young man."

"Come hither, you rascal!" said the baron to Gilbert, who affected to walk at his usual pace, "and tell me by what accident it happens you are here when you ought to be at Taverney."

Gilbert saluted Andrée and the baron a second time and replied:

"It was no accident which brought me to Paris, sir, I came hither of my own free will."

"Your free will, you scoundrel? Do you talk of your will to me?"

"Why not? Every free man has the right to possess it."

"Oh, ho! Free man? You imagine yourself free, do you, you little wretch?"

"Certainly I am; I have never sold my freedom to any one."

"Upon my word, this is an amusing sort of a scoundrel!" exclaimed the baron, confounded at the coolness with which Gilbert spoke. "Your free will led you to Paris! And how did you travel, pray? What assistance had you, may I ask?"

"I came on foot."

"On foot!" said Andrée, with a sort of pity in her tone.

"And pray, what do you intend to do in Paris?" inquired the baron.

"To get educated first—then make my fortune."

"Educated?"

"Yes, I am certain of being educated."

"Make your fortune?"

"I hope to make it."

"And in the meantime what do you do? Beg?"

"Beg!" exclaimed Gilbert, with lofty scorn.

"You steal, then?"

"Sir," said Gilbert, with a look so proud and fierce that it fixed Andrée's attention on him for a moment, "sir, did I ever steal from you?"

"What can your idle hands do but steal?"

"What those of a man of genius do—a man whom I wish

to imitate, were it in only in his perseverance," replied Gilbert. "They copy music."

Andrée turned toward him, "Copy music?" said she. "Yes, mademoiselle."

"You know music, then?" inquired she, with the same contemptuous tone in which she would have said, "It is false."

"I know my notes, and that is enough for a copyist."

"And how the devil did you learn your notes, you rascal?" cried the baron.

"Yes, how?" added Andrée, smiling.

"I love music, sir, passionately, and when Mademoiselle Andrée played on the harpsichord every day, I hid myself that I might listen."

"Good-for-nothing fellow!"

"At first I remembered the airs; then as they were written in a music-book by degrees I learned to read the notes from the book."

"From my music-book!" exclaimed Andrée, with the utmost indignation, "did you dare to touch my music-book?"

"No, mademoiselle, I did not permit myself to do so, but as it remained open on the harpsichord, sometimes in one place, sometimes in another, I endeavored to read in it, but without touching it. My eyes would not soil the pages."

"You will see," cried the baron, "that the fellow will assert next that he plays on the piano like Haydn!"

"I should probably have been able by this time to play," said Gilbert, "had I dared to place my fingers on the keys."

Andrée again glanced at that face which was animated by a sentiment only to be compared to the fanaticism of a martyr eager for the stake; but the baron, who did not possess his daughter's clear and comprehensive intellect, felt his choler rise on reflecting that the young man was in the right, and that he had been treated inhumanly in being left with Mahon at Taverney. It is not easy to pardon in an inferior the wrong which he proves you have done him, and the baron therefore became more furious in proportion as his daughter became calm.

"Wretch!" he cried, "you steal away, you go running about like a vagabond, and when questioned about your mode of life you utter such a tissue of absurdities as those which we have just heard! But it shall not be my fault if rogues and pickpockets infest the king's highways."

Andrée, by a gesture, entreated her father to be calm; she felt that ungoverned anger destroys all superiority in the person giving way to it. But the baron thrust aside her hand which she had placed on his arm, and continued:

"I shall recommend you to the notice of the Count de Sartines, and you shall speedily take a turn in the Bicetre, you scarecrow of a philosopher!"

Gilbert stepped back, crushed his hat under his arm, and, pale with anger, exclaimed:

"Learn, my lord baron, that since I arrived in Paris I have found protectors in whose ante-chambers your Count de Sartines would be glad to wait."

"Indeed?" said the baron. "In that case I shall take care, if you escape a prison, that you do not escape a good caning. Andrée, call your brother."

Andrée leaned forward out of the carriage, and said, in a low voice, to Gilbert, "Take my advice, Monsieur Gilbert, and retire."

"Philip, Philip!" shouted the old man.

"Leave us!" said Andrée again to the young man, who remained silent and motionless in his place as if in ecstatic contemplation.

An officer, summoned by the baron's cries, hurried forward to the carriage door; it was Philip, dressed in his captain's uniform.

The young man was splendidly attired, and seemed in high spirits.

"How—Gilbert?" he exclaimed, with a good-humored smile on recognizing the young man; "Gilbert here! How do you do, Gilbert? Well, what do you want with me, my dear father?"

"How do you do, Monsieur Philip?" replied Gilbert,

"What do I want?" said the baron, furiously, "I want you to take the sheath of your sword and chastise this scoundrel."

"But what has he done?" asked Philip, gazing by turns with increasing astonishment at the angry face of his father and the rigid and motionless features of Gilbert.

"Done? He—he—has—Beat him, Philip—beat him like a dog!" cried the baron. Taverney turned to his sister.

"What has he done, Andrée? has he insulted you?"

"Insulted her?" repeated Gilbert.

"No, Philip, no!" replied Andrée. "He has done nothing wrong; my father is in error. Gilbert is no longer in our service, and has a perfect right to go where he pleases; but my father will not understand this, and is angry at finding him here."

"Is that all?" said Philip.

"Nothing more, brother; and I cannot imagine why my father should be so angry, particularly on such a subject, and about things and persons that do not deserve even a thought. Philip, look whether the train is moving on."

The baron was silent, overcome by the lofty serenity of his daughter. Gilbert's heart sunk in his breast, crushed and withered under her contempt. For a moment a feeling akin to hatred darted through his heart. He would have preferred the mortal thrust of Philip's sword—aye, even a lash of his whip, to her insulting scorn.

He was almost fainting; fortunately, the address was now ended, and the cortége once more moved on. The baron's carriage advanced with the rest, and Andrée disappeared from before his eyes like a vision. Gilbert remained alone—he could have wept—he could have groaned aloud—he thought that he could no longer bear the weight of his suffering.

Just then a hand rested on his shoulder. He turned and saw Philip, who, having given his horse to a soldier of his regiment to hold, returned smiling toward him.

"Come, let me hear what has happened, my poor Gilbert," said he, "and why you have come to Paris."

His frank and cordial tone touched the young man's heart.

"Oh, sir," replied he, with a sigh, his stern stoicism melting at once, "what would I have done at Taverney, I ask you? I must have died of despair, ignorance, and hunger."

Philip started; his generous heart was struck, as Andrée's had been, by the misery and destitution in which Gilbert had been left.

"And you think, my poor fellow, to succeed in Paris without money, protectors, or resources?"

"I trust so, sir. A man who is willing to work rarely dies of hunger where there are other men who wish to do nothing."

Philip was struck by this reply; until then he had always looked on Gilbert as a commonplace domestic.

"But have you any means of buying food?" he said.

"I can earn my daily bread, Monsieur Philip. That is sufficient for one who has never had any cause for self-reproach, but that of having eaten bread not gained by his toil."

"I hope you do not say so with reference to that which you received at Taverney, my poor lad. Your father and mother were faithful servants, and you were always willing to make yourself useful."

"I only did my duty, sir."

"Listen to me, Gilbert. You are aware that I always liked you. I have always looked upon you in a more favorable light than others, whether justly or the reverse, the future will show. What others called haughty pride, I termed delicacy; where others saw rudeness and ill-breeding, I perceived only honest bluntness."

"Ah, chevalier!" said Gilbert, breathing more freely.

"I really wish you well, Gilbert."

"Thank you, sir."

"Young like you, and like you also in an unhappy position, I was perhaps on that account more disposed to feel for and pity you. Fortune has blessed me with abundance; let me assist you until fortune smiles on you in your turn."

"Thanks, sir, many thanks."

"What do you think of doing? You are too proud to accept of a situation as servant." _

Gilbert shook his head with a scornful smile, "I wish to study," said he.

"But, in order to study, you must have masters, and to pay them you must have money."

"I can earn money, sir."

"Earn money? How much can you earn?"

"Twenty-five sous a day, and in a short time perhaps thirty and even forty sous."

"But that is barely enough for food."

Gilbert smiled.

"Perhaps," continued Philip, "I am not taking the right way of offering you my services."

"Your services to me, Monsieur Philip?"

"Yes, my services. Are you ashamed to accept them?"

"Gilbert made no answer.

"Men are sent on earth to aid one another," continued Maison Rouge. "Are we not all brethren?"

Gilbert raised his head and fixed his intelligent gaze on the chevalier's noble countenance.

"Does this language surprise you?" said he.

"No, sir," said Gilbert; "it is the language of philosophy; but it is not usual to hear such from persons of your rank."

"Yet it is the language of the times. The dauphin himself shares in these sentiments. Come, do not be proud with me," continued Philip. "What I lend you, you can repay me one day or other. Who knows but you may yet be a Colbert or a Vauban?"

"Or a Tronchin," said Gilbert.

"Yes, or a Tronchin. Here is my purse, let me share its contents with you."

"Thank you, sir," said the indomitable Gilbert, moved, in spite of himself, by Philip's genial kindness, "but I do not want anything—only—only—believe me, I am as grateful to you as if I had accepted your offer."

And, bowing, he disappeared in the crowd, leaving the

young captain lost in astonishment. The latter waited a few minutes, as if he could not believe his eyes or ears, but finding that Gilbert did not return, he mounted his horse and returned to his post.

———

CHAPTER L.

THE DEMONIAC.

THE noise of the carriages, the prolonged and merry peals of the bells, the joyful beating of the drums, all the pomp and ceremony of the day—a faint reflection of that world now lost to her forever—faded from the Princess Louise's mind like an idle wave which had rolled up to the walls of her cell and then retreated.

When the king had departed, after having once more endeavored, but in vain, to win his daughter back to the world by a mixture of paternal entreaty and royal command, and when the dauphiness, who had been at the first glance struck by the real greatness of soul displayed by her august aunt, had also disappeared with her gay throng of courtiers, the superior of the Carmelites gave orders that the hangings should be taken down, the flowers removed, and the lace with which the convent had been decorated once more placed in its usual repository.

Of all the sisterhood of the Carmelites she alone was unmoved when the massive gates of the convent, which had for a moment opened to the world, closed heavily again on their solitude.

Then she summoned the sister who acted as treasurer of the convent.

" During these two noisy and bustling days," asked she, " have the poor received their usual alms ? "

" Yes, madame."

" Have the sick been visited ? "

" Yes, madame."

" Did the soldiers receive some refreshments before they departed ? "

"They received the wine and the bread which you ordered, madame."

"Then no one is ill or sick in the convent?"

"No one, madame."

The princess approached the window and softly inhaled the cool and perfumed breeze which was wafted toward her on the humid wings of the evening. The treasurer waited respectfully until her august superior should give her an order or dismiss her. Mme. Louise commenced to pluck the leaves of the roses and jasmine which twined around the windows, and climbed up the walls of the building. Heaven alone knows what were the thoughts of the poor royal recluse at that moment.

Suddenly the door of a detached building in the courtyard, close at hand, was shaken by the violent kick of a horse. Mme. Louise started.

"What nobleman of the court has remained after the rest at St. Denis?" asked she.

"His Eminence the Cardinal de Rohan, madame."

"Are his horses here, too?"

"No, madame; they are at the chapter-house of the abbey, where he is to pass the night."

"What noise was that, then?"

"Madame, it was caused by the foreign woman's horse."

"What woman?" asked Mme. Louise, endeavoring to recollect.

"The Italian who came yesterday to request the protection of your royal highness."

"Ah, true, I remember now. Where is she?"

"In her chamber, or in the church."

"How has she conducted herself since she came?"

"Since yesterday she has refused all nourishment except dry bread, and has spent the entire night praying in the chapel."

"Some great criminal, doubtless?" said the superior, frowning.

"I do not know, madame; she has spoken to no one since she arrived."

"What sort of a woman is she?"

"Extremely handsome, and with an expression at once gentle and haughty."

"This morning, during the ceremony, where was she?"

"In her chamber, close to the window, where I saw her, half hidden by the curtain, watching with anxious eyes every person who entered, as if in each she feared an enemy."

"She is some poor, erring creature of the world in which I once lived and reigned. Admit her."

The nun made a movement to retire.

"Ah! By the bye, what is her name?" asked the princess.

"Lorenza Feliciani."

"I know of no one of that name," said Mme. Louise, reflecting; "no matter, introduce her."

The superior seated herself in the chair of state, which was of carved oak, made in the reign of Henry II., and had been used by the last nine abbesses of the Carmelites. It was a formidable judgment-seat, before which had trembled many a poor novice caught on the slippery path between spiritual and temporal things.

A moment afterward the nun entered, leading in the strange lady, who was covered from head to foot with the long veil we have before mentioned.

The Princess Louise possessed the piercing eye peculiar to her family, and as Lorenza Feliciani appeared before her, she fastened a stern and searching glance on her. But she saw in the young woman's demeanor so much humility, grace and beauty, and in the large eyes, filled with tears, which she turned on her, such an innocent and supplicating expression, that her feeling of harshness gave place immediately to one of compassion and kindness.

"Draw near, madame," said the princess.

The stranger advanced hesitatingly, and was about to kneel, when the princess prevented her.

"Is not your name, madame," said she, "Lorenza Feliciani?"

"Yes, madame."

"And you wish to confide a secret to me?"

"Oh! I burn to do so."

"But why had you not recourse to the tribunal of penance? I have only power to console; a priest cannot only console, but pardon."

"I require only consolation, madame," replied Lorenza; "and besides, it is to a woman alone that I dare relate what I have to tell you."

"Then it is a strange story which you are about to narrate?"

"Yes, strange indeed. But hear me patiently, madame; it is to you alone, I repeat, that I dare confide it, both because you are a woman, and because you are all-powerful to protect me."

"Protect you? Are you pursued, then? Are you in danger?"

"Oh, yes, madame, yes!" cried the stranger, with wild alarm.

"But reflect, madame," said the princess, "that this is a convent, and not a fortress, that those worldly thoughts which agitate the breasts of men, penetrate not here; that strife and combat are here extinguished; that this is not a house of justice, of force, or repression, but simply the house of God."

"Oh! that is what I seek!" said Lorenza. "Yes, I seek the house of God, for there alone can I find shelter and repose."

"But God admits not of revenge. How then do you ask his servant to avenge you? Address yourself to the magistrates."

"They can do nothing against him whom I dread."

"Who is he, then?" asked the abbess, with a mysterious and involuntary dread.

Lorenza approached close to the princess in a nervous and excited manner.

"Who is he, madame?" said she.

"He is, I firmly believe, one of those demons who war against man, and whom Satan, their prince, has gifted with superhuman power."

"How? what mean you!" exclaimed the princess, recoiling as if to satisfy herself that she was not addressing a lunatic.

"And I—I—wretch that I am!" continued Lorenza, writhing her snow-white and rounded arms, which seemed modeled from those of some antique statue, "I crossed the path of that man—and now—I am—I am——"

"What? What?"

Lorenza again approached the princess, and, as if terrified herself at what she was about to utter, she whispered, hoarsely, "I am possessed by the demon!"

"Possessed?" cried the princess. "Take care, madame! Are you sure you are in your senses? Are you not——"

"Mad—you would say—no, no, I am not mad—but I may become so if you abandon me."

"But, madame," said the princess, recovering her firmness, "permit me to observe that you seem to me in all respects one of the favored of Heaven; you are rich and beautiful, you express yourself rationally, and I see in your countenance nothing betokening that terrible and mysterious disease called possession."

"Madame, it is in my life, it is in the adventures which have befallen me, that the baleful secret lies which I would willingly conceal even from myself."

"Explain yourself calmly. Am I the first to whom you have disclosed your sufferings?—your parents, your friends——"

"My parents!" exclaimed the young woman, clasping her hands with agony, "my poor parents! Shall I never see you again? Friends?" added she, bitterly, "alas! madame, have I any friends?"

"Come, let us proceed regularly, my poor child," said Mme. Louise, endeavoring to restore order to the stranger's incoherent words; "tell me all. Who are your parents? How came you to abandon them?"

"Madame, I am a native of Rome, and I lived in Rome, with them. My father belongs to the ancient nobility, but, like all our patricians, he is poor. I have also a mother, and a brother older than myself. In France, I believe, when a family such as mine has a son and daughter, the portion of the daughter is sacrificed to purchase the son's sword ; with us the daughter is sacrificed to put the son forward in the church. Consequently I received no education, as all our patrimony was required to pay for my brother's education, that, as my poor brother innocently said, he might one day be a cardinal ; and for this purpose my parents submitted to every privation, and decided on making me take the veil in the Carmelite Convent at Subiaco."

"And you—what did you say ?"

"Nothing, madame. From childhood I had been taught to look forward to such an event as inevitable. Besides, I was not consulted ; my parents commanded—I had only to obey."

"But yet——"

"Oh ! madame, we Roman girls are helpless instruments in the hands of others. Almost all my young friends, who had brothers, had paid this debt for the advancement of their families. I had therefore no reason to complain ; all that was done was in the ordinary course of things. My mother merely caressed me a little more than usual as the time for my leaving her approached. At last the day for the commencement of my novitiate arrived ; my father prepared his five hundred crowns, my dowry for the convent, and we set out for Subiaco. It is only about nine leagues from Rome to Subiaco, but the roads are bad, and our journey was slow and fatiguing. Nevertheless, it pleased me. I welcomed it as a last enjoyment, and whispered adieu to the trees, the shrubs, the rocks, and even to the withered grass which lined the road. How could I tell if at the convent I should see trees, rocks, or shrubs ? Suddenly, in the midst of my fancies, as we wound along between a wood and a mass of overhanging rock, the carriage stopped. My mother shrieked—my father seized his pistols. My thoughts descended suddenly to earth, for those who had stopped us were bandits."

"My poor child !" said the princess, becoming more and more interested in the narrative.

"Well—shall I confess it, madame? I was not much terrified, for these men had stopped us to take our money, and this money was the sum destined for my dowry to the convent. Consequently, if there was no dowry, my entrance into the convent would be delayed until my father could collect five hundred crowns more, and I knew well the time and trouble it had taken to amass these. But when the robbers, after having shared their booty, instead of permitting us to continue our journey, turned and seized me, regardless of the tears of my mother and the efforts of my father to defend me, I was struck with a sort of nameless terror, and shrieked aloud. They bound my hands in spite of my struggles, and held me there while they threw the dice to ascertain to whom I should belong. I had abandoned all hope; my mother had fainted away, and my father lay writhing on the earth. At this moment a man mounted on horseback appeared among the robbers. He had spoken in a low voice to one of the sentinels on passing him, and the man had allowed him to proceed, exchanging a sign with him as he did so. He was of the middle height, of commanding features, and with a fixed and resolute glance; he continued to advance calmly at the usual pace of his steed, and when he had arrived opposite me he stopped. The bandit who was holding me bound, turned suddenly at the first blast which the stranger gave on a little whistle fixed to the end of his whip, and allowed me to slip from his hands. 'Come hither,' said the unknown; and, as the man appeared to hesitate, he leaned forward, and whispering in his ear the single word 'Mac,' 'Benac,' replied the bandit; and then, like a lion subdued and crouching under the lash, he proceeded to untie my hands, as well as those of my father and mother. Then, as the money had been already divided, each man of the troop came forward in his turn to lay his share on a stone. Not a crown of the entire sum was wanting. 'Now, go!' said he to the banditti, and instantly every man disappeared among the surrounding woods.

" 'Lorenza Feliciana,' said the stranger then, addressing

me, and fixing on me a look which had more than human power in it, 'proceed on your way, you are free!' My father and mother thanked this stranger, who knew me, but whom we did not know, and entered the carriage again. I accompanied them with a sort of regret; for some strange, irresistible power seemed to attract me to the man who had thus saved me. He remained immovable in the same spot, as if to protect our retreat, and as long as I could distinguish his form my eyes were fixed on him, and it was only when he was lost to view that the oppressive feeling which weighed upon my bosom was removed."

"But who was this extraordinary man?" asked the princess, interested by the simplicity of the narrative.

"Deign to hear me further, madame," said Lorenza. "Alas! all is not yet told."

"I listen," said Mme. Louise.

The young woman proceeded:

"Two hours afterward we reached Subiaco. During the rest of the journey we never ceased conversing about this mysterious protector, who had come so suddenly, like an angelic messenger, to our assistance, and whose power seemed so inexplicable and unbounded. My father, less credulous than I, thought that he must be the captain of one of the numerous troops of robbers which infest the neighborhood of Rome; but in this I could not agree, although I dared not openly oppose my opinion to my father's, which was the result of years and experience. My instinctive feeling of gratitude toward this man who had so wonderfully saved me, revolted against the idea that he was a bandit; and every evening, in my devotions, I offered up a prayer to the Virgin for my unknown protector.

"The same day I entered the convent. I felt sadder, but also more resigned. An Italian, and consequently superstitious, I believed that God, by delivering me from the bandits, had wished to preserve me pure and unsullied for His service. I therefore gave myself up with ardor to the fulfilment of every duty of religion; and my father, learning this, drew up a petition to the sovereign pontiff to entreat him to shorten the period of my novitiate. I signed this document, which was expressed in terms so warm and earnest, that his holiness, seeing in it only the aspirations of a soul disgusted with the world, granted me a dispensation which fixed the term of my noviciate at a month instead of a year.

"This news, when announced to me, inspired me with neither joy nor grief. I was like one already dead to the world. For fifteen days I was kept closely confined, lest any worldly desires might arise in my breast. At the end of that time I was allowed to descend with the other sisters to the chapel. I entered and took my place behind the curtain which separated, or affected to separate, the nuns from the congregation. Looking through one of the openings, which seemed to me, as it were, a loophole from which I could obtain a last glance at the world I was leaving, I saw a man standing up alone in the middle of the kneeling crowd. He seemed to devour me with his eyes, and I felt again that strange sensation of uneasiness which I had before experienced, and which seemed to draw me, as it were, away from myself, as I had seen my brother draw a needle after a loadstone, even through a leaf of paper or a piece of wood.

"Overcome, subdued, without force to struggle against my feelings, I leaned forward, and with clasped hands I murmured, 'Thanks, thanks!' The nuns looked at me with surprise. They could not comprehend my words or gestures, and, following my glance, they rose on their seats, and gazed down the body of the church. I also gazed, trembling. The stranger had disappeared. They questioned me, but I only turned pale and red by turns, and stammered out some incoherent words. From that moment, madame," cried Lorenza, in a despairing voice, "the demon possessed me!"

"Nevertheless," replied the princess, smiling, "I see nothing supernatural in all that you have related. Calm yourself, my sister, and proceed."

"Ah, madame! it is because you cannot understand what I felt. Heart, soul, mind—the demon possessed all!"

" My sister, I fear greatly that this demon was only love,"
said Mme. Louise.

" Oh, love could not have me suffer thus ! Love would
not have so oppressed my heart—it would not have shaken
my frame as the storm shakes a slender reed ! Love would
not have whispered in my ear the sinful thought which
haunted me at that moment."

" What thought, my child ?"

" Ought not I to have disclosed all to my confessor,
madame ?"

" Doubtless."

" Well, the demon that possessed me whispered me, on
the contrary, to keep it secret. I feared what he would
think of me."

" An evil thought, indeed ; but it is often a very innocent
demon which puts such thoughts in the heart of a woman.
Proceed."

" On the following day I was summoned to the parlor.
I found there one of my neighbors of the Via Frattina at
Rome, a young married lady, who regretted very much the
loss of my society, because every evening we used to meet to
talk and sing together. Behind her, close to the door,
stood a man wrapped in a cloak, who seemed her servant.
He did not turn toward me, but I turned toward him ; he
did not speak, yet I knew him. He was my unknown protector. The same thrilling sensation I had already experienced shot through my frame. I felt my whole being
subdued by the power of this man. Had it not been for
the bars which held me captive, I should certainly have
followed him. Although enveloped closely in his mantle,
rays of light seemed to shoot from him which dazzled me ;
profound as was his silence, it had sounds which spoke to
me a harmonious language. I made a violent effort to
subdue my feelings, and asked my friend who the man was
who accompanied her. She did not know him. Her husband, who had purposed accompanying her, had been prevented by some engagement, and had brought this friend
of his. a stranger to her, to be her companion.

" My friend was religious, and seeing in a corner of

the parlor a Madonna who had the reputation of possessing miraculous powers, she would not depart without offering up a prayer before her. While she was engaged in her devotions, the man entered the room, approached close to me, uncovered his face, and fixed his glowing eyes on mine. I waited for him to speak—my bosom heaved as if in expectation of his words, but he contented himself with putting his arms through the bars which separated us, and extended them above my head. Immediately an inexpressible feeling of delight seized on my whole frame. He smiled; I returned his smile, closing my eyes, which seemed weighed down by an overpowering languor as I did so. Then, as if he had merely wished to assure himself of his power over me, he immediately retired. As he disappeared I recovered by degrees the use of my senses; but I was still under the dominion of this strange hallucination when my friend, having finished her prayer, rose, and, embracing me, took her leave. When I was undressing at night I found in my bosom a note containing these words: 'In Rome, the man who loves a nun is punished by death. Will you kill him to whom you owe your life?' From that moment the demon possessed me entirely, for I lied before Heaven, madame, in not confessing that I thought of this man much more than of my salvation."

Lorenza, terrified at what she had disclosed, paused to discover what impression it had produced on the mild and intelligent countenance of the princess.

"Still," replied the princess, firmly, "all this is not possession by the evil one; it is merely the result of an unhappy passion; and I must again repeat that such thoughts cannot be spoken of here, except to express regret for them."

"Regret, madame?" cried Lorenza. "What! you behold me in tears at your feet, beseeching you to rescue me from the power of this fearful man, and yet you doubt my regret? Oh, I feel more than regret—I feel remorse!"

"And yet," said Mme. Louise, "up to this point——"

"Ah, madame, you have not yet heard all. Wait till I have finished, and then, I beseech you, judge me mercifully.

Three days in the week we attended divine service in the chapel. The unknown was always present. I wished to resist him—I pretended that I was ill—I resolved not to go down. Alas, for human weakness! When the hour arrived, I descended with the nuns, as it were, in despite of my own will. If he were not in the church when I entered, I had some moments of calm; but as he drew near, I felt him coming. I could have said, ' Now he is a hundred paces off; now he is at the door; now he is in the church,' and that without even looking in the direction by which he came. Then, when he had reached his accustomed place, although my eyes had been fastened on my prayer-book, while I murmured the words before me, they turned involuntarily and rested on him. I could neither read nor pray; my whole looks—my whole thoughts—my whole being—were engrossed by this man. At first I could not look at him without fear; then I longed to see him; then my thoughts seemed to meet his; and often I saw him as in a dream in the night, and felt him pass beneath my window.

" The state of my mind did not escape the notice of my companions. The abbess was informed of it, and she in turn informed my parents. Three days before I was to pronounce my vows my father, my mother, and my brother—the only relations I had in the world—entered my cell. They came ostensibly to bid me farewell, but I saw plainly that they had some other motive, and when my mother was left alone with me she questioned me closely. And here the power of the Evil One may clearly be seen; for instead of telling all as I ought to have done, I denied everything obstinately.

"On the day when I was to take the veil, a strange struggle took place within me. I both dreaded and wished for the moment which was to give me up entirely to the service of God; and I felt that if the demon meditated a last effort to subdue me to his will, it would be at this solemn moment that he would attempt its execution."

" And had that strange man never written to you since

the first letter which you found in your bosom?" asked
the princess.

"Never, madame."

"And at that time you had never spoken to him?"

"Never, except in thought."

"Nor written to him?"

"Oh, never!"

"Proceed; you were at the day when you are to take
the veil."

"That day, as I have told your highness, I hoped was
to end my tortures, and I was impatient for the ceremony.
'When I belong to God entirely,' I thought, 'He will defend me against the demon who now wrestles with me for
the possession of my soul.' In the meantime the hour
arrived. I descended to the church, pale, restless, but yet
less agitated than usual. My father, my mother, my brother,
my friend from the Via Frattina, who had come before to
see me, and many other of our friends, were there. The
inhabitants of the neighboring villages also thronged the
church, for the report had been spread that I was lovely,
and a lovely victim, they say, is most acceptable to the
Lord.

"The service began. I would have hastened it by my
prayers; for he was not present, and in his absence I felt
that I was mistress of myself. Already the priest had
raised the crucifix before me, and I was just about to extend
my arm toward it, when the trembling which invariably
announced the approach of my persecutor seized me.
Forced by an irresistible attraction, I turned round and
saw him standing near the pulpit, gazing at me more
fixedly than he had ever yet done. In vain I endeavored
to keep my eyes on the priest—service, ceremony, prayers,
faded from my sight. I believe I was questioned concerning
the rite; I remember I was pulled by the arm to arouse me
but I tottered like some inanimate object trembling on its
base. I was shown the scissors, from which a ray of sun-
light was reflected back with dazzling brightness, but
I did not even wink. Then I felt the cold steel on my
neck, and heard its sharp point in my hair.

"From that moment it seemed to me as if all strength left me ; my soul rushed from my body to meet his, and I fell motionless on the pavement ; yet, strange to say, not like one who had fainted, but like one overcome by sleep. I heard a loud murmur, and almost immediately after became insensible. The ceremony was interrupted with a frightful tumult."

The princess clasped her hands with a gesture of compassion.

"Ah, madame, was not that terrible ?" said Lorenza ; "and is it not easy to see in such an event the intervention of the enemy of man ?"

"Take care, my poor girl," said the princess, in a tone of tenderness and pity ; "I think you are too much disposed to attribute to miraculous power that which is simply the result of human weakness. On seeing that man you fainted, that is all. Proceed."

"Oh, madame, do not say so, or, at least, wait till you have heard all before you judge. Had I fainted, should I not have come to myself in ten minutes, or a quarter of an hour, or an hour at most ? Should I not have been surrounded by my sister nuns, and have resumed courage and faith on seeing them ?"

"Doubtless," said Mme. Louise. "Well, was it not so ?"

"Madame," said Lorenza, in a low, hurried whisper, "when I was restored to consciousness it was night. I felt a rapid, jolting motion, which fatigued me, and I raised my head, thinking that I was under the vaulted roof of the chapel, or within the curtains of my cell. I saw rocks, trees, clouds ; then I felt a warm breath fanning my cheeks. I thought that it was the sick-nurse who was endeavoring to restore me, and I made an effort to thank her. Madame, my head was resting on the bosom of a man—that man my persecutor. I felt myself to ascertain whether I was really alive, or if I was awake. I could not restrain a cry of terror. I was dressed in white, and wore on my head a crown of white roses like a bride, or like a maiden dressed for the tomb."

The princess uttered an exclamation of astonishment. Lorenza hid her face in her hands.

"The next day," continued Lorenza, sobbing, "I made inquiries, and ascertained that it was Wednesday. For three days, therefore, I had remained insensible. I am ignorant of all that happened during that time."

CHAPTER LI.

THE COUNT DE FENIX.

A LONG and painful silence succeeded to this narrative, during which each of the two ladies seemed absorbed in her reflections. The princess was the first to break it.

"And you lent no assistance to this man to carry you off?" said she.

"None, madame."

"You are ignorant how you left the convent?"

"I am quite ignorant."

"Yet a convent is kept carefully guarded; there are bars to the windows; the walls are very high; there is a portress who keeps the keys of the gates always at her side. That is especially the case in Italy, where the rules are even more severe than in France."

"Madame, I can only reply, that from the moment of my awaking from my trance until now, I have searched my memory to discover any trace of what must have occurred; but in vain."

"But did you not reproach him for what he had done?"

"Oh, yes, madame!"

"What was his excuse?"

"That he loved me."

"And what did you reply to that?"

"That I had a horror of him."

"Then you did not love him?"

"Oh, no, no!"

"Are you quite certain?"

"Alas, madame, what I felt for that man was singular indeed! When he was present I was no longer myself; what he willed, I willed; what he commanded, I did; my soul had no power, my mind no will; a look from him subdued and fascinated me. Sometimes he seemed to inspire me with thoughts which were not mine; sometimes he seemed to draw from me ideas so deeply hidden that I had never even guessed that I possessed them. Oh! do you not see, madame, that there was a magic in all this?"

"It is certainly strange, if not supernatural," said the princess. "But after you had been carried off, how did you live with that man?"

"He displayed the warmest affection for me, the sincerest attachment."

"He was a vicious man, no doubt?"

"I do not think he was, madame; there was, on the contrary, something lofty and inspired in his manner of speaking."

"Come, come! you loved him; confess it!"

"No, no, madame," said the young woman, with mournful bitterness; "no, I did not love him."

"Then you ought to have left him—you ought to have appealed to the public authorities, and demanded to be restored to your parents."

"Madame, he watched me so closely that I could not fly."

"But why not write, then?"

"Wherever we stopped on the road the house seemed to belong to him alone, and every one obeyed him. Several times I asked for pen, ink, and paper, but those to whom I applied were doubtless desired by him not to obey me; for they never even answered me."

"And how did you travel?"

"At first in a post-chaise; but at Milan, instead of a carriage, we entered a kind of moving house, in which we continued our journey."

"But he must have sometimes left you alone?"

"Yes; but at these times, before leaving me, he

approached me and said, ' Sleep !' I slept and did not awake until his return."

The princess shook her head incredulously.

" You would have been able to escape," said she, "had you endeavored to do so with energy."

" Alas ! madame, and yet it seemed to me as if I did ; but perhaps I was fascinated."

" Yes, fascinated by words of love, and by his caresses."

" He seldom spoke of love, madame, and except a kiss imprinted on my forehead in the morning and one in the evening, he bestowed no caresses on me."

" Strange, strange, indeed !" murmured the princess ; then, as if some suspicion had crossed her mind, she said aloud : " And you are ready to assert again that you do not love him ? "

" I do assert it again, madame."

" And no earthly bond unites you to him ? "

" None, madame."

" Then should he claim you he would have no right over you ? "

" None, madame, none."

" But," added the princess, after a moment's reflection, " how did you escape at last ? I do not understand that."

" Madame, I took advantage of a violent storm which occurred while we were near a town called Nancy, I think. He left the part of the carriage in which I was, to go into another compartment of it, to talk to an old man who was with us. Then I leaped on his horse and fled."

" And why did you prefer remaining in France to re-turning to Italy ?"

" I reflected that I could not return to Rome, since my parents and friends there would certainly imagine I had been the accomplice of that man, and perhaps refuse to receive me. I resolved, therefore, to come to Paris, and to endeavor to remain concealed ; or to try and reach some great city, where no eye—and, above all, his—could dis-cover me. When I reached Paris, madame, every one was speaking of your retirement into the convent of the Carmelites. They lauded your piety, your charity, toward the wretched, your pity for the afflicted. A ray of hope darted through my soul, and I was struck with the conviction that you would be generous enough to receive me, and powerful enough to protect me."

" You appeal always to my power, my poor child. Is he, then, so powerful ?"

" Oh, yes, madame."

" But who is he, then ?   Through delicacy I have until now refrained from asking his name ; but if I am to defend you, I must know against whom."

" Oh, madame, even on that point I cannot enlighten you.   I know neither who he is nor what he is.   All that I know is, that a king could not inspire more respect, a deity could not receive greater adoration than he, from those to whom he deigns to reveal himself."

" But how do they address him ?   What is his name ?"

" I have heard him addressed by different names ; at present, however, I remember only two of them.   One is given him by the old man, who, as I told you, traveled with us from Milan ; the other he gives himself."

" What does the old man call him ?"

" Acharat.   Is not that a heathenish name, madame ?"

" And what is his other name ?"

" Joseph Balsamo."

" And what can you tell me of him ?"

" That he seems to know all persons, to penetrate into all things ; he is contemporary with all times, has lived in all ages.   He speaks—may Heaven pardon such blasphemies—he speaks of Alexander, Cæsar, and Charlemagne, as if he had known them, yet I am sure they have been dead a very long time.   But what is worse, he will talk of Caiphas, Pilate, and our blessed Saviour, as if he had been present at the crucifixion."

" He is some charlatan, I perceive," said the princess.

" I do not know exactly what that means, madame ; but what I do know is, that he is a dangerous, terrible man. All yield to him, all bend before him, all fall prostrate at his word.   You think him defenseless, he is armed ; you think him alone, and he causes men to rise out of the earth, and that without an effort ; by a gesture, a word, a smile."

" It is well," said the princess. " Whoever he be, take courage, my child, you shall be protected from him."

" By you, madame, by you ? "

" Yes, by me ; so long as you yourself do not abandon my protection. But cease from this time to believe, and above all cease to endeavor to make me believe, in the superstitious visions which are the offspring of your diseased imagination. The walls of St. Denis will guard you securely against infernal powers, and against powers even more to be feared, these of wicked men. And now, madame, what are your intentions ? "

" With these jewels, which belong to me, madame, I wish to pay my dowry to some convent—to this convent, if possible."

And Lorenza laid on a table precious bracelets, valuable rings, a magnificent diamond, and other jewels, the whole worth about twenty thousand crowns.

" Are those ornaments your own ? " asked the princess.

" Yes, madame.   He gave them to me, and I devote them to the church. I have only one wish with regard to his property."

" What is that ? "

" That his Arabian horse, Djerid, the instrument of my deliverance, be restored to him if he demand it."

" But with regard to yourself, you will on no account return to him ? "

" No ! by no means."

" Is it your intention to enter this convent and continue in the practise of those duties which were interrupted at Subiaco by the extraordinary circumstances you have related to me ? "

" It is my dearest wish, madame ; at your feet I supplicate its fulfilment."

" Be tranquil, my child ; from this day you shall live with us ; and when, by the exemplary conduct which I expect from you, you have shown that you deserve that favor, you shall take the vows, and I answer for it, no one shall carry you away from St. Denis while your abbess watches over you."

Lorenza threw herself at the feet of her benefactress, and poured forth expressions of gratitude the most tender and the most sincere; but all at once, rising on one knee, she listened, turned pale, and trembled.

"Oh, heavens! Oh, heavens!" she exclaimed.

"What is the matter?" asked Mme. Louise.

"My whole frame trembles. He is coming! He is coming!"

"Who is coming?"

"He who has sworn to destroy my soul."

"That man?"

"Yes, that man—do you not see how my hand trembles. Oh!" continued she, in a tone of anguish, "he approaches —he is near!"

"You are mistaken."

"No, madame, no! Hold me! He draws me to him against my will. Hold me! Hold me!"

Mme. Louise seized her by the arm.

"Courage! courage! my poor child," said she; "were it even he you are in safety here."

"He approaches! He approaches!" cried Lorenza, with despair and horror in her voice, her eyes fixed, and her arms extended toward the door of the room.

"This is madness. Dare any one, think you, enter unannounced the apartment of Madame Louise of France? To obtain admittance, he must be the bearer of an order from the king."

"Oh, madame, I know not how he procured an entrance," cried Lorenza, recoiling with terror, "but I do know that he is ascending the stairs—that he is scarcely ten paces distant—that he is here!"

At that moment the door opened. Alarmed at such a strange coincidence, the princess could not prevent herself from starting back. A nun appeared.

"Who is there?" asked the abbess, hurriedly, "and what do you want?"

" Madame, a gentleman has just arrived, who wishes to speak to your royal highness."

" His name ? "

" The Count de Fenix."

" Is that he ? " asked the princess, turning to Lorenza, " and do you know that name ? "

" I do not know that name, but it is he, madame—it is he ! "

" What does this gentleman want ? " inquired the princess, addressing the nun.

" Having been sent on a mission to the King of France by his majesty the King of Prussia, he wishes, he says, to have the honor of a moment's conversation with your royal highness."

There princess reflected for a moment ; then, turning to Lorenza, " Retire into that cabinet," said she—Lorenza obeyed—" and you, sister," continued the princess, " admit this gentleman." The nun courtesied low and left the room.

Having ascertained that the door of the cabinet was securely fastened, the princess seated herself in her armchair, and awaited the termination of the strange scene in which she found herself involved. Yet she could not subdue a certain degree of agitation.

Almost immediately the nun reappeared, followed by the person whom we have already seen, on the day of the presentation, announce himself as the Count de Fenix.

He was dressed in the same costume, a Prussian uniform, with the military wig and black stock. His large, expressive eyes were cast down at first in the presence of the royal abbess, but only in a manner to indicate the respect which any gentleman, how high soever his rank, was called on to exhibit before a princess of France, but immediately raising them again, with a look which almost implied that he had already shown too great humility.

" Madame," said he, " I thank your royal highness for the favor you have shown me ; but I did not doubt that I should obtain this favor, knowing that your royal highness is the generous patron of all the unhappy."

" Sir, I endeavor to assist all such ! " replied the princess with dignity; for she felt certain that he should, before the lapse of many minutes, put to shame this man who so impudently dared to claim her protection, after having deceived and ill-treated one confided to his care.

The count bowed, without betraying any consciousness of understanding the double meaning of her words.

She then continued, with something of irony in her tone: "In what way can I render you any assistance, sir?"

"You can aid me in a matter of the greatest moment, madame,"

"Speak, sir!"

"None but weighty considerations could have induced me, madame, to intrude on your royal highness in this retreat which you have chosen; but you have, I believe, given shelter here to a person in whom I am deeply interested."

"The name of that person, sir?"

"Lorenza Feliciani."

"And how does her fate concern you? Is she your relation, your sister?"

"She is my wife."

"Your wife?" said the princess, raising her voice so that she might be heard in the cabinet. "Lorenza Feliciani is the Countess de Fenix?"

"Yes, madame, Lorenza Feliciani is the Countess de Fenix," replied the count, with the utmost coolness.

"I have no Countess de Fenix in this convent, sir," replied the princess.

But the count was not to be so repulsed. "Perhaps, madame," said he, "your royal highness is not convinced that Lorenza Feliciani and the Countess de Fenix are one and the same person?"

"I confess, sir, that you have guessed my thoughts; I am not well convinced on that point."

"If your royal highness will but command Lorenza Feliciani to be brought hither, you will soon have all doubts on that head cleared away. I entreat your highness's pardon for urging the matter thus, but I am tenderly attached to the young lady, and she herself, I think, regrets being separated from me."

"Do you think so, sir?"

"Yes, madame, unworthy as I am, I think so."

"Ah!" thought the princess, "Lorenza was right; this is indeed a most dangerous man."

The count preserved the most perfect calmness of demeanor, and adhered to the most courtly politeness.

"I must temporize," thought the princess to herself. "Sir," said she, "I cannot give you up to a woman who is not here. If you love, as you say you do, the person whom you seek, I can easily understand why you thus persist in endeavoring to find her; but, believe me, to be successful, you must seek elsewhere."

The count, on entering the room, had cast a rapid glance on every article in it, and his eyes had rested for a single instant only, but that had been sufficient, on a table in a dark corner, on which Lorenza had placed those jewels which she had offered to pay as her dowry to the convent. He knew them again instantly.

"If your royal highness would have the goodness to recollect, and I venture to entreat you to do so, you will remember that Lorenza Feliciani was very lately in this room, that she placed on that table those jewels, and that, after having had the honor of conversing with your royal highness, she withdrew."

Just then he caught the eyes of the princess turning unconsciously toward the cabinet. "She withdrew," he continued, "into that cabinet, so that now I only wait for the permission of your royal highness to order her to return hither, which she will do immediately, I feel certain."

The princess colored with shame at the thought that she had lowered herself so far as to attempt to deceive this man, from whom, as it seemed, nothing could be hidden; and she could not conceal her vexation at the uselessness of all her efforts. She recollected, however, that Lorenza had fastened the door from within, and that, consequently, nothing but the impulse of her own free will could induce her to leave the cabinet.

"But even suppose she were here," said she; "what would she do?"

"Nothing, madame; she would merely tell your highness that she wishes to go with me, being my wife."

This last word reassured the princess, for she recollected the protestations of Lorenza.

"Your wife?" exclaimed she, with indignation. "Are you sure of that?"

"Your highness does not seem to believe me. Nevertheless, it is not quite incredible that the Count de Fenix should have married Lorenza Feliciani, and that, having married her, he demands back his wife."

"His wife!" she repeated, impatiently; "you dare to say Lorenza Feliciani is your wife?"

"Yes, madame, I dare to say so," answered the count, with the most natural air in the world, "because it is true."

"You are married to her?"

"I am."

"Legitimately?"

"Certainly; and if your royal highness thus persists in doubting my word, I shall place before your eyes the register of my marriage, signed by the priest who united us."

The princess started; so much coolness and self-possession shook all her convictions.

The count opened his pocket-book and unfolded a paper. "This is the register of my marriage, madame, and the proof that I have a right to claim that woman as my wife. If your royal highness will read it and note the signature——"

"The signature!" repeated the princess, in a tone of doubt more insulting to the stranger than her indignation had been; "but if this signature——"

"This signature is that of the Vicar of St. Jean de Strasbourg, who is well known to Prince Louis, Cardinal de Rohan, and if his highness were here——"

"His highness is here!" cried the princess, fixing her flashing eyes on the count. "He has not yet left St. Denis, and is now with the canons of the cathedral; so that nothing is easier for us than to ascertain the truth of what you assert."

"That is indeed a fortunate circumstance for me," replied the count, coolly putting up the paper again in his pocket-book. "When your royal highness has heard the cardinal's testimony, I trust that your highness's unjust suspicions will be dispelled."

"Sir, this impudent perseverance is most revolting to me," said the princess, ringing the bell violently.

The nun who had introduced the count appeared.

"Let my groom mount his horse instantly and carry this note to His Highness the Cardinal de Rohan; he will be found at the chapter of the cathedral. Let him come hither without a moment's delay—I wait his arrival anxiously."

While giving these directions, the princess wrote hastily a few words on a slip of paper, and, handing it to the nun, she added in a whisper: "Let a couple of archers of the guard be placed in the corridor, and take care that no one leave the convent without my permission."

The count had followed all the movements of the princess, whom he now saw determined to contest the point with him to the very last; but, evidently decided not to yield the victory to her, he drew nearer to the door of the cabinet while she was writing, fixed his eyes on it, pronounced some words in a low voice, and extending his hands toward it, moved them to and fro with a regular and steady motion.

The princess, turning, saw him in this attitude, and exclaimed: "What are you doing there, sir?"

"Madame," said the count, "I am adjuring Lorenza Feliciani to appear, and declare to you of her own free will that I am not an impostor nor a forger. But this is not to prevent your royal highness from requiring the other proofs you have mentioned."

"Sir!"

"Lorenza Feliciani!" cried the count, overpowering all opposition, even that of the princess, "leave that cabinet and come hither—come!"

But the door remained closed.

"Come forth! It is my will!" repeated the count.

Then the key was heard turning in the lock, and the princess, with inexpressible alarm, saw the young girl enter, her eyes fixed on the count without any expression either of anger or hatred.

"What are you doing, my child?" cried the princess. "Why do you return to the man from whom you fled? You were in safety here—I told you so."

"She is also in safety in my house, madame," answered the count. "Are you not, Lorenza? Are you not safe with me?"

"Yes," replied the young girl.

The princess, overcome with astonishment, clasped her hands and sunk back in her chair.

"And now, Lorenza," added the count, quietly, but yet with a tone of command, "I am accused of having made you act contrary to your wishes. Say, have I ever done so?"

"Never," answered the young girl, clearly and distinctly, yet without accompanying the denial by any movement.

"In that case," cried the princess, "what do you mean by all that tale of your having been carried off?"

Lorenza remained silent, and looked at the count as if life and speech hung on his lips.

"Her highness wishes doubtless to know how you left the convent, Lorenza. Relate to her all that happened, from the moment of your fainting until you awoke in the post-chaise."

Lorenza was still silent.

"Relate all that occurred from first to last—do not omit anything," continued the count; "it is my will that you should do so."

"I do not remember," she replied.

"Search your memory, and you will recollect all."

"Ah, yes, yes!" said Lorenza, in the same monotonous tone, "now I remember."

"Speak, then."

"When I fainted, at the very moment that the scissors touched my hair, I was carried back to my cell and laid on my bed. My mother remained with me until night, when, seeing that I continued in the same state of insensibility, they sent for the village surgeon. He felt my pulse, passed a looking-glass before my lips, and, discovering no sign of life in me, pronounced me dead."

" But how do you know all that?" asked the princess.

" Her highness wishes to know how you know that," repeated the count.

" Strange!" replied Lorenza, " I was able to see and hear; but I could not open my eyes, nor speak, nor move. I was in a sort of lethargy."

" In fact," said the princess, " Tronchin has sometimes spoken to me of persons who had fallen into a lethargy, and who, being to all appearance dead, were interred alive."

" Proceed, Lorenza."

" My mother was in despair, and would not believe that I was dead : she said that she would pass that night and the following day by my side. She did so ; but the thirty-six hours during which she watched over me passed away without my making the slightest movement, or without a sigh having escaped my lips. Thrice a priest came to visit my mother ; and each time he told her that it was rebelling against the will of God to thus persist in keeping my body on earth when He possessed my soul ; for, as I had died at the moment when I was pronouncing my vows, he did not doubt, he said, but that my soul had winged its flight to heaven. My mother, by her entreaties, prevailed on him to allow her to watch by me another night—that of Monday. On Tuesday morning they found me still insensible.

" My mother withdrew, vanquished, leaving me to the nuns, who by this time were loud in their exclamations against her impiety. The tapers were lighted in the chapel, in which, according to the custom, I was to be laid out during one day and night. As I had not pronounced my vows, the sisters dressed me in a white robe, put a crown of white roses on my head, crossed my arms on my bosom and placed my coffin on a bier.

" During this last operation, a thrill of horror ran

through my veins; for I repeat, although my eyelids were closed, I saw everything as if they had been wide open.

"The bier was carried into the church, and there—my face still uncovered, as is the custom in Italy—I was placed in the middle aisle, with lighted tapers around me, and a vase of holy water at my feet. During the day the peasants of Subiaco entered the church, prayed for me, and sprinkled my body with the holy water. Night came on, and, as the visitors had ceased, the doors of the church were closed except a little side door, and the nun who took care of the sick remained alone beside me.

"One terrible thought never left me during my trance, and now it became more dreadful; on the morrow I was to be buried—buried alive, if some unknown power did not come to my aid! I heard the hours strike one after another; first nine, then ten, then eleven. Each stroke found an echo in my trembling heart; for, oh, horror! I listened to my own death-knell!

"What efforts did I not make to break my icy sleep—to burst the iron bonds which held me down in my coffin! But Heaven at last had pity on me. Midnight struck! At the very first stroke, my frame was shaken by a convulsive shudder, like that which I always experienced when Acharat approached me; then my heart was stirred, and I beheld him appear at the door of the church."

"Were your feelings at that moment those of fear?" asked the Count de Fenix.

"No; they were feelings of happiness, joy, ecstasy! For I knew that he came to snatch me from the dreadful death which seemed before inevitable. He advanced slowly toward my coffin, looked at me for a moment with a melancholy smile, then he said, 'Arise, follow me!' The bonds which fastened me were broken at that powerful voice; I rose, and I put one foot out of the coffin. 'Are you glad to live?' he asked. 'Oh, yes!' I replied. 'Follow me, then,' said he.

"The sister who was appointed to watch the dead, had fulfilled this duty toward so many of the nuns that she had become careless and indifferent, and slept soundly in her chair. I passed close by her without awaking her, as I followed him, who, for the second time, had saved me from death. We reached the outer court, and once more saw the cloudless firmament, studded with stars, and felt the cool night-breeze, which the dead feel not, but which is so grateful to the living.

" 'And now,' said he, ' before leaving the convent, choose for yourself. Do you wish to be a nun or to follow me ?' 'I will follow you,' I replied. We reached the entrance gate ; it was locked. ' Where are the keys ?' he asked. ' In the pocket of the portress, on a chair near her bed,' I replied. ' Enter the lodge,' said he, ' and bring them without making any noise to awake her.' I obeyed, entered the lodge, found the key, and brought it to him.

" Five minutes afterward the gate was opened, and we were in the street. I took his arm, and we hurried toward the outskirts of the village of Subiaco. About a hundred paces from its last house a post-chaise was in waiting ; we entered it, and drove off at a rapid pace."

" And no force was used—no threat was uttered—you followed him voluntarily ? "

Lorenza remained mute.

" Her royal highness asks you, Lorenza, if by any threat, any violence, you were forced to accompany me."

" No."

" And why did you do so ?   Say, why did you accompany me ? "

" Because I loved you," said Lorenza.

The Count de Fenix turned toward the princess with a triumphant smile.

CHAPTER LII.

THE CARDINAL DE ROHAN.

STRONG as was the mind of the Princess Louise, all that she had just heard seemed so extraordinary to her, that she could not help asking herself whether the man who stood before her were not a real magician, disposing of hearts and understandings at his will.

But the Count de Fenix was not yet satisfied.

"That is not all, madame," said he ; "and your royal highness has only heard a part of our history. Some doubts might remain on your mind did you not hear the rest from her own lips."

Then turning toward the young woman :

"Do you remember, dear Lorenza," said he, "the rest of our journey ?—and how we visited Milan, the Lake Maggioro, the Oberland, the Righi, and the magnificent Rhine —the Tiber of the North ?"

"Yes," answered she, still in the same monotonous voice—"yes ; Lorenza saw all that."

"Dragged onward by that man, was it not, my child ? —yielding to an irresistible power which you did not yourself comprehend ?" asked the princess.

"Why should you think so, madame, after what your highness has heard ? But if you wish for yet more palpable and material proofs, here is a letter written by Lorenza to me. I was obliged to leave her alone for a short time at Mayence. Well, she regretted me and longed for my return ; for in my absence she wrote me these lines, which your highness may read."

The count took out of his pocket-book a note, which he handed to the princess. She read as follows :

"Return, Acharat ! When you leave me, all hope and joy depart. Ah, when shall I be yours through all eternity? "LORENZA."

The princess rose, anger flashing in her eyes, and approached Lorenza with the note in her hand. The young woman appeared neither to see nor hear her. Her whole soul seemed to hang on the count's lips.

"I understand," said the count, quickly, before the princess could utter a word ; "your highness doubts whether this note be really written by her or not. That point can easily be settled. Lorenza, speak. Who wrote this note ?"

He took the note, placed it in her hand, and she immediately pressed it to her heart.

"Lorenza wrote it," said she.

"Does Lorenza know what it contains ?"

"Yes."

"Then tell the princess what is in the letter, that she may believe me when I say you love me. Tell her—it is my will."

Lorenza appeared to make an effort; then, without opening the note, or turning her eyes on it, she read its contents.

"This is incredible," said the princess ; "I cannot trust the evidence of my own senses ; there is something inexplicable and supernatural in all this."

"It was this letter," continued the Count de Fenix, as if he had not heard what the princess said, "which determined me to hasten our marriage. I loved Lorenza as much as she loved me. We were in a position which might have given rise to unfounded suspicions. Besides, in the adventurous life which I lead, some accident might happen to me—I might be killed—I might die, and I wished in case of such an event that all my fortune should belong to Lorenza. On arriving at Strasbourg, therefore, we were married."

"You were married ?"

"Yes, madame."

"It is impossible !"

"Why so, madame ?" said the count, smiling. "What is there impossible in the fact that the Count de Fenix should marry Lorenza Feliciani ?"

"But she told me that she is not your wife ?"

The count, without replying, turned to Lorenza : "Do you remember on what day we were married ?" he asked.

"Yes," she replied ; "it was the third of May."

"Where ?"

"At Strasbourg."

"In what church ?"

"In the cathedral ; in the Chapel of St. John."

"Did you offer any opposition to our union ?"

"No ; I was only too happy."

"Because, Lorenza," continued the count, "the princess thinks that the marriage was forced on you—that you hate me."

As he said these words he took Lorenza's hand ; a thrill of rapture seemed to run through her whole frame.

"I hate you!" she exclaimed ; "oh, no! I love you; you are good, you are generous, you are powerful!"

The count turned toward the princess, as if he had said, "You hear."

Seized with a kind of horror, the princess had recoiled from the pair before her, and sunk at the foot of an ivory crucifix which was fastened against the black velvet hangings of the room.

"Does your royal highness wish for any further information?" asked the count, as he released Lorenza's hand.

"Sir," cried the princess, "do not approach me !— nor she either!"

At this moment the noise of wheels was heard in the courtyard, and a carriage stopped at the entrance door.

"Ah!" exclaimed the princess, "here comes the cardinal, and we shall now know the truth."

The Count de Fenix bowed, said a few words to Lorenza in a low voice, and waited with the patience of a man perfectly secure of his position. A moment afterward the door opened, and His Eminence the Cardinal de Rohan was announced.

The princess, reassured by the presence of a third person, resumed her seat, and desired him to be admitted. The cardinal entered ; but scarcely had he made his salutation to the princess, when, perceiving the count, he exclaimed, with surprise, "You here, sir!"

"Do you know this person?" asked the princess, more and more astonished.

"Yes, madame," said the cardinal.

"Then," cried she, "you will tell me what he is."

"Nothing is more easy," replied the cardinal; "the gentleman is a sorcerer."

"A sorcerer?" murmured the princess.

"Pardon me, madame," said the count ; " but I trust

that his highness will explain his words to your satisfaction."

"Has the gentleman been making any predictions to your royal highness, that I see you with a countenance of so much alarm?" asked M. de Rohan.

"The register of the marriage! The register, immediately!" exclaimed the princess.

The cardinal stared with the utmost surprise, not comprehending what this exclamation meant.

"Here it is," said the count, presenting it to the cardinal.

"Sir, what is this?" said he.

"I wish to know," said the princess, "whether the signature to that document be genuine or not."

The cardinal took the paper and read it.

"Yes," said he, "it is a perfectly legal register of a marriage, and the signature is that of Monsieur Remy, Vicar of St. John's, in Strasbourg. But in what way does that concern your royal highness?"

"Oh, it concerns me deeply, sir! So, the signature is correct?"

"Certainly; but I will not guarantee that it may not have been extorted——"

"Extorted?" cried the princess. "Yes, that is possible."

"And the consent of Lorenza, also?" said the count, with a tone of irony which was aimed directly at the princess.

"By what means, cardinal—by what means could this signature have been extorted? Do you know?"

"By means which this gentleman has at his disposal—by means of magic!"

"Magic? Is it you, cardinal, who speaks to me of magic?"

"Yes; I have said that this gentleman is a sorcerer; and I shall not unsay it."

"Your eminence must be jesting."

"By no means; and the proof is, that I am going, in the presence of your highness, to have a very serious explanation with him."

"I was myself going to request it from your highness," said the count.

"Excellent! But pray, do not forget," said the cardinal, haughtily, "that it is I who am the questioner."

"And do not forget, also," said the count, "that I will answer all your questions before her royal highness, if you insist upon it—but I feel certain that you will not insist."

The cardinal smiled contemptuously.

"Sir," said he, "to play the magician well is, in our times, a rather difficult task. I have seen you at work, and, to do you justice, you were very successful; but every one will not show the patience, and, above all, the generosity of her royal highness the dauphiness."

"The dauphiness?" exclaimed the princess.

"Yes, madame," said the count; "I have had the honor of being presented to her royal highness."

"And how did you repay that honor, sir? Come! Speak!"

"Alas! much worse than I could have wished; for I have no personal hatred against men, and, above all, none against women."

"But what did he really do before my august niece?" asked the princess.

"I had the misfortune, madame, to tell her the truth, which she demanded of me."

"Yes," said the cardinal, "a truth which made her swoon!"

"Was it my fault," cried the count, in that commanding tone which he could at times assume, "was it my fault that the truth was so terrible that it produced such effects? Was it I who sought the princess? Did I request to be presented to her? On the contrary, I avoided her; I was brought before her almost by force, and she positively commanded me to reply to her questions."

"But what, then, sir, was that truth which you declare to have been so terrible?" asked the princess.

"The truth which was hidden by the veil of futurity. I raised the veil, and then she beheld that future which

appeared so alarming to your royal highness, that you fled
for shelter from it to a cloister to offer up tears and prayers before the altar——"

"Sir, sir!" cried the princess.

"Is it my fault, if the future, which was revealed to her
as one of the sainted, was shadowed forth to me as a prophet, and if the dauphiness, whom it threatens personally,
terrified at the sight, fainted when I declared it to her?"

"You hear him acknowledge it!" said the cardinal.

"Alas!" sighed the princess.

"For her reign is doomed," continued the count, "as
the most fatal and disastrous to the monarchy of any on
record."

"Oh, sir!" exclaimed the princess.

"For yourself, madame," continued the count, "your
prayers have perhaps obtained favor, for you will not see
those events which I foretell; you will be in the bosom
of the Lord when they come to pass. But pray! Pray
always!"

The princess, overcome by his prophetic words, which
agreed too well with the terrors of her own soul, sunk again
on her knees at the foot of the crucifix, and commenced to
pray fervently.

The count turned to the cardinal, and, preceding him
toward the embrasure of a window, "Now that we are
alone," said he, "what does your eminence wish with
me?"

The cardinal hastened to join him. The princess seemed
wholly absorbed in her prayers, and Lorenza remained silent and motionless in the middle of the room. Her eyes
were wide open, but she seemed to see nothing. The two
men stood apart in the embrasure of the window, half
concealed by the curtains.

"What are your highness's wishes?" repeated the count.

"First, I wish to know who you are," replied the
cardinal.

"Yet you seem to know. Did you not say that I was a
sorcerer?"

"Yes; but when I met you formerly you were called

Joseph Balsamo, and now you are called the Count de Fenix."

"Well, that only proves that I have changed my name, nothing more."

"Very true ; but are you aware that such changes may make Monsieur de Sartines, the minister of police, rather inquisitive about you ?"

The count smiled.

" Oh, sir," said he, " this is a petty warfare for a Rohan ! What ! your eminence quibbles about names ? *Verba et Soces*, as the Latin has it. Is there nothing worse with which I can be reproached ?"

" You seem to have become satirical," said the cardinal.

" I have not become so ; it is my character."

"In that case I shall do myself the pleasure of lowering your tone a little."

" Do so, sir."

"I am certain I shall please the dauphiness by so doing."

" Which may be not altogether useless to you, considering the terms on which you stand at present with her," answered Balsamo, with the greatest coolness.

"And, suppose, most learned dealer in horoscopes, that I should cause you to be arrested ?" said the cardinal.

" I should say that your eminence would commit a very grave mistake in doing so."

"Indeed ?" said the prince cardinal, with withering contempt. " And pray, who will suffer from my mistake ?"

" Yourself, my lord cardinal."

" Then I shall give the order for your arrest this moment, sir, and we shall soon know who this Baron Balsamo Count de Fenix is, this illustrious branch of a genealogical tree not to be discovered in any field of heraldry in Europe !"

" But why has your highness not asked for information respecting me from your friend, the Count de Breteuil ?"

" Monsieur de Breteuil is no friend of mine. "

" That is to say, he is no longer so. Yet he must have

been one of your best friends when you wrote him a certain letter——"

" What letter ? " asked the cardinal, drawing nearer to the count.

" A little closer, Monsieur le Cardinal, I do not wish to speak loud, for fear of compromising you—that letter which you wrote from Vienna to Paris, to endeavor to prevent the marriage of the dauphin."

The prelate could not repress a gesture of alarm.

" I know that letter by heart," continued the count coldly.

" Then Breteuil has turned traitor ? "

" How so ? "

" Because, when the marriage was decided on, I demanded back my letter, and he told me he had burned it ! "

" Ah ! he dared not tell you he had lost it ! "

" Lost it ? "

" Yes, and you know that a lost letter may be found by some one."

" And so my letter——"

" Was found by me. Oh ! by the merest chance, I assure you, one day when crossing the marble court at Versailles."

" And you did not return it to the Count de Breteuil ? "

" I took good care not to do so."

" Why so ? "

" Because, being a sorcerer, I knew that, although I wished to be of all the service I could to your highness, you wished to do me all the harm you could. So, you understand ? A disarmed man who journeys through a wood where he knows he will be attacked, would be a fool not to pick up a loaded pistol which he found at his foot."

The cardinal's head swam, and he was obliged to lean against the window-frame for a few minutes ; but, after an instant's hesitation, during which the count eagerly watched every variation of his countenance :

" So be it," said he. " It shall never be said that a prince of my house gave way before the threats of a charlatan. Though that letter should be shown to the dauphiness herself—though, in a political point of view, it ruin me, I shall maintain my character as a loyal subject and faithful ambassador. I shall say what is the truth, that I thought the alliance hurtful to the interests of my country and my country will defend me, and weep for my fate."

"But if some one should happen to relate how the young, handsome, gallant ambassador, confident in the name of Rohan and the title of prince, and being most graciously received by the Archduchess, Marie Antoinette said so, not because he saw anything in the marriage hurtful to France, but because in his vanity he imagined he saw something more than affability in her manner toward him. What would the loyal subject and the loyal ambassador reply then ?"

"He would deny, sir, that there ever had existed the sentiments that your words imply : there is no proof that it did exist."

"Yes, sir, you mistake. There is the strongest proof, in the coldness of the dauphiness toward you."

The cardinal hesitated.

"My lord," said the count, "trust me, it is better for us to remain good friends than to quarrel—which we should have done before this had I not been more prudent than you."

"Good friends ?"

"Why not? Our friends are those who render us good offices."

"Have I ever asked you for any ?"

"No, and that is where you have been wrong; for during the two days you were in Paris——"

"I in Paris ?

"Yes, you. Why attempt to hide that from me who am a sorcerer ? You left the dauphiness at Soissons, you came post to Paris by Villers, Cotterets, and Dammartin—that is to say, the shortest road—and you hastened to request your kind friends there for assistance, which they all refused. After their refusals you once more set out post for Compiègne in despair."

The cardinal seemed overwhelmed.

"And what sort of assistance might I have expected from you," he asked, "had I addressed myself to you?"

"That assistance which a man who makes gold can grant."

"And what matters it to me that you can make gold?"

"Peste! when your highness has to pay five hundred thousand francs within forty-eight hours! Am I not right? Is not that the sum?"

"Yes; that is indeed the sum."

"And yet you ask what matters it to have a friend who can make gold? It matters just this, that the hundred thousand francs which you cannot procure elsewhere, you may procure from him."

"And where?" asked the cardinal.

"In the Rue St. Claude."

"How shall I know your house?"

"By a griffin's head in bronze, which serves as a knocker to the gate."

"When may I present myself?"

"The day after to-morrow, my lord, and afterward you may come as often and whenever you please. But stay, we have just finished our conversation in time, for the princess, I see, has ended her prayers."

The cardinal was conquered; and, no longer attempting to resist, he approached the princess: "Madame," said he, "I am obliged to confess that the Count de Fenix is perfectly correct; his register of marriage is authentic and valid, and he has explained all the circumstances to my perfect satisfaction."

The count bowed. "Has your royal highness any further commands for me?" he asked.

"I wish to speak once more to the young woman," she replied. Then turning to Lorenza, "Is it of your own free and unconstrained will that you leave this convent, in which you sought refuge?"

"Her highness asks you," said Balsamo, quickly "whether it is of your own free and unfettered choice that you leave this convent. Answer, Lorenza."

" Yes," said the young woman, " it is of my own free and unfettered will."

" And to accompany your husband, the Count de Fenix ? "

" And to accompany me ? " repeated the count.

" Oh, yes ! " exclaimed Lorenza.

" In that case," said the princess, " I wish to detain neither one nor the other ; for it would be doing violence to your feelings. But if there is in all this anything out of the common order of events, may the vengeance of Heaven fall on him, who, for his own advantage or profit, troubles the harmony, the proper course of nature ! Go, Count de Fenix ! Go, Lorenza Feliciani ! only take with you your jewels."

" They are for the use of the poor, madame," said the count, " and, distributed by your hands, the alms will be doubly acceptable to God. I only demand back my horse Djerid."

" You can claim him as you pass, sir. Go ! "

The count bowed low, and gave his arm to Lorenza, who took it, and left the room without uttering a word.

" Ah, my lord cardinal," said the princess, shaking her head sorrowfully, " there are incomprehensible and fatal omens in the very air which we breathe."

CHAPTER LIII.

THE RETURN FROM ST. DENIS.

AFTER leaving Philip, Gilbert, as we have said, had re-entered the crowd. But not now with a heart bounding with joyful anticipation did he throw himself into the noisy billow of human beings ; his soul was wounded to the quick, and Philip's kind reception of him, and all his friendly offers of assistance, had no power to soothe him. Andrée never suspected that she had been cruel to Gilbert. The lovely and serene young girl was entirely ignorant that there could be between her and the son of her nurse any point of contact either for pain or for pleasure. She revolved above all the lower spheres of life, casting light or shadow on them, according as she herself was gay or sad. But now the shadow of her disdain had fallen on Gilbert and frozen him to the soul, while she, following only the impulse of her nature, knew not even that she had been scornful. But Gilbert, like a gladiator disarmed, had offered his naked breast to the full brunt of her haughty looks and disdainful words, and now bleeding at every pore, his philosophy suggested nothing better than the consolation of despair.

From the moment that he once more plunged into the crowd, he cared neither for horses nor men. Collecting all his strength, he dashed forward like a wild boar with the spear in his side, and, at the risk of being crushed or trodden underfoot, he opened a passage for himself through the multitude. When the denser mass of the people had been crossed, he began to breathe more freely, and looking round he discovered that he was alone, and that around him was the green grass, the cool water, and solitude.

Without knowing whither he was going, he had advanced toward the Seine, and he now found himself opposite the Isle of St. Denis. Exhausted, not from fatigue of body but from anguish of mind, he sank on the turf, and grasping his head with both hands, he began to roar hoarsely, as if by these inarticulate sounds alone could he express his rage and grief.

All those vague and senseless hopes which until then had shed a glimmering light on the darkness of his soul, and whose existence he scarcely ventured to confess, even to himself, were now at one blow utterly annihilated. To whatsoever height genius, science or study might raise him in the social scale, he must to Andrée always remain the Gilbert that he had been ; a thing or a man—to use her own words to her father—not worth the slightest regard, not worth even the trouble of being looked down on.

For a moment he had thought, that, seeing him in Paris, learning that he had come on foot, knowing that he had determined to struggle out of obscurity into light, he had thought that Andrée would applaud his resolution ;

but instead of applause, what had he met with as the reward of so much fatigue and of such firm determination ? The same scornful indifference with which he had been treated at Taverney. Even more—was she not almost angry when she heard that his eyes had had the audacity to look on her music-book ? Had he only touched that music-book with the tip of his finger, he would have been doubtless considered only worthy to be burned at the stake.

By weak characters, any deception, any mistake, with regard to those they love, is quickly forgotten, and they bend under the blow only to rise again stronger and more persevering than before. They vent their sufferings in complaints and tears, but their resistance is only passive ; nay, their love often increases by that which should destroy it, and they whisper to themselves that their submissiveness will at last have its reward. Toward that reward they steadfastly advance, whether the road be easy or the reverse ; if it be unfavorable they will be longer in attaining their end, that is all ; but they will attain it at last.

It is not thus with strong minds, obstinate natures, and powerful wills. They are indignant when they see their own blood flowing ; at the sight their energy augments so furiously that they seem to hate rather than to love. Indeed, with them love and hate are so closely allied that they often are not aware of the transition from one to the other. So it was with Gilbert. When he flung himself on the ground, overcome by his feelings, did he love or hate Andrée ? He knew not ; he suffered intensely, that was all. But not having the virtue of long-suffering, he shook off his dejection of soul, and determined to carry into practise some energetic resolution.

"She does not love me," thought he, "it is true ; but had I any right to hope that she would ? The only feeling that I had a right to hope for was that kindly interest which attaches to the unfortunate who strive with energy to rise above their wretchedness. Her brother felt this ; she did not feel it. He said, ' Who knows ? perhaps you may become a Colbert, a Vauban !' If I became either one or other he would do me justice ; he would give me his sister as a reward for the glory I had won for myself, as he would now give her in exchange for my personal nobility, had I been born his equal. But as for her—oh, yes! I feel it—yes, although Colbert or Vauban, I should never be to her other than Gilbert! What she despises in me is what nothing can efface, nothing gild, nothing cover —it is the lowness of my birth. As if, supposing I attain my object, I should not then be greater, having risen to her level, than if I had been born beside her! Ah, sense-less, unthinking creature! Woman—woman! That is, imperfection! Do you trust in her open look, her expan-sive forehead, her beaming smile, her queenly carriage, her beauty, which makes her worthy to be an empress? Fool! she is an affected, starched country girl, bound up, swathed in aristocratic prejudices. The gay and showy young noblemen with empty heads—mere weathercocks—who have all the means and appliances for learning, but who know nothing—they are her equals; they are things and men on whom she may bestow attention! But Gilbert?— Gilbert is a dog—nay, lower than a dog! She asked, I think, for news of Mahon; she did not ask how it fared with Gilbert. Oh, she knows not then that I am as strong as they! That if clothed like them, I should be as hand-some! That I have what they have not, an inflexible will, and that if I wished——"

A threatening smile curled his lip, and he left the sen-tence unfinished; then slowly, and with a deep frown, his head sunk on his breast. What passed at that moment in his dark and gloomy soul? Under what terrible idea did that pale forehead, already furrowed with painful thoughts, droop? Who shall tell? Is it the boatman who slowly glides down the river in his skiff, humming the song of Henri Quatre? Is it the laughing washer-woman who is returning from the splendid scene at St. Denis, and who, turning aside from her path to avoid him, probably takes the young loiterer for a thief, lying, as he is, at full length on the grass amid the lines hung with linen.

After half an hour's reflection, Gilbert arose, calm and resolved. He approached the bank of the Seine, and re-

freshed himself with a deep draught of water ; then, looking around, he saw on his left the waves of people pouring
out of St. Denis. Amid the throng he could distinguish
the principal carriages forced to go slowly from the crowd
of spectators that pressed on them and taking the road to
St. Ouen.

The dauphiness had expressed a desire that her entrance
into the kingdom should be a family festival, and the good
Parisians had taken advantage of this kind wish to place
their families so near the royal train that many of them
had mounted on the seats of the footmen, and some held
on by the heavy springs which projected from the carriages,
without manifesting the least fear.

Gilbert soon recognized Andrée's carriage ; Philip was
galloping or, rather, we should say, reining in his prancing
horse, close beside it.

"It is well," said he, "I must know whither she is
going, and for that purpose I must follow her."

The dauphiness was to sup at Muette in private with the
king, the dauphin, the Count de Provence and the
Count d'Artois. At St. Denis the king had invited the
dauphiness, and had given her a list of guests and a pencil, desiring her to erase the name of any one whom she
did not wish to be present. Now, it must be confessed that
Louis carried his forgetfulness of the respect due to her so
far as to include in it the name of Mme. Dubarry. It was
the last on the list, and when the dauphiness reached it her
cheek turned pale and her lip quivered ; but, following
the instruction of the empress, her mother, she recovered
her self-possession, and with a sweet smile returning the
list and the pencil to the king, she expressed herself most
happy to be admitted thus from the first to the intimacy
of his family circle.

Gilbert knew nothing of all this, and it was only at
Muette that he discovered the equipage of the countess, followed by Zamore on his tall white charger. Fortunately,
it was dark ; and, concealing himself behind a clump of
trees, he lay down and waited.

The king supped with his daughter-in-law and his mistress, and was in charming spirits ; more especially when he saw the dauphiness receive the countess even more graciously than she had done at Compiègne. But the dauphin seemed grave and anxious, and, pretending that he suffered from a violent headache, retired before they sat down to supper. The entertainment was prolonged until eleven o'clock.

In the meantime the retinue of the dauphiness—and the haughty Andrée was forced to acknowledge that she formed one of them—supped in tents, to the music of the king's private band, who had been ordered to attend for that purpose. Besides these—as the tents could not accommodate all—fifty gentlemen supped at tables spread in the open air, waited on by fifty lackeys in the royal livery.

Gilbert, still hidden in the clump of trees, lost nothing of this spectacle, while he supped at the same time as the others on a piece of bread which he had bought at Clichy-la-Garenne.

After supper, the dauphiness and the king appeared on a balcony to take leave of their guests. As each person departed, he passed below the balcony to salute his majesty and her royal highness. The dauphiness already knew many who had accompanied her from Compiègne, and those whom she did not know the king named to her. From time to time, a gracious word or well-turned compliment fell from her lips, diffusing joy in the breasts of those to whom it was addressed.

Gilbert, from his distant post, saw the meanness of their homage, and murmured : "I am greater than those people, since for all the gold in the world I would not do what they are doing."

At last the turn of the Baron de Taverney and his family came. Gilbert rose on one knee.

"Monsieur Philip," said the dauphiness, "I give you leave of absence, in order that you may accompany your father and your sister to Paris."

Gilbert heard these words distinctly, which, in the silence of the night, and amid the respectful attention of all around, vibrated in his ears.

Then she added : " Monsieur de Taverney, I cannot promise you apartments until I install my household at Versailles. You can, therefore, in the meantime accompany your daughter to Paris. Do not forget me, mademoiselle."

The baron passed on with his son and daughter. They were succeeded by many others, to whom the dauphiness made similar speeches, but Gilbert cared no longer for her words. He glided out of the clump of trees and followed the baron amid the confused cries of two hundred footmen running after their masters and calling to a hundred coachmen, while their shouts were accompanied by the thundering of numerous carriages rolling along the paved road.

As the baron had one of the carriages of the court at his command, it waited for them apart from the general crowd. When, accompanied by Andrée and Philip, he had entered it, the latter said to the footman who was closing the door :

" Mount on the seat beside the coachman, my friend."

" Why so ? Why so ?" asked the baron, hastily.

" Because the poor devil has been on his legs since morning, and must be tired by this time."

The baron grumbled something which Gilbert did not hear, while the footman mounted beside the coachman.

Gilbert drew nearer. At the moment when they were about to start, it was perceived that the trace had become unbuckled. The coachman jumped down, and the coach remained for a few moments stationary.

" It is very late," said the baron.

" I am dreadly fatigued," said Andrée. " Are you sure we shall get beds ?"

" I hope so," said Philip ; " I sent on La Brie and Nicole from Soissons with a letter to a friend of mine, desiring him to engage a small garden pavilion for us, which his mother and sister occupied last year. It is not a very splendid abode, but it is suitable enough ; you do not wish to receive company—you only want a stopping-place for the present."

" Faith," exclaimed the baron, "whatever it is, it will be better than Taverney."

"Unfortunately, father, that is true," replied Philip, in a melancholy tone.

"Are there any trees?" asked Andrée.

"Oh, yes; and very fine ones, too. But, in all probability, you will not have long to enjoy them, for as soon as the marriage is over you will be presented at court."

"Well this is all a dream, I fear," said the baron; "do not awake us too soon, Philip. Have you given the proper direction to the coachman?"

Gilbert listened anxiously.

"Yes, father."

Gilbert, who had heard all this conversation, had for a moment hoped to discover the address.

"No matter," said he, "I shall follow them; it is only a league to Paris."

The trace was fastened, the coachman mounted his seat, and the carriage was again in motion.

But the king's horses go fast when they are not in a procession which obliges them to go slowly, and now they darted forward so rapidly that they recalled to poor Gilbert's recollection the road to Lachaussée, his weakness, and his fainting. He made an effort and reached the foot-board behind, which was vacant, as the weary footman was seated beside the coachman. Gilbert grasped it, sprang up, and seated himself. But scarcely had he done so when the thought struck him that he was behind Andrée's carriage, and in the footman's place.

"No, no," muttered the inflexible young man, "it shall never be said that I did not struggle to the last; my legs are tired, but my arms are strong."

Then, seizing the foot-board with his hands, he followed at full speed, supported by the strength of his arms, and keeping his hold in spite of jolts and shocks, rather than capitulate with his conscience.

"At least I shall know her address," murmured he. "True, I shall have to pass one more bad night; but tomorrow I shall rest while I copy my music. Besides, I have still some money, and I may take two hours for sleep if I like."

Then he reflected that as Paris was such a large place, and he was quite unacquainted with it, he might lose his way after the baron and his daughter should have entered the house chosen for them by Philip. Fortunately, it was then near midnight, and day would break at half-past three.

As all these reflections passed through Gilbert's mind he remarked that they were passing through a spacious square, in the center of which was a large equestrian statue.

"Ha! This looks like the Place des Victoires," cried he, with a mingled sensation of surprise and joy.

The carriage turned. Andrée put her head out of the window and looked back.

"It is the statue of the late king," said Philip; "we are now near the house."

They descended a steep street so rapidly that Gilbert was nearly thrown under the wheels.

"Here we are at last!" cried Philip.

Gilbert sprang aside and hid himself behind the corner of the neighboring street.

Philip leaped out, rang the bell, and turning, received Andrée in his arms.

The baron got out last.

"Well," cried he, "are those scoundrels going to keep us here all night?"

At that moment the voices of La Brie and Nicole were heard, and a gate was opened. The three travelers disappeared in a dark court, and the gate closed behind him.

The carriage drove off on its way to the king's stables. The house which had received the strangers was in no way remarkable in its appearance; but the lamps of the carriage, in passing, had flashed on that next to it, and Gilbert read over the gateway the words, "Hotel d'Armenonville."

It only remained for him to discover the name of the street.

He gained the nearest extremity, that by which the carriage had disappeared, and to his great surprise he found himself close to the fountain at which he was in the habit of drinking. He advanced a few steps further in a street parallel to that which he had left, and discovered the baker's

shop where he usually bought his loaf.   Doubting still, he
went back to the corner of the street ; and there, by the
light of a neighboring lamp he read the words which had
struck him when returning with Rousseau from their botanical excursion in the forest of Meudon three days before
—Rue Plastrière. Andrée, consequently, was not one
hundred paces distant from him—not so far off as she had
been at Taverney, when he slept in his little room at the
castle gate.

Then he regained his domicile, scarcely daring to hope
to find the end of the cord left out by which the latch of he
door was lifted.   But Gilbert's star was in the ascendant ;
a few raveled threads were hanging out, by which he
pulled the whole, and the door opened gently at his
touch.

He felt his way to the stairs, mounted step by step
without making the least noise, and at last put his hand
on the padlock of the garret door, in which Rousseau had
kindly left the key.

Ten minutes afterward, fatigue asserted its power over
his disquieted thoughts, and he slept soundly, although
longing for the morrow.

CHAPTER LIV.

THE GARDEN PAVILION.

HAVING come in late, and throwing himself hastily on
his bed, Gilbert had forgotten to place over his window
the blind which intercepted the light of the rising sun.   At
five o'clock, therefore, the rays of light beaming through
the window awoke him.   He sprung up, fearing that he
had slept too long.

Accustomed as he been to a country life, Gilbert could
guess the hour at all times with the utmost precision by
the direction of the shadows, and by the paler or warmer
tints of light.   He ran, therefore, to consult his clock.

The faintness of the morning beams, barely tingeing with their light the topmost boughs of the trees, reassured him; and he found that instead of having risen too late, he had risen too early. He finished his toilet at the garret window, thinking over the events of the preceding day, and exposing with delight his burning and oppressed forehead to the refreshing morning breeze. Then he remembered that Andrée lodged in the next street, near the Hotel d'Armenonville, and he tried to guess in which of all the houses that he saw she might be.

The sight of the lofty trees on which he looked down, recalled her question to Philip : "Are there any trees there ?"

"Might they not have chosen that uninhabited house in the garden ?" said Gilbert to himself.

This idea naturally led him to fix his attention on the garden pavilion, where, by a singular coincidence, a sort of noise and stir began to be apparent.

One of the window-shutters of the little abode, which had not been opened apparently for a considerable time, was shaken by an awkward or feeble hand. The wood yielded above, but held fast by the damp, no doubt, to the frame at the bottom, it resisted the effort made to open it. A second shake, more violent than the first, had a better effect ; the two shutters creaked, gave way, and, falling back quickly, exposed to view a young girl all in a glow with her exertions, and beating off the dust from her hands.

Gilbert uttered a cry of surprise, and stepped back. The young girl, whose face was still flushed with sleep, and who was stretching herself in the fresh air, was Mlle. Nicole.

There was no longer any room for doubt. The lodging which Philip had said La Brie and Nicole were preparing, was the house before him, and the mansion through whose gateway he had seen the travelers disappear must have its gardens adjoining the rear of the Rue Plastrière. Gilbert's movement was so abrupt, that if Nicole had not been completely absorbed in the lazy meditation so delightful at the moment of waking, she must have discovered our philosopher at his skylight.

But Gilbert had retired all the more speedily, as he had no intention that Nicole, of all persons in the world, should spy him out in so elevated a situation. Had he been on a first floor, and had his open window showed a background of rich hangings or sumptuous furniture, he would not have been so anxious to avoid her eye, but a garret on the fifth story declared him to be still so low in the social scale, that he took the greatest care to hide himself. Moreover, there is always in this world a great advantage in seeing without being seen. And then, if Andrée should discover that he watched her, would it not be sufficient either to induce her to change her abode, or prevent her walking in the garden ?

Alas ! Gilbert's pride still made him of too great importance in his own eyes. What was Gilbert to Andrée? Would she have moved her finger, either to approach or to avoid him ? But these were far from being Nicole's sentiments, and her, consequently, he must shun.

He hid himself carefully, therefore ; but as he did not wish to withdraw from the window entirely, he ventured to peep out cautiously at one corner.

A second window on the ground-floor of the pavilion, exactly below the first, just then opened, and a white form appeared at it. It was Andrée, seemingly just awakened. She was enveloped in a dressing-gown, and was occupied in searching for the slipper which had escaped from her tiny foot, and was lying beneath a chair. It was in vain that Gilbert, each time that he saw Andrée, vowed to build up between them a barrier of hatred instead of giving way to love ; the same effect was produced by the same cause. He was obliged to lean against the wall for support ; his heart palpitated as if it would have burst, and sent the blood in boiling currents through his whole frame. However, by degrees, his throbbing arteries beat with a calmer motion, and reflection resumed her sway. The problem he had to solve was, as we have said, to see without being seen. He took one of Therese's gowns and fastened it with a pin to one of the cords which crossed his window ; and, sheltered by this impromptu curtain, he would watch Andrée without running any risk of being discovered by her. The lovely young girl, following Nicole's example, stretched out her snowy arms, and then, folding th emon the window, she looked out on the garden. Her countenance expressed the liveliest satisfaction at all she saw. Lofty trees shaded the walks with their drooping branches, and everywhere verdure cheered her eye. She, who smiled so seldom on human beings, smiled on the inanimate objects around her.

The house in which Gilbert lived attracted her eye for a moment, like all the others which surrounded the garden ; but as from her apartment only the garrets of the houses were visible, and, consequently, from them alone could she be seen, she paid no further attention. How could the proud young girl take any interest in the concerns of a race so far removed from her sphere ? Andrée felt convinced, therefore, that no one saw her by whom it was of the least importance that she should not be seen, and that within the bounds of her tranquil retreat there appeared none of those prying or satirical Parisian faces so much dreaded by ladies from the provinces.

The effect was immediate. Leaving her window wide open, so that the fresh and perfumed air might penetrate to the furthest extremity of her apartment, she proceeded toward the mantelpiece and rang a bell.

Nicole appeared, undid the straps of a shagreen dressing-case of the reign of Queen Anne, took from it a tortoise-shell comb, and began to comb out Andrée's hair. In a moment the long tresses and shining curls spread like a glossy veil over her shoulders.

Gilbert gave a stifled sigh. At that distance he scarcely saw the beauty of her locks, but he saw Andrée herself, a thousand times more lovely in this déshabille than she would have been in the most splendid attire. He gazed, his whole soul in his eyes.

By chance, as Nicole continued to dress her hair, Andrée raised her eyes, and fixed them on Gilbert's garret.

"Yes, yes," said he, "look—gaze as much as you please; it is all in vain, you can see nothing, and I see all!"

But Gilbert was mistaken; Andrée did see something. It was the gown which he had hung up, and which, being blown about, had got wrapped round his head like a turban. She pointed out this strange object to Nicole.

Nicole, stopping in her complicated task, pointed with the comb which she held in her hand toward the skylight, and seemed to ask her mistress if that were the object which she meant.

All these gestures, which Gilbert devoured with the greatest eagerness, had, without his suspecting it, a third spectator. Suddenly a rude hand snatched Therese's gown from his head, and he was ready to sink with shame on seeing Rousseau beside him.

"What the devil are you doing there, sir?" cried the philosopher, with a terrible frown, and a scrutinizing glance at the gown borrowed, without leave asked, from his wife.

"Nothing, sir, nothing at all," replied Gilbert, endeavoring to turn Rousseau's attention from the window.

"Nothing? Then why did you hide yourself with the gown?"

"The sun hurts my eyes."

"This window looks toward the west, and the sun dazzles you when rising? You have very delicate eyes, young man!"

Gilbert stammered out some unconnected words, but, feeling that he was only getting deeper in the mire, he at last hid his head in his hands.

"You are speaking falsely, and you are afraid," said Rousseau; "therefore, you have been doing wrong."

After this terrible syllogism, which seemed to complete Gilbert's confusion, Rousseau planted himself exactly opposite the window.

From a feeling too natural to require explanation, Gilbert, who so lately trembled to be discovered at the window, rushed forward when he saw Rousseau standing before it.

"Ah, ha!" said the latter, in a tone which froze the blood in Gilbert's veins; "the garden-house is inhabited now."

Gilbert was dumb.

"And by persons," continued the philosopher, "who seem to know my house, for they are pointing to it."

Gilbert, trembling lest he had advanced too far, stepped back quickly; but neither his movement, nor the cause which produced it, escaped the jealous eye of Rousseau; he saw that Gilbert feared to be seen.

"No," cried he, seizing the young man by the arm, "you shall not escape, my young friend; there is some plot under this, I know, by their pointing to your garret. Place yourself here, if you please;" and he dragged him opposite the skylight, in the full view of those beneath.

"Oh, no, sir, no; have mercy!" cried Gilbert struggling to escape.

But, to escape, which for a young and active man like Gilbert would have been an easy task, he must have engaged in a contest with Rousseau—Rousseau, whom he venerated like some superior being—and respect restrained him.

"You know those women," said Rousseau; "and they know you."

"No, no, no, sir!"

"Then, if you do not know them, and if they do not know you, why not show yourself?"

"Monsieur Rousseau, you have sometimes had secrets yourself. Show some pity for me."

"Ah, traitor!" cried Rousseau. "Yes, I know what sort of a secret yours is. You are a creature of Grimm or Holbach's—you have been tutored to act a part in order to impose upon my benevolence; you have gained admittance into my house, and now you betray me to them. Oh, thrice-sodden fool that I am! Silly lover of nature! I thought I was aiding a fellow-creature. and I was bringing a spy into my house!"

"A spy!" exclaimed Gilbert, indignantly.

"Come, Judas, on what day am I to be sold?" continued Rousseau, folding Therese's gown tragically about him, and thinking himself sublime in his grief, when, unfortunately, he was only ridiculous.

"Sir, you calumniate me," said Gilbert.

"Calumniate you, you little serpent?" exclaimed Rousseau.

"Did I not find you corresponding with my enemies by signals? Making them understand, perhaps, what is the subject of my new work?"

"Sir, had I gained admittance to your house in order to betray the secret of your work, it would have been easier for me to have copied some of the manuscripts in your desk than to inform others of the subject by signs."

This was true; and Rousseau felt so plainly that he had given utterance to one of those absurdities which escaped him when his monomania of suspicion was at its height, that he got angry.

"Sir," said he, "I am sorry for you, but experience has made me severe. My life has been one long series of deceptions. I have been ever the victim of treachery; I have been betrayed, sold, made a martyr, by every one that surrounded me. I am, you must be aware, one of those illustrious unfortunates on whom government has put its ban. In such a situation it is pardonable to be suspicious. Now I suspect you, therefore you shall leave my house."

Gilbert was far from expecting this peroration. To be turned out? He clinched his hands tightly, and a flash of anger which almost made Rousseau tremble lighted up his eye. The flash was only momentary, however, for the thought occurred to him that in leaving Rousseau's house he should lose the happiness of seeing Andrée every hour of the day, as well as forfeit the friendship of Rousseau; this would be to add misery to shame. His untamable pride gave way, and clasping his hands, "Sir," said he, "listen to me. One word, only one word!"

"I am pitiless!" said Rousseau; "men have made me, by their injustice, more cruel than the tiger. You are in correspondence with my enemies. Go to them, I do not oppose your doing so. Only leave my house."

"Sir, those two young girls are not your enemies ; they are Mademoiselle Andrée and Nicole."

"And who is Mademoiselle Andrée ?" said Rousseau, who had heard Gilbert pronounce this name twice or thrice before, and was, consequently, not entirely unacquainted with it. "Come, who is Mademoiselle Andrée ? Speak !"

"Mademoiselle Andrée, sir, is the daughter of the Baron de Taverney. Oh, pardon me, sir, for daring to say so to you, but I love her more than you ever loved Mademoiselle Galley or Madame de Warens. It is she whom I have followed on foot to Paris, without money, and without bread, until I fell down on the road exhausted with hunger and fatigue. It is she whom I went to see yesterday at St. Denis, whom I followed, unseen by her, to Muette, and from that to a street near this. It is she whom by chance I discovered this morning to be the occupant of this garden-house ; and it is she for whose sake I burn to be a Turenne, a Richelieu, or a Rousseau !"

Rousseau knew the human heart, and felt assured that no one acting a part could speak with the trembling and impassioned accents of Gilbert, or accompany his words with gestures so true to nature.

"So," said he, "this young lady is Mademoiselle Andrée ?"

"Yes, Monsieur Rousseau."

"Then you know her ? "

"Sir, I am the son of her nurse."

"Then you lied just now when you said you did not know her ; and if you are not a traitor, you are a liar."

"Sir, you tear my very heart ! Indeed you would hurt me less were you to kill me on the spot !"

"Pshaw ! Mere phrases ! Style of Diderot and Marmontel ! You are a liar, sir !"

"Well, yes, yes," said Gilbert ; "I am a liar, sir ; and so much the worse for you, if you do not feel for one so forced to lie. A liar ! a liar ! I leave you, sir, but I leave you in despair, and my misery will one day weigh heavy on your conscience."

Rousseau stroked his chin as he looked at this young man, in whom he found so many points of character resembling his own.

"He has either a great soul, or he is a great rogue," said he to himself; "but if they are plotting against me, why not hold in my hand a clew to the plot?"

Gilbert had advanced toward the door, and now, with his hand on the lock, stood waiting for the fiat which was to banish or recall him.

"Enough on this subject, my son," said Rousseau. "If you are as deeply in love as you say, so much the worse for you. But it is now late; you lost the whole of yesterday, and we have to-day thirty pages to copy. Quick, Gilbert. Be on the alert!"

Gilbert seized the philosopher's hand, and pressed it to his lips; he would not certainly have done so much for a king's. But before leaving the room, and while Gilbert, still deeply moved, stood leaning against the door, Rousseau again placed himself at the window to take a last look at the young girls. Andrée had just thrown off her dressing-gown, and taken her gown from Nicole's hands. She saw his pallid countenance and searching eye, and, starting back, she ordered Nicole to close the window. Nicole obeyed.

"So," said Rousseau, "my old face frightens her; his young one would not have had the same effect. Oh, lovely youth!" added he, sighing:

> "O gioventu primavera dell' eta !
> O primavera gioventu dell' anno !"

and, once more hanging up Therese's gown on its nail, he went down-stairs in a melancholy mood, followed by Gilbert, for whose youth he would, perhaps, at that moment have exchanged his renown, which then rivaled that of Voltaire, and shared with it the admiration of the world.

CHAPTER LV.

THE HOUSE IN THE RUE ST. CLAUDE.

THE Rue St. Claude, in which the Count de Fenix had appointed to meet the Cardinal de Rohan, was not so different at that period from what it is at the present day, but that some vestiges of the localities we are about to describe may yet be discovered. It abutted then, as it does now, on the Rue St. Louis and the boulevard, to the latter of which it descended with rather a steep inclination. It boasted of fifteen houses and seven lanterns, and was remarkable besides for two lanes, or *culs-de-sac*, which branched off from it, the one on the left, the other on the right; the former serving as the boundary of the Hotel de Voysins, while the latter took a slice off the large garden of the Convent of St. Sacrament. This last-mentioned lane, shaded on one side by the trees of the convent-garden, was bordered on the other by the high dark wall of a house, the front of which looked toward the Rue St. Claude.

This wall, resembling the visage of a Cyclops, had only one eye, or if the reader like it better, only one window; and even that, covered with bars and grating, was horribly gloomy.

Just below this window, which was never opened, as one might perceive from the spiders' webs that curtained it over, was a door studded with large nails, which indicated, not that the house was entered, but that it might be entered, on this side.

There were no dwellings in this lane, and only two inhabitants. There were a cobbler in a wooden box, and a stocking-mender in a cask, both shading themselves from the heat under the acacias of the convent garden, which threw their broad shadow on the dusty lane from nine in the morning. In the evening the stocking-mender returned to her domicile, the cobbler put a padlock on his castle, and no guardian watched over the lonely street, save the stern and somber eye of the window we have spoken of.

Besides the door just mentioned, the house which we have undertaken to describe so accurately, had another and the principal entrance in the Rue St. Claude. This entrance was a large gateway surmounted with carved figures in relief, which recalled the architecture of the times of Louis XIII., and was adorned with the griffin's head for a knocker, which the Count de Fenix had indicated to the Cardinal de Rohan as distinguishing his abode.

As for the windows, they looked on the boulevard, and were opened early in the morning to admit the fresh air. But as Paris, at that period, and, above all, in that quarter, was far from safe, it occasioned no astonishment to see them grated, and the walls near them bristling with iron spikes. Indeed, the whole appearance of the house, at the first glance, suggested the idea of a fortress. Against enemies, thieves, or lovers, it presented iron balconies with sharp points ; a deep moat separated the building from the boulevard, and to obtain entrance on this side it would have required ladders at least thirty feet long, for the wall which enclosed, or, rather, buried, the courtyard was fully that height.

This house, before which in the present day a spectator would be arrested by curiosity on beholding its singular aspect, was not very remarkable in 1770. On the contrary, it seemed to harmonize with the quarter of the city in which it stood, and if the worthy inhabitants of the Rue St. Louis, and the not less worthy denizens of the Rue St. Claude, shunned its neighborhood, it was not on account of its reputation, which was then intact, but on account of the lonely boulevard of the Porte St. Louis, and the Pont aux Choux, both of which were in very bad odor with the Parisians. In fact, the boulevard on this side led to nothing but the Bastile, and as there was not more than a dozen houses in the space of a quarter of a league, the city authorities had not thought it worth their while to light such a desert region. The consequence was, that after eight o'clock in summer, and four in winter, the vacuum became a sort of chaos, with the agreeable addition of robbers.

It was, however, on this very boulevard, toward nine o'clock in the evening, and about three quarters of an hour after the visit to St. Denis, that a carriage drove rapidly along. It bore the coat of arms of the Count de Fenix on its panels. The count himself, mounted on Djerid, who whisked his long and silky tail as he sniffed the stifling atmosphere, rode about twenty paces in advance. Within it, resting on cushions, and concealed by the closed blinds, lay Lorenza, fast asleep. The gate opened, as if by enchantment, at the noise of the wheels, and the carriage, after turning into the dark gulf of the Rue St. Claude, disappeared in the courtyard of the house we have just described, the gate of which seemed to close behind it without the aid of human hands.

There was, most assuredly, no occasion for so much mystery, since no one was there to see the Count de Fenix return, or to interfere with him, had he carried off in his carriage the treasures of the Abbey of St. Denis.

In the meantime, we shall say a few words respecting the interior of this house, of which it is of importance that our readers should know something, since it is our intention to introduce them to it more than once.

In the courtyard, of which we have spoken, and in which the springing grass labored by a never-ceasing effort to displace the pavement, were seen on the right the stables, on the left the coach-houses, while at the back a double flight of twelve steps led to the entrance door.

On the ground floor, the house, or at least as much of it as was accessible, consisted of a large ante-chamber, a dining-room, remarkable for the quantity of massive plate heaped on its sideboards, and a saloon, which seemed quite recently furnished, probably for the reception of its new inmates.

From the ante-chamber, a broad staircase led to the first floor, which contained three principal apartments.

A skilful geometrician, however, on measuring with his eye the extent of the house outside, and observing the space within it, would have been surprised to find it contain so little accommodation. In fact, in the outside apparent house, there was a second hidden house, known only to those who inhabited it.

In the ante-chamber, close beside a statue of the god Harpocrates—who, with his finger on his lips, seemed to enjoin the silence of which he is the symbol—was concealed a secret door opening with a spring, and masked by the ornaments of the architecture. This door gave access to a staircase, which, ascending to about the same height as the first floor on the other staircase, led to a little apartment lighted by two grated windows looking on an inner court. This inner court was the box, as it were, which inclosed the second house and concealed it from all eyes.

The apartment to which this staircase led was evidently intended for a man. Beside the bed, and before the sofas and couches, were spread, instead of carpets, the most magnificent furs which the burning climes of Africa and India produced. There were skins of lions, tigers, and panthers, with their glaring eyes and threatening teeth. The walls, hung with Cordova leather stamped in large and flowing arabesques, were decorated with weapons of every kind, from the tomahawk of the Huron to the crid of the Malay; from the sword of the Crusader to the kandgiar of the Arab; from the arquebuse, incrusted with ivory, of the sixteenth century, to the damasked barrel, inlaid with gold, of the eighteenth. The eye in vain sought in this room for any other outlet than that from the staircase; perhaps there were several, but if so, they were concealed and invisible.

A German domestic, about five-and-twenty or thirty years of age, the only human being who had been seen wandering to and fro in that vast mansion for several days, bolted the gate of the courtyard; and, opening the carriage-door while the stolid coachman unharnessed his horses, he lifted out Lorenza in his arms and carried her into the ante-chamber. There he laid her on a table covered with red cloth, and drew down her long white veil over her person.

Then he left the room to light at the lamps of the carriage a large chandelier with seven branches, and returned with all its lights burning. But in that interval short as it was, Lorenza had disappeared.

The Count de Fenix had followed close behind the German, and had no sooner been left alone with Lorenza than he took her in his arms and carried her by the secret staircase we have described, to the chamber of arms, after having carefully closed both the doors behind him. Once there, he pressed his foot on a spring in the corner of the lofty mantelpiece, and immediately a door, which formed the back of the fireplace, rolled back on its noiseless hinges, and the count, with his burden, again disappeared, carefully closing behind him with his foot the mysterious door.

At the back of the mantelpiece was a second staircase, consisting of a flight of fifteen steps covered with Utrecht velvet, after mounting which, he reached a chamber elegantly hung with satin embroidered with flowers of such brilliant colors, and so naturally designed, that they might have been taken for real. The furniture was richly gilt. Two cabinets of tortoise-shell inlaid with brass, a harpischord, and a toilet-table of rosewood, a beautiful bed with transparent curtains, and several vases Sèvres porcelain form the principal articles, while chairs and couches, arranged with the nicest order in a space of thirty feet square, served to complete the decoration of the apartment, to which was attached a dressing-closet and a boudoir. These latter had no windows; but lamps filled with perfumed oil burned in them day and night, and let down from the ceiling, were trimmed by invisible hands. The sleeping chamber, however, had two windows hung with rich and heavy curtains, but, as it was now night, the curtains had nothing to conceal.

Not a sound, not a breath was heard in this chamber, and an inhabitant might have thought himself a hundred miles from the world. But gold, cunningly wrought, shone on every side ; beautiful paintings smiled from the walls, and lusters of colored Bohemian glass glittered and sparkled like eyes looking on the scene, when, after having placed Lorenza on a sofa, the count, not satisfied with the trembling radiance of the boudoir, proceeded to light the rose-colored wax-candles of two candelabra on the chimney-piece.

Then, returning to Lorenza and placing himself before her, he knelt with one knee on a pile of cushions and exclaimed softly, " Lorenza ! "

The young girl, at this appeal, raised herself on her elbow, although her eyes remained closed. But she did not reply.

" Lorenza," he repeated, " do you sleep in your ordinary sleep or in the magnetic sleep ? "

" In the magnetic sleep," she answered.

" Then, if I question you, you can reply ? "

" I think so."

The Count de Fenix was silent for a few moments ; then he continued :

" Look in the apartment of the Princess Louise, whom we left three quarters of an hour ago."

" I am looking."

" What do you see ? "

" The princess is praying before retiring to bed."

" Do you see the Cardinal de Rohan in the convent ? "

" No."

" In any of the corridors or courts ? "

" No."

" Look whether his carriage be at the gate ? "

" I do not see it."

" Pursue the road by which we came. Do you see carriages on it ? "

" Yes, several."

" Do you see the cardinal's among them ? "

" No."

" Come nearer Paris—now ? "

" Now I see it."

" Where ? "

" At the gate of the city."

" Has it stopped ? "

" Yes ; the footman has just got down."

" Does the cardinal speak to him ? "

" Yes ; he is going to speak."

" Lorenza, attend. It is important that I should know what the cardinal says."

" You should have told me to listen in time.   But stop ! the footman is speaking to the coachman."

" What does he say ? "

" The Rue St. Claude, in the Marais, by the boulevard."

" Thanks, Lorenza."

The count wrote some words on a piece of paper, which he folded round a plate of copper, doubtless to give it weight, then he pulled a bell, pressed a spring, and, a small opening appearing in the wall, he dropped the note down. The opening closed again instantly. It was in this way that the count, in the inner apartments of his house, gave his orders to Fritz, his German servant.

CHAPTER LVI.

THE DOUBLE EXISTENCE—SLEEP.

RETURNING to Lorenza, Balsamo said, " Will you converse with your friend now ? "

" Oh, yes ! " she replied.   " But speak yourself the most —I love so to hear your voice."

" Lorenza, you have often said that you would be happy if you could live with me, shut out from all the world."

" Yes ; that would be happiness indeed ! "

" Well, your wish is realized. No one can follow us to this chamber—no one can enter here ; we are alone, quite alone."

" Ah, so much the better."

" Tell me—is this apartment to your taste ? "

" Order me to see it, then."

" I order you."

"Oh, what a charming room!"

"You are pleased with it, then?" asked the count, tenderly.

"Oh, yes! There are my favorite flowers—my vanilla heliotropes, my crimson roses, my Chinese jasmines! Thanks, my sweet Joseph—how kind and good you are!"

"I do all I can to please you, Lorenza."

"Oh! you do a hundred times more than I deserve."

"You think so?"

"Yes."

"Then you confess that you have been very ill-natured?"

"Very ill-natured? Oh, yes. But you forgive me, do you not?"

"I shall forgive you when you explain to me the strange mystery which I have sought to fathom ever since I knew you."

"It is this, Balsamo. There are in me two Lorenzas, quite distinct from each other; one that loves and one that hates you. So there are in me two lives; in one I taste all the joys of paradise, in the other experience all the torments of hell."

"And those two lives are sleep and waking?"

"Yes."

"You love me when you sleep, and you hate me when you are awake?"

"Yes."

"But why so?"

"I do not know."

"You must know."

"No."

"Search carefully; look within yourself; sound your own heart."

"Yes, I see the cause now."

"What is it?"

"When Lorenza awakes, she is the Roman girl, the superstitious daughter of Italy; she thinks science a crime, and love a sin. Her confessor told her that they were so. She is, then, afraid of you, and would flee from you to the confines of the earth."

"And when Lorenza sleeps?"

"Ah! then she is no longer the Roman, no longer superstitious—she is a woman. Then she reads Balsamo's heart and mind; she sees that his heart loves her, that his genius contemplates sublime things. Then she feels her littleness compared with him. Then she would live and die beside him, that the future might whisper softly the name of Lorenza, when it trumpets forth that of—Cagliostro!"

"It is by that name, then, that I shall become celebrated?"

"Yes, by that name."

"Dear Lorenza! Then you will love this new abode, will you not?"

"It is much more splendid than any of those you have already given me, but it is not on that account that I shall love it."

"For what then?"

"I shall love it because you have promised to live in it with me."

"Then, when you sleep, you see clearly that I love you—ardently love you?"

The young girl smiled faintly. "Yes," said she, "I do see that you love me, and yet," added she, with a sigh, "there is something which you love better than Lorenza."

"What is it?" asked Balsamo, starting.

"Your dream."

"Say, my task."

"Your ambition."

"Say, my glory."

"Ah, Heaven! ah, Heaven!" and the young girl's breast heaved while the tears forced their way through her closed eyelids.

"What do you see?" asked Balsamo, with alarm; for there were moments when her powers of seeing the unseen startled even him.

"Oh, I see darkness, and phantoms gliding through it; some of them hold in their hands their crowned heads, and you—you are among them like a general in the thick of the battle ! You command, and they obey."

"Well," said Balsamo, joyfully, "and does that not make you proud of me ?"

"Oh, no, for I seek my own figure amid the throng which surrounds you, and I cannot see myself. I shall not be there," murmured she, sadly. "I shall not be there ! "

"Where will you be, then ? "

"I shall be dead."

Balsamo shuddered.

"Dead ? my Lorenza," cried he, "dead ? No, no ! we shall live long together to love each other."

"You love me not."

"Oh, yes ! "

"Ah !" continued she, "I feel that I am nothing to you."

"You, my Lorenza, nothing ? You are my all, my strength, my power, my genius. Without you I should be nothing. You possess my whole soul. Is not that enough to make you happy ? "

"Happy ?" repeated she, contemptuously. "Do you call this life of ours happy ? "

"Yes ; for in my mind to be happy is to be great."

She sighed deeply.

"Oh, could you but know, dearest Lorenza, how I love to read the uncovered hearts of men, and govern them with their own passions ! "

"Yes I serve you in that, I know."

"That is not all. Your eyes read for me the hidden book of the future. What I could not learn with twenty years of toil and suffering, you, my gentle dove, innocent and pure, you teach me when you wish. Foes dog my steps and lay snares for me—you inform me of every danger. On my understanding depend my life, my fortune, my freedom—you give that understanding the eye of a lynx, which dilates and sees clearly in the darkness. Your lovely eyes closing to the light of this outward world, open to supernatural splendors, which they watch for me. It is you who make me free, rich, powerful."

"And you in return make me wretched," she exclaimed, in a tone of despair, "for all that is not love."

"Yes, it is," he replied "a holy and pure love."

"And what happiness attends it? Why did you force me from my country, my name, my family—why obtain this power over me—why make me your slave, if I am never to be yours in reality?"

"Alas! why, rather," asked he, "are you like an angel, infallible in penetration, by whose help I can subject the universe? Why are you able to read all hearts within their corporal dwelling, as others read a book behind a pane of glass? It is because you are an angel of purity, Lorenza—because your spirit, different from those of the vulgar, or sordid beings who surround you, pierces through every obstacle."

"And thus you regard my love less than the vain chimeras of your brain? Oh, Joseph, Joseph," added she, passionately, "you wrong me cruelly!"

"Not so, for I love you; but I would raise you with myself to the throne of the world."

"Oh, Balsamo," murmured she, "will your ambition ever make you happy as my love would?"

As she spoke she thew her arms around him. He struggled to release himself, beat back the air loaded with magnetic fluid, and at length exclaimed, "Lorenza, awake, awake! It is my will."

At once her arms released their hold, the smile which had played on her lips died away, and she sighed heavily. At length her closed eyes opened; the dilated pupils assumed their natural size; she stretched out her arms, appeared overcome with weariness, and fell back at full length, but awake, on the sofa.

Balsamo, scated at a little distance from her, heaved a deep sigh. "Adieu, my dream!" murmured he to himself. "Farewell, happiness!"

CHAPTER LVII.

THE DOUBLE EXISTENCE—WAKING.

As soon as Lorenza had recovered her natural powers of sight, she cast a hurried glance around her. Her eyes roamed over all the splendid trifles which surrounded her on every side, without exhibiting any appearance of the pleasure which such things usually give to women.

At length they rested with a shudder on Balsamo, who was seated at a short distance, and was watching her attentively.

"You again !" said she, recoiling ; and all the symptoms of horror appeared in her countenance. Her lips turned deathly pale, and the perspiration stood in large drops on her forehead. Balsamo did not reply.

"Where am I ?" she asked.

"You know whence you come, madame," said Balsamo, "and that should naturally enable you to guess where you are."

"Yes, you are right to remind me of that ; I remember now. I know that I have been persecuted by you, pursued by you, torn by you from the arms of the royal lady whom I had chosen to protect me."

"Then you must know, also, that this princess, all-powerful though she be, could not defend you ?"

"Yes ; you have conquered her by some work of magic !" cried Lorenza, clasping her hands. "Oh, Heaven, deliver me from this demon !"

"In what way do I resemble a demon, madame ?" said Balsamo, shrugging his shoulders. "Once for all, abandon, I beg of you, this farrago of childish prejudice which you brought with you from Rome ; have done with all those absurd superstitions which you learned in your convent, and which have formed your constant traveling-companions since you left it."

"Oh, my convent! Who will restore me my convent?" cried Lorenza, bursting into tears.

"In fact," said Balsamo, ironically, "a convent is a place very much to be regretted."

Lorenza darted toward one of the windows, drew aside the curtains, and, opening it, stretched out her hand. It struck against a thick bar supporting an iron grating, which, although hidden by flowers, was not the less efficacious in retaining a prisoner.

"Prison for prison," said she. "I like that better which conducts toward heaven than that which sends to hell."

And she dashed her delicate hands against the iron bars.

"If you were more reasonable, Lorenza, you would find only the flowers, without the bars, at your windows."

"Was I not reasonable when you shut me up in that other moving prison, with that vampire whom you call Althotas? And yet you kept me a prisoner, you watched me like a lynx, and whenever you left me you breathed into me that spirit which takes possession of me, and which I cannot overcome. Where is he, that horrible old man, whose sight freezes me with terror? In some corner here, is he not? Let us keep silent, and we shall hear his unearthly voice issue from the depths of the earth."

"You really give way to your imagination like a child, madame. Althotas, my teacher, my friend, my second father, is an inoffensive old man, who has never seen or approached you; or, if he has seen you, has never paid the least attention to you, immersed as he is in his task."

"His task?" murmured Lorenza. "And what is his task, pray?"

"He is trying to discover the elixir of life—what all the greatest minds have been in search of for the last six thousand years."

"And you—what are you trying to discover?"

"The means of human perfectability."

"Oh, demons! demons!" said Lorenza, raising her hand to heaven.

"Ah !" said Balsamo, rising, "now your fit is coming on again."

"My fit ? "

"Yes, your fit. There is one thing, Lorenza, which you are not aware of ; it is, that your life is divided into two equal periods. During one you are gentle, good, and reasonable—during the other you are mad."

"And it is under this false pretext of madness that you shut me up ? "

"Alas ! I am obliged to do so."

"Oh, be cruel, barbarous, pitiless if you will—shut me up, kill me, but do not play the hypocrite ; do not pretend to compassionate while you destroy me !"

"But only reflect a moment," said Balsamo, without anger, and even with a caressing smile, "is it torture to live in an elegant commodious apartment like this ? "

"Grated windows—iron bars on all sides—no air—no air !"

"The bars are for the safety of your life, I repeat, Lorenza."

"Oh !" cried she, "he destroys me piecemeal, and tells me he cares for my life."

Balsamo approached the young girl, and with a friendly gesture, endeavored to take her hand ; but, recoiling, as if from the touch of a serpent :

"Oh, do not touch me !" said she.

"Do you hate me, then, Lorenza ? "

"Ask the sufferer if he hates his executioner. "

"Lorenza, Lorenza ! it is because I do not wish to be your executioner that I deprive you of a little of your liberty. If you could go and come as you like, who knows what you might do in the moments of your madness ? "

"What I might do ?   Oh, let me once be free, and you shall see what I would do."

"Lorenza, you treat the husband whom you have chosen in the sight of Heaven very strangely."

"I chose you ?   Never, never !"

"You are my wife, notwithstanding."

" Yes ; that indeed must have been the work of the demon."

"Poor insensate ! " said Balsamo, with a tender look.

" But I am a Roman woman," murmured Lorenza, " and one day I shall be revenged."

Balsamo shook his head gently.

" You only say that to frighten me, Lorenza ; do you not ? " said he, smiling.

" No, no ; I shall do what I say."

" Woman ! " exclaimed Balsamo, with a commanding voice, " you pretend to be a Christian—does not your re-ligion teach you to render good for evil ?   What hypocrisy is yours, calling yourself a follower of that religion, and vowing to yourself to render evil for good ? "

Lorenza appeared, for an instant struck by these words. "Oh ! " said she, "it is not vengeance to denounce to society its enemies—it is a duty."

" If you denounce me as a necromancer, as a sorcerer, it is not society whom I offend, but God ; but if I be such, the Deity by a sign can destroy me.   He does not do so. Does he leave my punishment to weak men, subject to error like myself ? "

" He bears with you," murmured the young girl ; " He waits for you to reform."

Balsamo smiled.

" And in the meantime," said he, " He counsels you to betray your friend, your benefactor, your husband ? "

" My husband ?   Ah ! thank Heaven—your hand has never touched mine that I have not blushed or shuddered at its contact."

" Oh, mystery !   Impenetrable mystery ! " murmured Balsamo to himself, replying rather to his own thoughts than to Lorenza's words.

" Once for all," said Lorenza, " why do you′ deprive me of my liberty ? "

" Why, after having given yourself voluntarily to me, do you now wish for liberty ?   Why do you flee from him who protects you ?   Why do you ask a stranger for pro-tection against him who loves you ?   Why do you threaten

him who has never yet threatened you, and say you will
reveal secrets which are not yours, and of which you do
not comprehend the import ? "

"Oh," said Lorenza, without replying to his questions,
"the prisoner who has firmly determined to be free will
be so sooner or later, and your bars of iron shall not keep
me any more than your moving cage kept me ! "

"Fortunately for you, Lorenza, the bars are strong,"
answered Balsamo, which a threatening calmness.

"God will send me some storm like that of Lorraine—
some thunderbolt which will break them."

"Trust me, you had better pray to Heaven to avert
such an occurrence. Do not give way, I advise you, to
the fancies of your overheated brain, Lorenza. I speak
to you as a friend."

There was such an expression of concentrated anger in
Balsamo's voice, such a gloomy and threatening fire darted
from his eyes, such a strange and nervous movement in
his white and muscular hand as he pronounced each word
slowly and solemnly, that Lorenza, subdued in the very
height of her rebellion, listened to him in spite of herself.

, "You see, my child," continued he, in the same calm and
threatening tone, " I have endeavored to make this prison
a habitation fit for a queen. Were you a queen, you could
here want for nothing. Calm, then, this wild excitement.
Live here as you would have lived in your convent.
Accustom yourself to my presence ; love me as a friend, as
a brother. I have heavy sorrows ; I shall confide them to
you ; I am often and deeply deceived—a smile from you
will console me. The more I see you kind, attentive,
patient, the more I shall lighten the rigor of your imprisonment. Who knows but that in a year—nay, in six months,
perhaps, you may be as free as I am, always supposing that
you no longer entertain the wish to steal your freedom ? "

"No, no !" cried Lorenza, who could not comprehend
that so terrible a resolve should be expressed in a voice so
gentle, "no ! More promises ! More falsehoods ! You
have carried me off, and by violent means. I belong to
myself and to myself alone ; restore me, therefore, to the

house of God, at least, if you will not grant me my full liberty. I have until now submitted to your tyranny, because I remembered that you once saved me from robbers ; but my gratitude is already weakened. A few days more of this insulting imprisonment, and it will expire ; and then—take care ! I may begin to suspect that you had some secret connection with those robbers ! "

"You do me the honor, then, to take me for a captain of banditti ? " said Balsamo, ironically.

" I know not what you are, but I have perceived signs, I have heard strange words."

" You have perceived signs and words ?" exclaimed Balsamo, turning pale.

" Yes, yes ; I have intercepted them, I know them, I remember them."

" But you will never tell them to any living soul ? You will shut them up in the depths of your heart ?"

" Oh, no !" exclaimed Lorenza, full of delight, in her anger, that she had found the vulnerable point of her antagonist, " I shall treasure them up religiously in my memory; I shall murmur then over to myself, and on the first opportunity shall say them aloud to others. I have already told them."

" To whom ? "

" To the princess."

" Well, Lorenza, listen ! " said Balsamo, clinching his hands till the nails entered the flesh. " If you have told them once, you shall never tell them again ; never shall the words you have spoken again cross your lips, for I shall keep every door closely shut, I shall sharpen the points on those bars, and raise the walls around this house, if need be, as high as those of Babel."

"I have already told you, Balsamo," exclaimed Lorenza, " that no prison can hold a captive forever, especially when the love of liberty is aided by hatred of the tyrant."

"Very well ; leave your prison, then ; but mark me, you have only twice to do so. The first time I shall chastise you so cruelly that your eyes will have no more tears to shed, the second time that your veins shall have no more blood to pour out."

"Great heavens! He will murder me!" screamed the young girl, in the highest paroxysm of fury, tearing her hair, and writhing on the carpet.

He looked at her for an instant with a mixture of anger and passion. At length compassion seemed to prevail.

"Come, Lorenza," said he, "be calm; some future day you will be rewarded for all you suffer now, or think you suffer."

"Imprisoned! imprisoned!" cried Lorenza, without listening to him.

"Be patient."

"Struck."

"It is a period of probation."

"Mad! mad!"

"You shall be cured."

"Oh, put me in a mad-house at once! Shut me up at once in a real prison!"

"No; you have too well prepared me for what you would do in such a case."

"Death, then!" screamed Lorenza, "instant death!" and, bounding up with the suppleness and rapidity of some wild animal, she rushed forward to dash her head against the wall.

Balsamo had only to extend his hand toward her and to pronounce, by his will, rather than his lips, one single word, to arrest her progress; Lorenza, checked in her wild career, staggered and fell into Balsamo's arms. She was asleep.

The strange enchanter, who seemed to have subdued in this woman all that belonged to her physical existence without having been able to triumph over the moral life, raised her, and carried her to her couch; then, having laid her on it, he imprinted a long kiss on her forehead, drew the curtains, and retired.

A soft and soothing sleep wrapped her in its embrace as the mantle of a kind mother wraps the froward child after it has long suffered and wept.

CHAPTER LVIII.

THE VISIT.

LORENZA was not mistaken. A carriage, after having entered Paris by the Barrière St. Denis, and traversing the faubourg of that name throughout its entire length, had turned the angle formed by the last house and the Porte St. Denis, and was rapidly advancing along the boulevard. This carriage contained M. Louis de Rohan, Bishop of Strasbourg, whose impatience led him to anticipate the time fixed upon for seeking the sorcerer in his den.

The coachman, a man of mettle and well accustomed to aid the handsome prelate in his gallant adventures amid the darkness and perils of certain mysterious streets, was by no means discouraged, when, after having passed the boulevards of St. Denis and St. Martin, still thronged with people and well lighted, he received the order to proceed along the lonely and dismal boulevard of the Bastile. The carriage stopped at the corner of the Rue St. Claude, on the boulevard itself, and, after a whispered order from its master, took up a concealed position under the trees about twenty paces off.

Then M. de Rohan, who was dressed in the ordinary costume of a civilian, glided down the street and knocked at the door of the house, which he easily recognized by the description of it given to him by the Count de Fenix.

Fritz's footsteps echoed in the courtyard, and the door was opened.

"Is it not here that the Count de Fenix resides?" asked the prince.

"Yes, monseigneur."

"Is he at home?"

"Yes, monseigneur."

"Well, say that a gentleman wishes to see him."

"His Highness the Cardinal de Rohan, is it not?" asked Fritz.

The prince stood perfectly confounded. He looked all around him, and at his dress, to see whether anything in his retinue or costume had revealed his rank ; but he was alone, and in the dress of a layman.

" How do you know my name ?" said he.

" My master has just told me this very instant that he expected your eminence."

" Yes—but to-morrow, or the day after."

" No, monseigneur—this evening."

" Your master told you that he expected me this evening ?"

" Yes, monseigneur."

" Very well ; announce me, then," said the cardinal, putting a double louis-d'or into Fritz's hand.

" In that case," said Fritz, " will your eminence have the goodness to follow me ?"

The cardinal made a gesture in the affirmative.

Fritz then advanced with a rapid step toward the ante-chamber, which was lighted by a massive bronze candelabrum containing twelve wax tapers. The cardinal followed, surprised and thoughtful.

" My friend," said he, stopping at the door of the saloon, " there must be a mistake, I think, and in that case I do not wish to intrude on the count. It is impossible that he can expect me, for he was not aware that I intended to come to-night."

" Monseigneur is the Prince Cardinal de Rohan, Bishop of Strasbourg, is he not ?" inquired Fritz.

" Yes, my friend."

" Well, then, it is monseigneur whom my master the count expects."

And lighting successively the candles of two other candelabra in the saloon, Fritz bowed and retired.

Five minutes elapsed, during which the cardinal, agitated by a strange emotion, gazed at the elegant furniture of this saloon, and at the eight pictures by the first masters which hung from the walls. The door opened, and the Count de Fenix appeared on the threshold.

" Good evening, my lord !" said he, simply.

"I am told that you expected me," exclaimed the cardinal, without replying to this salutation—"that you expected me this evening? It is impossible!"

"I beg your pardon, my lord, but I did expect you," replied the count. "Perhaps you doubt the truth of my words on seeing the poor reception I give you? But I have only lately arrived in Paris, and can scarcely call myself installed here yet; your eminence must, therefore, be good enough to excuse me."

"You expected me? But who could have told you that I was coming?"

"Yourself, my lord."

"How so?"

"Did you not stop your carriage at the Barrière St. Denis?"

"Yes."

"Did you not summon your footman to the carriage door, and give him the order, 'Rue St. Claude in the Marais, by the Faubourg St. Denis and the boulevard'— words which he repeated to the coachman?"

"Yes, certainly; but you must have seen me, and heard me."

"I did see and hear you, my lord."

"Then you were there?"

"No, my lord, I was not there."

"And where were you?"

"I was here."

"You saw me and heard me from this?"

"Yes, my lord."

"Come, come!"

"Monseigneur forgets that I am a sorcerer."

"Ah, true; I did forget that. But, monsieur, what am I to call you—the Baron Balsamo, or the Count de Fenix?"

"In my own house, my lord, I have no name; I am called THE MASTER."

"Yes, that is the hermetical title. So, then, master, you expected me?"

"I did expect you."

"And your laboratory is heated?"

"My laboratory is always heated, my lord?"

"And you will permit me to enter it?"

"I shall have the honor of conducting your eminence there."

"And I shall follow you, but only on one condition."

"What is that?"

"That you promise not to place me personally in contact with the devil. I am terribly afraid of his majesty Lucifer."

"Oh, my lord!"

"Yes, for in general you employ for such a purpose the greatest rogues unhung—discarded soldiers of the guards, or fencing-masters without pupils, who, in order to play the part of Satan naturally, treat their dupes to sundry fillips and tweaks of the nose, after first putting out the lights."

"My lord," said Balsamo, smiling, "my devils never forget that they have the honor of dealing with princes, and ever bear in mind the Prince de Condé's speech to one of them who would not keep still, viz., that if he did not conduct himself more decently, he would so rub him down with an oaken towel that he should never need washing again."

"I am delighted to hear that you manage your imps so well. Let us proceed to the laboratory, then."

"Will your eminence have the goodness to follow me?"

"Proceed."

CHAPTER LIX.

GOLD.

THE Cardinal de Rohan and Balsamo wound along a narrow staircase which ran parallel with the great staircase, and, like it, led to the apartments on the first floor. There, in a vaulted apartment, appeared a door which Balsamo opened, and a very gloomy corridor was disclosed to the cardinal's view, who entered it resolutely.

Balsamo closed the door behind them. At the noise

which this door made in closing, the cardinal looked back with a slight feeling of trepidation.

"My lord," said Balsamo, "we have now arrived. We have but one more door to open and close; but let me warn you not to be alarmed at the sound it will make, for it is of iron."

The cardinal, who had started at the sound of the first door, was glad to be thus prepared in time, for otherwise the grating noise of its hinges and lock would have jarred disagreeably on nerves even less susceptible than his.

They descended three steps and entered the laboratory.

The first aspect of this new apartment was that of a large room with the beams and joists of the ceiling left in their original state, and containing a huge lamp with a shade, several books, and a great number of chemical and other philosophical instruments.

After a few seconds the cardinal began to feel that he breathed with difficulty.

"What is the meaning of this?" said he. "I am stifling here, master; the perspiration pours from my forehead. What noise is that?"

"Behold the cause, my lord," said Balsamo, drawing back a large curtain of asbestos cloth, and disclosing to view an immense brick furnace, in the center of which two holes glared in the darkness like the gleaming eyes of a panther.

This furnace was situated in the middle of a second apartment, double the size of the first, which the prince had not perceived, hidden as it was by the asbestos curtain.

"Ah, ha!" cried the prince, retreating two or three steps, "that looks a little alarming."

"It is a furnace, my lord."

"Yes, but this furnace of yours has a very diabolical sort of a look. What are you cooking in it?"

"What your eminence asked from me."

"What I asked from you?"

"Yes. I think your eminence said you wished for a specimen of my handiwork. I had not intended beginning the operation till to-morrow evening, as you were not to visit me till the day following ; but your eminence having changed your intention, as soon as I heard you set out for my abode, I kindled the furnace and put in the ingredients for amalgamation ; so that now the furnace is boiling, and in ten minutes you will have your gold. Permit me to open this ventilator to give a current of fresh air."

" What ! those crucibles on the furnace——"

" Will in ten minutes give your highness gold as pure as that of the sequins of Venice or the florins of Tuscany."

" I should like to see it, if it is at all practicable."

" Certainly. But you must use some necessary precautions."

" What precautions ? "

" Cover your face with this mask of asbestos with glass eyes, otherwise your sight might be injured by the glowing heat."

" Peste ! I must take care of that. I attach a good deal of value to my eyes, and would not give them for the hundred thousand crowns which you have promised me."

"I thought so, for your eminence's eyes are very fine."

This compliment was by no means displeasing to the cardinal, who was not a little vain of his person.

" Ha !" said he, putting on his mask, " so it seems we are to see what gold is ? "

" I trust so, my lord."

" Gold to the value of one hundred thousand crowns ? "

" Yes, my lord ; perhaps even a little more, for I made a very abundant mixture."

" Upon my honor, you are a most generous sorcerer !" said the prince, with a joyous palpitation of the heart.

" Less so than your highness, who so kindly compliments me. In the meantime, my lord, may I beg you to keep back a little while I take off the lid of the crucible ? "

And Balsamo, having put on a short shirt of asbestos, seized with a vigorous arm a pair of iron pincers, and raised the cover, now red-hot, which revealed to view four crucibles of a similar form, some containing a mixture of vermilion color, others a whitish matter, although still retaining something of a purple, transparent hue.

"And that is gold!" said the prelate, in a half whisper, as if he feared to disturb the mystery which was being accomplished before him.

"Yes, my lord. These four crucibles contain the substance in different stages, some of them having been subject to the process twelve, others only eleven hours. The mixture—and this is a secret which I reveal only to a friend of the hermetic science—is thrown into the matter at the moment of ebullition. But, as your eminence may see, the first crucible is now a white heat ; it has reached the proper stage, and it is time to pour it out. Be good enough to keep back, my lord."

The prince obeyed with the promptitude of a soldier at the command of his captain, and Balsamo, laying aside the pincers, already heated by contact with the crucibles, rolled forward to the furnace a sort of movable anvil in which were hollowed eight cylindrical molds of equal caliber.

"What is this, my dear sorcerer ?" asked the prince.

"This, my lord, is the mold in which your ingots are to be cast."

"Ah, ha !" exclaimed the cardinal, and he redoubled his attention.

Balsamo spread over the floor a thick layer of white tow as a sort of protection against accidents ; then, placing himself between the furnace and the anvil, he opened a huge book, and wand in hand, repeated a solemn incantation. This ended, he seized an enormous pair of tongs intended for grasping the weighty crucibles.

"The gold will be splendid, my lord," said he—"of the very finest quality."

"What ! Are you going to lift off that flaming pot ?"

"Which weighs fifty pounds. Yes, my lord ; few founders, I may say it without boasting, possess my muscles and my dexterity. Fear nothing, therefore."

"But if the crucible were to break ?"

"Yes, that happened with me once, my lord—in the

year 1399. I was making an experiment with Nicholas
Flamel, in his house in the Rue des Ecrivains, near the
Church of St. Jacques la Boucherie. Poor Flamel was
nearly losing his life; and I lost twenty-seven marks of a
substance even more precious than gold."

"What the devil is that you are saying, master?"

"The truth."

"Do you mean to make me believe that you pursued
the *great work* in 1399, along with Nicholas Flamel?"

"Precisely so, my lord. We found out the secret together, about fifty or sixty years before, when experiment-
ing with Pierre le Bon in the town of Pola. He did not
shut up the crucible quickly enough, and I lost the use of
my right eye for nearly twelve years in consequence of the
evaporation."

"Pierre le Bon, who composed that famous book, the
' Margarita Pretiosa,' printed in 1330?"

"The very same, my lord."

"And you knew Pierre le Bon and Flamel?"

"I was the pupil of the one and the teacher of the
other."

And while the terrified prelate asked himself whether
the personage at his side was not the devil in person, and
not one of his satellites, Balsamo plunged his long tongs
into the furnace. The alchemist's grasp was sure and
rapid. He seized the crucible about four inches from the
top, satisfied himself, by raising it up a little, that his
hold was firm; then, by a vigorous effort, which strained
every muscle in his frame, he heaved up the terrible pot
from the glowing furnace. The handle of the tongs
turned glowing red immediately; then rippling over the
fused matter within, were seen white furrows like lightning streaking a black sulphurous cloud; then the edges
of the crucible turned a brownish red, while the conical
base appeared still rose-colored and silver beneath the
shade of the furnace; then the metal, on the surface of
which had formed a violet-colored scum, crested here and
there with gold, hissed over the mouth of the crucible,
and fell flashing into the dark mold, around the top of

which the golden wave, angry and foaming, seemed to insult the vile metal with which it was forced into contact.

"Now for the second," said Balsamo, seizing another crucible; and another mold was filled with the same strength and dexterity as the first. The perspiration poured from the operator's forehead; and the cardinal, standing back in the shade, crossed himself.

In fact, the scene was one of wild and majestic horror.

Balsamo, his features lighted by the reddish glare of the glowing metal, resembled one of the damned of Michael Angelo or Dante writhing in the depths of their flaming caldrons; while over all brooded the feeling of the mysterious and unknown.

Balsamo took no breathing time between the two operations; time pressed.

"There will be a slight loss," said he, after having filled the second mold. "I have allowed the mixture to boil the hundredth part of a minute too long."

"The hundredth part of a minute!" exclaimed the cardinal, no longer seeking to conceal his stupefaction.

"It is enormous in alchemy," replied Balsamo, quietly; "but in the meantime, your eminence, here are two crucibles emptied, and two molds filled with one hundred pounds' weight of pure gold."

And seizing the first mold with his powerful tongs, he plunged it into water, which hissed and bubbled around it for some time. Then he opened it and took out a lump of solid gold in the form of a sugar-loaf flattened at each extremity.

"We shall have some time to wait for the other crucibles," said Balsamo. "Will your eminence, in the meantime, be seated, or would you prefer to breathe for a few moments a cooler atmosphere than this?"

"And that is really gold?" asked the cardinal, without replying to the operator's question.

Balsamo smiled. The cardinal was his.

"Do you doubt it, my lord?"

"Why—you know—science is often mistaken——"

"Prince, your words do not express your whole meaning," said Balsamo. "You think that I am deceiving you, and deceiving you wittingly. My lord, I should sink very low in my own opinion could I act such a part, for my ambition, in that case, would not extend beyond the walls of my cabinet, which you would leave, filled with wonder, only to be undeceived on taking your ingots to the first goldsmith's you should meet. Come, come, my lord. Do not think so meanly of me, and be assured that, if I wished to deceive you, I should do it more adroitly, and with a higher aim. However, your eminence knows how to test gold?"

"Certainly. By the touch-stone."

"You have doubtless had occasion, my lord, to make the experiment yourself, were it only on Spanish doubloons, which are much esteemed in play because they are of the purest gold, but which, for that very reason, are frequently counterfeited."

"In fact, I have done so before now."

"Well, my lord, here are the stone and the acid."

"By no means; I am quite convinced."

"My lord, do me the favor to assure yourself that these ingots are not only gold, but gold without alloy."

The cardinal appeared unwilling to give this proof of his incredulity, and yet it was evident that he was not convinced. Balsamo himself tested the ingots, and showed the result of the experiment to his guest.

"Twenty-eight carats," said he; "and now I may pour out the two others."

Ten minutes afterward the four ingots lay side by side on the tow, heated by their contact.

"Your eminence came here in a carriage, did you not? At least when I saw you, you were in one."

"Yes."

"If your lordship will order it to the door, my servant shall put the ingots into it."

"One hundred thousand crowns!" murmured the cardinal, as he took off his mask to feast his eyes on the gold lying at his feet.

"And as for this gold, your highness can tell whence it comes, having seen it made ? "

"Oh, yes ; I shall testify——"

"Oh, no ! " said Balsamo, hastily ; "*savants* are not much in favor in France. Testify nothing, my lord. If instead of making gold I made theories, then, indeed, I should have no objection."

"Then, what can I do for you ?" said the prince, lifting an ingot of fifty pounds with difficulty in his delicate hands.

Balsamo looked at him steadily, and without the least respect began to laugh.

"What is there so very ludicrous in what I have said ? " asked the cardinal.

"Your eminence offers me your services, I think. Would it not be much more to the purpose were I to offer mine to you ?"

The cardinal's brow darkened.

"You have obliged me, sir," said he, "and I am ready to acknowledge it ; but if the gratitude I am to bear you proves a heavier burden than I imagined, I shall not accept the obligation. There are still, thank Heaven ! usurers enough in Paris from whom I can procure, half on some pledge and half on my bond, one hundred thousand crowns, the day after to-morrow. My episcopal ring alone is worth forty thousand livres." And the prelate held out his hand, as white as a woman's, on which shone a diamond the size of a small nut.

"Prince," said Balsamo, bowing, " it is impossible that you can for a moment imagine that I meant to offend you." Then, as if speaking to himself, he proceeded : " It is singular that the truth should always produce this effect on those who bear the title of prince."

"What mean you ? "

"Your highness proposes to serve me ; now I merely ask you, my lord, of what nature could those services be which your eminence proposes to render me ? "

"Why, in the first place, my credit at court."

"My lord, my lord, you know too well that that credit

is much shaken; in fact, I should almost as soon take the
Duke de Choiseul's, and yet he has not perhaps a fortnight to hold his place.   Take my word for it, prince, as
far as credit goes, depend on mine.   There is a good and
sterling gold.   Every time that your eminence is in want
of any, let me know the night before, and you shall have
as much as you like.   And with gold, my lord, cannot all
things be procured?"

"Not all," murmured the cardinal, sinking into the
grade of a protégé, and no longer even making an effort to
regain that of patron.

"Ah! true.   I forgot that your lordship desires something more than gold—something more precious than all
the riches of the earth.   But in this, science cannot assist
you; it is the province of magic.   My lord, say the word,
and the alchemist is ready to become the magician."

"Thank you, sir; but I want for nothing more—I desire
nothing further," said the cardinal, in a desponding voice.

Balsamo approached him.

"My lord," said he, "a prince, young, handsome, ardent,
rich, and bearing the name of Rohan, ought not to make
such a reply to a magician."

"Why not, sir?"

Because the magician reads his heart, and knows the
contrary."

"I wish for nothing—I desire nothing," repeated the
cardinal almost terrified.

"I should have thought, on the contrary, that your
eminence's wishes were such as you dared not avow, even to
yourself, since they are those of a—king!"

"Sir," said the cardinal, with a start, "you allude, I
presume, to a subject which you introduced before when I
saw you at St. Denis?"

"I confess it, my lord."

"Sir, you were mistaken then, and you are equally mistaken now."

"Do you forget, my lord, that I can read as plainly what is
passing at this moment in your heart as, a short time ago, I
saw your carriage enter the city, drive along the boulevard,

and stop beneath the trees about fifty paces from my house?"

" Then explain yourself ; tell me what you mean."

" My lord, the princes of your family have always aimed at a high and daring passion ; you have not degenerated from your race in that respect."

" I do not know what you mean, count," stammered the prince.

" On the contrary, you understand me perfectly. I could have touched many chords which vibrate in your heart, but why do so uselessly ? I have touched the one which is necessary, and it vibrates deeply, I am certain."

The cardinal raised his head, and with a last effort at defiance met the clear and penetrating glance of Balsamo. Balsamo smiled with such an expression of superiority that the cardinal cast down his eyes.

" Oh, you are right, my lord—you are right ; do not look at me, for then I read too plainly what passes in your heart—that heart, which, like a mirror, gives back the form of the objects reflected in it."

"Silence, Count de Fenix, silence !" said the cardinal, completely subdued.

" Yes, you are right ; it is better to be silent, for the moment has not yet come to let such a passion be seen."

" Not yet, did you say ?"

"Not yet."

"Then that love may in some future time bear fruit ?"

" Why not ?"

" And can you tell me, then, if this love be not the love of a madman, as it often seems to myself—and as it ever will seem, until I have a proof to the contrary ?"

" You ask much, my lord. I can tell you nothing without being placed in contact with the person who inspires your love ; or, at least, with something belonging to her person."

" What would be necessary ?"

" A ringlet, however small, of her beautiful golden hair, for example."

" Yes, you are a man profoundly skilled in the human heart ; you read it as I should read an open book."

" Alas ! that is just what your great granduncle, the Chevalier Louis de Rohan, said to me when I bid him farewell on the platform of the Bastilla, at the foot of the scaffold which he ascended so courageously."

" He said that to you—that you were profoundly skilled in the human heart ? "

" Yes, and that I could read it ; for I had forewarned him that the Chevalier de Preault would betray him. He would not believe me, and the Chevalier de Preault did betray him."

" But what singular analogy do you draw between my ancestor and myself ? " said the cardinal, turning pale in spite of himself.

" I did so merely to remind you of the necessity of being prudent, my lord, in obtaining a tress of hair whose curling locks are surmounted by a crown."

" No matter how obtained, you shall have the tress, sir."

" It is well.   In the meantime, here is your gold, my lord ; I hope you no longer doubt its being really gold ? "

" Give me a pen and paper."

" What for, my lord ? "

" To give you a receipt for the hundred thousand crowns which you are so good as to lend me."

" A receipt to me, my lord ?   For what purpose ? "

" I borrow often, my dear count, but I tell you before-hand, I never take gifts."

" As you please, prince."

The cardinal took a pen from the table and wrote a receipt for the money in an enormous illegible hand, and in a style of orthography which would shock a poor curate's housekeeper of the present day.

" Is that right ? "   asked he, as he handed it to Balsamo.

" Perfectly right," replied the count, putting it in his pocket without even looking at it.

" You have not read it, sir ? "

" I have your highness's word ; and the word of a Rohan is better than any pledge."

"Count de Fenix," said the cardinal, with a slight inclination, very significant from a man of his rank, "you speak like a gentleman; and if I cannot lay you under any obligation to me, I am at least fortunate in being obliged to such a man."

Balsamo bowed in his turn, and rang a bell, at the sound of which Fritz appeared.

The count spoke a few words to him in German. He stooped, and like a child carrying a handful of oranges—a little embarrassed, to be sure, but by no means oppressed with the burden—he carried off the eight ingots wrapped up in tow.

"He is a perfect Hercules, that fellow," said the cardinal.

"He is tolerably strong, indeed, my lord, but since he has been in my service, I give him every day three drops of an elixir compounded by my learned friend, Doctor Althotas. So, you see, the rogue profits by it. In a year he will be able to carry a hundred-weight with one hand."

"Wonderful! Incomprehensible!" murmured the cardinal. "I shall never be able to resist speaking of all this."

"Oh, speak of it by all means," replied Balsamo, laughing; "but remember that, by so doing, you bind yourself to come in person and extinguish the flame of the fagots, if by chance the parliament should take it in their heads to burn me alive in the Place de Grève."

And having escorted his illustrious visitor to the outer gate, Balsamo took leave of him with a respectful bow.

"But I do not see your servant," said the cardinal.

"He has gone to carry the gold to your carriage, my lord."

"Does he know where it is?"

"Under the fourth tree to the right, on the boulevard—that was what I said to him in German, my lord."

The cardinal raised his hands in astonishment, and disappeared in the darkness.

Balsamo waited for Fritz's return, and then entered the house, closing all the doors carefully behind him.

CHAPTER LX.

THE ELIXIR OF LIFE.

BALSAMO, being now alone, proceeded to listen at Lorenza's door. She was still sunk in a soft and gentle sleep. He half opened a wicket in the door, and contemplated her for some time in a sweet and tender reverie. Then, shutting the wicket, he crossed the apartment which we have described, and which separated Lorenza's apartment from the laboratory, and hastened to extinguish the fire in the furnace by throwing open an immense conduit, which allowed the heat to escape into the chimney, and at the same time gave passage to the water of a reservoir on the roof.

Then, carefully placing the cardinal's receipt in a black morocco case :

" The word of a Rohan is good," murmured he ; " but for myself alone ; and it is well that the brethren yonder should know how I employ their gold."

As these words died away on his lips three short, quick taps on the ceiling made him raise his head.

" Oh, ho ! " said he, " there is Althotas calling me."

Then while he continued his task of giving air to the laboratory and arranging everything in order, the taps were repeated louder than before.

" So ! he is getting impatient ; it is a good sign."

And Balsamo took a long iron rod and knocked on the ceiling in answer. He then proceeded to remove an iron ring fixed in the wall ; and by means of a spring which was disclosed to view, a trap-door was detached from the ceiling and descended to the floor of the laboratory. Balsamo placed himself in the center of this machine, which, by means of another spring, gently rose with its burden, with as much ease as in the opera the gods and goddesses are carried up to Elysium, and the pupil found himself in the presence of the master.

The new dwelling of the old alchemist might be about eight or nine feet high, and sixteen in diameter ; it was lighted from the top like a well, and hermetically closed on the four sides.   This apartment, as the reader may observe, was a perfect palace when compared with his habitation in the vehicle.

The old man was seated in his armchair on wheels, in the center of a marble table formed like a horse-shoe and heaped up with a whole world, or, rather, a whole chaos, of plants, vials, tools, books, instruments, and papers covered with cabalistic characters.

He was so absorbed that he never raised his head when Balsamo appeared.   The light of an astral lamp, suspended from the culminating point of the window in the roof, fell on his bald, shining head.   He was turning to and fro in his fingers a small white bottle, the transparency of which he was trying before his eye, as a good housekeeper tries the eggs which she buys at market.   Balsamo gazed on him at first in silence ; then, after a moment's pause :

"Well," said he, "have you any news ?"

"Yes, yes ; come hither.   Acharat, you see me enchanted—transported with joy !   I have found—I have found——"

"What ?"

"Pardieu ! what I sought."

"Gold ?"

"Gold, indeed !   I am surprised at you ! "

"The diamond ?"

"Gold ! diamonds ?   The man raves !   A fine discovery, forsooth, to be rejoiced at ! "

"Then what you have found is your elixir ?"

"Yes, my son, yes !   The elixir of life !   Life ?—what do I say ?—the eternity of life ! "

"Oh !" said Balsamo, in a dejected voice (for he looked on this pursuit as mere insanity), "so it is that dream which occupies you still ?"

But Althotas, without listening, continued to gaze delighted at his vial.

"At last," said he, "the combination is complete ; the

elixir of Aristæus, twenty grains ; balm of Mercury, fifteen grains ; precipitate of gold, fifteen grains ; essence of the cedar of Lebanon, twenty-five grains."

"But it seems to me that with the exception of the elixir of Aristæus, this is precisely your last combination, master."

"Yes ; but I had not then discovered one more ingredient, without which all the rest are as nothing."

"And have you discovered it now ? "

"Yes."

"Can you procure it ? "

"I should think so."

"What is it ? "

"We must add to the several ingredients already combined in this vial the three last drops of the life-blood of an infant."

"Well, but where will you procure this infant ? " said Balsamo, horror-struck.

"I trust to you for that."

"To me ?   You are mad, master ! "

"Mad ?   And why ? " asked the old man, perfectly unmoved at this charge, and licking with the utmost delight a drop of the fluid which had escaped from the cork of the vial and was trickling down the side.

"Why, for that purpose you must kill the child."

"Of course we must kill him ; and the handsomer he is, the better."

"Impossible ! " said Balsamo, shrugging his shoulders, "children are not taken in that way to be killed."

"Bah ! " cried the old man, with hideous coolness, "and what do they do with them, then ? "

"Pardieu !   They rear them."

"Oh !   Then the world is changed lately ?   It is only three years ago since we were offered as many infants as we chose for four charges of powder and half a bottle of eau-de-vie."

"Was it in Congo, master ? "

"Yes, yes, in Congo !   It is quite the same to me whether the child be black or white.   Those who were offered to us, I remember, were sweet, playful, curly-headed little things."

"Ah, yes," said Balsamo ; but, unfortunately, my dear master, we are not in Congo."

"Oh, we are not in Congo ?" said Althotas, "and where are we, then ?"

"In Paris."

"In Paris ? Well, if we were to embark from Marseilles, we could be in Congo in six weeks."

"Yes, no doubt. But I am obliged to remain in France."

"You are obliged to remain in France ? And why so, may I ask ?"

"Because I have business here."

"Business ?"

"Yes—important business."

The old man burst into a prolonged and ghastly laugh.

"Business !" said he, "business in France ! True, I forgot, you have your clubs to organize !"

"Yes, master."

"Conspiracies to set on foot ?"

"Yes, master."

"And you call that business ?" And the aged man again commenced to laugh, with an air of mockery and sarcasm. Balsamo remained silent, collecting his forces for the storm which was brewing, and which he felt approach.

"Well, and how is this business of yours getting on ?" said the old man, turning with difficulty in his chair, and fixing his large gray eyes on his pupil.

Balsamo felt his glance pierce him like a ray of light.

"How far have I advanced ?" asked he.

"Yes."

"I have thrown the first stone and the waters are troubled."

"Troubled ? And what slime have you stirred up—eh ?"

"The best—the slime of philosophy."

"Oh ! so you are setting to work with your Utopias,

your baseless visions, your fogs and mists! Fools! Ye discuss the existence or non-existence of God, instead of trying, like me, to make gods of yourselves. And who are these famous philosophers with whom you are connected? Let me hear."

" I have already gained over the greatest poet and the greatest atheist of the age. He is soon expected in France, whence he has been in a manner exiled, and he is to be made a freemason at the lodge which I have established in the old monastery of the Jesuits, in the Rue Pot-de-Fer."

" What is his name?"

" Voltaire."

" I never heard of him. Well, who else have you?"

" I am very soon to have a conference with the man who has done more to overturn established ideas than any other in this age—the man who wrote ' Le Contrat Social.'"

" What is he called?"

" Rousseau."

" I never heard of him."

" Very probably, as you read only Alphonso the Tenth, Raymond Sully, Peter of Toledo, and Albertus Magnus."

" They are the only men who really lived, because all their lives they were occupied by that great question—to be, or not to be."

" There are two methods of living, master."

" I know only one, for my part, viz., to exist. But let us return to your philosophers. You called them, I think——"

" Voltaire and Rousseau."

" Good. I shall remember those names. And you propose by means of these men——"

" To make myself master of the present, and to undermine the future."

" Then, it appears the people in this country are very stupid, since they can be led by ideas?"

" On the contrary, it is because they have too much mind that ideas have more power over them than facts. Besides, I have an auxiliary more powerful than all the philosophers on earth."

" What is that ? "

" Love of change. It is now some sixteen hundred years since monarchy was established in France, and the people are wearied of it."

"So that you think they will overthrow it."

" I am sure of it."

"And you would help them to begin the work ? "

"Aye ! With all my strength."

"Fool ! "

" How so ? "

"What will you gain by the overthrow of this monarchy ? "

"I ? Nothing. But the people will gain happiness."

" Come, as I am satisfied with what I have done to-day, I am willing to waste a little time on you. Explain, then, first, how you are to attain this happiness, and afterward what happiness is."

" How am I to attain it ? "

" Yes ; to this universal happiness of yours, or to the overthrow of the monarchy, which in your eyes seems to be the same thing."

" Well, there exists at this moment a ministry which is the last rampart of the monarchy, intelligent, industrious, courageous, and which might perhaps maintain this tottering and worn-out machine for twenty years longer—but they will assist me to overturn it."

" Who ? Your philosophers ? "

" No. The philosophers support it, on the contrary."

" What ! Your philosophers support a ministry which supports a monarchy, to which they themselves are hostile ? What fools these philosophers of yours are ! "

" It is because the prime minister is himself a philosopher."

" So I understand ; they mean to govern in the person of this minister. They are not fools, then ; they are selfish."

" I do not wish to discuss what they are," exclaimed Balsamo, who began to get impatient. " All I know is, that this ministry overturned, every one will cry havoc, and let slip the dogs of war on their successors. First, there will be against them the philosophers, then the parliament. The philosophers will blame, the parliament will blame; the ministry will persecute the philosophers and will dissolve the parliament. Then both mind and matter will combine, and organize a silent league—an opposition, obstinate, tenacious, incessant, which will attack, undermine, shake all. Instead of parliaments, judges will be appointed; these judges, nominated by the king, will move heaven and earth in defense of royalty. They will be accused, and with truth, of venality, of connivance, of injustice. The nation will arise, and then the monarchy will have against it the philosophers—that is, mind; the parliament—that is, the middle class; the people—that is, the lever which Archimedes sought, and with which he could have raised the world."

"Well, when you have raised the world, you can only let it fall back into its old place."

"Yes; but in falling back it will crush the monarchy to atoms."

"And when the monarchy is crushed to atoms—to adopt your false metaphors and inflated language—what will arise on its ruins?"

"Liberty!"

"Ah! the French will then be free?"

"They cannot fail to be so soon."

"All free?"

"All."

"There will then be in France thirty millions of free men?"

"Yes."

"And among those thirty millions of free men, has it never occurred to you that there might be one, with a little more brains than the rest, who, some fine morning, will seize on the liberty of the twenty-nine millions nine hundred and ninety-nine thousand nine hundred and ninety-nine, in order that he might have a little more liberty himself. You remember that dog we had at Medina, who ate up what was intended for all the other dogs?"

"Yes ; but you may remember also that one day the others combined together and strangled him ? "

"Because they were dogs ; in such a case men would have done nothing."

"Then you place man's intelligence below that of the dog, master ? "

"All examples prove it."

"What examples ? "

"I think you may recall among the ancients a certain Cæsar Augustus, and among the moderns a certain Oliver Cromwell, who bit rather deeply into the Roman cake and the English cake, without any great resistance having been offered by those from whom they snatched it."

"Well, and supposing that the man of whom you speak should arise, he will be mortal, he will die ; and before dying he will have done good even to those whom he may have oppressed ; for he will have changed the nature of the aristocracy. Being obliged to lean for support on something, he will choose that which is strongest—the people. Instead of an equality which degrades, he will establish an equality which elevates ; for equality has no fixed range ; it adapts itself to the level of him who makes it. Now, in elevating the people in the social scale he will have introduced a principle unknown until his time. A revolution will make the French free ; a protectorate under another Cæsar Augustus, or another Oliver Cromwell, will make them equal."

Althotas wheeled round in his armchair.

"Oh, the stupidity of man !" he cried. "Busy yourself for twenty years in educating a child—teach him all that you know—that at thirty he may come and tell you : ' Men will be equal.'"

"Certainly men will be equal—equal before the law."

"And before death, fool—before death, that law of laws, will they be equal, when one shall die at three days old and another at one hundred years ? Equal ? Men equal as long as they are subject to death ? Oh, fool ! thrice sodden fool ! "

And Althotas threw himself back in his chair to laugh

at ease, while Balsamo, grave and sad, sat with his head leaning on his hand.

The old man at length turned a look of pity on him.

"Am I," said he, "the equal of the workman who munches his coarse bread ? of the sucking babe ? of the driveling old man sunk in second childhood ?   Wretched sophist that you are !   Men can be equal only when they are immortal ; for, when immortal, they will be gods, and gods alone are on an equality with one another."

"Immortal !" murmured Balsamo.   Immortal !   'Tis a chimera."

"A chimera ?   Yes ; a chimera like steam—a chimera like the electric fluid—a chimera like everything which is sought—which is not yet discovered, but which will be discovered.   Rake up the dust of bygone worlds, lay bare one after another the superincumbent strata, each of which represents a social state now passed away, and in these human strata—in this detritus of kingdoms—in these slimy deposits of time, into which modern investigation has pierced like an iron plowshare—what do you read ?   Is it not that men have, in all ages, sought what I seek, under the various names of the highest good, human happiness, perfection ?   When did they not seek it ?   They sought it in the days of Homer, when men lived two hundred years—they sought it in the days of the patriarchs, when they lived eight centuries.   They did not find that highest good, that well-being, that perfection ; for, if they had, this decrepit world would now be fresh, youthful, roseate as the morning dawn.   Instead of that we have suffering, death, decay.   Is suffering good ?   Is death lovely ?   Is decay fair to look upon ?"

Here the old man was interrupted by his short, dry cough, and Balsamo had a moment to reply.

"You acknowledge," said he, "that no one has yet discovered that elixir of life which you seek.   I tell you that no one will ever discover it.   Submit to God."

"Fool !   No one has discovered it, therefore no one will discover it ?   By that mode of reasoning we should never have made any discoveries.   But do you think that

all discoveries are new things, inventions ?   Far from it ;
they are forgotten things found again.   Why should
things, once found, be forgotten ?   Because life is too
short for the discoverer to draw from his discovery all the
deductions which belong to it.   Twenty times has man
been on the point of grasping the elixir of life.   Do you
think that the Styx was merely a dream of Homer's ?
Do you think that Achilles, almost immortal, because vulnerable in his heel alone, was a fable ?   No ; Achilles was
the pupil of Chiron, as you are my pupil.   That word
Chiron means either best or worst.   Chiron was a sage
whom they have depicted as a Centaur, because by his
learning he had endowed man with the strength and swiftness of the horse.   Well, like me, he had almost found
the elixir of immortality !   Perhaps, like me, he wanted
only three drops of blood.   The want of those three drops
of blood rendered Achilles vulnerable in his heel ; death
found a passage—it entered.   Well, what have you to say
to that ? "

"I say," replied Balsamo, visibly shaken, "that I have
my task and you have yours ; let each fulfil his own at his
own personal risk and danger.   I will not second yours by
a crime."

"By a crime ?"

"Yes ; and by such a crime as would raise a whole
people with cries of indignation in pursuit of you—a
crime which would cause you to hang on one of those infamous gibbets from which your science has not secured
the best men any more than the worst."

Althotas struck the marble table with his dry and fleshless hands.

"Come," said he, "be not a humane idiot—the worst
race of idiots which exist in the world !   Let us just converse a little on these laws of yours—these brutal and absurd laws, written by animals of your species who shudder
at a drop of blood shed for a wise purpose, but gloat over
torrents of the vital fluid shed on scaffolds, before the
ramparts of cities, or on those plains which they call fields
of battle !   Your laws, ignorant and selfish, sacrificing the

future generation to the present, and which have taken for their motto, 'Live to-day, for to-morrow we die!' Let us speak of them, I say."

"Say what you have to say—I am listening," said Balsamo, becoming more and more gloomy.

"Have you a pencil? I wish you to make a little calculation."

"I can calculate without pen or pencil; proceed with what you have to say."

"What was this your project was? Oh, I remember. You are to overturn a ministry, dissolve the parliament, establish venal judges, cause a national bankruptcy, stir up rebellion, kindle a revolution, overturn the monarchy, raise up a protectorate, and hurl down the protector. The revolution is to bring freedom—the protectorship equality. Then, the French being free and equal, your task will be accomplished? Is not that it?"

"Yes; do you look on the thing as impossible?"

"I do not believe in impossibility. You see, I play fairly with you."

"Well, what then?"

"In the first place, France is not England, where what you wish to do has already been done—plagiarist that you are! France is not an isolated land, where ministers may be dismissed, parliaments dissolved, iniquitous judges established, bankruptcy brought about, revolt fomented, revolution kindled, the monarchy overturned, a protectorship established, and the protector then overthrown, without other nations interfering a little in these movements. France is soldered to Europe as the liver to the frame of man. It has roots in all nations; its fibers extend through every people. Try to tear up the liver of this great machine which is called the European continent, and for twenty, thirty, forty years perhaps, the whole body will quiver. But I shall take the lowest number, I shall say twenty years. Is that too much, oh, sage philosopher?"

"No, it is not too much," said Balsamo; "it is not even enough."

"However, I am satisfied with it. Twenty years of war,

of a bloody, mortal, incessant strife; let me see—I put down that at two hundred thousand dead each year. That is not too high a calculation, considering that there will be fighting at the same time in Germany, Italy, Spain, and Heaven knows where else! Two hundred thousand men a year, in twenty years make four millions. Allowing each man seventeen pounds of blood, which is nearly the natural quantity, that will make—seventeen multiplied by four—let me see—that will make sixty-eight millions of pounds of blood, shed for the attainment of your object. I, for my part, ask but three drops. Say, now, which of us is mad? which of us is the savage? which of us the cannibal? Well, you do not answer?"

"Yes, master, I do answer, that three drops of blood would be nothing were you sure of success."

"And you, who would shed sixty-eight millions of pounds, are you sure of success? Speak. If you be sure, lay your hand on your heart and say, 'Master, for these four millions of dead I guarantee the happiness of the human race!'"

"Master," said Balsamo, evading a direct reply, "in the name of Heaven, seek for some other means than this!"

"Ah, you dare not answer me!" You dare not answer me!" exclaimed Althotas, triumphantly.

"You are deceived, master, about the efficacy of the means—it is impossible."

"Aye? So you give advice, so you contradict me, so you give me the lie, do you?" said Althotas, rolling his gray eyes from beneath his white and shaggy eyebrows with an expression of concentrated anger.

"No, master—but I cannot help reflecting on the difficulties in your way—I, who am brought every day into contact with the world, in opposition to men—who have to struggle against princes, and who do not live like you, secluded in a corner, indifferent to all that passes around you, and careless whether your actions are forbidden or authorized by the laws—a pure abstraction, in short, of the savant and the scholar. I, in short, who see the difficulties, warn you of them. That is all."

"You could easily set aside all those difficulties if you chose."

"Say, rather, if I believed that you were in the right."

"You do not believe so, then?"

"No," said Balsamo.

"You are only tempting me!" cried Althotas.

"No; I merely express my doubts."

"Well, come; do you believe in death?"

"I believe in what *is*. Now, death *is*."

Althotas shrugged his shoulders.

"Death *is*," continued Balsamo; "that is one point which you will not contest."

"No, it is incontestable. It is omnipresent, invincible, too—is it not?" added the old man, with a smile which made his adept shudder.

"Oh, yes, master; omnipresent, and, above all invincible."

"And when you see a corpse, the cold sweat bedews your forehead, regret pierces your heart?"

"No, the cold sweat does not bedew my forehead, because I am familiar with every form of human misery; grief does not pierce my heart, because I attach little value to life. I only say in the presence of a corpse: Death! Death! thou art as powerful as God. Thou reignest as a sovereign, oh, Death, and none can prevail against thee!"

Althotas listened to Balsamo in silence, giving no other sign of impatience than that of turning a scalpel eagerly in his fingers; but when the pupil had ended his painful and solemn invocation, the master looked around him with a smile, and his piercing eyes, which seemed to penetrate nature's most hidden secrets, rested on a poor black dog, wdich lay trembling in a corner of the room on a little heap of straw. It was the last of three animals of the same species which Althotas had demanded for his experiments, and which Balsamo had procured for him.

"Take that dog," said Althotas, "and place it on the table."

Balsamo obeyed

The creature, which seemed to have a presentiment of its fate, and which had, no doubt, already been in the hands of the experimenter, began to tremble, struggle, and howl, as soon as it felt the contact of the marble table.

"And so," said Althotas, "you believe in life, do you not, since you believe in death."

"Certainly."

"There is a dog which appears to me quite alive. What do you think?"

"He is alive, assuredly, because he howls, struggles, is terrified."

"How ugly black dogs are! By the bye, remember the first opportunity to get me some white ones."

"I will endeavor to do so."

"Well, you say this one is alive? Bark, my little fellow, bark!" said the old man, with his frightful laugh; "we must convince my Lord Acharat that you are alive." And he touched the dog on a certain muscle, which made him bark, or, rather, howl immediately.

"Very well; now bring forward the air-pump, and put the dog under the receiver. But I forgot to ask you in which death you have the firmest belief."

"I do not know what you mean, master; death is death."

"Very just; that is my opinion also. Then, since death is death, make a vacuum, Acharat."

Balsamo turned a handle, and the air, which was inclosed with the dog in the receiver, rushed out by means of a tube with a sharp whistling sound. The little dog seemed at first restless, then looked around, sniffed the air uneasily, raised its head, breathed noisily and hurriedly, and at last sunk down—suffocated, swollen, senseless.

"Now, the dog is dead of apoplexy, is he not?" said Althotas; "a very good kind of death, as it does not cause much suffering."

"Yes."

"Is he really dead?"

"Certainly he is."

" You do not seem quite convinced Acharat."

" Yes, I assure you I am."

" Oh, you know my resources, do you not ? You suppose that I have discovered the art of insufflation, do you not—that other problem which consists in restoring life by making the vital air circulate in a body which has not been wounded, as in a bladder, which has not been pierced ? "

" No ; I suppose nothing. I simply believe that the dog is dead."

" However, for greater security, we shall kill him twice. Lift up the receiver, Acharat."

Acharat raised the glass shade. The dog did not stir ; his eyelids were closed, and his heart had ceased to beat.

" Take this scalpel, and, without wounding the larynx, divide the vertebral column."

" I do so only to satisfy you."

" And also to put an end to the poor animal in case it should not be quite dead," replied Althotas, smiling with that kind of obstinate pertinacity peculiar to the aged.

Balsamo made an incision with the keen blade, which divided the vertebral column about two inches below the brain, and laid bare a large, bloody wound. The animal, or, rather, the dead body of the animal, remained motionless.

" Ha ! by my faith, he was quite dead," said Althotas. " See, not a fiber moves, not a muscle stirs ; not one atom of his flesh recoils at this second attempt."

" I shall acknowledge all that, as often as you like," said Balsamo, impatiently.

" Then you are certain that you behold an animal, inert, cold, forever incapable of motion. Nothing can prevail against death, you say. No power can restore life, or even the semblance of life to this poor creature ? "

" No power, except that of God."

" Yes, but God turns not aside from His established laws. When God kills, as He is supreme wisdom, He has a reason for doing so ; some benefit is to result from it. An assassin, I forget his name, said that once, and it was well said. Nature has an interest in Death. Then you see before you a dog as dead as it is possible to be. Nature has taken possession of her rights over him."

Althotas fixed his piercing eye on Balsamo, who, wearied by the old man's dotage, only bowed in reply.

"Well," continued Althotas, "what would you say if this dog opened his eye and looked at you?"

"I should be very much surprised, master."

"You would be surprised? Ha! I am delighted to hear it." On uttering these words with his dreary, hollow laugh, the old man drew near the dog a machine composed of plates of metal separated by dampers of cloth : the center of this apparatus was swimming in a mixture of acidulated water, the two extremities, or poles, as they are called, projecting from the trough.

"Which eye do you wish him to open, Acharat?" asked the old man.

"The right."

He placed the two poles of the machine in juxtaposition, separated, however, from each other by a small piece of silk, and fixed them on the muscle in the neck. Instantly the dog opened the right eye and looked steadily at Balsamo, who recoiled with horror.

"Shall we now pass to the jaws?" said Althotas.

Balsamo made no reply ; he was overpowered with astonishment. Another muscle was touched ; and the eye having closed, the jaws opened, showing the sharp, white teeth, and below them the gums red and quivering apparently with life.

"This is, in truth, strange!" murmured Balsamo, unable to conceal his agitation.

"You see that death is not so powerful, after all," said Althotas, triumphing at the discomfiture of his pupil, "since a poor old man like me, who must soon be its prey, can turn it—the inexorable one—from its path." Then, with a sharp, ringing laugh, he suddenly added : "Take care, Acharat, the dog who just now seemed as if he would bite you, is going to give you chase. Take care!"

And, in fact, the dog, with its neck laid open, its gaping mouth and quivering eye, rose suddenly on its four legs, and staggered for a moment, its head hanging down hideously. Balsamo felt his hair stand on end, and he recoiled to the wall of the apartment, uncertain whether to fly or remain.

"Come, come, I do not wish to kill you with fright in trying to instruct you," said Althotas, pushing aside the dead body and the machine. "Enough of experiments like that."

Immediately the body, ceasing to be in contact with the battery, fell down, stiff and motionless as before.

"Could you have believed that of death, Acharat? Did you think it so kindly disposed?"

"It is strange, in truth—very strange!" replied Balsamo, drawing nearer.

"You see, my child, that we may arrive at what I seek, for the first step toward it is made. What is it to prolong life, when we have already succeeded in annihilating death?"

"But we must not assume that yet," objected Balsamo; "for the life which you have just restored is only fictitious."

"With time we shall discover the real life. Have you not read in the Roman poets that Cassidæus restored life to dead bodies?"

"Yes; in the works of the poets."

"Do not forget, my friend, that the Romans called poets *vates.*"

"But I have still an objection to offer."

"Let me hear it! Let me hear it!"

"If your elixir of life were made, and if you caused this dog to swallow some of it, he would live eternally?"

"Without doubt."

"But suppose he fell into the hands of an experimenter like you who cut his throat—what then?"

"Good! good!" cried the old man, joyfully, and rubbing his hands together; "this is what I expected from you."

"Well, if you expected it, reply to it."

"I ask no better."

"Will your elixir prevent a chimney from falling on a man's head, a pistol-ball from going through his heart, a horse from giving him a kick that shall destroy him?"

Althotas looked at Balsamo with the eye of a bravo who feels that he has exposed himself to his adversary's blow.

"No, no, no!" said he; "you are a real logician, my dear Acharat. No, I cannot prevent the effects of the chimney, or of the ball, or of the horse, while there are houses, fire-arms, and horses."

"However, you can bring the dead to life?"

"Why, yes—for a moment, not for an indefinite period. In order to do that, I must first discover the spot where the soul is lodged, and that may be rather tedious; but I can prevent the soul from leaving the body by a wound."

"How so?"

"By causing the wound to close up."

"Even if an artery be divided?"

"Certainly."

"Ah! I should like to see that done."

"Very well—look!" And before Balsamo could prevent him, the old man opened a vein in his left arm with a lancet. There was so little blood in his body, and it circulated so slowly, that it was some time before it issued from the wound, but at last it did flow abundantly.

"Great Heaven!" cried Balsamo.

"Well, what is the matter?" said Althotas.

"You have wounded yourself seriously."

"That is because you are so skeptical; you must see and touch before you will believe."

He then took a little vial which he had placed near him, and poured a few drops of its contents on the wound.

"Look!" said he.

At the touch of this magic fluid the blood ceased to flow, the flesh contracted, closing up the vein, and the wound became merely like the prick of a pin, too small an opening for the vital stream to issue from.

This time Balsamo gazed at the old man in amazement.

"That is another of my discoveries, Acharat. What do you think of it?"

"Oh, master, you are the most learned of men!"

"Yes; acknowledge that if I have not conquered death, I have at least dealt it a blow from which it will not readily recover. The bones of the human body are easily broken; I shall render them, my son, as hard as steel. It has blood which, when it is shed, carries life along with it. I shall prevent the blood from leaving the body. The flesh is soft and can be pierced without difficulty; I shall make it invulnerable as that of the paladins of the Middle Ages, which blunted the edge of swords and axes. But to do all that it requires an Althotas who shall live three hundred years. Well, give me, then, what I ask, and I shall live one thousand. Oh, my dear Acharat, all depends on you. Give me back my youth; give me back the vigor of my body; give me back the freshness of my ideas; and you shall see whether I fear the sword, the ball, the tottering wall, or the stupid beast which bites or kicks. In my fourth youth, Acharat, that is, before I have lived to the age of four men, I tell you I shall have renewed the face of the world—I shall have made for myself and for a regenerated race of men a new world, without falling chimneys, without swords, without musket-balls, without kicking horses; for men will then understand that it is better to live to help and love one another than to tear each other to pieces, and to destroy one another."

"It is true, master; or at least, it is possible."

"Well, bring me the child, then."

"Give me time to reflect on the matter, and reflect on it yourself."

Althotas darted on his adept a glance of sovereign scorn.

"Go," said he, "go! I shall yet convince you that I am right. And, in truth, the blood of man is not so precious an ingredient that a substitute for it may not be found. Go! I shall seek—I shall find. Go! I need you not."

Balsamo struck the trap-door with his foot, and descended into the lower apartment, mute, melancholy, and wholly subdued by the genius of this man, who compelled him to believe in impossibilities by accomplishing them before his eyes.

CHAPTER LXI.

INQUIRIES.

THIS night, so long and so fertile in events, during which we have been borne about, as in the cloud of the mythological deities, from St. Denis to Muette, from Muette to the Rue Coq Heron, from the Rue Coq Heron to the Rue Plastrière, and from thence to the Rue St. Claude, had been employed by Mme. Dubarry in efforts to bend the king's mind to her new political views. She insisted, in particular, on the danger there would be in allowing the Choiseuls to gain ground with the dauphiness.

The king replied to this, with a shrug, "That the dauphiness was a child, and the Duke de Choiseul was an elderly minister, and that consequently there was no danger, seeing that he could not amuse her, and she would not understand him." Then, enchanted with this bon mot, the king cut short all further explanations.

But if the king was enchanted, the countess was far from being so, as she thought she perceived symptoms of his majesty's throwing off her yoke.

Louis XV. was a male coquette. His greatest happiness consisted in his making his mistresses jealous, providing always that their jealousy did not assume the form of obstinate quarrels and prolonged sulkiness.

Mme. Dubarry was jealous; in the first place, from vanity, secondly, from fear. It had cost her too much pains to attain her present elevated position, and it was too far removed from her point of departure, for her to dare, like Mme. de Pompadour, to tolerate other favorites near the king. Mme. Dubarry, then, being jealous, determined to probe to the bottom this sudden change in the king's manner.

The king replied to her in these memorable words, in which there was not one particle of truth : " I am thinking very seriously about the happiness of my daughter-in-law ; I really do not know whether the dauphin will make her happy or not."

" Why not, sire ? "

" Because Louis, at Compiègne, St. Denis, and Muette, seemed to me much more occupied with any other woman than his own wife."

" In truth, sire, if your majesty had not told me this yourself, I should not have believed it ; for the dauphiness is lovely."

" She is rather thin."

" She is so young."

" Oh, as for that, look at Mademoiselle de Taverney ; she is the same age as the archduchess."

" Well, sire ? "

" Well, she is a faultless beauty."

A flash from the countess's eye warned the king of his mistake.

" And you yourself, dear countess," added he, quickly, " you yourself, at the age of sixteen, were as round as one of our friend Boucher's shepherdesses, I am sure."

This little bit of adulation smoothed matters in some degree, but the blow had taken effect. Mme. Dubarry therefore assumed the offensive.

" Ah ! " said she, bridling, " so she is very handsome, this Mademoiselle de Taverney ? "

" Handsome ! How should I know ? " replied the king.

" What ? You praise her, and yet you do not know, you say, whether she is handsome or not ? "

" I know that she is not thin, that is all."

" Then you have seen her, and looked rather narrowly at her ? "

" Ah ! my dear countess, you push me rather closely. You know that I am short-sighted ; a mass strikes me, but deuce take the details ! In looking at the dauphiness I saw bones and nothing more."

" And in looking at Mademoiselle de Taverney you saw

masses, to use your own expression ; for the dauphiness is an aristocratic beauty, Mademoiselle de Taverney a vulgar one."

" Oh, ho !" said the king, " by this mode of reckoning, Jeanne, you will never be an aristocratic beauty ! Come, you must be jesting, I think."

" Very good ; a compliment ! " thought the countess to herself. "Unfortunately this compliment only serves as the outer covering of another compliment which is not intended for me." Then aloud :

" On my honor," said she, " I shall be very glad if her royal highness the dauphiness chooses for her ladies of honor those that are a little attractive ; a court of old women is frightful."

" My fairest one, you need not tell that to me. I said the same thing to the dauphin yesterday ; but our newly fledged husband seems quite indifferent about the matter."

" And suppose for a beginning she were to take this Mademoiselle de Taverney ? "

" I think she has already chosen her," replied Louis.

" Ah ! you know that, sire ? "

" At least I fancy I heard some one say so."

" She has no fortune, I hear."

" No, but she is of an old family. The Taverneys Maison Rouge are of ancient descent, and have served the state honorably."

" Who patronizes them ? "

" I have no idea. But I think they are beggars, as you say."

" In that case it cannot be the Duke de Choiseul ; otherwise they would actually burst with pensions."

" Countess, countess, I beseech you, no politics ! "

" Do you call it politics to say that the Choiseuls are robbing you ? "

" Certainly it is," said the king, rising.

An hour afterward, the king arrived at the great Trianon, delighted at having awakened the countess's jealousy, but repeating to himself, in a half whisper, as the Duke de

Richelieu might have done at thirty, "Really, jealous women are very tiresome."

No sooner had his majesty left Mme. Dubarry, than she also rose and passed into her boudoir, where Chon awaited her, impatient to hear the news.

"Well!" said she, "your star has been in the ascendant these last few days—presented to the dauphiness the day before yesterday—invited to her table yesterday."

"A great triumph, truly."

"What! Do you speak in that tone? Are you aware that, at this moment, a hundred carriages are hastening to Luciennes, that their occupants may obtain a smile from you?"

"I am sorry to hear it."

"Why so?"

"Because they are losing their time. Neither the carriages nor their owners shall have a smile from me this morning."

"Ah! this is a cloudy morning, then, countess?"

"Yes, very cloudy! My chocolate, quick—my chocolate!"

Chon rang the bell and Zamore appeared.

"My chocolate!" said the countess.

Zamore retired, walking very slowly and with a most majestic strut.

"The wretch intends that I shall die of hunger!" cried the countess. "A hundred blows of the whip if you do not run."

"Me not run—me governor," said Zamore, majestically.

"Ah! You governor?" exclaimed the countess, seizing a little riding-whip with a silver handle which she used for keeping peace among the spaniels and monkeys. "Governor, indeed? Wait, governor, and you shall see!"

At this spectacle Zamore took to flight, slamming the doors behind him and uttering loud cries.

"Really, Jeanne, you are perfectly ferocious to-day," said Chon.

"I am at liberty to be so if I please, am I not?"

"Oh, very well; but in that case you must permit me to leave you, my dear."

"Why so?"

"I am afraid of being devoured."

Three taps were heard at the door.

"Well, who is knocking now?" said the countess, impatiently.

"Whoever he is, he will get a warm reception," muttered Chon.

"Oh! I should advise you to give me a bad reception," said Jean, throwing open the door with a majestic air.

"Well, and what would happen if you were ill-received? For, after all, the thing is possible."

"It would happen," said Jean, "that I should never come back."

"Well?"

"And that you would lose a great deal more than I should, by receiving me badly."

"Impertinent fellow!"

"Ah! I am impertinent because I do not flatter. What is the matter with her this morning, Chon, my beauty?"

"Don't speak to me about her, Jean. She is perfectly insufferable. Oh, here is the chocolate."

"Oh, well, never mind her, then. How do you do, chocolate? I am very glad to see you, my dear chocolate!" continued Jean, taking the tray from the servant, placing it on a little table in a corner, and seating himself before it.

"Come, Chon—come!" said he; "those who are too proud to speak shall not have any."

"You are quite delightful, you two!" said the countess, seeing that Chon, by a sign, gave Jean to understand that he might breakfast alone. "You pretend to be hurt, and yet you do not see that I am suffering."

"What is the matter, then?" said Chon, approaching her.

"No!" exclaimed the countess, pettishly. "Neither of them bestows a thought on what torments me."

"And what does torment you?" asked Jean, coolly cutting a slice of bread and butter.

"Do you want money?" asked Chon.

"Oh, as for money, the king shall want before I."

"I wish you'd lend me a thousand louis-d'ors, then?" said Jean; "I require them very much."

"A thousand fillips on your great red nose!"

"The king has positively decided on keeping that abominable Choiseul, then?" asked Chon.

"Great news that. You know very well that the Choiseuls are immovable."

"Then the king has fallen in love with the dauphiness?"

"Now you are coming nearer it. But look at that beast stuffing himself with chocolate! He would not move his little finger to save me from destruction. Oh, those two creatures will be the the death of me!"

Jean, without paying the least attention to the storm, which was raging behind him, cut a second slice, buttered it carefully, and poured out another cup of chocolate.

"How! The king really in love?" cried Chon, clasping her hands and turning pale.

Mme. Dubarry nodded, as much as to say, "You have hit it."

"Oh! if it be so, we are lost!" continued Chon; "and will you suffer that, Jeanne? But whom has he fancied?"

"Ask your brother there, who is purple with chocolate, and who looks as if he was just going to burst. He will tell you, for he knows, or at least he suspects."

Jean raised his head.

"Did you speak?" said he.

"Yes, most obliging brother—most useful ally!" said Jeanne. "I was asking you the name of the person whom the king has fancied."

Jean's mouth was so well filled that it was with great difficulty he sputtered out; "Mademoiselle de Taverney."

"Mademoiselle de Taverney! Oh, mercy on us!" cried Chon.

"He knows it, the wretch!" shrieked the countess, throwing herself back in her chair, and clasping her hands, "he knows it, and he eats!"

"Oh!" said Chon, visibly deserting from her brother's camp to enter that of her sister.

"I wonder," cried the countess, "what prevents me from tearing out his two great, ugly eyes! Look at them, all swollen with sleep, the lazy wretch! He has just got up, my dear, just got up!"

"You are mistaken," said Jean, "I have not been in bed at all."

"And what were you doing then, you glutton?"

"Why, faith, I have been running up and down all night, and all morning, too."

"I told you so. Oh, who is better served than I am? No one—no one—to tell me where that girl is!"

"Where she is?" asked Jean.

"Yes."

"Where should she be but in Paris?"

"In Paris? But whereabouts in Paris?"

"Rue Coq Heron."

"Who told you so?"

"The coachman who drove her; I waited for him at the stables and questioned him."

"He told you——-"

"That he had just driven the entire Taverney family to a little hotel in the Rue Coq Heron, situated in a garden adjoining the Hôtel d'Armenonville."

"Oh, Jean, Jean!" cried the countess, "this reconciles me to you, my dear. But now what we want is to know the particulars. How she lives? Whom she sees? What she does? Does she receive any letters? These are the important points."

"Well, you shall know all that."

"But how? But how?"

"Ah! Just so. Now try to find out how yourself. I have found out a great deal for my share."

"Oh," said Chon, "there might be lodgings to let in the Rue Coq Heron."

"An excellent idea!" exclaimed the countess. "You must hasten to the Rue Coq Heron, Jean, and hire a house. We will conceal some one there who can see every one that goes in or comes out. We shall know all. Quick! Order the carriage."

"It is useless—there is neither house nor lodging to be let in that street."

"How do you know?"

"Faith, in the surest way that one can know! I have inquired; but there are apartments——"

"Where—where?"

"In the Rue Plastrière."

"And where is the Rue Plastrière?"

"It is a street whose rear looks toward the garden of the hotel."

"Well! quick, quick!" said the countess, "let us hire an apartment in the Rue Plastrière."

"It is already hired," said Jean.

"Admirable man!" cried the countess. "Kiss me, Jean!"

Jean wiped his mouth, kissed Mme. Dubarry on both cheeks, and then made a ceremonious bow of thanks for the honor that had been done him.

"Was it not lucky?" said he.

"But I hope no one recognized you?"

"Who the devil should recognize me in a street like that?"

"And what have you engaged?"

"A little apartment in an obscure out-of-the-way house."

"But they must have asked for whom?"

"Certainly they did."

"And what did you say?"

"That it was for a young widow—are you a widow, Chon?"

"Of course I am," said Chon.

"Excellent!" said the countess. "Then it is Chon who shall be installed in the apartment; she will watch, she will spy—but not a moment must be lost."

"Therefore I shall set off at once," said Chon. "The carriage! the carriage!"

"The carriage!" repeated Mme. Dubarry, ringing loud enough to have awakened the whole household of the Sleeping Beauty in the wood.

Jean and the countess knew perfectly what they had to dread from Andrée's presence. She had, even on her first appearance, attracted the king's attention, therefore she was dangerous.

"This girl," said the countess, while the horses were being put to, "is not a true provincial if she have not brought some rustic lover with her from her dove-cot at Taverney; let us but discover the swain, and patch up a marriage at once. Nothing would cool the king like a marriage between country lovers."

"Oh, the devil! I am not quite so sure of that," said Jean; "I rather mistrust his most Christian majesty. But the carriage is ready."

Chon sprang into it, after having embraced her sister and pressed Jean's hand.

"But why not take Jean?" asked the countess.

"No, no; I shall go my own way," replied Jean. "Wait for me in the Rue Plastrière: I shall be your first visitor in your new domicile."

Chon drove off. Jean seated himself at his table again, and poured out a third cup of chocolate.

Chon called first at the family residence, and changed her dress, studying as much as possible to assume the costume and appearance of a tradesman's wife. Then, when she was satisfied with her labors, she threw over her aristocratic shoulders a meager black silk mantle, ordered a sedan chair to the door, and, about half an hour afterward, she and Sylvie were mounting the steep, narrow staircase leading up to the fourth story of a house in the Rue Plastrière. For in the fourth story was situated that lodging so fortunately procured by the viscount.

When she reached the landing of the second story, Chon turned, for she heard some one following her. It was the old proprietress of the house, who lived on the first floor, and who, hearing a noise, had come out to see what caused it, and was rather puzzled at beholding two women so young and pretty enter her abode. Raising her snappish countenance to the landing above her, her gaze was met by two faces whose smiling expression formed a strong contrast to her own.

"Stop, ladies, stop!" cried she; "what do you want here?"

"The lodging which my brother was to engage for us, ma'am," said Chon, assuming the serious air of a widow. "Have you not seen him, or can we have made a mistake in the house?"

"Oh, no," replied the old proprietress, "you are quite right; it is on the fourth story. Poor young creature! A widow at your age!"

"Alas! alas!" sighed Chon, raising her eyes to heaven.

"But do not grieve—you will be very pleasantly situated in the Rue Plastrière. It is a charming street; you will hear no noise, and your apartment looks into the gardens.

"That is just what I wished, ma'am."

"And besides, by means of the corridor, you can see into the street, when any procession is passing, or when the learned dogs are exhibited.

"Thank you; that will be a great relief to me," sighed Chon, and she continued to ascend.

The old proprietress followed her with her eyes until she reached the fourth story. Then Chon, after shutting the door, hurried to the window which looked on the garden.

Jean had committed no mistake; almost immediately below the window of the apartment which he had engaged was the garden pavilion which the coachman had described to him.

Soon, however, all doubts were removed; a young girl came forward to the window of the pavilion and seated herself before a little embroidery frame. It was Andrée.

CHAPTER LXII.

THE APARTMENT IN THE RUE PLASTRIERE.

CHON had not scrutinized the young girl many seconds before Viscount Jean, ascending the stairs, four at a time, like a lawyer's clerk, appeared on the threshold of the pretended widow's apartment. "Well?" said he, inquiringly.

"Is it you, Jean? In truth, you frightened me."

"Well, what do you say to it?"

"Why, that I shall be admirably situated here for seeing all that passes; unluckily, I shall not be able to hear everything."

"Ah! faith you want too much. By the by, I have another piece of news for you."

"What is it?"

"Wonderful!"

"Pooh!"

"Incomparable!"

"What a bore the man is with his exclamations!"

"The philosopher——"

"Well, what of the philosopher?"

"It is commonly said, 'The wise man is for all events prepared.' Now I am a wise man, but I was not prepared for this."

"I should like to know when you will finish. Perhaps this girl is in the way. In that case, Mademoiselle Sylvie, step into the next room."

"Oh, there is no occasion whatever. That charming girl is not in the way; quite the contrary. Remain, Sylvie, remain." And the viscount chucked the handsome waiting-maid's chin, whose brow began already to darken at the idea that something was about to be said which she was not to hear.

"Let her stay, then; but speak."

"Why, I have done nothing else since I have been here."

"And said nothing. So hold your tongue and let me watch; that will be more to the purpose."

"Don't be out of temper! As I was saying, then, I was passing the fountain——"

"Positively you never said a word about it."

"Why, there you interrupt me again."

"No."

"I was passing the fountain, then, and bargaining for some old furniture for this frightful lodging, when all at once I felt a stream of water splashing my stockings."

"How very interesting all this is!"

"Only wait; you are in too great a hurry, my dear. Well, I looked and I saw—guess what—I will give you a hundred guesses——"

"Do go on."

"I saw a young gentleman obstructing the jet of the fountain with a piece of bread, and by means of this obstacle causing the water to diverge and to spurt upon me."

"I can't tell you how much your story interests me," said Chon, shrugging her shoulders.

"Only wait. I swore lustily on feeling myself splashed; the bread-soaker turned round, and I saw——"

"Whom?"

"Who? Gilbert."

"Himself—bareheaded, his waistcoat open, stockings dangling about his heels, shoes unbuckled—in complete undress, in short."

"Gilbert! And what did he say?"

"I recognized him at once, and he recognized me. I advanced, he retreated. I stretched out my arm; he stretched his legs; and off he scampered like a greyhound, among the carriages and the water-porters."

"You lost sight of him, then?"

"Pardieu, I believe so. You surely do not suppose that I would start off and run, too?"

"True; it was impossible, I admit. And so we have lost him."

"Ah, what a pity!" ejaculated Mlle. Sylvie.

"Oh! most certainly," said Jean, "I owe him a sound thrashing; and if I had once laid hands upon him, he should have lost nothing for waiting, I promise you; but he guessed my kind intentions toward him, and made good use of his legs."

"No matter—here he is in Paris, that is the essential point; and, in Paris, if you are not on very bad terms with the lieutenant of police, you may find whatever you seek."

"We must find him."

"And when we have got him we must keep him, too."

"He must be shut up," said Mlle. Sylvie; "only, this time, a safer place must be chosen for the purpose."

"And Sylvie will carry his bread and water to that safe place—will you not, Sylvie?" said the viscount.

"It is no subject for jesting, brother," said Chon; "that lad saw the affair of the post-horses, and if he had motives for bearing us a grudge, we might have reason to fear him."

"And therefore," replied Jean, "I made up my mind, while ascending your stairs, to call on Monsieur de Sartines and inform him of my discovery. Monsieur de Sartines will reply, that a man, bareheaded, his stockings about his heels, his shoes unbuckled, soaking his bread at a fountain, must live near the spot where he has been seen in such a plight, and he will then engage to find him for us."

"What can he do here without money?"

"Go errands."

"He! A philosopher of that wild breed! I am surprised at you."

"He has perhaps found out a relation," said Sylvie, some old devotee, who gives him the crusts that are too stale for her lap-dog."

"Enough, enough, Sylvie! Put the house-linen into that old chest; and come you, brother, to our observatory."

Accordingly, the pair approached the window with the greatest caution. Andrée had quitted her embroidery, and extended her limbs carelessly upon an armchair; then stretched out her hand to a book lying on another chair within her reach, opened it, and was soon absorbed in what the spectators supposed must be a most interesting subject, for the young girl remained motionless from the moment that she commenced to read.

"Oh! the studious creature!" said Mlle. Chon; "what can she be reading there?"

"First indispensable article of furniture," replied the viscount, taking from his pocket an opera-glass which he drew out and pointed at Andrée, resting it upon the angle of the window for the purpose of steadying it. Chon watched his movements with impatience.

"Well, let us see; is the creature really handsome?" asked she.

"Admirable! She is an exquisite girl! What arms! what hands! what eyes—lips too tempting for St. Anthony—feet, oh! divine feet! and the ankle—what an ankle under that silk stocking!"

"Oh! I should advise you to fall in love with her; that would complete the affair," said Chon, peevishly.

"Well, after all, that would be no bad idea either, especially if she should grant me a little love in return; that would somewhat cheer our poor countess."

"Come, hand me that glass, and a truce to your gabble, if that is possible. Yes, in truth, the girl is handsome, and it is impossible that she should not have a lover. She is not reading—look, the book is slipping out of her hand. There, it drops—stay—I told you, Jean, she was not reading—she is lost in thought."

"Or asleep."

"With her eyes open! Lovely eyes, upon my word."

"At any rate," said Jean, "if she has a lover, we shall have a good view of him here."

"Yes, if he comes in the daytime; but if he should come at night?"

"The deuce! I did not think of that; and yet it is

the first thing that I ought to have thought of ; that proves how very simple I am."

"Yes ; simple as a lawyer."

"However, now that I am forewarned, I shall devise something."

"What an excellent glass this is !" said Chon. "I can almost read the characters in the book."

Chon had leaned forward out of the window, attracted by her curiosity ; but she pulled back her head faster than she had advanced it.

"Well, what is the matter ?" asked the viscount.

Chon grasped his arm. "Look cautiously, brother," said she ; "look, who is that person who is leaning out of yonder garret window on the left ? Take care not to be seen."

"Oh, oh !" cried Dubarry, in a low tone ; "it is my crust-soaker, God forgive me !"

"He is going to throw himself out !"

"No ; he has fast hold of the parapet."

"But what is he looking at with those piercing eyes, with that wild eagerness ?"

"He is watching somebody." The viscount struck his forehead.

"I have it !" he exclaimed.

"What ?"

"By heavens, he is watching the girl !"

"Mademoiselle de Taverney ?"

"Yes, yes ; that's the inamorato of the dove-cot. She comes to Paris—he hastens hither, too ; she takes lodgings in the Rue Coq Heron—he sneaks away from us to go and live in the Rue Plastrière. He is looking at her, and she is musing."

"Upon my word, it is true," said Chon. "Observe that look, how intently fixed, that lurid fire of his eyes. He is distractedly in love."

"Sister," said Jean. "let us not give ourselves any further trouble to watch the lady ; he will do our business."

"Yes : for his own interest."

"No; for ours. Now let me go and see that dear Sartines. Pardieu! we have a chance. But take care, Chon, not to let the philosopher see you; you know how quickly he decamps."

CHAPTER LXIII.

PLAN OF CAMPAIGN.

M. DE SARTINES had returned home at three in the morning, extremely fatigued, but at the same time highly pleased with the entertainment which he had got up on the spur of the moment for the king and Mme. Dubarry. Rekindled by the arrival of the dauphiness, the popular enthusiasm had greeted his majesty with sundry shouts of "Vive le Roi!" greatly diminished in volume since that famous illness at Metz, during which all France had been seen in the churches or on pilgrimage, to obtain the restoration to health of the young Louis XV., called at that time the well-beloved. On the other hand, Mme. Dubarry, who scarcely ever failed to be insulted in public by certain exclamations of a particular kind, had, contrary to her expectation, been graciously received by several rows of spectators judiciously placed in front; so that the pleased monarch had smiled graciously on M. de Sartines, and the lieutenant of police reckoned upon a handsome acknowledgment. In consequence, he thought that he might lie till noon, which he had not done for a very long time; and, on rising, he had taken advantage of this kind of holiday which he gave himself, to try on some dozen or two of new wigs, while listening to the reports of the night. At the sixth wig, and when about a third through the reports, the Viscount Jean Dubarry was announced.

"Good!" thought M. de Sartines, "here come my thanks. But who knows? women are so capricious. Show Monsieur le Vicomte into the drawing-room."

Jean, already fatigued with his forenoon's work, seated

himself in an armchair, and the lieutenant of police, who speedily joined him, felt convinced that there would be nothing unpleasant in this interview. Jean appeared in fact in the highest spirits. The two gentlemen shook hands.

"Well, viscount," said M. de Sartines, "what brings you so early?"

"In the first place," replied Jean, who was accustomed, above all things, to flatter the self-love of those whose good offices he needed, "in the first place, I was anxious to congratulate you on the capital arrangements of your fête yesterday."

"Ah! many thanks. Is it officially?"

"Officially, as far as regards Luciennes."

"That is all I want. Is it not there that the sun rises?"

"Aye, and retires to rest occasionally."

And Dubarry burst into a loud and rather vulgar laugh, but one which gave his physiognomy that good-natured look which it frequently required. "But," said he, "besides the compliments which I have to pay you, I have come to solicit a service also."

"Two, if they are possible."

"Not, so fast. I hope to hear you say so by and by. When a thing is lost in Paris, is there any hope of finding it again?"

"If it is either worth nothing, or worth a great deal, there is."

"What I am seeking is of no great value," said Jean, shaking his head.

"And what are you in search of?"

"I am in search of a lad about eighteen years old."

M. de Sartines extended his hand to a paper, took a pencil, and wrote:

"Eighteen years old; what is your lad's name?"

"Gilbert."

"What does he do?"

"As little as he can help, I suppose."

"Where does he come from?"

"From Lorraine."

"With whom was he?"

"In the service of the Taverneys."

"They brought him with them?"

"No, my sister Chon picked him up on the high-road, perishing with hunger; she took him into her carriage and brought him to Luciennes, and there——"

"Well, and there?"

"I am afraid the rogue has abused the hospitality he met with."

"Has he stolen anything?"

"I do not say that. But, in short, he absconded in a strange way."

"And you would now like to get him back?"

"Yes."

"Have you any idea where he can be?"

"I met him yesterday at the fountain which forms the corner of the Rue Plastrière, and have every reason to think that he lives in that street. In fact, I believe, if necessary, that I can point out the house."

"Well, but if you know the house, nothing is easier than to have him seized there. What do you wish to do with him when you have caught him? Have him shut up at Charenton—in the Bicetre?"

"Not precisely that."

"Oh! whatever you please, my dear fellow. Don't stand on ceremony."

"No, on the contrary, this lad pleased my sister, and she would have liked to keep him about her, as he is intelligent. If one could get him back for her by fair means, it would be more desirable."

"We must try. You have not made any inquiry in the Rue Plastrière to learn with whom he is?"

"Oh, no! You must understand that I did not wish to attract attention, for fear of losing the advantage I had obtained. He had already perceived me, and scampered off as if the devil was at his heels; and, if he had known that I was aware of his retreat, he would perhaps have decamped."

"Very likely. Rue Plastrière, you say. At the end, the middle, or the beginning of the street?"

"About one third down."

"Rest satisfied, I will send a clever fellow thither for you."

"Ah, my dear lieutenant, a man, let him be ever so clever, will always talk a little."

"No, our people never talk."

"The young one is cunning as a fox."

"Ah! I comprehend. Pardon me for not having seen your drift sooner. You wish me to go myself? In fact, you are right; it will be better; for there are perhaps difficulties in the way which you are not aware of."

Jean, though persuaded that the magistrate was desirous to assume a little consequence, was not disposed to diminish in the slightest degree the importance of his part. He even added: "It is precisely on account of these difficulties which you anticipate, that I am desirous to have your personal assistance."

M. de Sartines rang for his valet de chambre. "Let the horses be put to," said he.

"I have a carriage," said Jean.

"Thank you, but I would rather have my own. Mine is without arms, and holds a middle place between a hackney-coach and a chariot. It is freshly painted every month, and for that reason is scarcely to be recognized again. In the meantime, while they are putting the horses to, permit me to try how my new wigs fit me."

"Oh! by all means," said Jean.

M. de Sartines summoned his wig-maker. He was an artist of the first water, and brought his client a perfect assortment of wigs; they were all forms, of all colors, of all dimensions, and of all denominations. M. de Sartines occasionally changed his dress three or four times a day for the purpose of his exploring visits, and he was most particular with regard to the regularity of his costume. While the magistrate was trying on his twenty-fourth wig, a servant came to tell him that the carriage was ready.

"You will know the house again?" said M. de Sartines to Jean, when they were in the carriage.

"Certainly; I see it from this place."

"Have you examined the entrance?"

"That was the first thing I looked to."

"And what sort of an entry is it?"

"An alley."

"Ah! an alley: one third down the street, you say?"

"Yes, with a private door."

"With a private door? The deuce! Do you know on what floor your runaway lives?"

"In the attic. But you will see it directly; I perceive the fountain."

"At a foot-pace, coachman," said M. de Sartines.

The coachman moderated his speed; M. de Sartines drew up his glasses.

"Stop," said Jean; "it is that dingy-looking house."

"Ah, precisely," exclaimed M. de Sartines, clasping his hands; "that is just what I feared."

"What! Are you afraid of something?"

"Alas! yes."

"And what are you afraid of?"

"You are unlucky."

"Explain yourself."

"Why, that dingy house where your runaway lives is the very house of Monsieur Rousseau, of Geneva."

"Rousseau, the author?"

"Yes."

"Well, and how does that concern you?"

"How does that concern me? Ah! it is plain enough that you are not lieutenant of police, and that you have nothing to do with philosophers?"

"Pooh! pooh! Gilbert at Monsieur Rousseau's—what an improbable story!"

"Have you not said that your youth is a philosopher?"

"Yes."

"Well, 'birds of a feather,' you know."

"And supposing that he should be at Monsieur Rousseau's?"

" Yes, let us suppose that ? "

" What would be the consequence ? "

" That you would not have him. "

" Pardieu ! Why not ? "

" Because Monsieur Rousseau is a man who is much to be dreaded. "

" Why not shut him up in the Bastile, then ? "

" I proposed it the other day to the king, but he dared not. "

" What ! Dared not ? "

" No, no ; he wanted to leave the responsibility of his arrest to me ; and by my faith, I was not bolder than the king. "

" Indeed ! "

" It is as I tell you. We have to look twice, I assure you, before we bring all those philosophers about our ears. Peste ! Take a person away from Monsieur Rousseau. No, my dear friend, it will not do. "

" In truth, my dear magistrate, you appear to be excessively timorous. Is not the king the king ? Are you not his lieutenant of police ? "

" And, in truth, you citizens are charming fellows. When you have said, ' Is not the king the king ? ' you fancy you have said all that is necessary. Well, listen to me, my dear viscount. I would rather arrest you at Madame Dubarry's than remove your Monsieur Gilbert from Monsieur Rousseau's. "

" Really ! Many thanks for the preference. "

" Yes, upon my honor—there would be less outcry. You have no idea what delicate skins those literary men have ; they cry out at the slightest scratch, as if you were breaking them upon the wheel. "

" But let us not conjure up phantoms ; look you, is it quite certain that Monsieur Rousseau has harbored our fugitive ? This house has four floors. Does it belong to him, and does he alone live in it ? "

" Monsieur Rousseau is not worth a denier, and consequently, has no house in Paris ; there are probably from fifteen to twenty other inmates beside himself in yonder

barrack. But take this for a rule of conduct; whenever
ill luck appears at all probable, reckon upon it; whenever
good luck, never reckon upon that. There are always
ninety-nine chances for the ill and one for the good. But,
however, wait a moment. As I suspected what would happen, I have brought my notes with me."

"What notes ?"

"My notes respecting Monsieur Rousseau. Do you
suppose that he can take a step without our knowing
whither he is gone ?"

"Ha ! indeed ! Then he is really dangerous ?"

"No; but he makes us uneasy. Such a madman may
at any time break an arm or a leg, and people would say it
was we who had broken it."

"A good thing if he would break his neck some day."

"God forbid ! "

"Permit me to tell you that this is quite incomprehensible to me."

"The people stone this honest Genevese from time to
time, but they allow no one else to do so; and if the
smallest pebbles were flung at him by us, they would stone
us in return."

"Excuse me, but in truth, I know not what to make of
all these doings."

"And so we must use the most minute precautions.
Now let us verify the only chance which is left, viz., that
he does not lodge with Monsieur Rousseau. Keep yourself
out of sight, at the back of the carriage."

Jean obeyed, and M. de Sartines ordered the coachman
to walk the horses a few paces to and fro in the street.

He then opened his portfolio, and took some papers out
of it. "Let me see," said he, "if your youth is with
Monsieur Rousseau. Since what day do you suppose him
to have been there ?"

"Ever since the sixteenth."

"17th.—Monsieur Rousseau was seen herborizing at six
o'clock in the morning in the wood at Meudon ; he was
alone."

"He was alone ! "

"Let us proceed. 'At two o'clock in the afternoon he was herborizing again, but with a young man.'"

"Ah! ha!" cried Jean.

"With a young man," repeated M. de Sartines, "do you understand?"

"That's he, *mordieu!*—that's he!"

"'The young man is mean-looking——'"

"That is he!"

"'The two individuals pick up plants, and dry them in a tin box.'"

"The devil! the devil!" exclaimed Dubarry.

"That is not all. Listen further: 'In the evening, he took the young man home, at midnight the young man had not left the house.'"

"Well?"

"'18th.—The young man has not left the house, and appears to be installed at Monsieur Rousseau's.'"

"I have still a gleam of hope."

"You are decidedly an optimist! No matter, tell me your hope."

"It is that he has some relation in the house."

"Come! we must satisfy you, or rather utterly destroy your hopes. Halt, coachman."

M. de Sartines alighted. He had not taken ten steps before he met a man in gray clothes, and of very equivocal aspect. This man, on perceiving the illustrious magistrate, took off his hat and replaced it, without appearing to attach further importance to his salutation, although respect and attachment had been expressed in his look. M. de Sartines made a sign, the man approached, received some whispered instructions, and disappeared in Rousseau's alley. The lieutenant of police returned to his carriage. Five minutes after, the man in gray made his appearance again, and approached the door.

"I shall turn my head to the right," said Dubarry, "that I may not be seen."

M. de Sartines smiled, received the communication of his agent, and dismissed him.

"Well?" inquired Dubarry.

" Well ! the chance was against you, as I apprehend ;
it is with Rousseau that your Gilbert lodges. You must
give him up, depend upon it."

" Give him up ? "

" Yes. You would not, for a whim, raise all the philosophers in Paris against us, would you ? "

" Oh, heavens ! and what will my sister Jeanne say ? "

" Is she so much attached to Gilbert ? " asked M. de
Sartines.

" Indeed she is."

" Well, in that case, you must resort to gentle means,
coax Monsieur Rousseau, and instead of letting Gilbert be
taken from him by force, he will give him up voluntarily."

" As well set us to tame a bear."

" It is, perhaps, not so difficult a task as you imagine.
Do not despair ; he is fond of pretty faces ; that of the
countess is very handsome, and Mademoiselle Chon's is not
unpleasing. Let me see—the countess will make a sacrifice for her whim ? "

" She will make a hundred."

" Would she consent to fall in love with Rousseau ? "

" If it is absolutely necessary."

" It will perhaps be useful ; but to bring the parties together, we shall need a third person. Are you acquainted
with any one who knows Rousseau ? "

" Monsieur de Conti."

" Won't do ; he distrusts princes. We want a nobody,
a scholar, a poet."

" We never see people of that sort."

" Have I not met Monsieur de Jussieu at the countess's ? "

" The botanist ? "

" Yes."

" I'faith, I believe so ; he comes to Trianon, and the
countess lets him ravage her flower-beds."

" That is your affair ; and Jussieu is a friend of mine,
too."

" Then the thing is done."

" Almost."

"I shall get back my Gilbert, then ?"

M. de Sartines mused for a moment.   "I begin to think you will," said he, "and without violence, without noise. Rousseau will deliver him up to you, bound hand and foot."

"Do you think so ?"

"I am sure of it."

"And what must be done to bring this about ?"

"The merest trifle.   You have, no doubt, a piece of vacant ground toward Meudon or Marly ?"

"Oh ! no want of that.   I know ten such between Luciennes and Bougival."

"Well, get built upon it—what shall I call the thing ? a philosopher's trap."

"Excuse me, what was it you said ?"

"I said, a philosopher's trap."

"Pardieu ! and how is that built ?"

"I will give you a plan of it, rest satisfied.   And now, let us be off ; we begin to be noticed.   To the hotel, coachman."

CHAPTER LXIV.

THE TWO FETES.

THE important events of history are, to the novelist, what gigantic mountains are to the traveler.   He surveys them, he skirts their foot, he salutes them as he passes, but he does not climb them.   In like manner, we shall survey, skirt, and salute that august ceremony, the marriage of the dauphiness at Versailles.   The ceremonial of France is the only chronicle that ought to be consulted in such a case.   It is not, in fact, in the splendor of the Versailles of Louis XV., in the description of the court-dresses, the liveries, the pontifical ornaments, that our particular history, that modest follower who takes a by-path leading along the high-road of the history of France, would find anything to pick up.   Let us leave the ceremony to be performed amid the brilliant sunshine of a fine day in May; let us leave the illustrious spectators to retire in silence, and to describe or comment on the marvels of the exhibition which they had just witnessed ; and let us return to our peculiar events and personages, which also have, historically speaking, a certain value.

The king, weary of the ceremonies, and especially of the dinner, which had been long, and was an exact imitation of that given on the marriage of the great dauphin, son of Louis XIV.—the king retired to his apartments at nine o'clock and dismissed everybody. The dauphin and his bride had also retired to their apartments ; and the immense crowd of spectators of the ceremony thronged the courtyard and the terraces of Versailles, now one blaze of light, and waited anxiously for the fire-works, which were exhibited on a scale of unusual magnificence.

The evening, at first lovely and serene, by degrees became overcast, and gusts of wind, gradually increasing in violence, tossed the branches wildly to and fro, as if they had been shaken by some giant arm ; while immense masses of clouds hurried across the heavens, like squadrons rushing to the charge. The illuminations were suddenly extinguished, and, as if fate had determined to change the general rejoicings into gloom, no sooner had the first rockets been discharged, than the rain descended in torrents, as if the heavens had opened, and a loud and startling peal of thunder announced a terrible convulsion of the elements.

Meanwhile, the people of Versailles and Paris fled like a flock of frightened birds, scattered over the gardens, in the roads, in the woods, pursued in all directions by thick hail, which beat down the flowers in the gardens, the foliage in the forest, the wheat and the barley in the fields. By morning, however, all this chaos was reduced to order, and the first rays of light, darting from between copper-colored clouds, displayed to view the ravages of the nocturnal hurricane.

Versailles was no longer to be recognized. The ground had imbibed that deluge of water, the trees had absorbed that deluge of fire ; everywhere were seas of muddy water, and trees broken, twisted, calcined by that serpent, with burning gripe, called lightning. As soon as it was light, Louis XV., whose terror was so great that he could not sleep, ordered Lebel, who had never left him during the night, to dress him. He then proceeded to the bridal-chamber, and, pushing open the door, shuddered on perceiving the future queen of France reclining on a prie-dieu, pale, and with eyes swollen and violet-colored, like those of the sublime Magdalen of Rubens. Her terror, caused by the hurricane, had at length been suspended by sleep, and the first dawn of morning which stole into the apartment, tinged with religious respect her long white robe with an azure hue. At the further end of the chamber, in an armchair, pushed back to the wall, and surrounded by a pool of water which had forced its way through the shattered windows, reposed the dauphin of France, pale as his young bride, and, like her, having the perspiration of nightmare on his brow. The nuptial bed was in precisely the same state as on the preceding evening.

Louis XV. knit his brow ; a pain, keener than any he had yet felt, darted through that brow like a red-hot iron. He shook his head, heaved a deep sigh, and returned to his apartments, more gloomy and more affrighted, perhaps, at that moment, than he had been during the night.

*   *   *   *   *   *

On the thirtieth of May, that is, on the second day after that tremendous night, that night fraught with presages and warnings, Paris celebrated in its turn the marriage festival of its future sovereign. The whole population poured, in consequence, toward the Place Louis XV., where were to be exhibited the fire-works, that necessary accompaniment to every great public solemnity, which the Parisian accepts scoffingly, but which he cannot dispense with. The spot was judiciously chosen. Six hundred thousand spectators could move about there at their ease. Around the equestrian statue of Louis XV. had been erected a circular scaffolding, which, by raising the fire-works ten or twelve feet above the ground, enabled all the spectators in the place to see them distinctly. The Parisians arrived, according to custom, in groups, and spent some time in choosing the best places, an inalienable privilege of the first comers. Boys found trees, grave men posts, women the railing of fences and temporary stands, erected in the open air, as usual at all Parisian festivities, by gypsy speculators, whose fertile imagination allows them to change their mode of speculation every day. About seven o'clock, along with the earliest of the spectators, arrived several parties of police.

The duty of watching over the safety of Paris was not performed by the French guards, to whom the city authorities would not grant the gratuity of a thousand crowns demanded by their colonel, the Marshal Duke de Biron.

That regiment was both feared and liked by the population by whom each member of the corps was regarded at once as a Cæsar and a Mandarin. The French Guards, terrible on the field of battle, inexorable in the fulfilment of their functions, had, in time of peace and out of service, a frightful character for brutality and misconduct. On duty they were handsome, brave, intractable; and their evolutions delighted the woman and awed husbands; but when dispersed among the crowds as mere individuals, they became the terror of those whose admiration they had won the day before, and severely persecuted the people whom they would have to protect on the morrow. Now, the city, finding in its old grudge against these night-brawlers and sharpers a reason for not giving a thousand crowns to the French Guards—the city, we say, sent merely its civil force, upon the specious pretext that in a family festivity, like that in preparation, the usual guardians of the family ought to be sufficient. The French Guards, on leave, therefore, mingled among the groups mentioned above, and, as licentious as they would under other circumstances have been severe, they produced among the crowd, in their quality of soldier citizen, all those little irregularities which they would have repressed with the butts of their muskets, with kicks, and cuffs, nay, even with taking the offenders into custody, if their commander, their Cæsar Biron, had a right to call them on that evening, soldiers.

The shrieks of the women, the grumbling of the citizens, the complaints of the hucksters, whose cakes and gingerbread were eaten without being paid for, raised a sham tumult preparatory to the real commotion, which could not fail to take place when six hundred thousand sight-loving persons should be assembled on that spot and constituted so animated a scene, that the Place Louis XV., about eight o'clock in the evening, presented much the appearance of one of Tenier's pictures on a large scale, and with French instead of Dutch merry-makers. After the gamins, or street boys of Paris, at once the most impatient and the idlest in the known world, had taken or clambered up to their places, after the citizens and populace had settled themselves in theirs, the carriages of the nobility and the financiers arrived. No route had been marked out for them; and they therefore entered the place at random by the Rue de la Madeleine and the Rue St. Honore, setting down at the new buildings, as they were called, those who had received invitations for the windows and balconies of the governor's house, from which an excellent view could be obtained of the fire-works.

Such of the persons in carriages as had not invitations left their equipages at the corner of the place, and preceded by their footmen, mingled in the crowd, already very dense, but in which there was still room for any one who knew how to conquer it. It was curious to observe with what sagacity those lovers of sights availed themselves in their ambitious progress, of every inequality of ground. The very wide, but as yet unfinished street, which was to be called the Rue Royale, was intersected here and there by deep ditches, on the margins of which had been heaped the mold thrown out of them, and other rubbish. Each of these little eminences had its group, looking like a loftier billow rising above the level of that human ocean.

From time to time, this wave, propelled by other waves

behind it, toppled over, amid the laughter of the multitude, not yet so crowded as to cause such falls to be attended with danger, or to prevent those who fell from
scrambling to their feet again.

About half-past eight, all eyes, hitherto wandering in
different directions, began to converge toward the same
point, and to fix themselves on the scaffolding which contained the fire-works. It was then that elbows, plied
without ceasing, commenced to maintain in good earnest
the position they had gained, against the assaults of incessantly reinforced invaders.

These fire-works, designed by Ruggieri, were intended
to rival (a rivalship, by the way, which the storm two
evenings before had rendered easy) those executed at Versailles by Torre, the engineer. It was known in Paris
that Versailles had derived little pleasure from the royal
liberality, which had granted fifty thousand livres for
their exhibition, since the very first discharges had been
extinguished by the rain, and, as the weather was fine on
the evening of the thirtieth of May, the Parisians reckoned upon a certain triumph over their neighbors at Versailles.

Besides, Paris expected much more from the old established popularity of Ruggieri, than from the recent reputation of Torre.

Moreover, the plan of Ruggieri, less capricious and less
vague than that of his colleague, bespoke pyrotechnical
intentions of a highly distinguished order. Allegory,
which reigned supreme at that period, was coupled with
the most graceful architectural style, and the scaffolding
represented the ancient temple of Hymen, which, with
the French, rivals in every springing youth the temple of
Glory. It was supported by a gigantic colonnade, and
surrounded by a parapet, at the angles of which dolphins,
open-mouthed, only awaited the signal to spout forth
torrents of flame. Facing the dolphins rose, majestically,
leaning upon their urns, the Loire, the Rhone, the Seine,
and the Rhine—that river which we persist in naturaliz-
ing and accounting French in spite of all the world, and,

if we may believe the modern lays of our friends the Germans, in spite even of itself—all four—we mean the rivers, ready to pour forth, instead of water, blue, white, green, and rose-colored flames, at the moment when the colonnade should be fired.

Other parts of the works, which were to be discharged at the same time, were to form gigantic vases of flowers on the terraces of the temple of Hymen.

Lastly, still upón this same palace, destined to support so many different things, rose a luminous pyramid, terminated by the terrestrial globe. This globe, after emitting a rumbling noise like distant thunder, was to burst with a crash and to discharge a mass of colored girandoles.

As for the bouquet—so important and indeed indispensable an accompaniment that no Parisian ever judges of fire-works but by the bouquet—Ruggieri had separated it from the main body of the structure. It was placed toward the river, close to the statue, in a bastion crammed with spare rockets, so that the effect would be greatly improved by this additional elevation of six or eight yards, which would place the foot of the sheaf, as it were, upon a pedestal.

Such were the details which had engrossed the attention of all Paris for a fortnight previous. The Parisians now watched with great admiration Ruggieri and his assistants passing like shades amid the lurid lights of their scaffolding, and pausing, with strange gestures, to fix their matches and to secure their priming.

The moment, therefore, that the lanterns were brought upon the terrace of the building—an appearance which indicated the approach of the discharge—it produced a strong sensation in the crowd, and some rows of the most courageous recoiled, producing a long oscillation which extended to the very extremities of the assembled multitude.

Carriages now continued to arrive in quick succession, and began to encroach more and more upon the place; the horses resting their heads upon the shoulders of the rearmost spectators, who began to feel uneasy at the close vicinity of these dangerous neighbors. Presently the crowd, every moment increasing, collected behind the carriages, so that it was not possible for them to withdraw from their position, even had they been desirous to do so, imbedded as they were in this compact and tumultuous throng. Then might be seen—inspired by that audacity peculiar to the Parisians when in an encroaching mood, and which has no parallel except the long-suffering of the same people when encroached upon—French Guards, artisans, and lackeys, climbing upon the roofs of these carriages, like shipwrecked mariners upon a rocky shore.

The illumination of the boulevards threw from a distance its ruddy glare upon the heads of the thousands of spectators, amid whom the bayonet of a city official, flashing like lightning, appeared as rare as the ears of corn left standing in a field leveled by the reaper.

On either side of the new buildings, now the Hotel Crillon and the Garde Meuble of the Crown, the carriages of the invited guests—between which no precaution had been taken to leave a passage—had formed a triple rank, which extended on one side from the boulevard to the Tuileries, and on the other from the boulevard to the Rue des Champs-Elysées, turning like a serpent thrice doubled upon itself.

Along this triple row of carriages were seen, wandering like specters on the banks of the Styx, such of the invited as were prevented by the carriages of those earlier on the ground from reaching the principal entrance. Stunned by the noise, and unwilling, especially the ladies, who were dressed in satin from head to foot, to step upon the pavement, they were hustled to and fro by the waves of the populace, who jeered them for their delicacy, and, seeking a passage between the wheels of the carriages and the feet of the horses, crept onward as well as they could to the place of their destination—a goal as fervently desired as a haven of refuge by mariners in a storm.

One of these carriages arrived about nine o'clock, that is to say, a very few minutes before the time fixed for the commencement of the fire-works, in expectation of making its way toward the governor's door ; but the attempt, so warmly disputed for some time back, had at this moment become extremely hazardous, if not impracticable. A fourth row of carriages had begun to form, reinforcing the first three, and the mettled horses, tormented by the crowd, had become furious, lashing out right and left upon the slightest provocation, and already causing several accidents unnoticed amid the noise and bustle of the crowd.

Holding by the springs of this carriage, which was attempting to force its way through the concourse, walked a youth, pushing aside all comers who endeavored to avail themselves of this means of locomotion which he seemed to have confiscated for his exclusive use. When the carriage stopped, the youth stepped aside, but without losing his hold of the protecting spring which he continued to grasp with one hand. He could thus overhear, through the open door, the animated conversation of the party in the vehicle.

A female head, attired in white and adorned with a few natural flowers, leaned forward out of the carriage door. Immediately a voice exclaimed :

" Come, Andrée, provincial that you are, you must not lean out in that manner, or, mordieu ! you run a great risk of being kissed by the first bumpkin that passes. Don't you see that our carriage is swimming, as it were, in the middle of this mob, just as if it were in the middle of the river. We are in the water, my dear, and dirty water it is ; let us not soil ourselves by the contact."

The young lady's head was drawn back into the carriage.

" We cannot see anything from this, sir," said she ; " if our horses were to make a half turn, we could see from the door of the carriage, and be almost as well off as if we were at the governor's window."

" Turn about a little, coachman," cried the baron.

" It is impossible, Monsieur le Baron ; I should be obliged to crush ten persons."

"Well, pardieu ! crush away."

"Oh, sir !" exclaimed Andrée.

"Oh, father !" cried Philip.

"Who is that baron that talks of crushing poor folk ? "
cried several threatening voices.

"Parbleu ! it is I," said Taverney, leaning out, and
exhibiting as he did so a broad red ribbon crossed over his
breast.

At that time people still paid some respect to broad
ribbons—even to red ones. There was some grumbling,
but on a descending scale.

"Wait, father, I will alight," said Philip, " and see if
there is any possibility of advancing."

"Take care, brother, or you will be killed. Hark to
the neighing of the horses, which are fighting with one
another."

"Say rather, the roaring," resumed the baron.   " Stay !
we will alight. Tell them to make way, Philip, and let
us pass."

"Ah, father !" said Philip, "you are quite a stranger
to the Paris of the present day. Such lordly airs might
have passed current formerly, but nowadays they are but
little heeded ; and you have no wish to compromise your
dignity, I am sure."

"Still, when these saucy fellows know who I am——'

"My dear father," said Philip, smiling, " were you the
dauphin himself they would not stir an inch for you.   At
this moment, particularly, I should fear the consequences
of such a step, for I see the fire-works are about to commence."

"Then we shall see nothing !" said Andrée, with vexation.

"It is your own fault, pardieu !" replied the baron ;
" you were upward of two hours at your toilet."

"Brother," said Andrée, " could I not take your arm
and place myself among the crowd ? "

"Yes, yes, my sweet lady," exclaimed several voices,
touched with her beauty ; " yes, come along ; you are not
very large, and we'll make room for you."

"Should you like to come, Andrée?" asked Philip.

"Oh, yes!" said Andrée; and she sprung lightly from the carriage without touching the steps.

"Very well," said the baron; "but I who care not a straw about fire-works, will stay where I am."

"Yes, remain here," said Philip; "we will not go far, my dear father."

In fact, the mob, ever respectful when not irritated by any passion, ever paying homage to that sovereign goddess called beauty, opened to make way for Andrée and her brother; and a good-natured citizen, who, with his family, occupied a stone bench, desired his wife and daughter to make room for Andrée between them. Philip placed himself at his sister's feet, who leaned with one hand upon his shoulder. Gilbert had followed them, and was stationed about four paces off, with his eyes riveted upon Andrée.

"Are you comfortably placed, Andrée?" asked Philip.

"Excellently," replied the young girl.

"See what it is to be handsome," said the viscount, smiling.

"Yes, yes, handsome—very handsome!" murmured Gilbert.

Andrée heard these words; but as they proceeded doubtless from the lips of one of the populace. she cared no more about them than an Indian god cares for the offering which a poor pariah lays at his feet.

CHAPTER LXV.

THE FIRE-WORKS.

ANDRÉE and her brother had scarcely settled themselves in their new position when the first rockets pierced the clouds. and a prodigious shout arose from the crowd, thenceforward alive only to the spectacle which was exhibiting in the center of the place.

The commencement of the fire-works was magnificent,

and in every respect worthy of the high reputation of Ruggieri. The decorations of the temple were progressively lighted up, and soon presented one sheet of flame. The air rang with plaudits; but these plaudits were soon succeeded by frantic cheers, when the gaping mouths of the dolphins and the urns of the rivers began to spout forth streams of fire of different colors, which crossed and intermingled with each other.

Andrée, transported with astonishment at this sight, which has not its equal in the world—that of a population of seven hundred thousand souls, frantic with delight in front of a palace in flames—did not even attempt to conceal her feelings.

At three paces from her, hidden by the Herculean shoulders of a porter who held his child aloft over his head, stood Gilbert gazing at Andrée for her own sake, and at the fire-works because she was looking at them. Gilbert's view of Andrée was in profile; every rocket lighted up that lovely face, and made him tremble with delight. It seemed to him that the whole crowd shared in his admiration of the heavenly creature whom he adored. Andrée had never before seen Paris, or a crowd, or the splendors of a public rejoicing; and her mind was stunned by the multiplicity of novel sensations which beset it at once.

On a sudden a bright light burst forth and darted in a diagonal line toward the river. It was a bomb, which exploded with a crash, scattering the various colored fires which Andrée admired.

"Look, Philip, how beautiful that is!" said she.

"Good heavens!" exclaimed her brother, without making her any reply, "how ill that last rocket was directed! It must certainly have deviated from its course; for, instead of describing a parabola, it went off almost horizontally."

Philip had scarcely finished this expression of an uneasiness which began to be manifested in the agitation of the crowd, when a hurricane of flames burst from the bastion upon which were the bouquet and the spare fire-works. A crash equal to that of a hundred peals of thunder, crossing in all directions, bellowed through the place; and, as if the fire had contained a discharge of grapeshot, it put to rout the nearest spectators, who for a moment felt the unexpected flame scorch their faces.

"The bouquet already! the bouquet already!" cried the more distant of the crowd. "Not yet! it is too early!"

"Already?" repeated Andrée. "Ah, yes; it is too early!"

"No," said Philip; "no, it is not the bouquet, it is an accident, which in a moment will agitate this prodigious crowd, now so calm, like the ocean in a storm. Come, Andrée, let us return to our carriage—come along!"

' Oh! let me stay a little longer, Philip, it is so beautiful!"

"Andrée, we have not a moment to lose; follow me. It is the misfortune which I feared. Some stray rocket has set fire to the bastion. Hark! they are crushing one another yonder. Don't you hear their cries? Those are not cries of joy, but shrieks of distress. Quick! quick! to the carriage! Gentlemen, gentlemen, allow us to pass!"

And Philip, throwing his arm round his sister's waist, drew her toward the place where he had left his father. who, uneasy on his side, and dreading, from the noise which he heard, a danger of the nature of which he could form no conception, although he was thoroughly convinced of its existence, put his head out of the carriage door, and looked about for his children. It was already too late, and the prediction of Philip was verified. The bouquet, composed of fifteen thousand fuses, exploded, scattering about in all directions, and pursuing the spectators like those fiery darts which are flung at the bulls in the arena to provoke them to fight.

The people, at first astonished, then terrified, recoiled from the force of mere instinct with resistless impetus, communicating the same movement to the myriad of spectators in the rear, who, breathless and suffocated, pressed backward in their turn on those behind them. The scaffolding took fire ; children shrieked ; squalling women, almost stifled, raised them in their arms ; and the police, thinking to silence the screamers and to restore order by violence, struck right and left at random.   All these combined causes made the waving sea of people which Philip spoke of fall like a water-spout on that corner of the place where he was ; and instead of rejoining the baron's carriage, as he calculated upon doing, the youth was carried away by the mighty and irresistible current, of which no description could convey any idea ; for individual strength, increased tenfold by terror and anxiety, was again augmented a hundred-fold by the junction of the general strength.

At the moment when Philip drew Andrée away, Gilbert had resigned himself to the stream which carried them along ; but he had not gone above twenty paces, before a band of fugitives, turning to the left in the Rue de la Madeleine, surrounded Gilbert and swept him away, foaming with rage on finding himself separated from Andrée.

Andrée, clinging fast to Philip's arm, was inclosed in a group which was striving to get out of the way of a carriage dragged along by a pair of furious horses.   Philip saw it approaching swiftly and threateningly, the horses' eyes flashed fire, and they snorted foam from their nostrils. He made superhuman efforts to avoid it, but all in vain. He saw the crowd open behind him : he perceived the foaming heads of the two ungovernable animals ; he saw them rear, like the two marble horses which guard the entrance to the Tuilleries, and, like the slave who is striving to subdue them, letting go Andrée's arm, and pushing her as far as he could out of the way of danger, he sprung up to seize the rein of the horse that was next to him.   The animal reared a second time ; Andrée saw her brother sink back, fall, and disappear from her sight.   She shrieked, extended her arms, was hustled to and fro in the crowd, and in a moment found herself alone, tottering, borne along like a feather by the wind, and just as incapable of resisting the force that was hurrying her away.

The stunning cries, far more terrible than those of the battle-field ; the neighing of horse ; the frightful noise of wheels, grinding now the pavement, now the bodies of the slain ; the lurid flames of the scaffolds which were on fire ; the sinister gleaming of swords drawn by some of the infuriated soldiers ; and over all this insanguined chaos, the bronze statue, tinged by the ruddy reflections, and seeming to preside over the carnage—were more than was needed to disturb Andrée's reason and paralyze her strength. Besides, the power of a Titan would have been impotent in such a struggle—a struggle for life and limb— of one against all. Andrée uttered a piercing shriek ; a soldier, opening himself a passage through the crowd, was striking the people with his sword, and the weapon flashed over her head. She clasped her hands, like a shipwrecked mariner when the last wave is passing over him, and ex- claiming : "Oh, my God !" sunk to the ground. Who- ever fell in that scene might give himself up for lost.

But that terrible, that despairing shriek, was heard and answered. Gilbert, carried to a distance from Andrée, had by dint of struggling once more approached her. Bend- ing beneath the same wave which had ingulfed Andrée, he raised himself again, made a frantic leap at the sword which had unwittingly threatened her, grasped the throat of the soldier who was going to strike, and hurled him to the ground. Beside the soldier lay a female form dressed in white ; he raised her up and bore her off as though he had been a giant.

When he felt that lovely form, that corpse, perhaps, pressed to his heart, a gleam of pride lighted up his coun- tenance—his force and courage rose with the circumstances —he felt himself a hero !

He flung himself and his burden into a stream of people whose torrent would certainly have leveled a wall in its flight. Supported by this group, which lifted him up and bore him along with his lovely burden, he walked or rather rolled onward for some minutes. All at once the tor- rent stopped, as if broken by some opposing obstacle. Gilbert's feet touched the ground, and not till then was he sensible of the weight of Andrée. He looked up to ascertain what the obstacle might be, and perceived that he was within a few steps of the Garde Meuble. That mass of stone had broken the mass of flesh.

During that momentary and anxious halt, he had time to look at Andrée. Overcome by a sleep heavy as that of death, her heart had ceased to beat, her eyes were closed, and her face was of a violet tinge, like a white rose that is fading. Gilbert thought that she was dead. He shrieked in his turn, pressed his lips at first to her dress, to her hand, then, emboldened by her insensibility, he covered with kisses that cold face, those eyes swollen beneath their sealed lids. He blushed, wept, raved, strove to transfuse his soul into the bosom of Andrée, feeling astonished that his kisses, which might have warmed a marble statue, had no effect upon that inanimate form. All at once Gilbert felt her heart beat under his hand.

"She is saved!" exclaimed he, on perceiving the swart and blood-stained mob dispersing, and hearing the imprecations, the shrieks, the sighs, the agony of the victims die away in the distance. "She is saved, and it is I who saved her!"

The poor fellow, who stood leaning with his back against the wall, and his eyes turned toward the bridge, had not looked to his right. Before the carriages, which long detained by the crowd but now hemmed in less closely, began once more to move, and soon came on galloping as if coachmen and horses had been seized with a general frenzy, fled twenty thousand unfortunate creatures, mutilated, wounded, bruised one against the other. Instinctively they fled close to the walls, against which the nearest of them were crushed. This mass swept away or suffocated all those who, having taken up their position near the Garde Meuble, imagined that they had escaped the wreck. A fresh shower of blows, of living and dead bodies, rained on Gilbert. He found one of the recesses, formed by the iron gates, and stationed himself there. The weight of the fugitives made the wall crack.

Gilbert, nearly stifled, felt ready to loose his hold, but

with a last desperate effort, mustering all his strength, he encompassed Andrée's body with his arms, resting his head on the bosom of the young girl. One would have supposed he meant to suffocate her whom he was protecting.

"Farewell," murmured he, biting rather than kissing her dress; "farewell." And he raised his eyes to heaven as if directing a last supplicating glance to it for assistance. Then a strange sight met his vision.

Mounted on a post, holding with his right hand by a ring let into the wall, while with his left hand he seemed to be rallying an army of fugitives, was a man, who, looking at the furious sea raging at his feet, sometimes dropped a word, sometimes made a gesture. At that word, at that gesture, some individual among the crowd might be seen to pause, struggle, and by a violent effort strive to reach the man. Others who had already reached him seemed to recognize the newcomers as brothers, and assisted to drag them out of the crowd, raising, supporting, and drawing them toward them.

In this manner, by acting together, this knot had, like the pier of a bridge which divides and resists the water, succeeded in dividing the crowd and holding in check the flying masses.

Every moment fresh stragglers, seeming to rise out of the ground at those strange words and singular gestures, swelled the retinue of this man. Gilbert raised himself by a last effort; he felt that *there* was safety, for there was calmness and power. A last dying gleam from the burning scaffold, leaping up only to expire, fell upon his face. Gilbert uttered a cry of amazement: "Oh! let me die!" he murmured, "let me die, but save her!"

Then with a sublime forgetfulness of self, raising the young girl in both his arms, he exclaimed, "Baron de Balsamo, save Mademoiselle André ede Taverney!"

Balsamo heard that voice which cried to him, like that in the Bible, from the depths; he beheld a white figure, raised above the devouring waves, he leaped from his post to the ground, crying, "This way!" His party overturned all that obstructed their course, and, seizing Andrée, still supported in Gilbert's sinking arms, he lifted her up, impelled by a movement of that crowd which he had ceased to repress, and bore her off, without once turning to look behind.

Gilbert endeavored to utter a last word. Perhaps, after imploring the protection of this strange man for Andrée, he might have solicited it for himself ; but he had only strength to press his lips to the drooping arm of the young girl, and to snatch, with a wild and despairing grasp, a portion of her dress.

After that last kiss, after that final farewell, the young man had nothing left to live for ; he made no further struggle, but, closing his eyes, sunk dying upon a heap of dead.

THE END.

NOTE :—For the information of the reader the Marie Antoinette series should be read in chronological order as follows : 1st, Joseph Balsamo, 2d, Memoirs of a Physician, 3d, The Queen's Necklace, 4th, Taking the Bastile, 5th, The Countess de Charny, 6th, The Chevalier de Maison-Rouge.   These may all be found in Burt's Home Library.

CPSIA information can be obtained at www.ICGtesting.com
Printed in the USA
LVOW12s1220120114

369090LV00002B/115/P

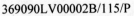